HER LOVER, A C...
WHISPERING T...
GIVE YOURSELF...
WE'LL BE TOGE...

And then the rush, the convulsion, her soul flying out as if caught on a hook. Now he had her, and she was lost, and she didn't care.

The dark powers of the earth were shifting around them. Clouds gathered, demons smiled, everything changed; but she didn't see. There was only this moment, like spilled jewels, a flight through paradise with an angel, her lover.

Divine, the memory.

But reality. Reality was hard, painful and full of blood.

The beauty of the memory pricked her with cruel claws. She'd slid into the Devil's satin trap. Forbidden pleasure must be punished . . .

ABOUT THE AUTHOR

Freda Warrington was born in Leicestershire and grew up in the beautiful Charnwood Forest area, which inspired a feeling for atmosphere, nature and fantasy. After training at Loughborough College of Art and Design, she worked in medical art, graphic design and illustration while writing in her spare time. Her first novel, *A Blackbird in Silver*, was published in 1986 and she is also the bestselling author of the vampire series *A Taste of Blood Wine*, *A Dance in Blood Velvet* and *The Dark Blood of Poppies*. *Dark Cathedral* is her eleventh novel. She now lives in Derbyshire and although writing takes up most of her time, she also enjoys music, reading, photography, art, tapestry, psychology, mythology, conventions and travel.

FREDA WARRINGTON

Dark Cathedral

A SIGNET BOOK

SIGNET

Published by the Penguin Group
Penguin Books Ltd, 27 Wrights Lane, London w8 5tz, England
Penguin Books USA Inc., 375 Hudson Street, New York, New York 10014, USA
Penguin Books Australia Ltd, Ringwood, Victoria, Australia
Penguin Books Canada Ltd, 10 Alcorn Avenue, Toronto, Ontario, Canada m4v 3b2
Penguin Books (NZ) Ltd, 182–190 Wairau Road, Auckland 10, New Zealand

Penguin Books Ltd, Registered Offices: Harmondsworth, Middlesex, England

First published 1996
1 3 5 7 9 10 8 6 4 2

Typeset by Datix International Limited, Bungay, Suffolk
Filmset in 10/12pt Monophoto Baskerville
Printed in England by Clays Ltd, St Ives plc

This book is dedicated to Mike, with love and thanks for endless inspiration!

With thanks also to Anne and Alan, for all their help and encouragement.

Prologue

THE memory was beautiful.

A male and a female, coupling in a Medusa-frenzy of limbs and hair and sheened bodies, of hot mouths and insistent hands. A bed of leaf-strewn moss, a canopy of branches; diamonds of white light peeping between the leaves like tiny eyes. Hearts leaping and blood rushing. The forest shimmering, spinning webs of hallucination across her astonished eyes. Another world opening up and the alchemic stars shining through.

Her lover, a god or a devil, whispering the lie in her ear: *'Give yourself to me now and we'll be together for ever.'*

And then the rush, the convulsion, her soul flying out as if caught on a hook. Now he had her, and she was lost, and she didn't care.

The dark powers of the earth were shifting around them. Clouds gathered, demons smiled, everything changed; but she didn't see. There was only this moment, like spilled jewels, a flight through paradise with an angel, her lover.

Divine, the memory.

But reality. Reality was hard, painful and full of blood.

The beauty of the memory pricked her with cruel claws. She'd slid into the Devil's satin trap. Forbidden pleasure must be punished. Not fair, but it must.

Tears ran down her face like rain down the ice-cold window of the bus. Yes, so wonderful, she thought. I know what it's like to trespass on heaven.

That was what got me into this mess.

She was fifteen, but she felt like a child. Alone, threatened, sick with fear, Beth stared out of the window and willed the bus to move off. The baby in her arms was four days old.

Come on, she thought. Please go before they guess where I'm going and come after me.

Nearly midnight. The bus was half empty so Beth had a seat to herself, but the people who were getting on unnerved her. There were green-haired punks with safety pins stuck through their cheeks and noses, women with tiny skirts and coarse, high-pitched voices, and several drunks. And then there were the solitary men who fixed the women with cold, intrusive eyes.

Beth had never been in the city centre so late at night before. It was a different world, hostile and aggressive. She rested her head against the glass and looked at her own white, worried reflection, tried to ignore the clouds of smoke, the swearing, the grainy metal stink of the bus. Outside, orange sodium lights shone on the concrete towers of Birmingham.

She wished she could ask someone for help. 'My mother wants to take my baby away and exorcize it. I'm afraid she's going to kill it. My mother thinks my baby and I are possessed by the Devil. And maybe she's right, because I'm scared and I have such strange dreams . . .'

Impossible. Who would believe her? Who would even care?

Beth's only chance to escape had been from the maternity ward. Her parents had kept her a virtual prisoner at home since the day they'd found out she was pregnant.

She had been meant to stay in hospital for a week. She hadn't wanted to leave; the nurses had been kind and she'd felt safe there. Today, though, Beth had begun to panic. What if Mum gets impatient and takes me home early? If I don't go today I may never get another chance.

So, after visiting time, Beth had put on her clothes under her dressing-gown. When it was quiet and dark, she had slipped out of bed, taken the baby from the nursery as if to feed her, dumped her dressing-gown in the ladies' loo, and walked out of the building. And no one had taken the slightest notice.

She'd taken almost nothing. A couple of disposable nappies and a can of Coke, that was all. She had ten pounds and thirty-eight pence after paying her bus fare.

But she was going to someone who would help her.

Three rowdy youths got on and came towards Beth, sensing a target for their drunken attentions. But when they saw the baby they backed off. One of them apologized.

Beth held her daughter closer and pressed into her corner. The baby, in a yellow Babygro and a white shawl, made soft cat-like cries, *mau, mau*. Her small, reddish face was serene; she smelled of talc.

Beth's parents had wanted to give the baby a Biblical name, but Beth called her Eirian. It was Welsh and meant silver. Beth had her reasons.

With a growling shudder, the bus moved into the night.

Beth let go of a held breath. The fear kept rising and falling in her throat with sickening insistence. She was too hot yet she kept shivering, her rock-hard breasts ached and her stitches were thorns pulling at her tender flesh.

I was crazy to run away, she thought. I feel lousy. I don't know how to look after this baby. What if she falls ill? The police'll come after us. We won't make it. But I must try, I must! Mum won't take her. Even if – even if she's right and Eirian has something evil in her.

Anguish and fear looped up, one after another.

Landmarks slid past; the Bullring, the Rotunda. The city looked bleak and full of menace. Behind the physical threats, Beth sensed something worse; a threading of psychic darkness, an ancient, shapeless realm of hatred trying to push through and seize her.

A police car screamed past the bus, blue lights flashing. Beth's heart accelerated wildly. But the car was off to attend to some distant crisis; not hers. Then they were away into the suburbs, heading northwards along an A road lined with dingy shops and houses.

Most of the city revellers got off before they reached the outskirts. The dozen or so passengers who were staying on to Tamworth were quiet. The growl of the engine was soporific. Too overwrought to sleep, Beth's mind kept dissolving into a muddle of images. The beautiful memories, and the ugly ones.

'You need help with the baby,' Beth's mother had said

ominously. 'The child of an evil father and a sinful act is bound to be born evil, but Pastor Blair says it can be cleansed. We will help you.'

Overlaid by earlier memories of her mother laying into Luke, Beth's brother; the terrible unhinged glare of her eyes as she beat the wickedness out of him.

Beth clutched the baby protectively, rocking her. Eirian's head was covered in thick dark hair and she had had a distinct personality from birth, placid, alert and watchful. Beth hadn't expected that. It was alarming, the weight of responsibility she felt when Eirian fixed her dark, bluish gaze on Beth's face.

'Even if Mum's right, I'll protect you,' Beth whispered. 'But it's nonsense, you're just a baby. How could you be evil?'

But Beth no longer knew what she believed. She was starving for a word of reassurance or love.

Please let us reach Rhianwen, and let Rhianwen help us. Please God – Goddess – I don't know – but *please*.

Beth began to feel faint. She should have been resting, thinking of O levels and God's forgiveness for her sins; trying to forget it had happened. While her mother took charge of Eirian's fate.

She breathed deeply to stay conscious. The wave passed, and she shivered. Fear all around her.

Eirian began to grizzle louder and louder. Feeling self-conscious and awkward, Beth surreptitiously fed her. The greedy mouth on her nipple hurt. They don't tell you how much it all *hurts*, Beth thought angrily. And this alien creature fastened to her seemed as ruthlessly demanding as a succubus.

Rhianwen must help, she's always been so kind to me . . . but why didn't I hear a word from her or Morgan, all the time I was pregnant? They must *know*.

Don't be stupid, she told herself. How could they get in touch? My parents wouldn't let them. It's my mother's fault, not Rhianwen's. I should've told Morgan months ago but I was so scared.

She isn't just my baby, she's his too. He must accept her. How can he not?

Sated at last, the succubus slept.

Beth dropped her head, touching her forehead to the baby's. 'Perhaps I should have you adopted for your own good, but I can't,' she whispered. 'You're ours.'

Darkness outside the windows now. Hedgerows and great shadowy trees in their June foliage.

And Beth fell asleep.

Darkness in the dream, as well.

Beth was running away but they were right behind her with hate-filled faces: her parents and Pastor Blair and Luke. Beth floundered in terror. '*Fallen from God's grace,*' hissed the voices. '*Tempted by the Devil. Fallen. Whore, witch!*'

The certainty of capture and punishment blinded her with pure blistering fire.

Beth stumbled, and the fall carried her out of herself and into another realm. Trees around her. All was still and silent but for the mournful note of the wind.

The forest was a great dark cathedral. Trunks towered into a vaulted roof of leaves, emerald and holly-green like stained glass. And like a cathedral the forest was full of solemnity, power and ghosts.

Beth was a disembodied witness. This was more a vision than a dream. She'd had many disturbing visions since the baby was conceived, but never one like this.

She saw a young woman running between the trees, dressed in the timeless garments of a peasant: a long dress, an apron tucked up into her belt, a neckerchief and a white hood. Her hair had escaped the hood and hung down to her hips, dull gold like corn stalks. She looked about eighteen. Her face was square and wind-reddened with coarse features, but her dark brown eyes shone with kindness.

In her right hand she carried a thick wooden staff.

This woman, too, was fleeing. Beth shared her urgency.

Beth watched her running deeper into the forest, along tortuous paths where a stranger would soon lose himself. At the heart, Beth saw an ancient, squat oak with branches sprawling to the ground. Grotesque yet beautiful, robed in its fretted leaves.

There was another figure standing by the tree. A girl of about eleven, poised and self-contained, with brown hair and a long, drab dress and apron. The sight of her, for no reason, sent shivers through Beth.

Seeing the girl, the woman stopped in shock. 'Where did you come from?' she cried.

'I don't know,' said the girl. 'I've always been here.'

The woman's expression turned to wonder. She rushed forward and fell to her knees at the girl's feet, laying the staff down like a sword.

'Mistress of the good people, aid me!' the woman cried.

Intuitive knowledge came to Beth; the child was a spirit, a faery, maybe a demon. Not human. The young woman knew it, too, yet she accepted it as if she had expected to meet spirits in the woods.

The girl's face was oval, with fine strong bones and green eyes the same shade as Beth's. These eyes were grave and bright, but they were not kind. Beth looked at the girl and suddenly knew, in a wave of chilling awe, *this is my daughter, grown up!*

'I'll aid you if I can,' the girl said softly, the faintest note of bewilderment in her voice. 'I am here to be your sister.'

'I'm Guendolen,' said the woman. 'Have you a name, good sister?'

A pause, as if the faery-child were thinking. 'I'm called Eirian.'

Guendolen lifted the staff. 'Then I beg you, Eirian, help me hide this!'

'What is it?'

'If I show you, you must never tell.'

'I promise I'll never tell,' said Eirian. How eerie, her emotion-less voice and bright eyes.

'Look,' said Guendolen. She pulled off the knobbly head of the staff and slid a long thin object out of the hollow shaft.

It was a slender horn of ivory, four feet long, with two

candy-stripes winding around it from base to tip. Beth saw it in crisp detail. One stripe was a frieze of tiny people, animals and trees with minuscule leaves, carved in fine detail; the other stripe was gold.

In the gloom, the horn shone. It was the loveliest thing Beth had ever seen, but it touched her with an electric needle of dread. The weight of these mysteries roped her down and the ropes were blood, lead and ice; she wanted to say, come away, Eirian, if you stay here you'll die! But she couldn't make herself heard, couldn't escape.

'It brings fertility to the land, and to the animals – and to men and women. It's sacred to us, Eirian. It's the Wand of Rebirth, the Horn of Power. It's *sacred*.'

'Why must you hide it?'

'There are men who would steal it from us. Cold men who want to take everything from us. They must never find it.'

'Never,' Eirian echoed. 'Climb the tree and hide it inside the trunk. It will be safe there. The tree is sacred, too.' Her face eerily lit by the Wand's shimmer, she added, 'Guendolen, *what* is it?'

'Don't you know, good sister? It's the Horn of the Unicorn.'

Guendolen slid the Horn back inside the staff and replaced the top. As she tucked up her skirts and began to climb the tree, revealing sores on her long naked legs, Eirian said in a tone of frost,

'How cruel to the Unicorn.'

Beth woke, with a jolt, to reality: the lurching motion of the bus, the grinding of the engine. Her neck and head hurt; she must have jolted her head against the glass when she dropped off. And she was tired, so tired, the shrinking of her womb like the worst period pains she had ever endured.

Eirian, cradled in her lap, slept on.

'I've always been here,' said the days-old baby in her sleep. Her unformed voice curled the words up, but they were clearer than a toddler's first attempts at speech. Terrifyingly clear.

Beth didn't react at first. She thought she was still dreaming.

'The tree is sacred, too,' said the baby.

Beth sat up straight, stricken by a wave of utter horror. This couldn't be happening! Babies didn't speak, unless, unless . . .

Petrified, she looked around at the other passengers. Surely they must have heard! But if they had, no one looked.

Is it me? Have I gone mad?

Unless she is possessed by . . . *something*.

'Cruel to the Unicorn,' the baby murmured, and fell quiet.

A black woman of about sixty, sitting behind Beth, was looking at her with a mixture of sympathy and concern.

Did she hear? Beth thought, quickly turning to face forwards again. I daren't ask her! Oh Goddess, God, help us.

The woman leaned forward and tapped her shoulder. 'How old is the child?'

'Four. Four months,' Beth lied, but she knew that even at four months, babies did not speak.

'Months?' The woman's eyebrows rose knowingly. 'She's small for her age – but advanced, eh?'

'She's just – babbling.'

'Let me see,' said the woman.

Obediently Beth held up the baby, supporting her head. She woke suddenly and gazed at the woman from sleepy eyes. A normal infant of four days once more.

The woman looked hard into Beth's eyes, seeming to read her mind. 'Are you all right? You need any help?'

Her attention, however well-meant, made Beth feel exposed and in danger. She wanted to be invisible. As a passenger rang the bell and the bus pulled into a stop, Beth panicked.

'No, I – we're fine. I have to get off here. Sorry. Thank you.'

Calling to the driver to wait, she hurried down the aisle as fast as her torn, stitched body would allow, and stepped down on to the pavement.

The bus, a two-tiered capsule of light, went on without her. Faces stared at her from the windows. Nosey, now they were safe from having to get involved.

Standing up made Beth feel she might pass out. She was in a street of shops and houses. She felt very alone and frightened, stranded with this tiny, demanding creature, shaken out of her wits by all that had happened.

Now she wished she'd let the black woman help her.

Beth put her shoulders back, hefted the bag in one arm and the baby in the other, and began to walk. *I won't give in. Even if Mum's right, I won't give in.*

But the terror remained inside her, a black stone.

At least Beth knew where she was. She'd come this way often enough with her parents, heading for her grandparents' house in the Staffordshire countryside. She was near the centre of Tamworth. She'd meant to stay on the bus until it terminated in the town centre; instead she'd alighted two stops early. It didn't make much difference. There would be no more buses out to the village, Lullingford, until the morning, anyway.

She had nearly five miles to go to her destination.

Common sense told her to take a taxi, but something stopped her. It was a pressure, a wave of command that seemed to emanate from the baby. *We must flee, we must not be separated, no one must find us!*

She didn't want a taxi driver knowing her destination. She wanted, simply, to disappear into the darkness.

'What are you?' Beth whispered. 'God, I hope Rhianwen knows what to do!'

Beth was wearing a long dress, jacket and boots. Her long brown hair was tied off her face. She was quite tall, so perhaps, from a distance, she did not look only fifteen.

She avoided the town centre, taking quiet side-streets. Her burdens grew heavier. Her soreness from the birth made her wince at every step. Beth knew it was a mistake, trying to walk, but there was no choice.

She followed a main road out of town for a time, then took a side turning. She was out into farmland. The only light was the orange glow of the town behind her. The roads grew narrow, with high banks on either side. When cars came – only a few – she pressed back into the hedge and hoped they would not see her.

When the baby began to caterwaul, Beth went into a farm

gateway to change her. The night was chilly and a thick dew was forming. She felt cold and unsafe, as if eyes were watching her from the darkness; she kept seeing shadow-figures from the corners of her eyes. *Cold men who want to steal everything from us.* Sinister words from the dream.

Beth took off her jacket, spread it on the damp grass, and placed Eirian on it. She removed the old nappy and stuffed it under the hedge, hating herself for leaving litter. And the baby, with a tell-tale noise and aroma, promptly soiled the jacket.

Beth almost screamed in frustration. Looking down at the small head with its curls of dark hair, for the first time she felt something close to hatred.

'Why did you have to come to cause all this trouble?' she said. 'It was so beautiful, before you ruined it all! What are you, repeating the words out of my dreams? *What the hell are you?*'

And immediately she felt guilty. She bit her hand until the tears of self-pity subsided.

'I can't cope with this,' she said, trying to clean both jacket and baby with handfuls of wet grass. Eirian began to wail in earnest. 'Maybe I should abandon you on someone's doorstep. For your sake.'

A surge of possessive denial drove the thought away.

Beth finished the task, put her coat back on, and somehow found the strength to continue.

'Rhianwen will help us,' Beth said, a chant to soothe the child and keep her own feet moving. 'You'll like her. She's your granny, but she's not horrible like your other granny. She's nice. She'll know what to do. She won't let Mum take you away. She'll look after us. And you're going to see your daddy. Won't that be nice? He'll be so proud.' *I hope.*

But the demon-child went on bawling insistently, wriggling powerfully against her mother like a cat demanding to be let down.

'Shut up,' said Beth in desperation. 'Shut up, or I'll leave you in the fields!' Then, 'Sorry. Sorry.'

Eventually the crying ceased.

'Sacred,' the baby murmured thoughtfully. 'Who would dare to take it from us?'

Her watch said two-thirty when they reached Lullingford. Beth was dying on her feet. Eirian slept, mute, a dead-weight in her aching arms.

Yet the scent and atmosphere of the village lifted her spirits. Here was happiness, freedom and safety. Rhianwen's house, now, was only a few minutes' walk away.

Rhianwen would not be expecting them, of course.

The darkness was not absolute; there was a brownish-orange glow on the horizon and a scattering of street-lamps around the village green. Beth passed a farmyard and breathed its evocative aromas. On the other side of the road was the church-yard with copper beech trees shimmering darkly against the sky. She passed a pub, rows of cottages, the post office, another pub. Through a gap, across the gardens, she saw the roof of her own grandparents' house. She thought longingly of going to them but she couldn't; they had been as furious as her parents about her pregnancy. They'd simply telephone her mother straight away and it would all be over.

Instead she turned into the rough lane that led to Rhian-wen's isolated house. Hawthorn loomed densely over her on either side. Cow parsley and nettles dragged at her legs. Beth was wide awake, all physical discomforts forgotten; but her heart was beating hard in anticipation of Rhianwen's shock.

'Once Rhianwen understands, everything will be all right,' Beth told Eirian. 'It's just embarrassing to stand on someone's doorstep at nearly three in the morning and beg for help, for *so much* help. But you *are* her granddaughter.'

Again the shadows, rippling in the hedgerows, like hooded priests.

'Nearly there,' Beth whispered. 'Nearly home.'

Eirian was unmoved.

'I did this for you and all you can do is sleep!'

She went through the gate in the tall hedge. Along the path between foxgloves, lavender and hollyhocks. The windows were dark. She thought of Morgan and Rhianwen asleep in their beds and her heart jumped.

Beth grasped the fox-head knocker and gave five sharp taps. Silence.

She waited. The thought of seeing Morgan made her breathless with anxiety. It would take them time to wake up, put on dressing-gowns, and reach the door . . . but not as long as this, surely?

She knocked again.

And again. Harder, more desperately now.

No one there. Beth couldn't believe it. She moved around the house, staring into dark windows, seeing nothing; or rather, seeing one bleak fact.

The curtains were open, even in the bedrooms.

Perhaps they were away; but Rhianwen never went away because of the animals. In the back garden Beth found the devastating proof that Rhianwen had gone for good. All the cages were empty.

As Beth returned to the front of the house, fighting to keep back her tears of disbelief, she saw something she hadn't noticed before. A post and board, stark in the softness of the hedge. Even in the gloom its message was unmistakable.

She started to sob in shock. Rhianwen had been her only hope.

Beth collapsed on the path and sat there in the damp, smelly jacket, hugging her daughter, spilling out all her misery. They had always been here, Rhianwen and Morgan, throughout those long, honeyed summers. But now, when she really needed them, they were gone.

She felt warm wetness between her legs and knew she had begun to bleed badly. Her womb and her heart, bleeding.

While above her the board spelled betrayal in two impersonal words.

For Sale.

PART ONE

Maiden

Lady of the Perfect Black

Chapter One

WHEN Beth was eleven, her grandparents' house represented an unexplored Otherworld, as if it were some mysterious Gothic mansion. She and Luke had only been taken there on day visits; they had never been allowed to stay for holidays. That would have kept them away from church.

'D'you think Mum'll let us stay this time?' Luke asked, pulling himself up on a window-sill and drumming the radiator with his feet. He was a year younger than Beth; a moody and nervous little boy.

'Well, we're here,' said Beth. 'You know how ill she's been; she's *got* to let Gran look after us so she can rest.'

'I know, but she keeps almost saying yes then changing her mind. She'll argue with Gran for half an hour then turn round and take us home.'

Beth sighed. 'Don't kick, you'll make marks.'

Luke kicked harder, then stopped. They had been left in the front room, but they'd crept upstairs to look at the view from the landing window. There were chestnuts and beeches in full leaf, gardens, hedges and fields glowing green in the July sunshine, a few roofs barely visible between the trees. A lush, enticing contrast to the suburb of Birmingham in which they lived. It wasn't often that Beth resented or even noticed the confines of her life, but at this moment she craved her freedom with unholy passion.

'Mum always does what God tells her,' said Luke. 'I hope he tells her to let us stay.'

'Come on,' said Beth. 'Let's sit on the stairs. Shh.'

Beth wasn't quite the angel her mother thought she was. She had learned tiny deceptions, like eavesdropping, because sometimes it helped her to protect Luke.

The house was an old rectory, with fascinating corridors and attics that the children had never had the chance to investigate. There were high ceilings, black and white tiles in the hall, stained glass in the front door. The house had atmosphere. As Beth seated herself half-way down the stairs, an eerie thrill went through her, like in the weird dreams she had sometimes, which were exciting but surely not Christian.

Beth's grandfather, Randolph Cross, was the village doctor; he and his partner shared a small modern surgery next to the school. Her grandmother, Heather, was a retired headmistress who devoted her time to dogs, horses and village business. They were both down-to-earth, practical people, Heather abrupt, Randolph rather aloof. Beth and Luke were in awe of them.

Heather and her daughter Olivia – Beth and Luke's mother – always shut themselves in the kitchen to argue. It was a tradition; Beth's father and grandfather would go for a stroll, leaving the women to argue in private. But Beth had discovered that from the stairs she could see as well as hear them through the fanlight above the kitchen door. Olivia was sitting at the kitchen table, cutting up tomatoes for tea; Heather was at the sink, rinsing lettuce.

'You can't get over an illness like that in a day,' Heather was saying. 'You need to rest. Anyone else would be glad to get rid of their children for a few weeks!'

Beth's mother had had an attack of hepatitis; she was still yellowish-pale and too weak to do much. 'Beth can look after me.'

'That wouldn't be fair on Beth. Look, we've already agreed that the children should come here for the summer.'

'I'm not happy about this, Mother,' said Olivia.

Beth's heart sank. Luke looked ready to cry.

'D'you think I've forgotten how to look after children?' Heather retorted. 'We never see them for more than a few hours. Really, not to let them stay with their granny is over-cautious, to put it mildly.'

'They need their routine.'

'Need a change from it, more like.'

'What is that supposed to mean?'

'They need to play,' said Heather. 'You never let them play.'

'They don't need that nonsense! They have church! I don't want them getting ideas.'

'Do let up, Livvy. This is hardly Soho.'

Olivia thrust her knife so hard through a tomato that the blade stuck in the chopping board. 'I can't let up! I don't want them growing up like other teenagers, in a revolting stew of sex, drugs and Satanic so-called music. I don't want them ending up like . . . They have *got* to be guided until they can think for themselves. The Lord has work to do through my children! They are temples of the Holy Spirit and that's how I intend them to remain.'

Beth's grandmother sighed. 'I know you have their best interests at heart, dear, but I'm sure God doesn't object to children having innocent fun. I'll keep them out of mischief.'

'They wouldn't be able to go to church while they were here.'

'Of course they would!' Heather retorted. 'What do you think the big stone building with the steeple is? Your father and I go every Sunday.'

Olivia made a *humph* sound, as if this didn't count; as if it were tantamount to paganism.

'There's a church youth group, you know,' Heather added. Silence. She went on impatiently, 'I hardly think a few weeks with Granny and Granddad is going to set them on the road to damnation.'

'Don't mock me, Mother! You don't understand!'

'I'm not mocking you. I respect your beliefs.' Heather was vigorously rolling the lettuce in a tea towel. A Labrador sat watching her, its thick tail thumping the quarry tiles. 'You used to call me Mummy. I wish you wouldn't be so formal.'

'Family relationships must not be allowed to come before one's relationship with God,' Beth's mother said quietly. 'That's one of the most important things Pastor Blair has taught us.'

5

Heather said something about Pastor Blair between her teeth. Beth didn't catch it.

'What?' Olivia snapped.

'Nothing.' Heather came to the table, threw the lettuce into a bowl, and began to shell hard-boiled eggs. 'Anyway, it's all decided. How long is the summer holiday, seven weeks? It'll pass in no time. And if you're so worried about the children, you can stay here with them. I'll look after you.'

'I can't. I need to be near church.'

'For heaven's sake, Livvy, you need a rest! I reckon you caught that ruddy hepatitis at church. All those germs on the chalice. Damned unhygienic.'

'You can talk, letting the dogs lick the dinner plates! That is disgusting, Mother! Don't fuss. People from church will help me out. We always help each other.'

'Good. The children can stay, then.'

'If it's God's will.' Olivia dropped her head. A nod. Beth and Luke hugged each other, rejoicing silently.

'You won't regret it,' Heather said with satisfaction.

'But you must promise to be strict with them!' Olivia said fervently. 'Especially Luke. Beth's a good girl but Luke – if you don't control him I'll have a demon on my hands in September!'

'He'll behave, don't worry. There's plenty to keep them busy. Beth loves the horses.'

'Make sure they read their Bible every day. I've made a list of the passages they must study.'

'Oh, must they?' Beth's heart was in her mouth, but her grandmother seemed to think better of arguing, for fear that Olivia would change her mind again. 'No, if you say so, it shall be done.'

'I'll test them when they come home, so they'd better do it. Don't let them watch television, especially not rubbish like *Top of the Pops*. Be careful where they go and who they meet. I don't want them going out alone.'

'They'll have to go out in the big bad world one day.' Heather filled the kettle and put it on the Aga.

6

'I don't want them mixing with the village children. And I particularly don't want them meeting *her*.'

'I'm sure there's no danger of that,' Heather said grimly.

'Well, I'm not leaving it to chance. Will you tell them or shall I?'

Their grandmother sighed. Finally she said, 'It's all so much nonsense. Ridiculous to give that woman more importance than she deserves. If you forbid children to do something, it's the first thing they'll want to do!'

What woman? Beth thought. She stood up and leaned out over the banister to hear better. Luke copied her.

'My children are obedient,' said Olivia.

Heather gave her a hard look, which meant something, though Beth wasn't sure what. 'As far as I'm concerned, that woman doesn't exist! Why wake their curiosity? They're most unlikely to show the remotest interest or even hear of her unless you deliberately draw their attention to her.'

'She's evil!' Olivia said passionately. 'This is like saying that if I don't warn them about the Devil, they'll be safe from him! Well, they won't!'

'I'd hardly call her that, dear,' Heather said drily. 'Heartless, calculating bitch would be nearer the mark. I know you have a right to strong feelings, but –'

'Yes, *evil*. She's a witch and a serpent, Mother. They worship Satan, these people. They lay themselves open to possession by demons! You *know* what she's like!'

A heavy pause. 'I still say that ignorance is bliss,' said Heather, banging tea-cups on to a tray.

'No. They must be told. And you must promise me that you won't let them anywhere near her, or I'll take them straight home now!'

'I don't want them meeting the bloody bitch any more than you do,' Heather retorted.

Then, by chance, their mother looked up and saw, through the fanlight, Beth and Luke leaning over the banister. Too late to hide. Olivia beckoned.

Beth's knees turned liquid with fear as they went sheepishly down the stairs and into the kitchen.

7

'Close the door behind you,' Olivia said calmly. Beth obeyed. 'Come here.'

They went to her chair and she took their hands, pulling them close. Olivia was tall and graceful with a long neck, oval face and firm mouth. Her hair, deep brown like Beth's, was parted in the centre and fastened back in a bun. She would have been pretty, if her expression had been less severe; her recent illness had deepened her frown lines and the pouches beneath her eyes. But her eyes, pale blue orbs, lightning conductors of her mood, still shone bright with the domineering force of her will.

Their grandmother, meanwhile, went on setting out the tea as if nothing were happening, her mouth thin with disapproval.

'Don't you know it's a sin to eavesdrop?' Olivia asked with ominous steel-sweetness.

They nodded, heads bowed. Then Luke blurted out, 'But is there really a witch?'

'It's just a nasty lady who doesn't like children,' said Heather.

Olivia snapped, 'Mother, leave this to me!' She drew her children closer. Beth regarded her with both love and terror. Her mother had seen visions, and had been possessed by the Holy Spirit. Her words were God's truth.

'Yes, there is a witch,' she said, low and intense. 'You remember me telling you about witches, don't you? What did I say?'

'They worship the Devil,' Beth whispered.

'But they don't have pointy hats or broomsticks!' Luke added, his eyes huge.

'That's right. You can't tell. Sometimes they seem so nice, you can't tell until it's too late. So I'm warning you now. Her name is Mrs Rhys and she lives in Farm Lane. Don't you *ever* go near her or God will punish you!' Beth glanced at Luke, saw him wince. 'That is, if you're ever seen alive again. Because witches drink the blood of children and hang out the skins to dry. They dance shamelessly in the moonlight to worship their master, the Devil. They copulate with Satan. If you go near

8

Mrs Rhys, she'll cast an evil spell on you, and you'll die and go straight to hell.'

'Won't Jesus save us?' Beth asked, almost crying.

'Jesus knows everything you do and think,' her mother said with soft menace. 'If ever he sees you with that woman, he will know you've disobeyed me. That will be very bad, won't it?'

Beth was shaking so violently she could hardly stand up.

Her mother drew a small black book from a pocket. She never went anywhere without it. 'Now put your hands on the Bible and swear, "I promise that I shall never go near or speak to the evil witch, Mrs Rhianwen Rhys, so help me God, Amen."'

They gripped the Bible and swore.

'Remember. If you break your word you'll burn in hell. Now pray with me.'

Their mother's passion was spent. Looking exhausted, she closed her eyes in prayer.

'Oh, Luke, for heaven's sake,' their grandmother said suddenly.

Beth followed her gaze to a pool of liquid on the tiles. Luke had wet himself.

Beth felt strange when her parents left after tea. It was weird, not to be getting into the car with them. Looking exhausted, Olivia hugged and kissed the children out on the gravel drive in front of the house; their father, Philip, only gave them a smile and a wave.

Philip Herne was a dentist. He was a quiet man, with an air of serenity and neatness about him; his light brown hair brushed just so, his spectacles gleaming bright as dental instruments. A slight smile always hovered about his lips but he never showed his feelings; Beth wasn't sure what his emotions were. He comes to church, she thought, so he must love God. Although he expressed affection for his children, it was in a very detached and distant way. Beth had never known anything else, but she still had a vague feeling that there should have been something more.

Heather had sometimes remarked that Philip's aloofness was actually shyness, though Beth couldn't see it. She was afraid of him, though not in the same way that she was afraid of her mother. It was a different kind of fear. She loved her father, but she didn't *know* him.

It was a wrench, to know she wouldn't see her parents for seven weeks.

'You can always come up at weekends,' said Randolph.

'We'll try,' said Philip, 'but Olivia isn't meant to travel. She shouldn't really have come today but . . .' He shrugged helplessly. 'We'll have to see how she is.'

'I'm perfectly all right,' Olivia said crossly, as she climbed into the passenger seat, though she looked dreadful.

'Baby,' whispered Luke, because Beth was crying and he wasn't.

As they waved the car off, Beth asked, 'Is Mum really ill?'

'She'll be fine if she follows her doctor's advice and rests,' her grandfather replied. Randolph didn't seem ancient, like other people's grandfathers: he was fifty-six and handsome, with hair and eyebrows the colour of charcoal. But he was very much a doctor, brusque and authoritarian, so Beth couldn't help being shy with him.

'We're a tough breed,' said Heather. 'But that church . . . I don't like the effect it's having on the children. Not even a proper church, y'know; they just meet in some hall.'

'Pastor Blair says it's the sincerity of worship that matters, not the place,' said Beth, but her grandparents went on talking over her head.

'I know,' said Randolph. 'They're the worst. Still, it means so much to her, and I suppose she thinks she's doing the right thing. The children seem healthy enough.'

'Oh, they're strong, like her. But they're so young, and she puts so much on them.'

'Mmm. Unfortunately it is up to her how she brings up her children. And you know what'll happen if they're any different when she comes to collect them,' Randolph said heavily. 'She'll never bring them to see us again.'

'Come on,' said Heather, propelling the children up the steps to the front door. 'Help me feed the horses, eh? Then we'll watch telly. I won't tell your mum if you don't.'

Beth's tears were swept away in a wild sense of freedom; that the green Otherworld was about to open its mysteries to her, and that anything was possible.

Images of the witch plagued Beth all night.

She had already built a very clear picture in her mind. It was rather like the villainess in *The Lion, the Witch and the Wardrobe*, a book Beth had read in secret, but much worse. This witch had long red hair and a long red tongue that she poked out lewdly as she lifted her skirts to let hordes of demons copulate with her.

Beth knew roughly what copulate meant, despite her mother's efforts to keep her in ignorance. The girls at school talked about it a lot. It sounded revolting.

She visualized disgusting potions brewing in a cauldron. Poisons and terrifying spells. A wicked, scarlet magic that could undermine even the power of God.

The bedroom in which Heather had put her seemed cavernous, chilly even though it was summer. Beth could imagine ghosts in the corners. As she lay awake, watching tree-shadows on her curtains and tormenting herself with half-formed fears, a figure appeared beside her bed. A little soundless shadow. Her skin prickled and she nearly screamed.

'Beth,' said the shadow, 'I want to go home.'

'Luke, you scared me!' she hissed.

'I didn't mean to. I want to go home,' he repeated, pulling at her pyjama sleeve.

'Why?'

'Because of the witch,' he said through tears. 'I'm frightened.'

'There isn't a witch,' said Beth.

'Mum said there was!'

Beth bit her lip. A dilemma. How could she comfort Luke,

without denying the truth of their mother's words? Their grand-mother had confirmed the woman's existence, after all.

'Come on, get in,' Beth said, lifting up the covers.

Luke hesitated, 'I think that's one of the things Mum says leads to uncleanness. Isn't it?' he asked worriedly. 'I wish I knew what she meant.'

Beth had a vague idea, but she wasn't sure. 'Just get under the eiderdown, then.' Luke obeyed, snuggling against her. He was trembling. Beth put her arm round him and said, 'There's no need to go home. It will be nice here. If there is a witch, I'll protect you from her.'

'Promise?'

'I swear on the Bible. I'll look after you, Luke. I'll never let you down. I'll always be with you.'

'Always?'

'For ever and ever, Amen.'

'And you'll never go away and leave me?'

'Never. Better now?'

Luke yawned. 'Yes, I don't know what I'd do without you, Bethie. I won't be frightened as long as you're here.'

'I will be.'

'Remember you promised,' he said softly. A few seconds later, he was asleep.

Beth lay with her arm over her brother's waist, brooding.

Luke and I mustn't change while we're here or we'll be punished. Mustn't meet the witch or we'll burn in hell.

She prayed to Jesus to help her. But a woman with pointed teeth and a long red tongue kept interrupting and desecrating her prayers, cackling and cavorting and kicking her black-stock-inged feet in the air.

The bloody bitch.

Chapter Two

I N daylight, Beth quickly forgot her nightmares. They seemed less real, at least. She and Luke said their morning prayers, washed, dressed and ran down to breakfast.

Luke kept yawning, almost falling asleep over his cornflakes. At least he went to sleep eventually, Beth thought in sympathy.

Randolph was reading a newspaper as he buttered his toast, and said nothing after, 'Morning.' He was an intimidating presence, but he intrigued Beth. She wished desperately that she knew what to say to him.

The dining-room was big and bright. All the rooms in the house were large, with high ceilings and big windows. There were polished wood floors, lots of rugs and a muddle of old furniture. It was comfortable rather than stylish. There were mysterious staircases, corridors and attics. Beth couldn't wait to explore, but felt too shy to ask.

'Well, what would you like to do today?' Heather asked. She had a strong face with broken veins mapping her cheeks, and short iron-grey hair. She always wore practical clothes: tweed skirts or trousers, plain jumpers, flat shoes; headscarf and wellies for outside.

Beth didn't know how to answer. She was used to being told what to do, not asked.

'You can please yourselves, you know,' said Heather. 'What d'you normally do in the holidays?'

'Erm,' Beth began, 'we have Bible study, go to church, do the housework, help Mum make lunch – and afternoon tea as well if she has friends round – and if someone's ill we visit them, and go to church again, and, well, things like that.'

'Don't you get bored?'

'No, I enjoy it,' Beth said honestly. 'Luke, well, Luke gets bored sometimes. He can't help it.'

'Things are a bit different round here. I know your mother doesn't want me to spoil you, but you are on holiday.'

Beth found her courage. 'Grandma, may we look round the house, please?' she asked.

Heather pulled a face. 'If you like. You can do whatever you want, within reason.'

Beth was overwhelmed.

'Luke, do stop yawning,' said Heather. 'I've been up since five-thirty to see to the hens and horses. Your grandfather has to start work at eight. You don't see us yawning, do you?'

But there was no menace in her voice. Beth felt a weight begin to lift from her shoulders. She hadn't realized it was there until she felt this wonderful lightness.

'Explore the house to your heart's content,' Heather continued, 'but there are more interesting things to do. There is an enormous garden out there. Surely you don't want to stay in while the sun's shining? There are animals to be mucked out and fed, horses to be ridden and dogs to be walked. There are fields and footpaths to be explored. Only stay together and don't get lost, eh? And don't go down Farm Lane.'

Beth stared at her grandma's reddish, no-nonsense face. 'Do you mean we may go out on our own?'

'Yes, if you're sensible, and I'm sure you will be.'

'But Mum said –'

'Who's going to know, if no one tells her?' And Heather winked solemnly. 'However, we do have some rules. Always come in the side door, wipe your feet and leave your boots or shoes in the scullery. No dirty shoes in the house. Always be home by half-five; tea is at six. No telly until after tea. Children need fresh air. Beth, you'd better change into trousers after breakfast.'

Beth blushed. 'I can't, Grandma.'

'Don't tell me you didn't bring any!'

'Mum doesn't let me wear trousers. I haven't got any.'

'Oh, good grief.' Heather sighed. 'We'd better go shopping.'

Luke brightened and colour came to his cheeks, as if he'd suddenly woken up. 'Can I get a football?' he exclaimed.

*

That was their first day. Shopping in Tamworth in the morning, just Beth and her grandma. Unlike Olivia, Heather let Beth choose her own jeans. She also bought her some riding clothes and a football for Luke, and in the afternoon, she gave Beth a riding lesson in the paddock behind the garden.

Beth's grandmother owned two sixteen-hand hunters, a bay and a chestnut. Beth rode the bay, Whisky. He was far too big for her, but well-mannered enough not to unnerve her.

Meawhile, Luke kicked his new football round the back garden, and seemed perfectly content.

For an hour before tea, Heather sat down with the children and helped them with their Bible study. She made it fun, a conspiracy. Let's fool your mother that we're sticking to her rules!

Beth thought it was the best day of her life.

After tea, they explored the nooks and crannies of the house. Heather had been right, though; the mystery had been more fascinating than the reality. It was the village that drew Beth now.

The days that followed were paradise. Beth loved helping Heather with the chores: feeding the hens, grooming the horses, cleaning tack. She loved the clutter of bridles, saddles and riding boots in the tackroom. She loved the smell of saddle soap, leather and hoof oil, which seemed to pervade not only the stables but the house itself.

Unlike Olivia, Heather was not fanatically tidy. Shocked at first, Beth soon grew pleasantly used to the idea that if she didn't leave things just so, she was not going to be shouted at.

Luke didn't take to the animals. He tried to play with the dogs, a collie and a Labrador, but he was too rough and the collie nipped him. Heather tried to show him how to handle them, but he'd lost interest. Apart from that, Beth had never seen him so happy: running, climbing trees and shouting like a normal boy.

Beth and Luke decided that when they grew up, they wanted to be just like Grandma and Granddad.

Every night, Beth guiltily asked God to make her mother

well again quickly, but not too quickly. She never wanted this happiness to end.

On Thursday evening, Heather let them watch *Top of the Pops*. They'd never seen it before; Beth had conjured only vague impressions from the murmurings of classmates. The groups were all dressed in sequins, make-up and ludicrous platform shoes, and had names like Slade, Sweet, Mud and T Rex.

Even at eleven, Beth thought the music dire. Afterwards, she and Luke agreed smugly that they had not been missing very much.

By Friday, they had gained the confidence to explore the village on their own.

'Remember the rules,' Heather said sternly. 'Don't go in farmyards because there's dangerous machinery and the farmer will get angry. Stay together and don't do anything obviously daft. Don't speak to strangers. *Don't go up Farm Lane.* Be home by half-past five. Have you got clean hankies? Good.'

Then she gave them each fifty pence and told them, ironically, not to spend it all at once.

It was like flying, to run down to the village shop and choose whatever sweets they wanted. They had never been allowed to do this before. Olivia said 'fleshly indulgence' was a sin.

Beth and Luke ate ice lollies with a massive sense of guilt which, strangely, added to the enjoyment.

As they ate, they walked past the surgery and the village school.

'Wouldn't it be nice to live here and go to school there?' Beth said wistfully.

'Don't be stupid,' Luke retorted. 'That school's only for babies.'

When they finished the lollies, Beth put the sticks in her jeans pocket. She became righteously angry when she saw people dropping litter.

Lullingford was a beautiful village with a green and winding roads lined with cottages of which no two were the same and all were pretty. Nothing like the drab rows of Victorian villas in

King's Heath where they lived. Beth saw a sign, pointing along a grassy path between two gardens. Public Footpath.

'Shall we?' she said.

Luke, over-excited, ran ahead of her. 'We might meet the bitch,' he said. 'Bloody bitch, bloody bitch, bloody *bitch*!'

'Shut up, or I'll take you straight home!' Beth said, mortified. Luke subsided and swished at the long grass with a stick.

The path led them over a stile and into lush fields of barley and wheat, with deep mysterious hedgerows and spreading trees. The sunlight was very soft through a veil of cloud; the day, hot and humid, seemed to shimmer.

Beth felt that she had stepped through the back of the wardrobe into the forbidden land of her dreams.

Heather had told them to stay at the edge of the fields and not trample the crops. They walked in silent reverence, trailing their hands through the dry silky wheat, picking grains apart to see the floury middles. The hedgerows were full of treasures; wild flowers, grasses jewelled with cuckoo-spit, with beetles and ladybirds.

When Luke started investigating in earnest, Beth had to keep restraining him from picking flowers or dissecting insects. She grew annoyed with him. No wonder Mum gets so angry, she thought, he won't *listen*.

Beth wished she were on her own. She wondered if there was some way of losing Luke, then felt guilty. Jesus, please forgive me, she said to herself; I didn't mean it.

They climbed over a stile and found themselves in a small, sloping meadow with two goats grazing on it. Bounded by thick hedges, with a wood at the top end, it seemed deliciously secluded.

How beautiful, Beth thought. She pointed down the hill to the bottom hedge, where a drift of buttercups shone. 'Let's go and look down there.'

There was a little stream crossing the far corner, and a mass of new flowers to study in the long, golden grass under the hawthorn.

'Ow,' said Luke, swatting at something. Beth took no notice.

He said it louder, '*Ow*!' and began, unexpectedly, to scream in pain.

She stared at him, too startled to react.

'What is it?' she said.

Luke went white, and collapsed.

Horrified, Beth knelt beside him. 'What is it? What's wrong?'

He was in too much pain to answer. He could only point at his ribs and grunt, 'Ah, ah.'

A wasp crawled out between the buttons of his shirt and flew off. Beth tried to see the sting, but he lay cramped around the pain, sobbing and shouting, not responding to her.

Beth stood up, feeling horribly powerless.

Then she heard a voice from the other side of the hedge. 'Hello? Hello?'

'Help!' Beth cried.

Silence. Then a woman appeared through a gap in the hawthorn a few yards away. She was slim, of medium height, about the same age as Beth's mother or a bit older. She was wearing a cheesecloth shirt, jeans, and boots. Her hair was tucked up under a man's cap, which half hid her face. But it seemed a fresh and kindly face.

'What's the matter?' the woman called, hurrying up to them. 'I heard someone crying.' She had a Welsh accent, a charming hesitation after consonants.

She looked like the kind of woman who would have a dog. Instead, a cat came after her: a grey, slim, Egyptian-looking cat with golden eyes.

'It's my brother. A wasp stung him. I don't think he can get up.'

The woman crouched down beside the white-faced Luke and gently prised his hand away from his ribs. The cat padded around, sniffing and exploring. 'Let me see.'

Luke shut his eyes and, whimpering, let her unbutton his shirt and look.

Beth heard the woman draw in a shocked breath. But when she spoke, her voice was light. 'Looks a bit pink, that's all. It's not an allergic reaction, just shock. Hurts like buggery, a wasp sting, doesn't it? Come on, let's get you somewhere more comfortable and I can see to it.'

'I don't think he can get up,' Beth said anxiously.

'Help me with him. It's not far. You're almost in my back garden.'

Between them they helped the fainting Luke along the hedge and through a small gate into a garden. The first thing Beth saw was a cloud of butterflies dancing round the purple spires of a buddleia. There were small lawns swamped by untrimmed shrubs, untidy bright flower-beds and winding paths. In the middle of it all was a cottage of flint, brick and slate. It would have looked severe, if not for the ivy and roses climbing its walls.

Immediately behind the cottage was a checkerboard of herbs, edged by lavender, which reminded Beth of a knot garden she had seen in a book. The scent was glorious.

In the far corner of the garden, to the left of the house as they approached the back door, there were several sheds in an L-shape. But they were half hidden by greenery.

The woman opened the door and took them through a large, brick-floored kitchen into a living-room. Three black kittens, like tiny hearthrugs, scattered under their feet. The woman sat Luke down on a sofa.

'Won't be a minute,' she said. 'I'll get something to put on the sting.'

Luke was shivering, his pale face screwed up. 'Bethie,' he said. 'It hurts.'

'I know. It's all right. The lady will make you better, then I'll take you home and Grandma will give you some of that chocolate cake you like. All right?'

He nodded, biting his lip.

The grey cat came in so they fussed it, and felt better.

The room smelled lovely, Beth noticed. Like flowers and newly-baked pastry and earthy spices. And it wasn't *ordinary*, like her parents' house. There were rush mats and huge colourful cushions on the floor, big tasselled blankets of black and gold thrown over the sofa and chairs. The walls were off-white and hung with exotic textiles, masks, pictures of moons and suns. Above the fireplace hung a painting of a strange Egyptian-looking creature. Beth could not make out whether it was meant to be a cat or a woman.

'Here we are,' said the woman, coming back with a bowl, cotton wool, a jar and a cup. 'Now, let's see.'

She had taken off the cap and her hair had come down. It was long, thick and auburn; dark, yet red like hot coals.

Luke resisted half-heartedly as she tried to open his shirt again, then submitted. As the woman bathed the sting and dotted ointment on it, Beth stared at her, feeling vaguely anxious.

But Luke seemed soothed by her touch. His colour came back, and Beth could see the pain had gone. 'I've got a little boy, too,' said the woman, buttoning up his shirt. 'Well, not so little. He's thirteen now.'

Luke looked interested. 'Where is he?'

'Off camping in the Lake District. I've forgotten what he looks like, he's away so often. There, all done.' The woman glanced at Beth and said, 'Don't look so worried! He'll be fine. Now drink this. It'll help with the shock, you see.'

She gave Luke a cup half full of a steaming dark liquid. He drank it without argument, looking brighter.

'How's that? Better now?'

Luke nodded. 'Yes, thank you.'

The woman looked pleased. She was pretty, in a fresh, unaffected way. Beth loved her accent. 'Will you stay for a cup of tea, or lemonade? You should have a bite to eat and a rest before you go home. I made some biscuits this morning but they're a bit of a disaster, like the last days of Pompeii. Taste all right, though.'

It would be rude to say no. 'That would be very nice, thank you,' Beth said politely.

'Come and help me then, dear.'

Beth left Luke playing with the cat and followed the woman back into the kitchen. Shutting the door behind them, the woman asked softly, 'I noticed your brother has some faded bruises on his ribs and back. Any idea how he got them?'

Their eyes locked, and Beth couldn't speak. The woman's eyes were the same colour as her own; green, like jade.

It didn't occur to Beth to lie. 'He wouldn't concentrate during Bible study. Mum says he has to be taught.'

There was an awful silence. Beth felt she'd said something terribly wrong; she always tried to protect Luke, but this time she felt she had to defend their mother instead. 'It's his fault, he knows he shouldn't fidget.'

'Does that happen very often?'

'No,' said Beth, realizing it was not advisable to tell the truth.

'Does it happen to you, too?'

'No.'

'Oh.' The woman sighed. At last she broke the terrible gaze and began to pour glasses of lemonade. 'Never mind. Put the biscuits on this plate. Don't tread on the kittens. Do you like cats?'

'Yes,' said Beth. She piled lumpy, singed biscuits on to the plate, then bent down to play with the tiny black kittens, enthralled.

'Because there are lots more outside. And hedgehogs, and a baby owl. I'll take you to meet them after, if you like.'

'Oh, yes please!'

Entranced by everything, not least by the woman herself, Beth wanted to stay here all afternoon.

The woman loaded a tray and picked it up. 'Open the door for me, there's a love.' As Beth reached the door, she added, 'He ought to see a doctor, your brother.'

Beth felt indignant, as if the woman assumed she knew nothing about doctors. As they went into the living-room, Beth said, 'My grandfather *is* a doctor.'

The woman didn't reply at first. Her silence was the unnerving sort you could almost *touch*. Beth wondered what she'd said wrong.

'Help yourselves. Don't mind the crumbs.'

Beth sat by Luke, and the woman sat on cushions on the floor. Beth had never seen an adult do this before.

The lemonade was real, not the fizzy sort. The biscuits, despite their resemblance to volcanic lava, tasted wonderful.

'So,' the woman said after a minute, 'you're Dr Cross's lot, are you? Staying for the holidays?'

'Yes,' Beth said, relieved that she still sounded cheerful. 'I'm Beth and this is Luke.'

'Well, I'm pleased to meet you, Beth and Luke. I'm Rhianwen Rhys.'

Beth's stomach gave a horrible jolt. Luke's mouth fell open and he put his lemonade down on the low table as if it were poison.

She could hear her mother's voice. *'You can't tell. Sometimes they seem so nice, you can't tell until it's too late . . . You'll die and go to hell . . . If you break your word you'll burn in hell.'*

'Oh,' was all Beth could say. She had gone completely numb. What was the appropriate reaction? To run out screaming?

She didn't. She only put her arm round Luke's shoulders and held him close as if to protect him.

And while half of her was terrified, the other half was telling her that it couldn't possibly be true. She couldn't bear it to be true, because she so wanted to stay and see the cats!

But perhaps it was too late. Rhianwen had already cast her spell, and they hadn't known. Who knew what potions she'd put in the food and drink? And what about the dark brew she'd given Luke and the ointment she'd rubbed on his skin?

She remembered the witch in the forbidden book, luring the children with Turkish delight and kindness.

'Oh dear,' said Rhianwen. 'What have they told you about me? Nothing good, obviously.'

'Mum said we weren't to come here,' said Beth, hanging her head.

'Well, you didn't come on purpose, did you?' Rhianwen said sadly. 'You weren't to know, so it's not your fault. I won't tell anyone. Come on, finish your lemonade.'

Luke didn't touch his. But Beth thought, it's too late anyway. She thought of Jesus, seeing her disobedience and forsaking her. Jesus won't help me now, she thought.

She raised the glass to her lips and drank.

Luke was fidgeting beside her as if he needed the toilet. His forehead was furrowed with distress.

'Bethie, we've got to go,' he whined. 'Bethie.'

'I wish you wouldn't go,' said Rhianwen. 'You don't have to hate me, just because your mother does. Did she tell you I was a witch?'

Beth froze. 'Are you?' she whispered.

'Not really. Well, sort of, but it doesn't mean what you –'

Luke suddenly wriggled off the sofa and stood up, animated by absolute terror.

'You're a witch!' he screamed, turning scarlet. 'Bloody – bloody – You copulate with the Devil!'

He span away and rushed to a door with a diamond-shaped window that looked on to the front garden. He wrenched it open and was away down the front path before Beth could stop him.

'He doesn't know what copulate means,' Beth said apologetically, compelled to be polite even to a witch. 'I'll have to go after him.'

She was on her feet and so was Rhianwen, facing her – but not cackling or cavorting or trying to imprison her.

'I suppose you must, but try to tell him . . . Look, Beth, I want you to understand. Your mother doesn't like me so she's tried to turn you against me, that's all. Will you come back and see me tomorrow, so I can explain? I'm not evil, whatever Olivia said. I can't make you believe it just by saying it, but . . . you won't get struck by lightning, I promise. Please? To see the cats, anyway?'

Beth hesitated, confused. Olivia had drilled it into them that the servants of Satan would sound utterly plausible when they tricked you into sin. But you couldn't believe a word they said! It was all deceit, all.

'Have you cast a spell on us?' Beth asked softly. Maybe she could uncover the truth by making the witch admit something.

'Of course not.'

'What was the stuff you made Luke drink?'

'Camomile tea and honey. Nothing sinister.'

'But what was in that ointment you put on him?'

'I've no idea,' Rhianwen said flatly. 'I bought it from Boots.'

They stared at each other. They were like sisters and enemies, bonded from the very first encounter. The golden-eyed cat wound round Beth's legs, purring.

'You'd better go after your brother,' said the witch. 'But tomorrow, Beth?'

She swallowed hard and heard herself saying, 'All right.'

Perhaps there was something in Beth that wanted to sin.

Chapter Three

LUKE ran.

He had never felt so terrified in his life, not even when his mother had that look in her eye and the belt in her hand. He knew what to expect then. But the witch was the edge of chaos.

Twenty yards along the lane he stopped and waited for Beth. He daren't go any further without her.

He'd almost wet himself again. He was in such misery he didn't know what to do. He had no clear thoughts. His mind was a whirl of confusion and terror, his eyes and nose thick with tears.

Then Beth appeared, striding towards him. Luke couldn't get used to seeing her in jeans, but she looked calm. Not scared. The mist cleared from his eyes and he began to feel better.

'I thought she'd got you!' cried Luke. He felt guilty for not going back to save her, and that made him resentful that she didn't seem frightened.

'Come on,' said Beth, taking his hand.

They walked in silence along the narrow lane between tall thick hedges, Beth in one of the vehicle ruts, Luke on the raised grass strip between them. They held hands tightly. It was better now she was there but he still felt bad.

At the end, where the lane gave on to a proper road, they saw the sign: Farm Lane.

'We weren't to know,' said Beth.

'What are we going to do?' Luke asked, wiping his eyes.

'Pray,' she said. She clasped Luke's hands between her own and they prayed. 'Dear Jesus, please forgive us for speaking to the witch. We didn't mean it. We didn't know. Please forgive us our trespasses, thank you Lord, Amen.'

They walked on, and found themselves in the far end of the village, near the church. Horse chestnut trees and copper beeches shaded the village green.

'Will God listen?' Luke asked anxiously.

'Of course he will.'

'But we broke our promise to Mum. We broke a vow we made on the Bible.' Luke thought of the terrible threats their mother had made. His fear of sin and damnation was formless but overpowering. 'I'm scared,' he said, and started to cry again.

'Don't, or you'll have red eyes when we get home.' Beth spoke reassuringly. 'She wasn't nasty to us. She didn't curse us. Grandma said she hated children, but she helped you, didn't she?'

'When she touched me the pain went away, like magic,' said Luke, panicking, 'so that proves she's a witch! I'm going to tell Granddad.'

Beth looked horrified. 'Oh, no you're not! We mustn't tell *anyone* about this, Luke. Jesus will forgive us but Mum will go *mad*.'

Luke felt angry suddenly. He didn't know why, but being frightened made him want to lash out. He glared sideways at Beth, his eyebrows drawn down. 'I'm going to tell,' he insisted.

But when they reached their grandparents' home, Luke found he couldn't say a word to contradict Beth's story. She was all he had. She was always there when he was upset, his shield against a cruel world; so how could he tell on her?

But he hated being so helpless. Hated it.

We went for a walk, Beth told Heather over tea. Luke got stung but he's all right now. We played in the fields. No, we didn't see anyone much.

Luke saw that Beth had her fingers crossed behind her back.

He hated it when she told lies, too.

When Beth woke the next day, she remembered that she was going to visit Rhianwen again, and she broke into a shivery sweat. Yesterday had been an accident, but to go again would be deliberately to break a sacred vow to God. But she was going to do it anyway. That was why she couldn't stop shaking.

Luke was a problem. If only she could slip away on her own! But she couldn't, it was her job to look after him, and they weren't allowed out separately. A more selfish sister might have 'lost' him somewhere, but Beth's sense of responsibility wouldn't let her. Luke, she felt, suffered enough without being abandoned by his sister.

If he makes a big fuss again, she thought, I don't know what I'll do. I love him but he's an awful nuisance sometimes.

And she longed instead for a friend. Someone like Rhianwen?

Beth didn't know what was possessing her to go completely against her mother's commands. She was risking going to hell; why?

Part of it was exactly as Heather had said. Forbid the children to do something and it's the first thing they'll want to do!

Beth wondered how far she could go before a thunderbolt from God struck her down.

That afternoon, after lunch, she came close to losing her nerve. She led Luke through the village, along the public footpath and across the fields, but her legs were trembling and she was thinking, I can't do it, I've changed my mind.

Luke wanted to go a different way, so she went along with him for a while. The day was sunny, the fields golden and clouded with insects. We're not going to Mrs Rhys's, she told herself. We're not doing anything wrong.

But somehow, by a more tortuous route, they found themselves in the meadow with the goats again. Approaching Rhianwen's cottage from the back didn't seem so much of a sin as blatantly walking up the lane to the front door. As if it could be an accident, again.

'Oh no,' said Luke. 'I might get stung again.'

'Don't be silly, wasps are everywhere.'

He stopped, but Beth kept walking along the hedge. Her knees were weak but she was in a kind of trance. Yes, I'm going to do it.

'You're not going *there* again, are you, Bethie?' Luke's voice was high and breathless. 'Bethie?'

She didn't answer. He came running after her and hung on her arm.

'You aren't, are you?' he cried. 'You can't, you can't! You know what Mum said! You only get forgiven if you stop sinning! *Beth!*' He sounded desperate, but she shut her ears. 'I'll tell on you, I'll tell!'

'Stop being such a baby!' Beth snapped, infuriated. She had never lost her temper with him before. Good girls were not meant to have a temper. 'You're coming with me and you'd better behave yourself this time!'

'But *why* are you going? *Why?*'

Even if she'd been able to articulate a reason, Luke wouldn't have understood. Yet God put an answer in her mouth. 'Why do we go out in town centres on a Saturday and try to get people to come to church?'

'To save their souls.'

'Well, if Mum's right, and Rhianwen's really a witch, it's our duty to save her soul.'

Luke went quiet and trailed behind her, so close he kept treading on her heels. She could hear his nervous, adenoidal breathing.

They found Rhianwen in the back garden, walking across the lawn towards the mysterious cages. She was wearing a long skirt of maroon brushed cotton and a cream kaftan.

'Hello,' she said brightly. 'Come to see the cats, have you? Come on.' And she seemed so nice, so pleased to see them, that Beth couldn't understand why she'd been afraid.

There were two long sheds in an L-shape, fronted with chicken wire, in which were tiers of large wooden cages. A few were empty, but most had occupants. There were two little tabbies like twins, a fat ginger tom, a sad-looking white and tortoiseshell curled up in a basket, a mother with three exquisite kittens, black, white and grey.

Beth was particularly entranced by the grey kitten, with its huge round eyes and adventurous temperament. Rhianwen opened the door and put the kitten in Beth's hands. She was in love.

Luke was poking his fingers into the cages.

'Don't do that, you might startle them and get scratched,' Rhianwen said mildly. 'If you want to stroke one I'll take it out.'

Luke blinked at her. He wasn't used to being spoken to so kindly.

'Are they all yours?' Beth asked.

Rhianwen laughed; she was merry, not mocking. 'Oh no, dear. I wish I could keep them but they'd eat me out of house and home. Didn't you see the sign on the gate when you left yesterday? This is a cat sanctuary. I take in strays and try to find new homes for them. Some I end up keeping because I can't bear to part with them. I'd let them all live in the house if I could but there're too many. And some of them have been ill and need to be quiet. The other shed's a cattery; I look after them while their owners are on holiday. Busy time of year, this. I never get away, but I'd rather do this than anything.'

One by one, she brought the cats out for them to stroke. 'People come from all over the place to bring me cats or to offer them a home. Such nice people. I look after other animals, as well; I've had foxes, ferrets, all sorts. Just got the hedgehogs and the owl at the moment. When they're better, I'll release them in the right habitat.'

'May we see?' Luke asked. To Beth's relief he seemed enraptured, all his misgivings forgotten.

There was a separate shed, half hidden behind a viburnum, next to the cat sheds. In the half-darkness, the children stroked the rough brown prickles of the hedgehogs and the fluffed-up feathers of a large, indignant-looking baby owl.

'So you make them better and let them go?' asked Luke.

'That's right. Fancy a picnic on the lawn? I've got cakes. Proper ones from the shop, this time. Don't taste as good but at least they don't look like an explosion in a mud factory.'

The three of them sat companionably on the grass in front of the cat-cages. Rhianwen was fun, making them laugh. Beth forgot – temporarily at least – all Olivia's and Heather's warnings.

When Luke began to fidget and look around, Rhianwen disappeared and came back with a bicycle.

'Can you ride a bike?' she asked.

'Yes, I learned at school,' said Luke.

'Well, would you like a go on this? It's Morgan's but he's outgrown it. You can ride on the paths, but keep off the flower-beds, there's a love.'

Luke appeared dumbfounded. He'd never possessed a bi-cycle of his own. What he usually received, in return for fidget-ing, was a beating.

While Luke amused himself with the bike, Beth had Rhian-wen to herself. Two cats came to join them: the slender grey Beth had met the previous day, and a huge, long-haired black and white tom, the biggest cat Beth had ever seen. 'What are they called?' she asked.

'The big one is Llew, which means lion, and the little one is Ankaret – Much-loved, which she is. Names are very impor-tant, I think.'

'My mum does, too.' Beth added impulsively, 'I wish I was called something different. I hate my name.'

'Elizabeth, is it?'

'No, it's Bethia. It's Hebrew, Mum says, and it means daugh-ter of Jehovah. But nobody's ever heard of it, so they think I'm making it up.'

'Ah,' said Rhianwen. 'But it's better to have an unusual name than a boring one.'

'I suppose so. The people at church say it's special.'

'Do you go to church a lot?'

'All the time.' Beth picked at a daisy in the grass.

'And what do you think of it?'

Beth didn't know how to answer. If her mother or father or Pastor Blair asked such a question, it had to be answered with joyful enthusiasm. But Rhianwen was different.

Rhianwen belonged to the other side.

Fortunately, Beth was saved from having to reply. A car had

pulled up by the front hedge and a small middle-aged woman with flyaway white hair appeared round the side of the cottage, carrying a basket.

'Oh, Mrs Rhys, can you help me?' she cried. 'It's Tim.' She came hurrying over and set the basket down on the grass. 'He can hardly walk,' she said tearfully. 'The vet wants to put him down. I know he's getting on, but I can't bear the thought.'

'Let's see.'

Rhianwen opened the basket and lifted out a big tortoise-shell cat. His back legs looked stiff, half paralysed.

'All right, Tim, come on,' said Rhianwen, gently examining the animal. 'Arthritis.'

Rhianwen sat down on the grass and held the cat on her lap, talking softly to it in a language Beth couldn't make out. Welsh, probably. She stroked the cat all over, pressed her fingers into its hips, then gripped the back limbs and stretched them out, one at a time.

The cat made a noise between a miaow and a purr.

Both Rhianwen and the cat seemed to have slipped into their own, private world.

After five minutes or so, Rhianwen set the cat on the grass. He stood up and yawned; he stretched languidly, front legs then back legs; walked a few paces then sat down, stuck one hind leg in the air, and began to wash himself. His owner was overcome.

'Oh, I don't know how to thank you!'

'A contribution to the sanctuary would be very welcome,' said Rhianwen, smiling. 'If he stiffens up again, bring him back. He might need regular treatment.'

When the overjoyed woman had gone, Beth said, 'How did you do that? Was it . . . magic?'

'Manipulation. I have a feel for it, see.'

Beth wasn't sure what manipulation was. She still thought it was magic. 'Can you heal people, too?'

'I only do animals. Otherwise I'd be trespassing on Dr Cross's territory, wouldn't I? It wouldn't do for the villagers to come to me instead of a proper doctor.' Rhianwen sounded

31

strange, and there was something in her eyes; secrets hidden in still green ponds. Beth became nervous.

'You healed Luke.'

'That was only first aid.'

'The Pastor says people can only do miracles if the Holy Spirit is working through them. Otherwise it's witchcraft.'

'There are no miracles in what I do. Only common sense. What exactly has your mother told you about me?'

Beth looked down. The habit of telling the truth died hard. 'That you – you were a witch, and you'd cast spells on us and drink our blood, and if we spoke to you we'd go to hell.'

Rhianwen gave a softly articulated *Ohh* of consternation. 'Beth, I know I've no right to say bad things about your mother, but you know that isn't true, don't you? You're not a little girl, you're almost a teenager. You can think for yourself.'

'You mean Mum's a liar?'

'No, I think she probably believes most of what she told you – but that doesn't make it true.'

'So you aren't a witch?'

'There are different kinds of truth.'

Rhianwen spoke in riddles, but at least she treated Beth like an adult.

'So why *does* Mum hate you?'

Rhianwen sighed. 'People fall out. It was an awful long time ago, before you were born. We used to be friends, believe it or not. We were in our twenties; Olivia was still living with her parents and I'd just moved here from Wales with my husband. I knew she went to church and she knew I didn't; it was okay. But then,' Rhianwen seemed to be choosing her words, 'she had some kind of problem, so she turned to this new church and your Pastor Blair for help, and she completely changed. It's a shame. I really liked her, until she got religion.'

Beth frowned, offended. 'It's not a disease! She was blessed by the Holy Spirit! That's what the Pastor says.'

'Whatever, we didn't see eye to eye about things any more. I tried to talk her out of it; big mistake. Your mother believes that people outside her church are going to hell, doesn't she?'

'They will, if they haven't been Saved,' Beth said emphatically.

'Well, I don't even believe in God, so she thinks I worship the Devil.'

Beth could hardly bear to ask. 'Do you?'

'Dear, I don't even *believe* in the Devil, so how could I possibly worship him?'

'He can still possess you!'

'Oh, can he?'

Rhianwen sounded so cynically confident that Beth didn't know what to say. Without stopping to think, she asked. 'Why does my Granny hate you too? She called you a –' Beth stopped, turning hot with embarrassment.

'I can imagine,' said Rhianwen, unmoved. 'It's just one of those family things. She takes your mother's side against me. She thinks I'm not respectable like her. But I'm harmless, honest, Beth. There's no need for you and me to be enemies, is there?'

Beth felt sudden tears choking her. 'You've got to tell Jesus you repent. Then it will be all right.'

'Why should I?'

'Because I don't want you to go to hell, Rhianwen. I don't.'

Rhianwen took Beth's hand and gripped it, seeming half way between laughter and tears. 'That's so sweet of you, dear. But you have your beliefs and I have mine; let's leave it at that, shall we?'

'The problem Mum had,' said Beth. 'What was it?'

'I don't know, love. People always have problems; some seem worse than others. Now I think you'd better find your brother and be off home, don't you?'

'All right.' Beth got up to leave, then said, 'You know that cat-person in the picture over your fireplace? Who is she?'

'Why do you want to know?'

'She looks interesting.'

Rhianwen gave her a strange, soft look. 'Well, she's an Egyptian cat-goddess and her name is Bast.'

'Is she, you know, for witches?'

33

'She's nothing to do with the Devil, if that's what you think. Bast is an aspect of the Great Goddess, in one of her many forms. The Egyptians revered the cat as an animal of the sun and the moon, and of nature. So Bast is an earth goddess, a bringer of life and fruitfulness. She's meant to protect women in childbirth. But she also reminds us to be playful, instinctive, graceful and independent, like a cat. She reminds us of our connection to nature. She's a goddess of joy. That's why she's my favourite.'

'Oh,' said Beth, dumbfounded.

'I painted it, by the way.' Then Rhianwen clasped her arms over her waist, seeming to shut Beth out. 'Look, it's not fair of me to make you disobey your mother. If you don't want to visit me again, I'll understand.'

'Don't you want me to come?' Beth was hurt, confused.

'Of course I do.' Rhianwen stroked her shoulder. 'I don't want you to get into trouble, that's all.'

At the gate in the front hedge, Beth turned to look at the sign: Blackthorn Cottage. Cat Sanctuary and Boarding Cattery.

For the second time, Luke and Beth guiltily left Rhianwen's house, and again God failed to strike them down.

Beth had a dream of cats that night. Beautiful grey cats like Ankaret, with huge golden eyes. They sat on the far side of a river, reflected like statues in the mirror-perfect surface, enticing Beth to cross over.

Come to us. Join us. Lovely here they purred seductively.

Beth put her foot in the water . . .

And woke with the wildest feelings of excitement, terror, and guilt. She had no idea what was happening to her. But she knew it was very, very wrong.

Beth knew a saying that meant if you had committed a small sin, you might as well commit a big one; you were going to be hanged anyway. So she and Luke went on visiting Rhianwen in secret, two or three times a week. All summer long.

Holy lightning didn't strike them once.

34

Although Luke had a wonderful time once he was there, he never wanted to go. Fear seemed to grip him, especially if their parents had rung up the previous day to check on them. Anxiety plagued Beth too, but it added a delicious edge to the excitement of having a forbidden friend. Nothing short of discovery would stop her now.

It was a strange reversal of roles. Luke had always been the naughty one, Beth as good as gold. But now it was Beth who set off along the path of damnation while Luke tagged nervously behind, constantly threatening to tell but never daring to do so.

After a while his threats became half-hearted, a mere habit, perhaps so he could say to God or Olivia, 'I didn't want to go but Beth made me!'

Heather showed no sign of suspicion about their long walks. 'Do you good, plenty of fresh air. Much healthier than sitting inside reading.'

Although Beth loved her grandparents, it was plain that they weren't used to having children around. They were relentlessly busy. Randolph was kind but rarely spent any time with them; if he sat down with Luke to watch sport on the television, he would usually be called away. Heather was good-natured but brusque, not really on a child's wavelength. Although Beth loved helping with the horses, it wasn't the same as having a real friend. Rhianwen, though, was friend, sister and mother all in one. A mother Beth could only have dreamed of.

Dreams. Beth's night visits from the cats grew more insistent.

She would be happy for days. Then, without warning, the guilt would dig its talons into her so hard she couldn't pray.

What could Rhianwen believe in, if not God?

At church, it was simple; all the answers to life were in the Bible. But Rhianwen's answers were different. They were never what Beth expected. Sometimes she didn't understand.

Even though Rhianwen wasn't Saved, Beth was convinced she wasn't evil. Her mother had been wrong about that – so Olivia *could* be wrong about things.

Beth began to wonder what other things she might have got wrong.

Like thrashing Luke. Mentioning Luke's bruises to her grand-dad would have been tantamount to suggesting that their mother was fallible, so Beth had kept her mouth shut. Impossible dilemma. Beth felt she was true to her birthsign, Gemini; always in two minds. But her mother said that horoscopes, too, were Satanic.

Rhianwen wouldn't explain precisely what she believed in instead of God. Apparently it was private. Strange and mysterious, it seemed to Beth, to keep a belief to yourself and not try to convert others!

'One day,' Rhianwen said. 'When you're older. If you're ready to understand. It would cause too many problems with your family if I told you now. Believe me.'

Luke, too, dreamed of cats; ones in cages.

He never wanted to go to Rhianwen's, even though he loved it when he was there. He was still afraid. There would be retribution any day now, and it would be terrible. He liked being there, but it was always Beth's decision to go, not his. He had no power. He wanted to make her stop but she wouldn't.

And then he hated Beth and Rhianwen a little, for making him like it so much.

Beth made me.

The cats made him feel funny. Cats had been witches' familiars in the old days, he'd read it somewhere, and he knew for certain that Rhianwen was exactly what his mother had said. She hid it, that was all.

A witch who tempted him with lemonade, cake and bicycles.

He enjoyed playing with the cats, too. He liked to make them flatten their ears and hiss at him; that meant they were scared.

Luke knew what it was like to be scared. So to frighten another living thing – that made him feel powerful. It made him feel as if he actually existed.

*

Every other day, Heather would take Beth out riding. Luke wasn't keen on horses, but he seemed happy to mess about in the garden. Beth, still inexperienced and nervous, thought Grandma expected too much of her sometimes. Luckily the dark bay, Whisky, was a smooth ride or she would have fallen off a dozen times instead of once or twice. Ginger Star, the chestnut Heather rode, was bouncy and hot-headed.

The summer seemed to go on for ever. It was only towards the end of the holiday that Beth realized, with dismay, that there were only a few days left before their father came to pick them up. Days. She thought in a kind of panic, will we ever be allowed to stay here again?

Beth had thought she was happy at home, because she'd never known anything else. But now their return loomed like a prison sentence. Luke felt it too. He became moody and badly behaved. Without physical discipline, he didn't seem to know when to stop.

At Rhianwen's, though, he calmed down, as if he felt safe there. So Beth felt bad for wishing she could have Rhianwen to herself.

One afternoon, Heather took Beth for a ride through the fields near Rhianwen's cottage. The sky was overcast, pregnant with rain. A humid breeze blew in their faces. And Beth felt miserable, because there were only two days left.

They were cantering sedately alongside a hedgerow. As they rounded a bend, Beth saw a boy walking along the bridle path a few yards ahead, with his back to them. She expected Heather to slow down; instead, to Beth's shock, she kicked Ginger Star harder and charged straight at the child.

Whisky leapt after his companion and Beth couldn't control him. She was suddenly breathless with fear, aware of the horse's massive strength and her own helplessness. She could only hang helplessly on to the martingale, praying he would slow down before she fell off.

'*Gooarn!*' Heather roared, whether at her horse or at the boy, Beth wasn't sure.

The boy was forced to jump out of the way as the two

horses thundered through. Beth caught a brief glimpse of his face as she was carried past him. He looked grim rather than shocked, as if it had happened before.

Fifty yards further on, Heather slowed to a trot. By that time, Beth was hanging on to the front of the saddle, shaken and trembling. She looked round, but there was no sign of the boy.

'Grandma, didn't you see him?' she cried.

'I saw him,' Heather said abruptly.

'Why didn't you stop?'

'S'bridle path, not a footpath,' Heather growled under her breath. 'Bloody people. Bloody hippies. Degenerates. Ought to be put down.'

'Who was it?'

No reply. All Heather said was, 'Sit down in the saddle, Beth. Heels down, hands down. Otherwise you'll come straight off if the unexpected happens.'

The next day, Beth and Luke went to Rhianwen's for the last time, to say goodbye.

There had been a storm in the night. Now the sun was peeping through and the world glistened silver. The hedges around the garden, the shrubs, the weeping trees and climbing plants, all were lush with rain.

When Beth and Luke slipped through the gate into Rhianwen's garden, he was there.

The boy her grandmother had almost ridden down the previous day.

He stood looking at them, a barrier between them and Rhianwen, as if he owned the place. Beth's heart faltered. His eyes, too, were green and he looked through her as if he thought she had tried to kill him.

He was dark, like Rhianwen, but there was no red in his hair. And he was very good-looking. Beth could see that, even though she wasn't meant to be aware of boys' looks. His hair was almost down to his shoulders and he wore black jeans and a white cheesecloth shirt, but he looked nothing like a 'degenerate hippie' or whatever Heather had called him. He was tall and slender, and he looked placid and very sure of himself. Next to him, Luke seemed a stocky, awkward little boy.

The sun blazed suddenly behind him and he became a silhouette half seen in the silver glare, black as an arrow tip.

He was like a cat, as elegant as Ankaret, but black instead of grey. Beth went dizzy, seeing the cats in her dreams. Cats that were really people, as poised as goddesses, but still, secretly, afraid of water.

No, she was the cat and he was her reflection in the water. *He* was the water, danger. And if she went a step closer to the edge she would fall in and slip down into the darkness.

Beth could feel the water all around her. Cold. Silvery bubbles trapped in her fur. She couldn't breathe.

'Hello,' he said. 'I'm Morgan.'

Chapter Four

'OH, you've met Morgan, have you?' said Rhianwen, appearing with Ankaret in her arms.

'We came to say goodbye,' Beth said nervously. 'We go back to school on Wednesday.'

'Me too,' said Morgan. He only had a trace of his mother's accent but it was still there; a charming inflexion. 'It's a bore, isn't it?'

Beth felt acutely shy, dazzled. 'Yes. I'd rather stay here.'

'And practise your horse-riding?' he said sarcastically. 'Learn to steer, you might get me next time.'

Rhianwen frowned at him, as if to say, *Don't*. Beth was mortified. She felt her face turning bright red. 'I'm really sorry. It was my gran. I don't know why she –'

'It's all right.' Morgan sounded amused. 'I know it wasn't your fault. It's a sort of village tradition, Mrs Cross trying to cull the peasants.'

When she looked up, he was grinning. It was the most beautiful and wicked smile she had ever seen.

'You don't have to rush off, do you?' Rhianwen turned to her son. 'Why don't you take Luke for a walk? It'll do him good to have someone to play with. You'll be companions for each other.'

Beth was relieved. This was perfect! She would have Rhianwen to herself for the last afternoon, with Luke and this intimidating young man out of the way.

'Okay,' Morgan said indifferently.

She thought Luke would be happy to go, but a change came over him. His chin went up and his eyes glittered. He came close to Beth, almost hiding behind her. 'I don't want to.'

'Don't be silly,' said Beth. 'Look, it's your last chance to go off and explore without me! You don't want your big sister with you all the time, do you?'

Luke clung stubbornly to her. 'No, I'm not going.'

Morgan shrugged. 'We can stay here. Makes no difference to me.'

Beth could have strangled Luke. She desperately wanted him and Morgan to make friends. The thought of having to spend any more time with Morgan around made her panic. 'Actually, we ought to be going. We just came to say goodbye, really, and thank you for letting us visit.'

Rhianwen looked disappointed, but Morgan appeared not to care either way. 'Oh, well, if you must,' said Rhianwen, letting Ankaret down on to the grass. 'I'm so glad we got to know each other. It will be lovely when you come next summer. Morgan and Luke will be company for each other. Won't you, boys?'

The boys didn't reply. Luke looked sulkily in the other direction. Beth sensed that Rhianwen had always wanted Luke out of the way so she could have Beth to herself. Beth wanted it too. But Rhianwen, being kind, wanted to manage things so everyone was happy.

'I don't know whether we'll be allowed to stay with Grandma again,' Beth said, feeling embarrassed.

'Why wouldn't you be allowed to stay with your gran?' Morgan asked in amazement.

'Mum prefers us to be helping out at church. We only came this year because she's been ill.'

Morgan stared at her with a kind of baffled pity. Beth resented the look. What did he know, anyway?

Rhianwen put her hand on Beth's shoulder. 'Come and see the cats before you go.'

Beth went eagerly, with Luke on her heels and Morgan following at his own pace. Rhianwen let them through the doors into the wire-fronted shed, opened a cage and took out a smaller version of Ankaret.

It was the grey kitten Beth had fallen in love with, the second time they'd come here. It was bigger now, with fur like

41

slate-blue silk and hypnotic, gold eyes. 'Would you like a cat, Beth?' asked Rhianwen.

Beth was moved to tears. 'I'd love one, but I don't think Mum would let me. The hairs and that. She's very house-proud. And she'd want to know where I got it. I'm sorry, I can't.'

The kitten purred as she caressed it, its warm body vibrating. Beth was concentrating hard on not crying in front of Morgan. He began to stroke the kitten too, and his fingers, sliding through the fur, touched hers. Beth quickly withdrew her hand.

'I know,' said Rhianwen. 'I meant I'll keep her here for you. Then you can come and visit. As soon as you're old enough to make up your own mind, you can have her; until then she can live in the house with me.'

'So you've got to come back,' said Morgan. 'It's like a binding spell. Witches are good at that.'

'Morgan!' said Rhianwen.

'I was only joking!'

'Well, don't. Some people don't think it's funny.' Rhianwen tilted her head towards Luke, who had his back to them and was staring out through the wire, arms folded. Beth wasn't sure whether he was sulking or genuinely upset by Morgan. 'So, d'you want me to keep her for you, Beth?'

'Oh, yes, please, it would be lovely,' Beth said, overjoyed. 'May I call her Bast, after your goddess?'

'Of course you can.'

'If you don't mind the nickname,' said Morgan. 'Little Bast –'

Rhianwen looked at him and shook her head. 'I'll lock you in with the cats if you don't shut up.' She replaced the kitten and ushered them out into the garden. Luke clutched Beth's hand, tugging gently to say, *Let's go.*

'Take care of yourselves,' said Rhianwen.

Morgan looked straight into Beth's eyes and she felt a lightning flicker through her nerves. 'I hope you can come next year.' He was talking only to her, not to Luke.

'So do I.' But next summer was a lifetime away.

'Can I write to you, Beth?'

'No!' she cried, alarmed. 'No, you can't. Mum would go mad if I had letters from a boy.'

Gripping Luke's hand, she began to pull him away towards the back gate into the field. She looked back once, to see them waving solemnly; two slim figures with cats around their feet, outlined by shimmering, watery sunlight, blurred by Beth's tears.

She was afraid she would never see them again, and even more terrified that she would.

'They've been angels,' Heather said, exaggerating slightly, when Philip came to collect the children. '*Do* persuade Livvy to let them stay again.'

'I'll do my best.' Philip sighed. 'You know how stubborn she can be. However, I think she rather enjoyed being without them. Meant she could spend even more time at church.'

There were no kisses and cuddles goodbye; they were not a demonstrative family. Emotion embarrassed them. But for all her grandparents' briskness, Beth had felt safe here. Loved. She felt loved at church, but that was different, like being smothered.

As the children climbed into the back of their father's brown Rover, Beth heard Randolph say to Philip, 'Can I have a word?'

They stood on the drive in a huddle with Heather, but Beth wound the window down an inch and listened. '. . . noticed some bruising on Luke's back shortly after they arrived,' Randolph was saying. 'Any idea how it got there?'

Their father's expression, behind the shining lenses, was unreadable. He clasped his hands in front, as if he were in church. 'The boy is always in the wars playing sports at school. I used to be permanently black and blue from rugby; weren't you?'

'I suppose so,' said Randolph. 'Just thought I ought to check.'

'Thanks,' said Philip. 'I appreciate it.'

Beth and Luke looked at each other.

'Bethie, I don't want to go home,' he said pitifully.

'Listen,' she whispered. 'Once we're home, we never mention you-know-who, all right? It never happened. Don't be frightened, nobody knows. We got away with it.'

'God will have seen what we were doing, though,' said Luke.

'Then we'll pray for forgiveness!'

'It doesn't work, if you know it's wrong and you keep on doing it!'

'All right. It's my fault, not yours, anyway.' She caught his hand. 'Pray with me: Almighty God, if you think we've been really bad, send us a sign, Amen! Now if nothing happens, we'll know God isn't angry.'

'You can't make bargains with God,' said Luke, jerking his hand away.

'All right in the back?' Philip said cheerfully as he got in.

'Yes, thank you,' they chorused.

Beth said, 'Did you miss us?'

'Of course we did. I hope you've been as good as your grandma says.'

'We tried,' said Beth.

No. We went to the witch's house, again and again and again.

Beth looked back at the rectory, her grandparents smiling and waving; watched Lullingford dwindling and disappearing behind a swathe of green fields. How she was going to get through the year, she had no idea.

The fields dissolved into main roads, factories and shops. There were traffic jams, people surging along the pavements, handsome old buildings and squalid warehouses side by side. And, at last, a long straight road of red-brick houses.

They were home; a big, semi-detached Victorian villa, ten minutes' walk from their school and seven minutes from church. The smell hit Beth as Philip opened the front door; polish mostly, mixed with old paint and cooking. Beth felt homesick for the smell of saddle soap and dogs; oh, and for joss sticks and burned biscuits at Rhianwen's. The pristine interior, with white embossed wallpaper, gold carpets and old-fashioned furniture with brocade and fringes, stifled her.

Their mother came sedately to meet them, in a flowery dress. She hugged and kissed them, stroking their faces and looking into their eyes as if for signs of spiritual pollution. She looked well, Beth noticed. Her colour had come back and she'd put on a little weight, though she was naturally thin.

'I missed you both so much,' she said with feeling. 'I hope you were good. Did you read your Bible? Oh, Luke, look at your fingernails! Go and wash. Beth, you can help me make tea. It was such a nuisance not having you to help around the house.'

Olivia was in a good mood. Beth and Luke exchanged a speaking look: *It's all right.* They could sometimes make her laugh, when she was like this.

That made the first few days bearable, if depressing. Morning prayers, school, Bible study, church, homework, chores, prayers, bed; the usual routine. Beth prayed the good humour would last, even though she knew from experience it wasn't likely.

One afternoon, when the children had been back at school a week, they came home to find that their mother's mood had changed. She seemed withdrawn and lethargic, and she looked straight through them when they spoke to her as if she couldn't understand what they were saying. Beth knew this was a warning sign. She felt sick with apprehension. The danger would last only until their father came home at about six, because Olivia never beat them in front of him.

Beth tiptoed around, trying to be extra helpful and to prevent Luke from doing anything provocative. Their mother's brooding tension lay on the whole house.

Luke felt it. He shadowed Beth, pestering her to distraction. But Beth daren't tell him off for fear of attracting Olivia's attention.

If nothing made her snap, they might get through this without incident. Beth checked her watch. Time for Bible study. A whole hour until their father came home.

'Mum, do you want me to get the Bibles ready?' she asked tremulously, standing in the doorway to the kitchen with Luke behind her.

Olivia, who was putting away crockery and obsessively cleaning the worktops, turned and glared at Beth with a hand pressed over her left temple.

Beth quailed, but her mother only said, 'Actually, I'm going to lie down. I've a dreadful headache. Read Hebrews tonight; I've marked the place. "My son, despise not thou the chastening of the Lord, nor faint when thou art rebuked of him: For whom the Lord loveth he chasteneth, and scourgeth every son whom he receiveth . . . for what son is he whom the father chasteneth not?" '

'Yes, Mum,' said Beth.

'Then you can make your father's tea. Do a fish pie.'

After she'd gone upstairs, Beth and Luke giggled soundlessly and punched each other with sheer, exuberant relief.

'She'll probably be better tomorrow,' said Beth. 'I think it's all right!'

They sat down to read.

'Luke,' said a voice from the hall, dull-cold like brass.

Beth turned sick with terror. They went sheepishly into the hall.

Their mother was at the top of the stairs, with a paperback book in her hand and the fires of hell in her face. Beth recognized her copy of *The Lion, the Witch and the Wardrobe*. She cringed; she thought she'd hidden it well enough under her mattress.

'Luke,' Olivia said thinly. 'I found this in your room.'

Then Beth realized that Luke must have found it and taken it. He knew her hiding places and he'd borrowed things from her room before; she'd asked him not to, but he still did it.

'Who gave you permission to read this?'

'No one,' he mumbled.

'No one. Come here.'

Luke, pallid and shaking, began to mount the stairs. He knew there was no point in resisting. Horrified, Beth ran up ahead of him. 'Mum, it's my book! I put it in his room. Punish me, not him!'

46

'It's no good trying to protect him.'

'Mum, it's a Christian book,' Beth said desperately.

'You mean the lion? It's blasphemy. To represent Christ as an animal is an abomination!' She ripped the book into pieces and threw it all over the hall. Beth nearly wept. 'Go downstairs, Beth. Luke, fetch the strap.'

Curled up on the sofa, with her head buried in a cushion, Beth could still hear the blows and the pitiful cries. This happened most weeks and it never grew any easier. Misery, terror, and the horrible dusty taste of the cushion in her mouth.

And having to be all normal and cheerful when her father came home from work. And her mother going into a frenzy of dusting and polishing afterwards, singing hymns, energized and cheerful now her terrible tensions had been released.

And Beth trying to comfort Luke in secret, without being able to hug him, because of his bruises – and for fear of committing some mysterious, unclean sin. Beth, clutching the cushion, knew everything to expect.

Olivia thrashed Beth occasionally, but Luke was the main target of her wrath. Beth wasn't sure why. Something to do with males being wicked, filthy beasts, even worse than women, if that were possible.

Beth would have given her life to protect Luke from this. She hated herself for failing.

When she heard her mother coming downstairs, she shot into the kitchen and frantically started fetching saucepans out. She could hear Luke crying very faintly upstairs, but Olivia looked fulfilled and radiant.

'Did you read the passage, Bethia? "Now no chastening for the present seemeth to be joyous, but grievous: nevertheless afterward it yieldeth the peaceable fruit of righteousness unto them which are exercised thereby." I hope you will remember that. Pass me the duster and the polish.'

'Yes, Mum.'

Welcome home.

*

47

Well, thought Beth, I asked God for a sign, and that must have been it, even though it was nothing new. God *is* angry. If only Mum knew what we've really been doing!

Flooded with remorse and guilt, Beth tried to be a good girl all year. She prayed fervently and did everything she was told. Pastor Blair and her parents were pleased with her and said she was blessed.

School was boring. Beth had no close friends there. She hung around with a group of other misfits, but she didn't have much in common even with them. She couldn't talk about television because her parents didn't possess one; she couldn't discuss pop music or films, magazines or books. She had nothing to say about boys. She would have liked to talk about deeper things to someone, but no one was interested. She was a good listener, so girls would confide in her; that was nice, but she didn't feel close to anyone. It was largely her own fault. She kept herself apart, and bullies had ceased picking on her years ago because she had learned to affect a chilling dignity. But it meant there was no one she could tell about Rhianwen.

She tried not to think of Rhianwen and Morgan, or of Bast; neither the goddess nor the grey kitten. But the dreams haunted her. The green and golden eyes of cats. Lotuses floating like stars on the silver water under a dark blue sky. *Cross over. You belong here with us.*

But she daren't cross the water. She was frightened of drowning.

She said to Pastor Blair one day, 'My friend said she had a dream about cats. Does it mean anything?'

'Cats represent the Devil,' the Pastor had replied. 'It means she's in serious danger of sin. We must pray for her, sister.'

Luke also dreamed of animals.

He dreamed of mice and voles and sparrows and beetles.

In his sleep he writhed in pain and confusion. It had been all right to be happy at Grandma's, but not at Rhianwen's. She was bad. It had been witchcraft, her making him enjoy himself. What the Pastor called Temptation. He hated Rhianwen for it.

He wasn't stupid; he knew she hadn't really wanted him around. He hated her for trying to take Beth away from him. He hated her for being Morgan's mother.

He dreamed of the times he'd pressed up against the cat cages, just looking. Looking. They'd scratched him sometimes and he was nervous of them, but that only made him hate them more.

He hated the witch for saying, 'Don't put your fingers through the wire.'

Hated Morgan for his rudeness and arrogance.

Telling him what to do, as if they had any right!

But they all told him what to do. Mother, father, even Beth. And nobody wanted him. Only Beth had ever wanted him, but now she wanted Rhianwen more. Beth thought of Rhianwen more than she thought about Jesus. Luke wasn't stupid. He knew.

One day I'll show them.

Something was walking across his bedside table in the dull light from the street lamps. A spider.

He got up, picked up a badge that lay on the table, and stabbed the spider with the pin. Its small death gave him a strange tingling sensation between his legs. He opened the drawer and looked at his collection; dead beetles, dead wood-lice, dead earwigs, dead moths.

Luke threw the spider in the drawer with all the others.

Feeling better, he stifled his giggles under the bedclothes. It took the pain away for a little while. That was good.

When the end of the summer term drew close, Beth almost hoped they wouldn't be sent to their grandparents' again. Last summer seemed so far in the past. She had settled back into ordinary life. To go back would stir everything up again: her unholy longings, her slide into deceitfulness. Better to avoid temptation.

They had made day visits to Lullingford during the Christmas and Easter holidays, but there had been no possibility of Beth and Luke sneaking off. Beth would look out of the

49

windows at the drizzle and think longingly of Rhianwen, wondering what she and Morgan were doing at that moment. So near, so far.

Now negotiations were taking place again; Heather saying, 'Let them stay, it did them no harm last time,' and Olivia protesting, 'Last year was different! It's out of the question, they have the Lord's work to do at home.'

Olivia held out until the last day of term, then caved in. It wasn't hard for Beth to work out: Olivia had enjoyed her freedom from the children and wanted it again, but because she felt guilty about it, she was honour-bound to argue until her conscience was appeased. If Heather persuaded her it was right, it must be God's will.

So they were to spend another summer in Lullingford.

As her grandparents' house, the old rectory, with its wrought-iron gate, broad gravel drive and handsome trees swung into sight, Beth felt apprehensive rather than overjoyed. She knew she was going to sin again, and she didn't want to. I don't have to see Rhianwen, she thought. I could repent and not go. Give up my cat and my friend; it's good to make sacrifices. I'd feel really cleansed and full of grace, then. Jesus would be proud of me.

The feeling lit a flame inside her.

Yes, I'll be good. I'll prove I can be strong!

'Remember all the rules from last year?' Olivia said, kissing them goodbye. 'Your conscience will guide you.'

'Yes, Mum,' said Beth, for once able to give her an open and honest smile. And she suddenly realized that her mother trusted her. What a wonderful feeling!

On the first full day of their holiday, Heather suggested that they take a walk in the afternoon. 'I've some dull ladies from the Women's Institute coming round; I'm sure you'd rather be outdoors.'

So Beth and Luke walked into the village, not speaking to each other. They went to the post office to buy ice cream; a ginger-haired girl served them, grinning insolently at Beth.

They walked slowly along the pavement outside. Luke

dragged his feet. Although he no longer held Beth's hand, he seemed slow to grow up; the gulf between them felt greater than one year.

'You're going to go and see *her*, I suppose,' he said.

'Do you want to?' asked Beth.

'We shouldn't. It's still wrong. She's still a witch.'

'Well, I'm not going,' she said firmly.

Seeing Luke's face light up, Beth knew she'd made the right decision. 'Why not?'

'Because you're right, it would be a wicked thing to do.'

'That's brilliant, Bethie! I didn't like her son, anyway.' Then his eyes clouded. 'What are we going to do instead?'

Beth felt hollow suddenly. 'I don't know,' she said, subdued. 'Just go for walks, I suppose. We could join that youth group at the church; Gran said that would be all right.'

'Mum says the C of E aren't Saved, though,' said Luke, dragging his hand through cow parsley in the grass verge. 'Maybe we can save them.'

They walked through the familiar sunny fields of wheat embroidered with poppies, hedgerows shaded by chestnuts and oaks. But Beth felt empty. There was no exciting forbidden destination now. Just an aimless circle. They entered a wood but she saw only a blur of green leaves and close-set trunks.

Clouds covered the sun. When they came out into a clearing on top of a hill, it was spotting with rain.

'I suppose we'd better go home,' said Beth.

'Look at this!' said Luke.

In the centre of the clearing was a huge boulder shouldering up from the ground, grey with rust-red streaks. It was about three feet high and fifteen across, giving the impression that its main bulk was concealed underground. Long grasses fringed it. Its surface looked smooth, weather-polished.

Luke leapt onto the stone and jumped triumphantly up and down, shouting. Beth walked round it, patiently ignoring him. Little boys, she thought.

'You shouldn't do that,' said a voice a few feet away. 'You'll wake up the demons.'

51

Beth looked round and saw Morgan coming towards her out of the woods. He was a bit taller but she recognized him instantly. He was in jeans, with a white T-shirt that revealed long, pale golden arms.

Her heart made frantic attempts to dive out of her chest. She couldn't avoid him unless she ran away, but that would look stupid and she had her dignity. But how could she keep her vow, if she spoke to him?

'Hello, Beth,' he said. 'How are you?' He looked pleased to see her. But he seemed so much older than her, so confident of himself, his beautifully expressive and satirical face seeming subtly to mock her.

'Fine,' she said.

'When did you get here?'

'Yesterday.'

'Are you going to come and see your cat?'

How on earth could she say no to that? 'Erm . . . yes,' she muttered.

'You should see her, she's absolutely beautiful.'

Luke had stopped jumping and was staring belligerently at Morgan. At least he didn't hide behind Beth this time.

'D'you know what this is?' said Morgan, coming closer and touching the stone.

'A bloody great rock,' said Luke.

'It's called the Hellstone. It's a site of pagan worship. It's sacred to some people. I'd get off it if I were you.'

Luke jumped down as if he'd been scalded.

'There are lots of sacred places if you know where to look,' said Morgan. 'Trees, wells and stones. Are you going to come and have tea with us? It's a really nice walk from here.'

Luke's face had gone patchily red and white. He began, 'Bethie, you said –'

'I know!' she snapped. 'Never mind. Yes, we'll come.'

She didn't know how to say no to Morgan. She felt ensnared.

'Mum will be so pleased I found you,' said Morgan. 'She

really likes you, you know. Your mother let you off for good behaviour, then?'

'No, just glad to get rid of us, I think,' said Beth.

Morgan led them into the woods. The light was strange, like the intense luminosity of a storm, as if they were underwater. Beth's hands were icy. She sensed God's wrath gathering.

She felt that if Morgan and Luke would make friends, as Rhianwen had wanted, it wouldn't be so bad; Luke would have made a decision of his own, instead of relying on Beth all the time. So she trailed along behind, trying to force the two boys together; expecting to be left out when they began to form a bond. But it didn't work. Instead Morgan kept waiting for her to catch up, and ignoring Luke.

The leaves were green jewels in the storm-light. She'd barely been aware of her surroundings before, but in Morgan's presence the woods took on a vivid intensity. He pointed out a delicate plant with nodding flowers. 'D'you know what this is?'

Beth wasn't sure. 'No.'

'Deadly nightshade. There are all sort of plants you can make medicines out of, even poisonous ones. But you can't just go round picking anything, you have to know what you're doing and the right time to take them.'

As they went on, Morgan pointed out scores of things she hadn't noticed before. Birds and small animals, insects and fungi. She became acutely aware that everything had a scent, fresh and green, musty or delicate. He drew her attention to tiny wild flowers that she would never have seen otherwise. He wasn't showing off; it was simply that he found all this fascinating, and wanted to share it.

The wood came alive for her, teeming with miracles. Beth began to forget her self-consciousness. She'd never met anyone like Morgan. When he wasn't being sarcastic he seemed quite nice; thoughtful and knowledgeable. Nothing like Luke, in whom – despite his upbringing – there was an ordinary, brash boy struggling to get out.

But she couldn't forget that Morgan, like Rhianwen, belonged to the other side. These were arcane things he was telling her, the sort of knowledge the serpent had whispered to Eve. Beth was walking away from God, and couldn't stop.

Luke trailed along behind, swishing at the undergrowth with a stick he'd picked up, his face sullen. He seemed determined to feel left out, and to resent it bitterly. Once or twice Morgan turned and said gently, 'Don't do that, Luke. You're damaging the plants.'

Morgan crouched down at the base of a tree and parted a curtain of leaves to reveal a magnificent shelf of ochre fungus. A huge, brightly patterned spider was traversing it, its body swaying between long legs.

'Look at this!' he said. 'You don't mind spiders, do you, Beth?'

'No, I quite like them,' she said. 'I've never seen one like that. Isn't it pretty?'

Luke came up between them and stabbed with his stick, crushing the spider and demolishing the fungus.

'Don't!' cried Morgan, seizing the stick. 'That was beautiful, and you've destroyed it!'

He was furious; so was Beth. 'Luke, for heaven's sake, behave or I'll –'

'You can't do anything!' said Luke. 'You can't even tell Grandma!'

The spider was still moving, its legs waving from the glue of its mashed body. Morgan stepped on it to end its suffering. For a moment, Beth thought he was going to punch Luke – but he was calm again. Beth found his self-possession stunning.

'Come on. Don't touch anything else.'

Luke went ahead, while Beth and Morgan walked side by side.

'I'm sorry,' she said. 'I don't know why he's behaving like this.'

'It's all right.' Morgan smiled at her. Dazzling. His combination of maturity, friendliness and equanimity bewildered her. 'He doesn't like me. Why should he?'

After a few minutes, Luke waited for them and asked rudely, 'Why isn't your father ever at home?'

'Luke!' Beth said, but he took no notice.

'Because he's dead,' Morgan said evenly.

'How did he die?'

'Car crash.'

'Was he Saved?'

'No, he died,' Morgan said drily, implying that he was only too aware of what Luke had meant.

'I expect he's in hell, then,' said Luke.

Morgan stared at him, as calm as ever. 'Is Luke short for Lucifer?' he said mildly.

'You're Lucifer, not me!'

Morgan's mouth curved up wickedly at the corners. 'I didn't finish telling you about the Hellstone. It's a good thing you weren't there after dark because the good folk come out and dance around it.'

Beth asked, 'What d'you mean, the good folk?'

'The fairies,' said Morgan. Luke made a *Huh* sound but Morgan went on in an eerie tone. 'Of course, you know the fairies aren't little creatures with wings at all; they're really the ancient gods of Britain. They have horns and tails and they drink the blood of children. Especially if you wake them up. You have to make a blood sacrifice to them or they'll get their claws in your soul and drag you down to the underworld.'

It sounded like a morbid joke, but there was still something in Morgan's voice that turned Beth cold. And Luke, who couldn't see the joke, had gone white.

'That's a load of rubbish,' Luke said shakily. 'How d'you know?'

'We see them all the time,' Morgan said offhandedly. 'They're all right if you make a pact with them. It's like you become one of them.'

'You're a liar.'

'Well, what do you think pagans do?'

'Worship the Devil.'

'That's right. We go up there, dance round the stone naked and worship the Devil. Didn't you see the bloodstains? The

55

infernal fire keeps us warm. That and the Satanic orgy afterwards.'

'Liar!' Luke screamed. 'You're a pig!' He rushed wildly at Morgan, pushed him, then went charging off through the trees.

'What's the matter with him?' said Morgan. 'I was only taking the piss.'

Beth was angrier with Morgan than she had been with Luke. He was her brother, after all. 'He's just a kid! He takes that kind of thing seriously!'

'Well, he was getting on my nerves.'

'I don't care!' she blazed. 'How could you?'

And she ran after Luke, feeling purged by the fire of her rage. She'd escaped temptation. She was free.

She caught Luke up at the edge of the wood, where it gave on to the meadow behind Rhianwen's house. It was raining. He faced her aggressively; with his grubby face and his hair sticking up, he looked about eight, but there was something age-old and poisonous in his eyes.

'You behaved like a little demon!' she said. 'Why were you so rude? I'm ashamed of you.'

'It was him!' Luke cried. 'He worships the Devil, he admitted it!'

'He was teasing you.'

'No, he wasn't, he meant it. You're stupid if you believe him instead of me. He's evil, I knew he was evil the first time we saw him!'

'Luke, you're in a state. Calm down and let's go home. We'll be soaked soon.' Beth put her hand on his arm, but he shook her off.

'You can sod off! I'm going to tell Mum about you and Rhianwen!'

'Oh no, you're not!' Beth was furious. This was the first real argument they'd ever had; it scared her, but she couldn't stop. Perhaps this was how he made Olivia feel. 'You won't say a word, or we'll both be in trouble, and you'll get it worst!'

Luke backed off, tears springing to his eyes. 'God will punish

56

you, Bethia. Go and see your stupid cat and lick the Devil's arse. But if you do I'll never be your friend again. And you'll go to hell!'

'Luke!' she cried, but he was away and running hard towards the stile in the hedge. Beth realized it was pointless going after him. Now they were going to arrive home separately, and probably wet through, and what would Grandma say?

'You all right?' said Morgan behind her.

Beth chewed her lip and didn't answer.

'I'm really sorry,' he said softly. 'Beth, *you* didn't believe me, did you?'

'Of course not.'

'It's just an old pagan site. My mum told me your mother had made you scared of witches and things, so I . . . sorry, it wasn't fair.' He looked contrite, and the rain shone in his dark soft hair like stars. In a pulse-beat, her perception of the woods changed; she could feel spirits moving in the trees, leaves dripping with dew, bark oozing sap like honey and the sweetness of it on her tongue; and the millions of diamond eyes watching her and the voices whispering, *Come to us, you belong* . . . and the rain warm and silvery on her skin . . .

'Beth, are you okay?' Morgan said anxiously. 'You went kind of blank.'

The world slipped back to normal, but her heart was racing. 'I'm fine.'

'You don't like me, do you?' He sighed. 'I thought so last time.'

'I like you,' she said weakly, 'but you're strange.'

'Not half as strange as you.' He smiled. She was beginning to realize that his teasing was not malicious after all. 'Don't be scared of me. I don't bite. Do you know you're incredibly pretty, Beth?'

'No, I'm not. My mum says I'm plain.'

'Oh, it must be me then. I am a bit short-sighted. I won't look too closely in case I get a fright.'

A laugh escaped Beth's lips. The rain grew heavier, hissing through the trees.

'Let's go in the house and dry off,' said Morgan.

As they walked down the slope of the meadow, she asked, 'You know what you said about your father? Was it true?'

'Yes. He died about two years ago.'

'I'm sorry.'

'Thanks, but I never met him, actually.'

'How awful! Why not?'

'Because he fell out with my mother and left her before I was born. I don't know how anyone can fall out with Rhianwen, but some people manage it. She has men friends, but never anyone serious. I'd hate it if she got married again. Is that selfish?'

Beth didn't know what to say. Morgan had a way of suddenly becoming wrapped in his own thoughts.

They were at the gate of Rhianwen's garden. 'Here we are,' he said. 'Bast is waiting for you.'

It was as if she'd never been away.

When Beth gained Morgan as a friend, she lost Luke.

Contrary to her fears, Luke didn't give her secret away. Arriving home a couple of hours after him – having got soaked again on the way back – Beth found he'd simply told Heather they'd had a quarrel. Heather dried her off with tea towels as if she were a wet dog, and wasn't cross in the slightest.

'Well, I don't see why you have to go about manacled together any more. You're both sensible enough to go out separately if you want. How're you going to grow up, otherwise?'

In the night, Luke came into Beth's room with glittering eyes.

'You don't care about me,' he said. 'If you're friends with the witches, you can't be friends with me.'

'Don't be daft. I'll always care about you. I am your friend, I'm your sister.'

'No. It's him or me. You promised you'd never leave me!'

'I haven't left you!'

'Oh yes you have.'

Secretly, Beth knew he was right. She was a sinner now.

She'd broken all her promises to her mother, Luke and God. She didn't like herself. But she couldn't turn back.

And then Luke spoke so plaintively she nearly repented there and then: 'I wish it was just you and me, Bethie, like it used to be. You promised you'd always stay with me.' His voice rose. 'You promised on the Bible and you lied. You bloody bitch! I'll never forgive you!' And he struck her with both fists and ran out of the room.

Beth thought Luke would forgive her in time, but he didn't. She saw a determination in him she hadn't known he possessed; he never told on her, but he never forgave her.

That summer, Luke joined the youth group in the village, while Beth went on visiting Rhianwen and Morgan. Her friendship with Morgan was completely innocent; it never crossed Beth's mind that it could be otherwise. Usually they stayed with Rhianwen around the house and garden, sometimes they went for walks. It seemed awful that they couldn't go into the village in case someone saw them together; that she couldn't invite him to her gran's for tea. This enmity between the families was galling Beth, though Morgan treated it as a joke.

Morgan enjoyed talking and Beth listening. She liked him a lot, yet she remained in awe, a bit uneasy. He might have been joking about the Devil, but who knew what pagans really did? Olivia would have said it didn't matter, it was all Satanic anyway.

All Beth's confusion seemed to crystallize in her love for her cat. Bast's affection was uncomplicated, pure and comforting, and when Beth sat on Rhianwen's sofa with the warm, furry body on her lap and Bast's contentment vibrating through her hands, Beth would think, what am I doing wrong? Yet she knew. This was a sensual pleasure. Cats were of the Devil. Bast was a temptation to surrender to all the fleshly evils of life.

Beth also made friends with the ginger-haired girl in the post office, Genette, and sometimes used her as an excuse when she was going to Rhianwen's. She wasn't found out, and there was no fire from God.

The second, perfect summer ended.

Home to grey skies, grey streets, church and schoolwork. Again Morgan had asked to write, but Beth daren't let him. She didn't think of Morgan as a boyfriend and didn't want to. She'd learned from girls at school that boyfriends only made you unhappy – and was reluctantly learning the sordid details of exactly how and why from the candid Genette.

As Luke grew older, Olivia was finding fewer excuses to beat him. He was becoming devout, too quiet. Turning into our dad, Beth thought.

On the occasions when Luke was punished, he would no longer let Beth comfort him.

'Go to your *friends*, Bethia,' he'd whisper. 'You like them better than me.'

He wouldn't relent. Her brother was gone from her, closed, lost.

Beth mourned, and blamed herself. She prayed a lot, which helped, but it didn't change anything. All that kept her going was the hope of next summer; in other words, the prospect of compounding all her lies, deceptions and sins.

'I worry about those children,' Rhianwen said, a few days after Beth had gone back to school. She stood watching Morgan, who had an injured bird in a box on the kitchen table, and was carefully feeding it with a dropper. Late sunlight came in, feathering his hair with gold. Rhianwen was proud of how attractive her son had turned out, but it also made her apprehensive. 'Trouble is, the more I try to help them – Beth, anyway – the more I risk getting them into trouble with their family.'

'They're all mad, if you ask me,' said Morgan. 'It's ridiculous Beth having to come here in secret. That Luke's a deranged little shit, and as for the grandmother –'

'Yes, well, I have you to thank for the fact that Luke won't come near us now,' Rhianwen said sharply.

'I didn't know he was going to take it so seriously!'

'You should have had more sense. You can be really cruel, sometimes, Morgan.'

He straightened up and looked at her. 'I've said I'm sorry,

Mum. He was appalling. I only gave him a little light torment; I didn't know he was going to run screaming for the hills.'

Rhianwen sighed. 'Well, it's his mother's fault he's like that. It's a miracle Beth seems relatively normal.'

Morgan leaned down to his patient again. 'I really like Beth,' he said.

'Morgan.'

'Yes, Mum?'

'She's a lot younger than you.'

'Only two years.'

'I want you to bear in mind that she's only a child. She needs a friend, a brother, someone she can trust. Treat her like a little sister, won't you?'

'Of course!' he said, wounded. 'What else?'

'Don't forget what I've said. With a mother like hers, she needs a friend. I don't actually think Olivia's fit to bring up children, but what can I do? It's none of my business.'

'What is it with you and her?'

'I told you, differences of opinion,' she said steadily. 'A long time ago, but her family can't forgive me. They'd like me out of the district so they don't have to think about me any more, but I'm not going.'

'Persecution of village witch. You should curse them and have done with it.'

'You know I don't believe in that kind of thing. If it doesn't work it's pointless, and if it does it's a hideous thing to do. I don't hate them, anyway. I like Olivia, in an odd way; she's so black and white. She doesn't patronize me like the vicar does, as if I'm some lost sheep who needs to be herded back into the fold. She tells me to my face I'm going to hell. She sees me as an adversary; in other words, an equal. I like that. Gives you a sense of purpose.'

'Oh yeah? What purpose would that be?'

Rhianwen smiled slowly. 'There are other kinds of magic. I can take Beth and turn her into Olivia's worst nightmare. It's very easy. Just tell her what we believe, and let her make a choice.'

Chapter Five

'**M**UM?'

Beth called out very softly, because it was one o'clock in the afternoon and she wasn't meant to be home from school – and because there was something strange and wrong in the house. Her father's car was outside, when he should have been at work. Yet there was no one about downstairs.

It was April, two months short of Beth's thirteenth birthday. She'd come home early because something dreadful had happened to her: her stomach had tied itself in agonizing knots, and when she had gone to the loo, she'd found blood.

Beth knew what it was, but it had still been a shock. Too embarrassed to tell anyone, even a teacher, she'd fled, feeling faint and shaky from the pain.

Olivia had to be told, but Beth had a premonition that she was going to be angry; irritated, at the very least. That was why Beth was creeping around. And if her father was at home, she wouldn't be able to mention it until she could get her mother alone.

Why did this have to happen? thought Beth, tiptoeing up-stairs. There was silence; maybe they were out. But then she heard the sound that sent shudders through her. A rhythmic *thwack, thwack, thwack.* The sound of Luke being punished. But Luke, surely, was at school.

The noise came from her parents' bedroom. Beth went closer, puzzled. The door stood an inch or two ajar, and through the gap she saw them.

Her mother and father, naked. She'd never seen them naked before! Her father was kneeling on the carpet, hands at his sides, a black cloth tied over his eyes. And her mother was lashing him with the same strap she used on Luke.

Beth stared at the welts on his back and buttocks. And the

prong of flesh, standing out in front! He was groaning, mouth distorted.

'This is for what you did,' said Olivia. 'This is for your weakness!'

Suddenly Olivia dropped the belt and pushed Philip backwards onto the carpet, uttering high-pitched gasps as if she couldn't breathe. She was bright scarlet. Beth put her hands over her face, and watched between her fingers.

Philip was on his back, Olivia on top, grunting, writhing.

Why did they do this if it hurt so much? It looked undignified, bestial. Horrific. Far worse than anything Beth had imagined.

Her mother's face, usually so composed, was beet-red and full of – what? Hatred, rage?

'Why can't you love *me*?' Olivia rasped as if in anguish. 'Why not me?'

She put her head back, gave a soundless scream, and collapsed on Philip's chest.

'I've punished you,' Olivia panted. 'Now punish me.'

Beth winced. She knew she mustn't witness this but it was too late, she was transfixed, eyes welded open.

Her father said weakly, 'I can't.'

'Do it!' said Olivia. 'Pretend you're betraying me, you bastard!'

Then she rolled on to her stomach and Philip, mute and blind in the black cloth, climbed on to her from behind. His head hung down as if he were in some kind of despair. Beth saw his hips stab forward. Olivia uttered a hoarse scream and her hands clawed at the carpet.

Beth shrank away. She couldn't watch any more. She skimmed noiselessly down the stairs, her throat full and her eyes burning.

No choice but to creep out of the house and walk the streets in misery until it was the usual time for her to come home from school. By then, she was exhausted from the stomach pain, sticky and soiled with the wretched blood.

As she let herself in for the second time, everything was

normal. Her father's car had gone. Her mother was all neat and prim in flowered cotton. And Beth felt another shred of innocence being torn away as she realized that it wasn't the first time it had happened. That it must have happened a thousand times in the past, on any normal schoolday like today.

Luke was already home, reading his Bible in the front room.

'Why didn't you and Luke come home together?' Olivia demanded. 'He says no one saw you this afternoon. What have you been up to?'

It was all Beth could do to speak to her mother, but she had become expert at pretending that certain things had never happened.

'Mum,' she said nervously, 'I think my periods have started.'

'What? Oh, God help us. Come upstairs. Are you sure?'

Beth could feel Olivia's temper, boiling like lava. She felt terrified and guilty, as if she'd committed a hideous crime.

'Get undressed. You'd better have a bath.'

Beth obeyed, while her mother ran the water. The blood had soaked through Beth's knickers and crusted on her thighs. Seeing it, Olivia gave a cry of exasperation. 'How did you manage to get into such a mess? You stupid, dirty girl!'

The blow took Beth completely off-guard. There was a ring-ing pain in her ear and she fell, striking her head on the corner of the bath, finding herself on the carpet with the room tilted at a strange angle. Her mother's face rose over her, contorted with rage. Just as Beth had seen it earlier.

'Why did you have to start with this filth so soon, Bethia? Why couldn't you wait?'

More blows stung her face, more shocking than painful. Olivia seized Beth's shoulders and shook her, then dragged her to her feet and hugged her fiercely.

'Get in the bath,' she said.

Dazed and trembling, Beth did so. The water was scalding; her whole body flushed red and she thought she might pass out. Was it hot enough to wash away her filth?

Olivia sat on the edge of the bath and began to talk to her.

64

Her anger had gone and her tone became warm and sorrowful.

'I am going to tell you something very important. It's a very dangerous time for you now. Girls are sinful but boys are beasts; all they are interested in is defiling girls – even plain ones like you, Beth – and they don't care what kind of mess they leave behind them. They can't help themselves' – Olivia sounded contemptuous – 'so it's your responsibility not to let anything happen. Do you know what I'm talking about?'

'Yes, Mum,' Beth croaked, tears of pain streaming down her cheeks. She had seen it demonstrated all too vividly, a few hours ago.

'You must never let a boy so much as touch you.'

'I wouldn't want to! It looks – sounds, I mean – it sounds too horrible to think about.'

'That's right. It is a beastly thing. Perhaps when you're a lot older, nineteen or so, you might meet a suitable, clean-living Christian boy at church and get married. But that's a long way in the future. Until then you must keep yourself chaste. Do you hear me, Beth? Never, ever say I haven't warned you!'

'I hear you, Mum. I will be good.'

'You will be perfect.' Olivia stroked Beth's hair, her expression wistful now. 'I'm hard on you and Luke because you're special. Most children drift into sin and ruin themselves, but I want something better for you! It doesn't have to happen. If you keep yourself pure you won't give the Devil a chance! You are a soldier of the Lord, Beth. That isn't going to be easy; it means taking up your cross and walking with Jesus, and that's a hard road. But I know you have the strength to do it. You know it too, don't you?'

'Yes, Mum.'

As Beth rose out of the water, Olivia wrapped her in a towel and pressed her hand over Beth's abdomen. 'This body is born in sin and filth: we can't help that, but we can change it. You have to work at driving out the filth and becoming a temple of the Holy Spirit. You can do it and you *will*.'

The command burned from Olivia's eyes into Beth's.

'I let you stay with your grandmother once a year because I trust you. My trust isn't earned easily, Beth. Don't let me down.'

'I won't,' Beth said, heat rushing to her face. 'I won't!'

'You're a good girl.' Olivia's face became passionate, beautiful like a saint's. Beth felt the searing ache in her chest that she always felt when she realized that, despite everything, she and her mother loved each other. 'But it's all too easy to slide back into the filth from which we try to raise ourselves. Don't ever make me think all my hard work has been in vain, Bethia!'

There were three months to get through before she could see Rhianwen. Beth never knew how she managed to endure it. She felt she would explode with confusion and self-loathing.

Beth's mind turned on a pivot around that day. She wondered about all the deceits and secrets there must always have been. All the guilt. No wonder they must pray constantly for forgiveness when there was so much sin, even in her parents.

She didn't know what it had meant, when her mother screamed at her father, '*Pretend you're betraying me!*' Didn't want to know, or even to guess.

And her mother's face haunted her, words stinging like blows. '*Born in sin and filth. Dirty. Filthy.*' Words reinforced by Pastor Blair's teachings and the Bible itself; that women were the gateway to hell, that menstruation was a pollution and a curse which they deserved, that the only perfect woman was the Virgin Mary; the rest must struggle permanently through punishment and self-abnegation towards the hope of being re-created male by Christ.

Beth had become convinced that she wasn't fit to live. Perhaps that wasn't what Olivia had intended, but it was what she had achieved.

There wasn't a soul she could tell. She could only do what she'd always done, when she'd been bullied, when she'd deceived her family with Rhianwen and when she'd fallen out with Luke; seal it deep inside and walk round with a frozen face and eyes of glass.

Being perfect.

When the end of term came, Luke announced that he didn't want to go to their grandparents'. Beth was glad, until their mother insisted that he go anyway. Olivia had grown to love her summers of devoting herself to the church without having to worry about the children. So Beth had to endure Luke's hostility and the snide remarks whispered in the back of the car on the way to Lullingford.

'I suppose you'll go and see *her*. Your friend, the bloody bitch. And her son the Devil-worshipper.'

Beth still wanted to mend their friendship. 'She was as nice as anything to you. I don't know how you can talk about her like that. She's just an ordinary person who had an argument with Mum once.'

Luke had changed a lot in a year. He'd increased dramatically in height, and was growing a shell of arrogance and secrecy. Beth had preferred the nervous and clingy little boy; at least he had loved her.

'You're stupid, Beth,' he said. 'The Devil *is* nice and he offers you everything; that's how he gets hold of you! You've gone to the Devil, Beth.'

'No, I haven't!'

'They're Satanists. Her son admitted it! You think he was joking but he wasn't.'

'I wish you'd shut up about it,' she whispered, annoyed. She was afraid their parents would hear, but the car engine drowned their voices.

'I don't care what you do,' Luke said offhandedly. 'I won't tell on you, don't worry. I don't have to. Your sins will find you out.'

When he smiled he looked thirty years old, not twelve.

The summer was relentlessly hot and dry, swimming in a heat-haze. On the first glorious day of freedom, Luke and Beth left the rectory together, then went their separate ways; Luke to the youth group at the village church, Beth to see Rhianwen.

Beth was nervous. She should be used to this by now, but the

67

dark excitement never wore off. Fear, too, that Luke was right; that she was being seduced into a chasm of evil, that her own secret parts were the mouth of hell and she would somehow fall through herself into a pit of turbulent blood and filth where devils with her parents' faces defiled and tormented each other. And one of the devils in her ghastly imaginings had Morgan's face, despite her efforts to blot him out.

Still her excitement had the edge on her fear.

It was Rhianwen she wanted to see, not Morgan; the thought of him made her feel hollow with anxiety, even though he'd been so friendly last year.

Even Rhianwen's lush garden was looking curled around the edges with the drought. Enveloped in the scents of rosemary, lavender and lemon balm, Beth ran through the herb garden, knocked on the kitchen door, and went in.

Rhianwen was there in jeans and an Indian top, drying dishes. Her hair was tied back, a thick auburn skein between her shoulder-blades.

'Hello, love,' said Rhianwen, looking delighted to see her. 'Welcome back.'

'Is Morgan here?' Beth asked anxiously.

'No, he's gone to France on a school trip. He won't be home until next week.'

'Oh good,' said Beth in relief. Then, without any warning signs, she found herself bursting into tears.

'Love, what is it?' Hurriedly drying her hands, Rhianwen took her into the front room and sat her down, hugging her and stroking her hair. The painting of Bast, the cat-goddess, watched over them. And the cats, Bast, Ankaret and Llew, stalked around them, mewing. 'Whatever's the matter? What's happened?'

'I need to talk to you. I've got no one else.'

'Go ahead. You can tell me anything.'

Bast remembered Beth, and climbed on to her lap, demanding love. She wasn't attenuated like Ankaret; she'd grown into a robust cat of a beautiful, solid slate-blue. As Beth stroked the vibrantly purring body, the wretchedness of the past few

68

months came pouring out; not what she'd seen her parents doing – that was too awful to mention – but all her horror at herself.

'Am I dirty?' she asked, weeping.

'Oh dear.' Rhianwen sighed. 'Oh dear. I should have known this would happen. I could strangle Olivia! Sorry, but it's plain wickedness for her to make you feel like this. Have you tried talking to your father?'

'I couldn't!' Beth gasped. 'He never discusses anything like that; I think he'd die of embarrassment if I tried – and so would I. No, it's impossible.'

'I could strangle them both, and that bloody pastor,' Rhianwen said grimly. 'Of course you're not dirty, love. And I can explain in great detail why you're not, so that no one will ever be able to make you feel dirty again; but to do it I will have to say bad things about what your parents believe. You might not feel the same about them after. You might not feel the same about God.'

She took Beth's face between her hands. Her eyes were so full of compassion that Beth loved her completely; love she should only have felt for God. How can they call her evil and my mother good?

'Please tell me,' said Beth.

'Are you sure? I don't want to influence you, see. You're too young to be told what's right and what's wrong. That's why I wouldn't say anything before. No one should have a religion forced on them before they're old enough to make up their own mind.'

'I'm sure.'

Beth was intensely aware of her surroundings: the lovely white room with its wall-hangings, big tasselled cushions, candles and incense; light coming in from the flowery cave of the garden, insects and dust motes as bright as tiny suns floating in the haze.

'All right,' Rhianwen began softly. 'I have sympathy for the Christian myth; it was like the last noble blaze of the vegetation deity against a world that was already a desert of hatred.

But I've no sympathy for the religious fascists it spawned; that goes for most other religions, too, and all the harm they've done down the ages. Oh, there's nothing wrong with being taught to love, to be kind, to think of others before yourself, and all that – but Christians don't have a monopoly on kindness and common sense. It's the baggage that goes with it that's so destructive.

'For thousands of years before other religions came into being, people worshipped a Goddess, the Mother of All Living. Have you heard of her?'

'There were goddesses when we did Greek and Roman myths at school,' said Beth.

'Oh, far too late; they were already destroying her then. Splitting her into smaller parts to take her power away. But the Great Goddess is far older than your God. If you had lived between five thousand and two hundred thousand years ago, a girl's first menstruation would have been cause for celebration, because in those days women's bodies were considered sacred. Women had power. They were priestesses, lawmakers, inventors and healers; each an embodiment of the Goddess. After all, our blood miraculously produces life, so it made sense to visualize a Goddess giving birth to the world. Sex wasn't shameful. It was a natural, ecstatic communion with the Goddess.

'It was only when male-dominated religions took over that sex, menstruation and childbirth were twisted to appear sinful and punishing. That's where the wickedness lies, Beth; not in our bodies.'

'But why would they want to do that?' Beth said, indignant.

'Fear. Only women had the power to produce life as if by magic. Men were afraid of their power, their sexuality, their mysteries. A mother is the all-powerful figure in a child's life; a daughter can become a mother in turn but a son cannot. And women induce desire and loss of control. And again, women are there at the end of life: the nurse, the funerary priestess. Women live on the shadowy boundary of the dying and the not-yet-born. So they became identified with death in men's eyes and men don't like to be reminded of death; they want to live for ever.

'So what do you do if you fear something? You dominate it. You belittle it. You make it seem small and dirty and, even better, you make it believe those horrible things about *itself*.

'Men learned to use weapons for killing each other instead of hunting, and from breeding cattle they discovered their own role in producing children. Then there was no stopping them. It was probably political, replacing the Goddess with a warlike God to stir people up to go out and conquer their neighbours. The Old Testament's full of it; the followers of the new God trying to suppress Goddess-worship. Not because it was evil, but because it was a threat. It was all about power, see. And that's the way they've all carried on, these male religions. Show me a church and I'll show you a man puffed up with power and wealth and a monopoly on the truth.'

Rhianwen sounded disgusted. Beth thought of Pastor Blair. True, she thought.

'Whether she exists or not, the idea of the Goddess was based on reality; the waxing and waning moon, the rhythm of the day, the cycle of the year. Her triple form represents the life of a real woman: Maiden, Mother, Crone. Initiation, achievement, wisdom. But God is a spirit who is separate from nature. Abstract, illogical. The Goddess was completely identified with nature, so the process of obliterating her meant despising matter, nature and flesh as corrupt and evil. Spirit, male and good; flesh, female and bad. The hatred of women that spills from Biblical writers and supposed saints isn't logical, it's pathological.

'Some saw the Holy Spirit as female; the early church put a stop to that. Nothing sacred was allowed to be female any more. An utter distortion of reality.

'Goddess-worship didn't seek to obliterate the male in the same way; everyone was sacred in her eyes. She had a consort, the Horned God, her son and lover. He wasn't a violent god; he represented strength, gentleness, fertility. Every year he was

71

sacrificed to bring new life, every year reborn in the spring. Does he sound evil?'

'I don't think so,' said Beth.

'No. But the church turned him into the Devil. It's what they call propaganda.'

'Why?'

'So they could make theirs the only true belief. So they could gather all the money, knowledge, power and land to themselves. The great thing about the Bible is that it's so contradictory, it can be twisted to mean anything. Picture it: the church would hold meetings, decide on official policy, then rush out and burn as a heretic anyone who disagreed with them. The only difference these days is that they can't burn you; just criticize and patronize you, warp your self-image, make you despise yourself.

'But the Goddess whose son is sacrificed and rises again – sounds familiar? It wasn't original, the story of Jesus. It was age-old. Mary was all that remained of the Great Goddess, with her sexuality and power removed, a passive vessel. But she was once the Goddess; God her consort and son. The corn king. The death and rebirth of the year.

'There was no Adam and Eve and no Fall, Beth. You can believe it if you like but I don't. It was invented to "explain" death and sin, and to prove woman's inferiority by blaming death and sin on her. But reading between the lines, you find the story of men and women being severed from their roots in the earth. The serpent wasn't Satan; she was the Goddess of wisdom, trying to win Eve back to the old ways. But the new jealous God wouldn't allow mankind the wisdom of the Goddess. Their exile from Eden was their loss of Mother Earth. Oh yes, tragic.

'The concept of the Devil, too, is very new; I mean, a few thousand years old against the hundreds of thousands that went before. But it's very useful for labelling anyone who doesn't fit in, isn't it?'

'Like my mum does to you,' said Beth.

'Quite. Everything you don't approve of, label it the Devil's work and you've dealt with it. Simple. We've had a supposed age of reason since the eighteenth century, but some people still have the same stereotyped ideas about witches and black magic.

'The idea of heaven and hell is useful, too, for making people believe. Everyone likes to think they can live for ever. But have you wondered how a loving God can condemn his own creations to suffer for *eternity*?'

'Well, yes.'

'Good!' said Rhianwen, as if this were a sign that Beth still had a mind of her own. 'In the personality of God you can see the personality of the men who invented him: jealous, absolute, life–death–judgement. But in the Goddess's eyes, life is cyclic. It doesn't go in a straight line, and spirit can't be separated from flesh. Nature's sacred, our bodies are sacred, death is only part of the cycle, so not to be feared. Sex isn't wrong, childbirth isn't a punishment, and Eve did not bring death into the world. Therefore, no reason for females to hang their heads in shame. All the illogic goes away. Make any sense?'

Beth nodded. 'Is this what witches believe?'

'Well, this witch does. You've noticed I don't wear a black hat or cast spells? It's a different way of looking at things, that's all – besides being the oldest religion in the world.

'I don't need Jesus – however wise and kind he was – to save me from sins that don't exist. But to know there's no saviour, that it's all up to *you* – that's not comfortable. Your religion labels me a devil-worshipper. But I can't possibly be, because he's an invention of your religion, not mine. It's a logical impossibility for me to worship him.'

Beth broke in, 'But my mum and the people at our church really believe it. They're always on about Satan being at large in the world. Anyway, people behave worse when they don't believe in God, not better.'

Rhianwen sighed. 'Because they've been cut off from their Goddess, then abandoned,' she said softly. 'They don't know what to believe; the church has spent centuries killing it. People are comfortable with what they know. Anything different-is alien. Men see women – like natives see foreigners – as *other*. Only the élite qualify to be saved, only *us*; all the nasty "others" can go in the pit. Maybe you think I'm alien because I'm Welsh, and when you get to heaven there won't be any Welsh people there, thank you very much.'

Beth laughed.

'That's better,' said Rhianwen. 'Doesn't do to take it too seriously.'

'You do, though, don't you?'

'I get mad when I still hear this mindless prejudice against paganism. Pure ignorance. The Middle Ages live on. D'you know when the last law against witchcraft was repealed?'

'Seventeen something?'

'Nineteen fifty-one. And people like your church would like to wake it all up again. I suppose they mean well. But I can't stand the way they *know* they're right and everyone else is wrong. They just don't *understand*. That can be very dangerous. Do you know the saying, "Thou shalt not observe times"? It means, don't respect the cycles of nature. Despise the earth and worship instead some disembodied God. Don't enjoy your body or have a joyful life, or you won't be saved. Treat women like shit. Treat *yourself* like shit. Talk about society shooting itself in the foot. It's the biggest mistake mankind has ever made.' Rhianwen gazed out of the window, inside herself, seeming to forget Beth was there. 'I don't think we'll ever recover.'

She got up and went into the kitchen; Beth stayed where she was with the cats. On her own, she cried again, but the tears were a clear stream now, not red sobs of agony. She felt worn out, but cleansed.

Yes, it made sense. She knew there was no sin in bleeding or in being female – and she was beginning to feel very angry at the church for making her feel unclean.

Rhianwen came back with glasses of apple juice. 'How are you feeling, love?'

'I'm not sure,' said Beth. 'Did you ever tell my mother this?'

'I tried,' Rhianwen said ruefully. 'She thought I was talking bollocks. Oh, well.'

Beth almost spilled her apple juice. Recovering herself, she said, 'Rhianwen, if my mother and the pastor could be wrong about this, how can I be sure of anything they tell me?'

'You can't,' said Rhianwen. 'That's why you have to learn to make up your own mind. That's too much for some people, of course; they need to be told this is true and that's false, because they can't think for themselves. But you can, Beth. You won't be a child for ever; in five years' time you'll be able to do and think exactly what you want.'

'You don't know my mother,' Beth said hopelessly.

'Oh, I do.'

In sudden despair, Beth said, 'But how am I going to get through another five years of church, after what you've told me? Because if I tell her I've stopped believing, she will kill me!' A memory came to her. 'There was a girl of about seventeen who tried to leave the church. Pastor Blair said she was possessed. We all had to go round to her house and pray over her. She looked terrified, like she was trapped. It was horrible.'

'What happened?'

'She repented, but a few weeks later she had a nervous breakdown and went to hospital. We never saw her again.'

'That won't happen to you.' Rhianwen looked sad, her eyes full of concern, and yet she seemed to be smiling a little.

After Beth had gone home, Rhianwen thought about her for a long time. A tall slender girl with glossy deep brown hair, leaf-green eyes, an oval, serious face with infinite potential for kindness and beauty. Rhianwen, as always, had felt delighted to see her. Seeing her only once a year, the changes were marked; her increase in height, and now the curves of her hips and her breasts budding.

Well, I've told her now, Rhianwen thought. I didn't mean it to be so soon but she needed it. And I saw every word fly to its mark, as I knew it would.

Rhianwen loved Beth. She wanted to see her free and happy, walking proudly through life instead of weighed down by religious neuroses. Oh, but the sweetness of taking her away from Olivia! That was a purely vindictive pleasure.

Rhianwen was aware of her own duality, compassion edged with cruelty. She didn't see it as a problem. She accepted the Crone's power to destroy as well as to create.

A few days later, when Morgan came home, she told him all about it.

'Beth's mother told her one sensible thing in a roundabout way,' Rhianwen concluded, 'which was not to start having sex too young.'

'Good for her,' Morgan said expressionlessly.

'I hope I don't have to say this again, but you will behave properly, won't you? I know you and Beth get on well. I don't want to treat you like children by refusing to trust you, but on the other hand I must know I *can* trust you. Imagine you're her older brother. Protect her.'

'Of course I will,' Morgan said indignantly. 'What do you think I am?'

'Well, love, you seem to be getting a reputation . . .'

'It's all lies,' he said.

'I hear you had quite a talk with my mother,' said Morgan.

He was looking golden, athletic and taller than ever. As they walked through the woods, Beth was intensely aware of him physically. She tried not to be but she couldn't help it. The length of his legs and the slimness of his hips in tight jeans, the lightly tanned skin and fine dark hairs on his forearms, which begged to be touched, like satin; his dark hair shining like glass, the light and humour in his beautiful green eyes – everything about him invaded her with tangible, unsettling energy.

'What did she tell you?' asked Beth.

'How horrible your mother was to you.'

Beth was mortified. 'Does Rhianwen tell you *everything*?'

'Most things,' said Morgan. 'Hey, don't be embarrassed. It's only nature. We're friends, aren't we? Friends can talk about anything. I have much better conversations with you than with the idiots at school.'

76

'Do you?' She felt curious – and flattered.

'Boys are so childish. I get on much better with girls. Always have.'

A pause. They went on climbing upwards though the trees. It was cool under the branches, but the sun burned overhead. Then he asked, 'Have you got a boyfriend, Beth?'

'You must be joking!' she cried. 'My parents would kill me!'

'Oh.'

'I suppose you have a girlfriend,' she said lightly, not caring what the answer was. Merely interested. That was what she told herself, anyway.

'Not really. Well, no one serious.'

'You have, then.'

'Girls I'm friends with, that's all.' He was being cagey; Beth didn't like that. 'You're fourteen, aren't you?'

'Thirteen,' said Beth.

Morgan said something under his breath; it sounded like, 'Shit, three years,' but she couldn't be sure. After a moment he asked, 'Have you thought about the things my mum told you?'

'All the time.'

'Well? Did it make sense?'

'Yes, it made sense.'

Morgan smiled at her; that always brought a strange heat to her stomach. 'You can tell your brother we don't really hold black masses and sacrifice virgins, then.'

'But what do you do?'

'Nothing much. Just observe the Sabbats: light candles, share wine and cake, say thank you to the Goddess. It's a bit like church, really. Mum's more into it than I am. I'm not superstitious, but I like the idea of a Goddess and I believe in showing nature some respect. What's wrong with that?'

'I have dreams about cats,' said Beth. 'What does that mean?'

'It's the Goddess trying to reach you,' Morgan said softly. 'Cats are her messengers. Shall we go and look at the Hellstone?'

'I thought that's where you were taking me,' said Beth.

' "Hell" means holy, actually,' he said. 'Bet you didn't know that.'

As they came up over the crest of the hill, through oak trees and long grass turning dry and yellow, Beth could hear people singing.

'What the hell's that?' said Morgan.

Half a dozen high voices were joined in a hymn. As Beth and Morgan came out into the clearing, Beth saw a group of three teenage boys, a girl and two women, standing by the far side of the stone. They were in a circle with hymn-books and crucifixes. A woman with short brown hair and severe glasses was scattering drops of water from a flask as they sang.

Luke was with them.

Beth's instinct was to slink away until they'd gone, but Morgan marched straight into the clearing and stood facing them across the silvery bulk of the stone. Beth hung back, but Luke looked up and saw her. His eyes were expressionless.

Morgan stood with his thumbs hooked in his belt. The group looked at him, but went on singing, as if hoping he'd go away.

'What the hell are you doing?' he demanded.

The hymn broke up raggedly.

'Kindly go away,' said the brown-haired woman.

'No, I'm interested,' said Morgan. Beth found his bravado both shocking and thrilling, in a perverse way.

'This stone has been used as a site of pagan activities,' said the woman. 'We're exorcizing the evil influences.'

'Sanctifying the area,' added the second woman, who was hugely overweight, with white-blond hair in a pony-tail and white eyelashes.

'Well, you can just fuck off,' said Morgan.

There was a horrified silence.

Beth heard Luke say, 'He's one of them.'

The white-blond woman gave Morgan a look of hard contempt. 'You're a very ignorant, silly young man. Don't interfere with what you don't understand.'

'You're the ones who don't understand.'

Morgan jumped up on the stone and walked towards them. Beth held her breath. She saw his narrow, gilded figure on the Hellstone; saw the faces of the hymn-singers, frozen with disgust. And then she saw . . .

Shadows, looming through the trees. Ghost-shapes that shouldn't be there, dark, transparent and overblown, towering over the humans. They were a procession, filling the clearing. Lumbering animalistic figures, swathed in flapping cloaks, with horns and antlers upswept to pierce the sky.

Beth shrank down in the grass, transfixed. Time had stopped turning as delicately as a music-box ballerina; nothing seemed to move except the flow of shadow-figures. All around, she felt the trees breathing, the leaves licking her like tongues, and some uncanny, honeyed fire running through her own body. And there was a silhouette, rippling and changing as if seen through water, with a single lethal horn like that of a unicorn.

In the burning heat of day, the dry grass turned crisp as frost, and the Hellstone to solid ice. Beth was in a fire, burning. But everything else was black winter.

The world shook itself, and the vision was over. It had happened between one breath and the next. Beth was overwhelmed, but she wasn't afraid; she wasn't even shaking. It had happened too fast for that.

Morgan was still walking across the stone. He halted and looked down at the group, with his back to Beth.

'Have you got the faintest idea what you're meddling with?' he said softly. 'If you have any sense you'll quit. Go on, *fuck off*.'

Beth didn't know what they'd seen in his face, or sensed in the glade, but she saw their expressions change. Sudden doubt, consternation, panic. Clutching their hymn-books, crosses and holy water, they began to hurry away into the woods on the other side, glancing back at Morgan and muttering angrily among themselves.

Morgan came back to Beth and jumped down, looking pleased with himself. 'They won't come back in a hurry. Stupid prats. I suppose Luke brought them up here.'

Beth could hardly speak. 'Did you see – did you feel cold, or see something?'

'What?'

'Shadows. People with horns.'

'No, Beth. Did you?'

She swallowed hard. 'It's nothing. I must have imagined it.'

'I shouldn't have told you about the good folk. I didn't expect you to start seeing them.' He sat down on the edge of the stone, and put his arm round her waist so she would sit down beside him. *Never let a boy touch you*, Olivia said in her mind, but the touch was impersonal and he took his hand away as soon as she had sat down. The stone was baking hot, the air heavy and hay-scented. 'Are you okay, Beth?'

'Yes, fine.'

'I'm sorry about that, but I can't stand these people. They call *us* superstitious! But there *is* something here, Beth, and it will take more than them to drive it away. You saw it, didn't you? And they felt it. Scared 'em shitless.'

Beth felt annoyed by his apparent callousness. 'You needn't have been so rude! I expect they're just like most of the people at my church: kind and well-intentioned and a bit lost.'

'You said it. Lost. It's a crutch. Saves them having to think for themselves.'

'I suppose you know everything!'

'Don't be daft.' He touched her shoulder, only briefly, as if trying to stop himself. 'I wasn't getting at you. I didn't mean to upset you, Beth. Sorry.'

'It's okay.'

Morgan leaned back on one elbow, but she remained sitting up. He said, 'I wish you'd talk to me.'

'I am talking to you.'

'No, I mean I wish you'd tell me what's inside your head.'

'Why?' she said, mildly horrified.

'You fascinate me, Beth. Your mother thinks you're one thing but you're not, you're a mystery. You're one of us, really. You ought to run away and live with us.'

Beth shivered, in spite of the heat. 'Don't be silly.'

'I think my mum would have liked a daughter. She keeps telling me to treat you like a baby sister, anyway. Do I treat you like a sister?'

'Yes, of course.'

Morgan looked at her with irises all green-gold flame, like a cat's. 'It isn't getting any easier, I can tell you.'

Beth's whole body flushed from cold to burning hot, because she had felt safe with him, and suddenly she didn't any more.

Chapter Six

THE fourth summer.

When Beth arrived with her parents, they found Heather in the kitchen, cleaning a shotgun on a table covered with newspaper and oily rags.

'Bloody rabbits all over the paddock,' Heather said by way of explanation. 'Make yourselves at home. Put the kettle on the Aga, Beth, while I finish this, there's a dear.'

Beth's grandfather came in, and immediately took her father for a stroll round the garden. Beth watched them through the window. Two aloof, handsome men without much in common, she thought, but their aversion to hearing her mother and grandmother bickering.

'Where's Luke?' Heather asked.

'He wanted to stay at home this time,' said Olivia, 'so I let him. We've got lots of new people at church and Luke's helping to organize a group for the children. The change in him this year has been remarkable. He's grown up so much. The Lord is really working through him now.'

'Terrific,' said Heather, squinting down the gun barrels. 'Shame to see the children have grown apart, though.'

Luke had never said a word to Beth about the incident at the Hellstone last year. He hadn't needed to. The glowering looks he had given her afterwards had been extremely eloquent. He was becoming ever more involved at church, so Beth left him to it. She didn't want to know why she sometimes heard him laughing through the bedroom wall at night. She was simply relieved that this year, at last, she had been allowed to come to her grandparents alone.

'Well, it wasn't healthy, the way Luke used to cling to Beth all the time,' Olivia said brusquely. 'They should be devoting themselves to God, not to each other.'

'Hmph,' said Heather.

Beth thought they were going to start arguing, but Olivia said, 'I must wash my hands,' and left the room.

Beth thought of her guilty secret, and was glad her mother couldn't read her mind. I'm friends with the witch and I'm going to see her the first moment I can get away! And her son, but we haven't done anything wrong, and we won't, because he's decent and he wouldn't fancy me anyway; I know he's only teasing me when he says I'm pretty.

'Beth, take your jacket off and make the tea,' said Heather. 'I don't know why you always hover about as if you're visiting the Queen when you first get here.'

Beth obeyed. While her mother was absent, she asked cautiously, 'Grandma, you know that Mrs Rhys you warned us about the first time we came?'

'What about her?'

'Is she still around?'

'Unfortunately, yes. Why d'you ask?'

'Nothing, it's just that I thought I saw her in the post office once.'

'Hmph.' Heather sounded disgusted. 'Dyed hair and hippie clothes?'

'Sort of, but she looked harmless; I wondered –'

'She didn't speak to you, did she?'

'No.'

'Good. She caused your mother a lot of grief; I know it's a long time ago but I can't forgive her. Oh, she's nice enough to speak to but she's a hard-faced bitch underneath. I don't ask much of you, Beth, but trust me in this, eh? If ever the woman speaks to you, ignore her.'

'Yes, Grandma. What about her son?'

Heather paused in her gun-oiling. 'How did you know she had a son?'

'Erm, I don't know; I thought you told me.'

'Maybe. Oh, he's as rotten as his dam. I heard he nearly got expelled last term. Typical.'

Before Beth could ask why, Olivia came back in. She was in a good mood, bright and breezy.

'Beth's been wonderful this year as well,' she went on. 'Haven't you, dear? Pastor Blair says my children have been touched by the Holy Spirit.'

Beth said nothing. She couldn't explain that she had been a solemn, angelic robot all year to hide the fact that her faith in the church was wearing very thin. Ever since that day with Rhianwen.

It wasn't easy, to feel her beliefs dissolving; it was agonizing. Between Rhianwen's gentle common sense and the pastor's strident conviction, Beth was still swimming in chaos. Perhaps other teenagers dealt with it by having screaming arguments with their parents or even leaving home, but that wasn't Beth's way. The worse she felt, the more deeply she buried it.

'I've been thinking,' said Olivia, putting an arm round Beth's shoulders, 'and the Lord has given me a very clear message. This is going to be your last stay with your grandparents.'

Beth was horrified, but managed to hide it. 'Why?'

'You're growing up. You have work to do at church, you can't waste seven weeks each summer. Luke's started without me having to ask him! The thing is, the pastor is planning to set up a church school for the children of the congregation. Won't that be exciting? Beth, we want you to teach there when you leave school.'

Beth was stunned. 'What if I –' she couldn't say, *don't want to do it*. 'What if I'm no good at teaching?'

'Then the Lord will call you to some other duty. Everyone has a vocation. But you're bright; you'll be a wonderful teacher! Just think, you might end up running the school! The Lord has called you to serve him, Beth.'

A headmistress, like Heather. Beth thought dully, I told Luke I wanted to be like Grandma; should've kept my mouth shut. If only I knew what I *do* want. To teach beliefs I don't hold any longer would be impossible, but how can I ever tell Mum?

Later, she waved her parents goodbye, feeling dead inside.

84

The future was abstract. Knowing that this might be her last summer of freedom was torment enough for now.

The next day, Beth took the familiar route across the fields to Rhianwen's, virtually running all the way. I hope Morgan isn't away, she thought. Hope he hasn't got some girlfriend with him!

Beth chastised herself for the thought. As Rhianwen insisted that Morgan behave like a brother – and he always had – what business had she to feel jealous?

Rhianwen, who was painting at an easel on the lawn, greeted Beth warmly. Morgan was there too, stretched out on the grass reading a book. Seeing Beth, he smiled and waved, as if he weren't much bothered to see her. She felt a bit hurt.

'Don't just lie there,' said Rhianwen. 'Go and make a cup of tea, or something.'

'Give us a hand, Beth?' said Morgan, getting up languidly. His hair was shorter and he was dressed all in black; narrow jeans, sleeveless T-shirt. He looked unconventional, rather punk-like; sinister and beautiful, with his fine-boned face and shaggy dark hair. He was nearly six feet tall, slender and clearly very fit.

As soon as they were out of Rhianwen's sight in the big, stripped-pine kitchen, Morgan threw his arms round Beth and hugged her. He'd never done anything like it before. Beth went dizzy, and his arms around her were so tight she couldn't get her breath. She felt flustered.

'Beth! I thought you were never coming,' he said.

'Same time as last year,' she gasped. Now he had one hand in her hair, the other drifting over her waist towards her hips. She extricated herself, alarmed.

Morgan stood looking at her. His eyes were too intent, too full of light. 'You look lovely,' he said. 'You know, it's really hard to get through the year without even being able to write or phone.'

Beth felt awkward suddenly. 'I bet you didn't even think about me.'

'I did. I'll have you know I gave up an exchange trip to Germany and climbing in Snowdonia to see you.'

Beth wasn't sure what to read into that: '*because I really like you*' or, '*so you'd better make it worth my while*'.

'You didn't have to!'

'But I wanted to see you. Didn't you want to see me?' He smiled teasingly. 'You're blushing.'

She pressed the back of her hand to her face. 'This might be the last holiday I can come and see you, anyway,' she said in a rush.

'How come?'

Beth explained.

'Your bloody parents!' Morgan cried.

'I didn't choose them!' said Beth.

'Don't get upset.' He slid his hand round her shoulders and kissed her cheek, and his touch felt anything but brotherly. 'You're here now. Let's make the best of it. There's this beautiful place we can go for a bike ride –'

Morgan let go of her rather suddenly, and Beth realized that Rhianwen was in the doorway.

'Put Beth down, Morgan,' Rhianwen said sternly; she was half joking, but she meant it.

'Her mother's upset her again. I was comforting her!'

'All right, but if you ever forget what I told you' – she pointed at a beam, where bunches of herbs were pinned up to dry – 'I'll nail you up there to make table decorations.'

'Is it true you nearly got expelled?' Beth asked.

'Who told you that?' Morgan exclaimed.

They had cycled five miles along country lanes – Beth having borrowed Rhianwen's bicycle – and now they'd left the bikes in a gateway and were climbing a long hill alongside a hedgerow. Bees and flies droned in swathes of golden heat. The scents of moist earth and sun-baked greenery were making her dizzy with pleasure.

Morgan was holding Beth's hand. She was so stunned and flattered that he liked her, she couldn't resist. Anyway, she didn't really think he would try anything else. He was too sensible to disobey Rhianwen. His hand felt affectionate and strong; she was rather shocked to find out how wonderful it felt.

'My gran told me.'

'She would.' He sighed. 'It was nothing. A misunderstanding. That's why I *didn't* get expelled.' He halted suddenly and kissed her lightly on the mouth. Beth's nerves leapt. She knew it was wrong but she didn't want to stop him.

'Sorry,' he said, walking on again. 'Mum keeps on about treating you like a sister but it's hard, if you know what I mean.'

Beth tried not to think about what he meant.

'Not far now,' he said. 'The view from the top is worth the walk.'

At the top of the hill there was a five-bar gate in a hedge. Beth could see a sun-flooded valley beyond.

'Climb up on the gate,' said Morgan. 'You can see better from there.'

He was right; there was a glorious view of woods on their right, a silken-green valley hazed with sunlight falling away to the left. Light shone through the trees. The grass was rich with wild flowers and insects.

While Beth sat on top of the gate, Morgan stood on one of the cross-bars behind her and put his left arm round her waist, his hand resting across her hips. With his other hand he brushed her hair aside and kissed her neck. Beth said nothing; shivers prickled her skin. As he stood holding her, with his chest pressed to her back and his chin on her shoulder, she was acutely aware of the heat and insistent tension of his body against hers. A need so strong he was almost trembling.

'Worth the climb, wasn't it?' he said lightly.

'It's beautiful,' said Beth.

Now what do I do? she thought wildly. I can't move without pushing him away but I shouldn't let him do this. There was a small sun dancing about in her chest. She knew perfectly well what Morgan wanted, though she tried to deny it, telling herself he was just being friendly. But Beth wanted something too; she loved the warmth of his hands on her, his energetic presence, the clean smell of his hair. Morgan was making her feel desirable and wanted after a lifetime of feeling she was a plain nonentity . . . and she found it madly intoxicating.

Rhianwen had told her, in her gentle way, that sex was nothing to be ashamed of – but it was Olivia's strident voice Beth heard loudest. Unnamed horrors would follow if ever she let a boy touch her.

Beth was utterly petrified. She daren't breathe.

The hand on her stomach slid lower. And then the fine strong fingers probed gently between her thighs.

'You shouldn't do that,' Beth gasped.

'Don't you like it?' Morgan had the sweetest expression.

'Yes, I like it, but you shouldn't do it.'

'I know. I'll stop if you tell me to.'

He took his hand away. Then he leaned around her, turned her slightly towards him and kissed her. The warm lips on hers made her feel weird, invaded. His tongue parted her closed lips; it was too intimate, too intrusive, and yet, and yet . . .

The sun inside her multiplied, shooting along her limbs and dropping hot and heavy into her abdomen. She opened her mouth to him. Thirsting.

His right hand, now, was undoing her jeans and sliding down again, flesh on flesh, into her secret, forbidden folds.

'Don't!' said Beth, breaking the kiss, but it was too late; his fingers were there, working gently between her lips, and she could feel them growing wet with her fluids, and she could have died.

'Shush,' whispered Morgan, holding her still with his left arm. 'All you have to do is sit here.'

The air was like amber, resinous and electric. His lips meandered over her ear and cheek in light kisses, hypnotizing her. Beth sat absolutely still, her breathing shallow and her heart thudding. Excruciatingly aware of the moist, moving pressure . . .

Actually it felt nice ... wonderful ... like an exquisite, demanding itch.

'Oh, God,' said Beth.

Her heart accelerated. Her blood seemed to be rushing in all directions at once. And then the sun exploded. She was on a golden thread; flying, dangling, caught.

Beth turned her face into Morgan's shoulder and sobbed for breath. She was trembling all over. Annihilated.

Very gently, Morgan drew his hand away, refastened her jeans, and cuddled her. When she could bear to glance at him, he looked highly amused. 'Are you all right?'

'What did you do to me?' Beth exclaimed.

'Beats holding hands, doesn't it?' he said, jumping off the gate.

And that was all. He didn't ask her to do anything else; didn't even try to touch her or kiss her again. But now she wanted him to. Morgan talked all the way back as if nothing had happened, while Beth didn't say a word, and afterwards couldn't remember a thing he'd said. She was melting with confusion, and with the echo of that indescribable sensation.

A few hours ago she'd been terrified of Morgan touching her. Now she craved his hands on her, wanted to rub herself all over him like a cat. But Morgan wouldn't play. All he gave her, when they said goodbye, was a very warm and knowing smile.

'See you tomorrow?'

This was not how things were meant to be.

The carrot-haired girl from the post office, Genette, had taken a liking to Beth and they sometimes hung round the village together. It was a one-sided relationship. Genette was totally self-centred and talked continually about herself; no input from Beth was invited or required. And all Genette talked about was boys.

She was fifteen and already on her third or fourth boyfriend; Beth had lost count. Genette's experiences were horror stories which she relished telling. The theme was that all boys were selfish, only wanted one thing, and would pester you until they got it. When it happened it was uncomfortable, crude, painful and disappointing. Then you had to worry about being pregnant or catching a disease – 'Me mam'd kill me!' – and then the boy would chuck you and, for an encore, tell all his friends you were a slag.

Genette's adventures were bringing Beth's fears to explicit life. She'd heard them last summer, as well as this. To hear first-hand accounts of degradation brought her to a state of frigid horror far more effectively than Olivia's direst warnings.

But Morgan's not like that, is he?

Beth sometimes felt like asking Genette why she went on doing it, if it was so awful, but it was hard to get a word in. Genette was in love with the sheer drama of it.

Beth was sitting with her on the village green, the day after the incident on the gate. For once, Beth was more concerned by her own feelings than anyone else's, and she broke forcefully into Genette's flow.

'What if – what if a boy did something nice to you, but didn't want anything for himself?'

Genette stopped, her freckled face a picture of disbelief. 'What d'you mean, summat nice?'

'You know,' Beth whispered, 'made you come.'

'What, you come and he doesn't? What planet are you from?' Genette gaped at Beth as if dumbstruck by her naïvety. Then she said flatly, 'That never happens.'

'But what if it did?'

'I'd marry 'im,' Genette said emphatically.

All the summers ran into one in Beth's mind; the years in between were a grey abyss, once she was here, living her secret life.

Beth daren't risk going to Rhianwen's too often. The more she went, the more risk there was of someone seeing her, and the news getting back to Heather. And now she was more nervous than ever of seeing Morgan. She was embarrassed, confused, terrified of what might happen.

But she went, anyway, two days after the fateful bike ride. It was a compulsion. Her fear of sinning had never kept her away before.

And so Beth found herself alone with Morgan again, walking in the woods behind Rhianwen's cottage. He held her hand firmly in his. His grasp felt reassuring; she hoped he couldn't feel her pulse leaping madly.

'I suppose you're studying for O levels, are you?' he asked.

'Starting next term,' she said, pulling a face. It wasn't quite so nerve-racking, now they were actually together; worrying about it had been worse.

'I'm doing A's. Then university, I suppose.'

'Botany?'

'No, I want to study zoology.'

'Are you going to be a vet?'

'I might,' Morgan said thoughtfully, 'but I really like whales and dolphins and that. What about you?'

'My mother wants me to be a teacher.' She sighed.

'Bethie,' said Morgan, 'I meant, what do *you* want to do?'

'I've no idea. I like animals, too. And I like art. No one's ever really asked me before.'

'Jesus,' Morgan said under his breath. His arm slipped round her waist. 'You know the other day – I didn't upset you, did I?'

'Of course not,' Beth lied.

'Have you never had an orgasm before?'

She swallowed the wrong way, and nearly choked. 'You're very outspoken, aren't you?' she gasped.

'Why not? I suppose your mother covers up the piano legs.'

Beth laughed, despite herself. 'She was always warning us not to touch ourselves so I didn't. And the pastor goes on about unnatural acts. I hadn't a clue what they were talking about until I was twelve. But I've had them in dreams, feelings like that . . . You're really embarrassing me, Morgan.'

'I know,' he said, 'but how are you going to get over being embarrassed, unless we talk about it? Look, Beth, I really fancy you, but I wouldn't dream of doing anything you didn't want.

So stop looking at me like I'm going to jump on you, okay? You're safe.'

'Thanks,' she said, relaxing a bit. She put her arm round his waist, and it felt heavenly.

'That's better,' he said.

'What about Rhianwen?'

'What about her?'

'Why does she keep telling you not to touch me?'

Morgan shrugged, in the endearing way he had. 'Because you're only fourteen, I suppose.'

Without warning, he pulled her against an oak tree and kissed her. Beth felt the molten sunlight running through her and she pressed herself against him. She wanted that feeling again, oh so badly.

Then it happened. The whole wood began to sway around her. It was as if she were underwater, drowning in glass-greenness, everything shimmering and breaking up around her, moving in slow motion.

She clung to Morgan and cried out, but her own voice was muffled.

There was a dark figure coming towards her through the water. Huge and ponderous, with a black hat and a flapping black coat, it rippled as it came, exuding formless menace.

The moment stretched out. Beth tried to scream.

The vision ended. She hadn't realized it but she'd slid down to a crouching position at the base of the tree. She was trembling violently. Morgan was kneeling behind her, holding her tight, his arms a cradle of safety around her chest and waist.

'What is it?' he asked anxiously.

'I saw someone,' she whispered.

'Was it one of the good folk again?'

'No, it was something really evil.'

'Describe what you saw.'

She tried. Morgan didn't laugh at her. He listened.

He turned her round in his arms and hugged her. His body felt wonderful against hers, slim and hard and warm. 'It wasn't the Devil, Beth. It was a vision of some sort. We'll tell Mum when we get home, eh? She'll know what it means. Don't be frightened now.'

He held her until she stopped trembling. His hands moved over her, stroking, soothing. He kissed her neck. 'Hush, Beth, hush. It's all right.'

She was warm now. Melting.

They should have stopped, but they didn't. One movement slid into another. There was a hollow beneath the oak and they eased down into it, cushioned by grass and leaves, shrouded by branches. A leaf-green bed, glistening with dappled sunlight.

Morgan undid her shirt and her jeans and ran his lips and tongue all over her stomach. Then he found the catch of her bra, and his hands and mouth were on her breasts. He gasped, as if he were on the verge of tears. Their legs were entwined, his pelvis hard against hers.

'Oh God, I can't wait any longer,' Morgan breathed. He pulled his T-shirt over his head and his hair fluffed out with static, like a black halo.

Beth was in a hot river, flowing.

It was awkward, taking off the rest of their clothes, but the awkwardness didn't matter. Didn't last.

But the stem of flesh that sprang loose as he dragged off his jeans; that was a shock. It looked red and moist and silky-hard, a fearful totem, but she'd gone too far to stop and she felt waves of heat and coldness sweep one after another over her with the enormity of what was going to happen.

Yet Beth felt no guilt. She didn't even think about what she'd seen her parents doing. This bore no relation to any horror story she'd heard. It was different. It was the first time in all the universe this had ever happened. Soft, gentle, beautiful and urgent . . . Morgan's lips and hands on her body, his naked legs between hers.

He'd done this before. He knew exactly what he was doing. Exactly. His hand was there, in her secret folds, making the golden thread sing . . .

'Wait,' he whispered. 'Must use this.'

He had a condom. Beth shut her eyes. Didn't want to see what he was doing, didn't care.

Then he was lowering himself between her hips, looking straight into her eyes; his lips parted, his face rapt, worried and breathless, just like hers.

She felt the domed pressure against her tender, innermost lips, painful and electric. Breeching a tight barrier, sliding deeper. Her virginity, gone in a heartbeat.

It hurt at first, but her wetness enveloped him and then it was like silk and satin. Urgent. His mouth was open on hers, his hair brushing her cheek, an impossible wild rhythm like a dance possessing them both.

'It's sacred, Beth,' he said in her ear.

She felt the explosion overtaking her again, and she clutched him shamelessly as the molten sun burst. Much stronger this time. So violent that she cried aloud in sheer amazement. And he wasn't gentle now but thrusting hard, helplessly pouring his body and soul into her.

Beautiful, yes. A fierce beauty that dragged them, whirling, up to the forest canopy and flung them back, transformed.

Then they lay dreaming, green eyes locked. He stayed inside her, moving gently, and she never wanted the melting sweetness of it to stop.

'Oh God, Beth,' said Morgan. 'I think I'm in love with you.'

Gently rebuttoning Beth's shirt for her and combing her hair with his fingers, Morgan felt passionately happy and pleased with himself. She looked beautifully flushed; she was languorous, satisfied and devastated, all at once. It felt thrilling to have done that to her; broken her shell of self-containment and introduced her to illicit pleasures her parents thought she should never experience. To have changed her for ever.

If Rhianwen ever finds out she'll kill me, he thought, but she won't find out. I know what she said but I don't care, I wanted this so much.

94

Beth's body was no longer nervously rigid to his touch but yielding and sensual. She was all over him, actually, and she made him want to laugh – out of affection, not mockery. Beth was weird, but she fascinated him; she saw things he had only sensed, and there was more going on in her head than she'd ever admit.

'Can you act like nothing happened in front of Rhianwen, when we go back?' Morgan asked.

Her eyes met his, gleaming with apprehension. 'I don't think so.'

'Well, we're going to have to. There's no hurry, anyway; I'd rather stay here with you. We'll wait until we've got over it, okay? Smile, Beth. Was it that bad?'

'It was wonderful,' she said softly. 'You know perfectly well it was wonderful.'

'It was the best thing that's ever happened to me,' Morgan said sincerely.

'But we shouldn't have –'

'Oh, look, God's waiting up there with a thunderbolt; he's got his eye on you, Beth.'

'Don't tease me.'

'By the way, do you always start seeing devils when you're about to do something wicked?'

'Stop it!'

'I'm cruel, I know. Don't feel guilty. No one will ever know.'

'Well, now I know why people do it, no matter how many times they're told not to.' Her mouth, deep-coloured with blood, almost formed a smile; her eyelids fell. Morgan couldn't resist kissing her. This had to happen again soon, had to.

'Now you know,' he said.

Morgan was grateful to a young woman who had told him that the infallible way to seduce a girl was to indulge her desires before his own. 'Never make her feel used,' she'd said. 'Be unselfish, and she'll want you so badly you won't have to twist her arm.' Then the young woman had shown him what she meant, several times, until he got it right.

And she'd imparted true wisdom. It had been agony, that

day on the gate, restraining himself while Beth gasped in his arms, but it had been worth it.

Your parents can go to hell, Beth.

I've got you now.

The dream again. Egyptian cats pacing, inviting Beth to cross the river. Boldly, without doubts, she put her foot on the mirror-surface.

And sank deep under the water. All was green, like Morgan's eyes, full of huge silvery bubbles that rushed up past her as she thrashed and drowned. Green with dark clouds, like blood in the water.

Once he's got what he wants, he'll despise you. Genette's words, harsh and cynical.

But the bad dreams and warnings didn't stop her.

The next time Beth saw Morgan she was withdrawn at first, so scared of rejection that she almost wanted to reject him first. But Morgan didn't behave like the boys in the terrible warnings. He was the same as ever; affectionate, teasing, delighted to see her. He soon joked her out of her mood. Rhianwen didn't seem to suspect anything. So Beth relented, and went to the woods with him again, as if drugged, and it was even more beautiful than the first time.

Heather gave Beth more freedom now she was older. She let Beth ride out alone on Whisky, or sent her out to walk the dogs, grateful for someone to exercise the animals. If Beth was on the horse, Morgan would meet her a couple of miles outside the village on his bike. They would go to the hill of the lovely view, tie Whisky up safely, and make love between the trees. If they were on foot, though, they'd go to the hollow beneath the oak; that was their place, sacred.

No one caught them. Beth felt herself opening up to the warm, moist rhythms of nature, transformed by Morgan's touch from an anxious child into a passionate, eager lover.

They always used a condom. Morgan was responsible, so Beth felt safe. He said he got them in town, never in the gossipy village.

'My mother's been on at me,' Morgan said one day, as they lay in long grass on the hill. 'She thinks I'm seeing too much of you.'

'She hasn't guessed, has she?' Beth was alarmed.

'No, she's just afraid something *might* happen; ha ha. I'll tell you what it is; she's jealous.'

'What of?' Beth exclaimed.

'She thinks I'm taking her little girl away from her.'

'I suppose it does look a bit selfish, the way we keep disappearing.'

'We ought to spend more time with her, if only to lull her suspicions,' said Morgan, 'but that's why Rhianwen doesn't know I'm with you today. She thinks I've gone cycling with some schoolfriends.'

'Funny,' said Beth, kissing his smooth, tanned chest. 'I've been deceiving my mother for years. I never thought you'd have to deceive yours.'

As they walked home along a narrow lane – Beth leading Whisky and Morgan wheeling his bike, so they could hold hands – five teenaged cyclists skimmed past in the other direction.

The leader turned and shouted over his shoulder, 'Who is it this time, Rhys? Dunno how you do it, you lucky bastard! It'll drop off!' Catcalls from the others rose and and fell in his wake.

'Who were they?' Beth cried.

'The prats I was meant to be cycling with.'

'What did he mean?'

'Nothing. He's an idiot. I'm not seeing anyone but you, Beth.'

She believed him, yet a thorn of insecurity slid under her skin. I don't really know him, she thought. Does he love me or am I just something to play with in the holidays? Beth found it hard to believe she could truly mean anything to him. Morgan made her feel scared sometimes, even oppressed; he could be almost too affectionate, too sexual, too intense, seeming to take her devotion for granted. Beth feared that he didn't know her, either; that he was loving an idealized version of her and not the real Beth at all.

Morgan asked suddenly, 'Can you get out of the house at night?'

'I shouldn't think so,' Beth said, startled. 'Why?'

He gave his seductive smile. 'Please try for me. There's something I've been longing to do.'

Anything for him.

Trembling, cold, and in a mild state of panic, Beth left her bedroom at one o'clock in the morning and crept downstairs, wincing at every creak. The dogs woke up and whined round her when she entered the kitchen; she tried to shush them. At any moment she expected the phone to ring and her grandfather to come rushing down to answer an emergency call. But tonight, as she let herself out of the back door, all remained silent.

Morgan, wearing a long dark coat, was waiting for her in a bus shelter a few yards from the rectory gate. They made their way to the footpath, across the fields and into the woods by the light of an egg-shaped waxing moon. Shadows of rabbits and hares bounded across their path. Trees, hedgerows and wheat stems rustled.

Morgan took her to the Hellstone. It shone like mica in the moonlight, rounded and silvery and crystalline. The rust streaks, which Beth knew were a mineral and not blood, glittered darkly.

'It's a bit cold,' said Beth.

'I'll keep you warm,' he said.

Morgan spread his coat on the centre of the rock. From a pocket he took matches and indigo candles, and began to light the candles in a circle, welding them to the rock with their own wax. The dancing flames turned the stone into an altar. The trees all around were breathing shadows, the sky beaten silver.

They undressed in silence, watching each other; Morgan's long slender body, golden in the sun, was ivory now, and so beautiful it took her breath away. He held out his arms and

Beth went into them, her long hair brushing his shoulders, his flesh folding smooth and warm against hers; and she was already aching to receive him, her fluids running like myrrh.

Morgan drew her on to the rock and made her kneel opposite him. To her amazement, he began to anoint her with oil from a small bottle. It smelled gorgeous, of frankincense and jasmine, sandalwood and musk and lavender. He stroked it on her face, smoothed it over her shoulders and breasts.

His fingers made trails of light on her skin, like tribal marks. Initiation.

'Dream of the moon,' he said softly, his face eldritch in the candle-glow. His fingers slid over her nipples, down her stomach, over the points of her hips and her small, curved buttocks. 'Dream of the Goddess.'

Beth smiled uncertainly. She was all gooseflesh with excitement. She took the phial from him and began to smear the oil over the contours of his chest. They anointed each other, hands sliding on a scented film, and she felt utterly pagan, sensual, animal; everything her mother dreaded.

Morgan pulled her down beside him.

'Do you believe in God?' he whispered, his oiled hand sliding between her legs.

'I don't know.' She folded her hand round his penis, loving the feel of it, rounded and hard and silky-warm, in her palm. He gave a soft laugh of pleasure.

'Do you believe in the Goddess?'

'Yes.'

'Give this to her.'

Morgan's reassurances that his beliefs were harmless were meaningless now. However innocent he seemed by day, in the darkness he was something else; a soft-eyed demon, seducing her with carnal pleasure into an abyss from which she'd never escape. He *was* the darkness, smiling not in love but in satisfaction at her downfall.

There had to be the sheath, of course. Even in this moment, he was effortlessly responsible.

When he slid inside her there was no pain, only gliding

sweetness and a star burning fiercer and fiercer in the red-veiled temple.

'The Goddess and the Horned God,' she whispered. 'Yes, yes.'

The moon shone hard into Beth's eyes. She saw an angel in white, plucked from a pedestal by a demon's claws and sent tumbling into the chasms of hell.

She saw rippling figures; there were men with wintry faces, walking round and round her, prodding her with sticks. The great crucifixes round their necks dazzled her. *She's guilty. She's one.*

Beth heard a fire crackling. The noise filled her ears like the rush of water; she was burning and drowning, falling, suffocating, with cruel mocking eyes all round her. She heard the distant sounds of someone running, bones breaking, a woman screaming.

But none of these visions chilled her pleasure. That went on through everything; Morgan's arms around her, one hand in her hair, one gripping her buttocks, and their mingled sweat, and the urgent essential heat melting them.

The horn of the unicorn pierced her, impaled her, split her into shards of diamond light.

They writhed against each other, crying out. She thought she would never breathe again. The visions died away with her breath.

Then calmness.

A pair of huge silver eyes were gazing down on Beth from a dark face, telling her, *All this must come to pass, you can bear it or fall*; coalescing to a single eye, the moon; and then she became aware of Morgan kissing her in the hollow of her throat, where the sweat and oil had pooled.

'Now you belong to the Goddess,' he said, his beautiful face rising over her; moon-washed skin and bewitching eyes.

'Yes, I felt her, I saw her.'

Morgan hugged her so tight she thought her spine would break. 'Oh Beth, I've never felt anything like this before. I wish I could stay here with you for ever.'

'You'll never come here with anyone else,' Beth said with

absolute conviction, as if the Goddess were speaking through her. 'And neither will I.'

She became aware of cold air on her skin. The initiation was over.

There was a strange moment as Morgan drew away from her, and sat on the edge of the Hellstone to pick up their clothes. She thought she heard him say, 'Oh, *shit*,' under his breath, and then he seemed to freeze for a second or two.

'What's wrong?' she asked. She felt a trickle of fluid come out of her and soak into the coat lining as she sat up.

'Nothing.'

Beth was concerned about the coat now. 'Your coat is going to stink of this oil. What will Rhianwen say?'

'It'll wash out.' He sighed, pushed his hair back, and smiled at her. 'It will be all right, Beth. Nothing to worry about.'

'You smell like a Turkish brothel,' said Heather at breakfast the next morning. 'What have you been doing?'

Beth cringed inwardly. She had tried to bathe the oil away, but it clung. 'They were trying to flog this perfume in the shop yesterday,' she said. 'The assistant sprayed it on me before I could stop her.'

'For God's sake, go and wash it off. You'll frighten the horses.'

Beth ran up to her room, then stood looking out of the window, smiling to herself. She had flown to another world last night. It had been terrifying – but, oh God, so thrilling.

She and Morgan made love twenty-seven times that summer. She counted and remembered every single one.

Not least the last time.

Arriving at Rhianwen's the day before she was due to go home, Beth couldn't find anyone at first. Then she heard Morgan calling her name from the direction of the animal pens.

He was in the smallest shed, in darkness, with an owl sitting on his arm. 'This chap had a broken foot,' said Morgan, smiling at her. 'Rhianwen put him right. We can let him go soon. D'you want to stroke him?'

It was at that moment, as she stroked the soft feathers and looked into the bird's huge black eyes, that Beth realized she was in love with Morgan. Strange that it hadn't dawned on her while they were making love, divine though that was; it was only now, seeing him with the owl on his arm and the rapt shine in his eyes, that she knew. It was a different feeling, much deeper. The revelation trickled through her from cell to cell, like petrol. Oh God, what are we going to do?

'Good news,' he said, putting the owl back into a cage. 'Mum's gone shopping in Nottingham with a friend. She won't be back for hours!'

Morgan took her hand and led her into the house. Beth had never seen his bedroom before; forbidden territory. Fascinating, because it was like glimpsing a hidden part of his soul. There was a sloping ceiling, ivory-washed walls with posters – mostly dolphins and sports cars, with a couple of rock groups – and a single bed with a patchwork cover. There were shelves of books, a few model cars, a battered teddy bear half-hidden in one corner, but it was surprisingly tidy.

'Who's this female?' Beth said, scrutinizing the posters.

'Sandy Denny. A folk singer. And that one's Marilyn Monroe; don't tell me you don't recognize *her*.'

Beth stuck out her tongue at him. 'Can I look at your records?'

'You can look at anything you like, my dear.'

She knelt down on the soft deep-green carpet. Some of the artists she'd heard of – Led Zeppelin, David Bowie, the Stranglers – but there were many others she didn't know; Planxty, Horslips, the Sensational Alex Harvey Band, Lou Reed, Dr Feelgood.

'The music of Satan,' said Beth, fingering through the album covers with relish. She was aware that this was an everyday experience for most teenagers, but for her it was like Christmas. She and Morgan seemed to be doing everything the wrong way round.

'Decided what you want to listen to?'

She pushed the Horslips album at him. '*The Táin*,' he said. 'Good choice.'

He put the record on a stereo that sat in a corner on the floor. An eerie, electric lament began, evolving into a throbbing rhythm; she'd never heard anything like it before.

'All these books!' she said.

'Never mind the books,' said Morgan, stretching out on the patchwork cover. 'Come here. Of all the strange places we've done it, we've never made love on a bed before. Do you want me to strew some leaves and grass around, make you feel at home?'

Beth made a running leap on to him and they wrestled, laughing.

'Do you really care about me, Beth,' he breathed into her ear, 'or do you just want me for my body?'

It was later, just as she was on the waterfall-edge of orgasm, that someone pounded on the front door. Beth couldn't stop; she went flying out over the edge, falling through the silver-sharp foam of ecstasy. But when it faded, she heard the pounding again.

She and Morgan both froze. The music had long finished.

'Who the hell's that?' he said.

'Don't answer it.'

'But if it's someone with a cat, I should see what they want. I told Mum I would.'

Holding their breath, they went to peer out of the window. There were a few moments of silence. Then a man in a suit walked away from the front door and along the path, turning and looking back at the upstairs windows as he went. Beth ducked. She thought she would die of shock.

'It's my father!' she gasped. 'What the hell's he doing here?'

'That's your father, is it?'

'Has he gone?'

'He's getting into a brown Rover. He's turning round in the lane.' Morgan exhaled. 'He's gone.'

Beth was shaking and wide-eyed. 'Had you seen him before?'

'Once or twice. I thought he was just some bloke Rhianwen knows; I think his name's Philip. I never made the connection. So, that's your dad.'

'Yes, but what would he be doing here?' she exclaimed.

'I've no idea! I've never spoken to him. Rhianwen's never said. I'm sure it doesn't mean anything; he couldn't possibly know you were here, could he?'

'I suppose if Rhianwen knows my mum, she must know my dad as well. I didn't think they were speaking, that's all.'

Morgan shrugged. 'It's a mystery to me. Would you rather we got dressed and did something innocuous?'

'No, come back to bed,' said Beth. 'You haven't finished.'

'It doesn't matter.'

'Yes, it does. I don't want you to be unsatisfied.'

'You're so good to me, Bethie,' he said, with a charmingly helpless smile.

Because it might be the last time, she thought, clinging to him, moved to overwhelming tenderness by the rapture he found in her. The last time. But she couldn't say it.

Afterwards, as they lay satiated with arms and legs tangled up together, Beth had a terrifying sensation that they were not alone. There was a presence with them. She lay motionless, not daring to breathe, chills sheeting over her.

A tiny noise made her jump so violently she banged her hand on the wall.

'Jumpy, aren't you?' said Morgan, holding her bruised hand. 'What's wrong?'

'There's someone there,' she whispered, looking at the door.

'Oh my God,' he said. He got up slowly, went to the door and turned the knob. Beth's heart tapped wildly at her breast-bone. She had no idea what she expected to see; Rhianwen, her father, or the Devil.

Morgan drew back the door a sliver. What insinuated itself through the gap was a slate-blue cat. Bast.

'Jesus, cat!' said Morgan. 'You scared the hell out of us!'

Bast jumped on the bed. Beth gathered her in her arms, laughing with nervous relief. 'Ouch, your *claws!*'

It was holding her cat that made Beth start crying. She'd been all right until then. Morgan sat down by her and put his arm round her.

'Don't, Beth.'

'I'm going home tomorrow. I don't want to.'

'Shit, I'm fed up with this!' Morgan exclaimed with sudden fervour.

Beth was alarmed. 'What, fed up with me?'

'Don't be silly, I mean I'm sick of having to meet in secret because of our stupid families! I can't wait another year to see you! You only live in Birmingham, for God's sake, not New Zealand! It's bloody ridiculous!'

'It's not my fault,' Beth said sharply.

Morgan hugged her. 'Sorry, Beth. I know that. Look, I love you, I can wait. We *will* be together one day, I promise.'

Beth wanted to believe it, but she daren't let herself. Life had made her a pessimist. 'My mother will never let me go willingly. By the time I'm eighteen and you're twenty, you'll have forgotten me.'

'No,' Morgan insisted, kissing her passionately all over her face and neck. 'Never, never.'

We got away with it, Beth thought one week later, as she stared out of the window of her classroom, seeing nothing but gilded memories of summer. Her overwhelming emotion was not of loving or missing Morgan, but of relief that they had not been found out. She felt too young to know what loving him really meant; too young to shoulder the immensity of all that had happened between them.

We got away with it. There was no thunderbolt from God, after all.

Beth had been back at school three weeks when she began to feel ill, and her breasts began to hurt, and her period never came.

In heaven, God pointed a finger, and the clouds turned black.

Chapter Seven

'Mrs Herne,' said the doctor. 'I'm afraid the cause of your daughter's symptoms is that she is approximately twelve weeks pregnant.'

Beth's mother made a small noise of exasperation. 'Doctor, with all due respect, I don't think you've listened to a word I've said. I brought the child in with a stomach bug. Every young woman who goes off her food is not automatically pregnant.'

The doctor tapped his pen on his desk. Beth's head drooped lower, her hair hiding her face. 'I am aware of that, Mrs Herne. However, having examined her, I find Beth to have all the symptoms of early pregnancy. A urine test will confirm things, but –'

'There's no need for a test,' Olivia said crisply, 'because there is absolutely no possibility whatsoever of Beth being pregnant.'

Please God, let me die, thought Beth. She was going to pass out, at the very least.

The doctor cleared his throat. 'Mrs Herne, would you mind if I spoke to Beth alone?'

'Yes, I would. Anything you have to say to her, you can say to me.'

'Beth?' Beth nodded. She daren't do anything else. The doctor went on, 'I know this must have come as a shock, but the important thing is not to judge Beth. She needs support. There are different options to consider –'

'I think you've wasted quite enough of our time already, thank you. We're leaving.'

Olivia took Beth's wrist, led her out of the surgery and along the street. Neither of them said a word. Beth's bones had turned to dough with terror.

She expected her mother to fly into a ferocious rage as soon as they were home. Instead, Olivia remained silent and closed, like a waxwork. She seemed to move in slow motion as she took off her coat and shoes. Beth longed to blurt out, 'Mum? Please listen, please try to understand!' but she was afraid that a single word would unleash a hair-trigger retaliation.

'Go to your room, Bethia,' Olivia said woodenly. 'I need to pray.'

Beth obeyed. She shut herself in and sat on the bed, her mind a blank. After a few minutes, she heard the key turn in the lock.

No prisoner in a condemned cell could have felt worse than she did at that moment.

Nothing to do but wait for the hangman. She couldn't pray. Nothing Rhianwen had told her had removed the image of a thunderous, punishing God from her mind. She knew her sins lay not merely in having sex, but in disobedience, lies, the breaking of solemn vows. Her pregnancy was the tip of a very dark and murky iceberg.

Will God tell Mum to believe the doctor? Will he tell her to forgive me?

She pressed her knees together and hugged herself. She was so cold she couldn't move.

How did it happen? We were so careful!

It was that time on the Hellstone. Beth was certain of it. The malevolent figures, the horn piercing her, the eyes of the Goddess . . . and the way Morgan had gone quiet after, as if he knew something was wrong and wouldn't tell her. Everything had been weird.

Hideous thoughts tormented her. *What if Mum was right? What if Rhianwen and Morgan bewitched me into thinking they were kind and loving, when really they belonged to Satan after all?*

Four hours passed. It was December so night came early. Beth walked around, tried to sleep, walked around again. She was growing frantic. She desperately needed the loo. The last thing she wanted was food, yet she felt sick and light-headed from lack of it.

She heard faint noises from downstairs; voices, doors opening and shutting. Things were happening behind her back.

The key turned. Beth drew a breath; she felt cold and brittle,
an icicle. Her father came in, alone.

He was still wearing his grey suit from work, and he stood
with his right hand cupped in his left. His face was composed
but his eyes, behind the sterile shine of his glasses, hung on her
like lead.

He'd never raised a hand to her, yet Beth was terrified of
him.

'Beth,' he said quietly, 'have you anything to tell me?'

'I really need the bathroom, Dad.'

'Go on. Quickly.'

She rushed along the landing, grateful for a few minutes'
reprieve. Her bowels were loose with sheer terror. When she
came back, feeling drained and shaky, Philip closed the door
and faced her.

His voice was soft and confidential, like the voice he used
with his dental patients. 'Just tell me, Beth; is there any possibility that you could be pregnant?'

Beth looked at the floor. Her throat went into a spasm which
she couldn't swallow away. After a few seconds she managed,
miserably, to nod.

Philip put a hand to his face; she heard a long sigh emerge,
muffled by his fingers. His eyes weren't even cold; they were
dead, as if he had no feeling for her at all, not even anger. As if
she'd ceased to exist.

'Can you tell me how this could have happened?'

She shook her head.

'I'm afraid you'll have to stay in here until you're ready to
tell us. God is deeply grieved by your behaviour, Bethia. I'll
pray for you.'

He went to the door. She blurted out, 'Dad, I'm sorry!' but
he was gone, locking the door again behind him.

Beth got on to her bed and shrank into the corner, looking
at the bare walls and the shelves with nothing on them but
Bibles and school books. Morgan had made her feel so grown

up, so free. The Devil's illusions. This was reality; she was a powerless, sinful child.

As she sat in the darkness, she made a decision. I'll never tell them about Rhianwen. I'll never tell them who the father is. I could pretend some boy in the village attacked me – but no, that would be another lie. My only defence, my only hope, is silence. Dear Goddess, help me!

It wasn't long before the door opened again, bringing a fan of yellow light from the landing. This time it was Heather.

'Grandma!' said Beth, sitting up. 'What are you doing here?'

'Brought you a cup of tea,' said Heather, sitting on the bed. 'Your mother called us. She's acting like there's been a death in the family.'

Beth swallowed the tea gratefully, clutching the mug in both hands for warmth.

'How did it happen?' Heather asked gravely, folding her arms. 'One of the village boys, was it?'

'Sort of, yes.'

'Who?' Beth didn't reply. 'You are a stupid little girl!' Heather was very much the exasperated headmistress. Beth sensed no sympathy; although she hadn't expected any, the lack of it stabbed her. 'I trusted you! I really thought you'd have more sense! Did it ever cross your tiny mind that I am going to get the blame for this? I was responsible for you!'

'That's not fair on you, Gran,' said Beth. 'It was my fault.'

'Well, it was at least half the boy's, as well. You're going to have to tell us who he was, you know. Drink your tea, Beth. They want to talk to you downstairs. Ready to face the world?'

Beth had no choice. She had been summoned.

'How's Mum?'

'Still trying to pretend it hasn't happened, though she knows damned well it has,' Heather said grimly, propelling her along the landing.

Her interrogators were waiting in the sitting-room: her father on his feet, Randolph and Luke sitting on the sofa, Olivia in an armchair. The room was stuffy and too bright, sweltering in the heat of the gas fire. Heather ushered Beth to the chair opposite her mother, then went to sit beside Randolph.

Olivia's countenance was pale and stiff with fury, and she was rigidly composed, hands in her lap. Beth quailed. Even the sight of Luke frightened her: he was like a replica of their father, serene and precise. Bizarre, the way their roles had reversed. Luke was now the saint, Beth the black sheep.

Beth felt blood rush to her face. How ghastly to face Luke and her granddad, knowing they knew. Randolph didn't look directly at her but he was a formidable presence in the room, another figure of disappointed, judgemental authority.

'Have you had anything to eat?' he asked as Beth sat down.

'I'm not hungry.'

He looked at Olivia. 'She must eat, or she'll be ill.'

'Father, can you stop being a doctor for five minutes?' Olivia broke in. 'She can eat after she's confessed.'

'Don't be afraid,' Randolph said gently. 'No one's going to shout at you. We just want you to tell us what happened.'

Beth couldn't make a sound.

'How long have you known you were – in this state?' asked Olivia. Her calm restraint was forced.

'I didn't know,' Beth whispered. She had, in her heart, but she'd been praying the symptoms would go away by magic.

'You must have suspected! Why didn't you tell us?'

'I couldn't. I knew you'd go mad.'

'Who was he?'

'Just a boy. It doesn't matter.'

'When did it happen? Where did it happen? Did he force you? You can't have consented!'

Beth squeezed her eyes shut. Philip said, 'You must tell us who he is so he can be punished.'

All through this, she felt Luke's eyes burning into her. *I know*, his eyes said. *I know*.

'It only has to happen once,' said her grandfather. 'One mistake. A boy tricks you, takes advantage of your innocence; you probably don't even realize what's happening until it's too late. His fault, not yours. Is that what happened, Beth?'

This was the scene they'd concocted in their minds, to try to preserve her innocence. Hating herself, Beth nodded.

'There, not her fault,' said Randolph.

'It doesn't matter, she's still been soiled!' Olivia cried. 'Oh, God Almighty, what have I done to deserve this? How could you, Beth, after all my warnings, my strict instructions to keep yourself pure? How could you let the Devil ruin you?'

'That's enough!' said Heather.

'I'm sorry, Mum,' said Beth, starting to cry. 'I'm really, really sorry.'

Olivia suddenly came to Beth, knelt beside her and clasped her hands. 'How could you let it happen, darling? I wanted you to be perfect in God's eyes. You were such a good girl. I knew I should never have let you stay at Mother's! It's my fault, I was selfish, I should have been looking after you myself.' They cried together, and Beth thought, it's going to be all right. She's going to forgive me! 'Just tell us who he is, darling,' Olivia went on. 'Tell us.'

'No, I can't. It doesn't matter.'

'You must.'

Beth shook her head stubbornly. She would have been admitting not one sin, but years of sin. The secret was all she had left.

Olivia sighed. 'Let's pray for guidance,' she said.

They all bowed their heads and clasped their hands, even her grandparents. There was a long moment of tranquillity. Into it, like a little knife, came Luke's voice.

'I know who the father of Beth's baby is.'

Beth felt a hideous jolt of coldness.

'Shut up!' she cried.

'It's that Morgan Rhys who lives up Farm Lane.'

Silence.

And then the worst sound she had ever heard, piercing her ears and shredding her nerves: Olivia, screaming. A hoarse, high-pitched wail of absolute horror and betrayal.

Beth shrank away, hands over her ears. A hand slammed into the side of her head; panicking, Beth scrambled over the arm of the chair but Olivia came after her, hitting, hitting. Beth fell on to the carpet; Olivia's face rose over her, eyes bloodshot, spittle flying from her mouth.

'You disgusting – vile – evil – wanton – stupid – little – *whore!*'

Beth shut her eyes, cowering. The blows stopped suddenly. Randolph was holding Olivia back and the others were all on their feet.

'For God's sake, Livvy!' said Randolph. 'Have some thought for her condition!'

'Have some thought, Dad?' Olivia shouted in his face. 'Have some thought?'

Grim-faced, Randolph pulled her away, forced her down on to the sofa. Philip helped Beth back to her chair, his touch impersonal. He offered her no comfort.

'Can we at least establish the facts?' Heather said briskly. 'Beth? Luke? *Is it true?*'

'Yes, it's true,' said Luke. 'She's been friendly with the witch and her son for years. Did she go out for a lot of walks, Gran? She was going to see *them*. That Morgan did it to her.'

Olivia turned on him now. 'You're lying!'

'I wouldn't lie, Mum! Ask her!'

They were all staring at her. Beth felt cornered. There seemed to be no point in denying it any more. 'Yes.'

'Jesus,' muttered Philip.

Her grandfather leaned his head on his hands and exhaled. 'Oh, God.'

And her grandmother exclaimed with a degree of viciousness that shocked Beth, 'That bloody boy. That bloody little bastard!'

'This is your fault, Mother!' Olivia shouted. 'You were meant to be protecting her!'

'What was I supposed to do? Keep her handcuffed? Good grief, as if we didn't tell her enough times to have nothing to do with them!' She looked hard from Luke to Beth. 'You'd better tell us precisely what went on.'

Between them, the story came out haltingly into a well of dark, disapproving tension.

'I only went to Rhianwen's house the first year,' said Luke, 'and only because Beth made me. I didn't want to tell tales on her so I prayed for her instead.'

Olivia, though, was no longer interested in Luke's sins. She stared at Beth with a frightful, contorted expression of incredulity, as if Beth had not merely betrayed her but stabbed her. 'You evil liar! After all I said! Every summer – you lying, evil *bitch*! Satan's got hold of you and he's working through you! Can't you see it? That boy belongs to the Devil! Did he force you, trick you, what? It happened just the once, did it?'

Beth was past lying. 'More than once, and he never forced me.'

'How many times?'

'Twenty-seven,' Beth said helplessly.

Olivia tried to leap up and would have slapped her, if Randolph hadn't held her back. 'You filthy whore!' Heather looked murderous.

Still terrified but stung to outrage, Beth cried, 'Why is Morgan worse than any other boy? Rhianwen isn't evil, she was nice to me. I know I did wrong, but – but –' she faltered, knowing they wouldn't listen. 'I love Morgan. We promised each other we'd be together when we leave school. We can get married and it will be all right!'

'Jesus,' her father said again.

'We'll have to get rid of it,' Heather said crisply. 'Pretend it never happened.'

'What?' Beth cried, aghast.

'No,' said Philip. 'That would be a crime against God.'

Olivia went white. 'Yes, it must be got rid of,' she whispered.

'I can arrange a termination,' Randolph said heavily. 'I'll speak to Beth's GP. The sooner the better.'

Beth couldn't believe her ears. Her mother had always been vehemently against abortion. Secretly, since knowing Rhianwen, Beth wasn't, and if it had been the child of any other boy she would have been relieved. But this was special, it was *Morgan's*.

'No!' said Beth. 'You can't make me do that. I told you, I love him.'

'What do you know about love, you silly girl?' Heather snapped. 'He was using you. He was nearly thrown out of school for being caught with some girl. He should be castrated with baling twine!'

'The Devil works through that family,' Olivia said, her voice low. 'That thing you're carrying is the child of the Devil.'

Beth's head was spinning. *Some girl. He was using you. The Devil.*

Olivia rose to her feet; Randolph tried to stop her but she shook him off, saying, 'It's all right, Father.' She stood over Beth with terrifying calmness, her face haggard, all her revulsion and condemnation gathered in the poisonous blue light of her eyes.

'*Bitch*,' she hissed. 'I nearly went against God's law for you. This is what you've brought me to!'

Beth shrank inwardly. She understood. Olivia had been prepared to go against her heartfelt beliefs to dispose of the baby; that was how deeply she loathed Morgan. The realization hurt Beth worse than any physical blow.

'No,' Olivia went on thinly, 'you shall have the thing, if only to make you understand that you cannot sin without punishment. You think you want it, do you? But it won't be a human being, it will be the fruit of your sins.'

'You'll have to have it adopted,' Heather said harshly.

'No, I'll look after it,' said Olivia. 'But can it ever be cleansed and live a Christian life? I doubt it. Can *you* ever be cleansed, Bethia? I won't have the Devil working through this family! You'll deliver the child into my hands, and I shall bring it to God.'

The room turned dark. The rest of her family didn't seem to hear the threat in Olivia's voice, but Beth was drowning, utterly alone. She could see nothing but her mother's burning eyes.

114

'What are you, Beth? I thought you were an angel, above the banal filth of the world. Instead I discover you've been rolling in it like everyone else. You're a stranger. You're not my daughter.'

Beth lay awake all night with the words walking round her head, as dark and physical as rats.

Not my daughter. The sense of total betrayal in Olivia's eyes tormented Beth. She thought, I didn't mean to do that to her; was what I did so very awful? It must have been. What am I, then? An orphan, a changeling, nothing. Not my mother's daughter. Just a piece of treacherous filth.

In the morning, her grandfather came in and sat on the end of her bed. He was wearing his overcoat, about to set off home.

'How did you sleep?'

'Not too well. I'm scared,' said Beth.

'Are you sure you want to go through with the pregnancy?'

'I don't know. I can't not. But Mum . . .'

There was some kindness in Randolph's eyes, under the thick charcoal brows. Perhaps she'd misjudged him. 'Your mother will forgive you. Give her time.'

'I don't think she will. Do you forgive me, Granddad?'

'These things are so difficult. Everyone does foolish things, Beth; I can't condemn you for falling in love. I'm not sure I can forgive the boy, though.'

'Will he get into trouble?'

'I don't know. He deserves to.'

She whispered, 'Granddad, would you post a letter to Morgan for me, if I wrote it quickly?'

He shook his head, looking sadly at her. 'I don't think it would be appropriate. Your mother wouldn't want it. I mustn't compound my negligence.'

'What do you mean?'

'I blame myself for what happened.'

Beth was stunned. 'Why?'

'I was never there for you. I was always working. If I'd

known you were so lonely with your grandma and me that you had to look for friends elsewhere . . . I should have realized what was happening, but I didn't. My fault.'

Desperate, she said, 'Granddad, don't leave me.'

'I have to go to work,' he said gravely. 'Olivia will look after you, don't worry.'

No one asked Beth how she felt.

Olivia kept Beth off school that morning. They passed the day in bitter silence as wide as a lake. That night, in utter exhaustion, Beth slept.

She dreamed of drowning in green water, with blood-clouds exploding all around her. She dreamed of a white horn piercing her in her side, her stomach, her womb. She saw dark figures flapping towards her through underwater forests, and she knew that when they reached her, she'd die.

She dreamed Morgan was pinning her down on the Hellstone, only he was really a demon in the shape of a black cat with fangs and claws. His penis, the ivory horn again, delivered a perfectly formed demon baby into her womb. She climaxed anyway, as if to show she had invited the sin.

Then the baby began to talk to her. *You can't let me go. We must stay together. We're in danger. Our kind have always been in danger!*

Beth woke, shaking and sweating, to find Luke leaning over her. He was growing into a stocky youth, stronger and taller than Beth.

'You dirty bitch,' he whispered venomously. 'I knew you were doing it with that Morgan.'

She sat up, shaken. 'You didn't know! You had no right to say anything!'

Luke was glaring at her, as if she were something he'd trodden in. Then he smiled coldly. 'Guessed right, though, didn't I? You let him fuck you.'

'Why did you have to tell them?'

'To save your soul, sister.'

'It wasn't fair!' Beth cried. 'You've never told on me before! I thought I could trust you! I never told on you when you did something wrong. I always tried to look after you.'

'Yes. Until you dropped me for *them*.'

'I didn't drop you.'

'It was me or them, Beth. You chose them. You chose the Devil. I used to really look up to you when I was little. I used to think you were a saint but you're not; you're just a common tart like all the others.'

'What others?'

'The girls at school. They're all prossies. I'll tell you what's unfair: Mum used to beat me for doing nothing, but she doesn't even beat you when you get pregnant. She didn't even slap you until I told her you did it with someone who worships the Devil.'

'He does not!'

'You know how witches are made, don't you? They go into the woods, make a pact with the Devil, then copulate with him to seal it. And that's what you did. That's exactly what you did.'

'No!'

'You're in for it now. You're damned. I told you your sins would find you out, didn't I? Serves you right.'

His eyes were merciless. She saw years of resentment there, burning. Luke had been storing up his hatred of Morgan for all this time and she hadn't realized, hadn't seen.

Now he was having his revenge.

In the morning, Beth tried to write to Morgan in the secrecy of her room. She tried, but the words wouldn't come. She was scared to set a single word on paper, in case her mother saw it; scared of what Morgan's reaction would be. What if he was horrified – or worse, utterly indifferent? What could he do, anyway?

The furthest she got was printing his address on the envelope. 'Morgan Rhys, Blackthorn Cottage, Farm Lane, Lullingford, Staffs.' The postcode, what was the postcode? Didn't matter. She sat and traced her fingers over the beloved address as if it were a photograph of him.

The door opened. Beth flung the envelope into a bedside drawer but it was too late; her mother had seen.

'What are you hiding?' Olivia snapped. She strode forward, wrenched the drawer open and seized the envelope. There was one second of bristling silence while she scanned it. Then she swung round and her hand felled Beth like a sandbag, knocking her across the bed.

'Jezebel!' she screamed, ripping up the envelope. 'How dare you? What will it take to teach you, you devious, addle-brained *bitch*?'

The strap.

There was no one else in the house. No one to stop Olivia laying into Beth until they were both crying with exhaustion, and Beth had bitten her mouth to shreds to kill the burning, throbbing pain in her back.

'If you ever try to contact that ungodly fornicator again,' Olivia panted, standing over Beth where she lay on the bed, 'you will wish you had never been born.'

Beth got the message. She lay on her stomach in agony, praying for her mother to leave her alone, praying to die.

'Jesus loves you, Bethia, but he hates the demon inside you,' breathed Olivia, eerily calm. 'I won't rest until I've driven it out. Cleanse it. Cleanse.' She walked away; a few minutes later, through sheets of pain, Beth heard the vacuum cleaner droning.

One afternoon in mid-December, while Rhianwen was contentedly doling out cat food for Llew, Ankaret and Bast, a storm arrived on her doorstep.

She answered a knock at the front door to find Olivia Herne standing there. Rhianwen was startled. For a moment she didn't recognize this handsome woman in a raincoat, with fierce blue eyes and brown hair gathered in a bun. Then her instincts kicked in, and she knew, ominously, that this was about Beth. They've found out Beth was coming here, she thought. Had to happen.

'Your bastard,' said Olivia, 'has got my daughter pregnant.'

Rhianwen felt the earth drop under her. She laughed in disbelief. 'I beg your pardon?'

'You heard me!'

Rhianwen controlled herself and said coolly, 'If you're referring to Morgan, you'd better come in.'

'You knew, didn't you?' Olivia shoved Rhianwen hard in the shoulder and walked past her into the cottage. 'You knew!'

'I have absolutely no idea what you're talking about.'

'Liar!' Olivia stood in the centre of the front room, glancing in contempt at incense burners and images of goddesses; in her eyes, signs of Rhianwen's inner pollution. Her tone was cold and savage. 'How long has he been corrupting my daughter? Was it just last summer, or for the past four years?'

Rhianwen was furious. 'Hang on, what right have you got to come in here accusing my son of molesting a child?'

'A child! Exactly! Don't try to defend him, because she's told me what he did to her. Taking her in the woods and doing those filthy things. You knew what was going on, didn't you? You encouraged it!'

'Of course I didn't!' Rhianwen flared. 'If you're telling the truth, I'll murder him. I thought I could trust him. I specifically told him to treat Beth like a sister. I warned him, countless times.'

'And I told Bethia to stay away from you,' said Olivia. 'If she took no notice of me, why should your brat listen to you? You must have known she wasn't allowed to come here but you didn't send her away, did you? You encouraged her. What gives you the right to usurp my rights as a mother? Did you think it was amusing, to get at me like that?'

'Yes,' said Rhianwen. 'It was more than amusing, dear. I was trying to save her sanity. She came to me one year, suicidal because her periods had started and you had given her the impression she was too filthy to live. Wonderful mother you are.'

'I did nothing of the sort!'

'Whatever you intended, that's the impression she'd got. So I put her right.'

'Oh, did you? And how are you going to put this right?' Olivia said contemptuously. 'Herbal potions, a spell?'

'Don't mock what you don't understand. You'd better tell me what Beth said.'

As Olivia acidly related Beth's confession, Rhianwen knew she was telling the truth. All those times I blithely let Morgan take Beth for walks and bike rides ... What a bloody fool I was. That was egotism, thinking no son of mine would break a promise! And why did I feel the need to warn him so often, if I didn't know in my heart he wasn't to be trusted?

'I'll give Morgan hell for this,' said Rhianwen. 'I never meant it to happen, Livvy, I swear.'

'Don't call me Livvy! This is what it's come to! You wanted to put the Devil into my daughter and you've succeeded. You'll burn in hell, you bitch!'

'Would you like a cup of tea?' Rhianwen asked sweetly. 'Olivia.'

'I won't touch anything of yours.'

'How is Beth?'

Olivia looked startled, as if the question had never occurred to her. 'She's learning her lesson.'

'Goddess,' Rhianwen whispered. 'I do know some very specific herbs . . .'

'She insists on having the damned thing,' said Olivia, tight-lipped. 'Let her have it. God did not mean women to have an easy escape from their sin.'

'Oh, shit,' said Rhianwen. 'Look, if you really can't bear what's happened, send her to me. I'll look after her.'

Olivia glared at her. 'You must be out of your mind! Send her to you, with that evil raping bastard in the house?'

'If you are referring to Morgan,' Rhianwen said icily, 'he wouldn't be here. I'll send him away to college, or some-thing.'

'I don't care. You won't have her. This is a battle for Beth's soul! You'll never win! She needs Christian guidance, not pagan immorality. Haven't you done enough?'

'Poor Beth,' Rhianwen said under her breath. 'Well, if I can't help, and you've finished shouting at me, you'd better go.'

'I haven't finished,' Olivia snapped. 'We want you to leave.'

'Leave my home?'

'Go away. Take the bastard with you.'

'Don't be stupid.'

'I'm deadly serious.' Rhianwen saw shadows from the corner of her eye, turned and saw the others standing in the open doorway: Philip, Heather and Randolph, staring her down with leaden eyes.

'You can't make me.'

'But if you stay, we'll make sure Morgan is prosecuted for child abuse, sex with an underage girl, anything we can throw at him. So if you don't want him going through life with a criminal record, get him out of here.'

'They won't do anything to a sixteen year old.' But Rhianwen's heart speeded up. She wanted to deal with him herself; the thought of him even being questioned by Social Services and the police made her feel ill.

'No? We can easily get Beth to say he raped her.'

'What?' Rhianwen gasped. 'Even you wouldn't sink that low!'

But Olivia's eyes were blue steel. 'Do you want to risk it? Even if he wasn't found guilty, mud sticks. Just go! And don't either of you make any attempt to contact my daughter, ever again. You owe it to us!'

Heather said from the doorway, 'You're meant to be wise, Mrs Rhys. You know Morgan and Beth can't possibly be allowed to see each other again.'

'I know,' said Rhianwen. She couldn't look at any of them. 'I know.'

'So take him away. For Beth's sake.'

Rhianwen glanced at Philip, then at Randolph. Their faces were sombre, resolute, only a touch ashamed. 'What am I supposed to say to this?' she said. '*Et tu, Brute?*'

Randolph only said sorrowfully, 'How could you let it happen?'

A couple of hours after they'd gone, Morgan came home from school, affectionate and cheerful as always. Rhianwen was slicing vegetables on a worktop. He threw his bag on a kitchen chair, slid up to her and kissed her cheek. 'Steady on, Mum, what have those poor carrots ever done to you?'

She threw the knife down, turned round, and whacked him as hard as she could across the face. He reeled away, gasping. 'For Christ's sake, what was that for?'

'Think about it. You were screwing her all summer. Oh, what a surprise, she is now expecting a baby.'

Morgan went absolutely white. Even the red mark she'd made bleached away. 'Oh, Christ. You mean Beth?'

'Yes, I mean Beth!' she shouted. 'How many more irate parents can I expect round here making threats? Get in the other room!'

He sat on the edge of the sofa under the onslaught, his head resting on one hand. Rhianwen paced about, so furious it was all she could do not to strike him again.

'How could you, Morgan? How many times did I tell you? Be a friend to her, I said. Treat her like a sister, I said. I said it about a thousand times. I thought I could trust you!'

'I'm sorry, Mum,' he said faintly. 'I didn't plan it.'

'*Beth* trusted you – so, you just took advantage of her, did you?'

'It wasn't like that. We're in love.'

'Oh, love, is it? You could at least have taken precautions!'

'We did!'

'Oh, did you? You have to use them every time, you know, not just when you think about it!'

'Mum, we did.'

'Even the first time? So how can you claim you didn't plan it? Just carry them round on the off-chance, do you?'

Morgan didn't reply. He was such a beautiful youth: who could blame Beth for falling? Yet it was his beauty that made her angry, because he thought he could have everything his own way, break all the hearts in his path and never be touched. 'So, these "precautions",' she said. 'What went wrong?'

'One of them split,' he murmured. 'I didn't tell Beth. I didn't want to worry her.'

'Well, I imagine she's worried enough now. I could have told you they're not infallible. For God's sake, what were you thinking of?'

'I told you, I love her.'

'But she's only fourteen! Fourteen, Morgan! What you did was against the law!'

'We didn't think. It didn't seem wrong.'

'Well, it was wrong, more wrong than you can imagine. If you'd really loved her, you would have left her alone.'

'If she'd said no, I would have done.' Morgan met Rhianwen's eyes, defiant. 'But she didn't put up much of a fight, I can tell you.'

Rhianwen gasped. 'Don't you dare blame her! I'm so ashamed of you!'

He stood up suddenly, folding his long bony arms. 'I can't believe you're going on like this. You're the one who always told me there was nothing wrong with sex. You told Beth it was sacred, too!'

'Yes, between consenting adults. "Sacred" means to be treated with respect, not indulged in at whim. I thought I'd explained that, too; d'you need your ears syringeing, or what? I've spoiled you. I have to beg your headmaster to reinstate you after you've been caught with some female in the school grounds – oh, he's a good boy, he's not really like that, she led him on – and now you do *this*!'

'I'm not that bad! I don't take drugs, I don't smoke, but you expect me to be sodding *perfect*. You're the one who wanted to take Beth away from her mother!'

'Yes, by making Beth strong. Not by ruining her life.'

Morgan went quiet, his face lengthening. 'She's not having it, is she?'

'Apparently she wants to. Her parents won't contemplate abortion, anyway. Goddess knows what will become of her.'

'But – oh, my God.' He half turned away, speechless for once. 'Oh, my God.' Then, 'I love her, I want to see her.'

'Well, you can't.'

'Why not?'

'Her parents won't let you. And neither will I.'

Morgan glared at her between strands of dark hair. 'I've never had a father. Is it going to be like that for Beth's kid, too?'

'Oh, listen to the voice of responsibility; you haven't a clue what you'd be taking on! You're both too young. You can't cope with babies, you'd end up hating each other. Her family are impossible!'

'You can't stop me seeing her.'

'If you try, her family will have you prosecuted. Unlawful sexual intercourse, I think they call it. Or even rape.'

'Christ,' said Morgan, turning pale again. 'That's not fair, I would never have forced her! She wanted it as much as I did. Oh, Christ.'

Rhianwen felt gratified to have shaken him up.

'You have got to learn that you can't have everything your own way. We're leaving. You can finish your A levels at college and forget about Beth. You have a very long way to go before you prove I can trust you again!'

'You can't stop me seeing her!' Morgan said fervently. 'Go to hell!'

He marched into the kitchen. Hearing the back door slam, Rhianwen shuddered. He'll be back, she thought. And one day, when he understands, I hope he'll forgive me.

Through wintry twilight, Morgan walked across the fields behind the cottage in no particular direction, brooding, furious with Rhianwen. It was as much the humiliation of being found out as anything. An illicit relationship was glamorous and exciting; the mess it created was not.

He wanted Beth as he remembered her, fresh, pretty and responsive. Wanted her, in defiance of his mother and her parents. But pregnant – maybe tired, preoccupied, her body swelling – he wasn't sure.

To think of being married with a small child, instead of looking forward to a life of freedom at university – Jesus, that was scary.

But Beth . . .

The truth was, Morgan didn't know what he wanted.

There was a figure coming along the hedgerow towards him through the gloom. A woman in tweed skirt, green Barbour jacket and headscarf, carrying a shotgun. Heather Cross.

He kept his head down, meaning to give her a wide berth, but she stopped in his path. And then she aimed the shotgun straight at his chest. Her eyes were psychotic with hatred.

'I should shoot you where you stand, for what you did,' Mrs Cross said quietly, 'you evil bastard.'

Morgan stared at her in unguarded terror. 'You'd be done for murder.'

'Do you think I care? They can lock me away; it'll be too late for you.' He heard the ominous crunch of the safety catch. Then she lowered the barrel to point at his loins. 'We geld horses humanely; that's too good for you. If you ever go near my granddaughter again, I'll blast your bollocks through the top of your head.'

Paralysed, he watched her finger squeezing the trigger. The moment was unreal, a nightmare condensed. Then there was a deafening bang and the earth at his feet exploded.

'If I *ever* see you again,' she hissed, 'I won't be shooting at the ground.'

Morgan backed away. He began to run. When he glanced back she was still there, staring after him.

'Maybe you're right,' he said, walking back into the kitchen, trying to act like nothing had happened. 'We should leave, after all.'

'What's come over you?' Rhianwen asked caustically.

'Nothing. Been thinking, that's all. And I'm really, truly sorry. I wouldn't have hurt Beth for anything.'

Softening, Rhianwen put her arm round him and stroked his shoulder. 'It was my fault, love. I should have guessed what was happening with you two, and stopped it. I suppose I did guess, but I didn't want to believe it. I won't let you ruin your life over one mistake. I know it hurts, but it's for the best. Believe me.'

'Yeah.'

'By the way, what was that shot?'

Morgan shrugged guiltily. 'Someone shooting at rabbits.'

'Come in, Bethia,' said the pastor.

There were ten members of the church waiting in the sitting-room, including Olivia. Their smiles were stern, sorrowful, condescending. Beth went in among them like a lamb among hyenas.

'You've fallen deep in sin, sister,' said Pastor Blair. 'The good news is that you can be purified and washed clean. But first we have to drive the Devil out of you.'

They were all around her, holding her, stroking her, talking, praying. 'Confess your sins, Bethia. Let it all spill out. You have to admit the Devil is in you before we can tear it out!'

'He wasn't a Devil,' she said defiantly. 'He loves me.'

'He deceived you,' said the pastor. He was stout and whiskery, and he smelled of stale tobacco. 'He tempted you into foul acts of fornication. That's the Devil's way.'

'No.'

'Repent, Bethia. Your soul is in peril.'

The exorcism was loud and violent. They began to throw her from one to another, praying and singing. The pastor repeatedly cast her to the floor, shouting for the Lord to take the evil out of this fallen soul. He yelled straight into Beth's face, commanding the demon to depart, shredding her nerves to rags.

Out of her wits with fear, Beth submitted. It went on all afternoon. At the end, weak with confusion and lack of food, she would have said anything to make it stop.

'Yes, there's a demon in me. He put it there. It talks to me. I repent, help me, help me.'

Afterwards, Beth realized the true purpose of the exorcism. She sat shaking, trying to drink a mug of sickly cocoa Olivia had made – as what, a consolation prize, a token of guilty love? – and she thought, they weren't trying to save my soul, they were trying to make me have a miscarriage.

It didn't work.

From the day her sins had come to light, Beth was kept prisoner at home. Her mother removed her from school. When the truant officer came round and pointed out that she couldn't do this, Olivia became devious and plausible, finally convincing the doctor to excuse Beth from school on medical grounds. Under her mother's direction, Beth complained of exhaustion, depression, half a dozen reasons why she couldn't face school, and she barely had to exaggerate. She had only to be careful, when the doctor prodded her abdomen, that he did not see the marks on her back.

Philip arranged for a tutor to come to the house instead; a retired teacher who was a fervent member of the church. Beth loathed him.

She was never left alone. If Olivia had to go out, people from the church would sit with her instead. The only time Beth went out was for her ante-natal checks. She was too sinful even to be seen at church, apparently. A social worker came to the house a couple of times; under Olivia's supervision, Beth assured her that everything was fine at home, her mother would be helping with the baby, she was perfectly happy, thank you.

Every day, as Beth's condition grew more blatant, she had to endure the contemptuous stares of her family whenever they glanced at her swelling stomach.

Olivia literally believed that the Devil had worked through Morgan. What could Beth say? She couldn't dismiss her mother as mad, because Beth had been surrounded by these beliefs from childhood. Lots of apparently sane people shared them.

Rhianwen had made these beliefs seem absurd. But Rhianwen wasn't here. And she had always been light-hearted about her Goddess, whereas the people who surrounded Beth now were heavy-handed and passionately convinced. Beth hadn't the strength to decide, *you are all crazy*. Not when her ghastly dreams seemed to be coming directly from hell.

Beth thought constantly of Rhianwen and Morgan, but she dared not make another attempt to contact them. Only an hour's drive away, they might as well have been on another planet.

At night she thought of Morgan. His lovely face and his hard slender body against her, inside her. She pressed her face into the pillow to muffle her groans of longing and pain.

Sometimes she could hear Luke giggling through the wall, and his inexplicable mirth chilled her.

She remembered when she and Morgan had been alone in the woods, and they'd been free, and in ecstasy.

Morgan, standing there smiling, with the owl perched on his arm.

He didn't know. She couldn't bear it that he had put this vibrant, throbbing life into her, and didn't know. But what if he didn't really love me? she thought, agonized. What if he lied, and used me, like everyone says? Would he chuck me, like Genette's boyfriends, and tell everyone I'm a slag?

That was the real reason Beth dared not write. To find out Morgan didn't care would kill her.

The day he'd heard about his sister's pregnancy, Luke had asked God what to do. God replied, tell the truth and shame the Devil.

Never, as long as he lived, would Luke forgive Beth for having sex with that wicked, depraved boy.

In the darkness of his room, after his parents and sister had gone to bed, he spread an old car rug, which he'd found in the shed, on the carpet. That was his church. He'd tried to shake out the worst of the mould and cobwebs.

Then he dragged a bulging carrier bag from under the bed; usually he kept it hidden under the compost heap, because it smelled, but tonight he'd smuggled it into the house. He began to remove the contents one by one and place them on the rug in careful rows.

Rats, mice, birds, beetles, frogs. All dead.

They formed his congregation.

Luke was their pastor. He had complete power over them. They hung on his every word as he preached in a whisper of good and evil, the supremacy of God, and the Apocalypse in which only the chosen would ascend to heaven.

Only those who follow me will survive! I am the prophet!

He touched the corpses in turn, blessing them. He remembered how each one had died.

I killed you but you will rise again, he told them. I killed you to save your souls.

Now it was time for the sacrifice.

He pulled the shoebox from under the bed. A scuffling sound came from inside.

Luke picked up his scalpel and lifted the lid.

This was special. It was a white mouse he'd stolen from a boy at school. White and pure.

'This is the sacrifice that will redeem you from your sins,' he whispered.

He held the mouse's head between his thumb and fingers, so it lay on its back in his palm. Its lips were drawn back from its tiny teeth and its whiskers quivered.

Luke drew the blade very delicately from its throat to its abdomen so that, when he pulled back the flaps to expose the organs, the glistening heart was still pulsing. He was a surgeon now, as skilful and precise as his father and grandfather. A real doctor, not a fake like Rhianwen.

The mouse squealed, but not very loud. Luke put the words in its mouth. 'My God, my God, why hast thou forsaken me?'

Luke's heart was beating as fast as the mouse's.

He put down the scalpel and pushed his finger into the mouse's guts. Hot and slippery with blood. He took the tiny heart between his thumb and finger and squeezed.

Now he was God. He had power over life and death. To this mouse, at least, Luke was God.

He laid the warm corspe down with the others.

Now, the sacrament.

Luke unzipped his trousers. His penis was already hard.

The semen would be the bread. And the wine . . .

This is my body, this is my blood.

With the tip of the scalpel he nicked the head of his penis, so the liquid bread and the wine flowed out together over his congregation.

Afterwards, with everything cleared away and bundled under the bed, he lay in bed and chewed the sheet to stifle his giggles.

Such was the ecstasy of power.

'I understand now,' Olivia said one afternoon, as she watched Beth preparing the tea. Beth's back ached and she needed to sit down, but she wasn't allowed to until the chores were finished. 'You are being used as a battleground between God and the Devil. That's why this has happened.'

Olivia had grown calmer as the pregnancy progressed, but her eyes were a china doll's, heartless.

'A battleground,' Beth echoed. To disagree would only invite her mother's wrath.

Olivia stared frigidly at Beth's swollen abdomen. 'So the sooner that abomination comes out, the better.'

'But you will help me look after it, won't you, Mum? You said you would.' Beth lived every day in the vain hope of forgiveness. She couldn't bear to give up.

'I told you; I will deal with it.' But Olivia's eyes stayed like glass, and Beth, suddenly and horribly, had to face the truth.

She is going to kill it. Even if she doesn't kill it, she is going to treat it worse than she ever treated Luke. And if I let her, it will be my fault.

Six months of imprisonment, shame, indoctrination and nightmares had made Beth crazy. But she wasn't as crazy as Olivia. She still had enough reason left to know that she had already let this go on too long. She could either run for it, or condemn the baby – and maybe herself – to death.

When the searing contractions began, Beth was almost relieved. She was going somewhere now, either towards death or freedom. Her father drove her to the hospital; Olivia didn't want to know. And Philip was quite kind, the kindest she'd ever known him.

But Beth gave birth alone with green-robed strangers in the cold lights of the delivery room. She screamed for Rhianwen. She screamed for Morgan, but he wasn't there. Wasn't there.

She prayed to the Goddess Bast, protector of women in childbirth.

At last the demon split Beth's pelvis apart, and came sliding out in a surge of blood. The demon was pink, helpless and innocent.

A kind midwife told Beth it had been a normal delivery and only nine hours. Beth knew one thing; she never wanted to go through it again. She cried when they put Eirian in her arms. She cried for hours, couldn't stop, and didn't even know why she was crying.

Philip smiled when he saw the baby, but the tears in his eyes were of grief, not joy. Her grandparents came once, trying to be nice but plainly uncomfortable. Luke never visited Beth in hospital at all.

Beth looked at the flowers and the cards around every bed but hers, the hordes of cheerful, chattering visitors hugging the new mothers. But her own family behaved as if attending a funeral, and she knew Eirian's arrival had brought no forgiveness.

She hoped Olivia would soften when she first saw the infant, but she didn't; she looked at it in its crib and her eyes stayed dead, like a fish on a slab.

Beth thought, she has already killed it in her mind.

Four days later, Beth was on the bus, alone with her terror and her unwanted burden.

And soon she was lying bleeding in the darkness, outside an empty cottage.

Betrayed.

All the sweetness and laughter, all the love, caresses and false promises she'd found here – gone. Snatched away, not only from her, but from the baby, who'd never hurt anyone; that was supremely cruel.

We will be together. I promise.

Beth stared through shadow-masses of overgrown vegetation, garlands and spider-ropes of neglected greenery silhouetted against an indifferent night sky. She felt the blood trickling out, hot as tears.

Nothing more to hope for.

They were demons in a fairy tale, Rhianwen and Morgan. They sucked you in and ruined you with pleasure, and then you woke up on a cold hillside and found the fairy palace an ancient, deserted shell.

PART TWO

Mother

Mater Dolorosa

Chapter Eight

BETH lay against the cottage wall in her damp, stinking coat for a long time, staring into space. The sky was a mirror of her own mind; cloudily dark and blank. The image of her grandparents flickered in the void, but they, too, were the enemy. They hated Morgan and Rhianwen, they had never tried to protect her from Olivia. If Beth went to them, they would simply call her parents and it would all have been for nothing.

In a trance, Beth climbed to her feet. She didn't know what she was doing, only that something was urging her to move. A compulsion, emanating from Eirian.

Gathering the baby close against her, Beth began to walk in a delirium of misery and pain. She went across the shadowy garden, through the back gate and into the meadow beyond. It wasn't pitch black; she could see through the gloom, but everything looked luminous and unreal, as if painted on glass.

Across the meadow and into the woods. Shivering with weakness, she could still feel the blood oozing between her legs, but she couldn't stop.

Staggering between the trees now. And there, oh Goddess, there was the sacred hollow beneath the oak where she and Morgan had loved each other all those times.

But the thread pulled her on. Up the hill between the blur of tree-trunks, Morgan's and Luke's voices echoing around her. *'We dance naked round the stone and worship the Devil.' 'Liar!'* and, *'If you go to them I'll never be your friend again.'*

The trees opened out. The Hellstone gleamed dully, like the petrified kneecap of some god who'd died and decayed under the earth.

Beth crawled on to the unyielding surface and collapsed, hugging the baby. Eirian began to cry. Her wails pierced the veil of semi-consciousness like physical pain. By instinct Beth put her daughter to one of her taut, painful breasts, but she hardly knew what she was doing. Reason had left her.

Beth remembered lying here with Morgan in her arms and the Goddess's eyes shining bright silver into hers. She'd named Eirian for their colour, silver. But the Goddess's eyes were closed. There was nothing left. Only the black figures, closing in all around the Hellstone.

Beth shut her eyes and waited.

You'll never come here with anyone else.

It seemed only right, if they must die, that Eirian should die in the place she was created.

The thunderbolt from God had finally struck, with a vengeance.

She slipped into unconsciousness and she saw . . .

Sunshine. A green meadow in a forest. Long lush grass, a profusion of spring leaves; a million flakes of green edged with light. Birds singing. A procession of men and women, stepping in a slow dance to the beat of a drum, all of them naked.

Beth, a bodiless witness, watched.

Their skins were crusted with ulcers, with flea-bites, rashes and pock-marks. Their stringy hair was crawling with vermin; she could even smell the miasma of their unwashed bodies. Yet in the forest they were transformed. The dew in the long grass bathed them. The pure air blew them clean. They were anointed with cuckoo spit, nectar and the sticky exudations of plants.

And they were laughing; celebrating life in defiance of disease and death.

But anxiety crawled through Beth as she watched. Darkness was closing in and she couldn't warn them. They danced on, oblivious.

A wedding procession. Beth knew intuitively. The couple leading the dancers were twined with leaves and crowned with ivy; the Green Man and his bride, the Goddess. A man covered in a deer-skin, with great antlers on his head, was cavorting around the revellers.

The scene filled Beth with a sense of something impossibly ancient, primaeval and terrifying, as if it cast a shadow into another dimension.

The priestess came out of the forest to meet the procession. She wore a pale green robe and a mask like a cat's face, but from the long syrupy skein of hair that hung down her back, Beth knew that this was Guendolen. Beth had seen her before, hiding the horn of a unicorn inside an oak tree.

And the brown-haired child, who had called herself Eirian?

Beth caught sight of her running towards the wedding party, hampered by her long skirts, urgently trying to reach them. It was as if Beth were a bird, gliding while Eirian struggled. Behind the child, at a distance, the men in black were coming through the trees. Dark, rippling figures in cassocks, carrying the weight of the law.

'They're coming,' Eirian gasped. Beth heard the words in her head. 'They're coming!' And she waved frantically at the priestess, but no one saw.

The figures came on, slowly, like spectres of death.

Guendolen lifted her wooden staff and drew out the long pale Horn of Power. The wedded couple knelt before her, and she touched the tip to their foreheads. A blessing. Their ivy-strewn flesh and the vegetation all around them glistened as if washed in a dew of fertility; nothing was ugly, nothing was out of place.

Then Eirian came rushing into the meadow.

'The men are coming. Go, quickly!'

Too late. Guendolen slid the Horn back into its disguising staff, and ran into the forest. She was gone, and no one had seen her face. But the dark figures flowed forward, and no one else could escape. There were five clerics and a band of men armed with staves; all their faces swollen with righteous contempt.

The sunlight bled away. The revellers, joyful no longer, shamefully tried to cover their nakedness. The armed men tore the deer-skin and antlers off the priest and flung him to the ground. Grinning, they waded among the others, aiming vicious blows at their unclad bodies.

One of the clerics unrolled a scroll of paper. Beth saw his face as if she were close enough to kiss him. Saw the bloated, fat-lipped, coarse spread of his features; saw every grease-brimmed pore and smallpox scar, even the tufts of hair in his nostrils. And smelled on him . . . death.

'*Under the law of God, your gathering is forbidden,*' his words echoed in her head. '*For it is an obscenity to go naked, and a devilish abomination to dress in the skins of animals.*'

Ravens were swirling overhead.

Eirian began to run into the forest after Guendolen. She kept looking back over her shoulder, her face contorted with terror. Run, Beth urged her. The scene broke up; Beth was spinning through fragments of memory.

She screamed soundlessly. The breath rasped through her throat but she couldn't make herself heard. The nightmare sucked her down into a feverish stormy sea of fear, blood, rejection. And of all horrors, rejection was the worst.

A face kept peering through the chaos. A dull gold face with a flare of light around it. The Goddess?

Beth became aware that she was lying in a drab, dimly lit confined place. There was some kind of narrow bed beneath her, odd flat cupboards on the walls, a small window with rounded corners.

She could make no sense of it.

It was a continuation of her nightmare. She felt drowsy, drugged, confused. Only one pricking of anxiety . . . my baby, where is she?

But Eirian was nearby. She was quiet but Beth could sense her; a forceful rose-red mote of life which would not let her surrender.

Eirian was safe. Beth could sleep.

She slipped down into the dreams.

Water again. A deep green, flowing ocean. Beth dived

through it, becoming part of it, a dark streak in the bubbling greenness. A shadow among shadows.

She heard Rhianwen's words in her head.

We are always under threat, Beth. We were in the past and we still are. Times have changed less than you realize.

A harpoon struck Beth in the side. It went deep into her, through thick layers of fat and muscle, into her womb. Hot, throbbing pain. Blood poured out, mixing with the water.

Like the blood and water flowing from the wound in Christ's side.

Flowing from Beth as she laboured to produce Eirian.

And the long white wand was torn from her, stained red.

Someone was bending over her, patting her face with a damp cloth. 'All right, now, lass. You're having a bad dream.'

There was a female face close to hers, wrinkled and tanned, with a fright of pale hair. A stranger.

'Eirian?'

'The babby's fine, love. It's you needs babying. Drink this; it'll take the pain away, help you sleep.'

The stranger helped Beth to sit up, held a cup to her lips. The liquid was warm, herbal, bitter-sweet.

Beth drowsed again. In her fever she felt that she was moving; the bed swayed under her and she could hear an engine. The place had an ingrained smell of diesel oil and cooking.

Eirian cooed. The sound came from a couple of feet away.

Beth slept.

She was at the bottom of the ocean, yet it was a forest, wind-blown and glowing with green fire.

'They can't do this,' said Eirian's small voice. 'It's wrong. They're mad. We must fight or they'll take everything away from us. Fight!'

It all ran together, vision and reality, dream and memory. Beth wept in her sleep, pricking the memories with her nails, washing them in tears. Salt water, sea water. And the salt stung.

*

When Beth had slept herself out, and her fever had subsided, she woke, clear-headed but confused.

She sat up weakly and looked around, baffled.

She was, apparently, in a tiny bedroom, in the lower of two bunks. Next to her, her baby lay in a carry-cot on the floor.

'How the hell did I . . .'

She looked through the window in the metal wall beside her. In the oblique light of early evening, she saw three caravans – modern white boxes in need of a coat of paint – parked along the edge of a wood.

The birds were singing. A dog barked. Those were the only sounds.

Beth pushed the covers back and sat up, feeling as if she'd barely come round from the worst attack of 'flu she'd ever had.

She was in a nightdress. Who had done that?

A sound came through the half-open door, someone moving around.

'Hello?' Beth said shakily.

There was a rustling noise like a newspaper being folded, and a figure appeared in the narrow doorway, clutching a copy of the *Daily Mirror*. A small, middle-aged woman with brown skin and curly, yellowish-white hair. Suddenly Beth remembered her face from the twilight of her fever.

'All right, love?' said the woman. Her eyes were bright grey. She seemed to be smiling, but Beth soon saw it was her permanent expression. A face screwed up against sun and wind. 'Back in the land of the living? Yer been out of it all day.'

'Who are you?' said Beth. She got up and leaned over the carry-cot. Eirian, apparently clean and contented, looked up at her with eyes that were already verging on green. Morgan's eyes.

'Mrs Primarola,' said the woman. 'I told you before, love; don't you remember?'

'I don't remember anything,' said Beth. 'I was at the cottage . . . but there was no one there so I started to walk. And then . . .' She shuddered, remembering more than she wanted to. 'Have you kidnapped us, or something?'

Beth didn't much care if the answer was yes. Eirian was safe and they were together. Did anything else matter?

Mrs Primarola chuckled. 'Sounds nice and dramatic, doesn't it? Kidnapped by the gypsies, heh-heh. No, we found you this morning, love. Our Emmy and Fred heard the babby bawling, found you dead to the world up in the woods on Broom Farm. Brought you in, nursed you, fed the child. No mystery.'

'If you hadn't found us . . .' Feeling dizzy, Beth sat down suddenly on the bed. 'Eirian might have died, and it was my fault.'

'*You* might have died, more like. Built like a tank, that 'un. Take more than that to kill 'er. Get back in bed.'

'But I can't stay here,' Beth said anxiously.

'Where d'you think you're going?'

'I don't know. I've run away.'

'I know,' said Mrs Primarola. 'You've been on the radio.'

'What?' Beth gripped the woman's thin arm. 'Oh, please don't tell the police! I can't go back to my parents, I couldn't stand it! They want to take the baby away and – and harm her, kill her, I don't know, but they'll do something terrible.'

'No one can take her against your will.'

'You don't know my mother,' said Beth.

She expected the woman to argue, but she only grinned, and patted Beth on the shoulder. 'Like to disappear, would you?'

'Yes. I'd like to disappear.'

'Well, you already have. We work the farms, see, move from one to another. We moved first thing. We're in Wiltshire now. All right? So don't upset yourself. No one'll find you unless you want them to.'

'Thank you,' said Beth. 'But why – why did you help me?'

''Cos you needed helping. Bathroom's next door. Y'can take a shower, if you must, but remember we're not on the mains. Then get back in bed. You were bleeding. I gave you something for it.'

And Beth knew. This was another healer, like Rhianwen.

Beth felt safe. She began to cry with relief. And with misery, because what she really wanted was to be with Rhianwen and Morgan, and they'd gone. They didn't want her. Didn't want her.

'Don't take on,' said her saviour. 'Bethia, isn't it?'

'Beth,' she said, trying to control her tears.

'Hungry, Beth?' Mrs Primarola stepped through the doorway and Beth followed, to find herself in a narrow corridor that served as a kitchen. It was cramped and shabby. 'You ought to eat.'

'I suppose so.' Beth went to look into the cot again. 'I'd better feed Eirian, first.'

'Why ever would your parents want to harm such a fine girl?' Mrs Primarola came back, tying on an apron.

The baby sneezed, then said, as if in response, 'Why would they do that?'

Beth's heart drummed, and she thought she was going to pass out. 'Oh, God,' she whispered, turning hot and cold. 'I thought I'd dreamed it. It can't be –'

Mrs Primarola, however, displayed no shock. 'I don't know,' she said softly to the child, leaning over the cot. 'Why would they?'

'Don't they understand?' said Eirian. A pause. The voice was babyish but the intonation was like that of an adult. Fully intelligent. She wasn't responding to Mrs Primarola, though, but conversing with an unseen companion. 'Oh, but they do. They're so clever. Make us look evil and they can take it all . . . I must get, must get . . .'

The baby kicked and waved her fists, as if struggling in a dream, then fell silent.

Mrs Primarola straightened up and breathed out heavily.

'Oh, we've got a problem here, ain't we?'

From the day his sister ran away, Luke became a much happier young man.

He discovered a new role; that of giving spiritual comfort to his mother. Through her initial shock at Beth's disappearance, the black rages that followed, her self-pitying grief and her fits of blaming everyone and everything around her, Luke stood by Olivia. He stoically absorbed all the fury she hurled at him, and when she was spent, he helped her to pray.

Luke was glad Beth had gone. He liked having his parents to himself. He had made the transformation from naughty little boy to model son, and for that he was receiving, at last, the respect and gratitude due to him.

His position was strengthened, naturally, by favourable contrast with his fallen sister.

Luke had hated Beth for betraying him, as deeply as he had once depended on her. But now she was gone, he merely pitied her. He prayed every night that the police would not find her; and with every day that passed without news, he thanked God. He added a small prayer for Beth, too. Poor soul, bound for hell; he'd foreseen it, the first moment she'd laid eyes on that depraved Devil-worshipper, Morgan Rhys.

Luke no longer lived in fear of Olivia beating him.

When he'd been small, he had prayed constantly for her to leave him alone, for Beth to protect him, but nothing had worked. Strangely, now his prayers had been answered, he missed those times.

Always, after Olivia had thrashed him, she cuddled and forgave him. 'I only do this because I love you,' she would say. 'I want to make you perfect in God's eyes. There is no perfection without pain. "If ye endure chastening, God dealeth with you as with sons; for what son is he whom the father chasteneth not?"'

Through that savage pain, Luke knew his mother loved him.

He missed it now, but he understood that their roles could not remain the same for ever. It was all part of God's plan. After all, Olivia had taught him a valuable lesson; that there could never be pleasure without punishment.

Chapter Nine

THE following day, Beth was in the newspaper. Just a small column tucked away on an inside page.

'Teenage Mother Missing. Schoolgirl Bethia Herne, aged 15, disappeared from a Birmingham maternity hospital on Friday night, taking her four-day-old baby girl with her. Police are concerned for her safety and say that both she and the baby may be in need of medical attention.

'Her parents believe she was making for the village of Lullingford, near Tamworth, where her grandparents live, but she never arrived. An extensive search of the area has so far proved unsuccessful.

'Her mother has made an impassioned plea for her return. "We can't understand why she would do this," Olivia Herne, 37, said last night. "We're a very loving, close family. We love Bethia and we won't be angry with her. We just want her to come home."

'Bethia was last seen alighting from a bus near Tamworth town centre at half-past midnight on Friday. She is five feet seven, with long brown hair and she was wearing . . .'

There was a blurred photo of Beth, in which she looked about ten.

'Sure you're doing the right thing?' asked Mrs Primarola.

Beth sat at the dining table in the living-room, her hand pressed to her mouth.

Eventually she said, 'My mother's a liar.'

'I didn't think you ran away for fun.' Mrs P – as she liked to be called – cleared away the breakfast things and dumped them in the sink in the narrow galley. Beth could see her through the doorway. The living-room, with a foldaway table, took up the front end of the caravan; it had blue bench-seats, a brown carpet, red and orange curtains, and a lot of clutter.

The galley ran along the right-hand side to the main bedroom at the back; on the left were Beth's room, the bathroom and a cupboard which served as a larder. The walls were pale greenish-grey, almost colourless.

'Don't you want to know why I ran away?' Beth asked.

'Can tell me if you want; don't have to.' She ran a fierce jet of water on to the dishes. 'There's too much talk, if you ask me. We just gets on wi' things in this family.'

'I must see to Eirian.'

Beth lifted the baby out of the carry-cot and cuddled her. At once a vision hit her; a transparent scene strung across the real world, like a double-exposure.

Writhing green shapes, trees or water. Flames, fear and anger.

With a cry, Beth jumped up and set Eirian down on the seat. The vision vanished. Eirian looked at her mother with a slight frown, as if to say, 'Why did you push me away?'

'You all right?' Mrs Primarola came in, drying her hands on an ancient tea-towel.

'I don't know. You heard her – speak, didn't you? What does it mean?'

'S'always got to mean something,' Mrs P muttered caustically. 'What do *you* think?'

Beth hung her head. Her mind couldn't encompass all that she'd been through in the past nine months. Out of self-protection, she'd become artificially calm. But sometimes, the horror of it would stab through her skin – just one thing, like the detached sorrow in her father's eyes as he turned away from her, or her mother saying, '*It's not a human being*' – and she would begin to shake uncontrollably.

'My mother kept saying she was possessed by the Devil. That was before she was even born! Why – why would she speak, if she wasn't? I don't know what to believe any more!'

Mrs P let out a loud sigh. 'Safe to say *something's* talking through her. Can't tell you what, gel; never heard owt like it before.'

Beth shivered. 'I thought you might reassure me that . . .'

'You've come to the wrong place for that. But.' Mrs P leaned on the table and looked into Beth's eyes. 'But you got a choice: y'can run screaming in circles until you have a nervous breakdown, or y'can stick around and find out what it means.'

Beth heard the Goddess's words again. '*You can bear it or fall.*' And Mrs P's face, a brazen sun-disc in a corona of light, was suddenly not human but an alchemic symbol, a smiling enigma.

'Will you help me?'

'Do what I can. But it's up to you.'

Gingerly, Beth picked up the baby again. Nothing happened. Eirian was warm, pink and harmless, and her gaze followed Beth's face as if she were fascinated.

Beth felt like weeping her heart out. But she was too tired to cry any more.

'I know what you want, gel,' said the woman, scrutinizing her.

I want Morgan, Beth thought. I want Morgan. Why is that so much to ask?

'A haircut,' said Mrs Primarola.

Beth sat on a stool outside, the scissors snipping close to her scalp, her long thick hair falling on to the grass near the caravan steps.

Mrs Primarola's daughter, Emmy, was cutting it. She seemed to think it was great fun.

Emmy was round and cheerful, with long blonde hair. She reminded Beth of someone, but Beth couldn't capture that elusive other face . . . oh yes, it was Guendolen, the girl in the dreams.

Emmy laughed a lot, but didn't say much. Beth was glad of that. She needed to be quiet, not to explain herself over and over again.

After Emmy had cut Beth's hair to within an inch of her scalp, she proceeded to plaster black dye on to it.

'Don't worry, I'm good at this,' said Emmy, painting dye on

Beth's eyebrows. 'Had mine all colours.' She shook her sun-coloured locks proudly. 'Looks natural, don't it?'

After Beth had sat with the stuff on her hair for an hour, Emmy rinsed it off with buckets of water, outside in the field. Beth came up spluttering, to find a circle of men, women and children watching and laughing. There was no malice in their amusement. When they broke into a round of applause, Beth started laughing, too.

Later, she examined her new self in a hand-mirror. What a shock this new Beth was. Short jet-black hair and emphatic eyebrows, making her face look white as crystal, her eyes like jade. She'd turned from an ordinary girl into a waifish punk.

Beth quite liked it.

'If anyone comes,' said Mrs Primarola, 'you're my daughter, Jean. All right? Had a Jean, once,' she added wistfully. 'Only lived a day. Now, Emmy's got a babby, couple of days older than your'n, a boy. If anyone comes, we'll swap 'em over.'

'You don't have to do this for me,' said Beth. 'I'm terribly grateful.'

'Can you talk like us, 'stead of a posh Brummie?'

'Reckon I can,' said Beth.

'Do it. All the time.'

More caravans had joined the first four. There were seven in all; five drawn by big, battered cars and two motor-homes. They parked in the edge of a field, with the farmer's permission. Here to help with the harvest, Mrs Primarola said.

Beth got to know most of the travellers within the first few days. Mr Primarola was a small, tough, grey-haired man like a twin of his wife. Beth was nervous of his monosyllabic manner at first, but she soon realized that he was good-natured, with no hidden side. She grew used to him; having to share a caravan with him, she had no choice.

Emmy and her husband Fred lived in another caravan with their baby and two older children; Fred was a big, cheerful teddy bear of a man. In a third were Mrs Primarola's two brothers, Arthur and Bernard; thin, bow-legged men with thick brown hair and sideburns which made them look ten years out of fashion. A fourth was occupied by Fred's parents, with his teenaged brother and sister. There was a family of six, another of four, and a group that consisted of Mrs P's elderly mother and assorted cousins.

There were twenty-seven people, not including Beth and Eirian, who all used the surname Primarola, regardless of relationship, like a badge of identity. A wiry, sun-tinged clan.

If Beth had approached them from outside, instead of waking up in their midst, she might have been frightened of them. But they were all right. Down to earth, neither over-friendly nor intrusive.

It was exactly what Beth needed, to be both accepted and left alone.

All around them rose great, curved sweeps of grass, soft as green silk in a silver-blue haze. Woodland ran down into the folds. The sunlight was misty and gentle. The birds piped angelically all day long.

This beauty made Beth feel sadder than ever. If only he could be here.

But Morgan wouldn't want me any more, she thought, with my shorn hair, my swollen breasts and stomach, shadows under my eyes, even though he did this to me.

Still, Beth told herself, she was lucky. She'd escaped and found good friends to help her. Women who knew about babies and understood. People who didn't bombard her with loving pity or with screaming insults, who could be kind without constant reference to the Bible.

Within three days of her arrival, Beth was expected to work. Everyone had to do something, even if it was only peeling vegetables. Beth didn't mind. She sat shelling peas with Emmy and Mrs P's mother – an intimidating, mischievous old woman known as Granny P – and they had a laugh.

Sometimes Beth would think, with helpless panic, about her O levels. She'd been clever at school. Her mother had wanted her to be a teacher at the proposed church school; Beth had hoped for something more. Oh, to have gone to university with Morgan and maybe worked with him one day . . .

Now I've thrown it all away, Beth thought, to shell peas and wash dishes.

A dog started barking. Bernard came running up to the caravan, out of breath.

'Police!' he wheezed.

'Get Emmy and the boy,' said Mrs P. 'Quick! Don't panic, Beth, and remember to call me Mam.'

'Keep Eirian awake,' Beth said to Emmy. 'Otherwise she might – you know, say something.'

As the white car drew slowly into the site, wheels crunching on the worn grass, Beth was sitting outside, peeling potatoes, with Emmy's boy asleep in a carry-cot beside her.

Beth ignored the two policemen who got out, but her heart was thumping, and she could feel sweat dampening her long white dress.

She could hear them talking to Mr and Mrs P. She tried not to look.

'We're looking for a group of travellers who were seen near Lullingford around the time the young woman disappeared.'

'Yes, that was us. Working at Broom Farm, we were. There every year, May, June,' said Mr Primarola.

'And did you pick up any strangers? A girl with a baby, perhaps?'

They shook their heads. 'Don't take in strangers. We're family.'

'Mind if we look around?' said the policeman. 'Any new babies?'

'Both my daughters, last week,' said Mrs Primarola proudly.

'Congratulations,' said the officer.

The policemen went in and out of caravans. The children banded together and followed them round. No one seemed perturbed.

'These are my daughters, Emmy and Jean,' said Mrs P.

'Not very alike, are they?'

'Sisters! Got to look as unlike as possible, ain't they?'

The policemen looked very hard at Jean. 'Mind if we look at the baby?'

Beth shrugged. 'Go ahead.'

'It's a boy,' one of the officers announced, struggling ham-handedly to refasten its nappy.

'Oh,' said the other, looking disappointed.

'Mine's a girl,' said Emmy. Eirian was alert and mute in her arms. 'Want to check?'

They declined, but they looked even harder at Emmy.

'Not tall enough,' one muttered. 'Sorry to have bothered you.'

'No trouble,' Mrs P said cheerfully. Everyone waved the policemen goodbye.

Beth almost passed out when they'd gone. The Primarolas sat her down and gave her tea. Bernard, who was at least thirty years older than Beth, was especially attentive.

'I don't believe we got away with it!' Beth cried. 'They didn't check anything!'

'Yup,' said Mr P. 'That's the police, bless 'em.'

They weren't tinkers. They weren't Romanies. They were the Primarolas, a clan apart.

Two weeks after they'd arrived in Wiltshire, they were on the move again. Another county, another farm. Harvesting, fruit-picking, anything that was needed. The farmers knew them and greeted them like old friends.

They went all round the country in a loop, Emmy explained, to the same farms at the same time every year. The farmers welcomed them, because they worked hard and caused no disturbance. When the Primarolas left a site, there was very little sign they'd ever been there. No rubbish, no dog mess. Only flattened grass.

'And they like us because we bless the land,' Emmy added mysteriously.

As Beth recovered her strength, she was glad to earn her

keep and not be in their debt. Her duties were mainly confined to the site; child-minding and cooking. 'When Eirian's older,' said Mr P, 'you can start on farm work, if you want.'

When she's older, Beth thought. My God, how long do they expect us to stay with them? Five years? A lifetime?

And where will Eirian go to school? she thought. Twenty different schools in a year, like these children? I know they seem happy enough but – I can't drag her round all her life like this.

'I don't know what I shall do,' she said to Mrs Primarola one day. 'I've got no money, no qualifications, nothing.'

'Y'got food and friends,' Mrs P pointed out.

It was enough for now. Not for ever.

Beneath the easygoing calm of everyday life, Beth existed in a silent state of panic.

But for now, who else would have looked after a shell-shocked, depressed girl without taking her baby away? Who would have tolerated a possessed baby that spoke in its sleep, if not these people?

In her parents' house, Beth had felt very close to madness. Away from them, somehow, she coped.

For the first few weeks, she would often burst into tears without warning, but no one made a fuss or said, 'Pull y'self together.' They let her get on with it, understanding. And as the weeks went by, her pain receded and the tears stopped.

Beth didn't like living in the caravan, though. Everything was so cramped, fiddly, inconvenient; there was no room to spread out and not much privacy. It wouldn't have been so bad if they'd all been women, but Mr P's presence embarrassed her.

Bernard was the only one Beth actually disliked. He had taken to hanging around, apparently thinking Beth must find him irresistible. And Beth had a ghastly feeling that Mrs P hoped she would make an instant wife and family for her bachelor brother.

Eirian, meanwhile, was thriving. It was as if she couldn't wait to grow, to move on. She always cried with purpose, never for the hell of it. Beth always knew what the matter was. The telepathy between them was as subtle as love.

To Beth's relief there had been no visions since the first few days, and the baby had not spoken now for weeks; only the odd strange phrase, at most. 'The Normans and the Planta-genets were kinder,' she had said one day, to Beth's mortifica-tion; no one else had heard, though.

There was no answer to the mystery of who or what Eirian was.

Beth loved her with almost sensual intensity, not because she was a baby, but because she was Morgan's. Yet Beth was also rather afraid of her. She looked at Beth with such knowing eyes. Sometimes, even if Eirian said nothing, Beth would feel the threatening darkness all around them, sense the shadows of lethal authority moving through the forest.

Eirian fed healthily, but Beth did not. She swiftly lost the weight she had put on in pregnancy, and more. Her hair grew, but she asked Emmy to keep dyeing the roots black. Beth began to dress in black also. It felt right. She was in a kind of mourn-ing, after all.

On a golden afternoon in late September, the workers re-turned early from the fields and Beth sensed an atmosphere of conspiracy and excitement. Sensing she was not meant to be part of it, Beth asked Mrs Primarola what was happening.

'If you know what today is, you'll know,' said Mrs P. 'If not, y'can stay back and look after the babbies.'

Beth thought. She hadn't forgotten what Rhianwen and Morgan had taught her. 'It's the autumn equinox. Mabon. That's all I can think of.'

'Ah, she knows,' said Mrs P, nodding in satisfaction. 'You can come. You're one of us.'

'Thank you, but I've hardly been with you long enough.'

'No, you're one of *us*.'

Yes, thought Beth in surprise, I am. Away from her mother, her terror of a punishing God and malicious Devil had van-ished, but her knowledge of the Goddess remained. It was the only belief that made sense to Beth. Even Rhianwen's betrayal hadn't damaged it; after all, Rhianwen was only a human being, not the Goddess herself.

They were in the south of England, in a valley between deeply folded fields and woodland. The harvests were in; the colours were beginning to turn to the copper and fire of autumn. The sun was a globe of melting red, the shadows like blue smoke.

Through this rich dusk, the adults and older children walked in procession through the trees, each with a lighted candle in one hand and a gift in the other: an apple, a pine cone, a potato. They were solemn, as if going to church. Beth was walking beside Emmy, not knowing what to expect. Eirian and the other young children were back at the site, being looked after by Granny P. Beth had the strangest feeling, though, that Eirian should have come with them.

In the edge of the woods they had changed into robes of pale violet, green and gold, like sun and shadows on the fields.

As the procession emerged from the woods on to the treeless peak of a hill, Beth saw that two of the travellers were already there, robed and hooded, their faces hidden by masks. And the masks were cat faces, tabby-marked in silver and gold. A bonfire burned behind them.

Priest and priestess.

'What should I do?' Beth whispered.

'Just follow,' replied Emmy. 'Don't worry. S'easy.'

The procession flowed snake-like up the hill towards the fire. Round it lay a wreath of wheat sheaves, bread, fruit and flowers. Each person in turn added their gift to the wreath and was greeted by the priest and priestess, 'Blessed be'. Their voices, muffled behind the masks, were unrecognizable.

Beth couldn't work out who they were. Who was missing?

Then all joined hands and began to circle slowly round the fire. The priest struck up a rhythm on a small drum; the priestess began to chant.

'This is the time of harvest, of fulfilment and thanksgiving. Now day and night are equal and we sail towards the darkness.

153

We thank you for the fruits that will sustain us through the winter. We sow the seeds and in the barren earth they are reborn. Come to us now, Queen of Heaven, Mother of All Living, Maiden, Mother, Crone, Isis Diana Cybele Artemis Ishtar Kore Cerridwen Demeter Hawwah Lilith Mary Inanna Rhiannon Persephone Selene Bast.'

Other voices took up the chant. The noise swelled, atonal. '*She changes everything she touches and everything she touches changes.*' Beth joined in. She felt light-headed.

'Come Mother come Moon come Goddess *come!*'

Then the priest began, 'Sower of seed, dying king, giver of grain and fruit, Horned One, come! Ever-dying, ever-living, reborn lord of winter, God of light, Green Man, Dancer, Hunter, Pan Osiris Eros Logos Dionysus Arthur Dumuzi Herne *come!*'

Dizzy from the whirl of figures round the flickering fire, Beth thought, if Mum could see me now, she would see her daughter in a coven worshipping the Devil. A lost soul.

But she's wrong. And it's her loss.

Beth felt the first tentative flame of joy she had experienced since losing Morgan. She knew this was where she belonged and always had. Rhianwen and Morgan had known, even while she couldn't see it for herself. It had been coming through in her dreams for years. Life should be lived in joy, not guilt.

The drum stopped.

'He is here,' said the priest.

'She is here,' said the priestess.

The dance stopped, but a cone of energy swirled between the dancers like the breathing of the earth. All was colour; red fire against the dark blue sky. And the dancers were transformed by grace into something deeper than their everyday selves.

The priestess came around the circle, placing a plaited cord round each person's neck. 'This is the cord of life, the circle of rebirth,' she said. 'Blessed be the life that comes from the Mother and returns to Her.'

The priest poured libations of grain and water on the fire. Fragrant smoke rose, hissing.

'The seed we sow in autumn shall live anew in the spring.'

A soft, improvised chanting went round the circle. A cup of apple cider came round, then a bag, carried by one of the girls, from which people took pieces of broken cake. Each one looked at his or her piece, then ate it.

Beth's piece was black. 'This is a bit burned, can I have another piece?' she asked. But the child began to jump up and down, shouting excitedly, 'She's got it! She's got it!'

The priest and priestess came and lifted her up. Beth still didn't know who they were.

'What's happening?'

'You got the black bit,' said the male voice, muffled behind the cat face. 'That means you are to be sacrificed to the Goddess.'

'What?'

'It's symbolic. You jump through the bonfire three times, that's all.'

'I do *what?*' she cried, but they only laughed.

The circle was breaking up and following Beth towards the fire, cheering her on. They threw the bread and fruits on to the flames; offerings to the God and Goddess.

A few people threw off their robes and were naked underneath. No one was shocked, no one was forced to join in. They were free to do as they wished. To feel the heat of the fire and the cool breeze on their skin, and to dance.

The drum began again. A violin and a flute followed.

Beth had seen more shocking displays at her own church, when worshippers possessed by the Holy Spirit had spoken in tongues. Her own mother had done crazier things than this in church.

The priest pushed the dying edge of the fire into a glowing line, no more than a foot high. It didn't look too terrifying. Gathering up the hem of her robe, and the dress she was wearing underneath, Beth ran and leapt over the embers. A

155

great cheer went up. She jumped again, exhilarated now. The third time, someone caught her and whirled her round.

It was Bernard, laughing, showing stained teeth. He was naked.

'C'mon, gel!'

Turning dizzy, Beth jerked abruptly out of his grasp. The music and voices began to echo, as if some drug had begun to work through her. All at once she was scared. Everyone else seemed manically joyful but she felt excluded, isolated in a vortex.

The hill began to sway like a wave, blue-green and crimson, shattering into diamonds of light. The grass beneath Beth rose and fell. Her breathing quickened; fear wove a breeze around her.

Something in the cider?

She had to escape.

Turning away, she began to walk down the hill, very carefully, as if through waves. With every step the ground sank or rushed up to meet her foot.

Someone was coming after her. Not revellers, but a man in a black, flapping robe and a dark hat. He was following her silently, breaking up and reforming as if seen through water.

She was in the trees now. Wading, struggling. Must escape—

Beth fell and he caught her. A sneering face under the dark brim; she thought it was Pastor Blair, changed, grown fatter and his skin punched with pock-marks.

Couldn't be, but –

He pushed her backwards with his hands clamped on her upper arms, until her spine slammed into the rough trunk of a tree. His breath stank. She was overwhelmed by a wave of weakness and sick terror.

'Well, Mistress Guendolen, and where are you going?' he breathed into her face. Beth tipped her head back to avoid him but he was too close. He was repellent, all sweaty flesh ingrained with its own grease and dead cells, bloated with self-importance. 'Away to worship your trees and stones, to open your fine legs to the Devil? I know what ye do in those woods.'

And he said a word so soft she could hardly hear it; coldly lethal, like the crucifix glinting on his chest. '*Witch.*'

Beth couldn't speak. She saw her own hair covering her shoulders and arms, but it was dark gold, not black.

She knew him. He was the leader of the clerics who had broken up the wedding procession. And she knew what he was called. Inquisitor Lacost.

'There's a way we can save your soul, Guendolen.'

Beth was breathing so hard she thought she would faint. She was in two places at once; here in the nightmare and there in her own past, being violently exorcized by Pastor Blair. *We must save your soul.*

'Lie with me, Guendolen.'

'No!'

He pressed against her and she could feel his member through the crusty material of his robe. Hard, bullying, profane. As if he'd stolen the Wand of Rebirth and twisted its sacred beauty into an obscenity.

The certainty of rape filled her with revulsion and bitter resentment.

'You know what will happen if you don't.'

'You have no proof!'

'You have bewitched me, daughter of Eve, Devil's gateway.' he said. 'That is proof enough.'

The fear that shuddered through her was fear of death; tortuous, agonizing, undeserved death. There was no escape. Nothing to cling to but her pride.

'You desire me, slut. All women are the same. You're longing to open your legs for me.'

'Never! I'd rather lie with a pig!' And she spat into his face.

The face, with a bubble of saliva dripping from eyelid to pock-marked cheek, shifted into a dangerous smile. His teeth were rotten, his lips like raw meat. 'That, you will regret. You'll beg me for salvation before you die.'

Beth's fear became wild panic. She dived sideways, and he let her go, and she fell –

And was whirled suddenly up into the air. She saw the scene

from above, as if through a lens; saw Guendolen stumbling to her feet and running away, long hair flapping in gold strings on her shoulders, and the Inquisitor watching her, hands on his hips. Laughing.

The laughter followed Beth, echoing, as the trees formed a whirlpool around her.

Beth emerged, shuddering, from the vision. She was lying against the base of a tree, but nothing around her made sense. The world was a shimmering mosaic of green, blue and black and she lay staring at it in a trance of mute horror.

It wasn't over.

A shape was coming for her, like a dark, fast-moving monkey. Lacost again.

She was petrified. She waited, mouth open, to die.

The shape came right up to her and gripped her shoulder. Beth screamed.

'Hush, love. S'only me. What's the matter? There, there. Come on now.'

That broke the trance. Her sight cleared. It was Bernard who had hold of her. He was naked, displaying a scrawny body and hairy, bowed legs.

She got to her feet. He placed his other hand on her left shoulder and pulled her closer to him. 'Come on, love,' he said, low and coaxing. 'Oooh, you're nice.'

Beth tried to pull out of his grip, but he was strong, his hands powerful from years of manual work. Whatever drug had been in the cider, it seemed merely to have overexcited him.

'Get off me,' she said.

'Just a kiss.' He smiled, showing long, yellowish teeth. Beth was more than revolted; she was still wild with the horror of the vision.

'Stop it!' she yelled. 'Don't!'

'C'mon,' he growled. He tried to get his arm round her. His chest touched hers, and his bristly sideburns pricked her face. His breath reeked of stale tobacco.

Beth brought her knee up, hard, into his unprotected scrotum.

Bernard collapsed, squawking, and Beth ran.

She couldn't find her way. The trees were a hallucinatory labyrinth, mocking her. Just as she began really to panic, she found herself back at the site, more by chance than anything.

No one around but a couple of small children, playing on Granny P's doorstep. 'Hello, Beth,' they called.

Beth's head ached. All she could think of was Eirian. She was terrified that Eirian had also experienced the vision – but what could her infant mind make of it?

Beth leaned against the back of Granny P's caravan until she had calmed down enough to go in and behave normally.

Beth knocked, then let herself into the dark interior; Granny P was there, knitting and listening to Radio 2 on a battered red plastic wireless. Both Eirian and Emmy's son were sleeping peacefully.

Weak with relief, Beth picked up her baby.

'How has she been?'

'Talkative,' said Granny P, looking at her with candid milky eyes. She seemed an immovable mountain of a woman with a squall of grey hair, but Beth knew she could move fast enough when the children needed sorting out. 'Very talkative.'

'Oh,' said Beth, dismayed. 'Thank you for looking after her.'

She fled to her own caravan and locked herself in.

Having settled Eirian down, she pulled off her robe and dress and put on jeans and T-shirt instead, and a heavy jumper for good measure. Protection from Bernard's attentions. Trembling, Beth sat curled up on the seat in the living-room, chin on her knees.

She felt in danger.

She'd felt safe here until tonight, but now she felt threatened.

Damn Bernard. Spoiling it all. There was always someone to spoil things. The man in the vision, hideous as it was, had been a hallucination – but Bernard was real.

Beth felt dirty, even though nothing had happened.

Morgan – Morgan had never made her feel dirty.

She breathed deep. Calmer now.

A soft noise made her jump. A thud, like a cat jumping down from a worktop in the kitchen.

Beth sat up straight, irrationally terrified that her would-be rapist had somehow got into the caravan.

The curtain across the doorway twitched. Then a cat appeared under it. An enormous black and white long-haired cat, like a lion.

Llew. Rhianwen's cat.

Beth jumped up, opened the curtain, and saw Ankaret, stalking out of the back bedroom. A slim grey reed with golden eyes. And following her came a plumper, slate-blue animal, Bast.

Beth stood with her mouth open. Perhaps the drug wasn't wearing off after all. She must be dreaming this but they looked so real.

The cats came round her, angling to be stroked. Llew pressed himself against Beth's leg, his chin on her knee. Beth hardly dared to touch them. She was afraid that if she did, she'd never be able to let them go.

Beth went to pick up Eirian and sat down again with her on her lap, but the cats came with her and jumped on her, fussing. She stroked them, gently pushing them away from the baby.

Beth had no idea how long she sat there. Not long. She was numb.

The caravan door opened, and someone came in. Beth froze. Either she hadn't locked it properly, or the lock was broken. Weighed down by cats and baby, Beth couldn't get up to see who it was. Had to wait, pinned, as the footsteps came along the galley and a hand pushed back the dividing curtain.

The priestess.

She was still wearing the green and violet robe, but she'd taken the hood and cat mask off, and her hair was a glowing auburn veil over her shoulders.

'Beth?' she said, and smiled.

Then her gaze lighted on Eirian, and she stopped smiling.

Her eyes went glassy. Beth could easily read her thoughts; so transparent.

Oh, Goddess, that's Morgan's baby. Morgan's.

Beth stared back at her, feeling strange. Almost cold, removed.

'Oh, Beth,' said Rhianwen, tears forming bright crescents on her lower lids.

'Where were you when I needed you?' cried Beth.

Chapter Ten

'I NEARLY didn't recognize you,' said Rhianwen. She came to Beth, smiling, seeming a little nervous; responding to Beth's question without actually answering it.

'Is Morgan with you?' Beth asked quickly.

Rhianwen looked sadly at her; she must have seen the hope in Beth's eyes. 'No, he isn't.'

'You were the priestess, weren't you? The priest –'

'It wasn't Morgan, Beth. It was the farmer's son.'

Beth's heart felt ready to break again and release a river of blood and water, even though she'd known it couldn't be Morgan. She would have recognized his hands, his touch, his voice. With an immense effort, she suppressed her tears. The moment passed.

'Where is he?'

'College.' Obviously the last thing Rhianwen wanted to talk about was Morgan. 'May I hold her?'

'If you like,' said Beth. 'Her name's Eirian.'

'Silver. That's nice. Why did you choose that?'

'I wanted to call her something Welsh. It was in a book of names. I just liked it.' Beth couldn't tell her about the Goddess's eyes.

Rhianwen sat down beside Beth. Passively, Beth let Rhianwen take the baby from her. 'Hello, Eirian,' said Rhianwen. Eirian responded with a smile, and kicked happily at the air. 'She's got your eyes.'

'I think she's got Morgan's eyes,' Beth said stiffly.

'Yes, well. You and Morgan both have beautiful eyes.' Rhianwen looked at Beth. 'Are you all right?'

'Fine,' Beth lied. 'Do you want a drink?'

'In a while. You're very angry with me, Beth, aren't you?' Beth said nothing. 'I don't blame you.'

'How did you find me?'

'I've known the Primarolas for years. They come and work on the farmland that backs on to my garden every summer. I asked them to look out for you. Just in case you came. I didn't really think you would, but –'

'So you knew I was with them?' Beth gasped. 'Mrs P never said.'

'You've probably found they don't say anything unless you ask a direct question. Mrs P sent me a message that they'd found you and you were safe – but she sent it to Blackthorn Cottage so it was a while before I got it.' Rhianwen spoke quietly, as if less than proud of her own conduct. 'You know it was in the papers when you disappeared? It's died down now, of course, though I suppose they're still looking.'

'Didn't you tell anyone you knew where I was?'

'No. Why should I? If your family are suffering now, it bloody well serves them right.'

Beth was shocked at the venom in Rhianwen's voice. 'I went through hell when they found out I was pregnant. Every day until Eirian was born. Hell. I don't know how else to describe it. I think Mum was planning to kill her when she was born, or make her life a nightmare, at least. I couldn't take any more. I really needed you and you weren't there!'

'I'm sorry. I had to take Morgan away.'

'Why?'

'Your family, dear. They came round and threatened me. If we didn't leave the area, they were going to make trouble for us.'

Beth was startled. 'How?'

'They were going to have Morgan prosecuted for having sex with an under-age girl.'

How cold that sounded. Clinical and disgusting. 'Who said that? My mother?'

'Yes, but your father and grandparents came too, to back her up. Didn't they tell you?'

'No,' Beth said angrily. 'They never told me anything. It's not fair, Morgan didn't do anything wrong!'

'But he did,' Rhianwen said very softly. 'And it's partly my fault. I didn't want to act like your mother by forbidding you to be friends. I thought if I warned Morgan not to touch you, that would be enough. I trusted him. Should have known better.'

'I hate my family,' Beth said under her breath. 'How dare they threaten you? I thought my gran was different but she's just as bad. But why didn't you stand up to them? How could you just give in?'

There was something Rhianwen wasn't telling Beth. Why else did she always pause before she spoke?

'I had to take Morgan away, settle him somewhere else. I'm sorry. There was nothing else to do. Your mother ordered us not to have any contact with you. Whatever I think of your mother, I've no right to go against her wishes where you're concerned.'

'Have you sold the cottage yet?'

'No, it's still on the market.'

'What about the cats?'

'I found homes for most, took the rest to a sanctuary in Loughborough.'

'Where do you live now? Where's Morgan?' Beth demanded.

'Beth, please. I can't tell you that.'

'Why not?'

Tears were threatening again. Eirian began to grizzle in response. Not wanting to upset her, Beth took her from Rhianwen and settled her back in the carry-cot.

Beth's mouth was dry. She was shaking. To regain her composure, she fetched a bottle of cider and two mugs from the tiny larder, poured them each a drink. She hoped the Primarolas would not suddenly walk in, or she'd never get the truth out of Rhianwen.

'Thank you,' said Rhianwen. 'Here's to happier times.' They drank. The cider was mouth-wateringly sour, but it helped.

'Does Morgan even know I was pregnant?'

'Yes, he knew.'

'What did he say?'

Rhianwen, once so open and candid, avoided Beth's eyes. 'He was very upset.'

'Worried about me, or just plain horrified?'

'Both.'

'Didn't he want to see me?'

Rhianwen sighed. Her long fingers played a tattoo on the china mug, as if she were debating whether to tell Beth the truth or white lies. Eventually she said. 'Yes. He wanted to see you.'

'Did he – did he ever say he loved me?'

'Beth, you're tormenting yourself with these questions.'

'There was a girl at school who got pregnant,' said Beth, 'in a higher form to me, so I didn't know her – but they said, when her boyfriend found out, he dumped her. Didn't want to know. Is that what Morgan's like?'

'No, my son is not like that, but your parents would never have let him see you.'

'I'm not with my parents now,' said Beth. 'Can I see him?'

Again a pause, a long breath. Rhianwen looked beautiful, her face half hidden between wings of dark-red hair. Beth had almost worshipped her; at this moment, she could have struck her.

'No,' said Rhianwen.

'Why not?' Beth cried, distraught.

'I told you.'

'But my mum wouldn't know! How can she do anything to him, if she doesn't know?'

'Beth, try to understand. You're both too young. You can't be together. It would ruin both your lives. Morgan wants to take his A levels and go to university; he's too young to cope with a family –'

'So am I, but I have to,' Beth said fiercely.

'I know, love, but boys are different. Bloody hopeless, actually.'

'So it's not just Mum keeping us apart. It's you.'

Beth felt betrayed, but Rhianwen was quietly intransigent. 'It would be no good, believe me. It's better to accept it's over now, before you're hurt even more.'

'You can't stop us doing what we want when we're both over eighteen! I'll find him!'

'No, I can't stop you for ever, it's true. But you'll both have changed by then. You'll be different people. You weren't Morgan's only girlfriend, you know, and there will be others. He likes girls. They're attracted to him because he makes them feel special – I suppose you know that. To be honest, if I were you, Beth, I wouldn't trust him as far as Llew can spit.'

A white-hot fire flashed through Beth. She couldn't speak or breathe.

'I know it hurts,' said Rhianwen, stroking her arm. 'I know.'

And Beth was in Rhianwen's arms, clinging to her. Not crying, but fighting for great gasps of air, as if she were about to drown.

Rhianwen held her. The cats climbed all over them, worried.

'I'm scared,' said Beth.

'It's all right. I'm with you now.'

'It's not all right,' Beth said into Rhianwen's hair. 'I had a horrible vision after the celebration. That's why I came back early. I suppose you think it was clever to drug the cider.'

Rhianwen drew back. 'Beth, there was no drug in the cider or the cake. Some people use hallucinogens in rituals to increase awareness, but I don't. Especially not when there are children there.'

'So I am going mad,' Beth said dully. 'It was so beautiful, the celebration. I felt as if I belonged. But after I jumped through the fire, it turned into a nightmare. And someone tried to rape me.'

Rhianwen looked horrified. 'Who?'

'Mrs P's brother, Bernard. It doesn't matter. He was being an idiot, so I kicked him where it hurt. The hallucination was worse.'

'What was it?'

Beth swallowed. She could hardly bear to think of it, let alone repeat it. She tried to describe it in a few words. 'It was the worst one I've had, but not the first. Mum thinks I'm possessed. She thinks Morgan put the Devil into me. And Eirian . . .'

'What?'

Beth suddenly realized she couldn't tell Rhianwen that Eirian led her into the visions, or that she talked. She wanted to, but she couldn't. If Rhianwen wouldn't let her see Morgan, wouldn't help her or even tell her the truth, how could Beth confide in her?

'Mum said she wasn't a human being.'

'Oh, Goddess help us.' Rhianwen sighed. 'Beth, she hasn't made you believe all that stuff again, has she?'

'It was hard not to, when she was on at me all the time. I've seen things that scared me, made me wonder if Mum wasn't right after all.'

'It's the stress you've been under.' Rhianwen hugged her again. 'That's all it is. Poor love.'

Beth was so glad Rhianwen was here that she was ready to forgive her anything. She felt safe with her cheek against the thick auburn hair, breathing in its scents of woodsmoke, incense and sandalwood.

'When I was with you and Morgan,' said Beth, 'it was easy to believe there was no God and no Devil, and nature was sacred, and all that. I felt free and happy. But when I was at home, I was always scared I'd got it wrong.'

'That we'd tricked you?'

'Something like that.'

'The Goddess encompasses all things, bad as well as good,' said Rhianwen. 'That makes her dangerous. Not always comforting. I never pretended I had all the answers. Don't expect me to be your guardian angel, Beth; I can behave as badly as anyone. I should never have let you keep visiting me for a start; I knew you'd get into trouble for it. I should have protected you from Morgan, but I failed you there, too.'

'Do you think Morgan's got the Devil in him?' Beth asked softly.

'I think he was irresponsible and selfish. He can be very wicked under the guise of behaving like an angel, yes.'

'So he was being wicked when he used to tell me that sex was a sacrament to the Goddess, was he?'

'Morgan said things like that?' Rhianwen seemed to wince.

'All the time,' said Beth. She was growing a little harder; she wanted to make Rhianwen feel bad. 'Great chat-up line, isn't it?'

'Great,' Rhianwen said grimly. 'So, you think my beliefs gave him licence to seduce you?'

'You told us sex was sacred.'

'Exactly. Not to be indulged in recklessly, and not at the wrong time. Like when you're too young. I thought Morgan understood that.'

'I thought he loved me.'

'I expect he thought he did, at the time,' Rhianwen said, sighing. 'Boys are like that; they have passions for a few months, then forget about them. That's why there's absolutely no point in you seeing him; you'd only get hurt.'

Again the arrow of pain pierced Beth. She was growing quite used to it.

'But it was so lovely,' Beth said, looking at Eirian. 'I could never explain to Mum, because she wouldn't listen. I can tell you, though. We had such a wonderful time. How can he just forget it, like it didn't mean anything? I never can.'

Rhianwen lowered her eyes. She had no answer, apparently.

Beth heard someone outside clear his throat and spit; she glanced up to see Bernard's face framed in the window. She started violently. The window was slightly open, which she hadn't noticed before. How long had he been standing there, listening to their conversation?

When Beth met his eyes, he gave a slight jerk of his head, a sort of sneer, and walked away into the darkness.

'Do you want me to speak to Mrs P about him?' Rhianwen asked.

'No,' Beth said hurriedly. She had a feeling that complaining would only make things worse. 'No, I don't want to make trouble when she's been so kind. How long will you stay with us?'

'I have to go back tonight,' said Rhianwen. 'I wanted to see how you were.'

'Can I come with you?' Beth asked rashly, desperately.

'No, Beth. I'm sorry. We're in the tiniest flat, we've got no money until I can sell the house, and as I explained, Morgan has to get on with his life.'

Rhianwen could never know how cruel that remark seemed to Beth. She felt reduced to a mistake, a nothingness, a would-be albatross round Morgan's neck.

Not part of his life. Just something he'd stumbled over on his way.

'You don't want me,' said Beth. 'I don't blame you. Why should you?'

'You've got friends here. You won't meet kinder people anywhere.'

'I know, but . . . You said sex wasn't a sin and childbirth wasn't a punishment. So why am I being punished?'

'I know it's hard.' Rhianwen stared down at her hands. 'But whatever we believe, we still have to live in the real world.'

'I don't want to stay here.' Beth felt herself losing control, beginning to plead. 'I've got no one. I can't cope, I need your help!'

'I'm sorry, Beth. Sorry. But you are not the only person in the world who has to suffer being separated from someone they love.' Rhianwen had turned pale. When she spoke again, there were controlled tears in her voice. Beth thought, does she still miss Morgan's father, after all this time? Or is it someone else? 'I'll leave you Bast. Mrs P said she doesn't mind. I only brought Llew and Anki for the ride; they hate it in the flat.'

Beth put a hand on her arm. 'Rhianwen, please . . .' tell me the truth, she was going to say, but the door opened and Mr and Mrs P came in, more than a little tipsy, and there was no further chance to talk.

Rhianwen seemed to jump at the excuse to end the conversation and leave. Beth was left feeling helpless and humiliated, wondering what she'd done wrong, or failed to understand.

They all went outside to wave Rhianwen off in her old, white Volkswagen Beetle. Mrs P must know where she's going, Beth thought; but what's the point of asking, when she doesn't want me?

Beth knew how it felt to be utterly powerless. No money, no choices. However kind the Primarolas were, she was trapped with them. She lacked even the power to sway a friend – if Rhianwen could still be termed a friend – into helping her.

When the Beetle had vanished into the night, Beth took the baby into her room and wept, her tears falling on to Eirian's sleeping face. Bast insinuated herself between Beth's knee and the baby, instantly at home. It was the cat's presence, more than anything, that made Beth cry. Bast had been there when Morgan had kissed her and promised they would be together.

Now I know he lied, Beth thought. Are there half a dozen other girls sitting crying because he lied to them, too? Or if he wasn't lying, Rhianwen is. I don't know which is worse.

Tears wouldn't make the pain go away. It stayed, a constant anguish, worse than anything her mother had inflicted on her.

'At least I've got you,' said Beth, kissing Eirian's tender forehead. 'Poor you. I know what it's like to have a mad mother.'

The baby frowned in her sleep, kicking and uttering faint grunts.

'The Horn of Fertility,' said Eirian, who hadn't said a word in Rhianwen's presence. 'The Wand of Power, they don't understand.'

'Did she say anything?'

Morgan needed to know, as soon as Rhianwen walked in through the door.

'Not much.' She released Llew and Ankaret from their basket and they padded around disdainfully, as if thinking, oh no, we're not here again, are we? Then she went to hang up her coat in the bedroom, but Morgan followed her. The flat was, indeed, cramped and rather claustrophobic with its relentlessly white walls. Rhianwen hadn't lied about that.

'But you found her?'

'Yes.'

'Is she all right?'

Rhianwen was trying to avoid confronting Morgan, but whichever way she turned, his anxious face was reflected in the mirrors. She'd had a tiring drive back to London; she didn't want to have this conversation.

'She's fine,' said Rhianwen.

'And the baby?'

'A girl.'

'I know that, Mum. It was in the papers, wasn't it? I mean, what's she like?'

'Like a baby, Morgan,' Rhianwen said sharply. 'Greenish eyes, brown hair, spends her time sleeping, crying and feeding.'

'I've got a right to know!'

'Have you?' She was tidying up now, throwing things into drawers. Then she stopped, feeling awful. 'Sorry, love. She's a very nice baby. Her name's Eirian. I wish I hadn't told you I was going.'

He hovered in the doorway; a figure in black from head to foot, with pale skin and too much brown-black hair. A heartbreaking beauty, her own son.

'But did she say anything? Beth, I mean. Didn't she give you a message for me?'

'No, love, she didn't.'

He looked incredulous. Baffled, and so disappointed that Rhianwen could hardly bear to do this to him.

'Didn't you give her my letter?'

Rhianwen shrugged. 'I couldn't force her to read it.'

'You've got to tell me where she is!'

'No. We've been through this a dozen times. You agreed it was right to leave.'

'I know, but I can't stop thinking about her.'

'Try!'

'I'll bloody well find her myself!' he exclaimed.

'You,' Rhianwen said sternly, 'have exams to think about. I'm not having you haring off across the country. You've got to forget her!'

'I thought I could, but I can't.'

'Morgan,' she said gently, 'she doesn't want to see you.'

Now his face went to stone. 'What?'

'She's had her fingers burned. She regrets what happened; I think she feels used, even if you don't think you used her. Hardly surprising. She was far too young to cope with sex and babies. She needs to be a child again. She doesn't want a man hanging around. All she wants to think about is Eirian, and quite honestly, I don't blame her.'

Morgan said nothing. He just looked at Rhianwen, then went away into the sitting-room. Making a calm and complete withdrawal into himself.

'By the way,' he said offhandedly, when she followed him, 'the estate agent rang. There's been an offer for the cottage. I wrote all the details on the pad by the 'phone.'

He went into the tiny kitchen; she heard him filling the kettle. Rhianwen sat down by the telephone, read through the details, and detached the sheet of paper from the pad.

Then she calmly tore it to pieces and dropped it into the wastepaper basket; just as, when she'd stopped at the first motor-way service station, she had shredded Morgan's letter to Beth.

Chapter Eleven

BETH had thought the Primarolas would stay in the south of England for the winter. Instead, they went to Scotland.

'Have to go where the work is,' said Mr Primarola. There were fences to be mended, walls to be built, all kinds of maintenance needed to make the land ready for spring.

Beth grew used to being cold all the time, to being constantly muffled in several layers of clothes, and trying to do everything with woollen gloves on. She even grew used to the darkness, but she didn't like it.

They had Christmas; the pagan version. Mrs P said that the decorations, the feasting and the exchange of presents were pagan customs anyway, until the church usurped them. Good enough excuse, they all agreed.

Mrs P gave Beth twenty pounds to spend on presents and she went into the nearest town with Emmy and Fred to shop. There was a long main street of grey buildings, with cold heathery hills louring all around.

The festive lights made Beth feel sad. Christmases had been happy at home. Olivia would call a truce with the world, Philip would be warmer than usual, and the carol services were beautiful and moving. Even Luke could play up without being punished. Their grandparents had come to stay – Olivia would never go to them, because it meant being away from church – so the house had been warm and alive, as it never was at any other time of year.

Perhaps time had put too rosy a gloss on the memories, but Beth was so homesick she thought she'd die of it.

She bought her parents a Christmas card, but didn't send it; if they saw the postmark, they might come looking for her.

She almost decided to go home. But then she remembered the craziness, and knew she couldn't.

Beth bought a teddy bear for Eirian, chocolates and soaps for Mr and Mrs Primarola. And Emmy bought a bottle of sherry, to cheer Beth up.

Things could have been worse.

At the winter solstice, they lit fires and celebrated on a freezing cold hillside the death and rebirth of the sun. On Christmas Day, the whole clan were invited to the farmer's house for dinner. Turkey, paper hats, a roaring fire making the room a golden-bathed sauna; all the traditional silliness. The Primarolas came here every year, apparently. The farmer said it wouldn't be Christmas without them.

Beth was glad she had stayed, after all.

The rest of the winter was hard. Everything around them was bleak; the iron ground, the bald grey hills, the water frozen to black flint. There were bitter frosts and snows; blizzards shook the caravan as they sat huddled in front of a paraffin heater.

Eirian seemed to withstand it better than Beth. But Beth, determined not to behave like a pampered city girl, tried not to complain.

There was beauty, too. Golden-white mornings under ice-blue skies, scented coldly with snow. Beth helped the children build a six-foot snowman, which they christened Hamish, in the middle of the camp.

Hamish melted, the brooks thawed and dashed down the hillsides, and the Primarolas began to move south once more.

The day they left Scotland, Beth posted the Christmas card after all. She sent it to her grandparents, not her mother. 'By the time you get this, I will have moved, so there's no point in looking for me,' she wrote. 'The baby and I are all right. Please don't try to find us. We're not coming home. Love, Beth.'

It was curt, but she had nothing else to say. At least they would know she wasn't dead, if they cared.

They spent the spring on farms in Cumbria and Yorkshire, early summer in the Midlands. Beth felt very weird when they stayed on Broom Farm again; so near Rhianwen's old house, so near her grandparents. She hated it, and didn't stir from the camp all the time they were there.

Eirian now occupied a tenth-hand cot, crammed into Beth's tiny room. She was a vigorous and cheerful child, fascinated by everything around her; so like Morgan, Beth thought. If only he could see her – surely he couldn't reject her, or me?

Now a year old, Eirian was beginning to walk and utter simple words. To Beth's relief, the babbling in her sleep had almost stopped. There were still visions; nothing as vivid as the wedding procession or the Inquisitor's attack on Guendolen, only meaningless scenes of forests, cottages or churches. Nothing happened, yet these silent images were suffused by an atmosphere of menace that Beth found unutterably disturbing. They came and went, but never faded completely.

Beth learned to live with it, but she would look at Eirian and think, are you seeing these images too? What can it be doing to you?

When they returned to Wiltshire, Rhianwen turned up again.

'Morgan sends his best wishes,' Rhianwen said. There was no other message from him. How cold it sounded: nice knowing you, goodbye.

Rhianwen seemed to be hoping that Beth had got over Morgan by now; Beth tried hard to pretend she had, but seeing Rhianwen stirred up all her anguish again.

'How is he?' Beth asked, as they sat on camping chairs in the watery sunlight.

'Fine. Very busy. He's got a place to study zoology, if he gets the right grades.'

'Which university?'

Rhianwen's bright expression clouded. 'Beth, you know there's no point.'

'I was only curious,' said Beth, trying to sound unconcerned.

Rhianwen took a camera from her tapestry shoulder bag. 'Do you mind if I take some photos of Eirian?'

'Yes, I do mind!' Beth exclaimed, her pain suddenly breaking its bonds. 'Why should Morgan get to see pictures of his child, if he doesn't want to see her in the flesh? Do you want to show them around, being the proud grandmother? Isn't that a little bit sick?'

Rhianwen sat back, looking stunned. 'They're only for me, Beth. And for you; don't you want any photos of her as she grows up? I know you're still angry but you won't feel like this for ever.'

'Won't I? How do you know? If Morgan really doesn't want me, why can't he come and tell me to my face?'

'Look, Beth,' Rhianwen said slowly, 'I'll make a deal with you. When you're sixteen, I'll tell Morgan where you are. Then it's up to him whether he wants to see you or not.'

'I am sixteen,' Beth said acidly. 'My birthday was on the fourth of June. Three days before Eirian's.'

Rhianwen exhaled. 'All right, I'll tell him. But he'll be getting ready for university.'

'And he won't want an old girlfriend and a kid to cramp his style,' said Beth. 'You don't have to spell it out.'

'I'm sorry. I don't want you to get your hopes up for nothing.'

'Go on, take the photos,' Beth muttered, picking up Eirian from a rug on the grass. 'What does it matter?'

This was the rhythm of Beth's life; bitter winters in the north, lush green-golden summers and harvests in the south.

She worked hard, trying not to think of anything but Eirian's welfare. Living completely within the cycles of nature, Beth found serenity there; and when she could lose herself in a long, sweeping blankness of mind – untormented by thoughts of her family or her yearning for Morgan – she was content.

At other times, it was hard.

Mrs Primarola was teaching Beth continually, not only about farming but also about animals, plants and healing. Much of it, Beth realized, could have been seen as witchcraft. Yet there was nothing particularly arcane in the knowledge. It was the folk science, Mrs P said once, that the mediaeval church had made such strenuous efforts to destroy.

'But y'can't get rid of the Goddess that easy,' Mrs P said. When they celebrated the Sabbats – urging the fertility of the land – Mrs P was usually the priestess, her brother Arthur the priest. Rhianwen rarely took the role; she only turned up once a year, to check on Beth and Eirian. But Mrs P was training Beth, too, to officiate.

Rhianwen should have been teaching me this, Beth reflected sometimes. Occasionally, when she had these thoughts, a great wave of pain would take her over and she'd have to sit on her own until it passed.

After Rhianwen had promised to tell Morgan where she was, Beth spent sleepless nights thinking of him. Did she really tell him? How could she know precisely which farm we're on, all year round?

Maybe he has to wait until half-term. Or the Christmas holidays, but he wouldn't travel to Scotland. Next spring, then . . . Excuses.

Beth waited, but Morgan never came.

Then her hopes turned to despair, all over again. Why can't I get over it? she asked herself. I've tried so hard but I can't stop thinking about him, remembering . . .

'I'm sorry,' said Rhianwen, when she eventually appeared the following year. 'I did tell him, but I didn't think he'd come.'

'Didn't he say anything – when you told him?'

'Not a thing. He's always tended to clam up on me, but it's only what I expected. Dear, I know he's sorry he hurt you, but it's in the past and he wants to forget it.'

'Is he . . . seeing someone else?'

Rhianwen shrugged. 'He has a lot of friends; no one serious. Too much work for that.'

Beth felt a little better then. If it was only work keeping Morgan away, perhaps there was still hope he might change his mind, and think fondly of her again. To hear he had a girlfriend would have destroyed her.

Beth went on, veering between optimism and despair.

When melancholy overcame her, Eirian would come and

climb on her knee, anxious to comfort her. Eirian always seemed to know when her mother was unhappy.

Beth was infinitely grateful for the kindness of the Primarolas, who never pestered or criticized her. They offered unconditional friendship – all, that was, except Bernard.

No one will ever be able to make you feel dirty again, Rhianwen had told Beth, but Bernard, somehow, managed it.

He never forgave Beth for the time she'd rejected him. Often, when she was engaged in some task outside the caravan, she would turn to find him watching her. Just staring, with a faint sneer on his face.

If he caught her alone – never in front of witnesses – he would belittle her, speculating lewdly on how she'd become an unmarried mother. But Beth felt she couldn't complain; she was sure Mrs P would believe no evil of her own brother.

Beth had grown to dread the sight of Bernard. Although he hadn't tried to touch her again, the threat was always implied. He used it to intimidate her. She feared that it was only a matter of time before he lost control.

Beth tried to show she wasn't afraid of him, but inside she was. She couldn't help it. She had Eirian to protect, too.

In spite of Bernard, life was bearable. Each year was reassuringly the same as the last; and each year was different, because both Beth and Eirian were growing up.

Eirian walked and talked early, and was rarely difficult, even as a toddler. She learned to read eagerly, sitting on Beth's knee, and her play tended to be creative rather than loud and destructive. She was affectionate, enquiring, and astonishingly sensible. But there was no answer to the enigma of the visions. It was as if some mysterious adult stranger had been born in her daughter's body. Sometimes Beth thought simple naughtiness would have been easier to cope with.

Five years had passed since the Primarolas had found her. Beth had accepted long ago that Morgan would never come. She spun a pearl around the pain and learned to live with it.

So here, before Beth, was an alarmingly bright five year old. Eirian was tall, with dark-brown hair – half-way between

Beth's original colour and Morgan's – and leaf-green eyes like both her parents. She was, one day, going to be stunning.

Beth adored and feared Eirian.

It seemed an eternity since Beth had given birth to Morgan's daughter, and it seemed like no time at all.

Luke was learning the knack of turning everything to his own advantage.

Beth's disappearance had given him a position of influence he'd never known before. Olivia still had spells of agonizing about having failed to save her daughter's soul; Luke helped her through them. As time passed, both she and Philip had grown resigned to the idea that Beth was not coming back. Especially since Randolph and Heather had received the sad little card from Beth.

Philip blamed himself. 'We drove her away,' he would say. Luke suspected that he cried in private. It seemed rather pathetic, his father crying like that.

Olivia blamed the forces of evil at work in the world.

Luke blamed Beth. She was female, after all, full of Eve's depravity and lascivious, serpentine sin. She and Morgan were as bad as each other.

And yet, he was also grateful to her. As a child, despite his mother's efforts, he'd been more fascinated by football than by the Word of God. Beth's sins, however, had brought him wholeheartedly back to the fold by demonstrating the snares set by the Devil.

Then there was school.

Luke had never fitted in. The others mocked his neat way of dressing, his carefully brushed hair and his good manners. He had been bullied, although thankfully that had stopped by the time he started A levels. Then, inexplicably, the girls started on him instead.

They seemed to think he was good-looking, whatever that meant. Luke wasn't vain; he didn't see beauty in others, either.

Different females kept fabricating excuses to meet him in odd places; the stationery cupboard, or behind the Lower

Fourth building. And then they'd try to seduce him. Bemused and mortified, he'd push them off and escape.

Luke found the girls revolting: red-lipped, unwashed harlots. And yet, when he went home, he was always painfully excited.

The Old Testament forbade him to spill his seed on the ground. But as a sacrament – that was all right.

It was best with a live animal; sometimes he bought a rat from the pet shop, and pondered the sacrifice of Abraham's son as its slippery insides spilled over his fingers. Then he made tiny nicks with the scalpel along the shaft of his penis – Jesus, that hurt – and the fluids ran red and white together.

My body, my blood.

Luke always felt a light shining from him when he came. It was the Holy Spirit working through him.

One day, a plump brown-haired girl called Susan cornered him in the cloakroom. Luke had had enough. Instead of escaping, he held her shoulders and pushed her against the wall, startling her.

'Tell me what's going on,' he said.

'Haven't you guessed? You're very naïve, aren't you?'

'That's not a sin. Christ instructs us to be as little children. Tell me!'

Susan had stopped grinning. Her gaze seemed to be skewered on his.

'There's a bet on to see what you're really like. You know, if you're a virgin, or queer, or what. First one who gets you to shag them, wins.'

Luke was furious and revolted for a few moments, but then he understood. God was presenting these harlots to him for a reason! Not as temptation, which they weren't, but so that Luke could save their souls.

He smiled and said gently, 'Have you really thought about what you're doing to yourself, Susan? You're treating your body as a cesspit. You should have more respect for yourself. Your body is a temple of the Holy Spirit. You probably think you know the Bible, but you've never really understood it, have you? Listen to the words of Paul in I Corinthians: "Flee fornication. Every sin that man doeth is without the body; but he that committeth fornication sinneth against his own body. What? know ye not that your body is the temple of the Holy Ghost which is in you . . . therefore glorify God in your body, and in your spirit, which are God's." Now let's talk about that.'

Susan sat down with him and listened, as if entranced. Luke spoke so movingly that she started to cry. 'I never looked at it like that before,' she kept saying. 'I hate the way I am. I never thought I could be forgiven for it.'

'You can be forgiven, and find grace, and be born again.'

Susan was Luke's first convert.

Others followed. Some of the girls he spoke to would fall about laughing – only to disguise their shame, Luke thought – but many listened.

They found Luke different from all the other boys in school. He was deep. He had answers. He was courageous. He didn't mock them with lewd remarks; he *cared* about them.

These girls stopped trying to get away with wearing lipstick and earrings to school. They tied back their hair and flocked around Luke every break-time, to hear him read from the Bible and discuss its meaning.

Boys joined, too. The loners, the ones who were too shy or too clever for their own good.

His band numbered only fifteen out of a school of six hundred, but it was a start. They began to come to church with him, but they looked on Luke as their leader, rather than Pastor Blair.

At last Luke had discovered his vocation.

He'd considered becoming a doctor, like his grandfather; he fancied that power over life and death. But God was calling him very clearly now.

Pastor Blair's church had reached a state of stasis, Luke felt. It was going nowhere. A fresh, new, crusading church was needed to take the Gospel on to the streets; a church of truth, the one and only Truth.

'And you will all be with me,' he told his eager followers, the day they left school and set foot in the outside world, 'there at the beginning of this great work for God.'

'How can we set up a church with no money?' a young man asked prosaically.

'The Lord will provide,' said Luke. He knew how guiltily generous people became with their life savings when their salvation was at stake.

There came a hot August day in Kent, when Eirian was five and Beth twenty; Beth was pegging out washing between the caravans when she saw Rhianwen's car, the same ancient white Beetle, pulling up at the edge of the site. Beth's heart gave a leap, as it always did, when Rhianwen got out. Beth still loved her, despite everything. Still hoped, hopelessly, that for once she would bring Morgan with her. But he lived in a different world now, of course.

Rhianwen waved as she came towards Beth, wearing a long brown dress of Indian crushed cotton, a floppy velvet hat the same colour. Her hair, too, glowed red-brown like autumn, and she was smiling broadly.

After a hug and the usual pleasantries, Rhianwen said, 'I've got some news, Beth.' She tried to sound serious, but she could hardly stop smiling, so Beth knew it couldn't be bad news. 'I thought you ought to know. Morgan got married last week.'

A chasm opened up in the earth. Beth was falling into it.

'Beth?'

She gripped the handle of the caravan door to stop herself falling, but she fell anyway, wrenching her hand. The sound of children playing receded. Rhianwen caught her, helped her sit down on the step.

'Oh, Goddess, you've gone white. Oh, Beth, I'm sorry, I didn't think you'd . . .'

Beth couldn't breathe. Thought she never would again. Then a breath whooshed into her lungs but she went on staring at the sky. Blue nothingness.

'I didn't think it would come as such a shock,' Rhianwen said. 'Not after all this time. I thought you'd accepted . . .'

No. Never accepted. How quiet and ordinary this moment was, the death of all her dreams.

After a few moments, Beth spoke, her voice breaking only a little. 'Who did he marry?'

'A Canadian girl called Marian who was on the same course. They're both going into marine biology. They're doing a project on whale conservation together.'

Beth could picture them. Two bright, happy people on a ship with the wind in their faces; Beth nothing more than a far distant memory in Morgan's mind. Not even that. Not even a shadow.

'So he did,' she said, 'forget me.'

'Eventually,' said Rhianwen. She produced a photograph, to grind the salt in, as if, under the guise of being sympathetic, she needed to be cruel.

A happy couple on the lawn outside a register office. Confetti snowing down. The bride was a nice-looking woman with blonde hair; the groom, slender and elegant in a dark suit, Morgan. She'd never seen him in a suit before. It wasn't a very clear photo, but he didn't seem to look any different.

Beth put her fingertip just below his face and kept it there. Trying to reach him.

'So you're happy now,' said Beth. 'The danger's over.'

'I'll make us some tea.' Rhianwen patted her shoulder and went past her into the caravan. Beth sat there.

Through a veil of flapping sheets, Eirian came running up. She knew, as always, that something was wrong.

'Mum? Why are you sad?'

Beth pulled Eirian onto her lap and held her. Bast came out and wove around them, mewing. 'Just am.' That was all Beth could say. He's changed, she thought. Now I have to change too.

'What's the picture?'

'It's your dad. With another lady.'

'Oh.' Eirian seemed to accept this quite sanguinely.

Then there was a shadow in the corner of her eye. Beth looked round and Bernard was there, grinning.

'Boyfriend done the dirty on yer?' he said.

'I thought you were out on the combine,' Beth said coldly.

'Tea-break. Came back to get me fags. So, kept y'self for him for nothing. Don't want soiled goods now he's got a nice new wife, eh?'

Bernard's shoulders shook with mirth.

Beth, suddenly, was not afraid of him any more. She'd had enough. Her own eyes felt like gelid green lasers as she stared him down. Eirian stared, too. And Bernard stopped laughing.

Rhianwen came out on to the step behind her. Bernard stood there a moment, jigging from foot to foot with a mixture of arrogance and discomfort. Then he said, 'Nyah, fuck you,' and walked off.

'You don't like that man, do you, Mum?' Eirian said gravely.

They walked up to the fields to watch the harvest; Rhianwen, Beth and Eirian. It was something to do, because Beth couldn't speak and Rhianwen had run out of consoling remarks.

Beth didn't see quite how it happened.

The workers hadn't finished their tea-break; the combine harvester was at a standstill, with no one at the controls while they stood about, drinking tea and beer. Then Bernard went and climbed up on it, maybe to fetch something, maybe for somewhere to sit while he had a smoke.

The big machine came to life and began to move, its huge blades threshing at the wheat. And Bernard slipped.

There was a mist of blood, a scream.

Beth saw quite clearly that he was trapped between the blades, that one of his legs was severed at the thigh. Blood was pumping freely from the ragged stump, blackening the remains of his trousers.

The machine went on moving; the blades turned, Bernard slid down between them and vanished.

The screaming stopped.

Crimson blood soaked into the earth, like the blood of the sacrificed corn king.

Beth grabbed Eirian and turned her away, so she couldn't

see, probably too late. And Rhianwen hugged Beth, while the others went running towards the combine, shouting.

Everyone cried out with horror, except Eirian, who smiled.

Afterwards, Rhianwen took Beth into a stand of trees behind the site, so they could talk alone.

It had gone on for hours: the ambulance, the police, the fuss. Bernard had lost an arm and a leg and bled to death before anything could be done.

Beth and Rhianwen had comforted Mrs Primarola in the caravan, but Rhianwen, looking pallid, had kept glancing at Beth over Mrs P's head. Terrible looks of suspicion.

Beth felt numb. She was shocked by Bernard's death, but she couldn't feel sorry. Whichever way her thoughts turned, they ran into a wall of knives.

But now things had quietened down. Beth left Eirian with Granny P, and went into the trees with Rhianwen.

'I don't know how to say this,' said Rhianwen, 'but when you looked at Bernard, I felt something.'

'What?' Beth said stiffly.

'An emanation. Power of will.' Rhianwen looked pale and shaken; Beth had never seen her like this before.

'Are you saying I ill-wished him, or something?'

'Did you?' Rhianwen looked straight into her eyes, challenging.

'Yes,' Beth whispered. 'I wished the bastard would fuck off and die. He promptly did. I'd be scared to death if I didn't think it was an accident, a coincidence. You don't think it's my fault, do you?'

'I think,' said Rhianwen, 'that you have a power, Beth, and Eirian's got it too.'

'So you are blaming me?' Beth gasped.

'No, no. I'm only trying to say that those of us who have this power must learn to use it responsibly. Never to curse or ill-wish.'

'But where did I get it? From Morgan? I was never like this

185

until Morgan – until I got pregnant.' But that wasn't quite true; Beth had had dreams and visions, long before that.

'Your mother's ideas about demon possession must be very hard to shake off.' Rhianwen sighed. 'Everyone has some kind of talent; I think Morgan's is charisma and the ability to fall on his feet, like a cat. I have a different kind of power, like my mother and grandma did. I use mine for healing animals; I keep it quiet, because even these days we can get persecuted for being different. You and Eirian are telepathic, aren't you?'

'How did you know that?'

'The way you look at each other, things I've noticed, comments Mrs P has made. It's part of the power. And having visions and hallucinations; it doesn't mean you're mad, it means you're picking up on something that's trying to reach you. It isn't necessarily evil as your mother would understand it, but it could be dangerous. The power wasn't planted in you by Morgan; it's been inside you all the time. Maybe that's why you and I were drawn to each other. I saw it the first time I met you, though you didn't know it yourself.'

'And now you think I'm dangerous?' Beth was incredulous. She didn't care that Rhianwen was trying to be diplomatic; all she could think was, Rhianwen is calling me a murderer.

'I'm only saying, be aware of your power and use it responsibly. You cannot and must not ever use it to cause harm. Don't even think about it, because if something happened you'll never know whether it was your fault or not.'

'So you really do believe that I –'

'I'm sure you didn't mean actually to kill him. But you cursed him, all the same. Be careful.'

What Rhianwen said was true. Beth had wished Bernard ill and it had happened. She should have been horrified at herself, yet all she felt was hard, cold rage.

'I will be very careful,' Beth said frigidly, 'next time.'

And Rhianwen drew away from her, as if in fear.

'Maybe I was right to keep Morgan away from you.'

'Maybe you were.'

This rage was all Beth's misery at the news of Morgan's

marriage coming to a volcanic head, but she didn't know it. All she felt was bitter fury and the need to reject, as she had been rejected.

'I want you to leave me alone, Rhianwen,' Beth said viciously, beginning to walk away. 'Do you really think I live for you coming here and torturing me once a year? I don't need it! Sod off out of my life. I don't give a toss if I never see you or your precious son again!'

Chapter Twelve

'I WANT to leave,' Beth told Mrs Primarola, a month or so after Bernard's funeral. She had been trying to say it for weeks.

'Leave us, eh?' Mrs P said noncommittally.

'You've been so kind. I can never repay you.'

'Don't want repayment, dear; you've always worked hard. But you're one of us now; why d'you want to desert us after all this time?' Mrs P's round, tanned face, with its halo of yellow-white hair, showed more concern than surprise.

'I'm not one of you, though. Not really,' said Beth. 'I miss living in a real house. And it's time Eirian went to school. I want her to be settled, not in a different school every month.'

'Does our lot no harm.'

That was a matter of opinion, Beth thought, but she didn't say so. 'I know, but – it's not what I want for Eirian. I'm sorry if you think I'm being ungrateful, but I want an ordinary life.'

She couldn't add the real reason; I ill-wished your brother and I think that's why he died. If it's true, I can't stay with you. I'm afraid of what else I might do.

None of them had ever accused her, though, or treated her any differently. Only Rhianwen. And she, thankfully, had kept her suspicions between herself and Beth.

Mrs P let out a long breath between narrowed lips, and concentrated on the potatoes she was peeling.

'Well, you're an adult. Nothing your parents can do to you now. S'pose you could go back to them.'

Beth shuddered. 'I couldn't. I wouldn't even ask my grandparents. Not after all this time. It's not just pride; either they'll reject me, or they'll try to control me again. The thought of my mother getting her claws into Eirian . . . No, never!'

Mrs P took this in without comment. 'S'pose the council would house you, single mother and child. Might only be a bed-sit for a long while, though. That'd be worse than this caravan. At least y'got freedom with us, and work. What job d'you plan on doing out *there*?' She jerked her head disapprovingly at the everyday world.

Beth's heart sank. She was trapped. The thought of being alone in a bed-sit, with no job and nowhere for Eirian to play, was unutterably depressing.

For a moment she hated Morgan, with his university degree and his wife and his pick of well-paid, exciting jobs.

She said nothing, but Mrs P read her expression. 'That bad, is it, love? Well, mebbe we can arrange summat.'

'What?' Beth exclaimed.

'Don't get too excited. It might take a while. Ye'll have to be patient.'

I should have an honours degree, Beth thought, in being patient.

Katy met the man as she was struggling out of the supermarket, arms weighed down with plastic carrier bags. The precinct was crowded with Saturday shoppers. She had to stop dead to avoid colliding with a woman, and as she did so some stupid youth cannoned into her from the side. One of the carriers was jolted out of her grasp and fell, spilling cans and cartons on the paving slabs. A bag of brown rice broke open. Katy howled, 'Shit!' and threw down her other bags in a fit of temper. Then she burst into tears.

As she bent down to pick everything up, he was suddenly there helping her; a man in a dark suit, with brushed-back dark hair, polished black shoes and black gloves. No one else had offered to help; only him.

'No consideration for anyone, these people,' he said, shaking his head. 'Godless, all of them.'

'Thank you.' Katy sniffed resentfully, as he repacked the bag. She didn't want to be helped. She wanted to go on being angry with the world.

He stood up, lifting all four bags effortlessly. 'May I help you to your car with these?'

'I haven't got a car,' said Katy. 'I'm going to catch the bus.'

The man looked at her. He was quite handsome, with a very sincere, caring sort of face. 'You're obviously upset, sister. You shouldn't go home until you're feeling better. Let me buy you a coffee.'

There was a bakery with a café just across from the supermarket. Katy went with him; her outburst had left her feeling shaky, and she needed to sit down. He seemed nice enough, well-educated, polite, and considerate – but what an odd way to address someone, 'sister', as if she were a nun! Far from it.

They made an ill-matched pair; a suited businessman and a forlorn-looking young woman dressed in an assortment of punky clothes, with long ginger hair under a beret.

'I can see you're troubled, sister,' said the man, bringing a cappuccino and sitting opposite her. He had bought himself a glass of mineral water. 'No one cries over spilled shopping unless there is something else wrong. Would it help to talk to me?'

Katy took out a tissue and blew her nose. 'I don't know.' But now she had a captive audience, she was beginning to feel better.

'Your secrets are safe with me,' he said, with a kind smile.

'It's my husband,' said Katy. 'He's so fucking *lazy*. All he wants to do is play his guitar and have his stupid friends round, and I have to do *everything* myself. Clear up after them, do the shopping, look after the kid –'

'You have a child?'

'A little boy. He's four. He's lovely, but,' Katy felt her mouth twisting down at the corners, the tears coming again, 'I don't love him. I feel guilty.'

'I'm sure you do love him,' said the stranger, 'deep inside.'

'It must be very deep.'

He leaned forward, his voice very low. 'Have you ever beaten him?'

'No!' Katy said, shocked by the question. Then she added,

'I've been tempted. They don't tell you how difficult it all is, and my husband doesn't help, and I get so mad . . .' and then I go out and find some bloke to sleep with, to make me feel free again. Katy couldn't actually bring herself to admit this, however. She sighed, twisting the damp tissue. 'It's not fair. I've no freedom any more. The doctor says I'm depressed, but I'm not. It's just that everyone around me is so fucking *selfish*!'

'Sister,' said the man, 'your problem is not a medical one. It's spiritual. Your depression is caused by the forces of good and evil battling for your soul.'

'You what?' said Katy. The stranger didn't look mad, but . . .

'It's true,' he said matter-of-factly. 'Look around you, and you'll see the Devil at work everywhere. But there's good news. You can be rescued. You feel unloved, don't you?'

'Yes,' said Katy, amazed by his perceptiveness.

'You don't have to feel like that. When you come to realize that Jesus Christ loves you, you can love yourself again.'

Katy wasn't religious. If he'd said this to her as she passed him in the street, she would have ignored him. But he was looking into her eyes, and he'd been kind, and she felt that he really *cared* about her.

Suddenly remembering the language she'd used, she felt her freckled face turning beetroot red.

'I'm sorry, I didn't realize you were a – a priest.'

He smiled softly. 'We're all sinners, sister. But there is a way for you to be born again. Don't take my word for it; why don't you come along to one of our meetings, and find out for yourself?'

Katy took a breath to make excuses, but nothing came out.

He took a leaflet out of an inside pocket and presented it to her. *The Church of the One Truth*, it read, *Pastor Luke Herne*. 'Here's the address and times of the main meetings. Don't expect a cathedral; it looks like an ordinary house. No obligation. Just come along and see what we have to offer. What have doctors and so-called professionals ever done for you? They don't care about you. Isn't that true?'

'Yes,' Katy said fiercely.

'But Jesus cares. He has the answer to every single problem in your life.'

How tempting it sounded, to unload all her guilt, misery and frustration on to someone else.

'All right, I'll come.'

'You won't regret it,' he said, beaming as if she'd made him overwhelmingly happy. That gave her a pleasant sense of power, and he was really not bad-looking. Studying him more closely, she realized that he was actually younger than her, only nineteen or twenty. But his assured manner made him seem older. 'What's your name?' he asked.

'Katy.'

'I'm Luke,' he said. 'Bring along your husband and son, too. Everyone is welcome. It could solve all your family problems.'

Katy stared into the foamy dregs of her coffee. 'They won't want to come.'

'Well, perhaps they won't,' Luke said in a low, strangely intense tone. 'Perhaps the Lord is calling you to leave your own family and join a new one. If so, you have no need to feel guilty. Your responsibility is to God; your only sin would be to ignore his call.'

Shivers ran down Katy's spine. She was suddenly, deliciously excited.

As Luke lifted his glass to his lips, looking at her over the brim, Katy noticed that he hadn't taken off his black leather gloves, even to drink his mineral water.

The cottage was nearly derelict. The water had been cut off and there never had been electricity. The furniture was worm-eaten and black with dust. The stone sink in the kitchen was full of leaves and chaff that had blown in through a broken pane, and the other fittings were primitive: a wooden drainer, a mangle, a huge, black wood-burning stove.

There were two rooms downstairs, kitchen and living-room, and three up, gained by precariously steep stairs. The rooms were a good size – to Beth, used to the caravan, they seemed palatial – but that was the best you could say about them.

Moving from one gloomy, cobwebby room to another, Beth felt depressed.

There were strange cupboards in the walls that gave her the creeps.

Can I really see us living here? she thought. Could I bear it?

The bathroom was an afterthought, a rough extension on the kitchen. It had a stone floor, a bath on legs, and a badly stained toilet with an ancient cistern. But at least there was a bathroom, of sorts.

The walls and floors leaned at disconcerting angles. The plaster was falling off and the bare boards creaked. There was dry rot and wet rot. The curtains at the tiny windows were held together only by cobwebs, Beth thought.

Bast padded around independently, passing her detached judgement on every detail.

'S'worse than I remember,' said the farmer. He scratched his head, looking embarrassed. 'Dove Cottage? Spider Cottage, more like. Haven't even looked in for the past ten years. Still, if you want it, it's yours. Just standing here, otherwise.'

Beth didn't know what to say. She had been offered a home of her own, for nothing, and she would not have asked a rat to live in it – although rats undoubtedly did.

'I don't know,' said Beth. 'I don't want to sound ungrateful but I'm thinking of Eirian. I can't bring up a child in a house with no water and no heating.'

'Mmm. Yeah,' said the farmer. He was a big, solid man, with dark hair going thin on top. Straightforward, decent. 'Well, we can get the water put back on, and I can help you clean the place up a bit. Got some tins of whitewash somewhere. Looks worse than it is. I'm not sure about the electric, though. Cost a fortune to have it wired, and if I start trying to get grants, they'll either want the whole place done up or knocked down.'

'I like it,' Eirian said brightly, running into the kitchen from the living-room. 'We can live here, can't we, Mummy? It feels right, like we belong here.'

Beth thought it felt haunted, as if there were skeletons

bricked up in hidden crannies, but she trusted Eirian's instincts.

'All right,' she said.

'Grand,' said the farmer. 'Sorry it's not nicer for you, Beth. But we can make improvements. And the wife will be so grateful to have you around. She doesn't need nursing but she does need help, in and out of the bath and that, and it's damned near impossible to find a housekeeper who'll do that. Last one wanted a fortune for doing fu— er, sorry, for doing nowt. She walked out without notice, few weeks ago. We need someone reliable!'

He looked plaintively at Beth, as if he wanted the best for his wife, and Beth was his last hope.

'I am reliable,' said Beth. 'I may not look it, but I am.'

'You wear what you want, Beth. It'd be a bit silly having dress rules in a farmhouse. Sorry there isn't room for you to live in, but I can't kick my son and my brother out, so . . .'

'It's fine,' said Beth. 'The view . . .' There were fields in front, a wood behind; exactly what her soul needed. 'The view is beautiful.'

Mrs Primarola had told Beth to be patient with good reason. It had taken them months to find Beth somewhere to live. At every farm they visited, Mrs P had enquired if they knew anyone needing a live-in worker – housekeeper, farm-worker, maybe a nanny. There had been a couple of offers but the people had changed their minds; one when they found out Beth had a child, one when they saw Beth's blackly gothic appearance.

It was early summer when their itinerary brought them to Dove Hill Farm.

The farmer and his wife, Gordon and Margaret Cleave, were good friends of the Primarolas. Margaret was wheelchair-bound after a car accident a few years ago; Mrs P had guessed she might be in need of help.

The Cleaves had welcomed the offer with enthusiasm. Beth would do the housework and cooking and help Margaret get about; in return, she would have a rent-free cottage and her keep.

If Beth could live without claiming state benefits, she was happy. She wanted no help. And she was becoming almost obsessive in her need to live secretly; to make her disappearance complete and permanent.

There was no one she wanted to find her, except Morgan, and that was a lost cause. Not even worth dreaming any more.

So, why not take Dove Cottage, ghastly as it was? Beth needed a new start. And Margaret needed her.

There was one problem. Dove Hill Farm's neighbour was Broom Farm, which backed on to Rhianwen's garden and Lullingford. Beth's new home was only five miles from her grandparents' house. It made her feel weirdly uneasy to know that she would be living so close . . . but part of her wanted, desperately, to be reconciled.

Beth cried the day she said goodbye to the Primarolas. She hadn't realized how strong her feelings for them were, until they parted company.

They'd each bought her a present, something useful for the house. Emmy wept her heart out as she, Fred and the children hugged her goodbye. Even Mr and Mrs P and Granny P, never ones for physical affection, gave her brief embraces.

'Blessed be,' said Mrs Primarola.

Emmy added, through her tears, 'Merry meet, and merry part, and merry meet again.' The witches' greeting.

Beth and Eirian waved them off; a ponderous convoy of off-white caravans and big, battered old cars. First time she hadn't gone with them for nearly six years. And she couldn't swallow.

She was remembering the celebrations round the bonfires, the Yuletides in Scotland. If she wanted to celebrate the Sabbats now, she and Eirian would have to do it alone.

'Are you all right, Mum?' Eirian asked, slipping her hand into Beth's. She hadn't cried.

'Let's go inside,' said Beth.

The Primarolas had helped her make a start on the cottage. They'd cleared out the rubbish, swept and scrubbed, laid rat poison. Gordon had had the water reconnected, lent her Calor gas heaters and got the stove working. A small larder kept the food cold.

For light, Beth was making do with oil lamps and candles. She had learned, over the years, to make do with very little.

They hadn't painted yet. The rooms were still grey, though clean. Beth stood in the sitting-room, looking at the beams, the low doorways with their crooked doors, the small, deep-silled windows.

She felt suddenly, devastatingly alone, despite Eirian's presence and Bast sitting by the fireplace. There was everything to be done – but nothing to do.

Not even a sofa to sit on.

'I'll make some cushions, like Rhianwen had,' said Beth.

'What were they like?' Eirian wanted to know.

'Big,' said Beth, 'so you could sit on them.'

Eirian went round the room, making plans. 'We could have a chair here. And another one here. And proper lamps. And a blue rug, with Paddington Bear on.'

'Yes, if we had any money.' Beth couldn't help smiling. The cottage would be wonderful, she thought, if I had about thirty thousand pounds to spend on it. She shook off her dark mood, thinking, well, I've got what I want, so we're going to make the best of it. 'Do you want to read your books, while I make tea?'

'Read them all,' Eirian said imperiously.

'Well, you'll be going to school soon. You'll have all the books you want there.'

'How can I go to school, if we haven't got any money?'

'You don't have to pay for it, darling. You can't not go, or Mummy will be in trouble. So I hope you don't mind.'

Eirian shrugged. Exactly like Morgan. 'I don't mind,' she said sanguinely. Then: 'Is Rhianwen really my grandma?'

'Yes, love, she really is.'

'Then why was she always horrid to you?'

The question stopped Beth short. When had Eirian noticed that Rhianwen was capable of being anything but kind?

'Horrid, how?'

'She wouldn't let you see my dad. I wanted to see him too. It's not bloody fair!'

'Eirian,' Beth said faintly, 'please don't say bloody at school or I'll be in even more trouble.'

Eirian lay in bed, huddled against her mother's side. There was only one bed, so they had to share, until they could beg another one. They both slept uneasily; so strange, to be in this cavernous room with its grey walls and static shadows. But Eirian could still sense, as she often had in the caravan, the swaying dance of the trees, the movement of the air through the grass, the light of the horned moon gleaming like milk through webs of branches. She heard an owl hooting, a fox circling the cottage, the footfalls of badgers in the woods, Bast sharpening her claws. The cottage walls might have been made of air; she felt open to every whisper of the world, unable to shut it out even if she wished to.

This acute awareness meant she was about to travel.

Eirian felt herself slipping away. The bed and her mother's warm slim body dissolved and the whispering filled her head. She saw the huge eyes of foxes and owls and the tender snouts of moles, saw every hair or feather, dewed with moonlight. The wind fluttered insistently at her back. *Remember, remember. Never forget the darkness.*

The moon was below her, a crescent reflected in a dark lake, like the Horn of Power distorted.

Eirian didn't want to go into the water but she must. The Goddess needed her.

She was diving into the lightless waters. Sinking, with green weeds waving and silver bubbles rising all around her. Sleek shadows raced past. She tried to catch them but they slid through her fingers and were gone.

Unconsciously, Eirian knew what this meant, but she couldn't explain it, even to herself.

There was pain and blood in the water.

The fear rose to the centre of her mind. She felt herself shift from dream into reality, and she was on firm ground; running through the forest.

Guendolen was ahead of her, the wooden staff in her hand, long hair escaping like honey down her back. The grass caught at their long skirts. Eirian breathed the wet scents of foliage, fungus, wild plants; plants she knew, healing or poisonous, invigorating or narcotic. All around them the vast green cathedral soared, with choirs of birds singing in its roof of branches.

Guendolen seemed a little older each time Eirian saw her, but Eirian herself was always the same age. Eleven. That was why, in her other life, she couldn't understand why she was only six. She was impatient with being small, couldn't wait for her body and intellect to catch up with the way she felt inside.

Eirian never had a sense of arrival, when she found herself here, only of slipping into a different, continuing stream of existence.

Guendolen turned to catch hold of Eirian's hand. 'Good sister, help me. It's dangerous to take the Horn of Power into the village but the Midwife needs it.'

Eirian, despite the sunlight dappling her green cloak and the birds piping in the treetops, felt cold with fear.

'They are closing in on us now,' Guendolen said. 'They have forbidden all our gatherings, all our visits to holy wells and sacred stones, all wedding revelry, and all healing. They say it is God's will, that women should suffer in childbirth and men die in pain. They won't let us bless the land or urge the crops. They would take everything from us and claim it as their own.'

'Who are they?' Eirian asked, though she could see the rippling figures in her mind. Great black wings of authority, swooping down, suffocating.

'The churchmen. Inquisitor Lacost and Judge Warbeck would take the Midwife as a witch if they had proof.'

'Don't be frightened, sister,' said Eirian. 'They can't hurt you.'

But she remembered when the Inquisitor had found Guendolen on her own and brutally threatened her. And Eirian had only been able to watch, not to help.

It had all become mixed up in Eirian's mind with the other man, Bernard, who'd been nasty to Beth.

Eirian was learning to recognize these men. They all had the same cold, arrogant, grasping spirit inside them, but they all claimed to be in the right.

Eirian's awareness of being Beth's child had begun only when she was a year or so old, yet her memories of being in the forest with Guendolen went back much further. Eirian found nothing strange in this. She could travel, that was all. Couldn't everyone? She had never tried to discuss it with Beth, though. Eirian's annoyingly six-year-old brain wouldn't seem to form the words – and anyway, surely her mother knew everything?

It was intolerable, being a child, having no power.

When they reached the village, Eirian had no memory of having come here before, and yet she recognized everything.

There were low cottages with thatched roofs drooping almost to the ground, hovels of sticks and clay. At the far end, Eirian could see a church steeple; in the centre was a pond, about thirty feet across, set in what must be the village green, although it was actually a mass of churned-up mud. Goats wandered freely, tearing at what little filthy grass was left.

A breeze blew the stench straight into Eirian's face. Excrement, decay, and eye-watering ammonia.

The path that wound between the dwellings was litter-strewn mud. Green liquid manure sat in the deep ruts. Eirian and Guendolen lifted up their skirts as they picked their way towards a tiny cottage.

An anxious-looking young man, standing outside, nodded at Guendolen but said nothing. From inside came groans of pain.

As they ducked through the doorway, a smell of animals and mouldering meat enfolded them, pierced by the sharper scents of sweat and fresh blood. Eirian saw in the gloom a naked woman sitting on the edge of a pallet, clasping her hugely swollen belly, her face contorted. Her hands were calloused and there was a raw-looking rash on her arms. The pallet on which she sat was jumping with fleas, stained with watery blood. An older woman sat beside her, rubbing her back.

'Clary sage. Ergot,' the older one was saying. 'That'll ease it along. Should have called me earlier.'

'Didn't want to cause trouble,' gasped the woman. Eirian noticed four dirt-encrusted pigs rooting in a pen in the rear half of the room.

'You don't have to suffer in childbirth, whatever *they* say.' The Midwife looked round at Guendolen and Eirian. 'Did you fetch him?'

'Yes,' said Guendolen, lifting the staff. 'He's here.'

'Right.'

Eirian was pleased with herself for realizing that the Horn was somehow to help the woman in labour. But the Midwife stood up and said to the woman, 'We have to leave you for a while. Won't be long. If it makes you feel better to walk about, you do it, all right?'

The woman nodded stoically.

'You can go back in,' the Midwife said to the man at the door. She wiped her sleeve across her perpetually running nose. 'Nothing'll happen until I come back, don't worry.'

Eirian followed Guendolen and the Midwife across the green. Ducks paddled in the edge of the pond, but the water was thick with rubbish: animal excrement, bones, old vegetables. A pig snuffled in a pile of rotting turnips, which gave off the rankest stink Eirian had yet noticed. Repulsive, yet strangely she was familiar with all this and accepted it.

Guendolen and the Midwife looked around surreptitiously as they went; watching out for the Inquisitor, Eirian thought.

The Midwife reminded Eirian of Mrs Primarola, although she was bigger-built and paler, without Mrs P's wind-browned complexion. But her unruly pale hair and her brusque kindness – they were the same.

On the far side, they entered another hovel. It was black inside, the air as thick as treacle with the smell of illness. Eirian made out a figure lying on a thin mat, with a log for a pillow.

In the other cottage, the woman's pain had been red and vigorous with life. But the pain here was a silent, stretched, unrelenting agony.

An old woman like a great black bolster sat hunched on a stool, watching over the man. She had a long nose that almost touched her chin, and tiny eyes, one of them welded shut by pus. As the Midwife came in, this crone pulled back the grimy square of material that covered the sick man. A foul, sickening stench wafted out. Eirian saw that his left leg was black and swollen, the skin split and oozing blood and plasma.

Guendolen nodded towards the doorway. 'Keep a look-out,' she said to Eirian. 'Tell us if anyone comes.' So Eirian stood in the doorway, glancing out, glancing in, missing nothing.

What they were doing was forbidden.

The man on the mat smiled weakly at the Midwife, but his face – Eirian could see, now her eyes had adjusted – was discoloured and drawn back against the skull. He might have been thirty, fifty, ninety.

'Still bad?' the Midwife asked gently.

'Very bad now,' he croaked. His eyes were lifeless, hopeless. 'Had enough.'

'I know. But we've got him here. Don't you worry. Guen?'

Guendolen pulled off the top of the staff and drew out the Horn. A streak of purity in the squalor. The Horn shimmered in the darkness like sea shells under the sea, leaving multiple images across Eirian's dazzled eyes.

The Horn of Healing. Wand of Rebirth.

The man's face turned to mother-of-pearl in its glow. The Midwife placed the long horn along his body with the tip pressing into his forehead, and folded his thin, weak hands around its shaft.

The sick man sighed and closed his eyes, bisected by white light.

Eirian waited eagerly for the miracle.

The dark tension in the room faded and was gone.

'His pain's over now,' the Midwife said gruffly. Gently she lifted the Horn out of his hands. The man, still smiling, didn't stir.

The hunched woman – the dead man's mother or wife? – who had been sitting motionless, suddenly came to life. She stood up, knocking over the stool, and glared at the Midwife. 'A healer, you said you were!' she uttered in a cracked voice. Then she hobbled out of the cottage, brushing past Eirian. The Midwife only shook her head.

Eirian realized the man was dead. Stricken, she moved into the room, whispering, 'But – but I thought –'

Guendolen stopped her with gentle hands. 'Sometimes the Wand can only take away the pain in this way. It's the Wand of Transformation. He suffered long and bitterly, with us forbidden to help him; but his sickness couldn't be healed. He desired and deserved an easeful death, did he not, good sister?'

Eirian understood. The healer was always a Midwife, in whatever she did, because she eased the passage of flesh and spirit from one state to the next. Like the Goddess, Eirian thought. Everything she touches, changes.

'Put him away,' said the Midwife. 'We have to go.'

Guendolen was sliding the Horn into the hollow staff, ready to take it back to its hiding place. It had shone like the moon, but it was dull ivory now, its work done; its transformative power spent.

'Like the Horned God,' Guendolen murmured. 'He rises, and spills his power, and falls back. Lives, and dies to bring us life, then lives again.'

The hairs stood up on Eirian's neck.

'I'll be getting back across the way,' said the Midwife. Eirian remembered the woman in labour. 'You be all right, Guen?'

'Yes. I have my good sister for company.' Guendolen smiled at Eirian. 'Want to help me hide him again?'

Eirian looked out at the green. The ducks were quacking and shaking their tails, a man was pushing a handcart full of turnips, jolting across the mud and filth. Otherwise, it was quiet.

'It's all clear,' she said.

Then the doorway went black. They must have come from the sides, the four men in cassocks with their hard, well-fed faces. They were a thorned hedge, garlanded with silver crosses.

A female voice croaked behind them, 'She killed him!'

And the long-nosed woman was there, pointing a shaking finger at the Midwife. 'She killed him! Witchcraft!'

'Take the women,' said the leader. He was the one who had lusted after Guendolen, Inquisitor Lacost. His face was a bloated, cratered moon, his eyes splinters of metal. 'And that – object.'

He pointed. One of his accomplices slid into the room, scooped up the Horn in its sheath, and seized the Midwife with one hand.

Eirian thought the Midwife would curse and fight; instead she seemed to collapse inside, all her power and assurance crumbling in a wave of terror.

'Don't. We've done nothing. We're innocent. Have pity on us poor women, Father.'

As she was pleading, another of the men seized Guendolen. Eirian turned and kicked him hard in the side of the knee. The man buckled, grunting in agony; and Guen burst from his hands and was out of the door, holding up her skirts so she could run, splashing through the mire.

Eirian sprang after her, but someone grabbed her. She bit the knobbled, warty hand; the man yelped, but wouldn't let her go.

He smelled of stale sweat and churches, and he was as hard and terrible as death. His breath was a plague.

One of the others started after Guen, but Eirian could see he was too fat to run far.

'Run, sister!' she cried.

'That,' said the Inquisitor, pointing at Eirian, 'is the girl's familiar. Don't mistake her innocent demeanour. That, in the shape of a child, is a demon.'

Lacost took the Horn out of his accomplice's hand, and grinned with plump satisfaction.

'Got it,' he said triumphantly. 'Take them.'

The men began to drag Eirian and the Midwife out of the hovel. Eirian stared at the Midwife's stricken face, and the precious Horn gripped in the Inquisitor's profane hand, and her heart almost burst with terror, rage and frustration.

Eirian began to scream. 'No! No!'

She came awake, screaming, shaking, sweating, in her mother's arms. The men were tall shadows all around them. And Beth, too, was crying out, 'No! Eirian, no!' and staring into the darkness with white, terrified eyes.

Chapter Thirteen

'No. Must go back there,' Eirian cried fiercely. Her eyes, unblinking, stared straight through Beth. 'We can't leave them! I must go back!'

Eirian struck out with clenched fists as Beth desperately tried to hold her. Beth couldn't drag herself out of the nightmare; this raging demon in bed with her was part of it. Shadows loomed round them, like the terrors her mother had planted long ago in her mind: *Morgan's put the Devil into you, the child will be evil.*

'Eirian, stop it!' Beth said, holding her off. 'Let me light the lamp!'

With Eirian clawing at her back, Beth struggled with matches, breaking three before one caught. Then the yellow light rushed up, and the shadows ran back into the walls and vanished.

Beth turned to see her daughter's face still wild with fear, her eyes white-ringed, as if she'd gone out of her mind. The tiny fists went on pummelling her.

'Stop it!' said Beth, overwhelmed by fear.

'No!' Eirian wailed.

Then Beth became aware of a warm wetness soaking into her pyjama leg and the sheet underneath. Eirian had wet the bed.

Fear flashed into rage. 'Oh, you stupid girl! For God's sake! Eirian, get out of bed. Get out!'

Beth pushed the covers back, climbed out and lifted her daughter bodily to the floor.

'Look what you've done! It'll take ages to dry that mattress out! What are we going to sleep on?'

Eirian backed up against the wall, her hair covering her face, and started to cry.

Beth's temper dissolved into devastating remorse. Eirian's pitiful sobbing broke her heart. She thought, she's only a little girl and I – I sound like my mother!

Beth rushed to her and hugged her, feeling Eirian's heart pattering arhythmically against her own.

'Sshh,' Beth soothed. 'I'm sorry. It's not your fault. It's all right. It was a nightmare.'

'Wasn't a nightmare,' Eirian said, her voice muffled in Beth's pyjama jacket. 'It was real.'

'Come on, let's find you some clean pyjamas and go down-stairs,' said Beth, combing Eirian's hair with her fingers. 'You can help me down with the mattress, and we'll put it to dry by the stove. Then I'll make some hot chocolate. A midnight feast, what about that?'

Eirian began to look more cheerful. She bounces back so easily, Beth thought; Goddess grant that she stay so resilient!

Beth felt stone-cold inside. This was the first time Eirian had ever been upset by the visions. Was it because she understood more as she grew older, or because the visions were becoming worse?

The kitchen was cosy in the lamplight. Sitting on rickety chairs with their elbows on a table topped with red Formica, they drank chocolate out of Eirian's favourite mugs, which were decorated with cartoon characters. In some ways, at least, she was a normal child.

'Tell me what happened.'

'They were going to take us away,' said Eirian. 'The ugly men.'

Beth knew what Eirian was going to say. She had seen it all, as if she were dreaming or watching a film – whereas Eirian, it seemed, had lived it.

'Did they take the Horn too, hidden inside a wooden staff?'

Eirian nodded miserably. 'It's sacred. They had no right. They took the Midwife away. A man got me but I bit him!'

'Guendolen escaped. You helped her, didn't you?' Eirian

206

looked up with sombre, deep-green eyes. 'I saw what happened, love. I know it wasn't a nightmare. I believe you.'

Eirian frowned, as if she'd never considered that anyone might not believe her. 'If you were there, Mum, why couldn't I see you?'

'I don't know, love. I've always followed you into your visions, even when you were a tiny baby. It was happening then, do you remember?'

'Of course I remember. Not being a baby, I mean, but going to the other place. I've always gone there.'

This was the first time they had ever talked about it, Beth realized in amazement. Something so profound, yet they'd never discussed it! Perhaps Eirian, until now, had been too young; or else, because of the subtle telepathy between them, they'd each assumed there was no need to mention it.

Or perhaps it was simply too disturbing to face.

'Can you visit the other place whenever you want?' Beth asked.

'No. It just happens. I can't make it.'

'Can you remember the first time you went there?'

Eirian shook her head. 'I think I can remember meeting Guendolen, but even then I felt I'd always been there, and like I'd seen her before. I'm always eleven in the other place, but Guendolen has got older. The Midwife was always old.'

Actually, she was fifty at most, Beth thought; ancient for those days. Those days? When?

'It used to be happy there,' Eirian went on, gazing at the rim of her mug, 'until the men came from the church. Now everyone's frightened. We must go back, Mum. We can't leave the Midwife with the horrible men! And what if they catch Guendolen?'

'They're things that happened in the past,' Beth said, thinking, does she know about the persecution of witches? Should I tell her, or will it put ideas into her head? She's too young to cope with this. Goddess, what else is she going to see? But how can I stop it? Beth went on, 'You might not be able to change what happens.'

'No!' Eirian said fiercely. 'It's happening *now*, and the other place is just as real as here!'

Beth put her hand over Eirian's, trying to calm her down. 'When you're there, you are really there, aren't you?'

'Of course I am, Mum. Aren't you?'

'No. I told you, I can see, that's all.' But even that wasn't completely true; she remembered with revulsion the time she had been in Guendolen's body, and the Inquisitor had nearly raped her. 'Eirian, what's happening to you doesn't happen to other people.'

'They can't . . . travel?'

'No. They can't travel.'

Eirian's face crumpled again. She had just been informed – and appeared to have understood the concept vividly – that she was different. A freak. Alone.

Beth hadn't meant to do that to her. 'It's a special gift,' she went on, trying to mend things, 'but I can't explain why it's happening. Can you?'

The small face cleared and became thoughtful. Eirian looked, in that moment, ageless. 'Because . . . the people in the other place need my help. They aren't allowed to believe what they believe, or do what they want. The ugly men from the church won't let them. Those men are evil, Mum. They tell lies. They talk about love but they practise hate. They are so full of hate for life that they have to torture it and cut it and burn it, and they will never stop because their hatred is insatiable.'

This creature that had come out of Beth's body was not a child. She clutched a cartoon mug and her small feet dangled over the edge of the chair, but her eyes were a thousand years old.

Beth's breath hung in her throat. 'I don't think you should go there any more.'

'I can't help it. I belong there.'

'But what can you do?'

'Stop them,' Eirian said emphatically.

Beth held her daughter's hand across the table. Her throat

solid, she thought, What's going to happen, my love, if they accuse you of being a witch? You came back to me this time – but what if, next time, you can't?

'She's a lovely little girl, isn't she?' said Margaret. 'Nice and quiet.'

Beth had pushed Margaret in her wheelchair out to the yard behind the farmhouse kitchen. Eirian was playing in the back garden, which was divided from the yard by a drystone wall and a gate. The sun gleamed on grass and trees and on the corrugated roofs of barns.

'Too quiet, sometimes,' said Beth. 'I don't think you'll find her any trouble; she isn't destructive or noisy, and she can always amuse herself.'

'That's good. I don't have much tolerance for children these days; this damned thing seems to have made me so irritable.' Margaret meant the accident, which had left her paralysed from the waist down and her left arm almost useless. She had a fleshy, intimidating face and stiffly curled brown hair, but beneath the stern mask she was, Beth sensed, good-natured. A once-active woman who hated being unable to cope. 'I do hope you won't take it to heart if I snap your head off.'

'I'll snap back,' said Beth.

Margaret laughed, and patted Beth's arm with her good hand. 'I really am very glad to have you around. Come on, I'll show you how to feed the hens and collect the eggs.'

'Eirian!' Beth called. 'Come and see the hens!'

'A bit pale, isn't she?' Margaret commented as Eirian came running. 'So are you.'

'We haven't been sleeping very well. Strange surroundings, I suppose.'

'You'll sleep all right once we set you to work, don't worry,' Margaret said ominously. 'And we'll feed you up. You need some flesh on you to work; mind you, I've gone too much the other way, this ruddy sitting about. Used to be slim like you, can you believe it?'

The hens ranged freely between a barn and a run at the side

of the yard. Beth opened the gate, eased the wheelchair through, and asked Eirian to close it after them.

The brown backs of the birds flowed around them like fleece, their clucking mingling to one ever-rising note. Eirian was captivated, and thrilled when Margaret showed her how to reach into the nests to find the warm eggs.

To Beth's relief, Eirian seemed unaffected by the horror of the previous night. Slightly tired, that was all. And to Beth, the vision retreated to the dimension of a dream. Haunting, but bearable.

We've got too much to do, she thought, to live in nightmares.

'I'm afraid I'll be asking a lot of you, Beth,' Margaret said brusquely. 'Hope you won't mind. All the cooking, most of the housework – I can do a bit of dusting, but that's all – and looking after the hens. And I need a bit of help, you know, in the bathroom.' Margaret looked embarrassed. 'My husband will help me when he's finished work of an evening, but during the day . . .'

'That's all right,' said Beth. She didn't mind what she was asked to do, as long as she and Eirian had somewhere to live. 'Don't the men help in the house at all?'

'Don't see why they should,' said Margaret, to Beth's surprise. 'You can call us old-fashioned, but when they've worked themselves to death on the farm all day, you can't expect them to come in and run round with a vacuum cleaner.'

'No. I suppose not.'

'By the way,' Margaret added in a low voice, 'you needn't worry about the men taking liberties with you. Gordon's brother Frank has never looked at a woman, and it looks like my son John's going the same way. They work hard and they're harmless; terrified of women, that's all.'

Beth was glad. The last thing she wanted was another Bernard.

As she pushed Margaret back towards the house, Eirian said, 'I'm going to school tomorrow.'

'Are you, now? Looking forward to it?' Margaret asked.

Eirian nodded, and ran off to stroke the sheep dog that was tethered at the top of the yard.

'It's a shame.' Margaret sighed.

'What is?' said Beth.

'You and your daughter, having to cope on your own. Oh, I don't mean to sound nosey. Take no notice of me.'

'It's all right,' said Beth. 'I don't mind you asking. I loved Eirian's father but we were very young. Our parents kept us apart and then . . . well, I suppose we grew up.'

'You're very cheerful,' said Margaret, 'but not very happy, underneath, are you?'

'I'm all right,' said Beth, 'as long as Eirian is.'

'It might help you to come to church with us of a Sunday.'

Beth's heart tumbled into a void inside her. She smiled faintly. 'I don't think so. I'm not a Christian. I hope that isn't a problem.'

'No one's business but their own, what they believe. Vicar says it's a test of my faith, this damned thing. It definitely helps me to believe in God; gives you someone to get angry with! I like to sit there behind the pews in my wheelchair, with three useless limbs, and say, well, here I am, Lord; happy now?'

Beth found looking after Margaret and the house exhausting work. She was expected to go to the farmhouse – a ten-minute walk along an overgrown lane – to make breakfast for the men at six-thirty every morning. Then she would take Eirian to school; another long walk to the bus stop on the main road, and a short ride to the primary school in the nearest village, Barton-in-the-Elms. Then Beth would return to Dove Hill Farm, help Margaret to bathe and dress, do the housework and make the lunch. In the afternoon, she would take Margaret out in her wheelchair and help her with the tasks she'd performed alone before her accident; feeding the hens and dogs, cultivating the vegetable garden. Margaret couldn't bear to feel useless. If the weather was fine, they would go for a stroll. If not, there was usually administrative work to be done.

Margaret, as she'd warned, had bouts of depression and bad temper, but Beth wasn't afraid of her. She developed the knack of easing Margaret out of it.

In the afternoon, Beth would collect Eirian from school, return to the farmhouse and make tea. Having eaten with the family, Eirian would watch television while Beth washed up.

Eirian liked programmes with animals or puppets, but to Beth's satisfaction, she wasn't that interested and never once complained that they couldn't have a television in the cottage. She preferred reading, painting and playing board games.

Finally, when Gordon had finished work, Beth was free to go home.

For the first few weeks, her evenings in the cottage were taken up by whitewashing, painting and cleaning. Gordon and his monosyllabic, grown-up son, John, helped her. She never felt nervous with them. She wasn't remotely attracted to John, nor he to her, yet the fact that she'd even thought of it made her realize that she had barely glanced at a man for seven years.

Gordon was not another Bernard, and neither was Frank nor John.

Beth didn't seriously believe she had killed Bernard by cursing him. If she had let herself believe it, she would have gone mad. It had been a horrible coincidence, and yet . . .

This power, if she possessed it, must be treated with respect.

Gradually Dove Cottage became, if not luxurious, bearable. Pieces of furniture turned up, donated by friends of the Cleaves; everyone seemed to know someone who was throwing something out. Beds arrived for Eirian and the tiny third bedroom, a sofa bed for the living-room, a couple of threadbare armchairs, an assortment of chipped crockery.

The plumbing made noises, the water ran brown for days, the chimney smoked even after a vigorous sweeping. The big wood-burning stove was messy, but at least it gave them heat and hot water. Having open fires in the living-room and bedrooms made a lot of work, too, but Beth loved their friendly glow and constant soft crackling.

After the vision of the Horn being stolen, Beth and Eirian had no more visions for a long time. Eirian never mentioned it, and didn't seem concerned; Beth guessed she would accept the next one with the same fatalism, if and when it came.

It was Beth who lay awake at night, dreading the continuance of the nightmare, until sheer exhaustion pulled her down into sleep.

As the days went by, however, her fear faded. If it happens, she thought, it happens.

Two stray female cats came to Beth, like iron filings called into a magnetic field. One was white, one creamy ginger. She called them Cerridwen and Eostre. Bast was disdainful at first, but accepted them as her courtiers.

Eirian was right, Beth thought one day. We do belong here. A cottage in the edge of the woods, like Rhianwen, like all the ones who were feared and accused.

If only my mother could see me now.

The glove was expensive and beautifully made. Hard-wearing brown suede; perfect. Luke hoped that this purchase would last him a good deal longer than usual. They wore out so quickly, the cheaper ones.

He had been on his way to buy it when he'd met Katy; that was a fruitful diversion. The Lord seemed to be dropping converts into his lap. The house wasn't big enough any more. The Church of the One Truth needed new premises; a second branch, a hundred branches from the first mighty trunk . . .

Locked in his tiny, austere bedroom in the church house, Luke inspected the glove. He had spent a long time choosing it in the department store; so long, fingering through sheaths of leather, plastic and suede that the assistants had begun to mutter to each other. Luke had ignored them. Foolish whores.

The left glove he chose had become detached from its partner; the assistant looked at him strangely when he put a single glove on the counter.

'Don't you want the pair, sir?'

'What? Oh, yes, of course,' he had said, fishing for the other one.

'Buy one, get one free,' she giggled. Luke smiled indulgently. He would have tried to save her soul, if he hadn't been so eager to get home.

In the privacy of his room, Luke dropped the right glove into his waste-paper basket. His right hand was to be kept unsheathed and pure, for blessing his flock. The right hand belonged to God.

His left, though . . . that was the hand through which the Devil could work, if Luke was not very careful.

The doctrine he'd learned from his mother and Pastor Blair had sunk very deep. '*Never touch yourself. It's unclean.*' That was why he had taken to wearing gloves when he went out, so that he should not touch anyone else either, or risk being contaminated by a Satanic world.

I should have learned this lesson years ago, he thought.

Luke had had a scare the previous year. The scalpel nicks he inflicted on his genitals had resulted in a major infection; he had prayed for recovery, and the Lord had directed him to an extremely discreet private consultant in London. Several weeks on antibiotics had left him cured, but shaken.

'Go a bit easier on yourself, old chap, eh?' the doctor had murmured confidentially. 'There are ways to obtain the necessary degree of pain without inflicting flesh wounds. There's this absolutely marvellous young woman I know, Members of Parliament swear by her; if you want the number . . .'

Revolted, Luke had declined.

Experimentation and prayer had brought him to a better solution.

First the glove must be made ready. He took a tin of drawing pins from his bedside drawer and began to slip them, one at a time, inside the glove. He worked meticulously, lovingly. A row of pins along each finger and the thumb, a cluster in the palm; the heads inside, the spikes sticking out through the tough suede. Not sharp enough to cut, unless he was careless; but sharp enough.

Luke eased his hand inside the spiked gauntlet. He felt the smooth metal heads sliding over his palm; relished the faint clicking and crunching as he flexed his hand.

He was already breathing fast through his teeth as he drew out his engorged member. The anticipation was divine. Then he positioned his armoured hand and closed it hard around the shaft. A grunt of pain exploded from him. Scores of pins dug into the tender skin, raking it as he began to move his hand. Agony. But it was the agony that made the act holy, made Luke aware of God's love pouring down on him and through him.

He didn't use animals any more. Animals were connected too much to his powerless childhood. Luke whispered the words of Paul. '"When I became a man, I put aside childish things."' Yet he missed their participation, their sacrifice.

But he had power now, and his congregation were human.

He pictured them as the fire and the wine and the Holy Spirit came bursting out of him.

The headmistress didn't like Beth.

When they first met, she scanned Beth's clothing with disdain, and expressed extreme disapproval that Eirian was starting school at six, rather than five.

Beth explained that because they'd lived with travellers, she had tried to educate Eirian herself.

The headmistress, Miss Townsend, sucked in her cheeks as if she'd swallowed vinegar. She was a relentlessly frumpy woman of about forty-five, with a flat voice, flat hair, and no sense of humour. She reminded Beth of an authoritarian social worker who'd come to see her when she was pregnant. 'I'll have to put her with the five year olds for the remainder of this term and probably the whole of next year. She will find it very difficult to catch up, *Mizz* Primarola.'

Eirian didn't like school, and said so. 'The other children are noisy and rough. And stupid, most of them.'

'Has anyone been nasty to you?' Beth asked. They were on the bus, on their way home.

'Some boys tried,' Eirian said disdainfully. 'I looked at them and they went away. How long do I have to go for?'

'To this school until you're eleven, then another one until you're eighteen. Sixteen if you like, but eighteen's better.' And I didn't even make fifteen, she thought.

Eirian looked horrified. 'Do I *have* to go?'

'I'm afraid so. You don't want to grow up knowing nothing, do you?'

'But I already know the important things,' Eirian said, half to herself.

When Beth waited for Eirian at the school gates, the other parents looked askance at her soot-black hair, now down to her waist, her long black skirts and ancient jacket. She wore solid boots – necessary for tramping the muddy lanes – and looked witch-like, poverty-stricken and intimidating.

Her style – which Beth had arrived at by instinct – might be common among students, but it was not approved of in the village. She felt the others either despised or feared her – if not both.

She smiled and was friendly; a few mothers realized she was not as alarming as she looked, and chatted to her, but Beth felt she had less in common with them than she'd had with the Primarolas. They talked about kids and husbands and soap operas and how they'd love a holiday, if only they could afford one, and why didn't Beth come to the aerobics class in the village hall? They never talked about the Goddess or even God, or collecting herbs under the full moon, or ecstatic sexual rites, or whether or not Eirian was possessed by the Devil.

In other words, Beth thought ironically, I'm even weirder than I actually realized I was.

Eirian survived school, as she seemed to survive everything.

When the new term began in the autumn, Beth began to notice a lone father waiting for his son every afternoon. He, like Beth, was an outsider. He had long, uncombed blonde hair that had tangled thickly into rats' tails, baggy jeans with zips, a brightly coloured patchwork coat. He and Beth would glance at each other and smile, recognizing a fellow eccentric. After a few days, they drifted together and began to chat.

'You've got a little girl, haven't you?' he asked, with a slight Black Country accent. He seemed shy and rather unsure of himself, and compensated by smiling too much.

'More like a creature from outer space,' said Beth.

'Bit of a handful?'

'Eirian's all right. Very opinionated, that's all.'

'I've got a boy called Sam. Oh, I'm Steve, by the way. Steve Pointon.' He took his hand out of a deep, patchwork pocket and, rather to Beth's surprise, shook her hand.

'How old? Sam, not you.'

They laughed. Steve was, she guessed, about twenty-five. Not bad-looking. Smooth fair skin, grey eyes, a nice smile – Beth stopped herself. Sam had a mother, naturally.

'He's five. Just started.'

'Eirian's six, but they've put her with the five year olds. She hates it. People must think she's backward, but she isn't.'

It became a routine, chatting every afternoon while they waited for the children to come out. Both Beth and Steve began to arrive unnecessarily early, so they could talk. And then they'd each take their child by the hand, and go their separate ways.

Barton-in-the-Elms was a bigger, less picturesque village than Lullingford, with a big council estate. Steve, although he'd trained at art college, worked as a gardener in a nursery on the edge of the village, and lived in a small, rented house in the main street. He talked about his work, but never mentioned a wife or girlfriend.

Beth didn't care either way. She didn't want a lover. She simply liked him.

One evening, when Eirian had been at school about six weeks, a teacher came hurrying out to Beth and said could she please come and have a word with the headmistress.

'I'll hang on for you,' said Steve.

'You don't have to.'

'No, I don't mind. You can leave Eirian with me while you go in.'

Beth trusted him. More importantly, so did Eirian.

Steve was waiting at the gate when Beth came out of Miss Townsend's office, so angry she could hardly speak. Sam and Eirian were playing on the grass verge a few yards away.

'Erhm, problems?' Steve asked nervously.

'Bloody woman!' Beth spat. 'Townsend says Eirian has a reading age of nine and is bright enough to move up a class.'

'What's wrong with that?'

'She says I've been pushing her too hard! Insinuating I shouldn't have taught her to read, because that's the school's job! Bollocks. Says she's too forward even for her proper age group, and gifted children have more problems than slow learners, and it's all my fault, and so on. Patronizing bloody cow!'

'Hey, calm down,' Steve said. 'I wish Sam was over-intelligent. Or even intelligent.'

'I don't know what to do with her!' Beth cried. She felt caught up in a rush of sheer, black panic at the strangeness of Eirian's whole existence.

Then Steve said, 'Who, Eirian or the patronizing cow?'

Beth laughed. 'If you know of some wet concrete, I know what to do with the cow.' The panic subsided. 'I wish this wasn't the only school.'

A pause. 'Do you, erhm, want to come for a drink?' he asked.

'How can we, with the kids in tow?'

'Not at the pub. They don't open 'til six, anyway. I meant at my house. I've only got lager or coffee, but . . .'

'What about Sam's mother?'

Steve looked at his feet. 'She . . . we don't live together.'

'Oh,' said Beth, not knowing whether to be sympathetic or relieved. 'I'm sorry. I can't. I have to go back and cook tea for the farmers.'

'Oh. Never mind.' Steve looked awkward, disappointed.

'But,' Beth said impulsively, 'you could come to mine, if

you've got transport. It's a bit out of the way. I finish about seven.'

Steve looked thrilled.

He arrived, about seven-thirty, with two bottles of wine and Sam, who was clutching a huge box of Lego.

Eirian jumped up and ran to meet Sam. She had taken to the sandy-haired, bespectacled little boy, and he seemed equally smitten.

'Couldn't get a baby-sitter,' Steve said apologetically. 'Sam won't be any trouble. He'll play for a bit, then go to sleep. I doubt if he'll even wake up when I put him back in the car.'

'It's all right,' said Beth. 'We'll put him in my bed when he gets tired. I have a hell of a job, getting Eirian into bed before nine, but she's never tired in the morning, so . . .' Beth looked out of the front window to see a dark blue Metro parked on the grass outside. 'Did you get your car up the lane okay? It's only fit for tractors, really.'

'I think I may have buggered the exhaust,' Steve said gravely. 'Never mind, it was only held together with sticking plaster anyway.'

The children played on the rug in front of the fire for an hour, building a Lego village, while Steve and Beth talked about nothing in particular. Then Beth ordered them to bed. She sensed that Steve wanted to be alone, as she did, so they could really talk.

Beth felt pleasantly drunk on the wine. The groups of candles she'd set on the mantelpiece and table – actually a crate with a rug draped over it – gave the room a mystical glow. For the first time, it felt like home. Her domain.

'It's great, the way you've done the candles,' said Steve. He was on the sofa, Beth cross-legged on a cushion on the floor.

'Gordon's not keen to get electricity put on,' said Beth. 'Thinks they might condemn the cottage if we try, and it would cost a fortune anyway. I don't like to make a fuss, when he's been so kind, and I'm living here for nothing anyway.'

Steve said, 'Wow. I think that's incredible.'

'What?'

'Well, I mean, the candles aren't a pose to create atmosphere. You really need them.'

'Yes, so?'

'All my friends are posers. So am I, I suppose. Trying to say something to the world. But you're real, Beth.'

She wasn't absolutely sure what he meant, but it seemed to be a compliment. 'No,' she said. 'I'm hiding.'

Steve leaned forward, elbows resting limply on his knees. He seemed fascinated, and she felt safe with him. 'What from? Eirian's father? He must've been mad to let you go.'

'Pour me some more wine,' said Beth, holding out her glass. And perhaps it was the wine that seduced her into telling Steve all about Morgan, things she'd never told anyone, flowing like burning oil from her tongue.

'We were so close,' said Beth. 'It wasn't just sex. Morgan was so affectionate. Always touching me as if he couldn't bear to let me out of his sight. Always glad to see me. He never made me feel bad. We talked all the time. We only ever quarrelled once or twice.'

'What about?' Steve needed to know every detail.

'He didn't like my family. But he was right, they were awful.'

'So how come he never came and found you, if he was so keen?'

Beth breathed in and out, wishing she didn't still feel that her whole life was lived inside that question. 'I don't suppose I'll ever really know. But I think Morgan was one of those people who needs to be liked, so they tell you what you want to hear. "Of course we'll stay together. I love you." And they probably mean it while they're saying it. But once he was back at school, he would be saying the same things to a dozen other girls.'

'Shallow, you mean,' Steve said thoughtfully.

'If I thought he was shallow, it would be easier to hate him,' Beth said, suddenly bitter. 'I do hate him, for not being what I thought he was.'

'Still hurts, though, eh?'

'Yes. It hurts.' She poured out more wine. 'Sounds pathetic, still pining for someone I haven't seen for six – seven years.'

'No. It's unfinished business, Beth; that's why you can't let it go. Maybe it's better this way; you can keep your dreams. If you'd stayed together, you might have been divorcing each other by now.'

'Yes, and he'd have hated me for tying him down. I think that's what Rhianwen was afraid of, actually. I'd rather he forgot me than hated me.'

'She should've left you to make your own mistakes, though,' said Steve. 'So, what do you think of Rhianwen now? After you told her to sod off?'

'I don't know. I should loathe her, but I don't. I had no right to assume she'd look after me when Eirian was born, but I'd built her up in my mind to be this infallible mother figure. Instead she let me down. My own mother behaved exactly as I expected her to; but I thought Rhianwen and Morgan loved me, so when I found out they didn't – oh God, it was worse, much worse than anything my own parents did.'

'Betrayal,' said Steve, nodding.

'I still don't know whether she was being deliberately cruel when she left me with the travellers, or just doing what she thought best. Sometimes I think she was only trying to protect Morgan and me from hurting each other, but sometimes I think she was every bit as bad as my mother and grandma said.'

'It's a bastard, not knowing,' said Steve. 'I hate that.'

'Yes, well. Maybe it's easy to blame Rhianwen when really it was Morgan's decision. I would just like to know, if I was only one of a dozen girls, what was so bloody special about the one he married?'

'Maybe he got her –' Steve went almost purple as he realized what he was saying, but Beth was too drunk to be upset.

'Pregnant? No, she had a brilliant career. A marine biologist called Marian. Marian the marine biologist. And I fucking hate her, even though I've never met her!'

'Hey.' Steve's hand came down on her shoulder. Understanding. And the wine cushioned her, so she didn't fall apart. 'I know how you feel. Exactly.'

'Sam's mother leave you too?'

'My wife,' said Steve. 'We were married, believe it or not. Yeah. Walked out about a year ago.'

'Another bloke?'

'Only the most famous bloke in the world. Jesus Christ.'

Beth went hot and cold. 'What?'

'She went religious. I don't know what it was with Katy; she was never satisfied. She always wanted more. It wasn't enough to live together, we had to get married. A flat wasn't good enough, had to be a cottage in the country. Then there had to be a baby; I wasn't keen, I thought we were too young, but she insisted. Then she found out Sam wasn't a toy, and she resented having to look after him. They said she had post-natal depression; in that case, she's had it as long as I've known her. I really tried to help, I looked after Sam every spare minute I had but . . . She didn't like my friends, didn't like me being in the band, said I was lazy. I don't know what she wanted. She was seeing other men, you know? She'd dump Sam with me, do herself up and make out she was off out with a girlfriend.'

'Maybe she was,' said Beth.

'No. She'd tell me what she'd been doing, after. I don't know if she made it up; doesn't matter, the point is she needed to hurt me. And I still forgave her, what a prat!'

'Why did you?'

Steve sighed. 'I dunno. I loved her. Katy had this energy, you know? She was this red-haired princess. I just wanted to please her. Getting the Metro was a last effort to keep her; she was always moaning about us not being able to afford a car. So much for that. Anyway, just over a year ago she changed. Went kind of serene and smug and glassy-eyed, and started lecturing me about letting Jesus into my life. She'd discovered this weird church in some backstreet in Brum. I thought it was just another way to get at me, but no, she was deadly serious. Three months of it then she announces that God has called her to

222

leave me and join this sect. I've hardly seen her for a year. Well, all right, maybe it was more exciting than living with me, but how could she walk out on her own son? That's what I don't get!'

Beth moved up on to the sofa beside him and put her hand on his arm. 'Religion can make people do insane things. I've seen it.'

'Anyway, I think she was screwing him.'

'Who?'

'The leader of the sect. Luke Herne, his name is. Bastard.'

'Oh,' said Beth, all the breath knocked out of her. 'Oh, God.'

'Beth? Are you all right?'

Couldn't be someone else with the same name, she thought. Do I tell Steve? What would be the point? Either he'll stop trusting me, or he'll think I can help, and I don't even know Luke any more.

'It's the wine,' she said. 'I don't drink, usually.'

'I'll get you a glass of water.' Steve stood up, swayed, and sat down again. 'I'm not sure I'm in a fit state to drive.'

'You'd better stay, then. This folds out into a bed,' said Beth, thinking, did he come here intending to stay the night? I don't mind. I suppose I wanted it too. The wine had made her feel relaxed, affectionate, sexy, if she could admit it. Such a long time since . . .

They looked at each other. Then Steve seemed to blink and start backwards. 'Look, Beth, I didn't mean *that*. It would be nice but,' he cleared his throat, 'I'm not ready.'

Beth was startled, but hid it. 'It's okay. I offered you a bed, not my body.'

'I'd feel guilty. I'm still married to Katy, even if she's gone; and you're still in love with Morgan, aren't you?'

'Not after all this time,' said Beth. But the familiar pain melted her from head to foot, as fresh as snow.

'Don't kid yourself,' Steve said morosely. 'If you meet the right person and lose them, you *never* get over it.'

Beth helped him to pull the bed out, and found an old eiderdown. She meant to go upstairs to her room, but Steve didn't seem inclined to sleep so she made coffee and they sat on the mattress, talking, and eventually, around two in the morning, Beth fell asleep where she sat.

They dragged her to a dark building that stank of urine and rotten meat, but Beth hardly noticed the stench; it was part of life. It was the clergymen she feared, with their dark robes and their coldly righteous eyes.

Obsidian men without emotions.

The Inquisitor, the one who'd tried to rape Guendolen, said, 'Let her confession be obtained without torture.' His breath was a brown miasma smoking out between the gaps in his teeth.

When they lifted Beth and strapped her into the chair, she felt as if she were falling. She flailed at nothingness. Tried to scream but she couldn't even breathe.

Someone was fastening beams across her calves and feet. Beth thought, they're strapping up my legs thinking I'm Margaret but I'm not, I don't need a wheelchair . . .

Tighter, tighter grew the pressure across her legs. That's tight enough! But it didn't stop. She heard the laboured squeaking of wood, the gasps of effort from the man who was tightening the beams. She smelled his sweat and filth.

Pain now. *Pain.* Her bones were creaking, a red fire ignited in the marrow. Blood was trickling from the torn flesh. Flies alighted on the fresh wounds, the tickling of their feet a distinct and subtle torture in itself.

With a silent scream, Beth broke through the pain, leapt out of the tormented body, and saw herself from outside, as if she were floating near the ceiling.

She saw an old woman, strapped in a chair, with some device of wood, metal and handles clamped round her lower legs. It was the Midwife. Her hair stood up from her head like a white flame. The men, hunched vultures, were all around, tightening the device notch by notch.

And this method, Beth realized, they did not count as torture.

One man stood apart, watching. He was tall, but stood

crookedly as if his spine were deformed. His face was too long, all the bones overgrown; his expression intellectual and utterly detached.

'Confess,' said Inquisitor Lacost. His broad, grotesque face was distorted, as if with sexual pleasure, and sweat trickled down his coarse skin. 'Confess, confess before God. You are guilty of witchcraft. You have the marks of the Devil upon you.'

The words came, rough as frayed hemp, from the Midwife's anguished mouth.

'I am a healer.'

Beth watched for an eternity, frozen, forced to watch the woman's slow, agonizing decline. Very distant in the back of her mind floated a thought: *My mother was right. I've died and been sent to hell.*

The once-kind light in the Midwife's eyes turned sick and mad.

'Sign the confession,' said Lacost, and an accomplice thrust a rag of paper and a quill pen under her face.

The crucifixes on their chests shone like scalpels.

'I am,' whispered the Midwife, 'guilty.'

Lacost grinned. The tall man in the corner raised his eyebrows and nodded, unmoved.

Beth was drifting away. She sank into thrumming darkness. There was a sickening stench of mould, rotting vegetables, manure. A barn of some kind.

Beth saw the two girls huddled in a pile of straw in the stinking darkness: Eirian and Guendolen. They were clinging to each other, eyes tight shut, oblivious to the rats running over their feet.

The Midwife's screams carried into their hiding place from outside.

'Don't cry, Guen,' said Eirian.

'She's my mother,' Guendolen sobbed. 'My mother.'

Beth woke, shrieking and trying frantically to scramble off the bed. She was out of her mind. But something, terrifyingly, was holding her back, like the shackles that had held the Midwife while they questioned her 'without torture'.

Steve's hand on her wrist.

Beth couldn't remember who he was, what he was doing there. She fought, panicking, as if his hand were a huge spider.

'Hey!' he said. 'Hey, Beth, calm down. It's me. What's the matter?'

Beth stared at him, and the fog cleared. 'They're torturing her,' she said. 'In the other place.'

His face relaxed into a smile, as if he imagined he understood. 'You've had a nightmare. Come on, it's over. Does this happen often?'

He tried to pull her down into his arms but she sat rigid on the edge of the mattress, sweat trickling down between her breasts.

'No,' she said, jerking free and making unsteadily for the stairs. 'Eirian needs me.'

The stairs were steep, dark, silent.

Perhaps it was just my own nightmare, thought Beth.

Then a terrible cry burst out, killing her hopes: Eirian's voice, shrill with terror. 'No! No! *Mother*!'

Chapter Fourteen

E IRIAN woke but Beth wasn't there.
The child stared into the darkness, clutching the edge of
the sheet. She was aware of the moon's presence; even in its
dark phase it was still there, a magnetic sphere, a plum-col-
oured shadow. Dark, like the Goddess's bitter rage and rejection. Like the Midwife's pain as the ugly men tortured her for
daring to help the sick.

But to be torn out of the other place now, when Guendolen
needed her!

'No!' she cried, her voice trembling. 'No! *Mother*!'

The crooked door opened, there was a wedge of lamplight,
and Beth was there.

'Mum,' Eirian cried, reaching out. Warm arms went round
her. Warm breasts and sweetly scented black hair enveloped
her. A man, Sam's father, was hovering in the doorway, but he
didn't matter.

'Did you see what happened to the Midwife?' Beth
breathed.

Eirian shook her head. 'I heard,' she said. 'I was with Guendolen. Hiding. But it isn't over.'

'No, Eirian! You can't go there again!' Beth spoke sharply,
looking alarmed. Beth didn't want to go back but Eirian knew
they must. She must wind her mother in her arms and pull her
back down into the darkness until it ended.

Eirian wasn't frightened. She was very angry, and very calm,
and in despair, and angry again, but not afraid.

The glass-green water, streaked with red, drew them down.

Eirian could no longer feel her mother's arms around her.
She was alone.

She was standing in the front of a crowd on a bare hill. On
its summit was a thin coronet of birches, and in the centre a

lone tree, leafless and stark as a cross. A group of men, dusty jackdaws, were gathered at its base.

Guendolen wasn't there; she had fled into the forest, Eirian knew.

A cold wind blew across the hill, chilling Eirian. Below lay the village, the striped fields, the sheep and goats grazing on the common land – and the forest. Was Guendolen hiding there now, living like a wild animal on berries and spring water? Eirian had always been at Guendolen's side before, but this time she was alone.

In the church steeple, a bell tolled.

The people carried the stench of the village with them, dried into their dun-coloured garments. Excrement and sweat, stagnant water and disease. Gusts of wind blew it away, but when the wind dropped, the smell rose again.

No one noticed Eirian, with her hair and half her face covered by her hood. She studied the faces of the men and women around her, and on their pock-cratered, haggard contours she saw fear, excitement, satisfaction, misery.

Some of these had once danced naked in the forest, paying joyful reverence to nature. No longer. They conformed piously to authority, lest they too be accused of witchcraft. They went with downcast eyes, glancing suspiciously at their neighbours, ready to denounce before they were denounced.

The raven-clad men around the tree held a prisoner. The Midwife, Guendolen's mother. She had seemed so beautiful in her age and wisdom; now, in defeat, she was a sad and terrified old woman, all her dignity gone.

The long-nosed woman who had betrayed her was there in the crowd, hunched bulkily over her stick, expressionless.

Inquisitor Lacost was reading from a document, his voice thin and piercing, a rusty needle.

'Matilda Agnew, you have been found guilty of witchcraft and have confessed freely and without torture the most heinous crimes and blasphemy against God our Father and against the divine ordinance, laws and acts of parliament of this kingdom; that you did deny your Christian faith and withdraw your allegiance from God; that you did deny your baptism and cleave to the Devil; that you did make sacrifice unto the Devil; that you did have several times carnal dealings or copulation with the Devil and so defiled that body of yours which should have been a temple of the Holy Ghost; that you did observe Sabbats; that you did heal without authority; that you did ease the birth pains of women whom God decreed must suffer; that you did blight a sick man and hasten his death; that you did endeavour to recruit diverse others into the service of the Devil. Of these foul blasphemies you shall be purged by hanging. May God have mercy on your soul.' The broad knobbly hand described a cross in the air. 'In the name of the Father, the Son and the Holy Ghost, Amen.'

A few yards away stood a tall, deformed man with an elongated face, watching with cold satisfaction. Eirian did not know how she knew him, but she did. This was Warbeck, the judge who had found the Midwife guilty.

As the Midwife was forced to climb on to a tall stool that stood beneath an overhanging branch of the tree, a strange low cry arose from the crowd, a kind of hysteria, an outrush of tension. '*Hang the witch. Kill the witch.*'

The same people who had once relied on her help now denied the Midwife and crossed themselves frantically.

A priest, standing beside the Inquisitor, said, 'Grant, we beseech thee, O Lord, that thy people may escape the contamination of the Devil, and may with a pure mind follow thee, the only God, through thy Son, Jesus Christ, Our Lord, for ever and ever, Amen.'

They put the noose round the Midwife's neck. Her face was blank, her hair a white halo.

'No,' said Eirian. Until this moment she hadn't believed they were really going to do it. Why am I here, she thought, if not to stop it? 'No! Stop!' she screamed.

People were turning to look at her.

Ruthless, she shouldered her way past a couple of adults who had drifted in front of her, and ran across the rough grass towards the Inquisitor.

'No!' she screamed with all the power in her lungs. 'Don't kill her! In the name of the Goddess, you mustn't kill her! You're wrong, you're mad, you don't understand what you're doing!'

A voice inside her head was screaming, *Eirian, don't!*

As Eirian ran towards the group, she saw one of the men wrench the stool away. The Midwife's body dropped, and jerked. Eirian heard her neck snap. The breeze blew her skirts up, and her thin, bowed legs kicked at the air.

The Midwife's face turned purple but she wasn't dead. Her breath wheezed out through her crushed throat and her eyes and mouth were open, bleeding pain into the air. Urine flowed down her legs and fell in a topaz stream to the ground. The stale scent mixed with all the other foulness.

Eirian fell to her knees, sobbing. She turned her head and demanded of the crowd, 'Why didn't you help her? She always helped you!'

But her voice was so thick with bitterness that only a few of them could have heard her.

It went on for ever, the Midwife hanging there in agony between life and death. Then she died. Eirian saw her life go out, like a candle kicked over, a jewel stamped into the mud.

'That is the one,' said Lacost, pointing at Eirian. 'The demon child. You heard her blasphemous objections! Bring her here!'

Eirian tried to run, but the men and women in the crowd caught her and handed her over. The ugly men held her with their bony, wart-encrusted hands and tied her wrists behind her back.

Time for me to go home, Eirian thought in terror, but she couldn't. The vision wouldn't end. This place was as real as life and she was trapped in it. The rope burned her wrists. Her mouth was dry and her heart was pounding as if it would burst.

She could smell the filth crusted in the men's clothes, stale food and fishy body odour and their foul breath. Paranoia rose from them like a black fog and there was no way to cut through it. They were beyond reason. They couldn't change, and only time could destroy them, time their victims did not have.

The men brought Eirian to Lacost, and he stared into her face. His eyes were slits of cruelty – and fear, she understood now.

Judge Warbeck also came to glare at her. There was no fear in his eyes. Only a cold, administrative spirit that held absolute conviction and power. Eirian despised Lacost, but it was Warbeck who made her shrivel to nothing.

'I shall not forget your face, demon,' said the Inquisitor. 'The works of the Devil are manifest everywhere.'

Goddess, let me go home. Eirian prayed with all her might. But the bare hill under the grey sky remained solid. Drizzle fell on her face. She could see every scab, every black pore and whisker on Lacost's face. She could feel the killing weight of the churchmen's combined will.

'You shall be drowned, then you shall be scourged, then you shall be burned, demon,' said Lacost. 'I command you, kiss the hem of my coat and thank me for saving your miserable soul!'

Eirian tried to pull back, revolted. But the two men who held her forced her down to her knees and pushed her forward with such force that her face went into the Inquisitor's groin.

The material of his breeches was thick and waxen with ingrained dirt and exudations. The stink almost made her sick. She screwed up her eyes and turned her face away from the foul touch of the material.

As they pulled her upright again, she felt the tickle of a louse running across her cheek.

Lacost's fat red mouth tightened with the merest touch of satisfaction. 'Bring her now, before she flees back to her master the Devil.'

They dragged Eirian down the hill, hurting her, with the villagers trailing behind. She remembered how they'd been united by joy in the wedding ritual long ago. Now they were united only by hate and suspicion. Divided by it, rather. No one trusted anyone now.

Ankle-deep in mud beside the village pond, they tied a muslin sash full of rocks round Eirian's waist, and slipped a rope round her.

Eirian knew she must say something, use this moment to make them understand the mistake they were making in denying the Goddess and defiling life, but she could hardly breathe for terror.

'I'm not a demon,' was all she could say.

'You shall receive a fair trial,' said Lacost. 'If you drown, it will prove your innocence. But if you live, it will prove your guilt. Then your demon shall be driven out by scourging and by fire.'

Eirian took a breath to attack him with words, only to be seized bodily and thrown out over the water. Her stomach looped in horror. The last thing she saw was Warbeck's granite-cruel face.

Green and thick with manure, algae and rotting vegetation, the surface received her.

Eirian went under, and sank. Sank.

A mouthful of the stuff went down her throat. She gagged, panicking. The water bubbled and clamoured in her ears. She saw the breath coming out of her mouth and vanishing, silvered, towards the surface; but she went down, down among the weeds and liquid excrement and decaying corpses of animals.

It was real – and unreal. A bad dream. All memories gone, no awareness of self. There was only the panic, the bursting of her head and lungs, the green darkness and a constellation of black stars exploding.

A thread of raw air went down Eirian's throat like a saw, and it *hurt*. She was choking, coughing uncontrollably. Lurching forward, she threw up a mouthful of pond-water. It began to soak into the floorboards beside her bed, leaving a stain streaked with pond slime.

Beth's arms were round her. Eirian had been numb with cold, but the sudden warmth made her shiver violently.

'We're home,' said Beth. She, too, was coughing and shiver-

232

ing, holding Eirian so hard that she couldn't breathe. 'It's all right, darling. We're all right.'

'But she's dead.' Eirian began to cry with shock. 'The Midwife. I couldn't save her!'

'I know, I saw,' said Beth. 'You did your best!'

'Wasn't enough.'

'You can't do any more. You can't go back.'

'No,' said Eirian. And she did not want to go back to Guendolen's village, ever again.

'It's over,' Beth said, rocking her. '*Now* it's over.'

There was nothing for Beth to do but hold Eirian, hold her to life, keep her pinned to this world.

Beth had seen everything through Eirian's eyes. Had felt it, too. She'd experienced Eirian's naïve bravery and its slow erosion by the witch-hunters' ruthlessness.

Beth knew that she had nearly lost Eirian tonight.

Vision or not, a few more minutes and Eirian would have died in her arms. The pond-water she'd thrown up, now no more than a dark stain in the twilight, was real.

'I'm not a demon,' Eirian said, still sobbing.

'You know you're not! Don't let those evil men make you believe their lies. They're cowards. You are brave.' And Beth went on, whispering into Eirian's ear, soothing her; trying to comfort herself, too.

After a few minutes, she became aware that they were not alone. She looked round to see dawn glowing in the window, and Steve standing in the bedroom doorway, looking baffled.

Beth had completely forgotten about him. For a moment she couldn't even think who he was or what he was doing there.

'What the hell's going on?' he demanded.

Beth felt cold towards him. He was an outsider; she didn't have to tell him anything!

'It's hard to explain,' she said.

'Well, try! You've been sitting there clinging to each other for half an hour, saying the weirdest things; I couldn't make you hear me! It was scary, Beth. I didn't know what to do.'

'I'm sorry,' Beth said, with an effort. 'I hope we didn't wake Sam.'

'He's okay. But you look terrible.' Steve's eyebrows were crimped with worry. 'And so does Eirian. I think you should take her to the doctor.'

'I don't want to go to the doctor!' Eirian said belligerently. 'I'm all right. Mum, can I have Mr Pepper, please?'

Beth took the large teddy bear – the one she'd bought in Scotland, for Eirian's first Christmas – from the dresser and gave it to her. Eirian hugged the bear, looking broodingly over its furry shoulder.

'She's like this all the time,' said Beth. 'An ordinary child one minute – and then a thousand years old.'

'What are you on about? This nightmare? Do you always have bad dreams in stereo?'

'It wasn't a dream. Have you got about a fortnight?' Beth said acidly. 'You'll still be none the wiser at the end of it.'

Steve pushed his hand through his matted hair. 'I'm not sure I can handle this.'

'You don't have to. Get Sam dressed and go home.' Beth didn't mean to be hostile but she couldn't help it.

'I didn't mean – look, I want to help, but –'

'Oh, shit, it's a quarter to six,' Beth said, seeing the clock. 'It's not worth going back to bed.'

'It's Saturday, Beth.'

'But I still have to work!' She cuddled Eirian. 'Come on, darling, you'll feel better after breakfast. You can watch telly at the farm, or help me feed the hens. Bring Mr Pepper with you, if you want.'

'Okay,' said Eirian, climbing out of bed.

Beth turned to Steve, trying to soften her voice, not quite succeeding. 'Look, Steve, I'm sorry about this but I really want to be alone. I shouldn't have let you stay. Just – make yourself a cup of tea and go, okay?'

'Stuff the tea,' Steve said sullenly, and walked out.

She heard Sam's voice from the other room as Steve helped him get dressed. Then their footsteps on the stairs, the front door opening and slamming, the Metro's engine whining into life.

'I wanted to say goodbye to Sam,' Eirian said plaintively.

Beth sighed. She was so tired she could hardly think. 'Sort out what you want to wear. I'll put the bath on.'

As Beth went downstairs into the sitting-room, she almost tripped over the Lego village on the rug. She bent down to move it, only to be arrested by the skill and detail with which the children had built it. Cottages grouped around a green and a church, and a make-up mirror placed on it for a pond.

Beth recognized it as Guendolen's village, reproduced in garish yellow, red and blue bricks. There was even a stepped mound for the hill beside the village. On the peak was a thin structure that could have been a pole with a cross-piece or a tree with a single branch.

The gallows.

'Are you still speaking to me?' Steve asked, sounding wary.

Monday afternoon; Beth was waiting for Eirian to finish school. All weekend she'd been mourning the end of her friendship with Steve, hating herself, hating everyone and everything. What has Eirian done, to deserve the ghastly things that had happened? Beth wondered. What have *I* done?

Once Eirian had calmed down, she had seemed her normal self, but Beth was worried sick. She'd been begging the Goddess, God, anyone who might be out there, to leave Eirian alone and let her grow up normally.

She had expected Steve to ignore her, but now he was at her shoulder, the usual shy smile on his lips.

'Of course I'm speaking to you.' Beth looked away, then met his eyes. 'I'm sorry I was so brusque on Saturday. It's just that I can't expect you to understand or even believe what's going on. Eirian and I don't need someone standing around looking baffled and telling us to see the doctor! It's too important for that. Too private. It's not your problem.'

'But I'd like to help,' Steve persisted helplessly.

'How?'

'I don't know. I'd like to be there if you need someone to talk to, that's all.'

Beth smiled ruefully, softening towards him. He was so eager to please; perhaps Katy had despised him for it. But I'd appreciate it, Beth thought defiantly. I need someone I can trust! 'I'd like that. But you'll think I'm crazy.'

'No, I won't,' Steve said indignantly. 'What does it matter what I think, or if you are crazy? Mad people used to be seen as visionaries. You're not mad, Beth, but you *are* a visionary.'

'Thanks.' She smiled grimly, then tried to explain something of what had happened. 'It's Eirian I'm frightened for. What is it doing to her, to see people tortured and hanged, all that squalor and cruelty? I wouldn't let her watch anything half as horrible on television, but I can't stop this! She seems all right. But what's it doing to her inside?'

'What you really need is someone who could explain what's happening. You know, like a . . .' His voice dropped. 'A witch. A Wiccan, I mean.'

'I had someone,' Beth said thinly. 'Morgan's mother. And Mrs Primarola. They couldn't explain it either.'

'Oh.' His shoulders rose and fell with disappointment. 'I don't want to lose our friendship, that's all.'

'Neither do I,' said Beth. 'But why should we? If you can put up with me going a bit strange sometimes. Don't look so worried, Steve. I think it's over; for now, at least. So, if you want to come round at the weekend?'

And their friendship was allowed to begin, at last.

Although Beth had to work seven days a week – the farmers rarely had a day off – her evenings were relatively free. Steve came round with Sam most Friday evenings, and often stayed until Monday morning.

Beth saw what Steve had meant about Katy complaining he was lazy. 'Laid-back' was the word, perhaps. He would do anything she asked him, even cooking the occasional meal – but nothing without being asked.

But Beth liked having Steve around. His company soothed

her and cheered her up. She could talk to him about anything. He never tried to seduce her; sometimes, when she'd had too much to drink, she wished he would, but in the morning she'd be grateful that nothing had happened.

Eirian mothered Sam, and Sam began to lose his shyness and do better at school.

The weeks went by, and there were no more visits to the other place; if Eirian went alone, Beth was unaware of it. But Eirian said nothing, and seemed too serene for anything to have happened. So Beth tried to put it all from her mind and go on with life; what else could she do?

Steve began to bring his guitar to the cottage, and then he began to bring his friends.

It came as a great shock to Katy, the day she discovered that the Church of the One Truth was not a game.

It had been simple fun to start with. People had welcomed her, showering her with love and attention without demanding anything in return – and above all things, Katy craved attention. There was a wonderful sense of community, lots of new friends, an intoxicating atmosphere of excitement. Knowing they were doing something to change the world!

Luke called his congregation his 'saints'. He said their discovery of the Lord was a 'wave of blessing'.

Katy wouldn't admit it to herself, but discovering God had been a new pose, something to alleviate her boredom, a way to get at Steve. She fancied Luke, too, comparing his congregation to groupies round a rock star; well, that was how they behaved, male and female alike. They needed someone to give them answers to all their problems – and Luke could.

Katy became rather drunk on it all, and that was when she made a terrible mistake.

The church had its headquarters in the suburbs of Birmingham, in a Victorian house with big draughty rooms. The décor was austere; white walls, green lino on the floors, a minimum of plain furniture. Two reception rooms, knocked into one, served as a place of worship. There was a pulpit on a dais at one end, but no altar and no cross; such things were graven images, Luke maintained.

Along the hall were the kitchen, a loo, and Luke's office. Upstairs, the rooms were crammed with bunk-beds for the church members who lived in. There was a common room on the third floor, for discussions and Bible study.

What was Luke doing, Katy wondered, when he gathered these impressionable young men and women to him, but creating a harem? It couldn't hurt to sleep with him, Katy reasoned. It was inevitable, really. Surely nobody could be as chaste as Luke appeared to be?

Full of herself, Katy slipped along to Luke's office one Sunday after the evening service. She was at her most flirtatious and seductive, tossing her long ginger hair around.

'I really want to learn everything you can teach me,' she said, moving round to his side of the desk and sitting on its edge, her lips and her legs slightly parted. 'I wondered if you would give me individual Bible study sessions. There must be so much you can teach me about love.'

Luke stood up, and pulled her to her feet, his gloved hands burning her wrist. Katy thought he was going to kiss her. Then she saw the cold rage in his face, and she was terrified.

He grabbed her hair and pulled it back, so tight her head went back and she gasped in pain. With his other hand he gripped both her wrists behind her back, and forced her on to her knees on the floor.

'You are a sinner, sister,' he said harshly. 'Jesus loves sinners, but you must repent! You have no place with us until you can give up your lascivious ways. Are you willing to repent?'

His anger frightened her nearly to death. Such power in his hands! A rash of gooseflesh broke out on her skin, and she came close to wetting herself. 'Yes,' Katy gasped. 'Yes. I'm sorry. I thought –'

'I know what you thought,' he said more gently, 'and you were wrong. You must do penance, before you can be forgiven.'

'All right. Please let me up.'

'Not until you've tasted the filth of your own sins.'

'What?'

'Wash the floor under my desk, so the place where I set my feet will be spotless.'

'How?'

'Lick it clean, Katy. Then dry it with your hair.'

She was at his feet and he towered above her, forceful and terrifying. If he'd told her to throw herself off the roof, she would have done it.

Gagging, her face twisted up with revulsion, Katy obeyed.

The house was kept immaculate by daily cleaning; Katy had mopped this lino herself, but she had been slapdash about the parts that didn't show. She regretted it now. Her stomach revolted and the taste of dust and detergent made tears run from her eyes.

At last, the torture over, Luke let her up. She managed not to puke on his suit. She was shaking violently. His right hand descended on her forehead; and as it touched her, a pure white light exploded in her brain, and she fell headlong on to the floor.

'The Holy Spirit is with you,' he intoned. 'God knows you, Katy.'

Then he prayed over her, and Katy was never the same again.

She was transformed, because Luke had shown her the truth; that he was serious and that, above all, he was genuine. God worked through him. Katy had never had clear rules and strict discipline before. Until Luke told her, 'No!' she hadn't realized how much she needed it.

No one had ever wanted Katy for her soul instead of her body, until Luke.

For that, she couldn't help but adore him.

At the next meeting, she had to stand up in front of everyone, confess all her faults, and tell them how Jesus had taught her humility and chastity by washing her clean in His blood.

The wave of approval and love that came from the others nearly knocked her over.

Now Katy was in, she could never get out. It was simple logic; to be rejected by Luke was death, but to be accepted was life, love, happiness, salvation. It was feeling special, and, well, superior to the unsaved masses who were going to hell on Judgement Day. Like Steve, and . . .

And Sam.

One Saturday, when they'd had been at Dove Hill Farm for six months, Beth cycled into Barton on John's bike to post some letters for Margaret. As she dismounted outside the post office and slipped the letters into the box, Beth saw her grandfather walking towards her on the other side of the road.

Perhaps he wouldn't have looked twice, if she hadn't stopped in her tracks and stared at him, her heart thumping. But because she caught his eye, he stopped too; and because she *was* eye-catching, all in black, he went on looking.

Randolph had hardly changed, although he was in his mid-sixties now. He'd gone greyer, but otherwise he was still handsome, tall and imposing, with a thick head of hair. He had a raincoat over a dark suit, and a briefcase in his hand.

Beth, though, looked very different from the girl who had stayed with her grandparents during those far-off summers. Surely it wasn't possible he could recognize her, with her dyed hair and funereal clothing.

Beth thought, I'll walk away and keep my head down – but she was rooted to the kerb by panic.

She hesitated too long. Randolph, frowning, was crossing over and coming towards her. It was a narrow road. A few strides and he was right in front of her, and it was too late to escape.

'Beth?' he said, peering at her, his thick, iron-grey eyebrows drawn together in doubt. He looked every inch the severe, aloof doctor she remembered. 'I do beg your pardon, I'm probably mistaken, but you so remind me of my – my grand-daughter. You don't look like her and yet . . .'

Beth couldn't breathe. All she could do was look at him, while her eyes confessed everything.

'Beth?' His eyebrows jerked up, transforming his expression to one of blank amazement. It was the first time she'd ever seen him display an unguarded reaction. 'It *is* you, isn't it?'

'Hello, Granddad.' Leaning on the handlebars of the bike, she gazed uncertainly back at him.

He tilted his head, as if he wanted to look underneath her disguise to find the Beth he remembered. 'I hardly recognized you.'

'That's the idea. I don't want to be recognized. You must be busy.'

'I was on my way to see Dr Bown. NHS bureaucracy. It can wait.' A pause. 'But you're all right?' he asked.

'Fine,' she said.

'And the – the little girl?'

'She's beautiful,' said Beth.

Randolph lost his colour, and for a moment he seemed to be near tears. But when he spoke his voice was clinical. 'Are you both eating properly? Has she had her inoculations? Are you registered with a GP?'

'Yes, yes. We see Dr Bown. She's very nice.'

'You are living locally, then,' he said. 'Well, how long have you been here?'

'Not long. Granddad –'

'I know, I know.' He sighed. 'I'm sorry, Beth. You're an adult, you have a right to privacy. But for God's sake, we've been frantic for – what is it? Six and a half years? And you were in the next village all the time?'

Suddenly Beth was in danger of weeping. She'd known how it would be, if ever she met a member of her family. Unbearable.

'Not all the time.' She looked behind her at the post office, a tiny shop that sold everything. 'I ought to go,' she said. 'I have some shopping to do.'

Randolph's hand fell on her shoulder. 'Beth, please. Don't run off. I'm not going to be angry, or start laying down the law, or even tell anyone I've seen you, if you don't want me to. I just want to talk. Will you come home with me? My car's round the corner.'

Beth shook her head.

'Let's go in the Swan, then,' said Randolph. 'I'll buy you lunch.'

The pub was small and traditional, with low ceilings, beams, dark furniture and a red carpet. Beth and Randolph drank halves of bitter and ate ploughman's lunches, seated in the corner on a plush crimson bench seat.

'How's Grandma?' Beth asked.

'Fine,' he said. 'Same as ever.'

'Good,' said Beth. She'd dreaded hearing that things had changed drastically in her absence. 'And the horses?'

'Getting on a bit, now. Heather still rides them, but they're all rather creaky now, Heather and me included.'

'I've missed them,' said Beth.

'We've missed you.'

A knot in her throat again, but the beer eased it.

'I'm sorry, but I had to escape,' said Beth. 'You know why. My mother would have killed Eirian. She was killing *me*.'

Randolph didn't try to deny it. Suddenly he looked his age. 'If only you'd come to Heather and me! We could have sorted something out.'

'But what? You and Gran hated Morgan as much as Mum and Dad did! I don't know why, I don't suppose there's even a logical explanation. It doesn't matter now, anyway. There was *no one* to help Eirian except me.'

Again he sighed. 'I'm so sorry you felt that. But was it really that bad?'

Randolph didn't want to believe it – so Beth, suddenly, wanted to make him understand. To make him suffer.

'You must have known how Mum used to beat Luke; she beat me too, sometimes. You must have known how she'd act when I got pregnant! She hit me in front of you, for God's sake! Why didn't you protect me?'

'I thought it was in the heat of the moment. I didn't realize –'

'I tried to write to Morgan one day. She found the envelope and thrashed hell out of me. I couldn't sleep on my back for a week. I don't know how I would have posted it anyway, because I was never allowed out without a bodyguard.'

Randoph's thick eyebrows indented. 'She beat you while you were —'

'Then there was the day the Pastor tried to cast the demons out of me. That was fun. They threw me all over the room and screamed at me non-stop for about six hours.'

'What?' He was beginning to look horrified, to her satisfaction.

'They were trying to make me miscarry, without admitting it; abortion without guilt, I suppose. They must've been so disappointed when I didn't. But the worst thing was the mental cruelty. Having Luke sneering, Dad trying to pretend it hadn't happened, and Mum glaring at me with those dead eyes day after day, telling me my baby wasn't human. Have you any idea how that feels? Even a prisoner of war knows why his captors hate him, but when it's your own family —!' Randolph looked down, shaking his head, unable to answer. 'It was indescribable! I couldn't take any more; I couldn't put my baby through it.'

'Your grandmother and I had no idea it was so serious,' Randolph said heavily. 'I swear we didn't. I know Olivia was strict, but she loved you.'

'She had a bloody funny way of showing it.' Beth was trembling. Agony to talk about her mother, but she had to ask. 'How is Mum?'

'Surviving,' said Randolph. 'We see less of her, now you and Luke have left. I think she felt she'd failed when you ran away.'

'Failed to save my soul, you mean? It was too late for that.'

'Well, she turned to the church to get her through it. They convinced her it was God's will that you'd gone, so she accepted it, eventually.'

'And my dad?'

'I understand he's left Pastor Blair's church and gone somewhere less evangelical, so your mother's not speaking to him. I don't know the details. We don't discuss it.'

'I thought you were going to say he'd left my mother,' Beth said. 'Did Dad ever say anything about me?'

'Not much. But Beth, with some people, the more upset they are, the less they say. Your father's like that.'

Beth felt a painful emptiness when she thought of her father. She'd never known him, really. 'And Luke?'

'He's quite an evangelist,' Randolph said sardonically. 'Your mother's very proud of him. Founded his own church in Birmingham; I understand it's very successful.'

Beth knew that from Steve. 'You don't sound very impressed. Aren't you proud, too? At least one of your grandchildren turned out all right.'

'Maybe one of them has,' said Randolph. He drained his glass. 'Another drink?'

'Yes, please.'

As Randolph came back from the bar with two more halves, Beth asked, 'How did my mum get like she is? You and Gran aren't that religious. You go to church, but you don't give everyone a headache about it.'

Randolph laughed out loud. She'd never made him laugh before. Beth was finding that her grandfather was actually rather charming, under the steel shell.

'Beth, I'm an atheist. You couldn't see what I saw in the war and still believe in a merciful God. It may be a cliché, but it's true. Your gran and I never tried to influence Olivia in any way. Perhaps she needed religion because she'd never had any; I don't know. When she started going to church we thought it was a phase she needed to go through, but it didn't wear off. She had, well, a bit of an emotional crisis, as young people do, and I think it helped her through. She met your father there. They met Pastor Blair just as he was creaming off the congregation to form his own church, and that was it. We lost her.'

'It scares me,' Beth said softly, 'what the church has done to Mum.'

Randolph held her hand. 'It scared Heather and me, too. But what can you say? If you try to argue with these people, they dismiss it as the arguments of the Devil. We just let her get on with it. We didn't like the way she brought up you and Luke, but how could we stop her, short of getting you taken into care? She's our *daughter*. We couldn't have her children taken away!'

'Do you know something?' Beth said bitterly. 'I wish you had. You don't know the half of it! She thrashed Luke every few days, for the flimsiest reasons or no reason at all; she just had to do it. And Dad did nothing to stop it! She did it when he was out of the house but he must have known; you must have suspected, too! And the miserable bloody lives we led, feeling guilty, hating ourselves, never having any fun. I think Mum was sick, actually. But who noticed, who helped her? No one!'

Looking distressed, her grandfather said, 'Beth, why didn't you ever tell us?'

'How could I?' Beth flared. 'That would have been to suggest Mum was capable of doing wrong, when she'd trained me to believe that everything she did was right! Complaining would only have got us into more trouble. I was so terrified of her! And you'd never have believed she could possibly be as bad as she was, because she's your daughter! You still don't believe me now, do you?'

Her grandfather rubbed his face. 'I don't know what to say. I suppose you're right, absolutely right. I could bear to believe Livvy was strict, but not that she was cruel.'

'You and Gran weren't there when I had Eirian. You abandoned us. Everyone abandoned us. Sorry if I sound bitter, but there it is.'

'You have every right. I really believed Livvy would accept the child, given time. She gave us the impression everything was all right; if only we'd known the truth.' He squeezed her hand. 'I would have interfered, but I can't turn back time. I regret it terribly. Lord, there's so much to regret.'

Realizing that her grandfather was genuinely sorry, Beth found it hard to stay angry. 'I suppose it's as much my own fault as anyone's,' she said. 'If only I'd shown my bruises to the doctor, or said something to the social worker – but I was too scared. Even when I escaped, I daren't turn round and fight my parents. All I could do was disappear.'

'You lost your faith in your family; any left in God?'

Beth laughed. 'Oh, that. I lost that a long time ago, not long after I met Rhianwen, actually. That's why she and Mum fell out, isn't it? Mum tried to save Rhianwen, but she wouldn't be saved. Rhianwen was everything Mum was frightened of – and now, so am I.'

Randolph said nothing to this. He asked, 'Have you any photos of the little one?'

Beth fished her wallet out of her black quilted jacket, and took out a photograph. 'This is Eirian about eighteen months ago. Rhianwen took it.'

'Oh, she's gorgeous. Is she sitting on the steps of a caravan?'

'Yes. We lived in a caravan.' Beth explained about the Prima-rolas. 'But I've got a house and a job now, and Eirian's doing ever so well at school.'

'Wait,' Randolph said suddenly. 'Did you say Rhianwen took it?'

'Yes,' Beth said evenly. 'She knew where we were. I knew I could trust her not to tell anyone.'

'Christ,' Randolph said through his teeth. 'She knew and didn't tell us? Typical.'

'Why should she, after you blackmailed her into moving?'

He lowered his eyes, as if ashamed. 'But you haven't seen –'

'No, I haven't seen Morgan since.'

'Well, that's something, at least.'

'Why?' said Beth, annoyed. 'Why is it something?'

'I only meant, well, a young man who is capable of behaving that irresponsibly would only have ruined your life.' Randolph looked at his watch. 'I'm sorry, Beth, I really *must* go and see Dr Bown now. May I keep the photo, to show Heather?'

'I'd rather you didn't.'

'Maybe you're right.' He gave it back. 'Can I tell them I've seen you? Not where you are, just that you're all right. You're over eighteen, there's nothing Olivia can do to you!'

'I know,' said Beth, 'but please don't. I'm not ready.'

Randolph nodded. 'As you wish. I won't say a word. I'm very good at keeping secrets, Beth. Patients' confidentiality, you know.'

They put on their coats and walked outside. Beth unchained the bicycle from the car park fence.

'I hope we'll meet again,' he said. 'You can come and see us any time, you know.'

Beth nodded. 'It was lovely to see you, Granddad.' As he bent to kiss her cheek, she asked softly, 'Why *do* you hate Rhianwen and Morgan so much?'

'*I* don't hate them. But Morgan shouldn't have done what he did to you. One of those unfortunate things, everyone's fault and no one's.'

Beth didn't know why she still felt the need to defend Rhianwen, after what had passed between them, but the old Rhianwen she'd idolized was still alive in her mind. 'Was that really a reason for my mum to force Rhianwen into selling the cottage? It was her *home*. She had the cats and everything. It's a horrible thing, to be forced out of your home for, well, for something that wasn't her fault. Just a mistake teenagers make all the time.'

Randolph looked puzzled. 'But you say you've seen her. Didn't she tell you?'

'What?'

'She didn't sell the cottage. She's living in it again. It stood empty for two or three years, then she took it off the market and moved back in. She's there now, I understand, so you needn't shed any tears for her.'

Chapter Fifteen

'I T must have been a hell of a shock,' said Steve, 'seeing your grandfather again after all this time.'

'It was,' said Beth. 'But I'm glad I saw him.'

'Will you go and see your gran?'

'Probably. When I'm ready.'

'What about your parents?'

'I don't know.'

'And Rhianwen?'

Steve was fascinated. He had to know everything.

'For heaven's sake, I don't know what to do!' she cried. 'Hold me, Steve. I'm confused.'

He held her tight. Two candles lit the room, flames dancing. Eirian and Sam were upstairs, asleep.

Steve kissed her. She could feel his heart beating where his chest pressed hard against her breasts. His hands went inside her shirt, and hers inside his, and his skin felt creamily smooth.

'Don't stop,' Beth whispered, as his fingertips moved over her spine, came up and round to enfold her breasts. She clung to him and bit his neck, leaving a bruise; licking and tasting the tender skin. Steve gasped. Beth felt the blood beating hotly through her, a desperate fire taking over from thought. Her hands slid down to caress his buttocks and thighs, to struggle with his zip. Steve kissed her again, more deeply now, his tongue and warm breath mingling with hers. Then he looked at her in a kind of helpless amazement.

'And please don't be gentle with me,' said Beth.

They undressed each other and made love there on the sofa without finesse, with a fiercely animal haste; stone-cold sober and utterly unembarrassed.

Beth had gone on the pill a few weeks ago, just in case.

Steve's body was thicker set than Morgan's but still as beautiful as ivory, long limbed and hairless. The hair that curled around the eager stem of his penis was blond; she barely had time to notice that as she drew him urgently into her.

It felt wonderful to have Steve inside her. Like the breaking of a seven-year spell. Beth came very fast, and so intensely that she almost threw him off on to the floor.

Then they had a fit of the giggles.

Finally they lay wrapped up in the glow of the fire, dreaming their private dreams. Did he imagine I was Katy? she wondered. Did I wish he was Morgan? I don't think so. Does it even matter?

Beth felt strangely melancholy then.

By the way, Steve, that bastard Luke Herne who stole your missus: I'm his sister.

She thought it, but she didn't say it.

In her room, Eirian heard her mother and Steve laughing downstairs and she hugged her knees to her chest, feeling isolated. She was meant to be in bed, but she was sitting instead on the floor of her room, her back against the roughly plastered white wall. Why was it that the sound of a man giggling chilled her? Nothing she could consciously remember.

Yet it made her feel cold and alone. She had felt like this, ever since they'd hanged Guendolen's mother, and tried to drown Eirian herself.

Eirian was good at burying her feelings. She got that from her father, though she didn't know it.

She couldn't let Beth know she was frightened, or Beth would worry. Nor could Eirian give in to her terror, or the ugly men would have won. Even after she'd heard the Midwife's dreadful screams and seen her dangling from the rope, even after she'd endured the thick green waters of the pond, Eirian couldn't let herself go under the waves of fear.

I must be strong, she told herself. Mum doesn't want me to go back to the other place, but she doesn't understand, I *must*. It isn't finished. Guendolen needs me.

Eostre, Cerridwen and Bast came to Eirian in the darkness.

They paced around her, white, gold, grey, rubbing their cheeks on her hands, placing their paws on her drawn-up knees.

'Goddess, please give me strength,' Eirian said under her breath, looking into the golden eyes of Bast.

Bast hissed, her lips drawn back from thin sharp teeth, her eyes terrible.

'Yes,' said Eirian. 'I know.'

The whispering began like a wave all around her and through her, the voices of all the lost ones throughout the unimaginable sweep of time.

She was drowning in the voices. Sinking through a black ocean full of blood.

A shape in the water. She saw a shadow creature gliding by, a brief flash of ivory like the Wand of Power. The unicorn, screaming, spilling its blood as the Horn was ripped from its forehead.

Then the face. A terrible, darkly glowing face with the eyes of a cat, seen through rippling water. Consuming Eirian. Demanding too much.

'I can't,' whispered Eirian, clinging hard to Bast so she didn't drown. She had an absolute terror of drowning now.

You must.

Eirian didn't know the face. Some deep part of her understood, but her conscious mind did not. Until her subconscious and her intellect connected, she had only instinct to guide her. A child's simple certainty.

'I must go back,' she said. 'I can't leave Guendolen.'

Bast, heavy in her arms, struggled and gave an angry, '*Mrrowr!*' Then she scratched Eirian's hand, and fled.

The pain brought Eirian back to reality, and she looked at the red scratch mark. It seemed to mean something. Blood, sacrifice, life, love.

'Mum wants it to be over. But it had no beginning, so how can it ever end?'

Every weekend, an assortment of Steve's friends would drop round, usually without invitation.

Beth didn't mind. She liked them. If she had minded, she would have said so.

There was a spoilt Pre-Raphaelite beauty called Cherry, a short, spherical girl called Bryony with black and pink hair, and a thin and very intense blonde feminist called Tash. Tash lectured Beth about a single mother's rights and child maintenance, and how wise she was to bring up her daughter without an oppressive male influence.

'Take the bastard to the cleaner's,' said Tash. 'He owes you seven years' upkeep for two minutes of self-indulgence!'

'It was rather more than two minutes,' Beth said drily, not knowing why she still needed to defend Morgan over anything. 'But I don't want to. I don't know where he is. I don't want anything from him.' Then she diplomatically changed the subject, and did so every time Tash tried to bring it up.

There were thin young men, called Zak, Tag and Chez, with long hair fountaining from half-shaved heads, ripped jeans and jewellery of teeth and skulls. These were the other members of Steve's alleged rock group.

There were a pair of goths with frantic black hair, black nail varnish and panda eyes. The female, who had an imposing presence and a dominant personality, called herself Isis; her boyfriend, Rob, seemed to have no purpose but to hang around looking sullen. These two came round less often, having business elsewhere; Isis was a Wiccan priestess with her own coven. Occasionally she brought some of the members with her, precious young people who would sit devotedly round her feet.

Beth sensed some antagonism from Isis, who seemed to see Beth as a rival. Beth, not remotely interested in competing with her, responded with unconcerned friendliness.

Steve had met most of them at art college; now they were librarians, bricklayers, gardeners or unemployed, but they wanted to be poets, writers, artists and musicians. They'd sit about on Beth's floor all weekend, drinking wine, smoking pot and discussing the meaning of life. Cherry and Bryony had convoluted relationships with Zak, Tag and Chez, which led to bitchy arguments, tearful exits, and emotional reconciliations. Tash remained above it all, an oracle of bitter wisdom.

Sam and Eirian would play quietly as if oblivious to all this, creating, as children could, a separate world.

Steve's group never actually seemed to rehearse. Occasionally while they sat around, they'd have a session with acoustic guitars, a saxophone and a bodhran. Actually they were quite good, Beth thought, but they rarely finished a song. They knew they weren't going to make it, so apathy had set in.

They were posers, as Steve had said. They were also disappointed dreamers, still young enough to have hope. Underneath their freakish masks, Beth found them gentle, harmless, rather lovable.

If Beth had had a neurotic temperament, they might have driven her mad, but she was developing a pleasant sense of serenity as time went on. She had to; it was self-defence against the craziness of the past, the relentlessness of day-to-day survival, and the lurking threat of Eirian's other life.

Eirian seemed to have put the experience behind her more readily than Beth had. It was as if Beth were drawing tranquillity from Eirian, rather than the other way round. Sometimes she wondered what effect her present lifestyle would have on Eirian, but what was the alternative? To banish her friends, and pretend to be respectable?

It wouldn't work. This was the way her life had evolved. Steve's friends kept coming round because they'd fallen in love with Beth.

'We think it's brilliant that Steve's met you,' Cherry said one day. 'That Katy was such a bitch, totally selfish, always putting him down. He deserved someone better.'

Beth didn't know why they were drawn to her. They seemed to see her as an earth-mother, a heroine, a genuine wise-woman of the woods, one of the faerie folk. They brought her gifts for the house: mirrors, cushions, rugs, incense. Clothes and jewellery, too. Maybe they were only projecting their fantasies on to her, but Beth certainly had the ability to make them laugh, to sort out their problems and dry their tears, even to cure their ailments with the herbs she grew in her garden. She couldn't help responding to their love. Playing the role of friendly witch.

I'm not turning into my mother, Beth thought. I'm turning into Rhianwen.

Steve brought a battery-powered cassette player, and introduced her to haunting music she had never heard before; the Sisters of Mercy, Joy Division, Dead Can Dance, the Cocteau Twins, All About Eve, and many others.

For the first time ever, Beth had a social life. On a Saturday night, as long as someone was willing to stay behind and look after Sam and Eirian, the rest would go to a gig in a nearby town, or maybe to a few pubs. Beth began to feel that she was rejoining the human race at last.

Sex with Steve was comfortable, affectionate and fulfilling. Beth found it hard to believe it could be so lacking in danger; there was no risk of pregnancy, no fear of being found out and punished. How things have changed, she thought. Great, I am now sleeping with a married man, but nobody gives a damn.

Steve was not demanding. Some nights he would have been happy to fall asleep, if Beth had not initiated love-making. Was this another of Katy's complaints? Beth wondered. At least he seemed to have got over his guilt about Katy.

With the encouragement of Cherry and Bryony, Beth was taking an interest in her appearance. On a Saturday, if Beth could get time off from the farmhouse, they would go shopping in Tamworth, Lichfield or Birmingham, scouring second-hand shops and markets in search of the velvet and lace and deep-dyed cottons they loved. Conventional fashions held no interest for them. Beth came out of plain black and began to experiment with dark jewel colours and styles that were less gothic than mediaeval, Victorian, romantic: fitted bodices and long skirts, velvet coats with slashed sleeves worn with high-heeled boots, lace shawls, crushed silks.

Arriving home after their first fruitful expedition, Cherry and Bryony dressed Beth, did her hair and make-up, and presented her to Steve, who almost fell over.

'Who is that masked woman?' said Tash.

'Look at yourself,' said Steve, ushering her upstairs to confront the long mirror, which had been a present from Bryony. 'You look stunning, Beth.'

Looking back at her was a creature she barely recognized. A tall, slim woman with black hair rippling to her waist, a pale oval face with red lips and exotically painted eyes; long legs encased in skin-tight black leather, high black boots, a tightly fitting frock-coat of plum velvet whose skirt, open at the front, came down to her ankles at the back. Necklaces and bracelets of bronze, with crimson stones. A shawl of midnight-blue lace, speckled with gold; mismatched earrings, a sun and a moon; heavy silver rings, set with garnets and amber, over black lace gloves.

She suddenly saw herself as striking and, maybe, even beautiful, in an unconventional way. She had transformed from scruffy goth to elegant Cleopatra.

'D'you think I dare go out like this?'

'You're joking!' said Steve. 'You've got to! You'll knock people's eyes out!'

Beth didn't look as if she had dressed up; she looked as if she couldn't dress any other way. This is me, she thought, pleased and allowing herself to be a little vain for once. The sorceress.

When they went out, crammed into Chez's van, on a tour of the local pubs – Tash nobly staying behind to babysit – Beth was stared at wherever they went.

Although her companions also dressed unconventionally, Beth was the most striking. Like-minded young people regarded her with admiration. The more conventional seemed taken aback, and those men who thought the measure of female beauty was a short skirt and a prodigious cleavage looked at her with outright disgust. This pleased Beth immensely. The last thing she wanted was to attract men like that. To scare them off, though, was fun.

And Beth knew she would continue to adorn herself for their shocked eyes. The time had come to re-create herself. Another disguise, perhaps, but the right one.

These rich colours were hers. These old-fashioned, lush materials and antique jewels connected her subtly to a mediaeval age that had only existed in the dreaming eyes of artists.

I haven't turned into Rhianwen, Beth thought. I've become myself.

Eirian felt the other place calling to her all the time, yet she couldn't pass through. She thought constantly about Guendolen; it was unbearable, not being able to reach her. Eirian was worried. The older she grew – she was eight now – the further away the other place seemed.

I don't want to grow up, she thought, if it means I can't help Guen!

Unless she was putting up barriers to protect herself. The last time had been so bad.

She dreamed and worried, her chin resting on her hand, seeing nothing. And suddenly a sharp voice was calling her.

'Eirian! I asked you a question! It's simple enough. Where was Jesus born?'

Scripture class, taken by the headmistress, who had never liked Eirian. They were sitting in a group round a table, while Miss Townsend taught them Bible stories.

Eirian had sat through these weekly classes in silence for months, not wanting to draw attention to herself. But today, something possessed her to stand up and stare the woman in the face. Some demon of mischief. 'Scholars can't prove that Jesus even existed,' said Eirian. 'The gospels are full of inconsistencies. Even the meaning of the word virgin has been misinterpreted. Why do you teach us myths as if they are facts?'

Miss Townsend gaped at Eirian, utterly stunned.

'Christians believe the Bible is true,' she said acidly. 'And we are Christians in this school, Eirian.'

'I'm not. I believe in older myths. They might not be true either, but they make more sense. The point of myths is –'

'That is enough! Sit down.' Miss Townsend had gone crimson, and the other children were silent, staring uncomprehendingly at Eirian.

'Millions of people have been killed because of the Bible,' said Eirian. 'It's not the word of God, it's a political weapon.'

The headmistress swooped, a cardigan-clad bird of prey, and seized Eirian by the arm, hurting her. 'Go and sit in the corridor outside my office. You can stay there until your mother comes for you.'

Eirian sat on a chair, looking at a white wall. She was shaking, but defiant. She knew she shouldn't have argued with her teacher but she just couldn't keep quiet.

The wall dissolved.

Eirian found herself looking at the door of a church. On the lintel was a carved face made of leaves, with laughing eyes, and fruits and sheaves of wheat flowing from his open mouth. The Green Man. The sacrificed king who died to bring life.

She moved into the cool shadow, and in the stone interior she saw two figures. Guendolen and a priest, a young man with gentle grey eyes who reminded Eirian of Steve.

He was clasping Guendolen's hands between his own as if in prayer, but he wasn't praying, and he was looking at her with something more than compassion.

'Tell me where they've taken the Horn of Power,' said Guendolen.

'I cannot,' the priest said, distressed. 'Nor can I give you sanctuary. If I do, they will hang me too.'

'I would not put a friend in danger,' said Guen. 'But as a friend, tell me: why have they brought this grief to us? Why do they distort and take away our beliefs, which never did harm to any?'

'To save your souls! There is only one Truth, one way.'

'But it is a distortion, to reduce our Goddess to a vessel, and elevate her consort and son above her!'

The priest couldn't answer. He was dazzled by Guendolen but he didn't understand what she meant, any more than Miss Townsend had understood Eirian's arguments.

'It's only a tipping of the balance,' said Guendolen. 'It will right itself. The teaching of love and forgiveness is good.'

'Yes,' the priest said fervently. 'To love and forgive is to create the Kingdom of Heaven.'

'So why do these churchmen not practise what the Son taught?'

The priest gripped her upper arms. His face was full of pain and contradiction. Finally he said, 'The Devil works through them.'

'But they claim God works through them, and the Devil through my kind. How shall we know what to believe? Either we believe what the men with authority and wealth tell us, or we die.'

'There is no Devil in you, Guendolen.'

'There is no Devil,' she said. 'The evil is caused by the reversal of the natural order.'

'God created the world.'

'Or the Goddess gave birth to the world. The god was her lover, not her lord and master. They have forgotten it, because they hate us and love power. If it took centuries to forget, it will take centuries to remember. We will never know the freedom of the Goddess again in our lifetime. But I can show you it, for a little while. Come out into the forest.'

The priest obeyed, walking meekly with Guendolen as she took his hand and led him outside into the greenwood. Eirian hid behind a tree-trunk and watched.

'I did not become a priest,' he said, 'to accuse innocent men and women of witchcraft and see them slain.'

'Kneel down with me,' said Guendolen. They knelt, hands clasped. 'This is the real cathedral. Hers. There is nothing else. Only the wind in the leaves and the moon in the lake and the seed in the earth. The son who dies and rises did not mean you to lose this.'

The priest was kissing her.

They took off their garments and lay naked in the grass, entwining convulsively, as instinctive and sinless as animals. Cleansed and made beautiful by ecstatic love.

Eirian watched. She felt a strange heat running all through

her from her mouth to the tips of her toes, but she didn't understand it.

Afterwards, the young priest wept on Guendolen's breast. 'I would marry you and keep you with me for ever, if I could. I've taken a vow – but I'd break it for you; priests do have mistresses.'

'Tell me where they've hidden the Horn of Rebirth,' she whispered.

'They took it to the cathedral in the town,' he said, 'but you cannot go there! They will capture you if they see you!'

'I am going to die anyway,' said Guendolen, 'but the Horn will endure for ever. We must take it back. It's sacred. Their touch profanes it, the men who hate life.'

'Don't go, Guendolen,' said the priest. 'If I lost you I should die.'

'Eirian?' said a voice.

She blinked. Beth's face came into focus above her.

'Were you day-dreaming? Come on, we've been summoned. What on earth have you been up to?'

'Nothing, Mum,' said Eirian, putting her hand in Beth's.

As they stood before the headmistress in her office, more like two naughty children than mother and child, Eirian couldn't put the scene in the forest out of her mind. Day-dreaming? If Mum needed to ask, Eirian thought, that must mean I went there without her! I don't want Mum to worry, so if I can go alone, it's better.

Eirian felt excited and terrified by the scene she'd witnessed. Guendolen is alone and in danger, she thought, but the priest helped her. They weren't all bad. Oh, let me out of this stupid school so I can go back and help Guen!

'I don't know what kind of ideas you are putting in your daughter's head,' Miss Townsend was saying, 'but they're dangerous, destructive and utterly unsuitable for an eight year old.'

'She's interested in religion,' said Beth. 'I try to be objective in discussing it with her.'

'Objective, indeed? It sounded to me as if she was parroting phrases she'd learned from an adult. A child of her age could not possibly have understood the complex and down-right bizarre things she was saying!'

'I do understand!' Eirian said indignantly.

Beth said, 'I can assure you, Miss Townsend, I haven't taught her to parrot anything. You said yourself she's intelligent. I don't know where she gets it from. But I do agree she's too young to be told one belief is right and another is wrong. She can make up her own mind when she's old enough.'

Beth was cool, polite and magnificent with her coat of chestnut velvet and her raven hair. Eirian felt proud of her. She made Miss Townsend look so dowdy!

'Do you *have* a religion, Ms Primarola?' the teacher asked sternly.

'Yes,' said Beth. 'Witchcraft.' Eirian had never heard her admit it before.

Miss Townsend looked as if she'd swallowed a marble. But she recovered herself and said, 'Would you like Eirian to be excused from scripture class on religious grounds? She wouldn't be the only one. We only have a few children from other cultures but we do try to accommodate them.'

'We're not from another culture,' Beth said stiffly. 'It's up to Eirian. She can learn about the Bible if she wants.'

'It's quite interesting,' said Eirian.

The headmistress glowered at her. Eirian wasn't afraid, but a sudden cold dizziness seized her, and she remembered the eyes of the Judge and the Inquisitor while they ordered her to be tied up with rocks and drowned. Their eyes had been impervious, like that.

'I can only teach her if she is going to pay attention and not argue with what she is being taught,' said Miss Townsend. 'It disturbs the other children.'

'I can't help it if she has a mind of her own,' said Beth. 'But I'm sure she didn't mean to cause any disruption. I'll talk to her.'

'I think you should.' Miss Townsend's voice lost its hard edge; she sounded almost awkward, and her eyes managed to be both concerned and accusing at once. 'To be frank, I don't know what we are going to do with her. I don't agree with labelling children prodigies, but her level of intelligence really is alarmingly high for her age. We aren't equipped to deal with children with special needs at this school.'

Beth looked dismayed. 'But this is the only school! I can't afford to send her to a better' – Beth clamped her lips over the offending word too late – 'I mean, to a special school.'

'I know,' Miss Townsend said acidly, 'and we'll do our best for her. The last thing we want is for Eirian to feel in any way abnormal. But you should be aware that over-intelligent children can have severe emotional problems in later life.'

'I'll bear it in mind,' Beth said, polite but frigid. 'Thank you.'

The meeting at an end, Beth marched Eirian out of the school, across the playground and along the road to the bus stop.

'Bloody woman,' Beth muttered. 'How can she take a gift and make it sound like a handicap or a deadly threat? Jealousy? She wants everyone to be exactly the bloody same, she can't bear anyone to be different!'

Her mother was angry, but she sounded just a little scared, too. Eirian said, 'Mum?'

'Yes, love?'

'Am I abnormal?'

'Of course you're not!' Beth was almost too fervent. 'There's nothing wrong with being bright. It just upsets people who are less clever, sometimes.'

'I didn't mean to be naughty, I said what I felt.'

'I know. They don't take kindly to being answered back, these people. I know it's annoying but you'll have to keep your thoughts to yourself until you're older. At least she didn't expel you.'

'What does that mean?'

'You know, throw you out of school. What's the matter?' Beth bent down and stroked Eirian's face, looking anxious. 'It's all right, darling, nothing's going to happen.'

'I thought she might drown me or hang me,' Eirian said softly. 'I mean, I thought they weren't allowed to do that these days, but then I thought, what if I'm wrong and they *can* do it?'

'Christ,' said Beth, looking stricken. 'You were thinking that? Of course they don't do it these days! Eirian, what am I going to do with you?'

'She can't do it, but she'd like to,' said Eirian.

'Darling, when I met you in the corridor, you weren't daydreaming, were you? You were – travelling.'

Eirian nodded. 'Didn't you come with me?'

'I felt something.' Beth sounded uncertain. 'But I wasn't with you. Was it as bad as before?'

'No.' Eirian sensed that her mother didn't want to hear what had happened: that Beth thought she could make it stop by pretending it wasn't happening.

'Eirian, I don't want you going there alone!'

'I can't help it, Mum. I must. Don't worry about me.'

Darkness drew in early that night, and Beth lit extra lamps, feeling oppressed. She'd been tempted to ask Margaret if they could stay at the farmhouse that night, with electric lights and television to ward off this eerie feeling, but she couldn't. Steve and the others would be arriving any minute.

Eirian seemed unaffected by Beth's nerves. She was in the other room, happily drawing by candlelight.

The kitchen door opened. Sam came running in, and disappeared into the sitting-room to join Eirian; Steve stood in the doorway, his arms folded over the bedraggled Indian cotton shirt he was wearing.

'Where were you after school?' he asked. 'I waited but there was no sign of you. I was worried.'

'I had to collect Eirian early.' Beth leaned across the sink to draw the curtains, but still the darkness bled in. 'She was in trouble again.'

'Oh, no.' Steve looked dismayed. 'What for, being too clever?'

'That's the understatement of the century.'

He came to her and they hugged each other. Steve felt solid and comforting. He was always there for her. Beth didn't know what she would do without him now.

As Beth put the kettle on the stove and began to relate her exchange with Miss Townsend, Chez's van drew up and disgorged the gang. So she had to start again from the beginning as they crowded into the kitchen, insisting on knowing what had happened. Isis and Rob were with them; must be a special occasion, thought Beth.

'What a bitch!' said Cherry as Beth related what the headmistress had said.

'Fascist,' said Chez.

'She's a victim of patriarchal brainwashing,' said Tash.

The others murmured in agreement and sympathy.

'We could do something about her,' said Isis.

There was a silence. The candle flames flickered, and Beth felt cold.

'Like what?' said Steve.

Beth looked at Isis, who was sitting beside Rob at the kitchen table. Isis stared back flatly. Her face was round and moon-white, her hair, eyes and lips drastically black against the pallor.

'No,' said Beth.

'Why not?' Isis stood up and came towards her. 'It works, you know. I've done things before.'

'Miss Townsend is just an old harridan.' Beth turned away to wash some mugs, feeling evasive. 'She doesn't know any better. She's trying to teach the children what she feels is right, that's all. It's not worth it!'

'What are you frightened of?' Isis asked.

'Nothing,' said Beth. But she was thinking of Bernard. All she'd done was to look at him, hating him, and he'd died. No, no. It had been a coincidence but, all the same, she couldn't take the risk.

Isis grabbed her wrist and Beth dropped a mug, splashing soapy water over herself. 'So why are you shaking?'

'"An ye harm no one, do what ye will,"' Beth murmured. '"*An ye harm no one.*" I don't do that sort of thing.'

'Suit yourself,' said Isis, letting go. 'All the same, we must do *something*. Tonight's special.'

'Why?' Cherry asked.

'Full moon, my child. We should celebrate the Esbat. You always wanted to know what we do within the coven; well, I'll show you tonight, if anyone's interested.'

'Yeah, why not?' said everyone, fascinated but trying to sound cool.

'So, why aren't you with your coven tonight?' asked Beth.

Isis shrugged. 'Only a couple of them could make it so I called the meeting off.'

Beth went on washing up, not speaking. She didn't want to celebrate the Esbat with Isis, but the idea had taken on its own momentum. It felt wrong, but she didn't know why.

'When are we going to do it?' Cherry demanded.

'Keep your voices down,' said Steve, pointing at the sitting-room door.

'After the children have gone to bed,' Isis whispered. 'We'll go out in the fields.'

'I'm not taking my clothes off,' said Zak. 'It's too bloody cold.'

Isis rolled her eyes. 'You don't have to.'

'But who's going to be the priestess, Isis or Beth?' Bryony asked guilelessly. 'It should be Beth.'

Isis gave Bryony a look that could have frozen flesh into stone; Beth turned, drying her hands on a towel, just in time to witness it.

'Why should it be Beth?' Isis said thinly.

'Because Beth – well, she's – it's her house and –' Bryony subsided, flustered.

Beth understood. Whether Isis was genuine or on a power trip, Beth wasn't sure; a bit of both, she suspected. Obviously she had relished being the wise woman of the group, the mystical one. But now Isis felt threatened and usurped by Beth, and she wanted to prove something tonight.

'Hey, let's be democratic,' said Steve. 'We'll take a vote. All those in favour of Beth . . .'

All the hands in the room, except those of Rob and Isis, began to rise.

'No!' Beth snapped.

They looked at her in surprise, and their hands sank down.

'Isis is the priestess, not me. Really, she's in charge. I wouldn't know what to do.'

They looked at her in disbelief, but Isis's face was sheet lightning. *They like me better, and she feels I've patronized her,* Beth thought. *Will she work a spell against me for this? Will it work? Damn this, I just want us to be friends. Oh, shit!*

'Who wants tea, who wants beer?' Beth said brightly.

Half an hour after the children had gone to bed, the adults filed softly out of the cottage. Tash willingly stayed behind to babysit, insisting that rituals weren't her scene. Beth had wanted to stay in with her, but Steve persuaded her to join in.

Beth had to admit she was curious. The Primarolas' celebrations of the seasons had been simply that; unthreatening and joyful. This was something else.

The moon was huge and low on the horizon, the colour of honeyed milk. The fields were grey and silver.

Cherry wanted to go into the woods behind the cottage, but Isis insisted they must work in the open. So they climbed the five-bar gate and went into the meadow on the other side of the lane. Now Cherry was sulking, and complaining that her feet and dress were soaked.

'You'd be even wetter if we were in the woods,' Bryony pointed out.

'Are you all right?' Steve asked, holding Beth's hand. 'You seem a bit distracted.'

'I don't know what it is. I'm fine. Do you often do this?'

He laughed softly, and said in her ear, 'This is the first time. Isis has always been mysterious about it before. She's doing it to impress you, Beth, so be impressed.'

'I am, I am.'

Isis favoured paraphernalia and portentous ritual. She had to lay a cloth in the centre of the field, and place on it her athame, censer, candles, herbs, cord and other tools before they could begin. Then she must consecrate the space, drawing pentagrams in the air with the tip of the athame, uttering invocations in some unknown language that, Beth suspected, she had invented herself.

None of this is necessary, Beth thought. To dance in the moonlight, to *feel*, that would be enough.

Still, Isis must do what she felt appropriate. It created atmosphere, at least.

'Now join hands,' said Isis. 'We will breathe together and meditate on the power of our Lady Moon.'

They formed a circle, Beth between Steve and Cherry. Immediately Beth felt electricity in the silence. The chilly autumn wind wove around them. After a few minutes, Isis began to chant syllables in a deep monotone. Other voices took up the chant, forming a weirdly moving dissonance.

Beth had felt this before. Energy, created by their joined hands, vibrating throats and their mutual will. It thickened the air between them like static. But it felt wrong. There was an underlying malice in it, not joy.

The humming grew stronger and wilder. Beth joined in, couldn't help herself; she tried to utter words of reverence to the Moon, mother Goddess, but the words wouldn't come. Only this savage atonal chant.

This wasn't a celebration. It was a Working.

Beth wanted to break away and leave, but she couldn't. She was woven firmly into the circle, couldn't break it without scattering the energy and calling down Isis's wrath upon her.

It was seductive, this singing up of power. She couldn't stop. The moon was coming down among them, not round and pure, but swollen, blood-dappled, and rippling as if through water.

Eirian lay in bed, unable to sleep. The moonlight through her curtains was dazzling.

She wanted to sleep, to slip back into the other place, to hold Guendolen's hand and say, 'I haven't left you. I'm here. I'll help you.'

But it wouldn't happen. Her brain remained stubbornly alert, tied to the present. She'd travelled easily once; now it was often hard.

There was a weird sound, more in the bones of her skull than in her ears. A vibration, like voices humming. It frightened her.

Eirian pushed the covers back and got out of bed. She felt unreal. The silver light and the eerie voices had caught her up in a trance. As if sleepwalking, she pulled on her jeans, trainers and sweatshirt. The three cats sat in a patch of moonlight, watching her.

If the other place wouldn't come to her, she must go out and find it.

Not a sound from Sam's room. Eirian tiptoed downstairs and peeped round the door at the base of the stairs into the sitting-room. Tash was there, lying on the sofa, her head hanging to one side so her short yellow hair glowed brightly in the lamplight. Fast asleep.

Eirian slipped past, ran across the kitchen and let herself out of the back door.

The chanting grew louder. She knew it was something to do with her mother, so that was all right. Yet how eerie it was! It made her feel as if she were floating.

Eirian climbed through the fence that bounded the back garden, and entered the woods. The chanting faded. Branches stroked and slapped her, coating her with dew. She couldn't see, so she kept missing her footing, and the grass seemed to twine round her ankles, as if the wood wanted to wrap her in its thin arms, to kiss her and soak her in its cold juices.

The cats were with her. She couldn't see them but she could sense them around her, guiding her.

The cats are the messengers of the Goddess, said a voice in her head.

Her mother's voice.

An owl screamed. No other sound. For a moment Eirian was utterly lost, and she lashed out at the foliage as if fighting unseen demons.

The thrumming in her head stopped her and her hand closed on a twig for support. The trees in front formed an oddly flat kaleidoscope of greys. The sound grew stronger. A rhythmic humming: no, a ringing, *dong, dong, dong.*

The grey kaleidoscope resolved itself into a great wall of stone. It wasn't undergrowth hampering her, but the weight of her long skirts and shawl. It was day, but the clouds were so low and thick it could almost have been night. The ringing of the bell was deafening and the twig in her palm became warm and solid – a human hand.

'The cathedral,' said Guendolen.

She looked down at Eirian and her square, ruddy face glowed; she wasn't beautiful like Beth but she was like a goddess in her strength. Behind her, Eirian could see worshippers walking in through the lych-gate and along the path between the gravestones. The trees swayed and the birds sang. The whole town, it seemed, was pouring into the cathedral from the mud-lined streets. They carried the stench of refuse on their skirts and boots.

'Will you help me, good sister?' Guendolen asked. 'I have never asked so much of you as I ask now, but it is our last hope.'

'I came to help you,' said Eirian.

'They hanged my mother,' Guen said quietly.

'I know. I saw. I tried to stop them but I couldn't!'

Guendolen touched Eirian's cheek with a tenderness that made Eirian want to cry. 'No one could stop them. I heard that they tried to drown a demon in the shape of a girl, but when they pulled up the rope, there was no one on the end.'

'Were they frightened?'

'They thought the Devil had been among them.'

'Good,' said Eirian. And Guendolen gave a faint, ghostly smile.

'The Horn of Power is in the cathedral, but they keep it locked away and only bring it out for the service. My friend told me.'

'The priest?'

'Yes,' said Guendolen, swallowing. 'They aren't all evil.'

'I know that,' said Eirian.

'So we must take it during the service, or we'll never get it back. And then we must hide it where they'll *never* find it.'

Guen took Eirian's hand and they joined the procession of worshippers; two sisters walking into the vaulted gloom with heads bowed.

Eirian had never been inside a church before. It took her breath away. So much stone, arching like the sky above them. The windows held coloured pictures. There were great pillars, rows of hard seats, and at the far end of the aisle the altar, railed off and unobtainably high and distant.

The cathedral smelled like a cave. But that smell, of damp stone and mortar, was swamped by the farmyard stench of the congregation. They brought with them the foulness of the streets, of homes infested by vermin, smoke and rotten food, of suppurating flesh and disease-clogged lungs. The solemnity was fractured by endless, racking coughs.

Then, through the fetor, Eirian caught a peppery, evocative note that thrilled her inexplicably. Clouds of frankincense from burners on thick brass chains.

The looming mystery of the cathedral made Eirian feel very small and isolated. As an expression of God's majesty, it was awe-inspiring, but this was a God of stone: aloof, unchanging, unyielding, sterile.

Eirian was not converted. She felt shocked and sad.

They found two seats on the central aisle, not as far forward as Guendolen had wanted, but the front pews were reserved for the wealthy, and the peasants must crowd in at the back.

A procession came in, to the exquisite chanting of unaccompanied male voices. The bishop in his splendid robes and mitre, his clerics, a choir of monks singing. Their deep, dark harmonies melted Eirian. She experienced again the strange feeling she'd had when she saw Guendolen and the priest making love in the forest. This grandeur was seductive.

A young priest went ahead of the bishop, carrying a candle

on a slim holder that was almost four feet long. Carved ivory, wound with a stripe of gold. Eirian tensed, recognizing the Horn of Power.

The Horn, reduced to a candlestick!

She shifted forward, but Guendolen's hand held her in place.

'When I move,' Guendolen whispered, 'don't come with me. Go down the aisle and wait by the door. Be ready to escape.'

'When?'

'Wait for the sermon. They'll start falling asleep then.'

The Horn had been placed in a holder near the pulpit. Candle wax dripped down its sides, filling the carving and covering the gold with blank white flux.

How painfully long-winded the service seemed. There were prayers and hymns and blessings, everyone sitting, standing, kneeling on cue. How sombre it all is! Eirian thought. They sing of joy and love but there isn't any.

She stared at the Horn, misappropriated and held hostage. It shimmered and divided in her vision, a pale flame.

Eventually the bishop mounted the pulpit and began to speak. He described the virtues of being meek, poor and humble, while the candlelight gleamed on the jewels in his robes and his plump, self-satisfied face.

Eirian's palms began to sweat. She could feel Guendolen shaking beside her, but Guen's face was smooth and intent.

'Now!' Guen whispered.

And she was out of the pew like a sprinter, racing towards the pulpit. Eirian's impulse was to follow and protect her, but she did as she was told and ran the other way towards the door, looking over her shoulder as she went.

The bishop and the congregation were so shocked by Guendolen running forward that they didn't move at first. The bishop stopped in mid-parable; no one realized what she was going to do.

Guendolen grabbed the Horn off its stand. The candle fell off and hit the flagstones. Guen began to run back along the aisle towards Eirian, holding up her skirts in one hand, and she seemed to be wading slowly through a lake as she came.

'Hurry!' Eirian breathed.

Men and women began to step out of the pews into her path, shouting indignantly.

Guen fought her way past the first few, but then there were too many. The shouts grew louder. The congregation were on their feet, the cathedral in uproar. Eirian saw the bishop's attendants hurrying down towards the struggling knot of people who held Guendolen in their midst.

Eirian's breath caught hard in her chest, painful. Guen was fighting gallantly but she couldn't break free. It was over.

Suddenly Guen's head and arms emerged above the crowd, a drowning woman rising briefly and desperately to the surface.

And Guendolen hurled the Horn like a javelin, clear over the heads of her captors. Eirian saw it coming, a bolt of creamy lightning. It flew the length of the aisle and landed, sweet and true, in Eirian's hands.

She was out of the door and running. Not to the lych-gate but along the cathedral's great buttressed walls, between the gravestones towards the trees, the undergrowth, and the copse that lay beyond.

They were slow to come after her, but they were coming.

Eirian looped up her skirts, scrambled over the wall and ran on, yanking her garments loose as they snagged on brambles. She'd never run so hard before and it was no dream, it was real. The breath rasping in her throat, the hammering of her heart, the stitch in her ribs. All real.

Run. Save the sacred Horn.

But what's the point? she thought in sudden despair. I will escape home sooner or later but I can't take the Horn with me. How can I hide it? I can't stop, they'll catch me, but I'll have to stop soon, I can't breathe.

Daylight ahead. The end of the trees. A lane, where horses and carts and cattle would run her down; and behind, the angry shouting men, gaining on her.

Eirian clutched the Horn to her, closed her eyes tight in pain, and felt the ground fall away beneath her.

The energy swirled and glowed within the circle. Beth could see it, in her mind if not with her eyes. It was full of sparks and colours, like a migraine. Building, it began to spiral, faster and faster. The voices rose. The energy span, narrowing towards the top, becoming a cone of impossible pressure, a whirlwind.

Isis, whether she had meant to or not, had called up real power. She was directly opposite Beth across the circle, her head back, her plump white arms raised.

She looked, Beth thought, both ecstatic and terrified.

Does she know what she's doing? The power must be released or it will harm us all.

In the taut pressure of the moment, Beth had a flash of terror, a premonition. Eirian!

Then she thought she heard someone calling from the direction of the cottage, faint but agitated. 'Beth! Beth, can you hear me?' Tash's voice. 'It's Eirian, she's gone!'

But Beth couldn't break free. The voice was drowned as Isis shrieked, 'Now!'

The chanting broke up into a series of hoarse screams. Cherry's and Steve's hands left Beth's as if torn loose. Beth felt and saw the cone of power break off and spin free, like a spear loosed through the vault of night.

It arched up and came down. Straight for Beth. A cone of black hatred.

Yes, Isis had needed to work against someone tonight.

Chapter Sixteen

E IRIAN was running on nothingness. She was being drawn home but she resisted. She couldn't go yet, not if it meant leaving behind the Horn and letting Guendolen down.

Eirian held the Horn to her chest, clutching it so tight that tears oozed from her eyes with the effort.

Guen's sacrifice couldn't be for nothing. Couldn't be.

The humming of voices began again. It reached her across the gulf of time, a beacon.

Eirian felt a cone of energy, like the shadow of the Horn, pulling at her. She hooked on to it, letting it concentrate in her hands, welding them to the Horn. Her palms burned. She sobbed with the pain.

The energy curled round her, like a whirlwind, and took her forward across the centuries. The Horn burned and dragged at her hands, trying to stay in its own time. It almost jerked her arms from the sockets. A rod of fire.

But the shadowy power she could feel in her own world . . . even as she seized on it, she sensed that it was destructive. Someone was in danger, but Eirian couldn't help. All she could do was to hang on with all her might.

The pain became searing, as if a red-hot rope were being dragged through her palms at speed.

Then the feeling stopped. Her feet struck solid ground. Still running, she tripped and rolled over and over on grass before colliding with a tree-trunk.

It was dark. Eirian lay stunned. She hurt all over and her chest was sore from running, but her hands were the worst, tingling so badly she could hardly breathe. She could feel grass beneath her, moisture soaking through her sweatshirt.

Her own clothes. So she was home. Moonlight gleamed wetly on the trunks of birches and oaks. She saw delicate stems of grass and brambles coiled like barbed wire in silhouette; she breathed the rank scent of nettles. She could sense the energy-cone thrumming, low and disturbing, like an engine barely within the threshold of hearing. It had saved her but it was about to destroy someone else.

It was coming from beyond the woods. Eirian pinpointed it in the meadow opposite the cottage; a cloud like an angry swarm of bees which wouldn't die until it had spent its venom in someone.

'Mum,' said Eirian. Suddenly she knew it was her mother in danger. She must run down through the trees, across the lane into the meadow, and use the Horn to protect Beth.

Then she realized her hands were empty.

Eirian hadn't brought the Horn through after all. Her strength of will hadn't been enough. With her hands clenched around nothing but crimson pain, she began to weep forlornly.

Beth turned and tried to escape, but the spear curved after her. It wasn't death but it was something ghastly; illness, despair, rejection. It would burn out some vital part of her and she'd never recover.

The meadow became a hill to her leaden limbs; the hedges and the cottage were flat, deformed shadows in the blood-tinged moonlight. Steve and the others were coming after her but she couldn't hear their voices, only the crashing roar of her own heart. No escape. She must let the power have its way, let it earth itself through her and endure whatever followed.

Run, run. The cathedral was behind her and the woods ahead but the men were catching up.

The vision flashed through her and vanished.

Beth was so shocked that she stopped in her tracks. Eirian's under attack too, she thought, but I can't help her! I must end this and find her *now*.

Beth turned to face the sending. The cone of power came down; she felt her strength failing, as if her nerves had short-circuited. By instinct she visualized a pentagram in front of her, the five-pointed star of birth, initiation, consummation, repose, death, and around it the circle of rebirth, the Goddess's cauldron.

The cone struck. The pentagram shone, a silver mirror; the power bounced off it, like a ball off a shield, and curved straight back to its source. Isis.

Beth, untouched but trembling, saw the energy hit Isis. It was invisible but real, like the wind. The priestess stopped as if she'd hit plate glass and stood there with static dancing over her skin. Then she staggered back and sat down heavily on the grass. Her eyes were wide open and she was twitching as if in a fit.

She's got no idea what to do, Beth thought. Summons it but can't control it!

The others, who were scattered between Beth and Isis, froze and stared; it struck Beth that they had no idea what was actually happening.

'Help her!' Beth called. 'Form a circle again. We must ground the power.'

They hurried to join hands. As they did so, she heard Tash shouting again, closer now.

'Beth? Are you deaf? Eirian's not in bed and I can't find her! For God's sake, what are you doing out there?'

Beth was desperate to find Eirian, but this must be finished first. She grabbed Isis's left hand, Rob her right, and the circle was made.

Beth felt power surge through her like electricity or a convulsing orgasm; out of Isis, through Beth, and into the ground.

Isis fell back, gasping.

'Is she unconscious?' Steve said anxiously. 'Shouldn't we put her in the recovery position?'

Isis's eyes snapped open. 'Don't touch me! God, my head. That was horrible.' She was gasping, shivering.

'Don't you know,' Beth said softly, 'that if you send harm it will come back on you with three times the force?'

'Fucking shut up!' said Isis.

'What happened?' said Cherry. 'It was so great, then it all went – horrible.'

274

Beth knew they should finish the ritual properly, or the negative energy would linger, leaving them bickering, not trusting each other, but there wasn't time. She broke away and ran to the gate, where Tash was shouting, 'Beth! Steve! Anybody!' Beth's long skirt didn't help; she wished she were wearing jeans.

'Hey, wait for us,' Steve called, trying to catch up.

'What the hell were you playing at?' Tash demanded angrily.

'Long story,' said Beth. 'Where's Eirian?'

Tash gave an anxious shrug. 'I went to check on her and she wasn't there. Sam's okay, Steve. I was asleep for a while, so Eirian must have sneaked out. God knows why.'

'Shush!' said Beth, listening.

In the silence, Beth heard the very faint sound of a child crying.

Beth was over the gate and past Tash. She ran round the side wall of the cottage, across the small back garden, and entered the woods, picking her way though the sodden undergrowth. 'Eirian! *Eirian!*'

The sound of sobbing drew Beth swiftly through the trees. The moonlight seemed static and unfriendly as if the Goddess had been disturbed by the working.

Beth found Eirian crouched on the roots of a beech tree, weeping steadily. Her clothes were soaked, her hair tangled. A surge of anger took Beth by surprise and she couldn't hold it back.

'Eirian, what the hell did you think you were doing, coming out here in the middle of the night?'

Eirian looked up, and cried harder, as if she couldn't stop.

Beth's anger died and her heart lurched painfully. 'What happened? It's all right, I'm here now. I'm not angry.' As she crouched down beside her daughter, Steve and Bryony arrived, out of breath. 'Just tell me what the matter is.'

Eirian extended her arms so they rested stiffly on her knees. Her fingers were clawed.

'My hands,' she wailed.

*

Steve carried Eirian down through the trees and into the cottage. They put her on her bed and lit lamps, then Beth dismissed everyone, saying she wanted to be alone with Eirian.

The cats came in and sat on the rug, three sentinels.

'Now, let's see these poor hands. Did you fall over?'

Beth brought a candle close so she could see. As Eirian opened her hands, Beth gasped. The palms were red-raw and oozing blood.

'It hurts.' Eirian bit her lip, trying to be brave. 'It really hurts, Mum.' A sob escaped; she tried to swallow the sound.

'Well, it will,' Beth said, trying to sound matter-of-fact. 'Wait here. Don't try to stroke the cats; elbow them off if they jump up.'

She brought a bowl of water, TCP, bandages and a healing ointment she'd made herself. Eirian gasped and tears ran down her face as Beth bathed and dried her hands; but as soon as she wrapped them in the ointment-smeared bandages, Eirian exhaled and her face cleared.

Beth remembered Rhianwen tending to Luke's wasp sting, his relief as the ointment killed the pain. 'I bought it from Boots,' Rhianwen had said afterwards. Beth thought, I should have known then she was a liar.

'Better?' said Beth.

Eirian nodded. Beth held a mug to her lips, camomile tea with honey, for shock; she'd made one for herself, as well.

'What happened?' Beth asked gently, as she dried Eirian with a towel and got her into her pyjamas.

Eirian began to sob again, and Beth suddenly realized she hadn't been crying over the pain at all.

Eirian told her. 'They got Guen,' she finished in a whisper. 'Guen knew they'd catch her. She sacrificed herself to save the Horn. I tried to bring it through, I really tried, but I couldn't. It tore out of my hands. So Guen gave herself up for nothing.'

'Oh, Goddess.' Beth groaned. She had been going to tell Eirian off for going outside at night, but what could she say after this? She and Eirian had never needed to put much into words, anyway. She thought, no child should have to face such hideous responsibilities as these! 'It's not your fault, love.'

Eirian hung her head. 'If I couldn't save the Midwife or the Horn, I can't save Guendolen.' Beth sat on the bed beside her and they hugged each other, both crying now.

'Goddess, what a night,' said Beth.

'I wanted to help you, Mum, but I couldn't.'

'Help me?'

'Against Isis.'

'How did you know?'

Eirian lifted her shoulders. Morgan's gesture again. 'I just know things. I knew she was attacking you but I sort of couldn't move. I'm sorry.'

'Don't be daft. I was all right. You've done enough.' Beth thought, with a ghastly wave of guilt, could we not have used the Working to aid Eirian, instead of wasting it?

'Not enough.'

Beth gave her a gentle shake. 'Now, you're not to be miserable about this. It's not your fault, the dreadful things the authorities used to do to people. You can't expect to change things that happened in the past!'

'Then what's the point of me going there?'

Beth couldn't answer that.

Eirian yawned. Her tears had subsided at last. 'I'm tired.'

'I should think so, too. Into bed, now. No more midnight expeditions!'

'Will you ask her to go?' Eirian asked as she wriggled down under the covers.

'Who?'

'Isis. I don't like her. She's not bad, just stupid, like Miss Townsend.'

'Oh, she's going all right.' Beth kissed Eirian on the forehead and turned down the lamp.

'They don't respect kindness,' Eirian murmured, falling asleep.

They were all in the kitchen, except Tash, who had unfolded

277

the sofa bed and fallen asleep on it. The others lurked by candlelight in the kitchen, not saying much. Cherry and Bryony were muttering in a corner, the men standing about drinking from cans of beer, Isis and Rob sitting at the kitchen table with their arms folded.

'How is she?' asked Steve, as Beth walked in.

'Exhausted. I think she'll sleep now.' She met Isis's gaze and said, 'I thought you would have left by now.'

'We would have done,' Isis said flatly, 'if Chez hadn't been too pissed to drive us. I'm not walking to Derby, thank you.'

'Right. Steve can take you, then. He's not pissed.'

Isis looked at Beth in surprise. She'd expected Beth to be conciliatory, as she usually was, but Beth had had enough. Eirian had said, *They don't respect kindness*, and Beth knew she was right. For kindness read weakness, condescension, fear, ingratiation. She'd humiliated Isis, and for that Isis would never forgive her; if Beth tried to be nice, Isis would only hate her more.

'Fine,' said Isis.

'It was incredibly bloody stupid, what you did out there. If you try to harm people, you know it will come back at you! Have you found that out at last? The Goddess knows what you've done to yourself.'

Isis's face remained stony, but the corners of her mouth were tight.

'You don't mess about with the Crone or she will devour you,' Beth went on. 'What have I done to deserve you attacking me?'

The priestess's eyes flashed. 'You think you're so superior! A witch who came to her Craft by instinct, not hard work.'

'Crap,' said Beth. 'I've worked. But I've never claimed to be anything I'm not. There's few enough of us already without trying to kill each other!' She remembered the Midwife's death, Guendolen's unavoidable fate, Eirian's bitter tears, and she bore down on Isis in fury. 'It's people like you who get us a bad name! Misusing the Craft, playing on outsiders' misconceptions. If you had the slightest understanding of the things that have been done to us in the past – if you'd seen a terrified old woman being tortured and hanged when her only crime was to help the sick – if there's anything in you that can *understand* – Christ, you'd think twice before attacking your own sisters!'

Isis went ashen under her chalky make-up. The others drew back; Beth realized she'd frightened them, and didn't care. She went on, less heatedly, 'I think you were good once, but power's gone to your head. If I were you, I'd go away and think hard about what I was trying to achieve. If anyone else wants to leave with you, fine; if they want to stay with me, that's up to them. At least we'll know where we stand.'

Isis stood up, Rob her sullen shadow. Steve was restlessly jingling his car keys. As they reached the door, Isis turned round; she clearly wanted to deliver a Parthian shot, but couldn't. She knew Beth was stronger, and she was afraid. There was nothing to be said.

When they'd gone, there was an empty space around Beth, as if no one else dared to approach her. It was a very strange sensation, to feel she had a power that she didn't even understand. She leaned on the kitchen table, exhausted.

'You all right?' Chez said eventually.

'Yes.' Beth sighed. 'Thanks for staying.'

'I'm not pissed,' said Chez with startling honesty. 'I was just shit-scared of sitting with Isis in the van all the way to Derby.'

Bryony approached and hovered warily at Beth's shoulder. 'Wher. you said those things – about witches being persecuted – it was as if you'd actually *seen* them.' Her small, serious face was set in a frown. 'You haven't, have you?'

'I can visualize how things were,' said Beth, 'all too clearly.'

In the morning, Sunday, Beth left the bodies to sleep, checked on Eirian, then went up to the farmhouse to make breakfast. It had been very late when Steve had returned from Derby, so Beth had left him dead to the world, too.

'You look knackered, love,' Gordon remarked jovially, as Beth stood over the stove, frying eggs and sausages. 'Everything all right?'

'Fine. Eirian fell over and hurt her hands; I had to sit up with her until she fell asleep.' Beth hated lying, but telling the truth was unthinkable. Quickest way to lose my job and home, she thought.

'Always in the wars, kids.' She expected him to sit down at the table but he stood there, clearing his throat. 'Er, your friends. They haven't moved in with you, have they?'

'Of course not.'

'Only Dove Cottage is just for you and Eirian, Beth. That's understood, isn't it?'

'Of course!' Beth felt quite upset, that he thought she would abuse his generosity. 'They only visit me at the weekend; sometimes they stay Saturday night. I can't really go to them because of having to be on hand here.'

'Yes, I can see that. Only we don't want, you know, squatters or hippies or something.' Gordon looked embarrassed, trying to express his fears without offending Beth. He had, but she wouldn't let him see it.

'They all have homes to go to. No one's moving in, not even my boyfriend. I wouldn't dream of abusing your kindness. If it's a problem, me having friends round, I'll ask them not to come so often.'

'No, no!' he exclaimed. 'I don't want to spoil your fun. Just making sure. I trust you, Beth. We wouldn't want to lose you, and you've made life so much better for Margaret. We appreciate that.'

As Beth made her way home along the lane, her morning chores completed, she looked over at the copse where they'd found Eirian last night. The leaves shimmered with rain and the trunks were silver. The undergrowth looked many-layered, mysterious, inviting. She found herself climbing through the wire fence at the side of the lane and entering the trees. Dressed more suitably this time in jeans, a long coat and boots.

She wanted to be on her own for a while, and the copse drew her. The trees were beautiful, shrouded in moisture and lit by slanting sunlight. The air was bitingly fresh with the scents of fresh earth and greenery. Silence, but for the chirping of birds and the hum of a distant motorway.

She remembered how she and Morgan had used to walk in the woods behind Rhianwen's house. Only a few miles from here, but so long ago. They had walked slowly, talking idly or not at all; electrified at being together. She hadn't been fully aware of it at the time, but it had been . . . electrifying, yes.

Especially that last summer, when Morgan had finally invaded her tender, willing body and they'd made love again and again.

No, don't think of that! For God's sake, you silly cow, she told herself sharply, it was a thousand years ago.

I've survived, and I think I'm all right; or I would be, if only Eirian was.

What made her come out here last night? Dear Goddess, I hope she's not going to start sleepwalking as well as travelling!

Here's where we found her, thought Beth. She recognized the place and the tall beech beneath which she'd found Eirian crying her eyes out. Beth visualized the scene, against her will; trying to exorcize it, maybe. She walked around the tree, kicking at the leaf mould and the long, tangled grass. It was like being stabbed, seeing her daughter in such hopeless grief.

'Why am I helpless?' She leaned back against the trunk, closing her eyes. 'Goddess, if you've given me any power at all, why can't I use it to help my daughter?'

The Goddess, not unlike God, didn't reply.

Yet Beth felt her presence in every leaf. It doesn't work like that, she thought. You don't pray for favours or forgiveness. She simply is. I have to work out what to do for myself.

When she opened her eyes, she saw something white in the grass. It could have been fungus, a bone or a stripped twig. Beth bent down and parted the dripping stems.

'Oh my God,' she gasped. 'Oh, *Eirian*.'

Eirian woke from an uneasy sleep to broad daylight; her clock said it was eleven, and she felt stale from too much sleep. She could hear Beth's friends and Sam's small piping voice downstairs, chatting as they always did over a late Sunday breakfast. Hope Sam wasn't upset by last night, she thought.

And saw her mother in the doorway, with her coat held strangely as if wrapped around a long thin cane.

'Are you awake?' said Beth. 'I've got something to show you.'

Eirian sat up, wide awake.

Beth came to the bed, laid the bundle on it, and let the sides of the coat fall away.

Inside lay the Horn.

Eirian put her bandaged hands to her face. She couldn't speak.

'I found it in the woods, where we found you last night,' said Beth. 'It was hidden in the grass. You must have brought it through after all!'

Beth's face was a picture of disbelief. Eirian was so stunned she couldn't even think.

'Is it all right to touch it?' Beth asked. 'I had to, to pick it up. Eirian?' She laughed, stroking Eirian's face. 'I know, it's incredible, isn't it?

Cautiously, Beth touched the Horn, then lifted it across her palms so they could both examine it.

'It's heavy,' said Beth. 'Look, there's candle wax down it. It's real. I can't believe it, but it's real.'

Finally Eirian managed to say, 'It's all right to touch it, if you do it respectfully.' She began to pick the disfiguring wax out of the bands of carving and of gold that spiralled around it; wax that had set there yesterday or centuries ago. The little men and women looking through leaves were a paean to life and joy; maiden, mother, crone, son, lover, sacrificed king. And there were stags and hares, boars and unicorns, dragons and dogs, carved in whisker-fine detail.

Eirian sensed no power in the Horn. It didn't shine or transmit tingling energy to her fingertips. But in its mystical beauty, it was amazing.

Suddenly her numb shock melted to exhilaration. 'We did it!' she said. 'Mum, we saved it!'

'Yes, love. You did.' Hugging her, Beth said softly, 'I've seen this in visions, through other people's eyes, like in a dream. But actually to be touching it — who would believe us? It can't really be the horn of a unicorn, but what on earth is it?'

'Did anyone else see it?' Eirian asked, worried.

'No. I charged in through the front door and straight up-stairs with it under my coat, so no one saw.'

'Good. We must keep it secret.'

'What are we going to do with it?'

'Hide it,' Eirian said firmly.

And then an icy gale of reality hit her. She had saved a thing, not a human being.

'If I could bring the Horn through,' Eirian said desolately, 'why couldn't I have brought Guendolen?'

Chapter Seventeen

S TEVE and the others wanted to talk about Isis; all Beth
could think about was Eirian.

'She was a bitch,' said Bryony. 'She had it coming. It was all
this big image, you know, being this scary Wiccan priestess
with black fingernails.'

Beth looked at her fingernails, which were pale and chipped
from housework. Hope they won't sit here one day bitching about me behind my back; I'll probably deserve it if they
do.

'But what *happened*?' Cherry demanded. 'What did she do to
you, Beth, and how did you stop it?'

Beth tried to explain, but her mind wasn't on it. Eventually
she asked them, as kindly as she could, if they wouldn't mind
leaving so she could be alone with Steve.

They all hugged her in turn as they piled into Chez's van,
even Tag and Zak, whose cynical outlook was incompatible
with hugging friends.

'We all love you, Beth,' Tash said into her ear. 'We'd do
anything for you. Just in case you didn't know.'

Beth was glad they left before she started crying.

Then she sat at the kitchen table staring into a mug of
coffee, while Steve tried to find out what was wrong. Eirian and
Sam had gone up to the farmhouse to watch television.

'Is it about the weird stuff with you and Eirian?'

'Yes, Steve. It's about the weird stuff.' She breathed in
deeply, let it go. 'I need some help.'

'I wish there was something I could do,' he said. 'Maybe Isis
could have helped, if she hadn't been such a prat.'

'Maybe, but I think it's out of her league. I think I have to
go and see Rhianwen.'

Steve's eyes widened. Beth had told him about their last

meeting. 'What, after she accused you of giving the evil eye to some old pervert?'

'I know.' The corners of Beth's lips twitched; for some reason she felt like laughing hysterically. 'But there's no one else I can even ask. I need to see her. Will you come with me?'

When Luke preached, he was like a prophet, a political leader and a rock star rolled into one. Katy, along with the rest of the breathless congregation, hung on his every gesture and nuance.

'It's all here in Revelation. God will sweep away the old world and bring in the new, and only the Chosen will be saved. The Lord is working through us to create a new, empowered church as God's means to bring a conclusion to history. But while we make ready for Judgement Day, we will be beset by enemies on all sides. We're in a battle. The Enemy will do anything to undermine us. My brothers and sisters, are you ready to engage in direct confrontation with the Devil?'

An exuberant shout went up.

Luke seemed to look straight into Katy's soul as he spoke, playing on her every emotion. The congregation were very vocal, responding with passionate cries. Katy had used to feel inhibited but now she joined in, crying, 'Hallelujah!' and, 'Praise the Lord!' with the rest. It was a marvellous release of tension. Better than sex, she thought. It had to do instead, anyway.

'We give thanks to the Lord for the light and revelation entrusted to us. Does not the Holy Ghost come to each of his saints in fresh ways to write reality on our hearts? If anyone feels the Holy Spirit within them, let him come forward now!'

Katy was first in the queue.

As Luke touched her forehead a white light burst into her brain and she toppled backwards to the floor, dead straight, like a tree falling.

Through her ecstatic trance, she remained aware of everything. Someone began to sing spontaneously and the other 'saints' joined in all around. Their voices wove a cradle. Katy felt filled with the Holy Spirit, completely saved and forgiven.

They sang 'Amazing Grace' to close the meeting, then people crowded round to help Katy and the others who had felt the Holy Spirit to their feet. They hugged Katy as if she'd achieved something great. Katy wanted to share her joy with the whole world, to rush into the streets and proclaim the good news that whoever followed Luke would share in this wonderful happiness.

First, though, she had floors to mop.

While Luke's assistants Mark and Jacob called a select few to a meeting to discuss recruitment strategy, Katy went upstairs to wash her face and comb her hair before she began her household duties.

Katy shared a room, crammed with bunk-beds, with five other women, an indignity she couldn't have imagined tolerating at one time. The change Luke had wrought in her, though, was incredible. She had realized she wasn't the most important person in the world. Luke was. Oh, and God, of course.

Her happiness should have been sublime, but there was always a niggling thought, like a stone in her shoe, to mar it. Her son, Sam. The image of his freckled, bespectacled little face irritated her to distraction, but it wouldn't go away.

As Katy combed her hair – now chopped short to avoid vanity – her room-mate, Meg, came bounding in.

'Wasn't Luke marvellous today?' Meg exclaimed, her friendly face glowing. 'The love just poured from him! I felt God telling me I could run a marathon if I wanted to!'

Meg was five-foot-nothing and weighed about fourteen stone. 'That *would* be a miracle,' Katy said artlessly.

Meg looked devastated. 'What's wrong with you?'

Katy remembered Luke's instruction to be kind and loving at all times. 'Sorry. I was thinking about things. You know, my husband used to really get on my nerves, going on about the sacredness of nature like some hippie born about fifteen years too late. But now I feel sorry for him.'

'Yes,' Meg said seriously. 'I really pity people who haven't found Jesus.'

'Oh, it's up to Steve if he goes to hell,' said Katy. 'But it's not fair on Sam.'

'No, you're right, it's not fair on children to be left out like that,' Meg said passionately. 'How can you bear to think of Sam being out in the world at the mercy of the Devil and everything?'

Katy nearly thumped Meg; she could feel herself going crimson with the effort of holding herself back. She'd wanted to be told she was doing the right thing, not to have her nose rubbed in her guilt. 'Shut up about Sam!' she snapped.

'You mentioned him first,' said Meg, wounded.

Katy held herself steady, trying to put her son out of her mind. The last thing she wanted was the kid round her neck. But Sam's poor little soul . . .

'The day you do something truly selfless, Katy,' said Meg, '*that*'s the day you'll really know what it is to experience God's grace.'

On an impulse, as Steve drove Beth and Eirian to Rhianwen's cottage, Beth asked him to divert to her grandparents.

'It won't take long,' Beth said. 'I want to see my gran. I've put it off too long. It won't be such a big deal, if I just drop in and say hi, as if nothing's happened.'

'Hope she hasn't got a weak heart,' said Steve, following Beth's directions; right at the village green, left, through the tall gates and along the gravel drive.

The big, handsome house looked exactly as she remembered. Eirian had her nose pressed to the car window, fascinated.

'Wow,' said Steve. Then, 'D'you want me to wait in the car?'

'No, come with me.'

Beth was going to lead them round the side to the kitchen, like the old days, but the front door opened and her grandfather was there.

'Beth!' he said, coming out to greet her. He clasped her shoulders, a physical gesture he'd never made in the past, and he looked delighted to see her, not in the slightest put out by her unconventional appearance. She was wearing a long, black, mediaeval-style dress which hugged her figure and flared to a full skirt from her hips; Steve was in ripped jeans, a purple shirt and embroidered waistcoat, his blond hair a tangled mass hanging to his shoulders. Eirian, in a sweatshirt and jeans, was the ordinary one. 'So you finally made it,' said Randolph. 'I was beginning to wonder if you ever would.'

'We can't stay long. This is Eirian and, erm, this is Steve. My friend.'

When Randolph looked at Eirian, Beth saw the briefest flash of a profound, hidden emotion surfacing on his face. Then he said, 'Hello, Eirian. I didn't realize you'd be so grown-up.'

'I'm eight,' she said. 'Hello, Granddad.'

'Great-granddad,' Beth corrected.

Randolph grimaced. 'Don't make me feel more ancient than I am!' he said, leading them through the house into the kitchen. The smell of wet dog surged out to meet them. Heather was on her knees, bathing a Labrador; her sleeves were rolled up and there was newspaper all over the kitchen floor. A familiar scene. Nothing had changed, except that Heather's hair had gone nearly white.

The dog shook itself, and through the cloud of spray, Heather looked up and saw the visitors.

'Good God,' she said, climbing stiff-kneed to her feet. Beth was shocked to see how much older she looked. 'Who's this?'

'It's Beth,' said Randolph, as if he couldn't believe she didn't recognize her granddaughter. 'And the not-so-little girl. And Beth's friend, Steve.'

Heather looked Steve up and down. She displayed neither pleasure nor surprise; her face was stern. A shiver of unease went over Beth. Maybe this was a mistake, she thought.

Eirian, though, went boldly up to Heather. 'Are you my great-grandma? I'm Eirian. May I stroke the dog, please?'

'He's wet,' said Heather.

'I don't mind.' Eirian caressed the dog's damp, sandy head with the back of her fingers; her palms were still tender. 'What's his name?'

'Fudge,' said Heather. And now she looked startled, at a loss, and rather grim.

'She likes horses, too,' said Beth.

'She's polite, at least.'

'Were you expecting me to drag up a foul-mouthed yob?'

'I didn't mean it like that,' Heather muttered, drying her hands on a tea towel which she then passed to Eirian. 'Do you want to dry him off, dear, before he catches cold? I want to talk to your mother in the other room.'

Heather steered Beth into the sitting-room, leaving Randolph with Steve and Eirian. Shades of the old days, Beth thought, Mum and Gran arguing in private.

Beth began, 'I'm sorry to descend on you like this, but I thought if I phoned first, I might lose my nerve and –'

Heather cut across her, 'How dare you flaunt her at me like this?'

'What?' Beth gasped.

'I suppose you thought if I saw the child I'd love her, but it won't work!'

Beth was astonished. She saw, with a jolt, that her grandmother was furious. 'Why not?'

'You know why!' Heather turned away suddenly, her hand to her mouth. 'Oh, God, this is such a shock. How could you, Beth, really?'

'I'm sorry. I thought you'd be pleased. Gran, are you okay?'

Heather turned back, calm again. 'Perfectly all right.' She was older but she wasn't frail; her intransigent spirit sat firmly in her eyes.

'It's not Eirian's fault she's, well, illegitimate.'

'It's not that. It's the blood,' Heather muttered. 'Family of degenerates, the Rhyses. She promised to leave but she's had the nerve to come back.'

'Who, Rhianwen?' Beth had to be careful not to admit she already knew.

'Yes. Incapable of making a promise and sticking to it; son's just the same. No doubt you're old and wise enough to have realized it by now. We tried hard enough to warn you at the time but children always think they know better.'

Beth drew a breath, outraged. 'I thought you were different from my mother; sane, that is. Eirian didn't choose to be related to Rhianwen! How can you hold it against her?'

'So, I'm insane, am I?'

Beth shook her head, frustrated. 'Sorry, Gran. I didn't mean it like that. I thought we could get beyond this, you know, forget the past.'

'I wish I could.' Heather placed a hand on Beth's shoulder. 'But how can I, when I'm presented with living, breathing reminders? Life is so bloody ridiculous. Not your fault, getting caught in the crossfire.'

'Haven't you forgiven me yet?' Beth asked.

Heather gave her a rueful look. 'I never blamed you. You were misled by that appalling boy. You were silly, not wicked.'

'I've paid for it,' said Beth, 'but I wouldn't be without my daughter for anything.'

She stepped forward and forcibly hugged her grandmother, something she'd never done before. Heather seemed startled, but returned the hug, patting Beth's waist. 'Good Lord, you're so tall. Do you mean to look like a witch? If your mother could see you!' She stepped back. 'This Steve, is it serious?'

'I suppose so.'

'Wedding bells?'

Beth winced. 'I don't think so. He's married. His wife left him before we met. It doesn't bother me whether he gets divorced or not.'

Heather rolled her eyes despairingly. 'Why people can't choose a partner and stick to them, I'll never know.' She looked contemplatively at Beth, her manner softening. 'I'm glad you came, dear. I always knew you would survive; I under-stand why you ran for it and I didn't blame you. You shouldn't have waited so long to come back, though. Where are you living?'

Beth hesitated. 'I work on Dove Hill Farm, near Barton-in-the-Elms. You won't tell Mum, will you?'

'Not if you don't want us to. Olivia pushed us away and she did the same to you; made a nice job of destroying the family, though I suppose it's not all her doing. I can't recommend you to go and see her. It would only stir it all up again.'

'I had a feeling it might,' Beth said regretfully. 'I come out in a cold sweat at the thought, actually.'

'Well,' said Heather. 'Well, now I've calmed down, will you stay for tea?'

'Thank you, but not this time.' Beth smiled. 'We have to go.'

'Come again,' Heather said stiffly. 'Bring the girl.'

At least she said it, yet there was still something very dark and very cold in Heather's eyes.

'Well, that wasn't too bad, was it?' Steve said brightly as they got back into the car. Randolph and Heather waved them off; it was all rather formal, a bit awkward, but bearable. 'Do you feel better now?'

'Yeah, not bad,' Beth said with a brief smile. 'But the truth is, I'll never really be free of all this until I can face my parents again.'

'Which way now?'

'Oh, back the way we came, turn left, follow the road round past the church. I'll tell you when we reach the lane.'

As they were approaching the turning into Farm Lane, a car pulled out in their direction and sped past them, a black XR2 with smoky windows. Beth caught the briefest glimpse of a blonde woman and a dark-haired man, mere shadows through the dark glass, gone. For a split second she thought nothing of it. Then her heart began to pound so hard she went dizzy.

That was Morgan, she thought. Morgan and his wife.

If we hadn't gone to see Gran, she thought, we'd have been here twenty minutes earlier and I would have met Morgan, and Rhianwen wouldn't have been able to do a damned thing.

Beth closed her eyes, caught on a wave of searing dismay and overwhelming relief.

Thank Goddess they've gone, she thought. It would have been excruciatingly embarrassing if we'd met! But her heart went on racing until she thought she might pass out.

'Are you okay?' Steve said, oblivious. 'You've gone dead pale.'

'Couldn't be better,' said Beth. 'Turn left here.'

The Metro bounced slowly along the rutted lane and drew up outside the gate in the hedge. The last time Beth had come here had been in darkness, with a baby in her arms, bereft and bleeding. The house had been deserted; now it was obviously occupied. The garden was tended, the cat sanctuary sign back in place. Suddenly Beth felt frantically angry. It was as if Rhianwen had only pretended to leave, specifically to avoid having to take any responsibility for Eirian.

'I can't do this,' Beth said. 'Let's go.'

'Too late,' said Steve. 'There's a woman in the garden staring at us. Is that her?'

Rhianwen was on the front path, in a long dark blue dress, denim waistcoat and floppy hat. The lines in her face had deepened, but she was still beautiful, her hair henna'ed as deeply red as ever. She had the kind of bone structure that was ageless.

'That's her. Oh, well.'

Unexpectedly feeling detached and calm, Beth climbed slowly from the car and tilted the seat so Eirian could get out. Eirian spoiled the aura of coolness by rushing through the gate exclaiming, 'Grandma!'

Eirian loved Rhianwen, whatever she'd done. That was the fearful thing about Rhianwen: whatever she did, she inspired love. Beth found it impossible to hate her.

Beth and Steve followed Eirian down the path. Rhianwen, now embracing Eirian, was the colour of paper as she looked at them.

'This is a surprise,' she said.

'Sorry if we've come at a bad time,' said Beth. 'Like if you've got visitors or something.' Just a slight dig.

Beth knew Rhianwen had gone pale, not because she was surprised to see Beth, but because if they'd arrived a few minutes earlier, they would have bumped into Morgan.

'How did you know I was here?' Rhianwen asked. Beth thought, does she look embarrassed? Yes!

'I've seen my grandparents. I understand you were away for about three years, so the last time I saw you, you must already have been back here for two years. I can't understand why you didn't tell me.'

The corners of Rhianwen's mouth tightened. 'You know why.'

'So I didn't try to see you-know-who?'

'I'm sorry, Beth.'

'So you keep saying.' Beth felt furious but very controlled. 'He was here, wasn't he? I thought I saw him leaving.'

Rhianwen sighed. 'Yes, he was here.'

'Does he often visit you?'

'Not often. They're working in Canada. They were just on their way to Heathrow.' *So you can forget any ideas of seeing him*, Rhianwen said between the lines.

Canada. *They.* Beth felt only a dull disappointment. Her hopes were long-dead, so what did it matter if Morgan lived in Canada, Australia or on Mars?

'What's she like, his wife?'

'Charming,' said Rhianwen. 'Very nice.'

And Beth thought, Rhianwen doesn't like her! Perhaps it was wicked to be pleased, but she couldn't help it.

There was a pause; Steve, behind Beth, cleared his throat.

'Oh, sorry, this is Steve,' Beth said, recovering herself. 'My boyfriend.'

At that, Rhianwen visibly relaxed, and smiled. 'It's nice to meet you, Steve,' she said, shaking his hand. 'You look wonderful, both of you.'

'I don't think my gran thought so.'

'Where are the cats?' Eirian asked suddenly. 'Can we see?'

'Come on.'

Everything was as Beth had remembered. The cages were occupied, Llew and Ankaret – elderly cats now – wandered in and out of the kitchen door, the herb garden was flourishing. A sensation akin to homesickness caught Beth in the chest.

Rhianwen let Eirian and Steve into the biggest cage to look at the cats in their boxes, but she and Beth stayed outside, talking softly so the others couldn't hear.

'You never had any intention of selling this place, did you?' Beth asked.

'I couldn't. It would have killed me. My whole life is here. It was a bloody nightmare, living in that flat in London. I just let things die down while I got Morgan established at university.'

'It's a good job we missed him,' Beth said acidly, 'or I might have cursed him. A nasty accident on the way to the airport.'

Rhianwen stared at her, and the suspicion in her eyes swam hard to the surface.

Beth said, 'You don't really think I cursed Bernard, do you? It was a coincidence! I can't believe you accused me of harming him! Harm comes back on the sender, doesn't it?'

'Not always. Beth, I'm sorry. I had no right to imply what I did. I was trying to make you understand that if you have power, you have to be careful with it.'

'You were frightened of me! That really hurt!'

'I couldn't help how I reacted. I never meant to hurt you. If I could make amends.' Rhianwen touched Beth's arm, cautiously.

'I had Morgan's baby and you wouldn't let me see him,' Beth said softly. 'Can you ever make amends for that?'

'I went to the Primarolas when they came to Broom Farm, the spring following Bernard's death,' said Rhianwen, 'but you weren't with them. And Mrs P said you'd made them promise not to tell me where you were. Well, one of the children did tell me, eventually, but it was obvious you didn't want to see me, so I didn't come.'

'Were you afraid I'd curse you?'

Rhianwen didn't reply. After a moment she asked, 'Beth, do you hate me?'

'You shouldn't ask questions like that. You might get an answer.'

Through the wire, Beth watched Steve and Eirian petting a tabby kitten, their heads bent together. She thought, I am so

294

lucky, really. And then she remembered why she'd brought them here.

'No, I don't hate you,' said Beth. 'And I didn't come here to make you feel bad. I really need your help. It's Eirian.'

'Why didn't you tell me this before?' Rhianwen asked. She was so dumbstruck by what Beth had told her, she hardly knew how to react. Beth, Steve and Eirian sat in a row on her sofa, all grave-faced; Eirian hadn't said much, but she hadn't denied anything. Sometimes she'd corrected Beth on details. And Eirian had claimed to have physically brought a sacred artefact from the past to the present. Rhianwen added, 'I know you told me about some of the visions you'd had but you never said it was coming from Eirian. I knew something was going on, but –'

'I wanted to tell you, every time I saw you,' said Beth, 'but I couldn't. You were the only person I could have told, but I didn't trust you; I felt you weren't there for me.'

Rhianwen experienced a familiar, heavy wave of regret. 'Did Mrs Primarola know?'

'Yes, I couldn't keep it from her because she'd heard Eirian speaking. But she didn't know what to do, either.'

Eirian said, 'There's nothing you can do. There's no point in worrying about me, Mum.'

Rhianwen found her captivating, this serious child with thick brown hair and Morgan's eyes. Yet something about Beth and Eirian frightened Rhianwen. She couldn't put her finger on it. A darkness, a combined force of will; rage at their unjust separation from Morgan. A wound that would never heal.

And something deeper and older than that.

Still, Rhianwen had to remain strong. She couldn't give in. She would have done the same again, to protect Beth from being hurt by Morgan, to punish them both – however unfair that was – but most importantly, to protect her son from letting a single mistake ruin his life. She loved Beth, but she loved Morgan more.

And she wished, for his sake, he could see this beautiful child once, but that, too, was impossible. Goddess knew how he'd react; and of course Eirian wasn't ordinary, she had this secret world moving inside her. Too dark, too dangerous. Morgan must never know.

Rhianwen desperately wanted Beth to love her, even though she'd had to be so unkind. The darkness in Beth drew her as much as it alarmed her, such a strange contradiction, because Beth was a kind, gentle person who would never hurt a soul. Yet there had been Bernard's death.

'I'll be honest, Beth. I've no experience of this kind of thing; I know of people remembering past lives, but never anything like this. I don't know what it means. If for some reason Eirian is meant to bear witness to the persecution we suffered in the past, I can't explain it.'

'That's a cruel fate to be inflicted on a child,' said Beth.

'It's all right, Mum.' Eirian looked down at her palms, which were pink and raw-looking, as if she'd had a fall. 'If it's what the Goddess wants me to do.' Rhianwen had never heard a child say such a thing before.

'It isn't all right!' Beth cried. She looked at Rhianwen. 'You probably think I've put ideas in Eirian's head, but I haven't. This is coming from her. If you'd seen her, breaking her heart because she'd let the Midwife or Guendolen down, and felt as helpless as I did to comfort her —'

'What do you want to do?' Rhianwen asked.

Beth sat back, calming herself; Steve took her hand. He's nice, Rhianwen thought, but he's weak.

Beth said, 'I took part in a coven meeting – that's another story – but we raised real energy. I thought, why can't we project energy like that to help Eirian? To help Guendolen?'

'It won't work,' said Eirian.

'You don't know that!'

Rhianwen broke in, 'Beth, my idea of witchcraft is reverence for nature and the power of healing. This is something else. And you mustn't make Eirian do anything she doesn't want to do.'

'Of course not,' said Beth. 'But I want to help her. I want her to be free of this damned thing!' She turned to Eirian. 'Don't you want to be free of it, love?'

Eirian's mouth tightened. Her eyes, wide and expressionless, turned shiny with unspilled tears. 'Yes.'

Rhianwen stood up, resigned. 'Come up to my bedroom. Steve, would you stay here in case the phone goes or anyone comes to the door? You know, women's work and all that.'

Eirian liked the bedroom, with its patchwork covers, old pine furniture and wooden candlesticks. Rhianwen closed the curtains and lit some candles. The atmosphere changed from day to mystical night.

'Stand in a circle and join hands,' said Rhianwen. Eirian remembered this from the Sabbats with the Primarolas. But this was dark, and it felt wrong.

'It won't work,' Eirian said again. 'You can't *make* yourself go there. It either happens or it doesn't.'

'Well, if nothing happens, no harm done, eh?' said Rhianwen. 'Close your eyes and breathe. Listen to the names of the Great Mother; Isis Astarte Ishtar Artemis Hecate . . .'

The chant raised the energy. It flowed up between them without effort, as if it was so strong in all three it couldn't be held back.

But we can't force ourselves to the other place, Eirian thought. It's not going to happen. It's not.

Dizziness, a nerve-jolt like a sensation of falling. Eirian was sinking down and she couldn't pull herself out of the trance if she tried. But it wasn't right. It wasn't colourful and real like the other times she'd been.

Instead the scene was grainy and grey, like an ancient film. It felt static and hostile, full of flickering shadows. Eerie, threatening. Eirian was there and yet she, too, was only half real, a ghost on the film grain.

She saw a stone room with an unglazed window and a pallet. There were heaps of chicken bones discarded in the corners, an uncovered slop bucket, rats and flies picking their way over the filthy stone floor. And on the pallet lay two heaving figures; Guendolen, her face stretched in agony, mouth open, and Inquisitor Lacost on top of her, fully clothed in his musty black cassock, thrusting hard between her legs. There was no sound. Guendolen screamed and sobbed in mime. Eirian felt unreal but she ran forward, struggling as if through water, and struck the rapist in the kidneys with her fists.

Lacost pulled himself out of Guen's body and turned. His face was grotesquely contorted, and his penis, sticking out from his infested breeches, was covered by some kind of cruelly studded leather sheath.

He stared in Eirian's direction, his eyes bulging. And she saw him mouth, 'Witchcraft. *Witchcraft!*'

He began to strike Guendolen across the face, again and again, as if to kill his own terror. The bruises and blood were black against her grey skin. A soundless nightmare.

Eirian felt energy gathering behind her eyes. She tried to control and project it but it was like grasping air. Then the Inquisitor climbed off Guen and came for Eirian.

His bloated, sneering face loomed towards her. She felt his fibrous hands on her shoulders, thrusting her up against an ice-cold wall. Caught the miasma of his foul breath and sweltering, unwashed body. A boil on his cheek, taut with yellow pus, hypnotized her.

One hand went under her skirts. Eirian's stomach lurched up into the back of her mouth but she couldn't stop him; his knee was between her thighs and the hard sheath was pressing against the tender lips where no one had ever touched her, poised to tear and desecrate.

He was mouthing something. 'Unclean. Devil's instrument. Gateway to Hell!'

Beth was Guendolen. She endured the tearing agony of the rape and the flowing of hot blood, worse pain than giving birth. Day after day she'd endured this – ever since they'd captured her in the cathedral.

Be my mistress and there will be no trial, Lacost had told her. But she wouldn't submit, not to him, no matter what he did.

So the Inquisitor kept her in his stinking room, raped her every day and would do so until she could endure no more; then she would be tried and put to death. To save her soul.

Guendolen tried to curse him but her curses had no power. She wanted only to die.

Then, over the Inquisitor's shoulder Guen saw the ghost-figure, her good sister, her familiar. Saw her rush forward and strike the rapist's back! Abruptly he climbed off Guen; her pain flared, then lessened, but now he was seizing Eirian instead.

My sister, my daughter!

Guendolen leapt off the bed, frantic. She grabbed the heavy wooden bucket, full of piss, and brought it down on Lacost's head.

The reeking urine splashed everywhere. His hands flew up in shock but he didn't fall. He begun to turn – then he gave vent to a hideous, high-pitched scream.

The wrath of the Crone possessed her. She struck again and again, her vision turning to a blizzard of black stars.

Then Beth-who-was-Guendolen turned and ran, blood chafing between her thighs.

They were pursuing her, her family; Olivia and Philip and Luke and Heather, screaming, 'Witch! Witch! Hang her! *Burn her!*'

Eirian felt her power surging. It lit her up like fury. She saw Guen, her lips drawn back from her teeth like a demon, rush forward and bring the heavy bucket down on the Inquisitor's head.

As Lacost flung up his hands through the revolting gush of liquid, Eirian seized his member and yanked at the leather sheath. The studs hurt her hands but she didn't care. She tugged hard, the sheath came off, and the leader screamed. She saw his rotting mouth come open, his larynx straining, his tongue wobbling between the black stumps of his teeth. His unsheathed penis was small and flaccid, scored with weals and suppurating sores.

Guen struck again. She brought the iron-bound edge of the bucket straight into the middle of Lacost's face, twice, three times. The first blow had been enough. Eirian didn't hear but sensed physically the crunch as his nose fractured and the splinters of bone slid up into his brain. Lacost slipped slowly down the wall.

And Guen – Guen fled.

Eirian looked at the Inquisitor lying on the floor amid the refuse of his gluttony. His eyes were open, his mouth slack. After a moment, a fly crawled out between his blubbery lips and flew up at the light of the window. A large, black fly.

The scene fluttered, bleached to white, and curled away. Eirian was falling through time . . .

And settling imperceptibly here. A rug, candlelight, a circle of three women. Golden reality. Beth turned and gripped Eirian hard in her arms. Rhianwen's arms went round them both and Eirian felt intense heat coming from her hands. Healing heat.

For those few seconds, in pain and bitterness and relief, they were one.

'I got away,' Beth breathed. 'Guen got away, I mean. The Inquisitor's dead. It's over.'

For now, Eirian thought. But she didn't say it. She was too tired to argue any more.

'It is over, love,' said Beth. 'You must believe it.'

Beth and Eirian seemed calm afterwards, like refugees deadened by war; they'd seen all this before. It was Rhianwen who was shocked, unable to stop trembling as she set out wine and cakes in the kitchen for the ritual sharing of food.

I had no idea, she kept thinking. No idea.

The scene she'd witnessed, bodiless, kept replaying across her mind, a horror film she'd never forget. And Eirian has been going through this since she was a baby? I thought I knew everything but I cannot begin to cope with this.

I only hope I've stopped it, healed the rift in Eirian's mind that was letting this stuff through. That's what I tried to do, to heal. 'If it's what the Goddess wants.' What a strange thing for a child to say!

But she's not a child. How much of this did she get from Morgan? Too much of the same blood.

Rhianwen carried the tray into the sitting-room and handed out glasses and plates. Eirian had wine; Beth didn't say she couldn't. Steve looked worried, a bit baffled, and seemed nervous of asking what had happened.

'Did you make these cakes?' asked Beth, holding up a brown lump.

'How did you guess?'

'Your baking hasn't improved, then.'

They laughed. Steve and Eirian looked at each other. And Rhianwen knew.

This was what she had wanted from Beth. This closeness, the sisterhood of witches, this warmth and understanding; and Beth a daughter–disciple to carry the knowledge on. Perfect friendship. With delicious revenge on Olivia thrown in.

Not Morgan, with his lust and his irresistible beauty, to take Beth away from her. Yes, Rhianwen had needed to punish them both for that. Jealousy, resentment and love all mixed up; there was no single, straightforward motive for the way Rhianwen had behaved. Although behind it all had lain the simple fact that Beth and Morgan could not be allowed to continue their relationship.

Steve said, 'So, er, are things all right, or what?'

Rhianwen and Beth left Eirian to answer. She nodded, not looking at anyone.

'It was hideous,' said Beth. 'But we came through.'

'I don't want to talk about it,' said Eirian.

'Well, then, we won't,' said Rhianwen. 'Have another cake, love.'

When they got up to leave, an hour or so later, Rhianwen

and Beth embraced with real warmth, like the old days. 'This is how we should be,' said Rhianwen. 'I never wanted us to fall out.'

'Neither did I,' Beth said warmly. 'I always loved you, however angry I was with you. Thank you for helping.'

'Come and see me again. Any time.'

'I don't want to see Morgan, you know. I'm over all that. It would just be embarrassing. So you can stop worrying.'

'Oh. Well, okay.'

Beth was smiling, but Eirian's eyes, as she stood in the doorway waiting for Beth, were cold green glass; exactly like Morgan's eyes the day Rhianwen had told him the lie that Beth refused to see him.

'It was Eirian's father, wasn't it, driving off just as we got there?' Steve said as they sat numbly exhausted in the car on their way home. It was dark, and Eirian was asleep in the back seat. Beth felt close to nodding off herself. 'That's why you went that horrible colour.'

'Did I?' Beth yawned, sighed. 'You don't miss a trick.'

'And there's been this big conspiracy to keep you apart.'

'That's how it looks from here.'

'Has it ever occurred to you,' he said, 'that there might be a perfectly simple reason for it?'

'It is simple. My family hate the Rhyses and Rhianwen thought I'd ruin her little boy's life.'

'No, simpler than that.'

'Like how?' Beth said, irritated.

'Like . . . maybe you and Morgan were related too closely to be having it off?'

'That's ridiculous.'

'Just a thought. Maybe his father had an affair with your mother.' Steve smirked, as if he found this idea amusing.

'Mother Teresa is more likely to have an affair than my mum!'

Rain began to fall. Steve switched on the windscreen wipers. Beth shivered, suddenly cold.

'Other way round, then. Your father had an affair with Rhianwen.'

'Oh, sure. My father is so shy he can hardly chat to his patients, let alone —'

Beth stopped, dazzled by an appalling memory; her father on his knees, her mother taking a whip to him again and again, her face red with passion, and her voice rasping. '*This is for what you did. This is for your weakness! Why can't you love me?*' And always the sense that Olivia held something over Philip, that he lived his life atoning for some dreadful transgression. Was that why he let Olivia have her own way in everything: guilt?

Beth remembered being in Morgan's room when her father had come to the door, how she'd crouched naked by the window, praying for him to leave. Was Dad still seeing Rhianwen? she thought wildly. Did Morgan know?

That's why Mum and Gran hate Rhianwen, and why Mum went insane when Luke told her who'd got me into trouble.

Beth remembered Rhianwen's words, long ago: 'It would be so nice for Morgan to have a sister.' And always to Morgan: 'Treat Beth like a . . .'

Sister.

That's what she wanted, Beth thought. Morgan and me to be brother and sister. Because we were.

'Beth?' said Steve, worried. 'Me and my big mouth. I was so busy playing the great detective I didn't realize I was upsetting you.'

'You haven't. It's crazy,' said Beth.

And it explained everything.

She went on staring through the rain rippling down against the darkness and the wiper blade cutting through, shivering so hard now she couldn't move. Why couldn't they have told us the truth? she thought. Oh, Jesus. Oh, *God*.

Guendolen was safe.

Eirian saw gentler visions when she lay in bed that night. The young priest who loved Guendolen was sheltering her in the little church on the edge of the forest. Sometimes she went to heal people in the night, when there was less danger of her being seen. The priest tried anxiously to convert her, but it was Guen who led him into her pagan ways instead.

Something woke Eirian out of her pleasant dreams. The buzzing of an insect circling the room, dive-bombing her head, tangling in her hair. Flicking it away, she saw a big, solid fly sailing towards the window and hitting the glass in silhouette against the moon.

When she got up to swat it, there was no sign of it.

But when she went back to bed it was there again. She lay staring at it, the covers drawn up to her nose, listening to the aggravating rasping sound the fly made as it bounced against the pane.

Chapter Eighteen

A FTER the working with Rhianwen, Eirian ceased mentioning her visits to Guendolen's village. Another lull; Beth
hoped with all her heart that it would be permanent.

'Are you still having the visions?' she asked Eirian very
gently, a few weeks later. 'You can tell me. I won't be upset or
angry if you are.'

'I see a vision sometimes,' said Eirian, 'of Guen with the
priest who helped her. He's hiding her. Sometimes she goes to
heal people in the night. She's all right.'

But there was no light in Eirian's eyes as she said this. Ever
since that day at Rhianwen's, she had become withdrawn;
rarely laughing or crying, too self-contained for her age. Her
eyes, emerald-cold and ageless, had become closed doors to
Beth.

Sometimes Beth would try to encourage Eirian to tell her
what she really felt; at others, anxiety made Beth angry with
her. Nothing Beth said seemed to have any effect on her daughter. Beth could only reassure her she was loved, and let her be.

The Horn, wrapped in blankets and polythene, lay in a
space beneath the floorboards in Beth's bedroom.

Sometimes Beth could hear a fly buzzing in Eirian's room,
but she could never find the damned thing.

Over the next couple of years, Beth's life followed a tread-
mill rhythm without holidays; seven days a week at the farm
with Sunday afternoon off, Steve and Sam to stay at the weekends, the company of friends and nights at the pub. Outside,
Beth could watch the seasons changing in the woods and fields.
There were bitter-cold winters and the endless labour of keeping fires burning so she and Eirian didn't catch pneumonia; the
delicious dawning of spring; autumns of red berries and mists.

Their friends came and went. Tash got a job in Leeds and

left them. Cherry married an accountant and rarely came round. Bryony pined for her friend; Beth sustained her through a near-nervous breakdown. Then Cherry began to show up again, unloading her marital problems on to Beth. Her marriage lasted all of eighteen months.

With Beth's encouragement, Steve's group had a successful year playing gigs in pubs and colleges around Birmingham. Then it fizzled out, but Chez, Tag and Zak kept coming round with various girlfriends. They made Beth feel part of the world, when her inclination was to become a recluse with cats. Like Rhianwen, maybe.

It seemed a logical step for Steve to move in with Beth, but when he broached the idea, Beth refused. She needed time alone with Eirian. So Steve and Sam stayed in their small house in the village and continued to visit Beth at weekends. Steve didn't seem upset. Beth suspected that he was still waiting for Katy to get bored with the cult and come home, but he waited in vain. He heard nothing from her.

Beth saw Rhianwen every three or four months at most. They were tentative friends again, but Beth kept her distance, determined to show Rhianwen that she didn't actually need her. And Rhianwen, it seemed, had the grace to feel guilty about the way she'd treated Beth in the past.

Morgan and Marian were working at a sea mammal research centre in Newfoundland, Rhianwen told her. Beth felt almost nothing at this knowledge, beyond a dull, formless ache; her life and Morgan's were so far apart that she couldn't even picture him any more.

To demand of Rhianwen, 'Tell me the truth; is Morgan my brother?' seemed not merely tactless and impossible, but pointless. How would it help, to know for certain?

Beth tried not to think of it. Spilled milk.

She saw Heather and Randolph occasionally. Heather seemed to find it difficult to spend much time with Eirian. She had developed a heart problem and needed a lot of rest: Eirian's presence seemed to sap her strength, so they never stayed long. A child of incest – was that why? Not Eirian's fault, the stigmas of illegitimacy, incest, paganism, and over-intelligence.

Beth wondered, often, what she had given birth to.

Heather's horses were enjoying a peaceful retirement. A woman from the village walked the dogs. Randolph, who showed no intention of retiring from his practice even as he approached seventy, coped without any sign of strain.

Margaret, though, was causing Beth anxiety. Lately she had been suffering a lot of pain in her spine, and although she got through the day on painkillers, she was constantly exhausted. She couldn't accept her condition, still railed against it. She became increasingly reliant on Beth for comfort, needing her so much that Beth couldn't have even considered taking an outside job. Beth began to worry that without her, Margaret would give up and die.

And Beth was growing restless. She'd been in the same place for close on five years without a break. Eirian was over ten and a half and would be going to secondary school next year, a new phase in her life; and Beth, too, craved a change, a holiday, something.

Steve and I are going nowhere, she thought. He just drifts, and I am trapped. But what on earth would I do without him?

Four months before Eirian's eleventh birthday, Beth woke suddenly on a wet February night, not knowing what had disturbed her.

She heard rain tapping on the windows, an odd bleeping like a car horn, and her name being called. A dream?

Then someone began hammering on the front door. She started, her heart racing, and got up to peer out of the window. Rain was sheeting down. Through it she saw the dim shape of Gordon, caught in the headlights of his Land Rover.

'Beth!' he shouted as she opened the window. 'Can you come up and see Margaret? She's in a lot of pain. She's asking for you.'

'Have you called Doctor Bown?'

'She's been and gone. Given her some stronger painkillers, but Margaret still can't sleep. I don't know what to do for her. She wants you!'

'I'm on my way,' Beth said. It was a Wednesday, so she and Eirian were on their own.

As she struggled into jeans and a jumper, Eirian came in, rubbing her eyes.

'I heard what Gordon said. Can I come with you?'

'Well, I'd rather not leave you on your own. Get dressed, love, quickly.'

Ten minutes later, Beth and Eirian were in the front seat of the Land Rover, bouncing along the lane in rain-filled darkness.

'I'm scared, to be honest,' Gordon said quietly. 'I think Margaret's dying.' Beth gasped, and he added hurriedly, 'Oh, not tonight! But slowly. I can see her getting a bit worse every day. S'pose you can, too.'

'She hasn't been well,' Beth said, trying to sound optimistic, 'but everyone goes through bad patches. I'm sure she'll pick up soon. Don't worry.'

Margaret was in bed, but the light was on, casting a bright yellow glow on the floral wallpaper and the brass bedstead. She smiled as Beth and Eirian came in, but she looked ashen and exhausted.

'It's good of you to come, dear. I'm so sorry to disturb you at this time of night but I feel so bad I don't know what to do with myself. Everything hurts.'

'It's no trouble. Is there anything I can do for you?'

'Just sit with me. That'll make me feel better.'

'Do you want the light left on?'

'If you don't mind.' Margaret's face squeezed up suddenly with pain; the backwash went over Beth as a wave of anxiety. 'I know it's childish, but I don't like lying in the dark.'

Gordon said from the doorway, 'Do you want me to stay, love?'

'No, go away and get some sleep,' Margaret said weakly. 'I only want Beth.'

'Can Eirian kip down on a sofa?' Beth asked. 'Otherwise she'll be too tired for school.'

Before Gordon could answer, Eirian interrupted, 'I want to stay here.'

'Let her stay,' said Margaret.

Beth relented. With Eirian sitting on the rug at her feet, Beth sat on a chair by the bed and held Margaret's hand. Agonizing, to watch her suffering and to be unable to help.

Margaret restlessly tried to push the covers back, as if she were too hot. The smell of talc and stale body heat rose from her. Beth folded back the blankets, and Margaret whispered, 'That's better.'

Beth began very gently to stroke the inert limbs, and to hum softly as she worked. Margaret seemed to relax. Beth stood up so she could work more thoroughly, running her fingertips over the woman's neck and shoulders, her arms, her fleshy legs. A feathery, hypnotic massage.

Eirian rested her head on Beth's thigh, as if falling asleep. Margaret's face had cleared and she seemed at peace, so Beth went on stroking her. This must distract her nerves from the pain, she thought. Whatever, as long as it helps.

Static crackled on Margaret's nylon nightie. Beth's hands became tingling hot, almost painful. Eirian shifted and gasped, as if she'd been holding her breath, then lifted her arm up to rest on Beth's waist.

The tingling faded. Margaret was sound asleep.

'She's dropped off,' Beth whispered. 'Lie on the bed beside her; you'd better get some sleep as well.'

Eirian, her face inscrutable, went round to the far side of the double bed and lay down. Beth switched off the light; a wedge of light from the landing remained. Soon she fell asleep, uncomfortably, sitting upright in the chair. When she awoke, by habit, at six, Margaret and Eirian were still fast asleep. Beth got up and stumbled downstairs, yawning, to start the breakfast.

Gordon, Frank and John were already in the kitchen, dressed for work.

'How's Margaret?' Gordon asked anxiously.

'Sound asleep.' Beth yawned again. She felt utterly exhausted. 'She had quite a good night, in the end. I'll take her some breakfast later.'

'You're a good girl, Beth,' said Gordon. 'I'll just go up and peep in on her. I won't disturb her.'

Beth switched on the kettle, took plates out of the cupboard and began to lay the table. Frank and John communicated in monosyllables. Radio 2 burbled tinnily in the background.

There came from upstairs a piercing scream.

Beth dropped a handful of cutlery. She fled into the hall and up the stairs, followed by Frank and John.

Gordon was in the doorway, flattened against the frame. Eirian was sitting up on the bed, her hair tangled, as if she'd just woken up. And Margaret —

Margaret was standing beside the bed, staring at her hands; first the fronts, then the backs, as if they didn't belong to her.

She was the one who'd screamed. Gordon was mute.

'Oh, *Goddess*,' Beth said under her breath.

Margaret's mouth worked. 'I, I,' she stammered, '*I can move*!'

'Sit down,' Beth said, putting an arm round her.

'Not likely! I might not get up again! Oh, Beth, Beth –'

'What exactly happened?'

Gordon said, 'I came in – I was trying to be quiet but I stubbed my toe on the chair leg, clumsy oaf – and Margaret sat up and screamed. I nearly had a ruddy heart attack, I can tell you!'

'He woke me up,' said Margaret. 'I sat up without thinking about it. And then I realized what I'd done. It was such a shock! Look, I can move my legs and my bad arm. I can walk!' She took a couple of steps forward, then swayed and sat down on the bed. 'Bit wobbly.'

'Do be careful,' said Beth. She was too stunned to feel joy. 'Are you still in pain?'

'No. I feel a bit creaky, you know. It sort of tingles.' Margaret clutched Beth's arm. 'It was you, Beth. When you were stroking me last night, I felt this heat. You healed me.'

Beth looked at Eirian, who looked back with no discernible expression. 'I –?' She thought, yes, I felt the heat. But I didn't know, it wasn't conscious.

Frank and John came awkwardly into the room, to scratch their heads and say things like, 'Blimey, Mags,' and, 'All right, Mum?'

Gordon fell heavily to his knees and clasped his hands.

'It's a miracle,' he said. 'Thank you, Jesus, thank you.'

'I didn't do anything,' said Beth. She sat at her kitchen table, clutching the thin white magazine Steve had brought. It was ten days since Margaret's recovery, and she'd shown no sign of a relapse.

'You must have done!' said Steve.

'I wanted to make her better, yes. That's not the same as thinking I actually could.'

'But you said you felt this heat.'

'It must have been a coincidence,' said Beth. 'Maybe she had a trapped nerve and it slipped back into place.'

'What's the matter with you? Why don't you want to believe it was real?'

'Because, because there was something not right about it!' Beth flared. 'I don't know. I really don't want to talk about it.'

'Well, you're going to have to.' Steve sighed, tapping the magazine.

'Since when do you get the parish magazine, anyway?'

'I don't. A bloke at the garden centre showed it to me and said, "Isn't this about your girlfriend?"'

Beth began to read aloud from the half-page article in the centre of the magazine. '"One of our parishoners reports the apparent miracle cure of his wheelchair-bound wife. Margaret Cleave, of Dove Hill Farm, Barton-in-the-Elms, who was paralysed from the waist down and had the use of only one arm after an accident nine years ago, woke up last Thursday to find she could walk again. Her husband Gordon credits divine intervention through the healing hands of their housekeeper, Beth Primarola. 'God works through Beth,' he said. 'She has healing hands. It's a miracle.' Whilst the Church must approach claims of miracles with extreme caution, all our parishoners will wish to join in giving thanks for Margaret's recovery, blah, blah, blah."' She looked at Steve, feeling slightly ill. 'How could Gordon do this?'

'I expect he wanted to share his good news with the world. You can't blame him for that.'

'I don't want people to know about it.'

'Well, only about six people read the parish magazine anyway. But what does it matter?'

Beth put her hand to her forehead. 'I'm not a healer.'

'Bollocks!' said Steve. 'You've been treating our coughs and colds for years!'

'With herbal remedies. There's science behind that. This is something different and I don't want people coming here thinking I can help them when I can't!'

Steve grasped her hand. 'You're scared stiff about this, aren't you?'

'You're perceptive.' Beth tried to smile. 'It's like the stuff with Eirian; having responsibility thrust on you when you don't understand what's going on. Don't get me wrong: I'm so, so happy for Margaret. But I've got to say something to Gordon before it goes any further.'

Alone, Beth left the cottage and marched along the lane to the farmhouse. It had turned cold; the hedges glittered with ice and the grass was crisply sheathed in frost. Sam and Eirian were at the farmhouse, watching television, as they often did at the weekends, under orders to come home before it got dark. They were still devoted to one another. Beth wondered, does Eirian tell Sam things she can't tell me? Bound to. And she'll soon be the same age I was when I first met Morgan! That is frightening.

Margaret was still weak, but she was walking with a stick and making progress every day. So now, Beth thought, I have to ask Gordon, tactfully, not to implicate me in the miracle.

Beth crossed the farmyard and opened the kitchen door. As

she did so, a voice said, 'Here she is!' and a flash of light blinded her.

Through the after-images, she saw Gordon and Margaret in their Sunday best, a man with a camera and a woman with a notebook.

Beth's heart jumped in dismay.

'Come in, love,' Gordon said cheerfully. 'These are people from the *Echo*. You don't mind talking to them, do you? This is Beth, this is our angel!'

His hand was round Beth's shoulder and he was propelling her towards the reporter. Beth looked sideways, shaking her head to indicate her reluctance, but Gordon was oblivious.

The reporter, a middle-aged woman wearing bright blue eyeshadow, shook Beth's hand. 'Ooh, dare I touch you?' the woman said heartily. 'Hope it does something for me bad shoulder. Lovely to meet you, Beth. If you wouldn't mind answering a few questions –'

'I would, actually,' Beth said coldly.

Their smiles faded.

'I'm sure you didn't mean any harm,' Beth said to Gordon, 'but I was horrified to see that story in the parish magazine. I came to ask you not to let it go any further, and I find this.'

He stared at her, crestfallen. Margaret said, 'Oh, but, love.'

Beth turned to the reporter. 'I've got nothing to say to you. There's no proof I did anything. I don't claim to be a healer. I would be most grateful if you forgot the whole thing.'

'But it's a lovely story,' the reporter said plaintively. 'Human interest.'

'I don't care,' said Beth. 'Leave me out of it.'

The reporter's over made-up face turned hard. 'It's up to you if you won't give an interview, but you can't stop the story. Margaret's given us all the information we need.'

The camera flashed again. Beth glared at the photographer but he was making for the door, hefting his camera bag on to his shoulder.

'Well, thank you for your time,' said the woman. 'If you change your mind, Beth, Gordon's got my number. Bye-bye.'

When they'd gone, Margaret and Gordon looked at Beth in dismay.

'I wish you'd kept this quiet,' she said.

'I'm sorry, love,' said Gordon. 'I had no idea you felt so strongly about it.'

'And I had no idea you were going to broadcast it! It'll be in the *News of the World* next! Sorry, Margaret. I don't want my picture in the paper, that's all.'

'We just wanted to share the good news,' said Gordon. They were so apologetic Beth felt guilty for making a fuss.

As she turned to leave, Margaret said worriedly, 'You're not in trouble or something, are you?'

'Yes,' said Beth. 'Faith healing without a licence.'

The story was in the local paper two days later, 'Wheelchair Wife in Miracle Cure.' There was a photograph of Gordon and Margaret beaming, an inset of a startled Beth. 'Beth Primarola – healing angel,' said the caption.

'Oh, shit,' said Beth. The copy detailed Margaret's experience, with a verification from Dr Bown that her spontaneous recovery was indeed inexplicable. It also explained that Beth lived on Dove Hill Farm with her ten-year-old daughter.

'What are you worried about?' said Steve, reading it over her shoulder. 'Your parents seeing it? They won't. This paper doesn't reach Brum.'

'I suppose not. Tell me I'm being paranoid.'

'You are.'

She read aloud. '"Beth herself plays down her role in the miraculous healing. 'There's no proof I did anything. I don't claim to be a healer,' she told our reporter. But Margaret's experience tells a different story." For God's sake. At least they didn't misquote me.'

'Wait until the nationals come round – only joking. They won't be interested. There's no scandal involved,' said Steve. Then he pointed at a story further down the page. 'Hey, here's a good one. "Church Leader's Sex Trial Verdict." Found guilty of an act of gross indecency with a seventeen-year-old boy in a public toilet.'

'Oh my God!' Beth cried, not knowing whether to laugh or cry.

'What?'

'It's Pastor Blair! My mother's pastor. The bastard who tried to make me lose Eirian. Gross indecency, after all those sermons about keeping ourselves pure!'

Steve's prediction proved right, thankfully. The story died out at local level; a couple of reporters rang the farmhouse but Margaret, respecting Beth's feelings, declined to give them the story. A handful of piteous letters arrived from sick people, begging for help; Beth cried, reading them, but replied politely to each that it had been a misunderstanding and she was not a healer.

'But how do you know you *can't* help them?' Steve asked.

That made Beth feel worse. But after a week or two, the letters stopped.

Rhianwen and Beth's grandparents had seen the newspaper. When Beth explained what had happened, they all accepted it sanguinely and said no more about it. Winter melted into spring; Margaret continued to make good progress; the newspaper article was forgotten.

Then Beth felt rather foolish for having made such a fuss about it.

Okay, so I am paranoid, she thought. What on earth did I think was going to happen?

Katy felt jumpy as she knocked at the door. She did not want to go through with this, but the more Christian she became, the less she could cope with her guilt over Sam.

The door opened and a large woman in a black djellaba looked out, her round, pallid face contrasted by stark black hair. Katy remembered her eyes being aggressively kohl-painted but now, without make-up, they looked pinkish and rather small. 'Yes?'

'Hello, Carol,' said Katy. 'Oh, sorry, you like to be called Isis, don't you?'

'Katy?' Isis frowned. 'It is you, isn't it? I never thought I'd set eyes on you again!'

'I know this is a bit unexpected, but can I come in? I need to talk to you.'

Looking taken aback and not very pleased, Isis let her into the narrow, dark house and led her through into the kitchen. Katy had always been frightened of Isis, and had coped with it by being bitchy. Now, armed with God's love, Katy saw – as she never had when she'd been with Steve – that Isis belonged to the other side, the Enemy. She was wishing she hadn't come, but Isis was the only one of Steve's friends who was not fanatically loyal to him.

'Can I ask you about Steve, without you telling him you've seen me?' Katy asked anxiously.

Isis folded her arms and her lips formed a downward bow. 'What about him?'

'I just wanted to know how he is, what he's doing, and that. I don't want to see him. I just need to know if he's looking after Sam properly.'

'I won't tell him, don't worry,' said Isis. 'I don't owe Steve a damned thing. Haven't even seen him for a couple of years.'

'Why not?'

'He's taken up with this female I can't stand. Thinks she's God's gift. I know you and I didn't get on too well, but I'd rather have you than her any day.'

Katy was outraged. 'What female? How long's he been seeing her? How dare he?' It didn't matter that she'd been unfaithful to Steve and left him; she'd expected Steve to remain the same for ever, devoted to her even in her absence.

'Been going on for nearly five years,' said Isis. 'I think she's a gypsy or something. She's a witch. I know that.'

'I thought you were one, too.'

Isis looked uneasily at the floor. 'I don't bother with it much these days. Anyway, as far as I know, Sam's all right. They were spending every weekend with this woman; Rob saw Cherry last week and she said it was still going on.'

'This witch is looking after my Sam?' Katy gasped.

'Since when have you given a damn about Sam?' Isis said harshly.

'That's not fair! Of course I care about him! It was God's will that I went away, but –'

'Now you're on a guilt trip, right?'

'No!' Katy gasped.

'It's okay, I don't give a stuff what you're after. I'd like to get back at them. I'll tell you whatever you want. Where Steve goes, what he does.'

'Tell me about this woman.'

Isis opened a kitchen drawer and began to rifle through it. 'Got a picture of her somewhere. She was in a local paper about three or four months ago. I cut it out.'

She presented Katy with a folded cutting. Katy gazed at a strong, fine-boned, very pretty face with large eyes and a mass of inky hair. She chewed at her lip. 'So, Steve's seeing a house-keeper with a kid, is he? He never had any ambition. Can I keep it?'

Isis pulled a face. 'If you want. Dunno why I saved it in the first place.'

In return, Katy gave her a leaflet for the church. It was her duty, although she fervently hoped Isis wouldn't actually come.

Later, when Katy returned to the church house, she showed Luke the article. It was not done to keep secrets from him. She didn't think he would be interested, but to her surprise he seemed riveted, smoothing out the cutting beneath his fingers on his desk, reading through it again and again.

'The woman who gave it to me says this Beth is a witch,' Katy said, nervous as she always was in Luke's dazzling pres-ence. 'You know what you said about direct confrontation with the Enemy.'

But Luke didn't reply. He said nothing for a very long time. The cutting seemed to have sent him into a trance. He kept tracing the picture of Beth Primarola with his finger.

'You've done well, Katy,' he said at last, very low and pre-occupied. 'God is definitely working through you.'

One Friday afternoon in late May, Beth was at the cottage alone; Steve had gone to pick up Sam and Eirian from school, and she was catching up on housework before returning to the farm to cook tea. As she swept the kitchen floor, there was a knock at the front door. Beth was surprised; she never had casual callers, because hardly anyone knew the cottage was there, let alone that someone lived in it. Her friends always walked straight in.

She opened the door to find a man in a suit, overcoat and gloves, with neat dark brown hair and a strong, square face. Double glazing or Jehovah's Witnesses, she thought. They can find you anywhere. Then, for a disorientating moment, she thought it was her father without his glasses. No, too young. His air of maturity had thrown her; surely he was only in his mid-twenties?

'I'm sorry to disturb you,' said the stranger.

One second of confusion, and she knew him.

'Luke?'

'Hello, Beth,' he said, with a reserved and ghostly smile, exactly like their father.

After astonishment, Beth's overriding emotion was joy. She'd thought she would be horrified if this ever happened, but she wasn't; she wanted to embrace him, to forgive him, to catch up on all their news, but all she could say was, 'How did you find me?'

'Someone showed me a cutting; a story of faith-healing and a photograph of you. You looked different and you were using another name, but I recognized you.' He looked her up and down, taking in her appearance; witch-black hair, a tight top with a black string vest knotted over it, black leggings laced up the sides. Beth wasn't wearing make-up but it didn't make much difference. She still looked every inch the demonic crea-ture her mother had dreaded her becoming. 'I made a few enquiries.'

'Have you joined the police, or something?' she said.

His smile almost became real. 'May I come in?'

'Yes, of course. I'll put the kettle on. It's wonderful to see you. How are you?'

'Very well, thank you,' he said. 'And you?'

'Oh, surviving.'

Luke came in, looking around. The evidence of her paganism was everywhere, in images and artefacts. She'd never felt awkward about it before. Yet Luke, just by looking, made her feel she'd done something to be ashamed of.

'You know, Beth, if healing isn't done through God it can indicate the presence of evil forces.'

Beth bit her lip so hard she tasted blood, to stop herself saying something she'd regret. 'Oh, it was blown up out of all proportion,' she said brightly. 'The lady had some trapped nerves that slipped back into place; it would've happened without me.'

'I see,' said Luke, apparently deciding not to pursue it. 'Where's the little girl?'

'At school,' said Beth. 'Would you like tea or coffee?'

'I don't take artificial stimulants,' said Luke. 'Water will be fine.'

'Our water tastes disgusting. Peppermint tea?'

Luke acquiesced. He waited silently on the sofa while Beth made drinks in the kitchen, still feeling childishly thrilled that her brother was here. She made herb tea for them both and carried it in.

'Don't get too excited,' she said, as she handed him the mug.

Luke, apparently, didn't think that was funny. He sipped at the tea as if it were pure lemon juice, then asked again, 'How are you?'

'Fine,' said Beth. 'You should see Eirian, she's so tall and beautiful.'

'Eirian is the name of the child.' Luke picked up a photograph from a side table and studied it. 'She looks like you, before you changed your hair.'

319

'Does anyone know you've come to see me?'

'No.'

'So you haven't told Mum where I am.'

'Not yet.'

'It doesn't matter if you do, anyway. I'm over eighteen. There's nothing she can do to me.'

Luke put the photograph down and breathed out audibly. 'Beth, our mother never wanted to *do* anything to you. I don't know what you were so afraid of.'

'Don't you?'

'It's up to the two of you, when and if you ever meet again.'

A pause. Beth's pleasure was fading to awkwardness. 'How are Mum and Dad?' she asked.

'Mother's been magnificent. It almost destroyed her, when you left. No one could find any trace of you, so we feared the worst, actually, until you sent that card. It was very distressing.'

'Oh, God.' Beth sighed. 'I really didn't mean to upset anyone. I was desperate. Can't you understand that? Surely you didn't want to see Eirian treated as badly as she used to treat us?'

Luke's face was too smooth. 'Her behaviour seemed harsh at the time, but I've come to realize that she acted with our best interests at heart. She only wanted to bring your unfortunate child to God. Happily, her faith gave her the strength to come to terms with your disappearance.'

'What, she saw it as God's will?'

'Naturally.'

'So she's all right?'

'Never better,' said Luke. 'So I hope that sets your conscience at rest.'

'What about Dad?'

'He's physically well; sadly he seems to have lost his faith, since you left. Your mother and I hope he will return to the fold, but it's in God's hands.'

'I suppose you heard about Pastor Blair?' said Beth. 'Gross indecency, who would've thought it?'

Luke shook his head, tutting. 'Very sad. A lesson that even the most holy of us can fall from grace. His church has fallen apart since he began his sentence.'

Marvellous, Beth thought, unable to stop herself gloating. 'But what about you? What have you been doing?' She didn't admit that she had already heard.

'I'm a teacher,' he said.

'What do you teach?'

'The Truth,' said Luke.

Beth thought, I bet that kills the conversation at dinner parties. 'To whom?'

Again the ghost-smile. 'I am the pastor of the Church of the One Truth, which I founded with some friends, by God's grace. Many of Pastor Blair's congregation have come to us, including our mother. We're flourishing.'

'Well done,' said Beth. 'I'm a housekeeper. Don't need O levels for that.'

'Beth, are you really happy, living like this?'

'Like what?'

'In virtual poverty, scraping a living by waiting on others?'

'I know, it's rather Biblical, isn't it?'

Luke didn't smile. There was a cold magnetism about him that Beth found positively disturbing. 'But what about your daughter? Is this spiritual desert really what you want for her?'

'Eirian is happy and healthy and doing very well at school, thank you,' Beth said shortly. 'You never used to talk to me like this, Luke. I was really pleased to see you, but if your only reason for coming here was to disapprove of me, I wish you hadn't wasted your time.'

His expression softened, and he looked down at his gloved fingers. 'I'm sorry, Beth. I was trying to express concern, not disapproval. I'm not making too good a job of it, it seems.'

'It's okay,' she said. 'Maybe we should start again.'

When he looked up, he reminded her of Randolph: a concerned but aloof authority figure, doctor or priest. The same darkly piercing grey-green eyes. Difficult to see the cowed little boy in him now.

'Forgiveness is the beginning of all things,' said Luke. 'We can forgive you, Beth, but can you forgive us?'

'I'm not sure I can ever forgive Mum for half killing me and my baby. Or Dad, for letting it happen.'

'A child born in great sin! She was trying to save your soul; the fact that she overdid it was a measure of her love for you. We want you to come back. We've missed you.'

'I've missed you, too. But I'm not ready. Please don't tell anyone where I am.'

'As you wish.' Luke stood up, and gave an understanding smile. 'God is patient, but don't stay out in the cold for ever.'

He pressed a leaflet into her hand. On it was the name and address of his church. Beth put it on the table beside the photograph of Eirian and stood up to show him out.

She felt she must make her position clear before he left. 'Er, Luke, I appreciate you taking an interest, but you ought to know I lost my faith a long time ago. When I was about thirteen, actually. I can't get it back. I've gone too far beyond it.'

'Rhianwen's poison, I know. But it's never too late.'

'I respect your right to believe what you want to believe,' she said, suddenly annoyed. 'Why can't you respect mine?'

Luke said nothing, only gave her a look of deep sadness and forbearance. Beth felt like hitting him. *How dare he pity me? Why can't he just be my little brother again?*

She said, 'If you come round again, please phone the farmhouse first. So I know to expect you.'

He went to the door and let himself out; she followed him. His car was a dark green Jaguar

'This is the way I am,' she said softly. 'If you can't accept it, that's too bad.'

Their eyes met and held across the low sleek roof of the car.

'Goodbye, Beth,' said Luke.

As Luke started the engine, the blue Metro pulled up and Steve, Sam and Eirian climbed out. Steve stared at the Jaguar; Luke looked sideways through the windscreen for a few moments, then drove off.

Steve sent the children into the house, then rushed up to Beth, looking agitated. She'd never seen him in such a state.

'What the hell was he doing here?' he cried, pointing down the lane after the Jaguar.

Beth, taken aback, wasn't sure what to say. 'Well, he . . .'

'Did he come to see me?'

'Why would he?'

'That was that bastard, Luke Herne!' Steve stood, clutching his head, as if he was about to leap back in his car and give chase. 'Was it about Katy?'

'No, It was nothing to do with her. Steve,' she glanced at the cottage to make sure the children were inside and not listening, 'I've got something to tell you.'

'What?'

'That bastard is my brother. My real name is Herne.'

He gasped. 'You're joking!'

'I should have told you before.'

'Damned right you should!'

'I didn't know how,' Beth said. 'It was never the right moment in the conversation. And I thought you wouldn't trust me if you knew.'

'Bloody hell,' he exclaimed, and walked away to lean on the meadow gate. After a minute or so he came back and said, 'Bloody hell, you poor thing.'

Beth laughed half-heartedly. 'Thanks. Luke saw that wretched article in the *Echo*. This is just the kind of thing I was afraid of, but . . .'

'You haven't seen him since you left home, right? What did he want?'

'Just to see me. He was quite nice, actually. I think he wants to reconcile me with our parents. But he can't stand the fact that I've gone over to the "other side": he looked at me with such pity I wanted to hit him.'

'Yeah, I hate that, the way they pity you. Katy used to do it to me.' Steve mimed putting his fingers down his throat.

'Is it going to be a problem, me being Luke's sister?'

Steve frowned, as if seeing her in a different light. 'Give me a while to get used to the idea. I don't think so. As long as he doesn't keep coming round here trying to convert us.'

Beth thought uneasily, is it a fault or a strength in Steve, that he can accept it so easily?

'I can't make Katy come back,' she said. 'I have no influence over Luke. I don't even know him.'

'Let's go in. I need a drink.'

In the sitting-room, Beth sat down beside Eirian and said, 'What homework have you got? If you bring it up to the farm you can do it after tea while I wash up.'

'Okay. It won't take long,' said Eirian. She had her nose in *Northanger Abbey*, and didn't look at Beth. Sam was on the rug, playing with a portable computer game. It was impossible to believe that he was only a year younger than Eirian; there seemed a gulf of years between him and this poised adult–child at Beth's side.

Steve had found the leaflet Luke had left, and was intently tearing it into shreds. He paused, looking at the side table where the photograph of Eirian stood. 'Hey, I thought I left a photo of Sam and me on here; I was going to frame it. Where is it?'

'I've no idea,' said Beth. She was suddenly, quietly drowning in the gulf that lay between her and Eirian; where had it come from, this terrible coldness in her daughter's eyes? We used to be so close. Where is she going, and will she ever come back to me? She answered Steve absently. 'Maybe it's fallen under the sofa.'

'Who was that man?' Eirian asked.

'No one. Someone I used to know. My brother.'

Eirian looked up, her ice-green eyes unreadable. 'But not the brother who is my father,' she said.

Beth found the following week with Eirian extremely difficult. Eirian became more withdrawn and aloof than ever; there was so much Beth wanted to say to her, but her daughter didn't want to know. Something dark and hard moved behind Eirian's eyes. She showed affection to Sam, but to no one else. It was like living with an unfriendly stranger.

The following Sunday, just as Eirian and Sam were setting off for the farmhouse to watch television, Beth took her aside and said, 'Look, darling, if something's wrong, will you please tell me? Whatever it is, we can talk about it. If you're angry with me, say so.'

Eirian met her eyes. The solemn, smooth shell of her face didn't change. 'I'm waiting for you to understand, Mum. There are so many things you should know, but you don't! So what's the use of talking to you?'

And she stalked off with Sam, leaving Beth speechless. She watched the two small, slender figures dwindling down the lane, gone.

'I don't know what to do with her,' Beth told Steve later. It was Beth's twenty-sixth birthday; a warm June evening, golden with late sunlight. Their friends had just left after a modest celebration, but she and Steve stayed out in the garden, drinking wine. Beth was slightly drunk, but she couldn't dull her foreboding. If anything, the wine had magnified it. 'Eirian won't talk to me any more. She looks straight through me when I speak to her.'

'Puberty,' said Steve.

'Not yet. She's still built like a little girl, even if she doesn't act like one.'

'I know, but they do start getting funny at this age. I'm dreading the day when Sam gives up toy cars and starts stealing real ones.'

'Don't!' said Beth. 'He's the dearest little boy. Eirian's more likely to steal cars than he is! Oh, I don't mean it. But she scares the hell out of me.'

'Don't be daft.'

'I mean it,' Beth said quietly. 'She really frightens me. And she remembers that conversation we had, after we left Rhianwen's that time,' said Beth. 'I don't know why you had to talk about it in front of her!'

'I thought she was asleep!' Steve protested. 'And it was nearly three years ago.'

'Yes, and she's remembered it all this time. Is that why she's gone so cold on me? She doesn't know it's only speculation, but she does know it's wrong to have sex with your brother, even if you didn't know.' Beth spoke bitterly. 'You know, I thought I could bring her up on my own and it wouldn't damage her. And I thought she could cope with her weird visions without cracking up, but now I'm not sure. Something dreadful's happened to her inside. Her only defence is to switch off her feelings and shut me out . . . and I feel so bloody helpless!'

Steve grasped her arm and gave her a shake. 'Don't let it get to you. Maybe she'll talk to you when she comes home tonight.'

'Maybe.' Beth looked at her watch, a hand-me-down from Margaret, and said, 'Talking of which, they're usually back by now.'

'Must be something good on.'

The blades of sunlight were fading, a cool twilight closing in. 'It'll be dark soon. I'm not having them walking back in the dark.'

'Well, shall we walk up and fetch them?' said Steve. 'Nice evening for a stroll.'

Beth's sense of foreboding was settling into a black depression. It was making her feel quite ill. Nothing could shift it; not Steve's company, not the blossom in the hedgerows nor the twittering of birds as they made the ten-minute walk to the farmhouse.

The sun was going down as they reached the kitchen door. Beth went in, calling, 'Hello! It's only me.'

Margaret came through the door from the front room, leaning on her stick; Beth could hear hymn-singing on the television. Not a programme Eirian would have wanted to watch.

'Hello, dear,' Margaret said, seeming surprised.

'I've come for the children. They're outstaying their welcome, aren't they? They are naughty, staying this late.'

Margaret blinked at her in confusion. 'But they haven't been here today.'

Beth felt the rush of shock all through her bones. Too soon to panic. 'They're not here? Haven't you seen them at all?'

'Not today.'

'But they came up here about four o'clock!'

'We haven't seen them,' Margaret insisted.

Now Beth panicked. She ran outside, looked up and down the lane, then ran to the main road, yelling Eirian's name. Steve followed her, shouting for Sam. Nothing.

'They've gone for a walk and got lost,' he said. 'Or they're trying to scare us on purpose.'

Ignoring him, Beth turned back and ran the length of the lane all the way to Dove Cottage, checked inside, then ran back up to the farmhouse again. She was gasping for breath, her throat sore. But the lane was silent and mockingly empty in the cold grey dusk.

As she entered the farmyard again, Gordon and John had come out to see what the commotion was.

'We'll search the farm. They'll turn up,' said Gordon.

Then John spoke slowly, thrusting a blade of terror deep into Beth's heart. 'I saw a car in the lane, 'bout ten past four. Thought nothing of it. A black car.'

PART THREE

Crone
The Horned Moon

Chapter Nineteen

'W'HAT sort of car?' Steve asked.

'Dunno,' said John. 'Escort, maybe.'

Beth's overwrought mind leapt to a wild conclusion.

'Was it an XR2 with dark windows?'

John shrugged, infuriatingly. 'Only saw the roof over the hedge. Took no notice.'

'Beth, what are you on about?' Steve said. He was shaking, and pushing his hands into his hair as he did when he was upset.

'The car we saw Morgan driving was black. What if he's taken Eirian?'

'Why would he?' said Steve. 'It was three years ago we saw him, so why –'

'She's his daughter. He's never seen her. Maybe he wanted . . . I don't know!'

'Then why the hell would he take Sam?' Steve shouted. She'd rarely heard him raise his voice before.

'Because Sam was there and they didn't want him telling anyone what had happened!'

'This is daft,' said Steve. 'I thought Morgan was in Canada.'

'He is.' Beth caught her breath and forced herself to think logically. 'Anyway, the car we saw him in that time must have been hired or borrowed. He wouldn't be driving the same one. And he doesn't know where I live, or even what Eirian looks like, unless Rhianwen's shown him photos, which I doubt.'

Beth was conscious of Gordon, Margaret and John staring at her in concern. 'Let's look at it the other way round,' Beth went on. 'Who would take Sam? Katy's parents? You said they don't like you.'

Steve was quiet, his expression undergoing changes. 'Or Katy,' he said eventually. 'Maybe she changed her mind about wanting him; it's exactly the sort of selfish thing she'd do!'

'Did she have a friend with a black car?'

'How should I know? But she wouldn't have taken Eirian, I just can't see it.'

'Well, who'd want both children?' Beth said in frustration.

They looked at each other. Beth felt sick, as if the sky were rushing blackly down to swallow her. 'Luke,' she said.

'That's it, Luke put Katy up to this!' said Steve. 'That photo of Sam and me that went missing – Luke must've nicked it, to check with Katy that it was really us.'

'Maybe they've been planning to take Sam for a while,' said Beth.

'At least Katy's Sam's mother,' said Steve, 'but what the hell gives Luke the right to take Eirian?'

Through a torrent of anger and fear, Beth could hardly answer. 'He wants to save her soul, of course.'

Gordon cleared his throat. 'The car might've had nothing to do with it. We ought to search the farm first. I always warn kids against going near machinery, silos, ponds and that, but you never know.'

Beth felt close to passing out. The shock was hitting her now, the terrifying reality that Eirian and Sam had vanished. She remembered the last sight of them, walking away down the lane and she grasped at it, thinking, if only I'd called them back, or walked with them! If only, if only.

Margaret said, 'I think we'd better call the police, don't you?'

Beth shivered. Steve supported her, his hands clammily hot.

'Don't let's rush into anything,' Gordon said reasonably, 'until we've had a damned good look round. Okay? Mags, can you go and prise Frank from in front of the box? I'll get some torches.'

'Perhaps they've run away,' said Beth. 'I wouldn't put it past Eirian, the way she's been.'

'They won't get far, if they have,' said Steve.

'But if they've been taken, if it wasn't Luke but some stranger, some pervert –'

'Stop it!' Steve shook her. 'I can't cope with this, Beth. We search the farm, okay, then –'

As he was speaking, the telephone shrilled out; there was a bell on the house wall, so it could be heard from the bottom of the farmyard. Beth jumped violently, her nerves shredded.

Margaret, tutting, went to answer it; she moved with laborious slowness on her stick, and Beth had to restrain herself from rushing past her into the house. Instead she followed slowly, and stood inside the kitchen as Margaret answered the telephone.

Beth watched her. Margaret looked gravely at Beth and said, 'It's for you.'

Beth took it. 'Hello?'

A female voice she didn't recognize said, 'The children are safe. I've got Eirian for you.'

Then Eirian's voice, high-pitched and shaky: 'Mum? I'm all right. Sam's with his mother. But –'

'Eirian?' Beth cried.

Then Luke's voice, smooth and deep: 'We've taken the children for their own good, Bethia. You will receive messages of their progress from time to time, but if you involve the police or try to get them back, you will never see them or hear from them again. Do you understand?'

'Luke!' Beth shrieked. 'This is against the law!'

A pause, then the voice spoke again, softer yet suddenly vibrant with danger. It shocked her, to realize suddenly what her own brother was really like: obsessed, ruthless. So hard to accept. 'I am aware that the authorities are too small-minded to recognize the sovereignty of God's law, so I'll say it again. If I catch the merest hint of the police you will *never* see the children again. They will disappear. Can you bear to wonder what happened to them for the rest of your sordid little life? Their lives are mine now. And their deaths.' As Luke spoke, Beth felt a deadly, bloodless chill spreading through her head, limbs and stomach. She thought she was going to throw up. An image of Luke, holding a sacrificial knife to Eirian's throat,

333

rose into her mind and stuck there. He hissed, setting her heart racing, '*Do you understand*?'

'Yes, yes,' cried Beth. 'But Luke, please –'

There was a clunk, a desolate electronic hum.

'Luke! Oh, Christ. he's hung up!'

A hand touched her arm. She jumped. Frank, John and Gordon had come into the room and were looking anxiously at her; Steve gripped her arm, demanding, 'Beth? Tell me!'

'We were right,' she said faintly. She was shocked at how ordinary her own voice sounded; she had to control it, or scream. 'Luke's got them. Er, Steve, have you got the phone number for his church? I'll try to phone them back.'

'I tore the leaflet up, didn't I?' he exclaimed. 'Oh, shit!'

'He said the children are safe, but if we call the police, they'll disappear.'

'Bastard!' said Steve, frantic. 'But he would say that! We must call them.'

'No!' Beth shouted, strangled. She put her hand to her mouth, swallowed a wave of sickness; rejection of what had happened. 'No, listen. You didn't hear him, but he means it. He really scared me. He implied –'

'What?'

Beth couldn't answer, but from Steve's expression, she saw she didn't have to. 'Do you want to risk it?' she said.

He shook his head. He'd gone deadly grey. Eventually he said. 'All right, we leave the police out of it for now. Never mind trying to phone Luke back; I know where the church is. Wait here, Beth. I'll go and get the car.'

As Steve rushed out, Margaret said, 'I'm lost, Beth. Who's taken the children?'

Beth explained. She could hardly get her breath. 'Luke found me because of that article in the paper,' she added.

'Oh, Lord. I'm most dreadfully sorry.'

'You weren't to know,' said Beth. 'Even I never dreamed he'd do something like this.'

Gordon said, 'You really should call the police, love.'

Again Beth felt like screaming. She was going to be under

334

this pressure, this impossible dilemma, all the time from now on. 'No,' she said emphatically. 'Promise you won't, either! As long as we keep this to ourselves, he'll allow us to have contact with the children. But if he thinks we've involved the police, God knows what he'll do. I know it's blackmail but he'll do it, he'll take Eirian away and I'll never –'

'Calm down, love,' Gordon said helplessly. 'Whatever you say.'

'But you say they're Christians, these people?' said Margaret, her tone soothing. 'Well, that's one less thing to worry about. At least you know they'll be kind to the children.'

'D'you know how to find it?' Beth said as she got into the car. 'I haven't got a map of Brum.'

'I know where it is.' Steve put the Metro in gear and pulled away as fast as the small engine and rutted track would allow. 'I went there a couple of times to talk Katy out of it: first time she wouldn't listen.'

'They never will.'

'Second time, they wouldn't let me see her. All I got was Luke and what looked like a couple of bouncers, warning me off.' Steve added grimly, 'If the children are being held at the church, at least they'll be all right. But if they're not there, then we'll *have* to call the police in, Beth.'

'Maybe,' Beth said, swallowing. She'd never quite shaken off the feeling that she was living outside the law. 'But not yet. Not yet. Even if they don't go charging in, however subtle they are, Luke will know.' She saw the image again: a policeman at the front door of the church, Luke in a back room with a knife to her daughter's throat.

'He's not fucking psychic,' said Steve.

'I feel like he is.' Beth shuddered. 'Look, we've been through this. While Luke's got Sam and Eirian we have to do things his way.'

'Okay, we get the children back ourselves, *then* prosecute the hell out of Luke.'

Beth wanted to share Steve's optimism, but her fear was like

335

black water churning in her chest. The motorway to Birmingham was monotonous, partly lit by soulless orange lights, partly sooty-grey. The car engine whined as Steve pushed it to its limit. Beth closed her eyes and tried to reach out to Eirian with her mind, but nothing would happen.

I'll never forgive Luke for this, she thought. He's turned out like Mum wanted. And he's going to do to Eirian what Mum tried to do to me: exorcism, brainwashing, oppression, to satisfy some fantasy of saving souls.

To make himself feel powerful. Yes, that's what he always wanted.

Goddess, if it were only a fantasy! But it's real to him and this is really happening.

The car slowed down. Beth opened her eyes to find Steve pulling off the motorway and on to a main road. The city looked grimly industrial and relentlessly ugly. Heartless, just as it had the day she'd fled on the bus eleven years ago. She sank down in her seat, rigid with tension.

They drove for what seemed at least half an hour; Steve swore to himself a couple of times.

'Are you lost?' said Beth.

'No. I can find it!'

They went in circles; Beth kept quiet. At last Steve drew up in a backstreet, lined with gaunt Victorian houses not unlike her parents' house. All was colourless under the street lamps.

They got out of the car to confront a big detached villa. There was nothing to mark it as a church but a small plaque beside the door: The Church of the One Truth. Pastor Luke Herne. Beth tried to look in through the bay window, but the blinds were down and there were no lights on.

Steve tried the door. Locked. He hesitated, then rang the doorbell.

'It looks deserted,' Beth whispered. She was trembling as they waited, but inside she felt angry, strong, and determined.

A light went on inside.

A young man with a beaky nose, receding chin and acne answered the door. He was wearing grey flannels and a tattered beige sweater. His eyes bulged when he saw Steve and Beth on the doorstep.

'We've come to see Luke Herne,' said Beth. 'Can we come in?'

'I'm afraid the pastor isn't here,' said the youth, in a Brummie accent. 'I can't let you in looking like that, sister.'

'You'd better,' said Beth. She put her hand to the man's shoulder and pushed past him into the hall. Steve followed.

'Where is he?' Beth demanded.

'I told you, Luke's not here. Please. I'll have to ask you to leave.'

'Do you know who I am?' Beth marched down the hall, opening doors; the rooms were dark and empty. 'I'm Beth Herne. Does that mean anything?'

'No.'

'Where are the children?'

'What children?' said Acne.

'Don't fuck around with me! You know bloody well what I'm talking about!'

Acne winced, but he answered calmly, 'There are no children here, sister.'

Steve said, 'We want to see Katy Pointon. I know she's here.'

'She isn't, I'm afraid.'

'Are they upstairs?' Beth began to mount the green lino treads. The place reminded her of her father's dental surgery. 'Steve, stay downstairs in case anyone tries to sneak out.'

Acne followed her, becoming agitated. 'There's no one here, sister, I don't know what you want! Please, you must leave or I'll call the police.'

'Do that,' said Beth. 'I wonder how long a sentence you'll get for aiding and abetting child abduction?'

In the frigid glare of the landing light, she opened doors to bedrooms crowded with bunk beds. They were all empty in the stark light from the street lamps; there was nowhere for children to be hidden, but she called, 'Eirian! Sam!' in every room.

There must be an attic, a cellar.

She ran up another narrow flight of stairs and threw open a

door on to a room with sloping ceilings. Bare light-bulbs shone on the faces of five startled people, two men and three women, who were reading from Bibles. It was some sort of common room.

'Will someone please tell me where Luke Herne, Katy Pointon and our children are,' Beth said. 'Come on! Or do you want your house of God desecrated by a fucking witch?'

They gaped at her; Beth knew she must look shocking with her raven hair and clothes, starkly black against the neutral surroundings. One girl clutched the silver crucifix round her neck, as if to ward her off.

Yes, it felt good to be feared.

Having gained their attention, Beth said quietly, 'Someone must know where Luke is holding the children. What he's doing is against the law. Tell me now, and you won't be in quite so much trouble later.'

There was a footfall behind her. Before she could look round, someone grabbed her. Hard, muscular arms held her in a vice; a hand grabbed her hair so she couldn't even turn her head. 'Jacob!' exclaimed Acne. Unable to resist or even see who'd grabbed her, Beth found herself being dragged painfully down two flights of stairs.

The attacker bundled her along the hall and thrust her hard out of the front door. She landed painfully on the doorstep and remained there, dazed, on her hands and knees. Steve was beside her, trying to help her up.

'Go home,' said a voice though a gap in the door. Not Acne; a stronger, harder voice. She caught a glimpse of short blond hair, broad shoulders, a hard, masculine face. 'You've seen for yourselves that the children are not here. They've been taken away for their own good. You were warned that if you tried to get them back, you would never see them again. Luke will be informed of this. He will be in touch, but only as long as you don't make any more stupid moves.'

The door closed emphatically.

'Bastards!' Steve shouted. Then, 'Beth, are you all right?

Some thug dragged you downstairs; I thought he was going to kill you!'

'The cellar,' Beth said weakly. He helped her to the car; she was dizzy and shaken. 'Haven't looked in the –'

'I looked while you were upstairs,' Steve said morosely. 'They're not here, Beth.'

She sat in the front seat, her head in her hands. 'There are only about seven people in the house,' she said. 'The cult must have another house somewhere. But where? How the hell are we going to find it?'

'Come on.' Exhaling heavily, Steve started the car. 'Let's go home.'

It was after midnight when they arrived back at the farmhouse, exhausted and disheartened. There were no further messages from Luke. Beth knew she wouldn't sleep; she and Steve sat with the family in the sitting-room, with the television burbling inanely in the background, and drank Horlicks. Her scalp was tender where her hair had been pulled, and she felt bruised all over.

The family tried to offer comfort, but eventually they ran out of things to say. One by one, Frank, John, Margaret and finally Gordon made their apologies and went to bed.

'It's all right,' Beth said as Gordon went. 'You need to sleep. I can't, that's all.'

She and Steve sat talking until dawn. The silence of the telephone hurt like nails down a blackboard, even though Beth didn't expect Luke to call in the middle of the night. Finally, she began to nod off out of sheer exhaustion.

'Come on,' said Steve. 'We'd better go home and get a few hours' kip. Gordon'll tell us if there's any news.'

It was growing light when they reached the cottage. The light shone strangely on the brickwork, in blobs and streaks of whiteness.

As they drew up, Beth saw that it wasn't light, but paint. She jumped out of the car, and stopped in disbelief.

Huge white crosses had been painted on the doors and

walls. The paint had run into ragged streaks. Words had been painted above the crosses: A witch lives here; Servant of Satan; and Burn the Witch!

'Oh, fuck!' Beth cried.

She went to touch the paint on the front door. Hard gloss paint, still sticky but drying fast.

'For Christ's sake!' Steve exclaimed.

'It'll take for ever to clean this off.'

'One of Luke's followers must have done it,' said Steve. 'They must have been watching the cottage from the woods, waiting for us to go out.'

Beth shuddered at the thought. 'This is meant to be a free country, isn't it?' she said tightly. 'Freedom of worship. If you ask me, nothing's changed. Nothing.'

'Never mind it now,' said Steve. 'Let's go in. I'm so knack-ered I can't think.'

Beth didn't think she would sleep, but she did, fitfully, until about ten o'clock. She dreamed she met Guendolen in the unspoiled wildwood of four hundred years ago, and begged her, 'If you see Eirian, make her tell you where she is! I must know where she is!'

But when she woke, she knew it had only been a dream, not a true vision.

'I've decided,' said Steve, sitting on the edge of the bed, still fully dressed. 'I'm going back to Birmingham and I'm going to watch the church.'

Beth sat up, her head aching, her mouth dry, a sick feeling of terror lurching through her. 'Why?'

'So if anyone leaves, I can follow them. They'll lead us to where Luke's holding the children. Or maybe Luke will turn up.'

'I can't see you as a private detective, somehow.' Beth meant it as a feeble joke, but Steve became furious.

'Look, Beth, Katy always said I was a wimp and I never got off my backside to do anything, but I'm damned if I'm just going to sit about waiting for something to happen! I'll get Sam back if it's the last thing I do!'

'All right,' she said, touching his arm. 'Sorry.'

There was nothing alarming or threatening in Steve's rage, and it evaporated too quickly. No fire behind it. Beth was afraid that after an initial outburst of defiance, he would collapse.

She said, 'Give me a few minutes to get ready.'

'No, I want you to stay here,' said Steve. She began to protest but he went on, 'I'm not being chauvinistic. One of us needs to be on hand in case Luke phones, or even turns up. And you can't drive.'

'Right.' Beth sighed. 'Okay. I can't stand waiting around, that's all. But if I was with you, I'd wonder if anything was happening here. I can't win.'

'We'll win,' he said.

'Be careful, won't you? We found out they're not above using violence. You ought not to go alone.'

'Are you okay, by the way? Any bruises?'

'A few, and a hell of a headache. I'll take a painkiller.'

'Haven't you got some arcane herbal remedy?'

'What's the point of that, when you can buy aspirin from the chemist?' Beth said mordantly.

'I'd better go,' said Steve. 'I'll see if Chez can come with me.'

They hugged. He left, and Beth got up, feeling shaken and numb. It was so hard to believe it had happened and that Eirian wasn't simply at school. And then Beth remembered that she hadn't made breakfast for the farmers.

Damn, she thought. First time I've ever let them down.

Half an hour later, when she'd had a bath and the aspirins had begun to work, there was a knock at the back door and she found Gordon and Margaret there.

'I'm so sorry about breakfast,' Beth said. 'I couldn't think straight. I just forgot.'

'Never you mind that,' Margaret said firmly. 'We don't expect you to work while this is going on! *I* made it.' She flexed the hand that had been useless.

'Any messages?' Beth asked anxiously.

'Nothing, love,' said Gordon. Her heart sank, although it was only what she had expected. 'We came to see how you are.'

Beth had stood back to let them in, but they remained on the step, looking up at the outside walls. 'But Beth,' said Margaret, 'who's made this terrible mess?'

Beth had forgotten about the graffiti. Her heart dropped down another step. 'I think the people who took Eirian did it.'

'It's disgraceful,' said Gordon. 'Why the devil would they – they ought to be locked up!'

Margaret came into the kitchen, using her stick but walking quite strongly now. 'I know you're not a believer, but that's no reason to call you a witch!'

'But I am,' Beth said quietly. She'd kept the fact quiet before; they'd never asked questions, but now they looked at her with a kind of baffled disapproval. 'Don't look at me like that. All it means is that I see the world as created by a Goddess rather than ruled by a God. I'm not a fanatic; I think people create the gods and goddesses that suit their temperaments. But Luke thinks it means I've made a pact with the Devil. You probably do, too; most people have completely the wrong idea.'

'No, no, we don't think that!' Gordon said quickly. 'It's a sort of nature religion, isn't it?'

'Sort of,' said Beth.

'Well, have you tried talking to Luke?'

'Even if I had the chance, it wouldn't make any difference. The trouble with people who think they've found the one and only truth is that they dismiss anything different as evil. And I think *that*'s evil, but what can you say? Luke genuinely believes he's saving Eirian's and Sam's souls.'

Gordon and Margaret fell quiet, looking uncomfortable. Finally Margaret said, 'Has Steve's wife ever challenged him for custody of Sam?'

'I don't think so. She walked out and never even came to see them.'

'It's just that if she does, she might win. And it's also possible that Luke might manage to have Eirian taken off you, if he's a mind.'

Beth went hot and cold. 'That's outrageous! How?'

'Because of this . . . occult thing, Beth.'

'I've just told you, it's nothing to do with Satanism, black magic or any of that nonsense!'

'I believe you, love.' Margaret clasped Beth's arm. 'Good Lord, we know you're a good girl, the best, but the courts probably won't see it that way. I mean, we've got nothing against the way you dress or the friends you have round, but it could be used against you. The courts'll see clean-living Christians trying to rescue children from an undesirable lifestyle.'

There was a chemical smell, and then there was blackness.

When Eirian began to come round, everything remained black. A band was chafing her eyelids, preventing her from opening them properly. A blindfold, tied so tight it hurt her head.

She went to pull it off, but her hands were also tied. She tried to cry out but there was sticky stuff over her mouth and she could only moan.

Her head hurt. The noise of a car engine filled her ears and she could feel the motion and smell the horrible leathery-plastic stink of the car.

Trying to shuffle sideways, Eirian came in contact with an adult leg. A hand pushed her off. Fingernails came scraping at Eirian's cheek, then there was a hot, sharp pain as the sticky tape was ripped off her mouth.

Eirian yelled, with fear and indignation.

A voice from the front said, 'What d'you take the gag off for?'

'She's woken up,' said a female voice. 'I was worried she couldn't breathe.'

'You haven't taken the blindfold off, have you?'

'I'm not stupid, Mark!'

343

'Sam,' said Eirian. 'Where's Sam?'

'He's here,' the woman said brusquely. 'Now shush. We've got a long drive.'

'Let me out!' Eirian roared. 'Let me out, let me out!'

'Put the gag back on her!' said the driver, whom the woman had called Mark.

The woman tried, but it wouldn't stick. Eirian bit her fingers. The woman yelped, 'You little c—'

'Susan! Language!' said Mark.

'Oh, shut up!' said Susan. Then, with forced sweetness, 'Just sit quiet, Eirian, because you're not going anywhere. The quieter you are the sooner we'll get there.'

Her memories were growing clearer now. She remembered the lane, the gilded blossom and the blackbirds singing as she and Sam walked towards the farmhouse. She remembered the black car reversing down towards them, its engine so quiet she could hardly hear it. She had thought it must be someone lost, using the lane to turn round.

Then the doors had opened, and Sam had been wrenched away from her, and there was the nasty smell that sent her mind humming down into oblivion.

Eirian was frightened, but this was not as bad as being drowned, or seeing Guendolen being raped. She saw a dark face with golden eyes in her mind, and ice-petals snapped around her emotions.

'Is Sam asleep?' Eirian asked.

'Yes.'

'Can you untie my hands so I can touch him? Then he'll know he's not on his own when he wakes up.'

'No,' said Susan.

'You'd better take his gag off, though.'

'Why?'

'He gets car-sick.'

'Shit,' Susan whispered. Eirian heard the tearing of the adhesive. Sam whimpered, regaining consciousness. A few moments later, he was duly sick.

'Oh, *Jesus!*' Susan wailed. And Eirian smiled, hoping fer-

344

vently that they would never get the smell out of the upholstery.

Sam started crying.

'It's all right, I'm here,' Eirian said gently. 'Some people are taking us for a ride. Are you all right, Sam? Don't worry.'

'I need to go to the loo!' he said.

'So do I,' said Eirian. 'I think I'm going to wet myself.'

'For God's sake!' Susan cried. 'Mark, can't you drive any faster?'

Eirian's dignity wouldn't let her carry out the threat, but Sam obliged.

She estimated that they were driving for about an hour; how long they'd been on the road before that, she had no idea. Then the noise of other traffic faded, and the car slowed down.

'Okay,' said Mark. The car came to a halt. 'Get them inside before you take the blindfolds off. The less they see, the better.'

Eirian was propelled forward, and promptly tripped over a step. The pain of falling shook her. A man's hands caught her under the armpits and she was lifted, carried and dumped on her feet.

A door closed and the blindfold came off. She blinked, her eyes stinging. They were standing in the hall of a big house with off-white walls and a grey marble floor. It was all absolutely plain; there were no pictures on the walls, and the only decoration was a cross painted on the wall of the stairwell.

The woman, Susan, had a plain round face, a pudding-basin hair-cut and a sour expression. She untied Eirian's hands; Eirian tried to hold Sam's hand, but Susan kept them apart. Sam, miserable and red-faced, was sniffing.

'Put his glasses on!' said Eirian. 'He can't see properly without them!'

'Bossy little madam, aren't you?' said Susan. But she took Sam's glasses out of her pocket and thrust them on to his nose.

'I want to go home,' he said.

'Well, you can't,' said Mark. 'You live with us now.'

Mark was ordinary-looking and wore a suit. He smiled as he

spoke to the children, but his eyes were too serene, as if they'd been emptied by some tranquillizer.

'I want my mother,' Eirian said firmly.

'So do I!' Sam wailed; meaning, she thought, he wanted Beth.

'But your mother's here!' said Mark. 'We've brought you to your mummy. So don't be afraid, Sam.'

'You'll go to jail for this,' said Eirian. Mark and Susan looked at her strangely, but said nothing. Doors were opening and more adults coming into the hall to view the captives. They had a look; short hair, plain unflattering clothes, a small silver cross round the neck. And they smiled as they came, exclaiming, 'Here they are! Oh, Mark, aren't you brilliant! Any trouble? Oh, praise the Lord!'

'Here's your mummy,' Mark said to Sam.

A slim young woman with a cap of ginger hair came rushing towards Sam. 'Darling!' she cried, throwing her arms round him.

Sam screamed and started hitting her. She leapt back, looking offended. 'I'm your mother! You can't have forgotten me!'

'Are you Katy?' Eirian asked. Susan had let her go, so she went and put her arm round Sam. 'He hasn't seen you for five years. No wonder he's forgotten you.'

'Leave my son alone,' Katy said stiffly, pulling Sam away. 'Darling, I've missed you! Have you missed me?' Sam remained stubbornly silent, and Katy seemed embarrassed, as if she hadn't a clue how to treat him.

'Come on,' said a blonde girl at Eirian's side. 'Let's get you settled in. Is your name Eirian? I'm Meg.'

Meg was a beach-ball of a woman with masses of wispy yellow hair and friendly grey eyes. Eirian immediately liked her. She was like Bryony: kind, vulnerable, eager to please.

'You can't keep us here,' said Eirian as Meg led her upstairs, following Katy and Sam. 'My mother will come.'

'I know you're a bit upset, but don't worry,' Meg said brightly. 'Do you need the loo?'

Eirian was taken to a bathroom with old-fashioned white

fittings, damp bubbling up beneath the plaster in places. There was no lock on the door; when she tried to open the window, which was sealed, Meg opened the door a crack and said, 'Don't take too long!'

So, she was to be allowed no privacy.

Acting cold and silent, Eirian let herself be taken along the corridor to a room. It could hardly be called a bedroom. There were two mattresses on a lino floor, a cupboard and a couple of hard chairs. Opposite the door was a large bay window; Eirian could see a flat landscape with trees, nothing she recognised. They seemed to be miles from anywhere.

Sam was already there. He'd stopped crying, but was stubbornly resisting Katy's efforts to get him out of his soiled clothes.

'Come on, Sam, you *smell*!' she was saying helplessly.

'Sam's mother never wanted him before,' Eirian said to Meg. 'Why does she want him now?'

Meg looked her in the eye; she was nervous and fluttery, but very sincere. 'Now, listen to me. Your name isn't Eirian any more; it's Faith. That's a Christian name. You're going to find things a bit odd at first, but you'll get used to it and you'll really love it here!'

'But why am I here?'

'Luke brought you,' Meg said gently, 'because your mum can't look after you.' Eirian felt a stab of unease; did Mum send me away because I wouldn't talk to her? She wouldn't do that, would she?

'Of course she can. This is wrong.'

'No, Faith. I know it's strange being taken away from your mum but you've got a new family now. She wasn't teaching you about how Jesus loves you. It's very important that you learn about Jesus and God or you won't be saved and go to heaven. That's why Luke brought you and Sam here. Because he loves you. We all love you here, Faith. We really love you and you're going to be so happy!'

Meg clearly believed every word, and assumed Eirian would believe it too.

347

'Don't keep calling me Faith,' she said.

'You'll soon get used to it. Are you tired? Would you like a lie down before supper?'

'I would like,' said Eirian, 'to go home.'

Katy wailed suddenly, 'I can't do a thing with this child!'

'Let me,' Eirian said brusquely. 'He knows me.'

She helped Sam out of his damp, puke-stained clothes and took him to the bathroom, with Katy and Meg in tow, to have a bath. They insisted he keep his underpants on in the bath, to avoid 'immodesty', which seemed to Eirian absurd.

'Don't be frightened, Sam,' she whispered, kneeling by the bath. 'I'm with you. Be strong, and we'll soon go home.'

'What are you whispering about?' Katy demanded.

When the children went back to the room – Sam swamped in an adult dressing-gown – a man was there, framed in the bay window. Like Mark he wore a suit and he seemed very calm and strong. Seeing him, Katy and Meg almost simpered, as if meeting royalty. He flicked a finger, and they went out, leaving the children alone with him.

This was the man Eirian had seen driving away from the cottage last week. Luke, Beth's brother.

'Samuel and Faith,' he said. 'Welcome home. God bless you.'

They stood like naughty children in front of a headmaster. When Luke smiled, his eyes weren't vacant, but full of passion and darkness. Just like the Inquisitor. Eirian went so cold she couldn't breathe.

'I wish to welcome you to the Church of the One Truth, and explain why you're here. We're very happy to have you with us at last. Do you know who I am?'

'Mum's brother,' said Eirian. 'Not my father.'

'No, but I have a right to guide your soul on to the path of salvation. You were born in sin, Faith.'

Eirian said coolly, 'That's strange. Mum said I was born in Birmingham.'

Luke stepped forward and smacked her across the face. It happened so fast she didn't see it coming. The pain shocked her like a blow to her soul and she began to realize that she couldn't cheek her way out of this, as she had with Miss Townsend. Luke was real, and strong, and terrifying. She sensed in him the monumental weight of doctrine, great wings as dark as the Bible flapping from his shoulders.

'You prove my point,' he said. 'Your insolence may be tolerated at home, but it is not tolerated here. Obedience, meekness and humility; these are what you need to learn. There is no easy way to grace.'

Eirian, furious, folded her arms and stood her ground.

'You are the man with the Word of God from on high, so you can tell me what to do,' she said acidly. 'And I can't argue because I am Satanic shit and filth. Is that it?'

Luke's face dropped, as if he couldn't believe such words had come from her lips. Eirian herself didn't know where the words came from.

She went on, 'I know why men like you have to believe the Bible. If you didn't believe it, you'd be scared to death. Scared, scared, scared. Well, you can pray yourself stupid. You won't stop the Black Crone coming to get you in the end.'

Luke glared at her, then his face lifted into cruel curves, as if she'd proved him right.

He went to the cupboard and took out what appeared to be a riding crop. Eirian ran to the door but found it locked. Luke came after her, pulled up her sweatshirt and, while she tried frantically to wriggle away, dealt her a single hard blow across the back.

She collapsed with the pain, tears flooding her eyes. Sam shouted in protest. She waited for more but Luke only stood over her, flexing the whip.

'Now you know how it feels,' said Luke. 'Imagine how *this* feels.'

He grabbed Sam, pulled up the dressing-gown, and struck him across the spine; one, two, three. Sam yelled pitifully and lay writhing on the mattress.

Eirian screamed, 'Leave him!'

Luke straightened up. His perfect hair was in slight disarray, but his face was as smooth as ever. 'Every time you spit blasphemy, Sam will suffer for it. Is that what you want?'

She shook her head, near to hysteria.

'It may seem harsh, but God's work is never easy. How else can I make you understand that the depth of your sin causes suffering to others, not just to yourself?'

Eirian faced Luke, but she couldn't speak. She was afraid, and in pain, and terrified for Sam.

Luke put away the whip and locked the cupboard.

'From the first moment you were conceived, the Devil has had uncontested possession of your soul, Faith,' Luke said intensely. 'Well, now he has a rival. Your soul is a battleground for God and the Devil; the question is, which of them are you going to aid?'

Later, Eirian was taken to an office and allowed to speak to Beth on the phone. 'Tell her you are all right,' said Luke.

Eirian obeyed. But as soon as she tried to elaborate, the phone was snatched off her. Then Luke told Beth not to try to find her daughter.

When Eirian and Sam were put to bed on the mattresses, on opposite sides of the room, the lights were left on and Meg and Katy sat up, watching them. Half way through the night, they left and Susan took over. Eirian got the message. They weren't to be left alone for a moment.

The fluorescent lights were bleak and cold. Eirian lay with her eyes shut, but she didn't sleep a wink.

I won't give in, she thought. Goddess, please tell me what to do! I can take it, but it's so unfair on Sam!

An absolute sense of helplessness came over Eirian. She thought of the Horn, lying hidden under her mother's bedroom floor; if only I'd got it with me, like a sword to fight my way out! But I haven't.

She'd never been so aware of herself as a child before, helpless among adults. She'd always had a sense of strength; even in the other place, even when she'd watched terrible things happening, she hadn't felt so bereft of power.

I can't escape like I could from the other place. It won't fade away when it gets too dangerous. Unless I do what they say and believe the things they're telling me, they're going to hurt me. And worse, they're going to hurt Sam. He can't look after himself like I can.

Eirian had been angry with her mother for not understanding, for letting things happen to her instead of fighting back, but at least Beth had loved her, and let her be herself.

The only person in all the world Eirian wanted now was her mother.

You must help us, she thought.

She closed her eyes and pushed the thought out further. *Help us.*

She thought, but what if Mum can't hear me? There must be someone else. Only half of me came from her.

She turned the thoughts into images and broadcast them hard, far and wide. Out on the wind, across mountains and oceans. She felt the Goddess's will surging through her.

You have never heard my voice, she thought fiercely. You had better hear me now! Help us. Help us. *Help us!*

Chapter Twenty

THE sea was full of grey walls, leaping, surging, dropping. The boat, riding the swell like a roller-coaster, was tiny under a huge louring sky. The clouds were dark and smoky, the ocean utterly desolate.

Morgan clung to the rail. The deck swayed and reared as waves exploded against the vessel, one after another. He was soaked, breathless, drowning. But as the boat surged on, faster and faster, he could only cling on, filled with foreboding. He knew that something terrible was about to happen. There was nothing he could do to stop it.

Water spouted hard into the air. There were huge fin whales all around the boat. Morgan saw their shiny wet backs curving out of the waves, the blow-hole of each pulsating like a great, honeycombed nostril. The sight of the whales only increased his formless, agonizing anxiety.

Morgan clutched the rail and leaned out, trying to see clearly, but all was vague, half veiled in stormy darkness and clouds of spray. The world was wild, unstable and hostile.

He saw a white streak, a horn or a harpoon, cleaving the waves.

Suddenly there was colour, down in the granite greyness. Clouds of crimson.

Blood in the water.

Red spray burst into Morgan's face. He cried out. The whole ocean was red and the black sky was rushing down to capsize the tiny boat.

Morgan saw a shape, mottled grey like a corpse.

And then he saw the girl's face floating under a wash of sea water, deathly white, like a china doll impaled on the horn. A face he seemed to know, pleading for help, too late. Calling to him from the world beyond death.

The boat turned over and he plunged into the salt sea,

sinking down among the corpses and blood and the huge shadow-shapes of the fin whales, drowning.

Morgan woke violently with a cry.

The cabin was dark. He felt the boat moving gently beneath him at its moorings, heard the creaks of the rigging and the eerie singing of humpbacks through the hull. His wife was lying beside him.

That was the third time tonight he'd had the same nightmare. Every time he fell asleep, it happened.

'You all right?' Marian said sleepily. 'What is it?'

'Did I wake you? Sorry. That damned dream.'

'Not again. What's wrong with you tonight?'

Morgan stared at the cabin ceiling. 'I've no idea. Can you hear the whales singing?'

'No. You must be hearing things. Look, we set sail for Greenland in the morning. You'd better not be coming down with 'flu or something.'

Morgan was silent for a few moments. Marian was so relentlessly practical; how could he make her understand? Eventually he just came out with it. 'I'm not going.'

'What?'

'I've got to go home. England, I mean. There's something really wrong there. It must be my mother, I can't think what else.'

'You've been working too hard,' Marian said firmly. 'Too many hours stuck in the laboratory. You need to get out on the ocean. We both do.'

'I'm not going,' he repeated softly. 'I'll get someone to drive me to the airport.'

'Go to sleep,' she said, turning her back. 'Phone your mom in the morning; I'm sure she's okay.'

Morgan couldn't face the dream again. As soon as Marian was asleep, he went up on deck and stood breathing the chill air. The harbour and the bleak Newfoundland coast rose to starboard; the waves were calm and solidly slate coloured. No blood, no child impaled and drowned. Only darkness.

*

The first day without Eirian was miserable and went on for ever.

Beth went up to the farmhouse with Margaret, oblivious to the blossom and birdsong which she usually loved. Spring had turned to winter for her. She felt helpless; Steve had gone back to watch the church, and without him to drive her, she couldn't go anywhere – unless she cycled – but where was there to go? Nothing to do but wait by the phone. So she did her usual housework with constantly shaking hands and her mind flying everywhere.

The farm couldn't be neglected, just because her world was upside down. The farmers' work went on as normal.

Gordon said, 'If I've got time later, I'll nip into Tam'orth and get some paint stripper.'

'What for?' Beth said blankly.

'So we can get that mess off the cottage.'

'Oh, yes, that. Thanks.'

At two o'clock, Luke rang. Beth gripped the receiver so hard she was in danger of breaking it.

'You were a foolish girl last night,' he said. 'You went to the Birmingham church and caused trouble, I hear.'

Beth tried very hard to stay calm. 'You can't seriously expect us to make no attempt to get our children back. What sort of mother would I be?'

'One who has bred a very wilful daughter.'

Beth thought, is Eirian being difficult? Good!

'One of your church members attacked me,' she said. 'That's assault. It's lucky he didn't put me in hospital. Look, Luke, please let's discuss this reasonably. You know you can't keep Eirian. If you tell me where I can pick her and Sam up, we'll forget all this, no hard feelings.'

A pause. 'You know that isn't possible. You aren't fit to raise a child. However, you will be allowed regular contact with Faith and Samuel.'

'I'm sorry, who's Faith?'

'Your daughter's name is now Faith.'

Beth held on to her anger so hard she thought she'd explode. 'Go on,' she said.

'You will receive regular news of Faith and Samuel, but only if you make no further attempts to find her. She is not at the Birmingham church, as you have seen. Her location is secret. She can be moved again at a few moments' notice, if you attempt to involve the authorities. By the way, if you are still tempted, consider this: even if they could find her and take her from us, it is likely that you wouldn't be allowed to have her back. I've seen how you live. A hovel with no electricity and a mother who takes part in Satanic orgies. No doubt you take drugs, too.'

'I don't even smoke!' Beth pressed her knuckles to her forehead, raging at the futility of the conversation.

'I was going to let you speak to Faith, but as you were foolish last night, I withdraw the privilege. I shall call again tomorrow.' He paused. 'You understand, don't you, that this is your punishment?'

'For what?' No answer. 'Luke, please!' she cried, but he was gone.

Beth dropped the receiver on its cradle, and burst into tears. Margaret fussed round her, but Beth was inconsolable.

'You know, if you told the police, they might be able to trace the calls,' Margaret said.

'I know, but I daren't,' Beth said, through a sodden tissue. 'If the police mess it up and I never see Eirian again, I'll never forgive myself. I don't know what to do! This is unbearable.'

'I wish I didn't feel so helpless,' said Margaret. 'If only we hadn't contacted that stupid newspaper!'

'It's not your fault my brother's a lunatic. Luke might have found me anyway.'

Margaret made a pot of tea, and put a cup in Beth's hands. 'But I can do things like this now,' Margaret said, flexing her once-paralysed arm. 'Thanks to you. You haven't eaten, have you? You must have something.'

'I can't eat. May I use the phone, please?'

'Of course, dear. You don't have to ask.'

Beth tried to ring Rhianwen, but she wasn't there. She tried again at hourly intervals; in between, she occupied herself frantically with chores, despite Margaret and Gordon's efforts to make her sit down.

At about nine in the evening, Steve arrived, looking ghastly with tiredness and disappointment.

'Nothing moved all day,' he said. 'No one came or went.'

'They'll probably go in the middle of the night, if they're going anywhere,' said Beth.

'Chez and Tag are still there in the van. Night watch.'

'Bless them,' said Beth, almost weeping again with gratitude. 'Come on, you look done in. We'd better go home to bed.'

'Have you told Rhianwen?' Steve asked.

Beth sighed heavily. 'I've tried. She's been out all day. What could she do, anyway?'

'I dunno. She might . . . consult a crystal ball, or something.'

'We don't do that kind of thing. You should know that by now.'

'Try again, anyway.'

Beth tried. This time, Rhianwen answered. Within half an hour she came rushing into the farmhouse kitchen, white-faced with anxiety, to hug and console Beth and Steve.

'I'm so sorry I wasn't home, I've been running errands all day,' said Rhianwen. 'That bloody little sod, Luke! There must be something I can do.'

'Not unless you know someone who knows where Luke's hiding,' Beth said grimly.

'Have you told your grandparents?'

'Not yet,' said Beth. 'I suppose I'll have to, if this goes on much longer. I don't want to worry them.'

'What about your parents?'

'You're joking!' Beth was horrified. 'They won't help me! They're probably on Luke's side!'

'I'll ring your father, if you like,' Rhianwen said calmly. 'He'll speak to me.'

'I bet he will!' Beth flared.

Rhianwen gave her a sideways look, frowning. 'What's that supposed to mean?'

'Nothing,' said Beth, turning away. 'I'm upset, that's all. Sorry.'

'Come on, love,' Rhianwen said, stroking Beth's hair. 'Don't lose hope. At least you know the children are alive, and not with a stranger. I'll stay with you tonight, shall I? At least I can be with you.'

'It's a bit spartan but I would appreciate it.' Beth thought, at least Rhianwen's here, at least she cared enough to come over! Beth went on, 'You can ring my dad if you like, but I gathered from Luke he has nothing to do with the church. Why should he help anyway? He never gave a damn about me in the past.'

Eirian found her first day at the church hateful, and she knew things could only get worse. She and Sam were woken at six – not that they'd slept – and Susan made them kneel down and pray. It was a childishly simple prayer, but Eirian refused to say it.

'You'll have no breakfast until you do,' said Susan. She stood over them, relentlessly severe.

Eirian gave in, because she didn't want Sam to starve, but she added, 'Goddess' under her breath whenever they said 'God'.

They were taken separately to the bathroom to wash and dress. Sam's clothes had been washed and dried. Then Katy brought a tray of porridge, bread without butter, and some chemical-tasting orange squash.

'I have tea at home,' said Eirian.

'Tea is an artificial stimulant,' said Susan. 'We don't drink it.'

Susan left, so they were alone with Katy. Katy seemed very young to Eirian; rather, she looked the same age as Beth, but she behaved like a wilful twelve year old. Eirian thought, I can play up to that.

She deliberately spilled her squash. When Katy rushed to fetch a cloth, Eirian spoke quickly to Sam.

'We've got to stick together and be strong. If they think they can grind us down they'll think they can do it to anyone. D'you agree?'

Sam nodded. He'd got over his tears, for the time being.

'Are you okay?' Eirian asked.

'Yes,' he said. 'But I miss my dad. It hurts where that man hit me. My mum doesn't like me, either. I want to go home!'

'We will. Remember I'm with you. I'll look after you.'

'I'm glad you're here, Eirian. I won't call you Faith, it's a stupid name.'

Then Katy came back. 'No talking!' she said, as if she suspected a conspiracy.

'Have you seen Sam's back?' asked Eirian, lifting up his shirt. The stripes looked red-raw. 'Do you think it's okay for Luke to beat your son?'

Katy's pale eyes widened and she seemed to bristle, as if she couldn't tolerate being in the wrong. Eventually she mustered an answer. 'If the pastor sees the need to chastise him, it must be right.'

'So everything Luke does is right, is it?'

'Yes!' said Katy. Eirian half expected her to stamp her foot.

'I don't think Jesus beat people and abducted children, did he?'

Katy looked furious, then her mouth crimped into a curve. 'Jesus said, "Suffer the children to come unto me, and forbid them not." Your mother and Steve were in the wrong, forbidding you to come to Jesus.'

'My mother is sleeping with Steve,' Eirian said casually. 'Did you know? He loves her much more than he ever loved you.'

'Liar!' Katy's freckled face went magenta, and she ran out. Eirian could hear her in the corridor, complaining to someone, 'I can't stand that child, she's got the filthiest mouth on her! I won't put up with her talking to me like that!'

Then Mark's voice, chiding. 'But you must; she can't help it, she's possessed. You can't give up, or you'll be letting Luke down. You don't want to let Luke down, do you?'

'No,' said Katy, as if this were a terrifying prospect.

'Go and pray for strength, sister.'

Mark and Meg came in and began, very slowly and patronizingly, to tell Sam and Eirian a gospel story. They sat on the hard chairs while the children sat cross-legged on the floor.

'We did all this at school,' said Eirian.

'But you didn't understand it,' Mark said patiently. 'That's why you're here. To learn to understand.'

'There is something I don't understand,' Eirian said, frowning. 'May I whisper?'

'Of course, Faith,' said Mark, opening his hands.

Eirian went into Mark's arms and murmured in his ear, 'You've got the hots for Luke, haven't you?'

Mark thrust her away, his face a storm. 'That devil in you must be cast out!' He pointed at her, his hand shaking. 'God deplores your insolence!'

Meg leaned forward, curious. 'What did she say?'

'Nothing!'

'It's not a crime to be gay, Mark,' Eirian said out loud. 'Well, it would be if you fancied Sam, but I'm sure it's all right with Luke.'

Mark strode out and shut the door so hard the walls shook.

'Eirian!' Meg gasped. 'Faith, I mean!'

'I don't know why he's upset,' Eirian said innocently, 'unless Luke doesn't fancy him back.'

'What are you talking about?' Meg squeaked. 'We are celibate here. Do you know what that means? We're pure, we don't –'

'Fuck each other,' said Eirian. 'Yes, I know what it means.' Sam began to giggle uncontrollably.

'Now look.' Meg took hold of herself, with obvious effort, and her voice fell back to its normal level. 'I know you're only doing this to shock us, dear, but it won't work. Bad language impresses no one. Settle down, because we've got to finish this story.'

'Why?'

'Because you won't be allowed out of the room until you do.

359

You won't get any lunch,' Meg said softly. She looked uncomfortable. 'The better you behave, the better you'll be treated.'

'Like dogs performing tricks for sugar lumps?' Eirian said caustically.

'Don't be silly.'

'I don't see why I should pretend to believe things I don't, just to earn lunch. Breakfast was horrible, anyway.'

'Faith, please.'

'This isn't fair on Sam! You can starve me, if you must, but leave him alone!'

'Oh, dear.' Meg bit her lip, looking upset. 'The thing is, Luke says if *you* won't do as you're told, both you *and* Sam will be punished.'

'Luke's a really nice person, isn't he?'

'He is!' Meg cried. 'You don't understand! It's a harsh and thorny path, having your soul saved; it's not *easy*.'

'Is your soul saved?' Eirian asked softly.

'I'm working at it.'

'But what have you done wrong? Why would a kind person like you go to hell?'

Meg looked down at the Bible in her hands, as if ashamed. 'I did a really terrible thing.'

'Committed murder? It can't have been that terrible.'

'It was,' said Meg.

'Tell me,' Eirian said softly.

'Well . . . When I was sixteen I got pregnant and I, I had an abortion. I felt so bad after, I was on tablets and everything. I couldn't cope, until I met Luke and he showed me how Jesus would take all the burdens off me. He really died for *my* sins, mine. And for yours, Faith.'

'I'm sorry you felt bad,' Eirian said gently. 'But millions of people are born, and millions of people aren't. We can't all be born, especially if the time isn't right. We come out of the stream of life and we go back into it. If I hadn't been born, I wouldn't know about it, so I wouldn't mind, would I? Don't feel bad, Meg.'

Meg said nothing.

'Shall we go on with the lesson?' said Eirian.

'In a minute.' Meg's shoulders shook. She was crying.

Katy knelt alone in the assembly hall, praying with all her might.

She was regretting ever mentioning Sam to Luke. All she'd wanted was a word of comfort to absolve her from feeling guilty; instead, Luke had begun to gnaw at the problem of Sam's soul like a tiger at a piece of fresh meat.

'If you want to bring your son to God,' Luke had told her, 'then God must be calling you to do so. When our second branch comes into operation, we will need new blood. Children. They are the way ahead.'

Katy had sat in meetings with Luke, Mark, Jacob and Susan as they discussed the best means of rescuing Sam from spiritual pollution. She'd felt miserable and uneasy, but totally unable to argue. You didn't argue with Luke! I don't actually want to look after Sam, Katy had thought, I don't want him here, but how can I stop them?

She couldn't. It was out of her hands. Plans were made behind Katy's back, while she and many of the congregation were installed in the new, secret house to await Sam's arrival. Presumably he would be the first of many children.

Luke had decided that the child of Steve's witchy girlfriend must also be removed from the evil influences under which she'd been brought up. This child, Luke explained, was possessed by the Devil. Luke had predicted a direct confrontation with the Enemy and, as always, he had been right.

Katy had heard a rumour that the witch, Beth, was actually Luke's sister, though Luke himself had never admitted it. It couldn't be true, anyway, could it?

Now Sam was here, it was even worse than Katy had feared. Sam was nothing but a nuisance, snivelling and whinging about wanting his dad. I knew I was better off without him, Katy thought, half pitying and half hating herself, and I was right!

But those stripes on Sam's back. That couldn't be right, but how could Luke do anything wrong?

I don't know anything any more, Katy thought. Almighty God, please forgive me for wishing Sam wasn't here! Please, please tell me what to do.

The Lord answered her prayer with a message of diamond clarity.

Luke is your leader. Put all your faith in him.

At about twelve, Eirian caught a gorgeous smell of beef stew and dumplings and potatoes baking. Both she and Sam had healthy appetites and were desperately hungry and thirsty after a tedious morning of being counselled by ardent believers. Eirian could see Sam falling under the spell, and she didn't see how she could save him, unless she got him on his own.

Their lunch, however, delivered by a middle-aged woman she hadn't seen before, consisted of an apple and a piece of bread and cheese each, and more of the horrible squash. Both children were still hungry after.

Later, Katy and Meg took the children out of the room to an assembly hall on the ground floor. Sam seemed more at ease with Katy by now; he was beginning to accept that she was his mother after all. Eirian wasn't sure this was a good thing.

There was a high ceiling, plain white walls, rows of chairs facing a dais at one end. Eirian was so glad to be out of the wretched room that she felt high spirited. She looked around for a means of escape. The windows were too high. Would the front door be locked, if she made a dash for it? But they were sitting in the front row, and other people were filing in.

I'd never get past them, she thought, thinking of Guendolen floundering through a sea of arms in the cathedral.

There were about fifty people, although there were chairs for three times as many. Luke was obviously planning to expand his congregation. Eirian noticed rather more women than men, including a clique of middle-aged ladies. They all looked ordinary, apart from the uniform drabness of their clothes – and the serene glassiness of their eyes.

They smiled and hugged each other as they came in, saying, 'Bless you, sister, bless you, brother,' non-stop. To Eirian's disgust they all insisted on hugging her and Sam, too, as if they were long-lost family.

Eirian found their kindness repellent, since they were keeping her prisoner. Once or twice, to particularly ardent advances, Eirian snapped, 'Get off me, I don't know you!' and was rewarded by hurt, baffled looks.

She realized they pitied her. How revolting.

Mark took the service, aided by three men who, Meg told Eirian, were deacons; there seemed to be no female ministers. They wore ordinary clothes and addressed each other by their first names. The deacons sat on the dais with Luke and a group of musicians with guitars, tambourines and flutes.

Eirian found the service the most extraordinary thing she'd ever sat through. Nothing like the maudlin service she'd endured in the cathedral with Guendolen, this was an explosion of cheerful music, handclapping, shouting. Not so far removed from the Sabbats with the Primarolas, she thought; a way of working themselves into a heightened state without drugs. But the Sabbats had been joyful. This was a form of hysteria.

Eirian remained stubbornly seated, despite Meg's attempts to make her stand up and join in.

The first burst of singing over, Mark addressed the congregation, in passionate tones, about avoiding sexual sin. Eirian smiled at him throughout; he faltered once or twice, then avoided looking at her.

Another hymn, then Luke spoke. He spoke of the roles of women and men, of original sin and the achievement of grace, of the end of the world and everlasting life. His tone was emphatic, passionate and repetitive. Eirian was transfixed, more by his delivery than the content. Yes, it was hypnotic. It was persuasive. It was designed indeed to put the fear of God into anyone who was vulnerable.

Sam looked frightened. Eirian wanted to hold his hand, but with Katy between them, she couldn't.

The congregation was transported, including Meg and Katy. Eirian was alarmed to see two relatively sane young women suddenly turning into slack-faced hysterics.

When the music began again, people were crying, screaming, giggling and talking gibberish. Eirian suspected a degree of competition among them. Luke pronounced that the Holy Spirit had come down among the saints; clearly no one wanted to appear left out.

It had been obvious from his sermon that Luke despised women. And yet these women accepted his view of them as weak, sinful and naturally subordinate!

Eirian thought they were all crazy. To see this mayhem among adults profoundly disturbed her, and she felt desperate to escape.

Luke came down among the congregation and began to touch individuals. When he touched Katy, she went rigid and sat lifeless in her chair, grinning at the ceiling, as if in a trance.

She's putting it on, thought Eirian.

Then Sam's terrified face appeared round his mother's body and he whispered, 'Eirian? Is Mummy dead?'

That finished it for Eirian. To inflict this on a child!

She was on her feet, gripping Sam's hand, pulling him determinedly towards the door. The others were so taken up in their ecstasy that the children were in the outer hall and half way to the front door before anyone followed.

Eirian reached the front door. It was solidly locked. Then two of the deacons grabbed her and dragged her upstairs to the dreaded room again. Sam was bundled up behind her.

She fought to reach Sam, but he was torn away from her. The last she saw of him was his freckled face, red with emotion, as another callous man dragged him along the landing. Sam was struggling and yelling, 'No! Eirian! Help me!'

The deacons shoved Eirian into the room and locked her in, alone. She ran to the window, struggled to open it, looked around for something to break it even though there was a sheer drop to the ground.

The door opened, and Luke entered. She saw an aura of white light round him, the energy he'd absorbed from the meeting. He exuded the menace of a scorpion.

'Faith,' he said heavily, 'have you heard the term, "tough love"?'

'No,' she said, folding her arms defensively.

'It means that because we love you, we must seem to be cruel in order to save you from yourself.'

'I don't want to be saved. I'd rather live in the underworld with Lilith and Persephone and Cernunnos; they're my friends, not you.'

Luke grabbed her shoulders and pushed her down to her knees. 'Blasphemy, Faith.'

'I have faith, but not in the deformed self-hating garbage you believe.'

He leaned close to her, pulling hard on her hair so she couldn't move. 'Now listen, you little bitch, I know what you think you're doing. You think you're very clever, don't you? But it isn't you speaking. It's the demon inside you. So you're not so clever after all. If you had any will of your own, you'd speak out against the demon. You would say, "I accept the Lord Jesus Christ as my only Lord and Saviour." Your pain will not stop until you say it, Faith.'

Her mouth opened in agony. She thought he would tear her hair out by the roots. 'You can't make me believe in God by torturing me!'

'Not torture. Tough love.' Luke flung her away and stood over her, laughing. He was like a lion, unassailable. The depth of her own hatred terrified her – because it proved Luke's power. 'The world is going to end very soon. God will sweep it away. Will you stand in Paradise glorying God with the Chosen, or will you spend eternity in the pit with the rest of the rubbish?'

A spider-cold thought betrayed her. What if it's true?

Eirian had no supper that night. The middle-aged woman

who had brought lunch came again, but this time she was carrying a Bible, not a tray. She was slender and imposing, with staring blue eyes, brown hair turning grey, and long hands clasped around the black book. She'd been beautiful once, Eirian observed, but years of distress or illness had scored her forehead with lines, hollowed her cheeks, drawn pouches under her eyes. She seemed uneasy as she came towards Eirian.

Susan was in the room, but she left as the woman came in. Eirian sat down on her mattress and ignored the intruder.

'Faith, do you know who I am?' The voice was quiet, but there was a steel cable within it.

'The Virgin Mary?' Eirian said flatly.

'I'm your grandmother,' said the woman.

Morgan could hear the droning of the boat's engine all around him. He watched as the horn arrowed through the darkly surging ocean, turning it all to blood, and the child's face came drifting up through the watery redness, paler and paler as it rose to the surface. Her lips were as white as her face. She had drowned. And then her eyelids flew open and she stared straight at Morgan with green eyes like lasers.

'Beef, chicken or vegetarian, sir?'

Morgan jerked awake to find a stewardess smiling expectantly at him from behind a narrow steel trolley. The droning was that of jet engines, not a boat.

'Oh, erm, beef, please.'

Morgan picked at the food in its tiny plastic trays, drank the complementary wine, and stared out at the glowing horizon beyond the aeroplane wing. He was worried now. He had tried to ring Rhianwen several times during the day. The last time had been from the airport at St John's, just before he'd boarded his flight to Heathrow. It would have been around one in the morning in England by then, yet Rhianwen still wasn't home.

He knew he was right to go home. But he was dreading what he would find when he got there.

Marian would be in mid-ocean by now, following whale mi-grations. She wouldn't have dreamed of abandoning the project, and Morgan hadn't expected her to; she'd thought he was crazy to fly home on the basis of a dream. He couldn't make her understand. Marian was a total sceptic where telepa-thy or the supernatural were concerned. That was partly why he'd married her.

As always, when Morgan flew home, he couldn't help wonder-ing about Beth. Where she was, what she was doing, whether she ever thought of him. He hoped she didn't hate him. And he wondered, often, what the child was like. Difficult to believe it was so long ago.

It had hurt, that Beth had never answered the letters he gave to Rhianwen for her, never even sent a message. My own fault, Morgan thought. I let Mum and Beth's family scare me out of trying to see her; she must've thought I didn't care, and by the time I did write, it was too late. Why did I write, anyway? Guilt?

I don't know whether I loved her or whether it was just the sheer excitement of seducing her, but if I didn't love her, why did she haunt me for so long?

Morgan had managed to put Beth out of his mind eventually. There had always been something to get in the way of trying to find her: life at university, work, exams, friends, travel. The more time elapsed, the less realistic the idea of seeing Beth became. Eventually Morgan had realized that it was only a fantasy; that she was part of the past, gone.

Marian had helped, of course. They'd drifted together through long hours spent in laboratories and lecture halls. She was outgoing, intelligent and beautiful, with long blonde hair; half the men at the university had been after her. Morgan remembered an evening when they'd been working late; one moment taking turns to peer down a microscope, the next kissing passionately and pulling off each other's lab coats.

Marian was utterly different from Beth. She wasn't naïve or vulnerable; she wasn't affectionate, either. She didn't see visions when they made love. Sex with her was magnificent, but it was only sex.

Morgan had been able to marry her – when he'd backed away from other relationships – because she demanded nothing of him emotionally. There was work, sex and laughter; and of those, work came first for both of them. Their partnership couldn't have been more perfect.

The flight was less than six hours. Morgan stayed awake, not wanting to face any more visions; couldn't have slept anyway. As the plane dropped in long steps through the clouds, all he could think of was how long it would take to get through customs so he could try to phone Rhianwen again.

Morgan came out into the main concourse at eight and found the public telephones. Still no answer. Shouldering his bag, he went out through the glass doors and jumped on the first shuttle bus to a car rental firm that came past.

He felt sick with worry now.

Rhianwen spent a sleepless night at Beth's cottage, in Eirian's bed. In the morning, she had breakfast with Beth and Steve, though none of them could eat much. They talked fruitlessly for a couple of hours; Rhianwen wanted to ring Beth's father, but Beth was against it.

'If we contact my parents, they'll just tell Luke straight away and God knows what will happen to Eirian then! Especially if it's you who calls them. Don't, Rhianwen, please. Not until everything else has failed.'

Rhianwen looked at her watch and gasped. 'It's getting on for eleven. I must go home and feed the cats. Will you be all right, Beth? I'll come back this afternoon.'

Beth nodded tiredly, trying to smile.

Rhianwen arrived home to find hungry, indignant cats mewing for their breakfast. With her mind constantly on Eirian she fed them, had a bath and got changed, then tried to meditate in the hope of picking up some clue. Nothing came. Only glimpses of the past, Guendolen being raped by a psychopath who believed that torture would save her soul.

Rhianwen brought herself out of the trance. Dangerous. Surely Luke isn't like that.

Yet she remembered, when he'd been a small, quiet boy who'd liked football and bikes, how she'd had to stop him tormenting the cats.

Giving up, she made herself some lunch, then tidied up after herself. It was while she was in the kitchen that she heard the front door open.

'Who's that?' she called, walking through. And there in the doorway was her son.

Rhianwen was stunned to see Morgan; even more amazed when he dropped his bag, rushed forward and threw his arms round her. 'Mum, thank God! Are you all right? I thought –'

'What? What is it, love?'

'I thought you'd had an accident, or something. That's why I came home. I tried to ring but you didn't answer.'

'No,' she said, trying to get her breath back. 'I stayed with someone last night, I haven't long been back. What made you think –'

'I suppose you'd call it a premonition.' He thrust his hands in his jacket pockets, looking anxious. 'I kept having nightmares. Kept seeing a girl's face, drowning in blood. Horrible. I just knew something was wrong here, don't ask me how. I knew you needed me.'

'Oh, Goddess,' said Rhianwen, turning away and sitting down on the edge of a chair. 'I don't believe this.'

'What?' He came to her and put his hand on her shoulder. 'Mum, tell me.'

Rhianwen thought, what do I say? He has a right to know. If things go badly wrong and he finds out I didn't tell him, he'll never forgive me. At last she said, 'There is something wrong, love. Beth's daughter has been abducted.' She almost started weeping as she said it.

Morgan gaped at her. 'She's what?'

'And they took a boy, too, the son of Beth's boyfriend. Luke took them.'

'Beth's brother Luke? The bastard! Why?'

Rhianwen explained what had happened. 'Look, Eirian's all right. Beth and Steve are doing everything to get them back. There's nothing you can do.'

'Nothing?' said Morgan. She sensed fury, indignation, dark emotions that had been held back for twelve years. 'Are you crazy? Of course I've got to do something! You'd better tell me where Beth is.'

Rhianwen was shocked by his tone. 'Morgan, it won't do any good, after all this time.'

His voice became as subtly dangerous as black ice. 'I've had enough, Mum. The child goes missing and you don't even let me know! I have to cross the Atlantic to find out!'

'I didn't see the point of worrying you.'

'Tell me where she is, Mother,' he said, gripping her shoulders.

Rhianwen exclaimed, 'You can't just go marching in on Beth out of the blue, after everything –'

'What the hell does the past matter at a time like this? Beth and I are adults, not love-struck teenagers; your obsession with keeping us apart is just a little redundant now, isn't it? The only person who matters is her daughter. *Our* daughter. Tell me!'

Rhianwen, chastised, felt the years of careful manipulation collapsing around her. Morgan was right, of course. They were adults, the past was dead. And she had no right to prevent something that might help Eirian. 'All right, love.' She sighed, defeated. 'Beth only lives a few miles from here. I'll take you over there later. Why don't you have a rest and a shower while I warn her?'

'What d'you mean, warn her?' Morgan seemed stunned to have won the argument; he'd gone pale.

'She's already in a state. I don't want her collapsing with shock.'

Beth had lain awake for most of a second, long night, while Steve slept soundly beside her. She was aware of the vast cold sky, the moon, the tangled branches; Hecate's domain. How can people believe in an impossible paradox like God? Luke thinks God is saving Eirian; from here, it looks as if God's abandoned her. And my Goddess? Is it any more use, praying to her?

In the morning, after Rhianwen had left, Steve came up with a fresh plan. 'I'm going to see some people. Katy's parents, for a start; they can't stand me, but she might have told them where she is.'

'Don't tell them about Sam though, or they're bound to call the police,' Beth said anxiously. 'Make out you just want to see Katy.'

'I'll have to play it by ear,' Steve said irritably. 'And I'll try Katy's old friends. One of them must know something. If that's no good, I'll go back to the church again. I don't know how long I'll be gone, so don't worry about me.'

'I can't help it. I hate staying here on my own!'

'But Luke might phone. And Rhianwen's coming back, isn't she?'

'Yes. We can go out in her car, anyway, if we need to.'

Steve drove Beth along the lane to the farmhouse, but as they pulled in, the telephone bell was shrilling out. It was about twelve-thirty. They looked at each other. 'Luke rang at two yesterday, didn't he?' said Steve. 'Could be anyone.'

'Come in, just in case.'

Beth ran into the kitchen, to hear Gordon saying, 'Hang on, she's just arrived.'

It was Luke. Beth listened grimly, then replaced the receiver and turned to Steve.

'Luke says, tell your friends to stop watching the church. There will be no contact with Sam and Eirian for two days as a punishment. And if it carries on, we won't hear from them again, ever.'

'Oh, shit!' Steve exploded. 'I've had it with this guy!'

'Just do what he says, Steve,' said Beth, shaken.

'Can't you put a curse on him?'

'Don't be an idiot!' she flared. Then Steve reached for her and they held each other, apologizing, while Gordon hovered in embarrassment.

'I'll still go and see the other people,' said Steve. 'I'll have to tell Chez to pull out, first.'

The telephone went again, and they both jumped out of their skins.

'Hello, Beth, how are you?'

It was Rhianwen. Beth took a breath and steadied her voice. 'Er, surviving, sort of.'

'I've got some news. Morgan's here. Turned up about half an hour ago.'

Beth felt a kind of emptiness, as if she'd missed a step. 'Why?'

'He knew something was wrong, without being told. Says he had a premonition, so he decided to come home.'

'Why are you telling me this?' Beth said dully.

Rhianwen sighed faintly. 'Because he insists on coming to see you.'

Beth sat down, heavily, on the chair by the phone.

'Do you mind?' said Rhianwen.

'Do you?'

'It really doesn't matter, does it?' Rhianwen sounded irritated and resigned. 'Anything that might help get Eirian back.'

'When, when is he likely to arrive?'

'Well, I've made him go to bed for a while; he hasn't slept properly for two nights and he looks dreadful. So I'll bring him over later this afternoon. About four, probably.'

'Would you rather I came over there?' said Beth. 'Oh no, I can't. Steve won't be here to drive me and the farmers are busy.'

'Don't fuss, we'll come to you. Shall we come to the farmhouse or the cottage?'

'Er, the cottage would be better.' Beth thought, the fewer people there are to watch me dying of embarrassment, the better. 'Is his,' Beth couldn't quite find her voice, 'is his wife with him?'

'No, he's on his own.'

After Rhianwen had rung off, Steve said, 'What's happened? You've gone scarlet.'

They were alone; Gordon had made a tactful exit.

'Morgan's coming to see me. Just like that.' Beth repeated what Rhianwen had said, and now she felt so strange she couldn't have described her emotions. She felt numb, weak, indifferent and scared, all at once.

Steve stared at her blankly, almost with hostility. 'The famous Morgan, and I won't be here.'

'You can stay. We'll be like strangers. I'm dreading it, actually.'

'No, I have to go.' His expression relaxed a little. 'Maybe he'll have a cunning plan; you always made him sound like fucking Einstein.'

'Steve, for God's sake.'

'Actually, it's probably a good thing for you to see him. He might be fat or bald, or chain-smoke, or have a cocaine habit. He might be a yuppy. He might vote Tory! That would break the spell, wouldn't it?'

'There isn't a spell!' said Beth. 'If all you can do is stand there bitching, you'd better go.'

'Sorry. I'm being paranoid.'

'Yes, you are. It will be very ordinary and I'll wonder why it used to matter so much.'

Steve kissed her. 'Well, good luck, anyway.'

'And you,' she said ruefully, and waved him off.

What the hell to do until four? Cooking the lunch wouldn't take long; Margaret was doing more and more, and Beth had already cleaned the house from top to bottom the previous day. She went out to collect the eggs, only to find that Margaret had already done it. As she came back, Gordon was in the yard, carrying cans and brushes.

'I've got that stuff for you, Beth. Brown paint for the doors – thought it would be easier than trying to remove it – and stripper for the walls. I'd do it for you, but we're so busy.'

'That's all right. Thanks, Gordon, I really appreciate this.'

Something to do, to save her from going mad.

Beth was up on a step ladder, at about three, painting her front door, when a large, smart estate car pulled up. Panic hit her: she had nowhere to go, had to stay there, trapped, as the man walked towards her.

He was in his late twenties, dressed in jeans, cowboy boots and a red lumberjack shirt, looking every inch a man who had just flown in from Canada. He had dark hair going thin on top, a thick woolly beard and a beer gut. Beth didn't recognize him at all but he was the right height, right age.

Oh, God, Steve was right, Beth thought. Her heart turned in loops of relief. It's bloody pathetic but it will be so much easier if I don't fancy him any more. She started to descend the ladder, telling herself to be very calm and offhand, even though her blood was thundering through her like an earthquake. Damn, he would be early!

She wiped her hand on her ancient dungarees. 'Er, Morgan?'

The man looked her over with indifference. Then he said, 'Cattle feed.'

'Pardon?' said Beth, dumbfounded.

'I've come to talk to Mr Cleave about cattle feed. They said he was down here somewhere.'

'Well, he isn't,' Beth gasped. 'He's out on the tractor.' She pointed at the horizon. 'On the other side of the farm. There's a footpath.'

The man grunted as if it were too much trouble. 'I'll drive round.' He got back in his car, and drove off.

Beth clung to the ladder, feeling a complete idiot.

Well, that's it, she thought. Morgan is not going to catch me in paint-covered dungarees and a headscarf.

She went inside, bathed and anointed her body, washed and combed her hair to a Cleopatra-black veil. She dressed in her favourite skirt of crimson velvet, a tight-fitting bodice and a deep black belt that emphasized her waist. She put on a couple of silver rings; nothing too elaborate. And she painted her face and eyes to look subtly exotic.

All the same, she felt that what she was doing was futile. What the hell did it matter what she looked like, when Eirian was suffering or, if not suffering, being seduced away from her?

But it was a compulsion. Something to do with pride, Beth thought; so that when Morgan sees me, he thinks, 'How could I let her get away?' and not, 'Christ, what a lucky escape!'

When Beth had finished, she sat down in a chair and was very calm. A goddess. We have both changed, she told herself. We both have other partners. It will be formal, friendly, and civilized, and it will all be about Eirian; nothing else.

I wish Rhianwen wasn't coming with him, she thought.

At five past four she thought, they're not coming. Rhianwen will have talked him out of it.

At ten past Beth heard another car draw up outside. She jumped to her feet, catching her breath. Of course, they were bound to come; I didn't finish cleaning the graffiti off the front! Sod's law.

She went to the window, and the man she saw locking the door of a dark blue Sierra was unmistakably Morgan. All alone.

'You're not my grandmother,' Eirian said contemptuously.

'I'm Luke's mother.'

'Beth's mother?'

'I had a daughter called Bethia, once. I'm your grand-mother, Olivia.'

'You're not my grandmother,' Eirian repeated. 'Rhianwen is.'

The woman stared at her. Colour spread slowly over her face and her eyes seemed to liquefy. 'You know Rhianwen?' she hissed.

A speck of spit landed on Eirian's lower lip. Obviously she was not meant to know Rhianwen. 'Of course,' said Eirian, wiping her mouth. 'We see her all the time. She's really nice. She looks after lots of cats. And my other granny is Heather, though she's really my great-grandma. But you are not my grandmother.'

'Heather's seen you?' Olivia took a step back, her face full of horror. 'I was right.'

'What about?'

'You are the child of the Devil!'

'You can't be Beth's mother,' Eirian said, gazing frigidly at her. 'Beth is wonderful, but you are an old bitch.'

The woman's lips drew back; she looked ready to explode with fury, and her fingers, crabbed around her Bible, were bloodless. Then Eirian saw a terrible exhilaration cresting over the rage.

'I have never seen anyone in such sore need of redemption as you, child,' said Olivia. 'I want to help you find the Lord.'

'Okay,' said Eirian, folding her arms. 'How did you find him, then?'

Olivia seemed to relax a little, as if she were on safer ground. 'I was in a sorry state when I was younger. One Good Friday I sat in church, meditating on the crucifixion, weeping for the Lord's pain and my own. I was staring at a great stained-glass window of Christ's Passion on the Cross and I suddenly understood. Only through suffering like Christ can any of us be redeemed!'

'Suffering,' Eirian said softly. 'Is that why you tortured Beth?'

'I did nothing of the sort! What has she told you?' Olivia leaned down, her odourless breath hot on Eirian's face. 'Let me tell you about your mother. She had every chance to be Saved. Instead she chose to walk with the Devil. She was a slut, a whore, a liar, a deceiver, a filthy, cowardly, depraved harlot. She caused me more grief than ever I caused her!'

Eirian drew back. Olivia smiled grimly, seeming to think she had shocked Eirian into submission. But Eirian met her gaze squarely and caught the imprint of Olivia's warped psyche.

'My mother is pure,' said Eirian. 'She's incapable of doing anything unkind or dirty, despite what you did to her. She's kind and loving and good. Now, let me tell you about yourself.'

'Shut up,' said Olivia. 'You can't be human, you don't talk like a child.'

But Eirian went on, unstoppable. 'When you tried to control Beth, you were trying to control yourself. All the filth you saw in her was the filth you saw in your own soul. When you

376

punished her, you were punishing yourself! What are you so afraid of? Why do you think you are so filthy and deserving of punishment? What gives you nightmares, *Grandmother*? All the nasty filthy demons inside you?'

'Shut up!' Olivia screamed, backing away. 'Luke! *Luke*!'

The door opened and Luke came in; obviously he'd been listening outside. 'I heard,' he said.

'You're wasting your time with this child,' Olivia rasped. 'She's turned out exactly like I knew she would! She should have been drowned at birth!'

Luke shook his head. 'Mother, you must have patience. No one is beyond redemption, not even Satan himself. Is she not the greatest challenge we've ever had?'

'She's evil.' Olivia was shuddering. 'You only have to look in her eyes! She's got eyes like that, that bastard who fathered her!'

She turned and rushed out. Eirian was alone with Luke.

'Well, Faith. You've upset everyone today, and you're a bad influence on Sam, so we've taken him away.' He gripped her arms painfully; when she tried to struggle, he pressed harder. 'Are you ready to say the words yet?'

'I'll never say them!'

'Oh, you will. But you seem intent on making things as difficult as possible for yourself. Let me remind you: for every word out of place, every little sin you commit, Sam will be brought in here and punished in front of you.'

Eirian forced down her rage and fear so hard they didn't reach her face. Her expression, like her voice, was a mask. 'I like it when you hit Sam,' she said coolly. 'It turns me on.'

The blow, crashing scarlet through her brain, knocked her out cold.

When she came round, Susan and a smiling man she didn't know were praying over her. Eirian tried to look at her watch, but it had been taken away.

It was dark outside and she badly needed to sleep, but they wouldn't let her. Her head ached, her throat was dry and she felt sick from lack of food, but still they wouldn't let her sleep.

Into the stark lights of the room came a procession of men and women in pairs, who talked non-stop of God's love and shook Eirian awake every time she began to nod off.

Outside the windows, blackness.

My blackness, Eirian thought. The night that belongs to Hecate and to me, the lovely soft dark powerful night. Mine.

The true darkness, the sort that held only lies and death at the centre, lay here, in the bright lights and the soft words and the sterile heart of Luke.

Eirian sent her thoughts spiralling out into the night; energy waves to call her sisters and brothers, the hags of the wildwood and the gods of carnal love, all those whom Luke's followers feared. She chanted silently, *Isis Artemis Diana Morrigan, all that I gave to you, give back to me now.*

But the ancient goddesses had no place here.

There was a fly buzzing against the fluorescent strip, bashing its fat, black body moronically against the plastic cover. The sight of it brought Eirian to despair. There was always a fly lurking around her, ever since that day Guendolen had killed the Inquisitor.

Doubt crept in as her spirit waned. What if they're right, muttered the treacherous thoughts, and I'm evil, and don't know it? All I have to do is tell a lie and they'll let me sleep.

She couldn't.

Exhaustion made her hallucinate that Luke was standing over her with searing red eyes and a spiked phallus sticking out from his trousers, willing her to confess, confess.

'You can't sleep yet,' said a voice.

Eirian woke, and Luke was really there.

Chapter Twenty-one

BETH moved away from the window as Morgan came to the door. She waited for him to knock and then she paused for ten seconds, not wanting him to think she was waiting behind it. It seemed the longest ten seconds of her life.

She collected herself, so that outwardly she would appear cold and businesslike. He's married and I'm with Steve. I must make it perfectly clear I'm over all that nonsense in the past.

Inwardly, every nervous response she possessed had gone haywire.

Beth opened the door and he was there: a man in black. T-shirt, black jeans, black leather jacket; neat and pristine as night. Morgan.

He looked different, and he looked the same. Slightly taller, still leanly muscular and slim. Older, but still young; faint lines around his eyes gave depth to his character. Same hair, thick raven silk hanging untidily to his collar. He was wearing glasses with thin black rims; that was different. Exquisite bone structure, dark eyebrows, green eyes . . . but to her shock she'd forgotten how beautiful his face was, forgotten its bewitching power to turn her weak with desire.

He looked like a young professor, and he looked – stunning.

They stared at each other.

'Beth?' he said, frowning as if he weren't sure.

'Hello, Morgan.'

'It is you. I didn't recognize you.'

'Come in,' Beth said offhandedly. She hoped he wouldn't notice that her hands were shaking so hard she could hardly close the door behind him. Her fingers were icy but her face was hot; she hoped she wasn't blushing. 'Did you find it okay?'

'No trouble.'

'I thought Rhianwen was coming with you.'

He gave a half-smile, not looking straight at her. 'I talked her out of it. You know how she takes over.'

'Did she – did Rhianwen tell you?'

'About – about –' Beth realized, to her surprise, that Morgan was as nervous as she felt. Strange; had she expected him to be a robot, emotionless?

She realized that he couldn't say Eirian's name. Couldn't say, 'our daughter,' or even, 'your daughter.' Just couldn't say it.

'Eirian.'

'Yes,' said Morgan. 'I thought I might be able to, you know, help. I had to come. Er . . .' An awkward silence. This was getting worse, not better. They really were total strangers to each other. Then he said, 'Did Mum tell you why? I had a premonition something was wrong.'

'Yes,' said Beth, clasping her hands to stop them shaking. 'Weird, isn't it?'

'Bit awkward, really.' He still had the Welsh lilt in his voice, like Rhianwen, that she'd found so seductive. 'We were about to set off on a sea expedition, part of this project we're doing on whale migration; I just walked off the boat and went straight to the airport. My wife thought I'd gone mad.'

My wife. Why did those words still make her shudder with horror? 'You must be tired, after your flight.'

He shrugged, exactly like Eirian did. 'I'm fine. I had a rest and changed into fresh clothes at Mum's.'

'The glasses are new.'

'Not really.' His smile still dazzled her. 'I've always been a bit short-sighted. Only use them for driving, really, so I can tell an old lady from a ten-ton truck.' He took the glasses off and put them in an inside pocket. She noticed he was wearing a wedding ring.

'They suit you, anyway.' But Beth thought, I wonder if he gets short-sightedness from my father?

'Nice cottage,' he said, inclining his head towards the front door, 'but did you upset your house painters, or something?'

Beth realized he meant the graffiti. 'Oh, that. Don't ask. I think Luke put his friends up to it.'

'Bloody hell.'

'How's Newfoundland?'

'Cold.'

Beth, shaking worse than ever, was running out of things to say. 'Er, tea?'

'I thought you'd never ask.'

Beth was turning away from him, edging towards the kitchen. She had to get away before she broke down and made a complete fool of herself. This was as awful as it could be.

'Make yourself at home,' she said.

'Beth,' he said gently. 'Oh, God, you look absolutely wonderful.'

She turned round. He'd followed her; he was almost touching her.

'So do you,' she said.

Morgan put his arms around her and she was crushed. Held. There at the centre of life.

For this moment she had waited twelve years. Would have waited sixty. Morgan's warm, hard body against hers. His arms binding her. To feel the passionate tension of his pain, his regret, not just her own. To know he hadn't been immune to the agony of separation and years of love unrequited.

'I'm going to be very stupid in a moment,' said Beth.

'It's all right,' he said. His mouth touched her ear and the shock arrowed down to her toes. 'So am I.'

Neither of them could let go. His leather jacket and some subtle musky-spicy fragrance he was wearing smelled delicious.

Morgan kissed her head, her temples and cheeks. And then, inevitably, his lips were on hers. Their mouths opened helplessly to each other and she felt soft flames melting her. Just like when she'd been fourteen but stronger now, much stronger. Steve had never made her feel this and never would.

Beth ended the kiss hurriedly. 'Oh, God, what are we doing?' she muttered. She pulled away and hurried into the kitchen, pressing her cold hands to her burning face. She could hardly walk straight, her legs were so unsteady. 'I'll put the kettle on.'

She meant him to wait in the sitting-room, but as she stood by the stove, waiting for the kettle to boil, Morgan followed her. He'd taken his jacket off. He stood behind her and put his arms round her.

Beth felt tears coming. This was unbearable.

She wondered, if we'd been together these last twelve years, would we have been on the verge of divorce by now? Or would we have still been in love?

When she tried to pour the boiling water on to tea bags in mugs, she spilled it everywhere.

'Let me,' he said, reaching round her to take the kettle off her. 'You'll scald yourself at this rate.' As Morgan poured the water, he spilled it too. 'Damn, I'm shaking like a leaf,' he said, and Beth felt a bit better then.

She got milk from the pantry; neither of them took sugar. Then Morgan picked up the mugs and said, 'Come on. Sit with me and tell me about Eirian.'

They sat together on the sofa, his arm round her, her head on his shoulder. It felt so wonderful to be touching him she could hardly breathe; could hardly keep her hands to herself, either.

But they drank their tea, and she told him about Eirian. Not everything; that would have taken hours. Only about her character, her intelligence, her singular personality. She showed Morgan a photograph and he said, 'She's lovely; she looks so like you at that age. She should have been here.'

'Rhianwen took loads of photographs; did she never show you?'

He shook his head. And then he went silent, his face mask-like. Beth could see that if he tried to speak, he would start crying. She wished he would, so she could cry too.

Pretending not to notice he was struggling, she told him how Luke had abducted Eirian and Sam.

'I feel so helpless,' Beth said, 'and so angry. At least Steve can go out and feel he's doing something. But I've just got to hang around waiting for Luke to phone.'

'I always knew there was something wrong with Luke,' said

Morgan, 'the first time I met him. Sorry, I know he's your brother, but –'

'Oh, don't be! I could kill him.'

'We ought to call the police.'

'I know, but I'm so scared if we do, I'll never see Eirian again.'

'Don't be scared, Bethie.' Morgan put his other arm round her and held her. The feeling was exquisite, like pain. All that had been between them twelve years ago was still there, magnified, because it was only separation that had made Beth realize what she'd lost.

'Do you know what tomorrow is?' Beth whispered.

'Wednesday.'

'It's Eirian's eleventh birthday.'

'Oh, Christ,' Morgan breathed. 'Sorry. I should have known.' His lean arms tightened around her. After a while, he asked, 'Did you ever think about me?'

'Only every day. Did you think of me?'

'Not every day,' said Morgan. 'Men are bastards, didn't you know? We put things out of our minds when it suits us. I only thought about you every other day.'

'As often as that?'

He let her go so she could sit back again, but he kept hold of her hands and stroked her hair as if he couldn't bear not to be touching her. Her memory hadn't deceived her; he really had been that affectionate. 'Are you angry with me?' he asked.

'I'm angry with someone,' she said. 'I don't know whether it's you, Rhianwen, my parents, or myself.' Beth was in agony, trying to talk about it; how could she admit she'd been heart-broken at losing Morgan, if he hadn't felt the same? She couldn't bear the humiliation.

'I promised you we'd be together when you were old enough,' Morgan said. 'I haven't forgotten. But I broke the promise.'

'I didn't think you meant it,' Beth said shortly.

He looked hurt. 'Why not?'

'Well, you never tried to find me. You let Rhianwen take you away. She promised me she'd tell you where I was when I was sixteen, but you never came. You couldn't even write and say sorry!' She was trying to sound indifferent, but she couldn't keep the pain out of her voice.

'Didn't you get my letters?' Morgan sounded horrified.

'What letters?'

'Ones I gave Mum to give to you.'

'I never got them,' Beth whispered.

'You mean she never . . .' He looked completely stricken. 'Oh, God Almighty, how could she? She made out you refused to read them. The bloody liar! Wait till I see her. I could kill her!'

'So could I,' said Beth. 'It would have meant everything to me to hear from you.'

'But Rhianwen told me you didn't want anything to do with me.'

'That was a lie. I was heartbroken, Morgan,' she said bitterly. 'I thought you didn't want me. She made out I was nothing to you, just one of a dozen girlfriends. I was frightened that if I found you, you'd reject me.'

'No, Beth. I don't know that I was fit to be a father, but I would never have rejected you.'

His words were knives. She couldn't tell whether he meant them or only thought he did. 'What did you say in the letters?' she asked.

'That I was sorry, and I hoped you were all right, and I wanted to see you. That kind of thing. Gripping stuff. So – you didn't hate me for what happened, after all?'

'Only once or twice,' said Beth. 'Maybe Rhianwen was right, though. Perhaps we were too young, and would've ended up hating each other. But I can't forgive her, for not letting us decide for ourselves! My mother was a nightmare, but it wasn't her who kept us apart; it was Rhianwen. It was her fault.'

'No,' said Morgan. 'It was mine.'

'Why?' Beth whispered.

'Because I didn't have to listen to her, but I did! All this time,

384

wasted. By the time she gave in and told me where you'd gone –'

'Oh, she *did* tell you?'

'Eventually. It was too late, really, and she knew it. I thought of trying to find you with the travellers, but it would have meant missing time at university, and I thought, am I going to throw away my career looking for someone who doesn't want me anyway? Rhianwen was so insistent that I was wasting my time. It was as if I'd break her heart if I didn't trust her. So I did what she said. I got on with my work and tried to forget. It worked, I suppose. Every year it seemed further away. Then I met Marian.'

'I never forgot,' Beth said fiercely. Her tears flowed freely. She felt so happy, and so miserable. Too much to bear.

'Beth.' He held her again. 'I'm so sorry. I thought I'd got over you, but the moment I saw you again – I couldn't believe my eyes when you opened the door. I've never met anyone like you. I wasn't wrong, I did love you all those years ago and I still love you now.' His green eyes held hers; they were hooks, thorns, demon eyes, and she was losing herself in them. Morgan had always been the gentlest of demons.

'You don't know me!' Beth cried, panic-stricken.

'Have you changed so much?'

He kissed her neck. Incandescent fires ran all through her from his lips. She was so aroused she almost came, just from the warmth of his mouth on her neck.

And then he stood up and left her sitting there.

'I'm sorry, Beth, I'm acting like an idiot. Of course you've changed. You love this Steve, don't you?'

'Er, yes.'

'I came here to help find Eirian, not to screw up your life.'

Morgan stood in the middle of the room, lean and dark, his hands hooked in his pockets, and Beth wanted him so much she was ashamed of herself.

She stood up, the fire cooling. 'What makes you think you have the power to screw up my life a second time?'

'Christ,' said Morgan. 'I asked for that.'

And now he wouldn't touch her at all, and she daren't touch him.

Beth tried to regain her composure. 'Tell me about this premonition you had.'

He relaxed. Something to talk about. 'I kept having this nightmare, every time I went to sleep. There was a stormy sea, something long and white like a horn passing through the waves, then the whole ocean would turn to blood. It started Sunday night.'

'That's the night they took Eirian,' said Beth, shivering.

'None of it made sense, but it was terrifying. I just knew I had to come home. I thought it was Mum, not –'

Beth broke in, 'Can you describe this horn?'

'Ivory coloured, very thin, maybe four feet long. I couldn't see it in any detail.'

Her heart went on pounding insistently. 'Can you keep a secret?'

'Runs in the family,' he said drily.

'Come with me. Have you ever seen a unicorn's horn before?'

Beth led Morgan up to her bedroom. She took a screwdriver from her dressing-table drawer, lifted the rug and removed a floorboard. She lifted the package, removed its covering, and let Morgan see the gold and ivory Horn inside.

He was transfixed. 'God, that's incredible.' He took it from her and sat on the edge of the bed. She felt he shouldn't touch it but it was too late, he was stroking the bands of carving. 'I know what this is.'

'What?' Beth gasped.

'It's not from a unicorn – well, obviously. This is a tusk from a narwhal, an Arctic whale.' He put a hand to his head. 'That's what I kept seeing, this kind of greyish shape; it was a narwhal! We've seen them around Baffin Island. Fairly dull whales, apart from the tusk. It's actually a tooth.'

'Don't give me a biology lesson,' said Beth. 'I think you've given me quite enough of those already.'

Morgan looked sideways at her; she had to bite her cheek to stop herself laughing. He was blushing, actually blushing.

'Yes, well,' he said, struggling unsuccessfully not to smile. 'This carving is amazing; it looks mediaeval. Where did you get it?'

'Now, that is a story.' Beth moved up beside him, so the Horn rested across both their knees. 'I didn't really think it belonged to a unicorn; I didn't know what it was.'

'Mediaeval hunters used to bring these home and pass them off as unicorn horns; no one ever saw the whales they'd come from, of course. They were meant to have magic and healing powers.'

'It must have been one hell of a trophy,' said Beth, 'and never mind the poor bloody whale.'

Morgan nodded sadly. 'You do realize that it's probably worth a fortune, don't you?'

'It's not for sale,' said Beth, taking it off him and laying it on the rug on its wrappings. 'It's Eirian's.' The Horn seemed to glimmer for a moment; a trick of the light, surely. But Beth felt a pressure all through her body and mind, demanding release. Desire, loneliness, anger, all of those.

Morgan's eyes were distant suddenly. Worried. Hesitantly, Beth put her fingers to his cheek. 'What is it? What else did you see?'

'Nothing,' said Morgan. He clasped her hand, kissed her fingers. Impossible to resist touching each other for long. Then his hands slid around her neck and he was kissing her mouth. Beth opened her lips and her whole self to him. All so easy, so natural, as if they'd never been apart.

His fingers, slender and strong, moved over her waist and came plucking at the hooks of her belt, the laces of her bodice. She pulled away to take the bodice off. As she stretched up, pulling it over her head, Morgan fell on her breasts with a sigh of pleasure that verged on relief; stroking the soft globes, kissing them, his hair deliciously stroking her chest.

She slid her hands beneath his T-shirt and felt his bare flesh at last. She closed her eyes and rested there a moment. In bliss.

Beth knew they shouldn't do this. They both knew, but it didn't stop them. They broke apart urgently to finish undressing, then they fell together on to the bed in a fever. And at last, at last, she had what she wanted: the feel of his silken skin and divinely firm body against hers.

She forgot he was married. She forgot everything.

His lips, tongue and teeth moved over her neck and breasts. She squeezed one of his long, hard thighs between her own, aware of her own wetness slicking his skin. The feel of his penis, trapped between his stomach and hers, hot and engorged, made her ache. She felt her heart hammering, blood flushing her face. If he had meant to suggest using protection she didn't give him a chance; she had to draw him into her, she had to be filled, surrounded and held, couldn't wait.

As Morgan slid into her, he kissed her, his tongue teasing between her lips. Beth burned and ached all over, outside herself. Gripping his buttocks, thrusting on to him, she climaxed so intensely that she almost passed out. The convulsion went all through her; body, heart, mind.

Morgan took longer, as if he didn't want it to end. She held him, felt him trembling with passion held back. When he came, his breath bursting in her ear, 'Beth, *Beth*,' she felt another spasm so poignant that she cried out.

Then he wrapped his arms round her and rocked her, covering her face with kisses. Their bodies were dewed with sweat and juices, but Morgan still smelled gorgeous. He whispered, his voice raw, 'Oh, Bethie, I've missed you so much. So much.'

And she knew he was speaking the unguarded truth. It was only the demon of doubt inside her that made her constantly mistrust him.

'We shouldn't have done that,' she said, pointlessly.

'Too late now.' Morgan smiled at her; his eyes were glittering and he was beautifully dishevelled. 'Don't be sorry.'

'I'm not.'

He stroked her face. 'Oh, Beth, what are we going to do?'

Luke was there. Just a man in a suit, but he was a mountain, a wall, a god. An immovable object with the Word of God in his chilling eyes.

'Are you tired?' asked Luke. 'Are you thirsty?'

'Well, I've been kept up all night and not given a drink,' said Eirian. 'Work it out for yourself.'

'God loves you,' said Luke. 'He wants you to have a drink of water and a sleep. Won't you admit your love for Him in turn, so He can give you those things?'

'It's your decision to keep them from me, not God's.'

'God is merciful. Won't you be merciful, so Sam can have his breakfast?'

'Sam is Katy's responsibility, not mine,' Eirian said icily. 'Have you heard the term child abuse?'

As Luke stood regarding her with his loathsome air of condescension, the fly wove aimless circles between them. Luke swatted it away; and at that moment, Eirian received a camera-flash of insight; a moment in Luke's past, frozen.

'That's what you like, is it?' Eirian murmured.

Luke, not knowing what she meant, smiled and withdrew from her prison.

Susan let her have a drink of water, eventually, but no breakfast and no sleep.

Eirian remembered seeing a documentary about political prisoners who had been deprived of sleep and food to make them give away secrets. She knew what Luke was doing. This was meant to make her malleable, so light-headed and confused that she'd believe anything.

And then, mystics had always used fasting to enter states of trance and induce religious experiences. She thought, does Luke hope I'll see an angel from heaven, and fall down crying, 'I was wrong, I'm a miserable sinner, I believe!'?

Is that what happens to people here?

The idea alarmed her. It would be a betrayal of all she'd ever experienced. Betrayal of Guendolen and the Midwife and the nameless millions like them.

I can't, she thought. I won't.

Eirian stared at the fly. Her eyes followed its meaningless

389

movements. She used it to focus her mind, to send a silent call
out into the crannies and attics of the house, out beyond the
walls into the moist roots of the grass and the fissured bark of
trees.

After a time, she heard the faintest dry tapping, all through
the house. Her call had been heard.

Meg came later, to continue Eirian's lessons. As soon as
she'd shut the door, Meg furtively produced a chocolate bar
and offered it to Eirian.

'No, thank you,' Eirian said politely, though she could have
fallen on it. 'I'm on hunger strike.'

Sheer panic filled Meg's round face. 'You can't do that!'

'They're starving me anyway, so what difference will it
make?'

'It's not for ever. I'll bring you food, secretly.'

'You'd be disobeying Luke.'

Meg looked desperately confused and worried. 'You'll make
yourself ill!'

'It would be embarrassing if I died, wouldn't it?'

'Don't talk like that!' Tears filled Meg's eyes. 'I wish I could
make you see how much we love you!'

'I think you mean it,' said Eirian, 'but Luke isn't like you. Is
Sam all right?'

'Yes, he's fine. He's coming along very nicely.'

That means he's given in, she thought. 'Are they feeding
him?'

'Of course, but you must be careful, or Luke will be angry
with him as well as you.'

'I'll be good,' Eirian said stiffly. 'I'll listen to my lessons. Go
on, tell me about the Bible.'

Meg tilted her head and gave Eirian that infuriating look of
pity. 'I wish you could find the happiness I feel! But to find it,
it's necessary to suffer. Jesus suffered.'

'The trouble is, you're missing the point, Meg. You tell me
that this or that is demonstrably true, because it says so in the
Bible. But I don't believe the Bible. I reserve the right to say
that the Adam and Eve story, for example, is crap. Do you

390

really think it's logical, that mankind should be punished for something two mythical people never did?'

'If you put it like that, it isn't logical, but symbolic things are still true.'

'So you believe in self-denial, the punishment of the flesh because it's sinful and evil?' Eirian spoke softly, and the words seemed to come from deep inside her. 'But imagine it isn't. Imagine your body is sacred. Then you could celebrate life instead of punishing it.'

'We do celebrate –'

'No, you don't, you despise it. You heard what Mark and Luke were saying yesterday! If you believe them, you must believe it's all right to whip a little boy.'

'Of course I don't, but –'

'Why do you hate yourself, Meg?'

Meg stared at Eirian, shocked. 'I don't. I used to.'

'No, you still do. That's why you're here. You need Luke and the Bible to take away your guilt and fear. But your punishing God is creating your guilt. Imagine if Eve's sin was invented to excuse men's hatred of women, not the other way round. Imagine if you could love yourself for being created in the image of the Goddess. Love Meg just for being Meg. Then you could feel your own power, even in the decision you made about your abortion; you'd realize that you possess the wisdom of the Crone, to know when it's time to create and when it's time to destroy.'

'Faith, stop it!' Meg was staring at her in fear.

'We're made in the image of the Goddess, Maiden, Mother and Crone; that's why men fear us. Their whole religion is built on the denial of death, but the Crone won't go away. That's why they try to make us hate ourselves. The Bible and the church are the works of man, not of God. God is deaf, dumb and blind but the Goddess is all around us. She is you, Meg. Your body and your blood are sacred; they produce life and death. Your pleasure is sacred, your kindness is sacred. Ask yourself: who has dared to tell the lie that Meg is bad and sinful?'

391

'No one. What you're saying is absurd.'

'Is it? I can say a lot more. For as long as you want to talk about the Bible, I can talk about selective editing and politics and inconsistences and invention and paranoia. I can show you men like Luke murdering millions of people like you and me, in the name of a man who preached love and forgiveness.'

'You *are* possessed,' said Meg. 'Where do you get this from? You're only ten!'

'I'm eleven tomorrow,' said Eirian. 'So what? I can't help what I know. If I listen to you, you must listen to me; that's only fair, isn't it?'

'Yes, it's only fair,' Meg said faintly.

'So, let battle commence.'

The trouble was, it was so easy with Meg that it was almost cruel to dig the roots of her faith away. But Eirian was gentle; she didn't leave her floundering in blackness but gave her images to replace those she was losing. She tried to give Meg her Self.

And something was changing within Eirian, too. Light-headed from fasting, she became an open channel; not to Luke's doctrine or holy visions, but to threads of a different energy. The shadow-light that had first drawn her to Guendolen's world.

As they talked, the delicious smell of cooking wafted upstairs, but Eirian was immune to it now. She smiled. A few minutes later there was a commotion downstairs, people screaming and shouting; Meg rushed out to see what was wrong, but Eirian already knew.

The kitchen had been suddenly overrun by rats, Meg told her later. They'd got into everything. Lunch had had to be thrown away. No one could work out where so many rats could have come from.

Eirian smiled serenely. 'Do you like spiders?' she asked.

'No, I can't stand them,' said Meg, shuddering.

'I'll keep them away from you, then.'

Meg went pale, and left hurriedly.

As the day passed, Eirian played on everyone who was sent

to brainwash her. As she'd played on Meg's niceness and gulli-
bility, she exploited Katy's selfishness and teased out Mark's
guilt over his lust for Luke. Susan she mocked until the poor
woman argued herself in circles. There were others, too. She
found out their weaknesses and tripped them up.

They no longer came singly but in pairs to protect each
other, but it made no difference to Eirian; she played them
against each other instead.

They were all damaged people, Eirian realized, in their different ways. They'd stumbled into Luke's cult from broken relationships, alcoholism, addiction, sexual guilt. They were lost
people who needed to be told what to think and do, needed a
leader to worship. When Luke explained, 'You are a hopeless
mess because the Devil is fighting for possession of your soul,'
it gave weight and meaning to their suffering. Without Luke
and the Bible, they would have been lost.

So Eirian led them out of the artificial light and into the real
darkness. She did so with anger, thinking, if you hadn't been
cut off from the Goddess, you wouldn't be lost in the first
place! She didn't hate them. She couldn't feel sorry for them,
though, because they'd made Sam suffer.

But Luke, oh, she hated Luke.

When Eirian's hunger strike became known, they tried to
force food on her, but she refused it.

Eirian was upsetting everyone.

Susan came back later, grimly determined, and reinforced
by one of the deacons, an overweight man called Paul, with a
chubby, bearded face. They sat down side by side on hard
chairs, beaming at Eirian. Then Susan opened her Bible and
fifty or so live centipedes came tumbling out on to her lap.

Susan leapt up, shrieking and frantically shaking her skirt.
The centipedes milled around on the lino. Paul performed an
undignified dance, trying to crush the creatures underfoot.

Eirian thought, what wouldn't I give for Sam to see this!

A little later, she heard Katy running along the landing,
loudly complaining that there were frogs in the bathroom.

Sound travelled in the house and Eirian could hear people

arguing about her in the corridor outside. 'It's her,' they all agreed. 'She is bringing these plagues into the house! The Devil is in her!' But how to treat her? To exorcize, to starve, to force-feed? Bullying or kindness?

Luke had taught them to believe in the literal reality of the Devil. That made it a lot easier for Eirian to drive them out of their neurotic wits with fear.

As the argument went on, Eirian heard Luke's crisp footfalls mounting the stairs. He silenced the arguing voices; he softly opened the door and came into the room with Mark. Mark stood by the door, his hands folded; Luke looked at Eirian. He seemed a towering shadow, a warning that whatever she was in spirit, her body and strength were only those of a child.

'I know what you are trying to do,' said Luke. 'You are very clever, demon, but not clever enough.'

Eirian was suddenly floored by ice-cold terror. She'd been calm until it hit her out of nowhere. It was the abyss of Luke's contorted, barbed, pitiless mind touching hers and nearly swallowing her.

But she clawed herself back from the edge and watched as Luke went to the locked cupboard where the whip was kept. Eirian was frightened of physical pain. What he'd meant to do to her, though, she never found out. As he opened the door, a great shoal of woodlice, spiders, beetles and mice came flowing out, alive and wriggling. Luke stood ankle-deep in the writhing mass, seeming paralysed by disgust. Mark exclaimed, 'Jesus help us!' and rushed out of the room.

'That's what you like, isn't it?' Eirian asked softly. 'Little, tiny defenceless animals to stick pins in. And to wank over afterwards.'

The ferocious blaze of hatred in Luke's face almost turned her to stone. She braced herself for an attack. But Luke quietly re-locked the cupboard door, stepped carefully out of the living mass, and came slowly towards Eirian.

His self-restraint was far more terrifying than an attack would have been.

'Well done,' he said. 'You have demonstrated to my flock

394

that you are an opponent worthy of me. Has it occurred to you how heroic I am going to look when I destroy you? It will be the perfect demonstration of God's invincibility.'

'I wouldn't put money on it,' said Eirian. But her heart was pounding.

'I would not put money on your demon,' he said, 'when we come to exorcize it. Tomorrow.' His authority crushed her, like the stony heartlessness in Judge Warbeck's eyes. Eirian wouldn't show it, but his power made her painfully conscious that she was only a child, physically defenceless. Secretly, she was turning rigid with fear.

'Don't leave it until tomorrow,' she said thinly. 'Do it now.'

'No. I'll leave you the night to lie awake and wonder what is going to happen. Enjoy the fruits of your devilry.'

He meant the insects and mice; he shut her in with them, but they held no fear for Eirian. She simply sent them scurrying under the door to infest the cult members' beds and food.

The fly, though, she could not banish. The fly hung around like her unknown fate. How vile, when she was Luke's spiritual superior, to be defeated by something as crude as physical violence.

Paul, Mark and Olivia, the old bitch who claimed to be Beth's mother, sat with Eirian all night, keeping her awake with hymns and Bible readings. Eirian switched off and sank into her own thoughts.

That night, her third, Eirian no longer felt hungry or tired. She felt like glass. The moon and the starry sky could shine through her. She called the Goddess through the moon and the Horned God through the Wand of Rebirth, visualizing its shell-light in her mind. All the powers that her captors feared, she called; she felt the ancient powers joining, flowing, swirling in silent ecstasy. Far away but moving closer.

But Eirian's mother and father hadn't heard. If they'd heard her calling they would have rescued her by now! She railed silently against their opacity, then took herself in hand.

If she couldn't make humans hear, she'd learned today that

she could reach animals. There were higher creatures she could command; the messengers of the Goddess.

Eirian wove her message and sent it looping out into the bleak, comfortless night.

'Do you always commit adultery the moment you're out of your wife's sight?' Beth asked. She lay with her head on Morgan's shoulder; he'd pulled the duvet over them. Blue dusk was filling the window.

'This is the first time ever,' Morgan said quietly. 'I've never been unfaithful before. I'm not like that.'

'At least you didn't call me Marian.'

'She didn't like it when I called her Beth, sometimes.'

'Did you, really?' Beth was perversely thrilled.

'It doesn't go down too well in moments of passion, I can tell you.'

'So she knows about me.'

'Yes, she knows about you. I didn't want her suddenly finding out I had a daughter I hadn't told her about.'

'What did she say?'

'She laughed and said something about everyone having skeletons in the closet.'

'She didn't see it as a threat, then?'

His eyes were distant for a moment, as if he were thinking affectionately about his wife. 'Marian doesn't let anything threaten her.'

Beth hated herself for asking, but she had to; it was like picking a scab. 'What's she like?'

'She's nice; she's from Kitchener, Ontario; she's blonde and slim, highly intelligent, likes animals, obviously; she's a lot of fun. Bit of a workaholic, though. Athletic type.'

'Really.'

'I mean she likes swimming, scuba diving.'

'I know what you mean,' said Beth. 'I bet she was a cheerleader.'

'I've seen the photographs,' said Morgan.

'Do you get on well?'

'Of course we do,' he said. 'I wouldn't be with her if we didn't.'

A shiver ran through Beth. I knew this was a mistake, she thought. He won't leave his wife for me; men never do. 'Do you love her?'

'Bethie, do we have to have this conversation?'

'As we have a daughter, and we're lying in bed together, and you keep telling me you love me, I think I have a right to know,' she said darkly.

'But however I answer, I can't win. If I tell you I love her, you'll feel betrayed; if I tell you I don't, you'll think I'm the sort of bastard who doesn't give a stuff about his wife.'

'You're wearing a wedding ring,' she said acidly. 'Is it so hard to tell me the truth, rather than what you think I want to hear?'

'This is the truth,' Morgan said quietly. 'I have never felt for anyone what I feel for you. The trouble was, I didn't realize it until I'd lost you. Yes, I'm fond of Marian; I suppose I love her, but it's not the same. I found it nearly impossible to have a relationship when I was at university. I don't know what I was scared of; making another girl pregnant, getting hurt or trapped. I suppose I was looking for another Beth, but you weren't there. I'd go out with someone a few times then run a mile. Marian and I kind of drifted together because we were working together. Marian's one of these very single-minded, self-sufficient people. She's an atheist; she thinks being a pagan is as daft as any other religion, so we don't discuss it. We work well together and we have a good time in bed, but . . .' he stared at the ceiling, pensive, 'tenderness; that's what's missing. She doesn't need it and she doesn't inspire it. But I miss it. I miss you, Beth.'

'Morgan, do me a favour.'

'Anything.'

'Don't bullshit me.'

'You're the one who never said, "I love you",' Morgan retorted. 'You've never said it, do you know that?'

'It's like a binding spell, isn't it? It's like putting yourself in someone's power and saying, "Here's my heart, trample on it."'

'How did you get so cynical?' Morgan said, dismayed. 'Is it my fault?'

'I don't know how you can still be so romantic.'

'Because it's not too late to make up for the mistakes we made, is it?'

'I don't know what you mean!' Beth said fiercely. 'You can't be telling me you'd leave Marian, just like that! How would she feel? No, don't answer. This isn't the time.'

'Well, what about your boyfriend?'

'Steve's wonderful,' Beth said with feeling. 'He's been my best friend for the past five years. I don't know what I'd do without him. He's never let me down.'

'Ouch,' said Morgan. 'That's put me in my place. I didn't realize the competition was so serious. But do you love him?'

'Do we have to have this conversation?' said Beth, mimicking him. 'I don't know. Yes I do but it's not the same, and all that.' She looked at Morgan's fingers, entwined with hers. 'Do I have to spell out how I feel? Isn't it obvious?'

'Unless you've been awarded a Nobel Prize for faking it.'

Beth smiled, but she was conscious of all the shadows between them; not only Eirian, Steve and Marian, but the fear that Morgan was her half-brother. Is it possible he knows, she thought, and made love to me regardless?

'Morgan, tell me something.'

After a few seconds he prompted, 'Tell you what?'

She couldn't go on. She must, but she couldn't. 'Are you hungry?'

'Yeah, starving,' he said. 'Is that what you wanted to ask?'

It was not, but Beth had lost her nerve. She said, 'Let's get up and have something to eat. It's only about eight, isn't it? Fancy an omelette?'

'Let me do it,' said Morgan. 'I've been complimented on my omelettes.'

'If you can do it without using every single kitchen utensil I possess.'

He looked wryly at her. 'If I didn't know you better, I would say that was a sexist comment.'

While they were downstairs in the kitchen, both dressed, there was a knock at the back door. Beth's nerves shrieked silently. She longed for messages, and dreaded them.

Gordon was there; she only opened the door half way, so he wouldn't see Morgan, at the stove.

'Sorry to disturb you, love. Steve phoned. Says he's on his way to Leeds, thinks he's on to something.'

'What?' Beth exclaimed, her heart accelerating.

'That's all he said.'

'And Luke hasn't phoned again?'

Gordon shook his head. 'Sorry, love. If there's any news, we'll let you know straight away. Er, your friend find you okay?'

He must have seen Morgan's car outside. 'Yes, thank you, he's here.' Beth opened the door fully; the scene looked innocent, she supposed, except that neither of them had combed their hair. 'Gordon, this is Morgan. He's Eirian's father.'

Gordon took a couple of long strides into the room; Morgan put down a spatula and shook his hand. 'I'm very sorry about the little girl,' Gordon said awkwardly. 'I'm sure you'll find her soon. Well. I'd, er, better be getting back. Get some rest, eh?'

When Beth had closed the door behind him, she asked, 'Have you got to go home?'

'Do you want me to?' said Morgan.

'Rhianwen might think –'

'I don't care what she thinks.'

Beth poured glasses of wine and they sat down to eat. The omelette was, after all, delicious.

'This is the first proper meal I've eaten for two days,' she said.

Morgan held her hand across the table. 'Eat it slowly, then. Must keep your strength up.'

When they'd finished, and Beth had a glass of wine inside her, she finally felt calm enough to ask the impossible question. 'Morgan, have you ever seen your birth certificate?'

He looked at her guardedly, puzzled. 'Of course I have.'

'Who does it say your father was?'

'Owen Rhys.'

'Has Rhianwen ever told you that he, erm, might not really have been your father?'

He became very still as he gazed at her, a slight frown shading his beautiful eyes. 'What's brought this on?'

She cleared her throat and twisted her wine glass between her fingertips. 'I'm worried that we might be . . . related.'

'Related? How?'

'Well, it's probably nothing, but there's just a possibility, I'm sure you can tell me it's not true, that we might, erm, have . . . the same . . . father.'

Morgan leaned his head on his hand and said, 'Oh, my God. Oh, Beth that's crazy.'

'Is it?' she said shakily. 'Oh, good.'

But Morgan looked deeply worried, not dismissive. 'What's made you think that?'

'If you can tell me Owen Rhys was definitely your father, I won't say another word.'

He looked at the table and exhaled slowly. 'Wish I could, but I can't. Oh, Christ.' Beth waited. Eventually he went on, 'When I told you Owen was dead, that was true. It was also true that I never met him. He divorced my mother ten years before he died. He left her while she was pregnant, or maybe before she was pregnant; Rhianwen is vague.'

'Is it possible he left because you weren't his?'

'I'm damn sure I wasn't his. Instinct. If she ever mentioned Owen, which was rare, she had this kind of indifference in her voice; not as if she hated him, just as if he meant nothing at all. Oh, she referred to him as my father but she never painted a cosy picture of him for me. He was an emotional blank. I've seen photos; I look nothing like him. And Rhianwen had something else going on; I've always suspected that.'

'Have you tried asking her about it?'

'Of course I have! She just changes the subject. Either she's taken a vow of secrecy, or she's too ashamed to admit that I was the result of an affair. But your father, Beth?' Morgan shook his head. 'Oh, no, anyone but him.'

'But it's the only logical reason for the sheer bloody hysteria when they found out I was pregnant. The reason for Mum and Gran hating Rhianwen, and forbidding me to meet you, and the reason for them keeping us apart. Because we were brother and sister. What I want to know is why the hell couldn't Rhianwen have had the decency to tell us?'

Morgan put the plates in the sink and poured more wine. She saw he couldn't respond, so she went on talking until he could. 'I saw my parents once . . . I saw my mother beating my father, and saying, "This is for what you did to me, this is for your weakness." He was always guilty about something. It must have been his affair with Rhianwen. It all made sense when I realized.'

'Oh God, Beth. I can't see my mother being attracted to a dentist, it isn't her.'

'My father's quite handsome,' Beth said indignantly. 'I thought he was inhibited; maybe I was wrong.'

'You can't tell why people are attracted to each other, can you?' Morgan sighed.

'Or what they're like inside. I suppose I didn't know my dad at all. We saw him coming to the house that time, remember?'

'Yes. And he came to see Rhianwen with your mother several times when I was small,' said Morgan. 'I didn't know who they were then. They'd have these quiet, stiff arguments behind closed doors. I never knew what was going on. If the affair came into the open when Mum was expecting me – God, no wonder your mother hated mine. And your gran, though why she didn't take it out on her son-in-law instead of me, I don't know. Did anyone ever tell you she nearly shot me?'

'What?' Beth gasped.

'Just after Mum told me you were pregnant. We had a row, I stormed out and there was your grandmother in the meadow with a shotgun. She shot at me.' Morgan grimaced. 'She said if I ever went near you again, she wouldn't miss. Inhumane castration was mentioned.'

'Oh, my God.' Heather's fervency only seemed to confirm Beth's fears. Her heart felt leaden. 'You can't tell me it's not true, then.'

'I wish I could. Trouble is, it seems to explain why Rhianwen kept saying, "Treat Beth like a sister," as if I was going to jump on you the moment her back was turned.'

'You did, though!'

Morgan smiled ruefully. 'I never thought she meant sister literally. But like you say, why else did she go neurotic about keeping us apart? I couldn't see any sense in it, when she's so fond of you. She doesn't like Marian, thinks she's cold.'

Beth was gratified that she'd guessed correctly, but didn't let on. 'I wish it didn't make so much sense.'

'If it's true, are you horrified?' he said, taking her hand again.

'It's a bit late to be horrified, isn't it? We've just been to bed together, despite everything.'

'I don't care, Beth. It doesn't make any difference to the way I feel about you.'

'But it's illegal.'

'Yes, but we didn't *know*. We still don't. Maybe it's better we don't ask.'

'And you're married. That makes it doubly wrong.' She drank more wine to subdue the waves of pain that kept hitting her. 'I almost died when Rhianwen told me! But it wasn't a surprise. It was easy to believe Rhianwen when she made out I meant nothing to you, because it rang true. When I was pregnant and I never heard from you, I assumed that when you'd said you loved me, you were just saying it. You know, in a rush of sentiment because you'd enjoyed having sex with me. You probably said that to all the girls.'

'Thanks,' said Morgan, sounding hurt. 'So we were best friends for four years and then you decided I was a promiscuous, insincere bastard?'

She didn't mean to sound vindictive, but her pain was surfacing ruthlessly. 'I was a virgin but you weren't. There must have been others. I didn't expect to be the only one; I didn't expect

402

anything. I was too young to know what I wanted. But it still hurts.'

Morgan stared at their entwined fingers, his head propped on one hand. 'I wasn't a saint. There were one or two girls at school; not many, truly, and never when I was with you in the summer. I'm sorry, Beth. I like sex. I can't help that.'

'So do I.' She sighed. 'Why shouldn't we?'

'But I only loved you. I don't know why you won't believe me. This sounds awful but when I was fifteen, this older girl took it into her head to give me some tuition and I went along with it, because I didn't want to be completely inept when you and I . . . I wanted to know what to do, so I didn't make a fool of myself. So you would think I was wonderful.'

Beth started laughing. She couldn't stop. 'Oh, it worked!'

'I should hope so. A teacher caught us once; nearly got chucked out of school for it. My friends nominated me school shagging champion, which was great for my image, but totally unjustified.'

'Oh, I don't know,' said Beth, laughing harder. 'I hope you didn't boast about me to them.'

'Hand on heart, I never, ever boasted about it. Never even admitted it, even after they saw us walking down the lane that time. Remember?'

'Every detail,' she said. 'So, you always planned to seduce me?'

'I took it for granted we'd stay together, when we were old enough and you got free of your sodding mother. Things just happened sooner than I intended. I should have waited until you were sixteen, but I couldn't; I don't know how I held out as long as I did. I've fancied you like crazy since you were twelve.'

'I wish we had waited,' said Beth.

'Do you really regret it?'

'I regret all the mess and pain it caused,' Beth said softly. 'But I don't regret loving you. I didn't realize how perfect it was until it was over and I found out there was no one else to compare. You know, first love; you don't expect it to last.'

'You go out and look for something different and better,'

said Morgan, 'only to realize it isn't there. You've already found it and lost it. I knew it was right. I wish I'd had the courage to tell my mother and your bloody parents to go to hell!'

'I don't regret having Eirian,' said Beth, 'even if she shouldn't exist. It was that time on the Hellstone.'

Morgan looked at her, green eyes tender and regretful. 'I know. Sorry. Great scientist I am, forgetting that oil rots rubber.'

'If only we'd been old enough to plan having a child, it would have been wonderful.'

He held her hands across the table. 'If only you hadn't been under age, and maybe my sister, and if only I hadn't deserted you and married someone else. If only I hadn't hurt you. I didn't plan any of that. I know I've done everything wrong. I've got a hell of a cheek even asking you to forgive me. But can you?'

'I don't know,' Beth said hopelessly.

'Do you want me to leave?'

'No,' she said, clasping his wrists. 'Please stay.'

'Come on, then.' Morgan's eyes were as seductive as the wildwood. 'Come back to bed, Beth.'

The Horn, lying where Beth had left it on the rug, had a distinct glow in the darkness. She began to rewrap it in order to put it back in its hiding place, and as her fingers brushed it, she felt the strangest sensation, like a wash of light going through her.

Oh, Goddess, she thought as she fitted the floorboard over the Horn, should I have done that? Beth had seen the Horn used in a ritual to bless a couple with fertility. Surely it can't stop the pill working, can it?

Don't be an idiot, she told herself.

Morgan had banked lamps and candles around the room, making the bed a bower of light. The cats came in and sat on the carpet at the foot of the bed. Beth watched Morgan bending down to fuss them, and she thought her chest would explode with the passion she felt for him. She sat with her arms resting on her drawn-up knees and her hair covering her like a rippled cloak.

She thought of Eirian, alone in captivity; prayed with all her heart to the Goddess, don't let her be suffering, please let us find her. And Eirian, please forgive me for making love to your father; it doesn't mean we've forgotten you – we haven't – but we need each other tonight.

Morgan took off his wedding ring and placed it on the chest of drawers.

And then he came to her, a long silhouette edged with white-golden radiance. Her demon lover.

It didn't matter how often he said he loved her, or how kind, ordinary and likeable he seemed. In the secret darkness he remained a wild, unknowable entity.

'Yes, love me,' whispered Beth. She almost wished he would get her pregnant a second time; an act of defiance against the world.

And again the warm silky hardness of him. Beautiful arms and legs and hair and the amber rod inside her. She was impaled like a red fruit and broken open with pleasure. All was joined flesh, swollen and glistening with juices; and starbursts, and lightning stitching the sky to the raw earth.

The cats sat in a triangle, watching with huge eyes, but Beth didn't care. They were part of the sacred rite. She noticed that they kept changing places; now Eostre would sit in front, now Cerridwen, now Bast. And they stared at Beth and Morgan all night with searchlight eyes.

Their love-making became hallucinatory. At one stage Beth thought there was no roof on the cottage; that they were out in the sky flying above the black webbing of trees, part of the blue-black sky and the moon. She felt the stream of ancient energies; Morgan felt it too, she didn't need to ask. They were god and goddess. Flowing in exquisite rhythm without words.

Alchemy.

Beth didn't count how many times they made love. Four or five? It seemed they didn't stop. One act ran into the next; and when she thought herself spent, Morgan would smile and weave webs of sensation with his hands and mouth and body, and she would be tumbling into the silver net of orgasm again.

And still she wanted more. Climaxes weren't enough, she wanted to grind herself to pieces against him, to devour him, and nothing would take away the ache but to hold him inside her for ever.

When Beth rose above Morgan, she wasn't the Beth he remembered, not the sweet-natured, naïve girl he'd seduced long ago. Instead she was a goddess, black and devouring. She was like night, dark and pale and blindingly lovely. She rose over him and he didn't know her; he felt her power and he was afraid, but still he craved her, loved her, would have given his life to keep her.

As she writhed snake-like on him, he seemed to see lights flickering over her skin, like the opal light of the Horn. But when she collapsed on him, spent, she was Beth again.

Towards dawn they rested, satiated at last. Morgan held Beth. It would be agony to let her go. As the light came into the window, the night magic faded, but it remained inside him. The cats jumped up on the bed and climbed over the angles of their entangled bodies; Bast put her nose against Beth's and stared into her eyes. Beth held the look, then her hands came up to fuss Bast and gently push her away.

'What happened?' said Beth, as if she'd come out of a trance. 'We were possessed.'

'The Goddess was with us,' he said, into her hair. 'How do you feel?'

'Strange. Sore. I wish you'd lie in the damp patch.'

'I'm already lying in several.' Morgan kissed her. 'Are you happy?'

'I would be, if Eirian was home.'

'I know who will know where Luke is,' said Morgan. He'd thought of it earlier in the night, but there had been no point in mentioning it until now.

'Who?'

'Your parents.'

'I've been through this with Rhianwen. They'll tell Luke!'

'Not necessarily. You're going to have to face them. Don't worry, I'll be with you.'

Beth was silent. Enchantment was gone, and the light of day was hostile and glacial.

Morgan had only told her half of his premonition, but he had no intention of telling her the rest; that he'd seen a child's face under the water. A child, dead.

Chapter Twenty-two

Beth opened her eyes and realized she'd been asleep. A sound outside had woken her.

'Are you awake?' she said. 'I haven't slept that well for days.'

'I thought I heard a car,' Morgan said sleepily. 'What time is it?'

'Eight.' A car door slammed. Beth sat up, then leapt out of bed and ran to the window. 'Oh my God, it's Steve! Oh, get up, quickly, put some clothes on!'

Morgan obeyed, having the grace to look worried. 'Is he going to kill me? Which deadly martial arts has he a black belt in? He doesn't carry a katana, does he?'

'Disposable razors in the bathroom,' said Beth, only half listening.

'He's going to slit my throat with a disposable razor?'

'No, I meant we've got some, so you can shave. Oh, shut up!'

'Sorry.' Morgan looked contritely at her. 'Seriously, is this going to cause a problem?'

'What do you think? Oh, don't worry, he'll be all right. The only thing I've ever known him get worked up about is Sam.'

When Steve came into the kitchen, Morgan had just disappeared into the bathroom and Beth was in her dressing-gown, putting the kettle on.

'Hi,' she said, trying to be nonchalant.

'Morning.' Steve slumped in and sat down at the kitchen table, looking exhausted and despondent.

'You look dreadful,' she said gently, anxious but trying not to panic straight away. 'Are you okay? What happened? Gordon said something about Leeds.'

'Wild goose chase.' Steve groaned and rubbed his forehead. 'I really could do with some lethal coffee, Beth.'

'Coming up.' The cats were mewing round her feet; she started the coffee, then opened a tin of catfood.

'I was ringing or visiting everyone I could think of who might have heard from Katy. When I rang Tash, she said some cult had just taken over a house not far from her. So I drove up to Leeds to look for it.'

'And?'

'We found it.' He sighed. 'They were Hare Krishnas.'

Beth was relieved there was no bad news; she hadn't expected good. 'At least you tried.'

'I stayed talking to Tash for a while, then set off home. Now my sodding car's knackered; I've crawled here at about thirty.'

'What's wrong with it?'

'I dunno. Fuel supply or carburettor. Jesus, Beth, I'm so pissed off with this.'

She thought he was about to start crying, so she went to hug him, partly out of her own guilt. 'I know, love,' she said, her arms round his neck, her head on his. 'So am I. We mustn't let it get us down. We *will* get them back.'

'Yeah,' he said, patting her arm. 'Christ, I'm knackered.'

'You ought to have a sleep.' Then Beth remembered the state in which she and Morgan had left the bed, and she went cold.

'I just need a coffee.'

As she busied herself pouring the drinks, Steve asked, 'Is that Morgan's car outside?'

'Yes.' Her craven first instinct was to avoid complications by denying everything. 'Well, we were talking for ages, and it was late, and I didn't want to be left on my own, so I said he could sleep on the –'

'Beth,' Steve said tiredly, 'was Morgan wearing some kind of aftershave or body spray with a sort of sandalwoody scent?'

'I think so. Why?'

'Because you stink of it.'

'Oh.'

'And you've got love bites all over your neck. Why can't you just admit you spent the night with him?'

'Oh, damn.' Beth sighed and clasped the collar of her dressing-gown, feeling more sad than guilty. 'Sorry.'

'I take it he hasn't turned into a twenty-stone coke-snorting bald git, then.'

Beth put Steve's coffee down in front of him. 'It will probably turn out to be a terrible mistake,' she said. 'We both thought we'd got over it, but when we saw each other, we hadn't.'

'How surprising. Great,' said Steve, apparently too tired to express anything stronger than sullen sarcasm. 'I suppose I'm in the way. Do you want me to leave?'

'Of course not! Don't be stupid!' She sat down opposite him to drink her tea. 'Don't be like that.'

'You're still in love with him, aren't you?'

'Yes.'

'And did you establish whether or not you're related?'

'Not as such, but it doesn't look too hopeful.'

'So you've just slept with someone who is probably your brother.'

'Looks like it,' Beth said offhandedly.

'Jesus, Beth.' Steve dropped his head on to his hand.

'I'm really sorry, Steve. You don't deserve this. I suppose it sounds awful; I don't blame you if you're disgusted with me.'

He shouted at her, making her jump. 'I don't give a toss about your sex life, Beth! All I care about is getting Sam back! Christ, how could you? When Eirian and Sam are God knows where, and I'm flogging my guts out all night trying to find one miserable clue? You and Morgan can go to hell! I'll find Sam on my own.'

He leapt up and strode towards the door; distraught, Beth rushed after him and caught his arm.

'Don't, Steve. I'm really sorry, I didn't mean it to happen. I had no idea I was going to feel like that, and neither did Morgan.' He stood sullenly as she put her arms round him and kissed his cheek. 'Come on, Steve, please. Don't run out on me. We've got to help each other. We've more chance of finding them together.'

She felt the breath go out of him; she took his hand and led him back to the table. 'Right,' he said under his breath as he sat down. 'Just don't expect me to be thrilled about this, okay? First Katy, now you!'

Beth leaned against the sink and stared at her feet. She felt awful now. 'I know. But can we please save the recriminations until after we've found the children?'

That was the moment at which Morgan came out of the bathroom, dressed. He gave Beth a slight grimace, as if to say, is it safe to come out?

Steve had his back to him, but he saw Beth look up, and he turned round with a sullenly hostile expression.

'Tea or coffee?' Beth said desperately. She had a ghastly feeling she was about to start laughing hysterically.

'Tea, please,' said Morgan. He gave Steve an apologetic smile and extended his hand. 'Hello, Steve.'

Steve gave the hand a brief and reluctant shake. 'Hello.'

'Like Beth says,' Morgan said in a conciliatory tone, 'we need to help each other now. We can do the Uzis at dawn bit later, eh? It happened and I'm not sorry, but don't blame Beth, blame me.'

Steve said nothing.

'Steve's got a problem with his car,' Beth said brightly. 'D'you know anything about engine trouble?'

'I know where the gas goes in. Sorry, petrol,' said Morgan. 'That's about it. Well, we can use my car, anyway, but what's wrong with it?'

That got them on to safer ground, at least. As Steve began to explain, Beth said, 'I'm going to have a bath,' and fled.

As she lay soaking – however unwelcoming the bathroom was, with its cracked tiles and mildew, at least there was hot water – she felt increasingly guilty about Steve. He really doesn't deserve this, she thought. First Katy, now me. He's been my best friend for years, I know I can trust him. And the truth is, one night of lust with Morgan doesn't prove we have any future together.

We were appallingly selfish last night. How could we even think about sex when Eirian's in this plight? But we did.

Beth felt guilty, and then she began to feel angry. Steve's done enough. It's my turn now. I am going to get the children back if it's the last thing . . .

She remembered, suddenly, the cats' eyes blazing into hers. Especially Bast's. Telling her something. A wordless message, another kind of energy, like the Horn of Power's light, like the delirium of making love.

While Beth was drying herself, she heard their voices through the door.

'You'd better not do anything to hurt Beth,' Steve was saying. 'I'm warning you.'

'You really care about her, don't you?' said Morgan.

'Everyone loves Beth,' said Steve. 'She's the best person I've ever known. She doesn't deserve to be messed around!'

'I'm not going to mess her around,' said Morgan. 'I love her.'

'You'd better prove it, because I think you're using her.'

Oh God, they're going to start fighting, Beth thought in dismay. But Morgan said mildly, 'You can think what you like. I know you want to protect Beth; so do I, so we've got something in common, haven't we? And we've both had our children taken by this lunatic. So come on, Steve, don't let's argue.'

Steve mumbled something like, 'Yeah, right.'

When Beth came out, a few minutes later, Morgan was making breakfast and having a civilized, if stilted, discussion with Steve on the best route to take to Birmingham. A dark-haired beautiful demon and a scruffy blond angel; she loved them both.

They sat down at the table together, Beth still in her dressing-gown. Morgan put his hand on Beth's leg under the table; Steve pretended not to notice. Beth nibbled at some toast and drank more tea. Then she said, 'Steve, I think you should stay home and get some rest. We're going to see my parents. They must know where Luke is.'

'I'd rather come with you,' said Steve.

'But what if Luke phones?'

Morgan said, 'Well, ask the people at the farm to take a message. We can always ring them from a call box to see if there's any news.'

'Okay,' said Beth. 'But I'm not staying at home today. I can't stand it. I'll get dressed, then we can go.'

She meant to put on jeans and T-shirt, to look relatively ordinary. But some strange impulse stopped her. It was a weird unease, the same energy she'd felt all night, defiant anger – against Luke, against herself, even against Morgan and Steve, though they didn't deserve it. But she needed anger now.

Beth dressed in skin-tight shiny black leggings, high black boots with solid heels, a baroque black top with lacing, panels of net and jet beads. The love bites weren't that bad; she covered them with make-up. She gave herself a pale face, Egyptian eyes, and red lips, and brushed and sprayed her hair to a state of wildness. She put snake bracelets on her wrists and a silver pentagram round her neck.

When she went into the kitchen, both Morgan and Steve stared at her with eyes on stalks. She felt strong.

'I'm ready,' she said.

As Morgan drove along the lane, Beth saw Gordon's Land Rover coming towards them. Gordon immediately backed up to the farmyard, beckoning wildly.

'Park in the yard,' Beth said, her anxiety flaring. 'There must be a message.'

'Luke phoned,' Gordon shouted as Beth, Morgan and Steve got out of the Sierra. 'I told him to phone back in ten minutes, after I'd fetched you.'

They rushed into the farmhouse kitchen. 'Tell him I want to speak to my wife!' said Steve.

Gordon vanished diplomatically while Beth and the others hovered anxiously, waiting for the phone to ring. When it did, Beth almost hit the ceiling. She grabbed the receiver and said, 'Luke?'

'Your friends have stopped watching the church,' said Luke's metallic voice. 'That is good. You can tell Sam's father that Sam is adjusting very nicely. However, I have to express the deepest concern over your daughter, Bethia.'

'What do you mean?' Beth said, breathless.

'Faith is a witch and a demon. I do not mean it symbolically. You have literally produced the child of the Devil.'

'If that's what you think of her, let me have her back!'

Luke laughed. 'That isn't the point. The point is that I saved her from you not a moment too soon. She is in even greater need of cleansing than even I had realized.'

Beth had no idea how to respond. 'Luke, what do you want?'

'I want you to understand that Faith is shortly going to be released from her bondage to the Devil and come joyfully to God. That's all I want from you, Bethia; to understand that you've lost.'

Beth tried to sound controlled. 'May I speak to her, please?'

'That's impossible. You have both been disobedient.'

'Steve would like speak to Katy.'

'Also impossible.'

'Look, what do you want us to do?'

Morgan said, 'Let me speak to him.'

Beth knew she was getting nowhere. Apprehensively she passed Morgan the receiver and pressed her ear to the other side so she could hear both voices. She whispered, 'He calls Eirian, "Faith."'

'Hello, Luke, this is Eirian's father.'

There was a deathly silence at the other end. Beth could almost touch Luke's shock.

'Are you still there?' said Morgan.

Luke, Beth realized, had begun to laugh. To snigger, rather. 'Oh, so you're her father now, Rhys? After all these years, you think venting your revolting lust on my sister qualifies you to call yourself the child's father? She has no father but your master, the Devil!'

Very matter-of-fact and calm, Morgan said, 'Luke, you know perfectly well that either we or the police are going to catch up with you sooner or later. You can't play games with children's lives. We can sort this out amicably. Tell us where to pick them up and we'll come and fetch them.'

'Don't you know where they are?' Luke said mockingly. 'Hasn't your master given you that information?'

'Are you telling me that a twenty-five-year-old man still believes the garbage about Devil-worship fed to him when he was eleven? I was taking the piss, Luke. It was a joke.'

'If you believe that, you are stupid as well as evil,' Luke said softly, 'because Faith has the Devil in her and you don't even know it. She is a witch.'

'You're out of your fucking mind,' said Morgan.

'When I was I child,' said Luke, 'I was afraid of you, Rhys. But your evil woke me out of my stupor and I know now that with God on my side we shall grind you and your sort to dust in the earth.'

'I've had enough of this.'

'Too bad. You daren't put the phone down, while I hold Faith.'

'Her name's Eirian!' Morgan's tone became so chillingly vicious that Beth went cold. 'Listen to me, you bastard; if you want to believe I serve the Devil, believe it. Remember that time at the Hellstone?' Beth recalled Luke and his friends trying to exorcize the shadowy pagan forces they didn't understand – running in fear from something they'd seen in Morgan's eyes – and she shivered at the memory. Morgan went on, his tone lethal, 'Think about that while you're waiting for us. Because I'm coming for you and when I find you I'm going to stick your fucking Bible so far down your fucking throat it'll meet the crucifix coming up your arse. I'm sure my master would like to see your throat ripped out, your muscles flayed off the bone and your balls fed to your congregation. When I've finished with you, you sick fucking pervert, no one will love you but the flies. We're on our way, Luke.'

Luke broke in, chanting, ' "And the devil that deceived them was cast into the lake of fire and brimstone, where the beast and the false prophet are, and shall be tormented day and night for ever and ever ... And whosoever was not found written in the book of life was cast into the lake of –"'

Morgan slammed down the phone. He was shaking.

'He's out of his tree,' said Morgan. 'He's barking.'

Steve was staring at Morgan. 'We know.'

'This has got us nowhere,' said Beth. 'I'm really scared now. He's just playing with us.'

They waited a few more minutes in case Luke rang back, but he didn't. As they walked out to the car, Beth asked Morgan, 'Are you okay?'

'I couldn't quite believe it was real, until I spoke to Luke,' he said in a low voice. 'Oh, Christ. I'm sorry, Beth, I didn't know how bad –'

'It's okay.' She put her hand on his arm. It seemed strange, having to comfort Morgan instead of him consoling her.

'Well, now you know,' Steve said bitterly. 'Welcome home.'

They took Eirian to the assembly hall, where they'd put the chairs in a circle. The light through the high windows was bleak. Eirian felt dislocated, trapped, abandoned.

The whole congregation was there; some sat around the edges of the circle and watched, others crowded in on her, smiling down on her with glassy eyes. Luke, Mark, Susan and the deacons were immediately around her; Meg, Katy and Sam near the back. The 'saints' sang a hymn, swaying with joined hands.

Eirian made a break for it, just to test them, but they caught her and held her down on the floor. Then Luke began to shout.

He seemed to be praying. Calling down the Holy Spirit. The others joined in and the chant was atonal, forceful, nerve-jangling.

Pressed in agony to the floor by Mark, Paul and others, Eirian thought, why do they think that they're so different and so superior to us?

She felt the energy of their massed will. It felt white. Not pure; simply colourless. She felt claustrophobic. She could smell their sweat, their cheap soap and toothpaste and bad breath in a suffocating cloud around her. She was hot and shivering.

But the power that came from Luke was real, heavy and grey and draining. He smelled of ice and mothballs.

'Begone, foul demon, from the body of this innocent child. In the name of Jesus Christ our Lord, *begone*!'

Eirian was lifted up to her knees. Luke clutched her forehead, working her head round and round. She hated this. She began to gasp for breath.

Everything went black, and she was in the past.

She was in darkness, in Guendolen's arms. They were clinging to each other in mutual terror. Eirian could smell the body odours and smoke and dirt crusted in Guen's unwashed clothes, the ever-present stink of those times, but it smelled as good as the earth after the clinical stench of Luke and his followers.

'Sister,' Guendolen breathed. 'Sister, it's over. They have found us out.'

Eirian looked up and she saw a scene, frozen like a photograph. A forest in winter, bare branches dusted with snow. A small church in a clearing with the Green Man carved on the lintel. But the carving had been mutilated, the face obliterated. And lying across the threshold of the porch was the body of the young priest, Guen's lover. Neck broken. His tongue protruding, swollen. Signs cut into the flesh of his forehead which she knew meant, *Witch. Lover of witches.*

The scene darkened. A winter blizzard blew in.

'They're coming for me,' Guendolen whispered.

Eirian felt the dark shapes all around, leaning over her. *Begone, demon.*

'Sister, help me,' said Guen.

'I can't,' said Eirian. 'They're coming for me too.'

'Even in your spirit-land, you are not safe?'

'We will never be safe. We will always have to fight.'

'Yes, fight,' Guen breathed. 'You have always aided me; take my strength to aid you now!'

'No, Guen. You need your power to fight the witch-finders.'

'I shall die anyway. Take my strength, sister.'

Eirian was shivering with the cold, but she felt her hands turning hot. She felt herself spiralling away; saw Guen huddling by the trunk of a tree, a shapeless bundle under her woollen cloak. She saw snow crusting on Guen's back. She saw the men in their clerical robes coming; she willed Guen to run and hide, but Guen stayed where she was, too weak to move because her strength now burned in Eirian.

The blizzard swept the scene away. Eirian opened her eyes and found Luke's face staring into hers. His face was like a gargoyle's, sanded smooth.

She turned her head away, shuddering. She was on her knees and Luke was holding her there, his hand gripping the neck of her sweatshirt.

'Has the demon gone?' someone whispered.

Luke dropped her. She sprawled on the bare floorboards. 'Who will test her?'

No one spoke. They were afraid of Eirian. She sat up, looking around their nervous, excited faces.

She felt the power burning inside her. She was angry now.

'I will,' said a woman.

It was Olivia who stepped forward, Eirian's alleged grandmother. Eirian stood up to face her, arms folded.

The long face, with its ravaged beauty, came questing towards her. 'Now, child,' Olivia said, as if approaching a strange dog. 'Have you felt the love of the Lord in your heart? Are you cleansed, washed clean in the Blood of the Lamb?'

'Blood?' said Eirian. She was trembling with the blue-black energy erupting in the marrow of her bones. She heard the ticking of filamental feet coming closer.

'Have you seen a vision to free your soul? Have you been touched by the Holy Spirit?'

'Ah, visions,' said Eirian, thinking, this woman is quite mad. 'How is this for a vision?'

A shape of glowing light appeared in the centre of the

circle. Some of the women gasped. They didn't all see it; Luke clearly could not, but Olivia could. It was the Virgin Mary.

Olivia fell to her knees, mouth and eyes gaping.

The Virgin began to transmute. She threw off her sculpted robes and danced, her long hair writhing. She stood, powerful and sexual and terrible, above the world.

'This is who your Virgin really is,' said Eirian. 'The Goddess. You tried to take her power away but you can't. She'll have her revenge!'

The shape changed again. It became a hideous old woman, a witch in a cloak of storm clouds. Olivia screamed.

'You have the power of the Crone,' said Eirian, pointing at her. 'The power of destruction. That is all you know, isn't it? Destruction of your husband, your daughter, your son, and now me.'

As Eirian spoke, she *was* the Crone. Olivia's face elongated with horror as if the scales had been ripped from her eyes, forcing her to stare into the ghastly abyss she had made.

Olivia pitched forward on to the floor, eyes glazed and foam collecting in the corners of her mouth.

In the same moment, huge spiders began to drop from the ceiling on to the congregation. Men and women alike leapt up, hysterically swatting at their clothes and hair.

A spider fell on Eirian but she brushed it away, unconcerned. People were rushing for the exit, but Luke remained where he was, glaring at his adversary.

'What is this?' Luke rasped, pointing at his mother. 'What have you done to her?'

'She wanted visions. I gave her one,' Eirian said lightly. She held out her wrists. 'Better tie me up and lock me away, if you dare.'

She was all rage now. The others receded. There was only Eirian and Luke, matched opponents on a bleak, frozen plain.

Of all things, Beth dreaded meeting her mother again.

As they drew up outside her parents' house, she felt deadly

calm. It wasn't like meeting Morgan, no violent trembling or palpitations. It was pure dread, cold as sludge.

'They might not be in,' she said. 'My father's almost certainly at work. But if Mum's not there, we'll go to his surgery instead.'

'I suppose I'd better stay in the car,' said Steve. He had volunteered to sit in the back, but he plainly resented Morgan being in control of the car and in possession of Beth.

'If you don't mind,' said Beth. 'This is going to be awful. But I want Morgan to come with me.'

Morgan didn't argue. Steve stared pointedly in the other direction as they got out of the car.

'Steve doesn't like me, does he?' Morgan said as they walked along the short garden path. How familiar the house looked; it hadn't changed at all. Same neat lawn, same pristine paintwork edging the Victorian brickwork.

'Well, don't sound so pleased about it,' said Beth, thinking, I don't belong to either of you! 'Mum had better be in, I can't go through this twice.'

'I'm with you,' he said, putting his arm round her waist.

Beth rang the doorbell and waited.

Footsteps; the door opened, and there was her father in a casual jumper and trousers, not his work suit. He looked just the same, apart from a few grey hairs; serene face, shiny glasses, quiet manner.

'Yes?' he said, plainly not recognizing either of them.

'It's me, Dad,' said Beth. 'And, and Morgan.'

Her father put his hand to his mouth.

'Sorry to give you a shock,' said Beth. 'It's really important. Can we come in?'

His hand fell and he said, 'Beth!' His face was unreadable; he had rarely expressed any emotion in the past, and it seemed he hadn't changed. 'This is incredible. I'd given up hope of ever seeing you again. Yes, come in.'

He stood aside and they went into the hall. The forgotten scent of polish hit her, rousing thousands of memories, mostly unpleasant.

'You know who Morgan *is*, don't you?' Beth said.

Philip cleared his throat. He avoided Morgan's eyes and his face seemed frozen. 'Yes, of course I know who he is.'

'He's my daughter's father.' She spoke pointedly, but he still didn't show any reaction.

'I know that, Beth.'

'I thought you'd be at work.'

'I've caught a cold. Don't want to infect the patients.'

They entered the sitting-room. Same furniture; it all looked rather shabby and old-fashioned now. But her mother wasn't there, and Beth couldn't hear her in the kitchen.

She took a breath. 'Isn't Mum here?'

'I'm afraid not.'

'What about Luke?'

'Good Lord, no.' Philip gave a half-hearted laugh. 'We hardly see him these days.'

'But you must know where he is?'

'Er, won't you sit down, have a cup of tea? I hardly know what to say to you. It's wonderful to see you, but I don't understand why you've come now or why' – he made a minimal gesture towards Morgan – 'why he's with you.'

Beth remained on her feet. She felt her rage smouldering under her heart, but she controlled it. 'Hasn't Luke told you?'

'Told me what?'

'Luke has abducted my daughter, Eirian. He's also taken the son of a friend of mine.'

Philip's face, unguarded, revealed such shock that she saw he genuinely hadn't known. 'He wouldn't do a thing like that!'

'He's done it, Dad.'

Morgan said, 'We've been to his church in Birmingham and we know he's not there. We think he has another place somewhere.' Morgan was polite but he had presence and authority; Beth kept seeing Eirian's qualities in him all the time. 'Would you know where he is, Mr Herne?'

Philip turned away, scratching at his chin. 'I know he was setting up another branch of the church, but I've no idea where it is.'

'You must have!' Beth cried. 'The least you can do is help us find Eirian!'

Morgan touched her to quieten her; Philip turned, and looked coldly at Morgan's hand on his daughter's shoulder.

'I swear, I don't know. Luke tells me nothing.'

'Would Mum know?'

Her father exhaled, looking old and tired suddenly. 'Beth, your mother is with Luke.'

'What? Then she must know!'

'Yes, but I don't see her. Our old church has disbanded; Pastor Blair had an unfortunate crisis in his life.'

'I'm sure he'll soon be up for parole,' said Beth. 'Yes, Dad, I know.'

Her father went quiet and, to her surprise, blushed faintly. 'Anyway, your mother had joined Luke before that. I haven't seen much of her, since. I've virtually been living alone.'

'She's left you?' Beth gasped.

'Not officially, but as good as.'

'I'm sorry, I didn't know, but . . .'

'I'm managing. It was never much of a marriage to begin with. Such is life.'

Beth didn't know whether to be sorry or pleased for her father. She persisted, 'But you must know where she's gone!'

'All I know is that Luke was establishing a headquarters somewhere up North.'

'Where up North?'

'Somewhere near Stockton-on-Tees, I think, but I can't be absolutely sure. That's all I know, Beth, I swear! It was all deadly secret.'

'So you didn't know Luke was planning to take my daughter?'

'I had no idea! Have you called the police? I really don't know what to say. I can't believe Olivia would go along with such a thing.'

'Come off it! You know I ran away because I was terrified she was going to kill Eirian, didn't you?'

'Beth, don't get upset,' Philip said awkwardly. 'Please, let's discuss this over a cup of tea.'

'Luke's as crazy as Mum is and now they've both got Eirian, and all you can talk about is tea?'

She felt Morgan's hand pressing her shoulder, and she subsided. 'All right,' Beth said more calmly. 'But I think I've a right to be upset, don't you?'

When her father went into the kitchen, she followed him, leaving Morgan in the sitting-room. Morgan could probably overhear their conversation, but she didn't care.

'Dad,' she said softly to his back, 'you're running away from this, aren't you? Like you ran away from everything.'

He filled the kettle, not answering.

'It's at least half your fault that Luke turned out like he did. And half your fault I ran away. You never raised a finger to help us. Not a finger.'

'I know.' He plugged in the kettle, assembled cups and saucers.

'Why?'

'Do we have to talk about this now?'

'It might be your only chance to explain yourself! I know Mum never beat us in front of you, but you must have known what was going on! Why did you turn a blind eye?'

'These things are complicated,' he said wearily. 'There isn't a simple answer.'

'Try!'

He exhaled helplessly. Beth had never cornered him like this before, but she wasn't afraid any longer. 'Your mother was only trying to bring you up according to a moral code. I agreed with her. Our church required children to be brought up with strict discipline and your mother took that role within the family. I received corporal punishment as a child and it did me no harm.'

'I get it,' said Beth. 'You condoned what she did, but you were too soft actually to beat us yourself! Is that it? You must have known in your heart it was wrong, but you were too much of a coward to stop her, too. I suppose if you didn't actually witness it, you could pretend everything was all right!'

He appeared to wince with genuine pain. 'Perhaps you're right. It's easy with hindsight, isn't it, to see one's mistakes. It's not so easy at the time, Beth, believe me.'

Beth stood watching him, her arms folded. 'I didn't come here to criticize you,' she said stiffly. 'I just need to find my daughter.'

The tension in his shoulders lessened a little. 'What's she like, the girl?'

'Lovely,' said Beth. 'Very intelligent, difficult sometimes, but I wouldn't be without her for anything.'

'What about him?' Philip inclined his head towards the other room. 'I thought he was married, living in Canada.'

'Did Rhianwen tell you that?' Beth said acerbically.

'We heard, indirectly. You're not seeing each other again, are you?'

'Would it matter if we were?'

He fell silent again, stirring the tea in the pot vigorously. 'I don't know. I suppose it's too late, really.'

Now I've got to ask him, thought Beth. If I don't ask, Morgan and I could go on pleading ignorance – but we have to face it. 'Dad, will you answer a question truthfully?'

'I'll try.'

'Are you Morgan's father?'

He took off his glasses and turned to face her, rubbing his eyes. He might have been crying, she wasn't sure. 'God, what a thing to ask.'

'You had an affair with Rhianwen. Wasn't that what it was about, Mum punishing you?'

He was no longer emotionless. He looked horror-struck. 'Beth, what are you saying?'

'Dad, it's all right, I'm not going to judge you or hate you for it. If Morgan's my half-brother, I need to know. So does Morgan!'

He said quietly, 'The idea of me having an affair with Rhianwen is preposterous.'

'Why? Men and women do, all the time. She and Mum used to be friends. Isn't it why they fell out?'

424

'Not exactly.' He replaced his glasses and began to put things on a tray.

'Dad!' Whatever was wrong, he had no intention of talking about it. But Beth realized, suddenly, that what she felt was not merely anger but power, the energy of the night. She caught his arm and made him look at her. And when their gazes met, her eyes caught his like the mirror-eyes of Bast. 'Tell me the truth. I came home from school early one day and I saw Mum beating you and saying things like, "This is for your weakness, why can't you love me?" Sorry, I know it's embarrassing, but what was that about, if not Rhianwen?'

He'd gone crimson. This was something he couldn't bear to confess, but her power was forcing him. 'Good God, Beth, do I have to spell it out?'

'Yes, please spell it out. I haven't a clue what you're on about!'

'They have a nice word for it now. Gay. When I was younger it used to be queer, bent, homo. Pass me the sugar bowl.'

Beth obeyed automatically, stunned. 'You're not talking about yourself . . . are you?'

'Yes, Beth,' he said, so quietly she could hardly hear him. 'That's why I joined the church, because I couldn't bear the guilt. I still can't. If my parents had ever known they would have disowned me. That's why I married your mother, to deny it, to "get over" it, as if I could. Pastor Blair pushed us to-gether. I shouldn't have gone through with it. I betrayed your mother. I never told her, you see, but she found out, not long after Luke was born. Someone I had thought was a friend gave me away. Horrendous mess. She's never forgiven me. How can she? The Bible calls it an abomination.'

'So you just took it from her, letting her beat you?' She felt herself turning hot. 'I'm sorry.'

Yes, he had tears in his eyes, now. Beth felt compassion for him now, mixed with her bitterness.

'I wasn't unfaithful to her,' he said. 'Well, not after she found out, anyway. I controlled my inclinations, as Godly people should. Yes, I let her punish me; it was the only way I could

425

deal with the guilt. And we'd play games, pretending she was a man. She made me do that, to stop me straying, she thought, and to punish herself. But she hated me for it, and I hated her, because she couldn't understand that it wasn't the same. And now she's gone I don't know what to do.'

'You mean, you don't know whether to indulge your instincts or not?'

'It never gets any easier.' He swallowed, and his voice was thick. 'I should be grateful to your mother for keeping me on the straight and narrow, or God knows what punishment would have been visited on me by now. That disease . . .'

'Don't say it, Dad! If you say AIDS is a punishment from God, I'll hit you!' Beth leaned on a worktop, her head in her hands, until she could speak again. 'It's guilt that's made you unable to cope with it! And what's made you feel guilty? The Bible, the church. And what about Pastor Blair? I bet he made you feel guiltiest of all, the sodding hypocrite! I tell you, these bloody religions have got so much to answer for!'

'I don't know how you can still speak to me.'

'Dad, if you need me to punish you like Mum did, forget it! You need to talk to someone who understands, someone who won't judge you! There are organizations you can contact, you know.'

'It's a private matter,' he murmured.

'God, no wonder we're all so screwed up!'

'I hoped you'd never find out.'

'And I wish you'd been honest about it. I don't condemn you, Dad. For heaven's sake, you're not the first person this has happened to. I forgive you, if you need forgiving, okay? What I can't forgive is . . .'

'What?'

'The lack of honesty.'

Philip's expression was composed, but there was too much colour in his cheeks, and his eyes betrayed an inner rawness, a collapse. 'All right. What else can I tell you?'

'You are *my* father, aren't you?'

'Yes, of course I am.'

'Do you know who Morgan's father is?'

He looked down, and Beth had a sense of foreboding. 'Yes,' he said heavily.

'If it isn't you, how bad can it be?'

'This isn't fair. Rhianwen should have told him, not me.'

'Yes, but she hasn't! Oh, forget the tea, Dad. Come in the other room and tell us both together.'

Morgan looked at her as they went in, and she knew he'd heard every word. And every time she saw him, the delicious shock of his presence made her heart race.

Philip looked ill, it was so hard for him to discuss anything personal. He said shortly, 'It's Beth's grandfather.'

Beth's heart missed several beats. 'Oh, shit,' she said under her breath.

Morgan went very still, but he didn't betray surprise or shock. 'You do mean Dr Cross, don't you?'

Philip sat down, exhaling heavily. 'I'm afraid so. It was Randolph who had the affair with Rhianwen. I understand Rhianwen's husband left her because of it.'

Morgan said, 'But how can they be sure I was Randolph's?'

'Rhianwen's husband left her a long time before she fell pregnant. He left her because of the affair.'

Beth felt dizzy. 'I can't believe my grandfather would do that; he's so devoted to Heather, so *respectable*.'

'We're all respectable, Beth,' said Philip, less uncomfortable now the worst of it was over. 'The whole thing hurt Olivia more than it hurt Heather. She worshipped Randolph; she simply couldn't believe her own father would do such a thing. She had a nervous breakdown over it, actually; her faith got her through. Heather just soldiered on. I don't know what else to tell you. Randolph had to make a choice in the end, and he chose Heather. But Morgan was there, the walking evidence. Rhianwen should have gone away, but she wouldn't.'

'Good for her,' Morgan said under his breath. 'But you used to visit my mother, didn't you, Mr Herne?'

'I used to go and talk to her, sometimes. That's all. I mean, the whole row was nothing to do with me, really; Rhianwen was the only person I could go to when Olivia was driving me insane. I could understand what Randolph saw in Rhianwen. She's such a warm person. She couldn't help me get over my problems because she wasn't speaking from a Christian viewpoint, but she did try.'

'And that's really why Mum and Gran hated Rhianwen — the affair, I mean?' said Beth.

'That and her paganism. Olivia saw her as a witch who'd wantonly tempted her father to betray her mother. You can imagine how they felt when they found out that you and Morgan —'

'But why wouldn't anyone tell us?' Beth exclaimed.

Philip shrugged. 'They made a pact of secrecy, to avoid scandal. You know what villages are like. You weren't to know. We thought we'd taught you to stay out of trouble, but,' he shook his head, 'teenagers make these stupid mistakes, don't they?'

'It wasn't half as bad as the mistake Luke and Mum have made!' Beth snapped.

Her father's voice was raw, all its clinical restraint gone. 'Does this give you some idea of why your mother convinced herself that your baby had the Devil in her? Olivia really believed it. She thought Morgan was the child of an evil woman, an evil act.'

'Did *you* believe it?'

'Not as such, but I accepted Olivia's viewpoint as logical.' Philip was staring unfocused at the carpet. He looked broken. 'But when I lost my faith I could look back and see that I had been mad, in a way. Luke and your mother still are. It's not pleasant knowledge to live with.'

And it wasn't pleasant for Beth to feel pity for her own father; and to despise him, for the disasters he'd allowed to happen.

Silence. Then Morgan said, 'Beth, we ought to go.'

She started. 'Oh, damn, I'd forgotten about Steve! He'll think we've abandoned him. Look, Dad, if Mum calls, will you find out what's going on and where she is? Without saying you've seen us. You can get me on this number.' She wrote the farm's number on a scrap of paper and gave it to him.

'I'll do my best. But she doesn't phone very often,' Philip said resignedly. 'Beth, I'm glad you came. Come back, won't you? If there's anything I can do . . .'

'Yes, well, thanks. Er, do you mind if I use the loo before we go?'

'I'll wait by the car,' said Morgan.

As Beth came downstairs again she looked into the sitting-room and saw her father tearing up his Bible, shredding the pages into a waste-paper bin. He worked methodically, without emotion. Then he struck a match and orange flames came dancing over the lip of the bin.

Beth let herself out without saying goodbye.

Steve, far from being agitated, had fallen asleep in the back seat. Morgan said nothing as they got into the car. But he reached for Beth's hand and held it, tight.

'Are you all right?' she asked. 'Was it a shock?'

'A bit. It had to be someone, didn't it? But he must be twenty years older than my mother.'

'So?' said Beth. 'She was in her twenties and he was in his forties; what's strange about that? He's still handsome now. Now I know where you get it from.'

Morgan leaned on the steering wheel. 'She used to be his patient, you know. His patient. He gave me my vaccinations, for God's sake!'

Beth asked softly, 'Is it still incest?'

'I'm not sure,' said Morgan. 'I think it must be.'

'Our families obviously thought so.'

'I thought your grandmother was a psychopath,' Morgan said, with a grim smile. 'I was terrified of her! She must've wished Rhianwen had got rid of me; she was still trying to perform a late abortion on me when I was sixteen.'

'Is there anything you won't make a joke about?' said Beth.

'Only Eirian.' Morgan leaned over and rested his head on hers. Steve shifted. He was awake; he'd probably been listening. 'You took your time, didn't you?'

429

Morgan drew away from Beth, unhurriedly. 'Sorry, it got complicated,' she said.

Steve roused himself, looking anxious. 'Find anything out?'

'Luke might be near Stockton-on-Tees. My mother's with the cult, too. That's all my dad knows, but he'll try to find out where she is, if she ever phones.'

'Let's go and get a coffee before we rush into anything,' Morgan said, putting on his glasses and starting the car.

They found a coffee shop in the High Street, and Beth telephoned the farm from a call box outside. Rhianwen had rung to see where Morgan was, but there was no other message.

When Beth entered the café, Morgan and Steve were at a table in the window. As she sat down beside Morgan, he took her hand and kissed her cheek. 'Are you okay?' he said tenderly, as if Steve wasn't there.

'Fine. Nothing from Luke. Rhianwen wants to know where you are.'

'I'd better call her.' Morgan took a handful of change from his pocket, and went out to the phone box.

Steve looked thoroughly fed up. Tilting his head in Morgan's direction, he murmured, 'He can't leave you alone, can he? I don't keep kissing you in front of him!'

Beth felt annoyed with Morgan for upsetting Steve, and annoyed with Steve for being upset. 'I'll have a word with him.'

'Don't bother.'

There wasn't much Beth could say to that. They sipped their coffee and were silent for a few minutes. Finally she said, 'Is this jealousy, or do you really not like him?'

'I don't trust him. I think he's arrogant. One of those people who thinks he knows everything.'

Beth sighed. 'Steve, don't do this. Not now.'

'Sorry,' he said flatly. He put his hand on hers, still concerned for her despite everything. He was too soft-hearted to be truly angry with her. 'Was it really bad with your father?'

'It was okay. I found out some things I never knew.'

'About –?' Steve glanced at Morgan, who was coming back into the café, threading his way between tables. 'Well?'

'It's not as bad as we thought. He's not my brother. His father's my grandfather so he's only, well, my mother's half-brother.'

'Only?' Steve's sleepy eyes opened wide. 'Oh, well, that's all right then. I'm sure it's all right for an uncle to screw his niece!'

'Steve!' she hissed. Morgan showed no sign of having heard, though she was sure he had; Steve had meant him to. He kissed the top of Beth's head and sat down beside her.

'I tried Directory Enquiries,' said Morgan. 'No luck.'

'What for?' said Beth.

'To find out if there's a listing for a Luke Herne or a Church of the One Truth around Stockton. There isn't. We'll have to go up there.'

'Yes, and then find out the bloody place is probably in Cornwall,' Steve said despondently.

Beth said, 'It's the only lead we've got!'

They drank their coffee, Morgan and Steve discussing places to try, people to ask. But Beth felt energy rising inside her again. It had been simmering, ever since she'd first shown the Wand of Power to Morgan. It was like a separate entity. As if sparks were firing in every single cell of her body.

She knew what to do. The cats had already given her the message.

She said, 'We already know who can tell us; the people at the church. We'll go there again.'

'After what Luke threatened?' Steve said, aghast.

'Luke thinks he can make us do anything by threatening the children. I've had enough. We're going to the church.'

She had made up her mind; they couldn't argue with her.

'I'm with Beth,' said Morgan.

'Yeah, we noticed,' Steve murmured. 'Okay, whatever you say.'

Beth wasn't nervous as Morgan drove north through Birmingham's tortuous roads and traffic, following Steve's directions. She was calmly furious. And she felt detached from both Morgan and Steve, no longer needing either of them.

She was going into the house alone.

'Park here,' she said, as Morgan turned into the street. 'You can just barely see the church house from here. See that roof with the yellow-painted eaves?'

'Yes, I see it,' said Morgan.

'I don't want them to see our car. I'll go on foot from here.'

'We're coming with you,' said Steve.

'No!' said Beth. The force of her own will shocked her; it shocked them, too, because they seemed unable to argue with her. 'I've got to go in alone.'

'Are you sure?' Morgan's eyes, behind the black-rimmed glasses, seemed to look straight inside her and she felt the echoes of their love-making, alchemic fire. He understood.

'Yes. Just be ready to drive off when I come back.'

'This is a mistake,' said Steve, who didn't understand. 'Be careful, Beth!'

Alone, Beth began to walk along the pavement towards the church house. This was why she had not wanted to look ordinary. She was a witch-queen in shades of black; the embodiment of the sinuous female serpent-energy that all male religions dreaded.

She knew what to do. The Goddess inside her knew. The Goddess had spoken to her through Bast; her sexual ecstasy with Morgan had woven power; the Horn had enabled her to focus the power against her enemies.

Beth tried the front door and found it open. There was no one in the hall, but she could hear a voice in another room.

'Women do not actually enjoy sex,' the voice was saying. 'They use it as a weapon to enslave men to the Devil. This is why the Apostle Paul tells us, "It is good for a man not to touch a woman . . . He that is unmarried careth for the things that belong to the Lord . . . But he that is married careth for the things that are of the world". He speaks against marrying and begetting because he knew, as we do, that the time of the Apocalypse and the Second Coming are very near. Their approach is signalled by the intensifying of enemy activity, and women are in the very vanguard of this activity. It is more important than ever before, brothers and sisters, that we remain aware of our own potential for corruption and remain pure in our hearts. We must not cower and cringe in the face of the Devil's bellowing!'

Beth's rage leapt to a higher level. This is the garbage with which they want to infect my daughter, is it?

She peeped round a door and saw the long bare room in which they must hold their services. There was a group of eleven people, mostly women, seated round the speaker, a big blond man. She recognized him as the thug who'd hit her, the one Acne had called Jacob. And Acne was at the edge of the group, biting his nails and looking decidedly uneasy.

No one saw Beth. She slipped past and tiptoed up the stairs.

She glanced in the rooms as she went, but they were deserted. She went up the second flight to the common room, found it empty. Walking to the centre, she looked up at the ceiling and breathed deeply, grounding herself like a lightning rod between earth and sky, drawing down the moon.

She felt a shutter in her mind turning transparent, dissolving to let currents of force run through her. It was an energy she'd often sensed but never quite grasped. But now it was hers. It came through as colour: indigo, violet, darkest magenta, black and midnight blue, threaded with silver and opal. The colours of the night goddesses.

And it was sexual magic. An energy that she and Morgan had created between them as they'd created Eirian. There had been purpose in their passion beyond mutual gratification; they had both felt the fearful powers of the Goddess running through them.

These people fear me so much they had to deface my house with crosses and insults. Well, I'll give them something to fear.

Beth closed her eyes, head back, lips parted. She felt an icy wind blowing right through the house. She felt the delicious darkness flowing into every room. Friendly forces to her; but to these people, spectres, devils and demons.

When she'd finished, she calmly walked down the stairs once more.

From the hall, she could hear concerned voices.

433

'What *is* that?' a man said.

'It's gone really cold!' exclaimed a woman. 'I'm freezing!'

'I saw a ghost once,' said another female voice. 'It went cold, just like this.'

'Is this house haunted?'

'Don't! I'm scared, I don't like it.'

They were working each other up towards panic.

'Keep calm,' came Jacob's deep voice. 'Demons love to attack holy work! This is proof! We'll join hands and pray.'

Beth pushed open the door and walked in.

The disciples gaped at her, almost falling over each other with shock. Acne fled, rushing past her and out of the door, but no one followed him.

'It's her!' said a woman, pointing at her with a trembling hand. 'She's doing this!'

'I can do worse,' said Beth, 'if you don't tell me where I can find Luke. My brother.'

She'd seen most of these faces before; the others were obviously newcomers who had no idea what was happening. What a wonderful introduction to the Church of the One Truth!

Jacob bellowed, 'Don't cower in the face of the Devil, I said! I'll get rid of her.'

He came towards Beth menacingly, one fist clenched. He was about six feet five, with a wrestler's build and intimidating presence. Beth felt tiny before him.

He put up a huge hand and began to shove her towards the door.

'You have been warned, sister.' He spoke with an arrogant, menacing grin. 'You're in a sad way, but you've no place here unless you're ready to repent. We don't want your pagan pollution here! Get out, demon. Out, in the name of Our Saviour Jesus Christ.'

'Don't touch me,' Beth said sharply. 'I'm not leaving until you tell me where to find Luke.'

Jacob pushed her again. 'Out.'

The smirking male arrogance on his face inflamed her. Beth

felt power convulsing her suddenly, like an orgasm. 'I said, don't touch me.'

Jacob lurched backwards violently as if she'd pushed him with incredible strength. He fell over a chair and went sprawling on to the floor with a grunt of pain. Yet she hadn't laid a finger on him.

The others gasped and clung together.

Jacob struggled up, gasping, his mouth slack with amazement. The air was stiff with unspent power.

'Tell me.'

'You evil bitch!' And to Beth's amazement, he made the sign of the cross at her.

'You labelled me,' she said, calmly and completely furious. 'So I'll be what you want me to be. Exorcize this.'

She lifted her hands and the ice-winds blew ghosts out of the walls.

A few minutes after Beth had gone into the house, Morgan saw a figure come hurrying out of the church house and along the pavement in their direction. Not Beth; this was a thin young man in a polo-necked sweater. As he came closer, Morgan could make out his face: a large nose, no chin, an acne-marked red complexion.

'I know him!' said Steve. 'He's from the church. He tried to stop us going in the first time. Dunno his name, we call him Acne.'

'Well, let's get him in the car,' Morgan said matter of factly.

'I hate violence,' Steve said unhappily.

'I don't think this wimp is going to give us any trouble.'

They both got out, ready to grab the youth. But when he saw them he stopped dead and exclaimed, 'You've got to help me! I want to leave the church.' And he virtually threw himself on Steve.

'Get in,' said Morgan.

Acne climbed into the back seat with Steve, his head whipping from side to side as if he suspected enemies on all sides.

'Well, just leave,' Steve said contemptuously. 'What's your problem?'

'You don't understand. They're wonderful people while you're going along with them. But I've lost my faith. I want out. I tried to leave before; they come after you, it's like the Gestapo.'

Morgan said, 'If we help, will you tell us where to find Luke?'

'I don't know, I swear!' said Acne, rubbing his palms. He was so scared, Morgan almost felt sorry for him. 'It's deadly secret, you don't find out until you get there, and then you don't come back. But I can tell you who does. The big blond bloke. His name's Jacob. I tell you, I wouldn't leave your witchy friend on her own with him. He gets violent.'

That was enough for Morgan; Beth had been in the house long enough. 'I'm going after her,' he said, beginning to climb out. 'Steve, stay here with –'

'I'm Peter,' said Acne.

'You'd better be telling the truth, Peter,' said Steve.

'I swear, I just want out. You don't know what they're like!'

Morgan ran down the road, jumped over the front wall rather than waste time going through the gate, and entered the hall.

There were strange sounds. There was a heavy coldness in the air. He went to a doorway, and inside the room he saw Beth with her back to him; simply standing there, magnificent in skin-tight black, her hair a rippling black waterfall, her hands open as if she were giving a blessing. Faint sparks crackled around her, like static.

Nine or ten people, huddling together, were staring wild-eyed around them. And the blond hulk, who must be Jacob, was shouting an incoherent prayer, as if that could stop her.

'Morgan,' said Beth, turning towards him. Her eyes were green lasers, like the child's eyes in the vision.

There was a feeling of something unspeakably old, shapeless and dark, lurking behind the thin veil of the world.

Morgan felt weak and cold suddenly, and had to support himself against the doorframe. Beth was taking energy from him to add to her strength. And he was afraid of her, suddenly, in the pit of his stomach, deeply afraid.

Then she came towards him, her hand outstretched. 'It's time to go,' she said calmly.

The veil was tearing.

Morgan felt the room – the whole house – thrumming with ancient energy; fugitive firelight licking the walls, strange lights glowing, spheres of primaeval radiance drifting like spores beneath the ceiling. Wordless voices chanted. Flickering ghost-images haunted the rooms; crones and horned men, griffins, wolves and gargoyles. Tall, shadowy figures in animal skins moved past, crowned with branching antlers. All the horrors of the pre-Christian world.

Huge serpents writhed and blood ran down the walls.

Hand in hand, Beth and Morgan left the house and ran towards the car, pursued by the horrified cries of Jacob and his followers.

Beth felt drained, now it was over. She could barely believe what she'd done. And she was glad Morgan had come, even though she'd asked him not to; his presence had given her that extra thrust of power to raise the ghost-world.

Morgan slipped back into the driving seat, Beth into the passenger seat.

'Start the car,' she said. 'They'll be out in a few minutes. They won't be able to stand it in there.'

She looked round and saw the spotty young man sitting next to Steve. Acne shrank away from her, wrapping his arms round his lanky body and clutching the cross that hung round his neck.

'What's he doing here?'

'This is Peter,' said Steve, gazing at her wide-eyed. 'He says he wants to help. What have you been doing?'

'Nothing to advance the cause of pagan–Christian understanding,' Beth said drily. 'I've contaminated their house with

437

all their worst fears. Drive further up the street, Morgan. They'll have to go to Luke now.'

Morgan drove slowly towards the church. As Beth had predicted, the disciples were now on the pavement. They were agitated; clinging to one another, breaking apart, gesticulating.

'I tell you, there's only one of them who knows where Luke is!' said Peter. 'Jacob. The one who looks like a wrestler.'

'He's the one to follow, then,' said Morgan.

'There he is!' said Beth.

Jacob was the last to come running out of the house, panic informing every line of his muscle-bound body. He ignored the disciples. Beth caught a glimpse of his face as he turned to look back at the windows of the house; his eyes were blank, his heavy face contorted with terror.

He stayed too long, Beth thought with a thrill. His mind's gone.

The others were crowding round him, crying, 'Jacob, tell us what to do! Jacob!' but he thrust them off so hard that one woman went flying over the garden wall. Then he ran.

Morgan drove just fast enough to keep him in sight. But Jacob veered off down a pedestrian alley and disappeared.

'Shit!' said Morgan. 'Why the hell did he have to go down there?'

'Go straight on,' said Peter. 'Take the first left, then second left. He's gone to get his car, he keeps it in a lock-up down there.'

Morgan followed his directions. They came to a thin gravel drive leading to a courtyard of ramshackle garages. Morgan stopped short of the entrance; Beth ducked down in the front seat so Jacob wouldn't see her.

'What sort of car is it?'

'Green Mini,' said Peter.

'A Mini?' Morgan exclaimed, sounding pleased.

'But he's done things to it. New engine, turbo-charged or something.'

An acid-green Mini came swerving out of the drive and roared away on fat tyres, expelling a cloud of exhaust.

'Bloody hell, I see what you mean,' said Morgan, hurriedly accelerating after him.

It wasn't easy, keeping the car in sight in the city traffic. Jacob switched lanes and jumped lights as if he had a death wish. Morgan was a fast driver, but he only just managed to keep Jacob in sight. Steve, Beth knew, would have lost him.

'Christ, Morgan, are you trying to kill us?' Steve said, clinging on as the Sierra swerved in front of a lorry.

'Just wait until the bastard gets on the motorway,' Morgan said with wicked glee. 'We'll have him then.'

'The police'll stop him if he carries on like this,' Steve said morosely. 'They'll stop us, too.'

'They won't,' Beth said quietly. 'He'll take us where we want to go.'

Because she could feel Jacob's thoughts, his fears, hitting her in a deluge.

All the old things are still there. Why hasn't the Saviour destroyed them? Why are they still there? My faith. I have no faith. Luke. Luke will come and destroy them. I must find Luke. He will know. Oh, God, oh, God, though I walk through the valley of the shadow of death – oh, God. Luke, save me . . .

Chapter Twenty-three

WHEN Luke looked into Eirian's eyes, he knew he was facing the ultimate opponent. Satan himself.

No child could utter the poison that came from Eirian's mouth, no child could have made his followers doubt their faith or question their leader or conjure visions to drive his own mother out of her mind, unless the Devil himself spoke and worked through her.

This was his destiny, appointed by God; to fight and vanquish the Enemy, the father of lies, Lucifer.

Luke was apprehensive; he could admit that, for even the Lord had been afraid at times. But he was also furious – and excited.

'Take the child to her room,' he said.

No one obeyed. They shrank away, shaking their heads fearfully. Meg had helped Olivia to a chair, but she sat there with blank eyes, as if she'd seen a vision of hell.

'Cowards!' Luke shouted. 'We are the chosen of God! What is there to fear? *I* am not afraid!'

He seized Eirian himself, gripping her hands behind her back. She was slender, with bones that might snap like twigs. There was nothing she could do to him, as long as he did not look in her eyes.

'Bring the other child to the room also,' Luke said, as he marched the girl towards the stairs. 'Mark! Do it!'

This time, Mark obeyed. He wrenched Sam from Katy's side and dragged the frightened, unprotesting boy up the stairs.

They pushed the two children into the room together and locked the door. Luke told Mark, 'Stand guard outside; I must go to my room to prepare.'

His disciples were gathering on the landing and in the stairwell, anxious to see what was going to happen. Much as Luke despised their weakness – and would admonish them for it later – at this moment it was irrelevant. Olivia was there, too, glassy-eyed and being supported by a trembling Meg. The sight of his mother in this state gave Luke an extra frisson of excitement. To remember her, all-powerful as she thrashed his young body, to remember the excoriating pain of her love, and now to see her drained and powerless – for some reason Luke found the juxtaposition incredibly arousing.

This was his destiny, to vindicate his mother and to obliterate the hideous evil that Beth and Morgan had brought into the world.

Luke faced his followers. 'Go downstairs,' he said. 'Go down into the assembly hall and pray as you've never prayed before. Go on, all of you!'

They obeyed, wide-eyed. When the landing was empty, apart from Mark guarding the door, Luke continued to his own bedroom.

Mark would think he was going to pray. In fact, there was an item Luke needed. A secret between him and God.

Some of the tools he needed were already in the room, locked in the cupboard; the Bible, the whip, the knife. But there was something else he required, his very personal instrument of self-immolation, to make this an ultimate ritual of sacrifice, cleansing, blessing and rebirth. Luke felt himself becoming hard at the thought of it.

The glove.

He was going to break Eirian now.

As the door slammed and the key turned, Sam ran to Eirian and clung to her.

'I hate it here!' he said. 'My mum is so weird. She doesn't cuddle me like Dad and Beth do. She just tells me off all the time. The food's horrible. And all they teach you is things from the Bible, it's really boring. I want my dad. I want to go home!'

'I know,' Eirian said, hugging Sam tight against her, rocking him. He was so vulnerable.

'I prayed to Jesus like they told me, but he hasn't done anything to help us get away.'

'We have to help ourselves,' Eirian said into his fine sandy hair. 'I am going to get us out of here, Sam, I promise.'

Sam sniffed loudly. Eirian found a clean tissue in her pocket and wiped his nose.

Then she felt the cutting metallic coldness of Luke outside; heard him say, 'Leave us now, Mark. Join the others.' She heard the key turn, the door opening with a menacing click. And Luke appeared. He stood there, watching Eirian, who was hugging and fussing Sam.

Sam was her weak spot, and Luke knew it.

Luke slammed the door and locked it.

'It's Judgement Day, Faith,' he said, taking something from his pocket. A small key. He went to the cupboard, took out the whip and a Bible, and turned towards her. A few wood-lice came dribbling out, like the last spasm of Eirian's power, and a devil's coachhorse, a great black beetle with a scorpion tail.

Luke's eyes were serene and his smile a torturer's. He crushed the beetle underfoot without blinking. Its entrails left a red streak on the floor.

Seeing the whip, Sam burst into tears and tried to hide behind Eirian.

Luke brandished the Bible at her. 'God's Word,' he said. 'The One Truth. Demons must be cast out and witches must die and only through suffering can we be Saved.' He pointed at Eirian and his voice was rusting iron. '"Ye are of your father the devil and the lusts of your father ye will do. He was a murderer from the beginning, and abode not in truth, because there is no truth in him. When he speaketh a lie, he speaketh of his own: for he is a liar, and the father of it."'

He put the Bible down on one of the hard chairs, and flexed the whip. 'Which of you shall it be first?'

Eirian searched desperately inside herself for the dark face of the Goddess, the waves of blue sexual energy or the Wand of Power's glow, but the powers scrambled away between her fingers. She threw visions at Luke but he didn't see them. He was blind.

She put herself in front of Sam and said, 'Hit me. I'm bigger than Sam, but a lot smaller than you.'

She wanted to shame Luke, but nothing could shame him.

'Very well,' he said. 'You think yourself brave, but you are a weak little fool.'

'"But God hath chosen the foolish things of the world to confound the wise,"' said Eirian, '"and God hath chosen the weak things of the world to confound the things which are mighty."'

To hear Eirian quoting the Bible seemed to inflame Luke. He grabbed her by the neck of her sweatshirt and flung her down on to a mattress. His physical strength shocked her, knocking all her breath out. He pulled her sweatshirt up at the back and she felt the blows on her bare flesh; stinging pain that made her cry with rage and agony.

Sam was wailing. She pictured Meg and Katy and thought, why don't they come in, why don't they help?

But no one was going to help.

And Eirian, writhing helpless in a cloud of pain, knew that she couldn't keep her promise to Sam. Her only powers were words and visions, but Luke was blind and deaf to their meaning.

The blows stopped suddenly.

Coughing and sobbing for breath, her back fire-blistered, Eirian looked up and saw Luke turning to Sam. She couldn't move. Her vision was clouded with stars and she was too dizzy to stand up.

Luke's expression was different when he looked at Sam. Not contemptuous and dismissive as it had been when he'd beaten Eirian. He looked contemplative, tender and intensely excited.

Luke touched Sam with the whip.

'Stop crying,' he said quietly. 'Take down your trousers and underpants.'

Sam obeyed, terrified and gulping back tears as if he dared not make a sound. Luke pushed a hard chair up to the wall with its back facing outwards. 'Now, lean on the chair with your back to me.'

Sam did so, his elbows and chin resting on the back of the chair. He looked so little and skinny. Luke traced his thighs and small buttocks with the end of the whip, drew his arm back.

'Don't!' said Eirian.

Luke dropped the whip.

She caught her breath. I stopped him!

But she hadn't. He was doing something else. First he fetched a thin object of grey metal from the cupboard and placed it on the seat of the chair in front of Sam, alongside the Bible. Now he was taking a glove out of his jacket pocket, a thick leather glove with spikes sticking through the fingers and palm. He was sliding the glove onto his hand. And with his other hand, Luke was unzipping his flies.

Eirian caught a wave of Luke's thoughts like a sticky, ugly heat. And she understood a grotesque truth which at her age she should not have had to face, but must face anyway; that the things Luke wanted to do were far more vile than simple beating, and he wanted particularly to do them to Sam. Maybe to her as well, after Sam, to complete his barbaric victory.

Eirian knew that it wouldn't matter now if she threw herself at Luke's feet and proclaimed her abject repentance. Because Luke was now out of his mind, and his desires were nothing to do with saving Sam's or Eirian's soul.

It was easy for Morgan to keep the green Mini in sight on the motorway, even though Jacob drove between eighty and ninety all the way, when the traffic allowed.

'Do you think he's guessed we're following him?' Steve asked.

'Doesn't matter if he has,' said Morgan. 'He'll still go to Luke, because he'll think Luke can deal with us. Eh, Beth?'

'He's probably too wrapped up in his own panic to notice us,' said Beth. 'But if he has, you're right.'

'He could lead us in circles until we run out of petrol,' Steve observed.

'Nah,' said Morgan. 'He hasn't got the brains.'

Peter huddled in a corner, clutching his crucifix and saying nothing. Beth knew he was wishing he hadn't got himself into this.

'My dad was right,' she said. 'He's heading for Stockton or Middlesbrough, definitely.'

The Mini diverted on to an A road and turned off towards Yarm. Morgan pursued it along the broad, graceful main street of the town and out the other side, over a bridge, and along a country road.

Five miles further on, in the midst of flat, open country-side, the Mini turned left through a gateway into a private drive.

'Wait,' said Beth.

Morgan pulled up at the gates, and they looked along the drive to see a park with a scattering of trees and a plain eighteenth-century mansion; the sort of place that might have been converted for use as a school or a rest home. Or the headquarters of a cult.

The only sign was a plaque etched with a discreet cross on one of the gateposts. The Mini was speeding towards the house.

'This is the place,' said Beth.

'I think we ought to get the police,' said Steve.

'No,' she said, feeling certain of herself, as she had when she'd entered the other house. 'There isn't time. They'll let us in.'

Let this child be a sacrifice to you, Lord. Luke prayed, as he slid the glove on to his eager left hand. *Let this act consecrate Sam's soul, let my body and my blood spill into him and cleanse his wretched sinfulness, let his pain and my pain bring the Holy Spirit among us.*

Luke no longer knew what he was praying for. He only knew that this act must be made sacred, that it mustn't be a sin, but how could it be, it was holy, it was the holy rite of blood and wine and it was the only way to drive out the Devil.

Animals, God's lesser creatures, had only been a rehearsal.

All of it had been leading up to this. A human boy, a pure little soul like a lamb in this corrupt body.

Luke wanted to feel himself in the boy's body. He needed to feel *himself*. Wanted to plunge his gloved hand through the living tissues and feel the spikes in his own member even as it gave the last sacrament to the boy.

This, this, he knew through the white fire in his brain, would bring them all salvation.

Eirian still didn't comprehend quite what Luke intended to do, even as he unleashed the large, stiff penis from his trousers. The member looked red and ugly with scabs and gashes; she thought of the witch-hunter raping Guendolen, but Luke had the cruel spikes in the palm of his hand, not on his prick.

She watched, paralysed, as Luke ran the spiky glove over Sam's bare stomach and between his thighs. She seemed to be looking through fogged glass. Sam whimpered. Luke positioned himself against Sam's buttocks. Then he thrust forward and Sam screamed, as if he'd been impaled on white-hot metal.

That scream of grief and violation would live with Eirian for ever.

She was on her hands and knees now. She no longer cared about her own pain. She was crawling forward.

She saw Luke thrusting. He looked ludicrous.

She saw that the grey object on the chair was a scalpel.

Sam, she thought, get the knife and stab him! But she daren't speak aloud in case Luke hurt him worse. Instead she crawled forward, her eyes fixed on the lethal blade.

But Luke's naked right hand came round to pick up the knife. He reached up under Sam's shirt and seemed to draw the blade very lightly down the length of his body, from neck to abdomen. As if making a tentative dummy run. Or as if heightening his own anticipation.

The next time he did it, Eirian knew in a sickening rush of terror, he would slit Sam open.

She forgot her own pain. Her head cleared and strength fountained inside her, born of pure despair.

'Get off him!' she screamed, lunging at Luke. She caught hold of his trousers, which slid down around his knees. He grabbed at them by reflex, dropping the knife as he pulled them up again. Then he turned to stare at her with psychotic loathing.

Eirian seized the scalpel and slashed at his thigh. Luke yelped in pain, withdrawing from Sam, who collapsed to the floor. Blood sprayed from somewhere.

'Bitch!' Luke snapped. He kicked her wrist, and the scalpel went flying. Her whole arm thrummed with pain. Then, his eyes white-ringed with fury, Luke turned away from Sam and came towards her. He picked up the scalpel as he advanced.

Luke was going to do it to Eirian instead. Me first, she thought in abject horror, then back to Sam. And Eirian could see he didn't care that when he'd murdered two children they would lock him away, because his eyes were two empty wells of insanity.

'God told me to do it.' That's what it would say in the newspapers, while people cried about Sam and Eirian, too late.

Today, she thought, I come into my power.

Eirian backed up to the cupboard as Luke came towards her with the knife in his hand and his ugly puce penis swaying in the air.

Eirian spoke, her voice cold and thin. 'So, that's the kind of thing you like, is it?'

'Shut up!' he hissed.

'I can do it, but it doesn't come cheap.'

'You're an evil witch like your mother. Jezebel. "And I gave her a space to repent of her fornication; and she repented not."'

'I'm eleven today,' said Eirian. 'I told you, you should have done it last night.'

As Luke came towards her, Eirian thrust a needle of power into his mind and showed him what she was going to do to him.

Luke stopped dead.

His face stretched like dough; she saw what was left of his reason fleeing in front of mindless fear. He put up his ungloved right hand, as if to ward her off, his lips moving in soundless prayer. Then he fled, fumbling frantically with the key and throwing the door back so hard it cracked plaster off the wall.

His glove had fallen off. Eirian picked it up.

Luke surged out on to the empty landing, so fast he slipped on the lino and cannoned into the opposite wall.

Eirian stood in the doorway and said one soft word.

'*Luke.*'

He froze. There was no one there to help him. Luke turned slowly, pressing himself back against the wall by the stairwell; seeming unable to resist her will, unable to flee downstairs or even to move. He could only watch Eirian coming. His unfastened trousers began to slide down around his hips, but his erection had shrivelled to a wrinkled plum.

Eirian pointed at Luke. His shirt split open, scattering buttons. A red dot appeared over his heart. She drew her finger down in the air and the dot became a line, running down his sternum, over his stomach, down to his abdomen.

He scratched at the wound, as if it merely itched. Then he winced with unexpected pain, and looked down at himself.

'What . . .'

Blood was running down the slit. He pawed at the blood, stared in disbelief at the redness on his fingertips.

The slit widened. Luke began to pray. His screams ran hoarsely up the register. He clawed at his stomach, as if trying to hold the sides of the slit together, but he couldn't. He held his hands out like claws, screaming and staring down at himself.

The huge wound gaped open from throat to genitals. Blood was pouring out of him, yet he lived; his internal organs were undamaged. She could see them, pulsing, shining obscenely through veils of membrane and the moving veil of blood. But his intestines were beginning to slip down under the force of gravity, pinkish-blue ropes.

'Help me,' he rasped. '*God help me.*'

'May God strike me down where I stand,' said Eirian, but God did not help Luke.

She moved forward. She held up her left hand; she was wearing the glove.

Luke began gasping for breath in grunts. '*Ah, ah, ah.*'

'Is this what you like?' she said, her voice velvety. 'You seemed to think Sam would.'

Eirian reached into his body cavity and stroked his stomach and liver with the back of the glove. She let her knuckles trail gently over the soft, glistening organs, finding her own actions revolting yet horrendously fascinating. A deeper force than her own will was driving her.

Luke had stopped breathing. His blood was pumping everywhere. Somehow it had got on to his face, and his eyes gleamed madly white through the red.

Eirian had a glimpse of his thoughts.

He saw the Crone coming for him. Saw Eirian a hundred years old, with weed from the drowning pond for hair, her burned flesh falling away, her neck broken and her face swollen and purple from being hanged. But still she came.

'You can't avoid the Crone of Death,' said Eirian. 'She devours all she brings forth. There is no eternal life in paradise for the chosen, Luke; you have deluded yourself and your followers. Everything you have done is in denial of death but in denying death you deny life. Turn against the Great Mother and she will turn against you. Listen to the names of the Death Goddess; Hel Cerridwen Anath Macha Hecate Erinys Nemesis Skadi Kali.'

As she went on chanting, Eirian turned her gloved hand round, so that the tips of the pins faced towards him. She caressed his raw organs with the spikes. She bore down and squeezed. 'This is for my mother. This is for Sam. And this,' she squeezed again, staring hard into his eye, 'this is for my father. The Lord of the Flies.'

Luke screamed until his breath was no more than a rasp, but Eirian was not merciful.

When she saw he was losing consciousness, she thrust her hand up under his rib cage and closed her fingers round his heart.

Luke convulsed. He was sliding down the wall, leaving long red streaks.

Eirian gripped, twisted and wrenched. She felt the aorta burst, the other vessels stretching and popping. Great gouts of blood fountained out. The heart came free.

Luke, the fount of wisdom, was silent.

Letting the glove slide off, Eirian dropped to her knees beside Luke's gore-soaked corpse and began to go through his pockets. She quickly found what she wanted: a bunch of keys. Then she went back into the bedroom, quickly refastened Sam's clothing, and led him across the landing. He was bent double and crying with pain, but he could walk.

'Close your eyes, Sammy,' she said gently, hiding his eyes as they passed the body. 'It's not nice.'

She had thought everyone was inside the assembly hall, but where the stairs turned a corner, half way down, they bumped into Olivia. She was just standing there; Eirian had no idea how long she'd been there, how much she'd heard or seen, but her eyes were as madly white-ringed as Luke's had been.

Olivia stared at the blood on Eirian's clothes and her mouth came open. 'What have you done?' she hissed. 'Demon!'

Eirian pushed past her and hurried Sam down the rest of the stairs into the hall. She could hear chanting from the assembly hall; the doors were shut, and their own voices must have drowned Luke's screams. Rushing to the front door, Eirian began to try one key after another with trembling hands. The strength she'd poured out against Luke was waning; she knew it was not infinite.

A shrill, heart-rending scream came winding down the stairwell. A moment later, Olivia rushed shrieking down the stairs, her hands held out stiffly and the palms red with blood.

Eirian went on struggling with the lock, not helped by Sam clinging piteously to her arm. Olivia flung open the doors to the assembly hall and ran inside, sobbing; the chanting broke up; there was a lull, in which Eirian at last found the right key and the lock gave with a satisfying crunch. She wrenched the handle; the door stuck. Bolts. Oh Goddess, please.

Pandemonium had broken out behind her. The congregation were coming into the hall, some running upstairs, some heading for her and Sam.

She flung the bottom bolt back, but couldn't quite reach the top one. In a flash of sheer panic and frustration, Eirian aimed her will and the bolt shot back on its own. She glanced round; Mark and Paul were only feet from her. Then the door burst open without her touching it, and she and Sam stumbled out into the open air.

Behind her, she heard people screaming and sobbing that their beloved Luke was dead. The cacophany chilled her: how could they wail for him, after what he'd done? But it seemed to arrest her pursuers. She and Sam walked out into the open air and for a few moments they were alone, free.

Outside there was a park with trees, and a long drive leading into the distance. Eirian began to walk briskly along the tarmac, but Sam was in pain and he couldn't keep up. He was weeping.

Eirian's burst of power was over. She was beginning to shiver, and the flesh of her back was throbbing and stinging. It looks such a long way, I don't know where I am, and Sam can't make it.

She tried to pick him up, but she couldn't carry him far. He sobbed with pain.

'Come on, Sam, we've escaped. We must go on. Please, a bit further.'

'I can't.' He sniffed. He was absolutely white. 'It hurts.'

But while they spoke the cult members came flowing out of the house behind them, catching up and surrounding them easily. Eirian felt their rage, confusion, grief and terror assaulting her from every direction, waves of coloured fire. She saw Katy's and Meg's distraught faces. Mark, Paul and a couple of other big men were closing in slowly with grim expressions.

However frightened they were of Eirian, they were much too angry to let her escape.

Eirian clutched Sam. She glared at her captors.

'Don't touch us,' she said, 'or what happened to Luke will happen to every one of you.'

They hesitated, scared. They weren't sure what she was capable of. Eirian held her breath, trying to gather her power, and praying that their fear would vanquish their outraged grief.

In the fraught silence, a small green car came hurtling towards them. As everyone looked up, Eirian took the chance and began to pull Sam sideways on to the grass. The car screeched to a halt, a big fair-haired man leapt out and rushed to meet Paul and Mark. Everyone began shouting at once, pointing at Eirian.

'Jacob, be careful!' cried Susan. 'She's got the Devil in her!'

Jacob, Eirian sensed, was as unhinged as Mark and Paul, but they seemed to give each other courage. She and Sam didn't get far before their path was blocked, large hands closed on their shoulders and hate-fired eyes burned into hers.

And at that moment she saw another car, long and deep blue, sweeping along the drive towards them. Eirian caught her breath with a wild thrill of instinctive knowledge.

I called him across an ocean and he came!

But Jacob, holding Eirian, was pointing at the blue car with a knotted, trembling hand. 'Those scum have desecrated our church. Don't let them have the children. Luke must punish them!'

As they drove towards the house, Beth saw figures on the drive outside. A loose group of adults – and in their midst, two children.

'There they are!' she cried.

Eirian was struggling in Jacob's hands, Sam stooping in his captor's grip as if hurt. Morgan accelerated towards the centre of the group then stood on the brakes, forcing people to scatter as the Sierra swept to a halt.

He and Beth leapt out of the car, closely followed by Steve.

'Mum!' Eirian cried. Beth thought she would pass out with relief at the sight of her daughter, and with shock when she saw the blood that covered Eirian from head to foot.

Morgan said, 'Let the children go. You know it's over.' His voice was even and commanding. The cult members stared at Morgan and Beth, all in black, personifications of the witch-haunted darkness they dreaded. But Jacob and a dark-haired man held on to Eirian and Sam with the menace of cornered, rabid dogs.

To Beth's amazement, it was Steve who waded straight in and grabbed Sam from his captor, shouting, 'Get your hands off him, you bastard!'

The man seemed so astonished that he let Sam go. But as Steve gathered his son in his arms, four or five suited men closed around Eirian.

'Get Sam in the car and wait for us,' Morgan said grimly. As Steve obeyed, a ginger-haired woman detached herself from the crowd and rushed after him, exclaiming, 'Steve! Steve, you don't understand!' Steve walked away, ignoring her, but she followed him to the car, pleading. Beth took a deep breath. Katy.

To the others, Morgan said, 'Come on, give her up.'

'We can't,' said the dark-haired man, who was wild-eyed and sweating, with tears rolling down his face. 'Come a step nearer and we'll hurt her! She must be punished for what she did to our leader!'

Eirian spoke in a clear, assured voice, 'You can't hurt me now my parents are here. Your beloved leader liked raping little boys, Mark. He liked cutting and whipping children. And you – all of you – just walked away and let it happen!'

A round, blonde woman at the edge of the crowd started crying.

'She's a liar,' said a female voice. Beth tore her gaze from her daughter and saw, with a ghastly rush of shock, her own mother coming towards her. Olivia looked so crazed that Beth hardly knew her, but she clearly recognized Beth. She held clawed, blood-caked hands out towards Beth. 'Look what she did. This is what you created, this abomination. I was kind to you, I was far too kind to you, letting you bring this horror into the world!'

Speechless, Beth stepped back, felt Morgan's hands clasping her upper arms. 'What the hell's she talking about?' Beth gasped.

'Christ knows. She's crazy,' said Morgan over Beth's shoulder. 'Mrs Herne, why don't you tell these thugs to let our daughter go?'

Olivia glared at Morgan, like a snake gathering venom in its fangs. Then she spat at him. Beth felt him go rigid. 'In that case,' Morgan said thinly, 'why don't you just fuck off and die, *sister*?'

Olivia backed off as if he'd slapped her. 'You've done this to my daughter, you serpent, you lover of Satan! Corrupted her!'

'Yes, and I enjoyed every minute and I'm going to go on doing it just as soon as your sick fucking friends have given us our daughter back.'

'Come on, grab them, get them in the house!' Jacob shouted suddenly. Beth sensed that he was burning for revenge through his fear. 'There's fifty of us and three of them! Luke will deal with them!'

'He can't, brother, you stupid bastard. Don't you understand?' yelled the dark one, Mark. 'Luke's dead, he's dead! Go and look if you –'

'No!' Jacob roared. And he let Eirian go and punched Mark in the jaw. Eirian made a break for freedom; Beth and Morgan leaped forward and caught her in their arms. A man jumped on Morgan and tried to pull him off; Morgan spun round and punched his attacker in the throat, sending him crashing backwards into someone behind him.

Then Beth, Morgan and Eirian were fighting their way towards the car through a morass of clawing hands. These people are all in a state of hysteria, Beth realized, and in this state they don't care what they do or who they hurt.

Beth felt a flow of blue-black power. It was as if she, Eirian and Morgan worked as one instinctive entity, like her three

454

cats. As Morgan picked up Eirian and bundled her into the car, Beth turned and faced the cult members. The force that surged through her was Eirian's and Morgan's as well as her own. The Goddess's rage.

'Leave us!' Beth shouted, raising her hands. 'Jacob knows what we can do; we'll do worse, if you don't let us go!'

There was a silent, rolling flash of light, and Luke's followers fell away as if they'd run into a brick wall. Most of them began to surge back into the house in terror. There had been something in that power to open their minds to the darkness and damage their memories, and that had come from Eirian, not Beth.

Beth leapt into the passenger seat next to Morgan. Eirian was settling herself in the back next to Steve and Sam; Katy was clinging to the off-side of the car, shouting at Steve through the closed window. Peter had remained huddled in the back all through the confrontation, but when he saw the blood on Eirian, he panicked.

'Christ! Let me out! Oh, Jesus!' Peter gasped, fumbling frantically with the door handle and flailing his way out of the car. He almost knocked Katy over as he went but she bounced back, crying, 'Steve, listen to me!'

'Sod off, Katy!' Steve yelled, in tears. 'How the hell could you let this happen?'

He slammed the door against her as Morgan steered off the road and drove in a circle on the grass to turn round. Jacob, Mark and the others stared after them with blank eyes; Beth felt a wave of madness and unbearable loss from them, but she quickly shut it out. Then a woman came rushing forward and threw herself on the bonnet of the car.

'Shit!' said Morgan, braking.

It was Beth's mother. As the car stopped she dashed along the side and opened the back door, which Eirian hadn't locked.

'Give me the demon!' Olivia cried, clawing at Eirian, trying to pull her out of the car. 'I must purge it, destroy it!'

'Oh, Christ,' said Beth, struggling to unlock her own door.

Steve held on to Eirian's arm, while Eirian and Olivia wrestled for possession of the door.

Before either Beth or Morgan could leap out to help, Eirian spoke in a low, unchildlike, petrifying tone, 'Go back to the house. You belong there.'

Olivia's face emptied. The door slid out of her hands. Eirian shut and locked it; Morgan, breathing out grimly, put his foot down and the car shot away. Beth looked back to see the dwindling figure of her mother watching them; then turning slowly back towards the house.

'Sam's hurt,' Steve said hoarsely. 'We need to get him to a doctor. Someone's beaten him, and cut his stomach.'

'There must be a casualty not too far away,' said Beth. 'We'll stop and ask.' Tears were streaming down her cheeks. She reached into the back and gripped Eirian's hands. 'Love, are you all right? Whatever happened?'

'Don't fuss, Mum,' said Eirian. 'It's not my blood.'

She wandered back into the house and up the stairs as if reeled on an invisible line, and knelt by the body of her son. Knelt in the pools of blood where he lay like a gutted fish, and watched over him.

'I did this,' said Olivia.

It made sense. She was the Virgin whose son was sacrificed so others could live. And she was the Crone who devoured her own children. Eirian had shown her this.

Beth's offspring could only be from the Devil, to do what she'd done. All her life Olivia had blamed those around her for every misfortune; Eirian had opened a little window of cruel reality to show her that certain things, at least, had been Olivia's fault, after all.

And if some things, she thought blankly, why not everything? Therefore I must have killed my son. I made Luke as he is, therefore I destroyed him.

The glove with the drawing pins stuck cruelly through it was lying by his corpse. She fingered it, and somehow it slipped onto her left hand. It was heavy and wet with blood, but it felt right. She touched it to her lips and tasted the holy blood.

A large fly came droning through the air and landed on Luke's intestines. It dabbled its feet in the blood, then vanished under a flap of skin. Olivia watched it, but it meant nothing.

'I did this,' she said again and again. 'I killed my son. It's my fault. I killed him.'

The scalpel, too, had found its way into her right hand and lay thinly cold in her palm.

She was still there when the police came and took her away.

Chapter Twenty-four

As Morgan stopped the car outside the accident and emergency department, Steve climbed out with Sam in his arms and rushed straight inside through the automatic doors. Beth helped Eirian out of the back seat, anxiously studying her daughter's face.

'Are you hurt?' Beth asked. 'All this blood.'

'No, I'm all right,' said Eirian. She dived into Beth's arms. 'Mum, I'm sorry I was horrible to you.'

'When?'

'Before Luke took us away. I wouldn't speak to you, remember? I'm really sorry.'

'Oh, that.' Beth gasped. 'Oh, love.'

Standing on the pavement beside the ambulance bay, they hugged each other, weeping, regardless of the dark red gore plastered on Eirian's sweatshirt. Morgan looked on, struggling not to cry with them.

'Ow,' said Eirian, wincing. 'Mind my back, Mum.'

'What's wrong?'

'Nothing, just a bit sore.'

'I put a sweater in the car,' said Beth to Morgan. 'Can you pass me it, so we can get this ghastly thing off Eirian?' Morgan obliged, passing Beth the violet-blue garment.

Beth caught her breath as she removed Eirian's blood-caked sweatshirt and saw the raw stripes on her daughter's lower back. 'You said you weren't hurt! Who did this?'

'Luke,' said Eirian. Although there were tears running down her face she seemed self-possessed. 'But it's all right, Mum, he won't do it any more.'

Beth glanced at Morgan as she threw the soiled shirt into the car. 'Someone said Luke was dead. Is it true?'

Eirian didn't reply. She slipped into the sweater, which was far too big for her, and looked at Morgan as she disentangled her hair from the neckhole. 'You're Morgan, aren't you?' she said.

'Yes,' he said, his voice unsteady. 'Hello, Eirian.'

'He's your dad,' said Beth.

'I know,' Eirian said matter-of-factly. She reached for Morgan's hand, and he came to hug both his daughter and Beth, in tears but smiling in amazement. Eirian added, 'You heard me.'

'How do you mean?' said Morgan.

'I called you. I knew you'd come.'

'Oh, God,' he breathed, staring dumbfounded at Beth.

'I know,' said Beth. 'I should be used to it by now, but she's still a shock a day. I told you she wasn't ordinary.'

Eirian said very softly, 'I'm going to tell you something now; I'll never tell anyone but you, and if the police ask me I won't say anything at all. I killed Luke.'

'You can't have done!' Beth exclaimed by reflex.

'Where do you think the blood came from? It's his.'

Beth and Morgan stared at each other over her head, baffled and horror-struck. Beth thought, she must be fantasizing! 'How?'

Eirian frowned, as if she wasn't sure. 'With my hands. And the Goddess's power. I did it because he was hurting Sam. He would've killed us both.' She fixed her unavoidable gaze on Morgan. 'I did it for you and Mum.'

Morgan looked more horrified than ever. 'I threatened Luke but she carried it out,' he said softly. Beth thought, I don't think he can handle this. And I'm not sure I can, either.

'You can't leave your car there, sir,' said an ambulance driver. 'Public car park round the back.'

'Oh, sorry, I'll move it,' said Morgan. 'You go in, Bethie, I'll find you.'

The children were seen quickly, queue-jumping a waiting room full of casualties. Beth hated the echoey, bustling atmosphere of tension; all she wanted was to go home. But there were doctors to be seen and questions to be answered.

When the doctor told Steve that in addition to his other injuries, Sam had been buggered, Steve tried to hit the doctor. Beth and Morgan held him back, and Beth cradled him as he wept tears of bitter rage into her shoulder.

'I'm going to kill Luke,' Steve kept saying. 'And Katy. How could she let him do it?'

The police were called. A police doctor examined the children; Beth, Morgan and Steve were questioned. The detective seemed to be implying that they had caused the children's injuries themselves. Then it was Beth who had to be held back. But in the end, their story was accepted.

The children were kept in hospital overnight. Sam was quiet and tearful; Eirian was in trouble with the nurses for constantly leaving her bed to comfort him. Morgan phoned Rhianwen, Beth phoned the farm and her father, then she and her companions spent an uncomfortable night trying to sleep in the waiting room. In the morning Beth felt as if she had been under a steam roller. Before they could leave, they were required to make a statement at the local police station.

Steve went first, then Beth and Morgan, while Steve stayed with the children. Beth didn't want them left alone, even in hospital.

She and Morgan told the whole story. There was nothing to hide, now the children were free. Yet they were made to wait in an interview room for another hour. Beth had washed off her make-up, tied back her hair and put the violet sweater on, so at least she looked less startling.

'What's going on?' said Beth. 'They can't charge us with anything, can they? What have *we* done wrong?'

'Nothing,' said Morgan. 'You're being paranoid.'

'Do you blame me?'

Eventually a detective came in and told them that the cult leader, Luke Herne, was dead. The other cult members had been arrested; some would be released after questioning, others would be charged with the abduction and unlawful detention of the children.

Beth felt numb at the news of Luke's death. She felt no joy, no regret. Only dull grief in the pit of her stomach.

'You do understand that the children will have to be questioned about Luke Herne's death,' said the detective. 'Your daughter must have been close by when it happened, to have got so much blood on her. No one else seems to have witnessed the event. However, a woman has confessed to the killing; she was found beside the body with what appear to be the murder weapons in her hands. It seems she's extremely mentally disturbed; she's been taken to a psychiatric unit. Unfortunately, Ms Herne, it appears the woman is your mother, Olivia Herne. I'm sorry. Too early to draw conclusions but it may be that she killed her son to protect the children.'

This news, too, was only another wave of greyness. Beth rested her head on Morgan's shoulder while he hugged her, but she didn't cry.

Beth had to go to the morgue to identify Luke. As she looked at the smoothly waxen face – the rest of him was covered up – she thought she heard one policeman saying to another in the corridor outside, 'Good riddance. Did you hear what he did to the little boy?'

Afterwards, they took Beth to see her mother. Morgan went with her, while Steve stayed with Sam and Eirian.

Olivia was in a private room on a psychiatric ward, with a policeman guarding the door. A policewoman and a male nurse came in with Beth; she didn't want them, but they insisted. Morgan waited outside.

The woman in the bed looked bonily gaunt and her uncombed hair was full of grey. Beth's throat closed up. Olivia's face was slack, her eyelids half lowered over eyes that were dead with sedation. She showed no sign of acknowledging Beth.

'Mum?'

Beth stood over the broken figure with tears spilling down. I could have loved you so much, if only you'd let me, she thought. I really wanted to love you.

'Mum, can you hear me?'

The blue eyes swung towards her without recognition.

'It's me. It's Beth.'

Still nothing. Beth felt desperate. She wondered, can they do anything for her?

The nurse said, 'We had to sedate her rather heavily, I'm afraid.'

Beth tried again. 'Mum, I'm Beth. I'm your daughter.'

Suddenly Olivia lurched forward, clawing convulsively at Beth, as if some fierce energy within her overrode even the sedatives. Words fell slurred and ugly from her mouth. 'Child of Satan! Whore! God will punish your incest! "Babylon the great is fallen, is fallen, and is become the habitation of devils, and the hold of every foul spirit, and a cage of every unclean and hateful –"'

The nurse rushed over to quiet Olivia while the police-woman quickly ushered Beth out of the room.

They took Beth to an office, where she sat shaking, with Morgan holding her. A doctor came and gave her a Valium.

'At least your mother will get treatment now,' Morgan said gently.

'I can't hate her,' Beth whispered. 'I feel so sorry for her.'

'I know. Come on, let's go home.'

On the way back to the children's ward, Beth went into the hospital shop and bought some new clothes for Eirian and Sam. The children needed rest, the doctor said; their physical injuries would soon heal as long as they were kept quietly at home for a few days. But he also made ominous remarks about psychological damage and the need for counselling.

Then, at last, they were allowed to go home.

Before they left, Beth rang her father again, and her grand-parents, to tell them about Luke and her mother. Randolph and Heather reacted with quiet sorrow rather than outright grief, almost as if they'd expected something like this to happen. As if, expecting it, they'd long ago separated them-selves emotionally from their daughter and grandson. They'd never been particularly open anyway, Beth thought. At least the fact that they could cope with the news had made it easier to tell them.

Eirian, washed and dressed in her new T-shirt and jeans, seemed composed and cheerful as Morgan drove them all home. Sam began to chatter, already beginning to forget what had happened. Steve was promising him treats, cinema trips, visits to his grandparents.

'Resilient, aren't they?' Morgan said softly to Beth. 'We're the ones who fall apart.'

Beth badly wanted to hold Eirian on her lap all the way home, but the seat belts made it impossible. Instead, Steve sat in the back with the children, and Beth turned round in the front seat to hold Eirian's hand. Uncanny, how unmoved Eirian seemed by everything. Her green eyes were the same: cold, watchful, ageless.

Morgan drove from Stockton-on-Tees to Staffordshire rather more sedately than he had driven up there. After half an hour, the children fell asleep.

It was mid-afternoon when they got home, and they were all exhausted, but there was a welcoming committee at the farm. As well as Margaret, Gordon, John and Frank, Rhianwen was there. Their joy at the children's arrival barely touched Beth through the veil of exhaustion.

'I hope you'll forgive me if I cut this short,' said Beth, 'but Eirian needs to rest, and so do I. We'll tell you about it another time, okay?' Preferably never, she thought.

Morgan took Beth and Eirian to Dove Cottage, then Steve asked him to run him and Sam back to their own house. Steve wanted to be alone with his son now; Beth understood. At this moment, Steve could not have been less interested in Beth's relationship with Morgan.

While Morgan was gone, Beth and her daughter crashed out on Beth's bed and both fell sound asleep. Beth opened her eyes suddenly and found it was five o'clock; two hours had passed. She felt more human, at least. Leaving Eirian asleep, she changed into jeans and a long black Indian top, combed her hair and staggered downstairs.

Rhianwen and Morgan were in the kitchen, drinking tea; Rhianwen jumped up and hugged Beth. The cats had their noses in their bowls as if they'd never seen food before; either Rhianwen or Morgan had, apparently, just fed them. Morgan's chin was shadowed with stubble and he looked worn out, but more lovable than ever in Beth's eyes.

'How are you feeling, love?' asked Rhianwen. 'How's Eirian? Morgan's been telling me what happened.'

Beth grimaced. 'Good, I don't feel like going over it again. Eirian's fast asleep. As long as she's all right, so am I.'

'Well, you don't have to talk about it if you don't want to,' Rhianwen said gently. 'The children are safe, that's what matters.'

'I don't know whether to laugh or cry,' said Beth. 'Sorry if I'm not very good company. I feel totally shell-shocked.'

Morgan poured her a mug of tea, but when he gave it to her it was at arm's length, with an impersonal air. Beth and Rhianwen sat at the table but Morgan stayed on his feet, leaning against the sink, arms folded.

Even through her tiredness, it took Beth one second to work it out. Morgan was trying very hard to reassure his mother that nothing had happened between him and Beth. Beth wondered if she had actually asked directly, forcing him to lie. She felt annoyed that he hadn't had the courage to tell Rhianwen the truth; but not wanting to embarrass anyone, Beth decided to play along with it.

'Morgan's been great,' she said lightly. 'We'd never have found the children without him. I'm really grateful.'

She saw Rhianwen's gaze flicking between them; looking for clues but trying not to make it obvious. Beth and Morgan tried to appear physically indifferent to each other.

'By the way,' Rhianwen said to her son, 'have you called Marian with the news?'

'I can't,' said Morgan. 'She's somewhere off the coast of Greenland for the next fortnight. I could 'phone work; they'd be able to get a message to her.'

'Well, do you want to come home with me and do that?' Rhianwen said insistently.

'I suppose so. I could have a shower and fetch some clean clothes, too.'

'Aren't you staying with me tonight?' Rhianwen asked. Beth stared into her tea and said nothing. Oh, God, here it comes, she thought; the point at which either Rhianwen kills Morgan, or I do.

'I don't think Beth should be here on her own, do you?' he said.

'As long as you didn't find the sofa bed too lumpy,' Beth said with the perfect degree of offhandedness.

'No, it's fine,' said Morgan.

'Well, it's up to you,' said Rhianwen. And she seemed reassured that nothing was going on. 'I'm glad you two are friends again.'

'Just like brother and sister,' Beth said under her breath.

As Rhianwen went out to her own car, Morgan whispered to Beth in the doorway, 'See you later.'

'You are coming back, aren't you?' said Beth. She had a sudden, heart-rending fear that he was deserting her again.

'Of course I am.'

'Why did you make out there's nothing between us?'

He looked apologetic. 'It was hardly the time, was it?'

'I suppose not,' she sighed. 'Are you going to ask your mum about my grandfather?'

'Yes, but it's not something you can just come out with, is it?'

'You're scared of her!' said Beth. 'You're still scared of your mother!'

Morgan pulled a faintly ironic face. 'See you this evening.' He kissed her on the cheek, and left.

Beth went back upstairs and found Eirian awake, looking drained. She's not as strong as she makes out, Beth thought. She gives the impression of being invulnerable but she isn't, she's still a little girl.

'I'm starving, Mum,' said Eirian. 'What's for tea?'

'What do you want?'

'Spaghetti on toast and poached eggs. Is my dad still here?'

'He's gone to Rhianwen's. Be back later.'

'Good.' Eirian smiled, like the Mona Lisa. 'I like him. I really, really like him.'

'So do I,' Beth murmured. 'Happy Birthday for yesterday, love; I'm sorry it was so rotten, but I will make it up to you at the weekend, I promise.'

'That's all right. I want to tell you what happened with Luke,' Eirian said gravely, 'and I will, both of you; but not yet.'

'Whenever you want, love,' Beth said, stroking her hair. 'I'm always here.'

'It doesn't upset me to talk about it. But I won't tell you until after Olivia's been locked away for killing Luke. So that when you tell the police you don't know anything, you really don't.'

This calculating intelligence knocked Beth sideways. Again she thought, what is this creature in my daughter's shape?

'Don't look at me like that, Mum,' said Eirian. 'If you'd seen what Luke did, you'd have killed him too. He and his followers don't matter. But Guendolen . . .'

'What about her?'

'I think she's going to die.' Eirian's jade eyes gleamed with tears that didn't fall. 'The Inquisitor's men caught her, because she gave her strength to help me.'

No, Eirian isn't heartless, Beth thought heavily. She has her priorities right, and I'm a mess.

At about six, to Beth's surprise, Steve turned up with Chez, Tag, Zak, Tash, Cherry and Bryony. They came rushing into the kitchen to smother her with outpourings of love, condolence and relief. Their emotion made Beth start crying again. She was so glad to see them.

Steve said, 'My mum and dad have come over to look after Sam, so he's happy. I didn't tell them much, but I s'pose it'll all have to come out eventually.' Beth had met Steve's parents: lovely, friendly, ordinary people. Why, she thought, couldn't my family have been like that?

She and Steve hugged each other and talked for a while, like loving friends, but Morgan was not mentioned.

Beth felt better in company. She began to feel normal again. Eirian, still tired, went back to bed; Beth poured drinks and they had a low-key celebration.

At seven, Morgan came back.

All their friends knew was that Morgan was Eirian's father; neither Beth nor Steve had told them that anything else had happened. When Beth introduced him, they were friendly and welcoming, treating him like a long-lost friend. Cherry flirted shamelessly with him, to Beth's displeasure. But later, catching Beth alone in the kitchen, Cherry cuddled up to her and whispered, 'Beth, he's absolutely *gorgeous*. How did you let him get away? Is he married?'

Beth didn't know what to say. 'Erm, didn't he tell you?'

'All he seems to talk about is you.' Cherry frowned. 'You're not getting back together with him, are you?'

'I don't know.' Beth sighed.

'Oh. I wouldn't blame you, but what about Steve?'

Beth tried to appear indifferent to Morgan, but it was impossible. The looks, body language and affection between them were all too obvious to the others. Steve left early, saying he wanted to get home to Sam. He was polite to Beth but offhand, almost hostile. She felt wounded, even if it was her fault.

'Steve, we need to talk.'

'Yeah,' he said. 'When Morgan's fed up of stringing you along and he fucks off back to Canada, come round and cry on my shoulder.'

Beth watched, stunned, as Steve got into his ailing car, brought the engine to reluctant life and drove slowly away. Bryony appeared at her shoulder, giving her a look of deathly accusation.

'How can you do this to Steve?' said Bryony. 'You're betraying him, just when he needs you most! We all feel the same.'

'Do you?' Beth said distantly, thinking, am I going to lose all my friends over this? 'Well, I'm sorry. I didn't mean to hurt him.'

She went into the other room and quietly asked them to

467

leave. 'It's lovely to see you but we're really tired,' she said. 'I'm sure you understand.'

That night, Beth slept with Eirian in her bed while Morgan slept in Eirian's room. They were too exhausted even to think about making love; mentally too drained to think as far as the next day. A mass of complications and problems to be faced. But for now, what bliss to feel her daughter's flank under her hand, and to fall into oblivion.

When Beth woke up, with daylight streaming through her curtains, Eirian wasn't beside her. She leapt up in a panic and rushed downstairs, only to find Eirian and Morgan sitting on the rug in front of the fireplace with the three cats climbing over them.

'. . . because Bast is the boss and she won't let the others have their own way,' Eirian was saying. 'Bast likes Mum best but Eostre likes me. So you can have Cerridwen, only she is fickle.'

Beth collapsed against the door-frame in relief, her hand to her forehead. She was half hidden by the stairs, so they didn't notice her at first.

'Anyway,' said Eirian, 'why haven't you come to see us before?'

Morgan smiled very sadly at her. 'I wanted to. It's complicated. I'll explain one day.'

Eirian knelt up and hugged him. And Beth felt the rush of an unexpected and deeply unpleasant emotion: jealousy. She'd never had to share her daughter before. She thought, Morgan just walks in after all this time and Eirian immediately, unconditionally adores him!

Eirian looked up and saw her. 'What's the matter, Mum?'

She let her breath go. 'Nothing. I thought you'd disappeared again. Oh, God.'

Eirian and Morgan both came to her and embraced her.

'I was talking to my dad.'

'Come and sit down,' said Morgan. 'Did you know it's nearly midday? I didn't like to wake you up.'

'You should have done,' she said, yawning.

'How are you doing?'

'What do you think?' she said, looking at Eirian, who was playing with the cats on the rug. 'I'm fine now.'

But she wasn't. Beth thought that she should have felt euphoric – she had Eirian home, she had Morgan, Sam was going to be all right – but instead she only felt depression, restlessness, sorrow.

Morgan, too, seemed quiet and uneasy. This is it, she thought; he's got cold feet about all the things he said in a rush of lust. I'm going to lose him. Again.

'We've hardly had a chance to talk,' he said, weaving his fingers with hers. She loved his hands, with their long fingers and fine dark hairs and beautiful bones.

'We will,' said Beth.

'Are you okay? You seem distant. You're not having second thoughts, are you?'

'About what?'

'Us staying together.'

'Are we?' said Beth. 'You'll be going back to Canada.'

'I don't have to. I can get a job here. You could do wonders with this cottage; renovate it, extend it, build a conservatory, do something with the garden.'

What about your wife? Beth thought dully. Morgan seems to be presuming so much; that I automatically want him back, that he can walk in and take over my life and Eirian, that Marian won't fight for him. But she will and he'll probably give in. He couldn't even tell Rhianwen he still loves me!

Beth should have felt happy but she only felt a dull pain, like fear. All she could see was the face of Luke, on the big filing cabinet drawer in the morgue; and the face of Olivia lunging at her, slurring curses from the Book of Revelation.

She remembered the nervous, clingy boy Luke had once been, devoted to Beth. What happened to him? Beth wondered. Where did my little brother go?

She put her head in her hands.

'Hey, what is it?' Morgan said gently. Eirian came and leaned on Beth's knees, concerned.

'I'm just tired,' said Beth. 'My brother's dead, my daughter says she killed him, my mother's barking mad, I've just found out my dad's gay and I've been sleeping with a close relative. There's going to be some kind of ghastly court case and they want Eirian to see a child psychologist. Isn't that enough?' She smiled weakly. 'I don't know, Morgan; one moment you're quietly saving whales, the next you're dropped into all this. I don't blame you if you want out.'

'I'm staying, Beth,' Morgan said firmly.

'But when are you going to tell your mother? And your wife?'

'Soon.'

'We've got to sort this whole mess out once and for all,' said Beth. 'I want to go out, I can't face staying in all day.'

'Sure. Wherever you want. I'll take you and Eirian out for lunch.'

She released a long breath. 'That sounds wonderful, but there are other things we need to do. I must tell the school Eirian won't be back for a few days, and apologize to Margaret for not working – and I think we should go and talk to my grandparents.'

'Will you give yourself a break?' Morgan said, kissing her. 'Of course we'll go and see them, but we still need to eat.'

'If Eirian really killed Luke,' said Beth, 'can you live with it?'

They were in a pub car park after lunch, waiting while Eirian stroked a horse at the gate of an adjoining field. It was a perfect June day, gleaming with fresh green leaves and spring flowers.

'I would have killed him myself,' said Morgan.

'Yes, but you're a fully fledged acolyte of Satan. She's just a little girl.'

'We don't need DNA testing to prove she's mine, then, do we?' Morgan grinned at her. 'Seriously, I don't know. Whatever she's done, I love her.'

'I haven't told you the half of it, yet,' Beth said grimly.

470

'Are you sure you want to go and confront your grand-parents about me?' said Morgan. 'They're not going to like it.'

'But I need to know *why*. I'm sick of being kept in the dark as if we're kids. We'll take Eirian back to the farmhouse first; Margaret likes looking after her and she'll be safe there.'

'Hey, I know it's hard, but don't get too over-protective, will you?'

'Thanks for the parenting lesson,' Beth said sharply.

'Ow,' said Morgan, wounded. 'You've obviously taken the sarcasm lessons to heart.'

Beth tried to smile. 'Sorry. Anyway, I don't want Eirian with us in case it gets acrimonious. But today, I want everything out in the open.'

Morgan put his arm round her. His scent and touch always turned her nerves to silver. 'Just don't be too upset if they won't tell us everything we want to know, okay?'

'They'll tell us,' said Beth.

All the same, she felt like the fallen, humiliated girl of twelve years ago as she stood on her grandparents' doorstep with Morgan beside her. Habit. She suppressed the feeling and re-solved to be strong.

Heather answered the door and looked at Beth with raised eyebrows. But when she saw Morgan, her face transformed. The naked hatred Beth saw there was horrifying; as hideous as the expression on Olivia's face, even without the sick light of insanity.

'Get him off my property,' Heather said viciously.

'Gran, please don't be like this,' said Beth, shocked. 'We want to come in and talk.'

'I have nothing whatever to say to him.'

Morgan began, 'Mrs Cross —' but she broke in.

'Get him out!'

'Gran, please! Just listen —'

'I'll listen to you. Not to him. I won't stand here arguing, just get him out!'

'All right,' Beth said. 'Morgan, would you mind wait-ing in the car for now?'

'On the road,' Heather added.

Looking grim but resigned, Morgan got back into the driver's seat, and Heather let Beth into the house.

'Isn't Granddad here?' Beth asked.

'He's at the surgery. What is it you want, Beth? I don't know what you think you're doing, bringing that creature –'

'Trying to find out why you hate him!' said Beth. Heather walked into the front room and Beth followed. 'Gran, please. This has been going on for years and no one will tell us the truth! I've had enough. I want to sort this out once and for all.'

'I knew this would happen one day.' Heather looked out of the window at the Sierra pulling out of the drive. Her face was bleak.

'Is it true that Granddad is Morgan's father?'

Heather stiffened; cold lights moved in her eyes. 'Who told you that?'

'My dad. He only told us because we thought *he* was.'

'Been doing too much thinking, have you? Very well, yes, it was Randolph,' Heather said shortly. 'Happy now?'

'Gran, I'm sorry, but why couldn't someone have told us?'

Heather folded her arms and went on gazing out of the window. 'Rhianwen deliberately set out to seduce my husband,' Heather said contemptuously. 'Oh, Randolph couldn't resist. She was so very beautiful, twenty years younger than him, and he's only a man, after all. I couldn't really blame *him*. But she tried to take him away from me and when she couldn't, the tramp got herself pregnant. Still didn't work. He stayed with me. Really, someone should have told her that men do these stupid things, but they stay with their wives.'

A fearful tremor went through Beth, the echo of her own insecurity. 'You must have been terribly hurt,' she said.

Heather's shoulders rose and fell tiredly. 'One gets on with things. I'll tell you who suffered: Olivia. She was devastated. She's always had a religious bent but this drove her completely over the top. She began seeing visions, saying God was telling her to fight against witches like Rhianwen. Do you know . . .'

'What, Gran?'

472

'Olivia got angry *for* me. So I didn't have to.'

'You were angry though, weren't you? You forgave Grand-dad but you couldn't forgive Rhianwen.'

'For hurting my daughter. For firing up this lunacy that drove her away from us. For refusing to move away and parading her brat under our noses. Do you think I wanted it to be common knowledge that my husband was the father? The least she could do was promise to keep her mouth shut!'

'Even to Morgan?'

'Especially to him!'

'But it's not Morgan's fault! Why can't you forgive him?'

'What does it matter to you?'

'I love him. He's staying with us.'

'For God's sake. He is so lacking in principles he seduced a fourteen-year-old girl and ruined her life!'

'It was Mum who ruined my life! And you lot, forcing Rhianwen to leave! You even shot at him, didn't you? That is crazy.'

Heather grunted. 'Wish I hadn't shot to miss. He's just like his mother, can't you see it? Married, isn't he? How can you trust a man who would leave his wife and expect you to take him back, just like that? For pity's sake, Beth, don't do it.'

'He's made mistakes but he's a good person.'

'Like hell.'

'But he's Eirian's father.'

'Eirian has grown up quite satisfactorily without a father. Why does she need him now? Stick with that Steve, Beth; he may be a scruffy devil but he'll never let you down.'

Beth took her grandmother's hand, convinced that she could mend things if she tried hard enough. 'Gran, if you'd only speak to Morgan, you'd find out what he's really like. He's nice, he's kind, he really cares about us and Eirian loves him.'

'No.'

'Oh, damn this!' Exasperated, Beth left the house and beckoned Morgan to come in. As she stood there waiting for him to walk up the drive, she had a bad feeling, as if a chilly wind were blowing through her. Nerves. She ignored it.

'Are you sure?' said Morgan.

'Come on.' Taking his hand, Beth led him into the front room.

'Look, Gran. He's not the Devil. You're going to have to get used to this; it's silly to go through life not speaking to each other.'

Heather stared at Morgan, at Beth's hand in his. Her face remained contemptuous, hostile. Then it changed. Her lips parted, her eyes and forehead seemed to crumple with devastating pain.

For one blinding second, Beth saw it. Heather's pain.

Morgan saw it too; he looked sideways at Beth, worried.

'Beth,' he said. 'She's ill.'

He started forward suddenly, and as he did so, Heather collapsed, one arm folded across her chest.

Morgan barely caught her, let her down onto the carpet. 'I'll call the surgery,' he said.

Beth felt for a pulse, listened for a heartbeat or a sign she was breathing. Nothing. Not even believing she had healed Margaret, she despised herself for being helpless now.

She said quickly, 'Morgan, I think you'd better call an ambulance.'

When they arrived back at Dove Cottage, several hours later, Beth's mood was so black she couldn't speak. Heather had died in the ambulance without regaining consciousness. There was nothing to say.

Randolph, who had arrived while the ambulance was there, had been shocked and distraught, but he'd asked them to leave him alone. So there was nothing to do but come home.

Morgan had tried to comfort Beth but she was beyond being comforted. Rejected, he stopped trying, and now he was quiet too, slowly distancing himself from her. She saw he was capable of cutting himself off and withdrawing. She didn't like it, even if it was her fault. It only made her feel worse.

Morgan dropped Beth at the cottage, but stayed in the car.

'Where are you going?' Beth asked.

'To fetch Eirian from the farmhouse.'

'Oh. Thanks. Then I want to talk to you.'

'Do you?' he said. 'Good.'

While Beth was on her own, she leaned against the sink and didn't even bother to take off her shoes. She couldn't move. She felt that she was standing in a wasteland.

Of all the people this has hurt, she thought, Gran was hurt the worst. Gran, who seemed so strong, as if nothing could touch her; she was the one who must have been dying inside for years. And I – I have to go and rub her face in it! Thinking I could make it better. How could I be so arrogant?

Beth's mind was ice and lead. This was the darkness that had been haunting her. After her grandmother's death, she had no love left. None for Steve, none for Morgan, none even for Eirian.

She sat down and waited for them to come back.

Eirian came in crying. Morgan had told her. Beth hugged her briefly and said, 'Go up to your room, love. I need to talk to Morgan. I'll come and talk to you in a few minutes, okay?'

Eirian did as she was asked without argument.

'She didn't know her great-grandma that well,' said Beth. 'Heather could barely tolerate her, actually.'

Morgan stood looking at her, his hands in the pockets of his leather jacket. 'What did you want to say to me, Beth?' he asked, as if he already knew.

She couldn't look at him any more. She said gently, 'It isn't working. This feeling between us is infatuation, Morgan. It's the novelty of being together after we've been separated all these years! When it wears off in a few weeks' time, you'll be straight back to Marian. You're already restless.'

'No!' Morgan looked stunned.

'You can't even tell your mother! I didn't mean to say this, but you'll never know how I felt when I ran away to you and Rhianwen only to find you'd gone. I was desperate and you deserted me! Have you ever felt betrayed like that? It's like having your guts ripped out. You ignore me for twelve years then you walk in and think you can take over my life – and just

475

share Eirian as if you've always been there! But you haven't! And I don't think I can ever forget or forgive that sense of betrayal. It would poison us.'

'Beth, please, if I'd had any idea what was going to happen I'd have broken your parents' front door down.'

'But you didn't!'

'I can't change the past! At least let me try.'

Morgan was distraught, but Beth felt quite ruthless. 'You're not being realistic!' she said. 'What about your work? You can't give it up, you'd go mad! What the hell would you do around here? And if I break up with Steve, all his friends will go with him. I don't want to lose the people I love. You're asking me to give up my life. I can't come with you and save whales, I don't know the first thing about what you do! We've lived utterly different lives. It can't work, it's a fantasy!'

A change was coming over Morgan's face. A kind of blankness, as if he was so hurt he had to shut it out.

'I wouldn't ask you to give up anything, Beth,' he said. 'You don't trust me! You think I'm playing with you. Have you any idea how bloody insulting that is? I always loved you, and you know it!'

She had to fight very hard then to stay strong, but she'd made up her mind.

'I didn't mean to insult you. But I still think our relationship is borderline incest. It might even be against the law. I don't think I can live with that. Imagine what it will do to Eirian, if people find out! I think Rhianwen did the right thing, keeping us apart, whatever lies she told to do it. I really think she did the right thing. I couldn't forget you because there was unfinished business between us, but now we've seen each other, it's over.'

'Over. So that's it?'

'Think how Marian would feel, if you left her.'

Morgan turned side-on to her, as if he couldn't look at her any more. 'I don't want to hurt her. I didn't want to hurt you. Very noble of you to put Marian before us, when you don't even know her. But what about my feelings, Beth? Don't they count?'

'I know it's hard.' Beth was calm, but there seemed to be too much air in her lungs, making her dizzy. 'But you know I'm right. Don't you?'

'So you don't love me.'

'No, I don't love you. And you don't love me either.'

'You've made up your mind?'

'Yes.'

'Right,' Morgan murmured. And he was gone from her; mentally, if not yet physically. His face was now quite composed. 'Well, I'll be off then. Say 'bye to Eirian for me; I can't. Erm . . .' He hesitated in the doorway a moment, as if trying to find the right way to say goodbye. Beth watched him, wishing he'd go before she broke down.

'No hard feelings?' Beth said faintly.

'Shit, I can't think of anything that isn't a cliché either.' Morgan sighed. 'What's the point?'

And he turned and was gone. Beth listened to his car pulling away, and she didn't break down after all.

Chapter Twenty-five

WHEN Morgan had gone, and Beth was certain that she was in control of herself, she went to call Eirian. But Eirian was already running downstairs. She and Beth collided in the doorway between the sitting-room and kitchen. Eirian stood back and looked at her with grave and accusing eyes.

'Why has my father just driven off?' asked Eirian. She looked accusingly at Beth as if she already knew.

No point in lying; it was impossible to treat Eirian like a child. 'I've sent him away, love.'

'He's not coming back, is he?' Eirian started to cry. Then Beth felt like dying, but she didn't show it.

'No. He's not coming back.'

'Oh, Mum, what have you done?' Her tears stopped with frightening abruptness; her eyes were frigid green jewels. '*What have you done?*'

Beth's intention to explain seemed hopeless in the face of Eirian's bleak anger, but she had no other defence. 'I'm sorry, dear. I had to.' She stroked Eirian's shoulder, but Eirian shook her off.

'Why?'

How to explain this to a child – even to one like Eirian, who was wiser than Beth? 'A lot of reasons. For one thing, we're too closely related. When we had you we – we didn't know it was wrong but it was. His father is my grandfather. That's why our families didn't want us to be together, and maybe they were right.'

'You mean it's incest.'

'Yes,' said Beth, wondering how anything Eirian said could still surprise her.

'So?' Eirian said reasonably. 'The ancient Egyptians used to marry their brothers and sisters. It's a social taboo. And you're not meant to have children in case there's something wrong with them, but I'm all right, aren't I?'

Beth thought, I don't know what you are! She put her head in her hands, not knowing whether to laugh or cry. 'Goddess, where did you come from?'

'I want my dad,' Eirian said flatly, like a five year old. 'You should be together.'

'It's not that easy, love. He lives in another country. He can't just leave. He's married to someone else.'

'So? Why can't we all live together? Steve and Sam, too.'

'You are priceless, Eirian.' Beth began to laugh so hard that it hurt. A kind of hysteria. Tears came to her eyes. 'I'm not laughing at you. I'm just –'

'We could have done, in the past,' Eirian said stubbornly. 'In the Goddess times.'

'But things aren't like that now.'

'They should be!' Eirian cried, with a sudden fierce anguish that pierced Beth's heart. 'They should be! I want my father, Mum! You had no right to do this without asking me! No right!'

She stormed away from Beth and went to stare out of the window, as if by staring she could bring Morgan back. She was so angry Beth could almost see static sparks coming from her; a physical barrier that said, *Don't touch me!*

Beth was desperate, but she was also a little angry.

'You can't always have exactly what you want,' she said.

Eirian said nothing, but her back was eloquent.

In the silence, Beth heard a noise in the kitchen, and jumped nervously.

'Who's that?' she said, walking through to see.

Steve was there, in his patchwork coat, looking sheepish.

'I knocked, but I don't think you heard,' he said.

'You don't have to knock.' Beth sighed.

'Where's Morgan?' Steve said warily, as if Beth kept a dangerous dog in the house. 'I didn't see his car.'

'Gone. It's over between us.'

Steve looked stunned, then pleased, then dismayed. 'Christ, really?' Then very gently, 'Are you okay, Beth?'

She was touched that he thought about her feelings before his own. Steve had always been so kind, so considerate, so sweet to her, but . . .

But she didn't love him.

'I'll live,' she said.

'So what happened? Did he decide to go back to his wife? I had a feeling –'

'No, he didn't. I sent him away before he had the chance. I could see it wasn't going to work.'

Far from being thrilled, Steve looked distressed. 'Hurt him before he hurt you? But are you sure that was the right thing to do?'

'It wasn't just that,' said Beth. 'My gran died today.'

'God, I'm sorry. I didn't know.'

'It's a long story. I'll tell you sometime.'

'You are still speaking to me, then?'

'Of course.'

'Look, I'm sorry I got so worked up,' said Steve. 'I feel a bit stupid about it, now he's gone. I was upset.'

'You had every right. I behaved badly.'

But Beth didn't want to have this conversation; she had no feelings of affection or reconciliation to offer. She wanted solitude. 'How's Sam?' she asked.

'He's doing fine. I wanted to thank Morgan for helping us find him. Oh well, maybe I can phone him at his mother's, or something. D'you want to hear something priceless? Katy asked me to take her back.'

'What?' said Beth.

'She was arrested and released. I don't think they've decided yet whether to charge her with anything, like taking Sam without my permission. But it really shook her up, you know? She phoned me, all pathetic, wanting me to help her.'

'Will you?'

'You must be joking!' Steve said with feeling. 'I don't think I ever completely stopped loving her until I found out what she let Luke do to Sam. After that,' he shook his head. 'I hope she rots in hell. With Luke.'

'I'm glad he's dead,' Beth said suddenly. 'I don't even feel he was my brother now. He's a stranger. Sometimes I imagine – I know I shouldn't but I can't help it – I imagine the children dead and Luke alive, in Broadmoor or somewhere, watching television and doing art therapy and trying to get an early release because he's discovered God.'

'I know,' said Steve. 'I do it too, imagine all sorts of things. But we shouldn't. It's over.'

He came and hugged her, but Beth didn't want affection. She didn't want anything but Eirian's understanding.

'Is there any chance of us starting again?' Steve asked cautiously. 'I don't want us to stop being friends. I still want you, Beth. And Sam needs Eirian.'

Beth pushed him away, very gently. 'I know, but . . . we are friends, Steve, but I'd like you to leave, if you don't mind.'

'Why?'

'I don't want anyone at the moment. I just want to be on my own with Eirian. Just the two of us. I hope you understand.'

'Yeah, sure,' he said, looking sad and mildly bewildered. 'You need some time to think.'

'That's it.'

'Okay. Right, well, you know where we live. Anytime, when you feel . . . I'm sorry about your gran. Really sorry.'

Beth closed the door behind him, and exhaled, the weight of twelve years falling away from her. Outside, she heard Steve's car coughing into life and pulling away.

Beth felt exhausted, sad, and cleansed.

Now we can start again, she thought, just Eirian and me. Maybe we should move away, now Margaret doesn't need me so much, and I can get qualifications and a job. After Gran's funeral. I'll be able to think straight then.

She made some hot chocolate, and took it through with a plate of sandwiches to the sitting-room.

'Steve was here,' said Beth.

'I know, I heard him,' said Eirian, still leaning forlornly on the window-sill. 'You sent him away, too.'

'Are you speaking to me now?'

'Of course I'm speaking to you, Mum.'

'Come and eat, then.'

Eirian turned round, and came into Beth's arms.

'I don't understand adults,' said Eirian, 'why they do these cruel and stupid things.'

Like sending Morgan away, betraying partners, tormenting children, persecuting heretics. Beth knew she meant all those things.

'I don't understand either, love,' Beth said, holding her tight.

'I won't be cruel,' said Eirian, 'but I will be fair.'

'And will you be honest?' said Beth, who still didn't believe she had killed Luke.

'People don't like it if you're too honest,' said Eirian. 'It hurts them. But I will be, anyway.'

Beth thought Eirian was going to make some kind of confession then, but she didn't. She drank her hot chocolate, and was silent. The three cats slept in front of the fire. They had a fire most evenings, even in summer.

'What would you like to do tonight? Just the two of us.'

'Let's play Coppit,' said Eirian. It was a board game, her favourite, with pieces like witches' hats, which chased and captured each other.

Beth smiled to herself. At least Eirian hadn't said, 'Nothing!' and stormed up to her room again. Soon, maybe, Beth could explain about Heather and Randolph and Morgan; when it had stopped hurting.

Because, Beth realized, it had only just begun to hurt.

Sitting side by side on the sofa in front of the fire, with the game on a small table, they threw dice and chased each other round the board. When Eirian played with Sam, they never stopped laughing, but tonight she played with a strange concentration, outwitting Beth at every turn. She is such a strange girl, Beth thought; so passionate and so self-possessed. And I love her to distraction.

I'm sure she'll never let herself fall stupidly in love, like I did.

*

Morgan saw the blue Metro pass his car, slow down and pull up in front. Steve got out and came to the Sierra, so Morgan pressed the button to wind down the window.

'What are you doing, sitting here in the middle of the village?' Steve asked, puzzled.

'Thinking,' Morgan said tiredly. 'Best man won, eh? Congratulations.'

'What are you talking about?'

'Beth's just kicked me out,' said Morgan. 'Didn't she tell you?'

'Yes, she told me,' said Steve. 'But she's kicked me out as well.'

'Oh, God, I'm sorry.'

'She wants to be alone with Eirian, she says.'

Morgan was quiet for a moment. He didn't want to talk to anyone; couldn't go back to Rhianwen. Steve leaned on the side of the car, shaking his head. Eventually Morgan asked, 'Did Beth seem all right?'

'No,' said Steve. 'I don't think so.' He sighed, looking aimlessly up and down the street. 'D'you fancy going for a drink, mate?'

'Yeah,' said Morgan. 'Why not.'

The ache in Beth's chest grew stronger. She tried to ignore it.

It began to rain as darkness drew in, around nine. It rattled on the roof, tapped at the windows and dripped from the leaves. Beth shivered once or twice.

The air was too cold, but the fire felt too hot.

Beth turned round a few times because she thought she saw flames from the corner of her eye, as if they had spread right across the wall. They had not.

She was becoming more and more jumpy, when tonight she should have felt happy with her daughter, the cats, the fire, the silly game. She heard twigs scraping at the windows. First in the kitchen, then the front window in the sitting-room, then across the side wall and round to the back window. But there were no trees that close to the cottage.

It sounded as if something outside were moving around the house.

The ache in Beth's heart became fear. She looked at Eirian, but her daughter was concentrating on taking three of Beth's pieces into captivity.

The cats got up and began to pace around. Eostre's tail bushed out like a squirrel's; Cerridwen uttered a raw-sounding, *mrrow*, making Beth's heart beat faster; Bast's hair stood on end.

Beth had an overwhelming urge to look out of the windows, but she didn't want to transfer her nervousness to Eirian.

'They can't want feeding,' Beth said, meaning the cats.

'Mum, they're scared,' said Eirian. 'Don't pretend.'

Beth looked at the fire again. She began to shiver with the cold and yet the fire seemed to scorch her, making sweat trickle down her back. The flames began to obsess her; the leaping tongues of white and yellow and the searing scarlet heart, the orange sparks and the little blue or green spurts igniting on the logs. Its crackling became terrifying to her. She imagined the flames on her skin, her sweat pouring out, her flesh melting and running down with the sweat, the smoke, fumes and ash making her cough and gag.

'Mum,' said Eirian.

Beth looked at her. Eirian's face was like a shell, lit from below, eerily unhuman. Her eyes were drops of green glass, molten.

'What is it?'

Eirian said softly, 'Mum, they're burning Guendolen.'

'No!' Beth said firmly. 'It isn't happening.'

'But it is. That's what we can feel. Don't tell me you don't feel it; I can see it in your face!'

Beth gripped Eirian's hand. 'Now listen to me. It happened hundreds of years in the past; we can't stop it.'

'It's my fault.' Eirian's voice was low but intense. 'Guen gave her strength to help me, that's why they caught her.'

'You don't know that! Love, we have to be strong until it's

over. We'll go on playing the game. Your turn. You're winning, come on.'

'I can go back there and help her,' said Eirian. 'If I close my eyes.'

'Don't close your eyes!' Beth snapped. 'Stay here!'

'I must help her!'

'No! If you go now, they'll try to burn you, too.' Beth knew, because she could see the images moving faintly across the real world; the young woman trussed up in the centre of a bonfire, the crowd around it, the clergymen in their drab charcoal cassocks with their hard faces in a row like the secret police. Loving to watch the suffering of heretics. She saw Judge Warbeck with his heartless eyes in his long-boned, arrogant, soulless face.

They had nearly drowned Eirian once. That had been real. The Horn and her torn hands had been real. Beth knew that if she let Eirian go this time, she would lose her. Knew it.

'I must! You don't care about Guen!' Eirian cried.

'I do, but I care about you more. I'm your mother, you have to do what I say and I'm telling you to stay here!' Beth spoke so fiercely that her daughter shrank back a little. But Eirian's gaze was unblinking. 'Shake the dice,' said Beth. 'It's your go.'

Eirian obeyed, stiff and unspeaking. Beth felt the flames leaping up around her. She couldn't breathe. Her hands were shaking so hard she could barely move her pieces around the board.

'I can't, Mum. I've got to.'

'Go on playing,' said Beth. 'Hold my hand. Don't think about it.'

Eirian's eyelids began to flicker and fall.

'No!' Beth cried, shaking her. 'Stay with me!'

The candles flickered and windows rattled in turn, all around the house. Then there was a knock at the front door, sharp and hard, making them both jump violently. Beth shot to her feet and the board-game went flying.

Eirian's eyes opened wide and she said, 'Don't answer it, Mum.'

Beth's heart was pounding thickly. 'But it might be, it might be Gordon.' And if there's someone else here, anyone, it will help keep Eirian with me.

'Come to the door,' said Beth, holding her hand firmly. 'I'm not leaving you alone.'

The fire receded and the room felt cold and black as she walked to the front door.

Eirian said faintly, 'Mum.'

Beth opened the door. Rain blew in from the blackness. And the man who stood on her doorstep was Luke.

He was the same. The dark suit, the gloves, the brushed-back hair framing the serenely knowing face.

But she had seen him, dead.

Ludicrous and terrible possibilities ran through her mind. I made a mistake, the police made a mistake, oh Goddess, what the hell does it matter? He's here, what does he want?

Clutching Eirian, she tried to push the door shut but he put his right hand up and stopped her. He wasn't a ghost. He was real and solid.

'You know why I'm here,' he said. He pointed at Eirian. 'I've come for her.'

Beth put her foot against the door, but he barged in. There was a smell on him of icy air, of entrails, and a sourness like stagnant water. He was the same yet he was different; something odd in the way he moved, as if he were overweight and stiff. Then he raised his left hand and she saw that it was sheathed not in an ordinary glove but in a thick, cruelly-spiked gauntlet.

She couldn't get her breath for terror, but she pushed Eirian behind her and said, 'Go upstairs. Shout out of the window, Gordon might hear.'

Beth hadn't expected Eirian to obey, but she did. She was gone, her feet thudding lightly on the treads.

'It won't help,' said Luke. 'She stole something from me.'

'Your life?' said Beth. Unconsciously she gripped the pentagram round her neck and called on the Goddess with all her mental strength. 'Your faith?'

Luke laughed.

He turned towards the stairs as if to follow Eirian. Beth seized his arm to stop him. It horrified her to touch him, but it was all she could do. He felt strong and physical.

He stopped, turning his attention to her.

'There is a hell, Beth,' he said. 'I want you to see it.'

He flexed the gauntlet; the spikes glinted like a spiteful little forest of brass nails. With his right hand he reached in his pocket and took out a scalpel with a narrow, vicious-looking blade. It looked worse than any dagger. It looked mean, crude and painful.

Beth's mouth was sour with fear. The cats were on the back of a chair, hissing, welded together like a freak with twelve legs and three heads.

'Put it down, Luke.' She tried to hold her ground but he came closer. 'How have I hurt you?'

'By existing. Women – women are all of the Devil. You opened your legs for the Devil and that's where the demon-child came from.'

'You're frightened of us,' said Beth, drawing him into the room. She felt his power, like the creaking authority of the church down the ages. Intolerably heavy, impossible to resist. She tried to call up her own power; she tried to create a mental mirror to throw his power back at him.

'What are you scared of?' she said provokingly. 'We're only women. God is on your side. Daren't you argue with your own sister without a knife in your hand?'

He swung the scalpel at her. She didn't realize it had caught her across the shoulder until she felt the itching pain and the blood trickling down. She froze with shock and sickly terror. Then he flung the knife at the cats; it stuck in the chair-back and they scattered, yowling.

'No. God is my weapon.'

'Come on, then. What would you like to do to me? Tell me how I should be punished and how I can be saved.'

Beth withdrew, taunting him, and he followed. To keep him away from Eirian, that was all that mattered.

'I want to repent,' she said. 'God will forgive anything, won't he? Even raping little boys. So I'll see you in heaven.'

She wove her power but she couldn't aim it. It made nets in the air like dark lace, nothing she could catch and throw at him.

'Abomination!' he said. 'Your soul is damned!'

His spiked hand shot out and gripped her throat. Pin-pricks of bruising pain choked her. Beth kneed him hard in the groin but he didn't even wince. He was a ghost of granite. She gripped his arm with both hands and couldn't shift him; she groped behind her and found a glass vase on the mantelpiece but it broke like sugar on his head, cutting her hands.

Her throat was being crushed. She felt heat on her legs. Her sight filled with red, yellow and white flames.

The fire rushed up all around her.

'It's the only way your soul can be saved,' said Luke. 'In the fire.'

'I curse you.' Beth couldn't speak, but she thought it and mouthed it through her pain. Her hands came up and gripped his head. With all her will she pushed images of his own fears into him: of sex and mothers and witches, of goddesses and death-hags. But she slipped and lost herself and fell into him; into all the horrors of his poisoned mind. Dying animals, sobbing children, a thousand small torments and mutilations, the Midwife's death and Guendolen's rape, all the loathing of life that had made him crave a sterile, transcendent God.

Through the roar of flames, Beth heard Eirian's feet on the stairs.

The front door's open, thought Beth. Run, run while I hold him here. And she held on to Luke through her agony as if he were her lover.

Eirian ran upstairs to Beth's room, but she didn't shout for Gordon. She flipped back the rug, then searched for the screwdriver in the top drawer of the bedside table. It wasn't there, why wasn't it there?

She looked round, frantic, then saw it. It was on top of the table instead, half hidden by a paperback. Eirian seized it and struggled to loosen the screws. Everything conspired against her. The screwdriver slipped in her hands, the screws wouldn't turn. An archetypal nightmare of struggling in slow motion against danger. But Eirian had never had nightmares. She couldn't dream anything worse than the things she had seen in real life.

The screws came out, but the floorboard stuck. Luke hadn't come after her so he must still be with Beth. And Beth was brave but she didn't *understand*.

Eirian stuck the shaft of the screwdriver under the board and levered it up. A nest of spiders scurried away. She lifted out the long parcel and ran towards the door, struggling with the knots of string and the layers of polythene and cloth.

The wrapping came free as she reached the bottom of the stairs. The Horn looked dull, ancient and lifeless. She gripped the shaft and reached into herself for strength. Not to Guen this time, Guen couldn't help her any more. She only had herself now.

Eirian saw Luke with his armoured hand on her mother's throat, Beth holding his head as if she were healing him. Firelight shone around them. Its glow bounced brightly off the gold spirals on the Horn.

'Is this what you were looking for?' said Eirian.

Luke threw Beth down. She fell back along the hearth, her shoulders up against the blazing fire. He turned towards Eirian and smiled.

'You stole that,' he said. 'We want it back. Our symbol of purity. The unicorn's horn represents God's mystic impregnation of Mary, though you wouldn't know that, pagan. It signifies the One Truth of the Gospel.'

'Tell the Goddess,' said Eirian. 'She likes a good laugh. Impregnation without sex; only a man could think of a deformed idea like that.'

'You will have your reward in hell,' Luke said calmly. 'Give it to me.'

'If I do, will you leave us alone?'

'God will be your judge.'

'Come and take it, if you can.'

Eirian moved slowly forward, with the point of the Horn towards his heart. Luke came to meet her, grinning now. He grasped the end of the Horn.

And Eirian unleashed her power, thrusting it with all her will down the shaft. The Horn lit up like fire through diamonds: a column of milk-white light, gathering all Eirian's power and all the nets of power Beth had left floating, channelling them along its length to slam into Luke's mind.

Eirian saw everything. And knew for certain that this wasn't only Luke, it was also a creature that had pursued her across centuries in the body of a fly to take back what she'd stolen. The witch-finder in Luke's shape. He'd stolen Luke's form because he had no form of his own; now he was both Luke and Lacost and all the men who had ever inflamed hatred against women, nature and freedom of thought.

Eirian saw endless ranks of women and men, children and animals, their bones crushed in intruments of torture, their skin flayed off, cheeks and tongues pierced by the scold's bridle, the turgid pond water pouring into their lungs, the noose and the flail and the flames blistering their skin.

And she turned it back at Luke–Lacost and she made him feel every second of every torment.

He began to scream. There weren't enough screams in eternity to express his agony.

Then she touched the Horn to his forehead and drew it down the length of his torso, bisecting him with a long red seam. The entity divided like some grotesque amoeba; one ragged half was the Inquisitor, the other Luke – no longer pristine in his suit but as Eirian had last seen him, with his guts spilling out in glistening, membranous ropes. The two spectres turned on each other, still screaming, destroying each other with the force of their hatred.

Eirian seemed to be falling through the bloody chasm she'd cut between them.

She saw a bonfire on a hillside, spiralling closer. There were

490

crowds of the prurient and the cowardly around it, shouting for the witch's death. She saw the close-knit, all-powerful group of men in cassocks, their callous eyes narrowed with excitement. Inquisitor Lacost wasn't there; he was dead, battling in another dimension. But Judge Warbeck was at the very front, the tiniest smile crimping his withered lips as he watched the flames leaping around Guendolen's skirt.

Eirian pointed the Horn.

Blue-black clouds congealed. A wind rose. A great gust blew hard at the bonfire; it quelled the flames around Guendolen but swept fire and kindling straight into the group of church men.

The fire caught on Warbeck's cassock as if he'd been doused in petrol. His eyes opened wide. He began to shriek and beat at his own limbs, while everyone turned to stare at him. 'Witchcraft!' they cried.

Flames burst out of Warbeck's body. He fell to the ground, burning, his skin erupting in great crimson blisters as the flames licked over him.

The other witch-haters, too, were burning.

While Guendolen, in the middle of the fire, was untouched. A cool rain began to fall, only for her; the Goddess's libation.

Eirian saw her shake off the ropes and walk out of the pyre. Guen's face was black with smoke but her eyes were silver spoked with gold. The crowd fell away in terror as she came. She walked away into the forest and no one dared to touch her as she went.

One moment there was furnace-heat and choking fumes; the next, the reprieve of wind and rain. Beth-as-Guendolen felt a wonderful coolness enveloping her suddenly and she understood. *Eirian gave back to me the life I gave to her.*

Guen stepped down and walked away. Her tears ran down through the soot. They dared not touch her and they never would again.

Judge Warbeck went on writhing in fire as she walked away.

She felt for him neither pity nor hatred. Only the Goddess's dispassionate justice.

The scene dissolved.

She was Beth again. She was prostrate on the hearth, staring at two spectral figures locked in combat: her brother and the Inquisitor. One had been impeccable, one grotesque, unwashed and vermin-ridden. And yet they were the same. The whole room thrummed with their anguish and their sick loathing of all that was living, earthy, sexual and female. But now they turned their loathing inwards, where it belonged.

Eirian made a tiny thrust with the Horn. Light spiralled along it and yellow flames ran all over their bodies.

'You love giving pain so much,' Eirian whispered. 'Give it to each other.'

She stepped back. In a ripple of ghost-light, Beth saw Lacost and Luke struggling; two rapists locked in grisly conflict. As the fire consumed their clothing, Beth saw a spiked phallus protruding obscenely from the Inquisitor's fat groin. It was bigger and more vicious than she remembered. Pinioning Luke's arms, Lacost manoeuvred behind him and buried it to the hilt between Luke's buttocks.

His hideous screams rang in Beth's ears.

'Make it stop,' she said, but Eirian seemed not to hear. Beth's own power, which she'd wielded with such effortless confidence against Jacob, had deserted her now. She felt helplessly human. 'Eirian, make it stop!' she said again, but it went on.

Somehow the scalpel was in Luke's hand again. He forced it between his buttocks and Lacost's groin, severing Lacost's tiny member but leaving the phallus wedged inside his own body. Their bodies came apart and blood spurted from the stump. But somehow Lacost had Luke's spiked glove on his own hand and he swiped it down Luke's face, leaving gaping red slits.

Screaming their throats to rags, they wrestled manically while the flames began to blister their flesh. Eirian stood aside, leaning on the Horn, a cold-eyed witness.

Beth stared, petrified, thinking, this is never going to end; I am going to wake up, please Goddess let me wake up – or give me the strength to stop this horror.

And then there came the sound of someone pounding at the front door.

Another ghost, another walking nightmare to plague them. Beth couldn't bear any more. Her fear thickened to rage.

Beth saw the scalpel lying on the rug. She crawled forward and seized it. And then she crouched, breathing hard, clutching the weapon and waiting as the intruder opened the door and walked softly into her domain.

Chapter Twenty-six

'WHY didn't you argue with her?' Steve asked. The Swan was busy, hot and full of smoke. They sat on a red plush bench at a corner table.

'I tried. I couldn't,' said Morgan. He sat with his arms folded and legs stretched out, staring into a half-empty glass of bitter. 'There was nothing I could say to what she was telling me. She'd made up her mind.'

'So you just walked out?'

'That's what she wanted.'

'Like hell,' said Steve. 'D'you always do that? Just walk away, when someone tells you to?'

'What else? It's so undignified, arguing with someone who's already made a decision.' But Morgan thought, that's what I did with Rhianwen, just gave in to what she wanted, and I lost Beth and missed Eirian growing up.

'And that works for you, does it? Just wash your hands of it and forget it. I suppose you'll go back to your wife like nothing happened.'

'I suppose so,' Morgan said. 'I can't stay around here.'

'Christ, what is the matter with you?' Steve put his head in his hands.

'I don't know what you're getting so worked up about, Steve. I thought you wanted me out of the way, so you can have Beth back.'

'I want what Beth wants,' Steve said. He drained his glass. 'I just want Beth to be happy. For heaven's sake, she's in love with you, she worships you, can't you see that? God knows why. You know why she threw you out, don't you?'

'She doesn't trust me. She thinks I won't stay anyway,' Morgan said flatly. 'How the hell can I prove her wrong, if she won't let me?'

'Morgan, she threw you out because she was upset about her grandmother. Beth seems to think she's got to be a martyr, that she doesn't deserve to be happy because she never has been. Don't let her get away with it. Don't go straight back to Canada. Stay around for a few days. Go and see her again. Okay, if she throws you out again, maybe she means it, but at least give it a try.'

'Doesn't it bother you, the way Beth and I are related? It seems to bother Beth now.'

'Yeah, well, that's your problem,' Steve said bluntly. 'Think about it, while I get some more drinks in.'

'Just a Coke for me,' said Morgan. 'I don't want to lose my licence.'

'You don't have to drive. You can kip on my floor. My house is only five minutes' walk away. My mum and dad are there, but they won't mind.'

'No, it's all right. I can't think straight if I'm pissed.'

'I thought that was the whole point,' said Steve as he stood up.

Beth was so determined, Morgan thought. It was like she couldn't stand me near her any more because I'm always going to remind her of the past. Maybe I haven't got the courage to face her again.

'I know what Beth sees in you,' Morgan said as Steve came back from the bar and sat down. 'You're totally unselfish. I'm not.'

'Katy had another word for it,' Steve said self-mockingly. 'Doormat.'

Morgan confessed, 'If this was the other way round, I wouldn't be so willing to give up Beth for you, even if you are better for her.'

'I won't be giving her up, that's the point,' said Steve. 'There are more important things than sex. I mean, sex with Beth was wonderful, it was the best sex I've ever had, she was incredible –'

'Okay, you've made your point.'

'But I can live without it. It means more to me not to lose

495

her friendship. And Sam needs Eirian, to help him get over that crap with Luke. Beth's someone special; she could have anyone she wants. But do you want *her*?'

'I've never wanted anyone else,' Morgan said quietly.

'Then listen to me, for Christ's sake.'

They stayed in the pub until closing time; by then Steve was less than coherent and unable to walk straight. It had begun to rain. Morgan, coldly sober, drove him home to his small, terraced cottage on the main street.

'Sure you won't stay? Go and see Beth in the morning.'

'No, it's all right.'

'Going to stay with your mother?'

'I expect so. 'Night, Steve. And thanks.'

Morgan walked back to his car through the rain. In fact he had no intention of going home to Rhianwen. He meant to sleep in his car, if he could sleep at all.

As he put his key in the lock, Morgan felt a wave of intense fear pass over him. Exactly like the visions. The night was a block of indigo glass, shot through with silver rain, and through this medium he saw a dark figure coming towards him, rippling.

The illusion passed, but Morgan knew. It couldn't wait until morning. Eirian was calling him again. He had to go to Beth now.

The feeling of cold dread persisted as he drove out of the village to the farm, down the rough track towards the cottage. The farmhouse was an oasis of light, but the lane led past it into darkness.

There was firelight flickering in the window as Morgan drew up and leapt out of the car. His terror was so strong he almost wept, certain that something terrible had happened, that he was going to find Beth and Eirian dead; and he was thinking wildly, if only I'd stayed with them!

He pounded on the door, then tried the handle. The door swung open. He strode into the sitting-room and the world overturned into chaos.

Outlined by a watery glow of fire, a black-haired fury came rushing at him, hoarsely screaming, '*No! No more!*'

It was Beth, her face contorted like the death goddess Kali. She raised her hand and a tiny, deathly blade glinted in the light.

'Beth!' Morgan cried. 'Don't, it's me!'

But she came on, sweeping the blade down as if hurling a javelin towards his heart.

Morgan twisted away, caught Beth's wrist and turned the scalpel aside, more by panic and luck than anything. She went on struggling to wound him, her face wild. Her strength was incredible.

'It's me,' Morgan said desperately. Maybe she knew perfectly well it was him and meant to stab him. 'Beth, stop it!'

The blade clattered to the floor. Her expression changed to dismay, horror. Then she collapsed against him, shuddering. Morgan held her, feeling her body warm against his and her black hair spilling over his hands. And over her shoulder he saw a hideous scene of fire and blood, incredible but real.

He stared at two figures tearing at each other in ripples of flame. Their clothes were ash, their flesh bubbling red raw under a black crust, their fat boiling and blue veins popping. Yet they lived, and the aura of their twisted, life-loathing soul flowed out to Morgan like the stench of a crematorium.

And Eirian, silhouetted against the hellish light, simply watched, leaning like a shepherdess on the Horn. Morgan thought he heard her speak, then realized the words were only in his head.

'I won't be cruel,' she said, 'but I will be fair.'

But the Crone's justice was terrible to witness.

'Eirian,' Morgan said firmly, 'it's enough. Make it stop now.'

Eirian neither argued nor ignored him. She raised the Horn. Beth turned in Morgan's arms to watch.

Eirian thrust the Horn between the two figures; they broke apart as if from a jolt of electricity and collapsed, still screaming and writhing, to the floor. Then she drew the tip of the Horn, like a scalpel, along the Inquisitor's blistered torso.

His fingers, clutching at the Horn, were naked bones.

A slit appeared down the length of his body. Skeletal hands

came out of it. Thousands of hands, clawing at him from inside, pulling, dragging him down into their own hell to share their anguish. The fire stripped the Inquisitor's body to a skeleton; his ribs became a cage of blackened twigs against baleful embers; and the hands came fingering up through the embers to crumble the cage to ash. His bones sank to ash, to dust, to nothing; drawn down through the floor by the spidery fingertips, gone.

Eirian watched without expression. She wasn't happy, she wasn't sorry.

Now Morgan believed she was capable of killing.

Then Eirian loomed over the writhing, bloody mass that had been Luke. She pointed the Horn, only to put it aside and to kneel down by Luke's head. His eyes, in the suppurating flesh of his face, still showed a lingering, raw intelligence.

'No, you enjoy pain,' Eirian said aloud. 'But the one thing you despise, the one thing that will shrivel your mean soul to nothing with horror, is the love of the Goddess.'

Eirian leaned over Luke and kissed him full on the mouth.

A death rattle came from his throat. The entity that had been Luke desiccated, vaporized, fell away. There was nothing to show he had ever been there. Not even a mark of melted fat on the rug.

Morgan held hard on to Beth. Their breath suspended, they both stared as Eirian stood up, holding the Horn like a staff of office. The cats, self-contained again, came to sit in a triangle around her. She smiled, but it was the smile of a deity, not a child.

'Now it's over,' said Eirian. 'I only gave them what they deserved.'

'We know,' said Morgan.

'So don't look at me with horror, wondering what I am. You know what I am. You are my parents, you created me.'

Beth, with her arms wrapped round Morgan's slender, firm body, was so glad he was there she could have wept. There was no sign of the scalpel anywhere, but the shallow, itching cut in her shoulder and the bruised soreness of her throat were real enough.

'I'm sorry I went for you,' she said. 'The last time someone knocked, Luke was standing there. I thought you were – I don't know.'

'It doesn't matter. It's forgotten.' Morgan said gently. 'Are you okay?'

'Yes,' said Beth. And she meant it. Feeling strong again, she knew she wasn't going to fall apart. She held out her hand to Eirian, and her daughter came obediently to her. 'Shall we put the Horn away? I think it's served us well.'

Eirian nodded. She was no longer a Goddess, just a child, to Beth's relief.

'Come on,' said Morgan. 'Get some things together. I'm taking you back to Mum's.'

'We're perfectly all right,' said Beth.

'Maybe, but I still don't think you should stay here tonight. Will you please stop arguing with me? We have to talk, Beth, but we can do it tomorrow. I'm not putting you under any pressure. Just let yourself be looked after for once, okay?'

Beth gave in. Morgan was right; it was a relief to take Eirian away from the cottage and go to Rhianwen's where there would be company and light. If they'd stayed at home, they would never have slept for the haunting of images and bad memories.

When they arrived at Blackthorn Cottage, Rhianwen had already gone to bed.

'I won't disturb her,' said Morgan. 'We can explain in the morning.'

'Are you sure she won't mind us staying?' Beth asked.

'Tough if she does.'

Morgan showed Beth and Eirian to a guest room with two single beds. It was a lovely room, with a sloping ceiling, fresh creamy walls, dried flowers and Rhianwen's sure touch for creating a welcoming atmosphere.

'You know where the bathroom is, don't you?' he said.

'I remember.'

499

'Well, good night.' Morgan stood smiling at her, stroking her face and her hair. Beth tried not to let his seductive eyes, his delicious touch and his beauty dissolve her judgement, but it happened anyway. All the reasons for which she'd asked him to leave still stood, but logic had no defence against love.

'Good night,' said Beth, and watched him walk along the carpeted landing to his own room.

She recalled the time they'd made love on his bed, sensing a presence in the room with them. She realized now that she had already been pregnant then; the presence had been Eirian.

Later, as Beth and Eirian lay in their beds in darkness, Eirian said, 'Mum?'

'Yes, darling?'

'It's finished now. Guendolen's safe. I don't have to go back there any more. You know that, don't you? Even though there's so much you don't understand.'

'What don't I understand?'

'Your power,' said Eirian. 'You have it, but you daren't use it, because you think you killed Bernard with it. But you didn't. It was me. I cursed him because he was upsetting you.'

Beth exhaled, stunned but not wholly surprised. 'Christ, Eirian.'

'And who do you think healed Margaret? I did it. Through you. You do have power, Mum, but not as much as me and you don't know how to use it! I don't know why you couldn't see it! That's why I was angry with you, before Luke took us away.'

'I'm sorry, love, but I'm not a mind-reader and I'm not infallible,' said Beth, dismayed. 'But why use your power through me?'

A pause. Then Eirian said softly, 'Because I was scared of it, too. You were like a shield. I can heal people and I can kill them. It's frightening. You don't think I'm human, but I am.'

'Oh, Goddess,' Beth breathed.

'Yes,' said Eirian. 'She has chosen to work through me. I don't know why, but I can't stop it.'

A few hours later, when Eirian was asleep and Beth still

lying awake, she heard the bedroom door opening softly. Morgan's voice whispered, 'Beth, are you awake?'

'Yes,' she said, turning over. 'What is it?'

He came to her and knelt by her bed. 'Nothing. I couldn't sleep. I missed you.'

'Get in,' she said, lifting the covers.

'I only want to hold you,' he whispered. He slid down beside her in the narrow bed, keeping his cotton dressing-gown on. 'I'm not going to misbehave.'

'Oh, damn,' Beth breathed, smiling. Morgan, though, was true to his word. With his arms around her she fell asleep quickly, feeling warm and safe. Supremely happy, if she dared to admit it.

But in the depths of the night, as Morgan lay behind Beth with his arm over her waist, she became aware of the domed head of his penis resting, deliciously warm and heavy, between the tops of her thighs. Still half-asleep she moved backwards against him so he glided between her thighs, between her soft lips. Her juices flowed. The shaft slid fluidly inside her; his hand came over her hips to clasp the outer, downy folds around her clitoris. Beth rested her own hand on his, to keep him there. Barely moving and in total silence they came, falling together along a line of searing, silver electricity. It was like a dream, secret and almost unbearably erotic. Neither of them said a word. Beth didn't even open her eyes. They fell asleep again, still coupled, as if it had happened beyond their conscious wills.

Eventually Beth became aware of daylight glowing behind the curtains, Morgan kissing her cheek and leaving the bed.

When Beth woke up properly, a few minutes later, she felt different. Her depression had lifted. She could smell fresh coffee from downstairs. Eirian was still sound asleep; Goddess knew, she needed it. Trying not to wake her, Beth put on the dark blue towelling robe she'd brought with her, visited the bathroom, and went downstairs. How weird it felt to wake up in Rhianwen's house, the first time ever after all these years.

It was sunny and the world felt real again; solid and

501

wholesome, full of leaves and blossom and birds chirping. We survived, she thought. The evil's gone. Or at least, the part of it that touched us has gone.

She thought of Guendolen, walking away from the fire while her persecutors died in the agony they'd meant for her. We saved one life out of millions, Beth thought. Just one.

She entered the large, old-fashioned pine kitchen to find Morgan, in his black cotton robe, standing over the coffee maker. Beth stopped dead in the doorway, staring at Morgan, his beautiful lean body in black, his slender arms, untidy hair, the seductive green eyes looking sideways at her. She couldn't move. She seemed to have melted into the door-frame.

'Where's Rhianwen?' she asked.

'Still in bed. It's only seven. I was going to bring you a coffee.'

'Why did you come back last night?'

He looked wary, as if he were unsure of her reaction. 'I couldn't just leave it like that,' he said. 'I know what you said, but . . . Well, I met Steve and he convinced me I should come back and talk to you again. I would have left it until this morning but I had such an intense feeling there was something wrong last night.'

'You can say that again.' Beth peeled herself off the door-frame and sat down at the scrubbed pine table. The two elderly cats, Llew and Ankaret, were lying in a pool of sunlight.

Carrying two mugs and a milk jug, Morgan sat beside her. 'It's very hard to leave you when something keeps pulling me back.' His smile, as usual, demolished her. As they drank their coffee, Morgan told her what Steve had said in the pub. Beth listened, shaking her head in bewilderment.

'Steve thinks I'm an idiot,' said Morgan.

'We're both idiots,' said Beth. Very soon she was either going to laugh or cry.

Morgan took Beth's hand. His arm went round her shoulders and her hand on his thigh; their heads rested together. It was like the blissful relief of pain, to be touching each other.

'If you send me away a second time,' he said, 'I'll know you mean it.'

'I only had the strength to do it once. I meant it when I said it, but that was yesterday. All I could think about was Gran, and what she must have felt every time she saw you. A reminder that Granddad had been unfaithful, maybe that he loved Rhianwen more than her. She pretended it didn't matter, while all the time she was in agony. Furious, at least. But us being miserable won't give Gran back her life, will it?'

'No,' said Morgan. 'And I don't know what I can say to prove I'm not a heartless bastard. Nothing I can say, is there? I can only prove it, Beth, if you'll let me.'

'You're still going to look like one to Marian, though,'

He cared; he looked troubled. 'I know. She's going to go crazy, but she's not the kind of person who falls apart.'

'Not like me,' said Beth.

'I didn't say that. You're strong, Bethie.'

'Not as strong as Eirian,' she said. 'Maybe I needed to believe you were a bastard so it wasn't so hard to lose you. If I let you back in now, I'm laying myself open to having my heart broken again.'

'But so am I, Beth! I'm willing to take the risk. I always knew, from the very first time I met you, that we should be together. Didn't you? I hated your parents for making things impossible. I don't know how I got through the year, not seeing you. I shut it off, I suppose. But I couldn't wait for the summer holidays.'

'Didn't you ever worry I might not turn up?'

'Never,' he said. 'I couldn't imagine you not being there. We had such a good time, didn't we? Honestly, I didn't mean to seduce you when you were fourteen. Like I told Steve, I'm selfish. But I thought, if we could just get through two more years until you were sixteen, we'd be together and no one could stop us.'

'You took a lot for granted, didn't you?'

'But you were the one who had no faith! My mother told you I was a womanizer so you just believed it!'

'And she told you I didn't want to see you,' said Beth, 'and you believed it.'

'Sorry,' he said into her hair. 'Sorry, sorry. Don't cry.'

'It's all the time we've lost that we can never get back.' Beth wiped the tears away, but more came. 'You not being there when Eirian was born. All the letters you would have sent me if I hadn't had to say, "Don't write". Letters I could have re-read when I felt unhappy. Instead I had nothing; I don't even know what your handwriting looks like! We can never get those times back.'

Morgan fetched a pen and notepad from a Welsh dresser. 'Mum writes love notes to the milkman on this,' he said. He tore off a page and wrote, Dearest Beth, I love you, one extra pint please, I suppose sex is out of the question?

'I can't read that,' said Beth. 'Are you sure you're not a doctor?'

Laughing, he wrote, I love you, emphatically, several times over. Beth would take that scrap of paper later and keep it somewhere safe.

'I'll write you all the letters you want,' he said. 'Look, we're in our twenties, not our seventies. If we'd only just met, we'd have nothing in the past but everything to look forward to. But think of what we've had; three summers together, and a gorgeous child; that isn't nothing, is it?'

'Talking of which,' Beth said, straight-faced, 'you owe me eleven years' maintenance for Eirian.'

She said it to see how he'd react. To see if romance could survive the stone hand of reality.

Morgan paused, turning rather pale. 'Oh, fuck,' he said. Then: 'I owe you a lot more than that, Beth. I'm not that well off, but I'm doing okay. I don't want to take over your life but I want to look after you both. You've never been abroad, have you?'

Beth gave a hollow laugh.

'There are so many places I'd love to take you and Eirian. A holiday in America, she'd love that.'

'Holiday?' said Beth. 'What's one of those?'

He smiled, but his eyes were serious. 'Look, I'll have to go back to Canada to tell Marian. I can't do it over the phone, it wouldn't be fair. And there are things to sort out at work.'

'But you can't just resign, can you?' Beth said anxiously. 'I mean, it's a vocation, not a job, isn't it?'

'It can be a very depressing job, Bethie, watching species of whales becoming extinct. And I get seasick. It'll take time but I'll sort something out. Maybe Birmingham University would have me.'

'We don't have to stay around here,' said Beth.

'But Eirian needs to be settled until she finishes school.'

Beth was touched that he'd thought of that, but she still wasn't convinced. 'I'm afraid if you see Marian again, you won't come back.'

'Come with me, if you don't believe me.'

'No. I must be able to trust you.'

'I will come back, Beth, I promise. Then can we please get to know each other, at long last?'

His mouth met hers, exquisitely warm, his tongue igniting mercuric responses all through her body. When it ended, Morgan rested his cheek against hers.

'Are you going to be all right with this?' he said softly.

'What, you going to Canada?'

'No, I meant with knowing who my father is. You said you felt it was wrong.'

'So what if it is?' Beth said defiantly. 'I don't care. I was trying to be unselfish. I was thinking of your wife, your mother, my grandmother, Steve, what people would think – everything except you, me and Eirian. Well, I've had enough of being noble. And if anyone tries to split us up and tell us what we're doing is wrong – they can mind their own business and go to hell. I'm going to be selfish now.'

Rhianwen came down into the kitchen at seven-thirty, yawning, and saw them; Morgan and Beth, sitting close together at the kitchen table. They were facing towards her but they were too wrapped up in each other to notice her. Their heads were together, dark hair mingling as they kissed and caressed with all the bewitched intimacy of lovers. Rhianwen stopped in her tracks, dismayed, quietly enraged and a touch embarrassed.

'Oh, great,' Rhianwen said, tight-lipped. 'I knew the moment you two set eyes on each other again, this would happen.'

She went to pour herself a coffee; when she turned round, they were still entwined and looking at her with coolly defiant eyes.

'Why shouldn't it happen?' said Morgan, a strange edge of sarcasm in his voice. 'We're not children any more. Is there some other reason I shouldn't be with Beth? What could it be, Mum? It can't be much, since you've never said. Well, I'm sorry if you don't like it, but there's nothing you can do about it.'

'What about your wife?' Rhianwen cried, her voice rising. It was helplessness that made her angry; the failure of all her efforts to keep them apart. 'Goddess, do you ever stop and think?'

'I've been thinking a lot,' Morgan said thinly. 'Don't talk to me about Marian when all she's ever been to you is a device to keep me away from Beth! I've made a choice I should have made when I was sixteen. What are you going to do about it, have us prosecuted for incest?'

Rhianwen went hot and cold. She felt as if he'd struck her. How the hell had he found out? Beth was beginning to look embarrassed.

'Who told you?'

'Beth's father. Her grandmother confirmed it, just before she died. I suppose you know Mrs Cross died yesterday?'

'Yes,' said Rhianwen. 'Someone told me last night. I'm terribly sorry, Beth.'

'Thanks,' Beth said faintly.

'Is it true, about you and Dr Cross?' Morgan persisted.

'Why ask me? Sounds like you know everything.'

'Mother!' Standing up, Morgan came towards Rhianwen and, for one terrible moment, she thought he was going to hit

506

her. Instead he put his arms round her in a tight embrace, as if to squeeze the truth out of her. She resisted, but after a moment she let her hands relax on to his back. 'Just tell us the bloody truth, will you?' he said, his voice muffled. 'What does it matter? We need to know.'

Rhianwen closed her eyes. She breathed in and out and knew she was defeated. At last she said, 'All right. I suppose now Heather's gone there's no need to keep it secret any longer. Oh, Goddess.' Rhianwen extricated herself, trying to tidy her hair. 'Where's Eirian?'

'Upstairs, asleep,' said Beth.

'Okay. Let's get some more coffee and sit in the other room. Come on, Beth, I'm not going to bite you.'

Beth curled up on the sofa next to Morgan, Rhianwen on a floor cushion. Early sunlight made the room sweetly fresh and bright; Rhianwen had made a special effort to tidy up and place fresh flowers everywhere, after she'd heard the news about Heather last night.

Now Rhianwen had made up her mind to tell them, she felt calmer.

'Nobody's going to prosecute you,' she said. 'I checked the law after Beth's family threatened us with God knows what. It's only illegal with your parent, grandparent, child or sibling. Not between uncle and niece. You can't get married, but it's not actually illegal.'

'You still think it's wrong, though, don't you?' said Morgan.

'Well, don't you?' Rhianwen exclaimed. 'Think how it looks from Randolph's point of view, his son seducing his grand-daughter! Of course it's wrong.'

'But we didn't know!'

'I thought I made it clear enough, the number of times I told you to behave yourself.'

'I thought that was because Beth was so young. If you'd told us the real reason —'

'What difference would it have made?' Rhianwen folded her arms, unable to stay as calm as she wished. 'The fact that Beth was too young didn't stop you, why should anything else? I should have kept you apart from the beginning. I didn't want to behave like Beth's mother, that's all.'

'But that's all beside the point,' Morgan said, agitated. 'What I'm asking is why the hell you wouldn't tell me who my father was? Why, Mum, why couldn't you tell me?'

'I'm sorry,' Rhianwen said quietly. 'I know it wasn't fair. It's really hard to know the right or wrong thing to do in that situation. You think you're doing the right thing but twenty-eight years later you realize you weren't. I don't know.'

'The longer you keep something secret, the harder it is to admit it anyway,' Beth put in.

Rhianwen nodded. 'Oh, that's true, all right. I can't explain unless I tell you the whole story.'

'Go on, then,' Morgan said intently. 'We're not going anywhere.'

'All right. If you insist.' Rhianwen looked out of the window at the garden as she spoke, trying to ignore their eyes on her. 'We came here from Wales because Owen was transferred to a company in Lichfield. I was twenty, I couldn't settle, I wanted to go home; Owen thought I should shut up and have babies. I shouldn't have married him, but that's another story. Anyway, we registered as Dr Cross's patients but I was never ill so I never saw him. Randolph came round here . . .' Rhianwen hesitated, caught on memories. 'People in the village had started coming to me for healing, instead of going to Randolph. He was incensed, naturally. He would come round and we'd have these civilized but truly dreadful arguments. I hated him to start with. It was a matter of principle; it was like the approved paternal authority versus the village witch, you know, Beth?'

Beth nodded grimly. 'At least they can't burn you at the stake for it these days. Only deface your house.'

'But he wasn't really like that. I didn't realize but Randolph was a healer, too. More than a doctor, I mean. He was one of us.'

'My granddad?' Beth gasped.

'He kept quiet about it, naturally. Anyway, we stopped arguing and started to understand each other and we came to an agreement; I would stick to animals and he would stick to people. But while all this went on I fell in love with him.

'Randolph was such a lovely man. Older than me, but I didn't care. I set out to seduce him. He was very strong and he resisted for ages, but I wouldn't give up, even though I knew he was married. Even though I was friendly with his daughter. Olivia wasn't so crazy then. She was always trying to win me for Christ but she wasn't so fervent, it was almost a joke between us. I liked her.'

Beth started to cry silently. Morgan squeezed her hand.

'Anyway, I was determined to have Randolph, regardless of anyone else. I'd go to the surgery with invented chest infections. Eventually he surrendered. Oh, I did a lot of things I shouldn't have done. We both did. We even did them in the surgery sometimes. Oh, you look shocked, Beth. Did you think I was a saint? Randolph knew how risky that was. I suppose it was the excitement. He'd come to see me, while Owen was at work. House calls. But we were in love. I thought he'd leave Heather for me, like a fool.'

Beth leaned her forehead on her hands. 'I can't imagine Granddad doing any of this.'

'Or my mother,' said Morgan. He looked more shocked than Rhianwen had expected.

'Believe me, we did. Well, Owen caught us and told Heather; turned out she'd guessed anyway, but she'd pretended nothing was happening. When Owen walked out I was relieved. I felt nothing for him. Heather tried to stop the affair, naturally, but we carried on. And about six months after Owen had gone – so the child couldn't possibly have been his – I found I was pregnant. It wasn't on purpose, although I would have done anything to marry Randolph and have his children. Well, maybe it was on purpose, subconsciously.

'Randolph felt he had to tell Heather. I think that was the closest he came to leaving her but she decided to hang on to him like grim death.'

'She loved him, too!' said Beth. 'She must have been devastated!'

'I know that. I was selfish, but it's very difficult to be unselfish when you're blindly in love. But it was Olivia who went off her head about it. I became the Whore of Babylon in her eyes. I suppose I understand. If my father had had an affair with my best friend, I'd be pretty bloody upset about it too. Olivia was unbalanced, actually, but she wouldn't see a doctor; she thought this Pastor Blair had all the answers. He egged her on to regard me as the instrument of the Devil. To be fair, though, I acted up to it, I was that angry.

'The thing about Randolph is that he's an atheist with a pagan soul and Christian principles. The baby forced him to choose, so he chose his wife. What else could he do? He had to be the respectable country doctor with wife and daughter. If he'd come to me he'd have lost his livelihood and his social standing.' Her tone was acerbic. 'Doctors aren't meant to screw their patients, they get struck off for it. He loved Heather, he didn't want to hurt her. And he stayed for Olivia's sake, of course. He said he was worried she might actually kill herself if he came to me. I said that was emotional blackmail. Oh, I didn't give in gracefully. I fought like hell to get Randolph. I had no scruples. I was a bitch to Olivia and Heather and I scared them. I'm not proud of the way I behaved. I just thought you should know, Beth, they had every reason to hate my guts and forbid you to see me.'

Beth, looking stricken, said nothing.

'Anyway,' Rhianwen went on, 'Heather won; I lost. Naturally I put Owen as Morgan's father. I had a choice: move miles away and tell Morgan the truth, or stay here and not tell him. I stayed, because I couldn't bear not to see Randolph.'

Morgan said, 'But you used to take me to him, and he'd be absolutely poker-faced. I'd never have guessed I was anything to him.'

'Neither would I,' Rhianwen said acidly. 'Yes, I stayed on his list for a few years. I thought if he saw you often enough, he'd weaken and acknowledge you. But he didn't. And I had to suffer Heather and Olivia coming round and nagging me until I had to find another doctor. I could treat most of Morgan's ailments myself, of course, but healing doesn't work for everything. I can't give vaccinations or do emergency operations. Heather and Olivia tried to make me leave the village altogether but I drew the line at that. So we came to an uneasy agreement; they'd tolerate me staying, as long as Morgan never knew who his father was. Imagine the embarrassment it would cause if Morgan insisted on seeing Randolph when he got older! So we all agreed to act like it had never happened. Whatever you think of me, I had consideration for Heather and Olivia's feelings, even if they had none for mine.'

'So you never saw Randolph?' said Beth.

'Oh, we saw each other. He even wanted to carry on our affair, have his cake and eat it, but I said no. We met, but we weren't lovers. As far as I was concerned he'd taken his family's side so he wasn't my friend any more. But we didn't stop loving each other. It was agony, if you must know. It was just one of those impossible bloody situations you have to put up with for years. You cope. He gave me an allowance for Morgan, secretly, so I could send him to a good school and that.'

'But you loved him,' Beth said. 'Heather called you a manipulative tramp, or words to that effect.'

'Well, I was in her eyes. If I'd left him alone it wouldn't have happened, I know that. But yes, I loved him. Still do.'

'That's it,' Morgan said, his voice quiet but so cutting it made both Rhianwen and Beth jump. 'That's why you kept Beth and me apart. Revenge.'

'What?' said Rhianwen.

'Well, you'd suffered for years so you wanted us to suffer too! And Beth suffered the most. I was all right, I had university and Marian and money. But Beth had nothing! You bloody –'

'Stop it!' said Beth, pressing her palm to his chest. 'Morgan, for God's sake!'

'Well?' he said. 'Isn't it true?'

'No,' Rhianwen said. 'I was thinking of you. Everything was wrong. I wanted to end it before you got too involved and had more kids. I thought if I split you up once and for all you'd both get over it faster. And I was really afraid you'd hurt each other if I let you stay together, because you were just too young to cope! Better to make a clean break. I was thinking of Randolph, too. How would he feel if I'd condoned his son and granddaughter having a relationship?'

'But that was up to us!' said Morgan. 'You had no right! Wasn't it revenge against Olivia, subverting her daughter? Maybe you meant me to seduce Beth; that really stirred the shit, didn't it?'

'Of course I didn't!' said Rhianwen. She'd never seen Morgan so upset before.

'I didn't see my daughter for eleven years because of you!'

'Whatever I did, I didn't mean to hurt either of you. I'm sorry. I did what I thought was best. I still think it was for the best, but if it hurt you, I am truly sorry.'

'I didn't have "nothing",' Beth broke in indignantly. 'I had friends and I had Eirian. Everywhere I've been, I've met good people who've helped me. Can't you forgive your mother, Morgan?'

'How can you?'

'Because I know how she feels. Think about it; she's lived with this pain all your life and *you didn't even know.*'

Morgan went quiet. 'Shit,' he said under his breath. And after a few seconds, 'Mum, I'm sorry I shouted at you.'

'If you want to be with Beth,' said Rhianwen, 'I won't try to stop you. Do what you want to do. I want you to be happy.'

'The past is over,' said Beth. 'Everything's all right – well, most things are all right, and I don't want to fall out with Rhianwen again. Not now. Do you?'

'Of course I don't,' said Morgan.

'Well, then.'

Morgan held out his hand. Rhianwen moved up on to the sofa beside him and he kissed her, forgiving her reluctantly.

'Are you still angry with me?' Rhianwen asked.

'How can anyone stay angry with you?' said Morgan.

'You've got the charm of the Devil. Isn't that where I get it from?'

'Very funny,' said Rhianwen. 'D'you know something? Now you know the truth, I don't know why I was so scared of telling you.'

As Rhianwen finished speaking, Beth heard the back door opening and a deep, familiar male voice calling, 'Rhianwen? It's only me. Sorry to come by so early, darling, but I've so much to organize today and I had to see you.'

Rhianwen shot to her feet and rushed towards the kitchen, just as Beth's grandfather appeared in the doorway, dressed smartly in a dark suit. As Rhianwen almost collided with him, Randolph put his arms round her and held her, his eyes closed and face half hidden in her auburn hair.

Rhianwen was tapping his shoulder; Randolph looked up and saw Beth and Morgan. His thick, dark-grey eyebrows rose in consternation; he held Beth's gaze for a moment, then Rhianwen pushed him back into the kitchen and closed the door behind them.

Beth put her head in her hands. 'Oh, I see. Oh, my God. Oh, fine.'

'It isn't over, then,' Morgan said flatly.

'Are you all right, after all this?'

'Sure,' he said sarcastically. 'What else can happen?'

There were whispering voices for a few minutes. Morgan held Beth's hand; they waited. Eventually Rhianwen and Randolph came back, arm in arm.

Beth and Morgan stood up, looking at each other.

'Hello, Granddad,' Beth said helplessly.

'Hello, Beth.' Her grandfather looked worn out and under strain, but still poised, resigned rather than embarrassed. And she could really see Morgan in him now: the fine bones and thick dark hair, his charisma and bitter-sweet personality. He was still elegant and distinguished, his grey-green eyes still full of life. 'Hello, Morgan. I gather you know all the, erm, sordid details.'

Morgan didn't speak; Beth, touching his arm, could feel his hostility as physical tension. Beth said, 'Couldn't you have waited until after the funeral? Gran hasn't been dead a day!' She was shocked to realize how angry she felt.

Her grandfather looked her straight in the eye, grave and apologetic but not in the least ashamed. 'Beth, I mean no disrespect to your grandmother. But I am seventy-one years old. Rhianwen and I have waited – what is it? – twenty-eight years for this. We may have twenty years together or we may have two, who knows? We can't afford to waste a day.'

'I suppose not,' said Beth. Beside her, Morgan was speechless.

'This must have come as rather a shock to you both.'

'You could say that. It's all true, is it?'

'Yes, it's true. Beth, I wouldn't have betrayed your grandmother for anything. I loved her. But try to understand. Rhianwen and I love each other too. It wasn't just an affair.'

'That's just it, isn't it?' Beth exclaimed, feeling there was no one to defend her grandma but her. 'If it had been "just an affair", Gran could have got over it. She couldn't get over knowing you loved someone else. And why couldn't *you* have told me who Morgan was? Even when I was pregnant, you still didn't tell me!'

Her grandfather sighed, looking at the carpet. 'Beth, this is so difficult.'

Rhianwen broke in, 'I think I should leave you alone to talk for a while. Will you excuse me while I have a shower and get dressed?' And she went quickly up the stairs, leaving Beth and Morgan awkwardly alone with Randolph. They remained on their feet. Morgan folded his arms and stared at Randolph.

'I can't understand why my mother's still speaking to you,' Morgan said frostily, 'after the way you've treated her. You rejected her, you wouldn't acknowledge me, you forced her to lie to me and Beth. You even made us leave home! On top of that I had your wife trying to kill me every time she saw me. I don't know how you dare show your face after all that.'

Randolph nodded grimly. 'I know. I was in an impossible

situation: I had to be loyal to Heather, even if it meant being unkind to Rhianwen at times. But that's between Rhianwen and me. We've sorted out our differences and she's forgiven me.'

Morgan went to stare out of the window, arms clasped over his waist.

'You were round here last night, weren't you?' said Beth. 'That's why you didn't want Morgan and me to stay with you.'

'Yes,' he said gravely. 'I didn't stay the night. We only talked. I know how it looks, but in the space of a week I've lost my wife and my grandson, while my daughter's been put in a psychiatric ward. Can't help wondering where I've gone wrong . . . and Rhianwen's been my only comfort.'

Beth reached out to him. 'What about me?'

Randolph clasped her hand, half smiling. 'But Rhianwen knows all about me. My faults, everything. We talked for hours last night. She knows I've always loved her.'

'You treated her like shit, but that's okay, she knew you loved her,' Morgan said acidly. His eyes were glacial.

'I understand your bitterness.' Randolph met Morgan's gaze and his tone hardened. 'But you are hardly in a position to judge me, after your behaviour towards my granddaughter.'

'Nobody told me who she was,' Morgan said thinly.

'Would it have stopped you?'

'Probably not.'

'Quite so. I regret not being in a position to make you aware of the damage you caused. Imagine you had a brother, and that brother seduced Eirian. How would you feel?'

'Right,' said Morgan, smiling bitterly. 'I'd want to kill him. Point taken. I've treated Beth badly – but it's okay, she knows I love her.' Then his sarcasm faded. 'And I hope she still loves me like that when I'm seventy-one.'

Beth was still holding her grandfather's hand, thinking, so this is where our powers come from, from him and Rhianwen. I must ask him about it later. Is that why Eirian's like she is, because she has two lots of the same blood?

Randolph breathed out softly. 'Morgan, I hope we can

515

forget the past and be friends,' he said, 'because Rhianwen and I are going to live together. We plan to marry as soon as possible. I hope you can come to terms with the idea.'

'As long as you don't mind me being with Beth,' said Morgan.

'I can't say I'm happy about it. It seems, well, bizarre, from my point of view. But it's your decision,' said Randolph. Soon Beth was going to get annoyed with that tone of understanding sadness from everyone.

'We love each other,' Beth said defiantly. 'We don't care what anyone thinks.'

'And I am hardly in a position to criticize, having behaved so badly myself,' Randolph said heavily. He looked at Morgan. 'I know this is difficult for you, but I hope you can come to terms with it.'

'It's wonderful,' Morgan said sardonically. 'I'm twenty-eight years old and my parents are getting married. D'you want me to be best man, or what?'

'Well, yes, actually.' Randolph's gaze met Beth's and she saw a gleam in his eye. She went to Morgan and slipped her hand through his intransigent arm.

'Come on, love,' she said. 'If your father can forgive you, why can't you forgive him?'

'You seem to be doing enough of it for both of us.'

'Well, why not?' said Beth. 'Don't you want your mum to be happy?'

Morgan sighed. He pushed his hand through his dishevelled hair. Then he went to Beth's grandfather and rather brusquely shook his hand.

'You don't mind if I go on calling you Dr Cross, do you?' Morgan said coldly. 'I don't think I can get used to calling you Dad.'

As Rhianwen climbed the stairs, she felt cleansed and light of heart. It was such a relief to have told Beth and Morgan the truth at last. It hadn't achieved much, if they insisted on staying together, but at least there would be no more lies and deceptions. Now Rhianwen had Randolph – however late in the day it was – Morgan's love for Beth no longer distressed her. She could accept it. They could all be loving and forgiving to each other, because they were all happy now.

As she reached the top of the stairs, Rhianwen had a shock. Eirian was sitting on the landing, looking through the banisters. And Rhianwen realized that she must have overheard everything.

'Morning, love,' Rhianwen said warmly. 'Did you sleep okay?'

Eirian stood up, a tall, poised child, brown hair cloaking her shoulders. But there was no reciprocal warmth in her face.

'You were listening, weren't you?' Rhianwen said sadly. 'It's all right, no one's going to be angry. You have a right to know, so if there's anything you want to ask, just ask us.'

Eirian didn't respond. Rhianwen had expected a change of expression or a question, but she saw no curiosity or affection in her granddaughter's demeanour. Eirian's expression was blank and hostile, like polished ice, and her pupils were flints caught in green amber.

Then Eirian spoke at last and Rhianwen felt the wintry breath of the Crone freezing her to the core.

'You stopped my mother seeing Morgan; you would have kept my parents apart for their whole lives if you could. You really hurt them. Beth and Morgan may have forgiven you for what you did to them, but I haven't. I never shall.'

Envoi

EIRIAN sat in the centre of the Hellstone.

The sun poured down, insects sang, the summer air was motionless. Her parents were sitting on the edge of the stone, hand in hand like teenagers, whispering about something they seemed to find highly amusing. But Eirian took no notice. She divorced herself from them: the world receded until there was only the smooth silvery stone, the rustling trees, the sky.

A weirdly glowing gloom enveloped her, and through it she saw the Goddess's silver eyes. She could hear a strange deep chanting, very faint but growing louder.

I did my best, Eirian told the Goddess. I did everything you required of me. I shall do more.

Then it seemed the Goddess lifted the hem of her robe and beyond, as if through muslin or a crumpled photograph cracked and starred with whiteness, Eirian saw a circle of women chanting. They seemed infinitely far away, ghosts of the distant past; not Guendolen's past but a time primaeval beyond imagining. Eirian saw them across a blizzard-torn vortex that turned her dizzy. Hundreds of thousands of years, yet the force of their will hit her with searing, urgent intensity.

The end of the Goddess times is coming when men will hate us and turn against us and deny their own Mother but men can never destroy her. She will endure through all and there must be a child, a warrior, a witness to the crimes that will be committed against the Great Mother in the name of the life-denying gods, a child to hear us and work for our Good Mistress, to bear her name and love and justice through all denial, all oppression, all abomination.

The chant went on for ever; it had no words but Eirian understood it perfectly. It lived in every cell, bone, fibre and nerve of her body, throbbing and instinctual. The force of female magic, blood and sexuality against the cold, life-hating authority of the male gods.

Eirian put back her head and breathed the fresh air, the Goddess's will; breathed the sultry aromas of sun-baked stone, moist grass roots and aromatic leaves. She felt strong and happy. She felt utterly invincible.

A loud, droning buzz startled her. Something chitinous bumped against her cheek; she instantly flicked it away, but it circled her, annoyingly persistent. Her eyes came open. She felt insect feet pricking her skin. She looked down to see a huge, bristling black fly crawling on the back of her left hand. Sun-drowsy, it rubbed its filamental forelegs together as if sharpening knives.

Eirian froze. It was just a fly, ugly and banal, yet it seemed to shoot a warning into her mind as if it had stuck its proboscis like a hypodermic needle through her skin.

You think you are invincible, witch? You think you've destroyed us? But there are always more of us and one day we will grind you on this stone like the speck of filth you are.

In horror, Eirian shook the fly off her hand. Her reflexes were sharp with revulsion. As the insect buzzed in a lazy arc to land in front of her, her fist hammered down and squashed it. Then she sat staring at the repulsive mash of legs, broken wings and innards on the rock. Her confidence was badly shaken, if not shattered. The fly was dead. But there were always more flies.

'Eirian?' Her mother's voice. The lush sweetness of summer rushed back in, but the chill stayed deep inside; more a thorn of grim knowledge than a mere premonition. Something to be borne. 'What are you looking at?'

'Nothing,' Eirian said lightly, wondering if she would always have to lie to protect Beth. 'Nothing.'

SIGNET

Published or forthcoming

KISS A BEFORE DYING

Ira Levin

Dorothy, Ellen and Marion: three attractive sisters with a very rich father.

Dorothy meets a handsome young man with an eye for her inheritance while she is at college. They are to be married and her life will be blissful; but Dorothy is pregnant and her fiancé's plans are ruined, for Dorothy will be disinherited if her father discovers the truth.

So the young man provides his bride-to-be with some pills that will solve the problem. Soon there will be no baby – and perhaps no Dorothy either …

SIGNET

Published or forthcoming

THIS PERFECT DAY

Ira Levin

Chip is a good, obedient citizen of the brave new world. A world where sex is programmed and regular treatments keep people docile. A world where everyone is scheduled to die at the age of sixty-two, for efficiency.

But Chip encounters a group of subversives who tempt him with ideas of freedom, original thought and love. The dilemma that ensues is both horrific and irresistible.

'A futuristic nightmare' – *The New York Times*

SIGNET

Published or forthcoming

ROSEMARY'S BABY

Ira Levin

When the truth is more sinister than imagination …

Rosemary and Guy Woodhouse's new apartment in the Bramford was everything the young couple wanted. Yet as soon as they'd signed the lease Rosemary began to have doubts.

The neighbours were quaint but friendly. Too friendly. Especially after Mr and Mrs Castavet learned that Rosemary was planning to have a baby.

'A darkly brilliant tale of modern devilry that induces the reader to believe the unbelievable. I believed it and was altogether enthralled' – Truman Capote

'This horror story will grip you and chill you' – *Daily Express*

'Diabolically good … the pay-off is so fiendish it made me sweat' – *Sun*

'A terrifying book … I can think of no other in which fear of an unknown evil strikes with greater chill' – *Daily Telegraph*

SIGNET

Published or forthcoming

LOOSE AMONG THE LAMBS

Jay Brandon

In the endless heat of a San Antonio summer, three children are abducted and abused. As the city howls for justice, a man steps forward to offer his confession. An innocent man ...

District Attorney Mark Blackwell and Prosecutor Becky Schirhart get on the case and begin to peel back the complex web of lies and deceit protecting those who think they are beyond the law. Starting with their own department ...

'The pace is effortlessly sustained to produce a gripping story whose outcome is uncertain till the final pages' – *Sunday Telegraph*

Published or forthcoming

Host

Peter James

Like Dr Frankenstein, brilliant scientist Joe Messenger will stop at nothing in his quest for immortality.

Through a combination of artificial intelligence and the freezing of bodies, Joe hopes to be able to defeat death itself. When he meets and falls for Juliet Spring, a gifted young researcher who claims to have stumbled on a way to transfer human consciousness into a computer, he believes the final breakthrough is near.

'Easily James's best book to date; a thought-provoking menacer that's completely techno-logical and genuinely frightening about the power of future communications' – Christopher Fowler in *Time Out*

SIGNET

Published or forthcoming

Prophecy

Peter James

They met by chance but archaeologist Frannie
Monsanto was soon deeply involved with handsome Oliver Halkin and Edward, his young
son. Yet, unknown to them, their paths have
crossed and recrossed over the years.

As their relationship develops – and slides into
a bizarre nightmare – Frannie realizes that if
she is to survive, she must prevent her own terrifying fate. Too late she discovers the real
meaning of the Halkin family motto, *Non Omnis
Moriar – I shall not altogether die* ...